Actual reader comments from a pre-release version of the Believing Magic series I posted briefly on Bookrix.com:

Reader comment:
Ummm. I read a lot, but never has a book kept me outside in freezing weather, gripping the edge of my seat as an unending chain of smokes dangles from my trembling teeth. I have laughed and cried and loved and died along with the characters you so richly brought to life and as corny as it sounds, I feel changed. Thank You for the best week and a half of late nights in a long time. I am 'praying' that Garden of Wrath is not the last in the series, because I am surely addicted, and having just finished the last page of the fourth book, I am already feeling the withdrawal.

Author reply:
A Piece of my Soul. Dear Reader - This book has cost me a lot. For countless hours it has literally consumed my existence. That time and that part of 'me' has not vanished into thin air, it has simply moved onto a page where I shaped that part of myself with loving hands into 'Friends'. I sympathize. I have been trapped before my keyboard, up sometimes all night long as these people lived their lives, first in me, and now - in you. I hold duel residency. A part of me lives in Amen Hale. I have more friends there than here.

Reader comment:
I'm about to start the 6th book and i have to say I'm kinda sad about it, i have been able to lose my self in ur books over the last few weeks and I hate to know its coming to an end. Every time I think there is no way u can make me want to be at Amen Hale myself u do, and the way u have incorporated the real world into the story makes it so much better.
Please, please take down my email XXXXXXXX and please, please let me know as soon as ur books are ready to be sold, id love to be one of the first to buy the entire set.
Ok here I go jumping into the last book, thank u so much for the entertainment ur books have brought me, I've actually got my coworker reading the series as well, I love coming to relieve her from work she is just now on the first book and so excited to talk about it every time I come in!!!!! AGAIN THANK U

BELIEVING MAGIC

BELIEVING MAGIC

MAGIC

SHANE WESLEY SHELTON

Believing Magic Books

This is a work of fiction. Names, characters, places, and incidents are either products of the author's imagination or, if real, are used fictitiously.

Copyright © 2014 by Shane W. Shelton

First U.S. edition 2014

ISBN 978-1-941570-04-3

Printed by Amazon CreateSpace

Artwork for all covers in the Believing Magic series purchased on Shutterstock.com

Grammatical and line editing for all books in the Believing Magic Series by:
Karen Robinson – Freelance copy editor and proofreader
Bachelors, English & Masters, English | Texas A&M University, Doctorate, English | Perdue University, Faculty Fellow | Ivy Tech Community College teaching English and Composition

Second Editing and Final Read Through Proofing for all books in the BM series:
Sherri McDougald – English major at University of North Florida
Artist: acrylics, ink, pencil/charcoal, and glass etching
Contact for any work requests at: sherrir30@yahoo.com

Interior book design and ebook conversion by:
Jimmy Sevilleno – professional interior book designer and ebook conversion specialist

Cover artwork tweaked and adjusted and prepped for print by:
Jeesun Hwang – Graphic artist and designer

Believing Magic Books
13 Kingfish Avenue
Ponte Vedra Beach, Florida 32082
visit us at **www.believingmagic.com**

Also by the Author

Contents

To my friends:
Thank you for everything.

I Believe.

Jane Miller

Dr. Burgis fought and failed to stifle a yawn. It was the final, grueling day of screening acne-ridden, emotional teens for twelve study patients, and the selection process had been brutal. Dr. Burgis was in his mid-fifties, sporting a salt and pepper beard, wire rim glasses, and a few extra pounds around the middle. He looked like someone's grandfather. Someone's tired and less than thrilled grandfather in this case.

The teenage girl perched on the exam bed stared at him with the same startled expression he'd seen on a blur of other faces. The face of an introverted, self-conscious teen being uncomfortably daring. The girl had attractive features, perfect teeth, a delicate nose, large hazel gray eyes framed by high cheekbones, but all anyone would notice when they first laid eyes on her would be the acne-stricken cheeks and brow.

Despite her desperately pleading eyes Burgis had already made his decision. All that remained was to find, or engineer, some reason to set her aside so he could move on to the next applicant. The Doctor licked his index finger and thumbed through the pages of the file in his hands, eyes scanning, searching for something that tickled at his mind about the girl. He made a grunt of satisfied discovery and asked his last question.

"One final question, Jane, and I believe we'll be finished with your psychological evaluation. I noticed you were reading a book in the waiting room when I called you back. May I ask what you were reading?" He arched an eyebrow and forced a reassuring smile onto his face.

"Oh, it's nothing, just a silly teen book," the girl shrugged.

Burgis frowned. "But, Jane, in your bio you said that you didn't read books or novels of any kind. Obviously, you do read books." He sounded less than pleased. "I know that the online questionnaire was long and horribly tedious. There were a large number of questions. Mistakes and even omissions were bound to happen."

Instantly Jane flushed with dread. If the Doctor thought she'd been deceptive in her answers, she was done! She threw her explanation at him before he could say another word because she knew what his next words would be.

"Oh no!" she practically shouted. "It's not a mistake! I answered all the questions myself, and no one helped me or answered for me. And I took my time. I'm not a reader! Not normally anyway." Jane gave the book lying on her purse a hateful, angry glare. Stupid book! She turned her pleading eyes back to Burgis. "Honestly, I told the truth in my bio. And I don't like books, but one of my best friends, Stacy, she's been pestering the living crap out of me all summer to read the Midnight books and I finally said I'd do it just to get her to shut up! She even made me promise not to cheat and watch the movies first. Stacy said the books were better than the movies and it would mess me up if I watched them and make the books suck."

Burgis was smiling.

Jane cocked her head back in surprise. What did it mean?

"You haven't read any books or novels just for the pleasure of reading before today?" he asked, eagerly awaiting her response.

"No, sir," Jane answered, too relieved that Dr. Burgis seemed to be happy with her again to give too much thought to how weird the question was or what it had to do with anything.

"Surely when you were little you read books just for the pleasure of enjoying a good story," Burgis pressed.

Jane's relief began to turn to suspicion. Was he *still* trying to catch her in a lie about her reading habits? He must be. She answered as if she were stepping through a mine field of words, her reply filled with hesitant pauses, as if any wrong word might explode and ruin everything.

"Well, my mom would read me books… to put me to sleep when I was a baby… and… I'm pretty sure I read a couple of books when I was little… I sorta remember one about a rabbit. Edward something… I remember it was really sad… and—" she swallowed and faced him squarely. "Honestly, Dr. Burgis, if it's not a book I have to read for a book report or some school book, I don't read – at all." She ended with an apologetic face.

Dr. Burgis pursed his lips, picked up her book, and studied the cover art.

Jane summed up her "booklessness" with the standard cop-out statement, "Books take too long to read. I'd rather just watch a movie."

"What's it about?" Burgis asked as he opened the book to where her bookmark held her place.

"Vampires."

He nodded and turned a page or two, like this was an expected theme for teen reading. "As I guessed from the cover, but give me more details than that," he urged warmly. "Who is the main character in the book? Is it a boy, a girl, or some vampire? You're well over a hundred pages in, what's happened so far?"

Dr. Burgis was watching her so closely, Jane felt a little like a bug in a box. She could tell he was still in psych evaluation mode. Pressure!

"Well, the main character is a girl named Sarah, and she just found out that the guy she likes is a vampire."

"And are you like this Sarah in the book? Same age, same hair color, same interests?" Dr. Burgis looked over the top of his glasses at Jane, striking a classic "teacher" pose as he lectured. "The best way to read a story is to imagine yourself as the main character and let yourself be part of the story. Let your mind create the world of the book instead of some director and a movie screen. Your imagination is far better than the movie will ever be, so in this I agree wholeheartedly with your annoying friend—" he searched his memory for a moment, "Stacy, you said."

Jane nodded and Dr. Burgis handed her back the book and asked again, "Are you like Sarah in the book, Jane?"

Jane reached up self-consciously to her red pimply face as she answered. "No, I'm not like Sarah. I mean, she—Sarah is pale and has real fair skin—in the book she has perfect skin." She wouldn't meet the doctor's eyes as she answered but studied the book in her hands and the cover art.

Jane tried not to let the tight knot she felt in her stomach creep up into her eyes. Not the best time to cry, during a psych evaluation, but it didn't look like she was going to be able to stop it. It was getting hard to see. Her eyes were filling up. Dr. Burgis coughed and cleared his throat and rubbed at his own eyes which made Jane blink, which was like flushing two toilets! Everything that she'd managed to keep pooled in her two aquatic orbs hosed down her face.

"Good grief!" she moaned. She was ruined! Now she was crying, and she had the doctor crying!

Burgis chuckled and smiled. "We're done. And, Jane, you're in the drug study if," he held up a finger, "you agree to all the trial restrictions, and one very important condition."

Jane's watery eyes got huge as she processed this. *I'm IN!* She let out a happy "Yea!" and bounced around on the exam bed in celebration as she wiped her tears away with the palms of her hands.

Dr. Burgis cleared his throat again and wiped quickly under his glasses at his own eyes with a tissue he'd grabbed from the box on his desk. He handed the box to Jane.

"All right now, let's get this wrapped up." He harrumphed, cleared his throat a final time, and busied himself, organizing papers and handing them to Jane as he talked. "I know you're already aware that this drug study is very special. We're trying to make changes to your genes, the very most basic parts of what makes you 'uniquely' you, and that is very serious business, so you'll have to follow our directives to the letter. You understand, Jane?" He looked at her expectantly and waited.

"Yes, sir."

"You will be back here, in my office, this coming Monday to start the five-day course of the Derm 513 pills. You will take the Derm 513 pill in my presence and will let me know each day if you are experiencing any side effects, changes in mood, diet, sleep patterns, or any other adverse or unusual reactions. Although we don't expect anything severe to happen, we're still going to be keeping an extremely close eye on you. You'll have to give up any travel plans you may have made for the last weeks of summer vacation before school starts as well. We can't have you going out and getting into trouble, getting hurt or catching a cold from someone. Gene therapy medicine is still a new science, and we must treat it with care. You must abide by the following restrictions—without fail." He paused again, waiting until she nodded her understanding and acceptance.

"First is the drug testing. Before you leave, you'll have to provide a urine, blood, and hair sample to Nurse Ann. I'm sure you've read the restriction on prescription drugs, over-the-counter drugs like pain and cold pills, and of course illicit drugs, but we'll still do testing to make sure you're drug free, and we will be testing all five days of the study to make sure you stay that way. Also, no excessive physical activity starting today. That means no working out, no stressing out, and you'll have to stay home and indoors as much as possible till the end of the study next Friday.

"Second. Avoid direct and prolonged sunlight. Absolutely no tanning till the end of the study.

"Third." Dr. Burgis took out a white bottle of pills from his pocket and wrote her name on it. "You'll be taking a weak antibiotic for the next ten days to make sure you don't catch a cold. There are ten pills in this bottle, take two today and two each day after lunch so these" he shook the bottle "will be gone before I see you in my office on Monday. When you come on Monday, I expect you to bring me back this bottle, empty." He handed her the bottle of pills with her name on it.

Dr. Burgis leaned over and used his pen to point at RESTRICTION #4 on the paper he'd given her for emphasis as he went on. "Fourth, final, and also, I'm sure, the most egregious restriction to you and any teenager, absolutely no soda or other sweetened drinks or energy drinks for the next ten days. Only water. Yes, that's plain old H_2O. And no excessive sweets like candy bars or doughnuts. Sugar on your corn flakes is fine but don't overdo it."

"How many others are in the drug study, Dr. Burgis?" Jane was almost afraid to know how lucky she was.

"There are only twelve teens in the clinical trial, Jane, and as I have informed your parents, there are no placebo slots. All twelve of you will be getting the same treatment – no sugar pills – not for this particular trial, just the real drug."

Jane was relieved to hear this again. "Good, I'd hate to think that I was lucky enough to get in only to get a fake pill." She wiped at her eyes with one of the doctor's tissues as she thought about the waiting room filled with other teens who were trying to get into the drug study. A sad, crowded room packed with desperate kids with bad skin, all of them dreaming of getting it fixed–permanently–by five magic pills.

"Dr. Burgis, how many open spots are left in the study?" Jane asked, thinking about the waiting room.

"You were the last one, Jane. Study patient number 12." As if he could read her thoughts, he continued, "Yes, you are very, very fortunate, Jane. Hundreds have come here hoping to be a part of this clinical trial and I have selected you, and this reminds me of my one condition for you to be part of this drug study." Burgis leaned in, "You remember?"

Jane nodded, worried again.

"About your book," Dr. Burgis said, "your vampire book with the young girl named Sarah."

Jane still had it in her hands, and she hugged the book to her chest as her emotions from earlier threatened to wash back over her. She didn't want to cry again. She was done with that! She sat up straighter and listened carefully as the doctor spoke.

"Jane, you're in the study, but in exchange I want you to do something for me. I want you to read your book and I want you to picture yourself as Sarah, with perfect pale skin. The heart and the imagination are very powerful, Jane. Your heart and your mind can change what you are, not just on the inside, but also on the outside if you only believe. So here is what I propose. First, you will read these – Midnight books." He tapped the book she held tight in her arms.

He scratched his head with his pen as he thought, then picked up a brown envelope off his desk, opened it, and took out a new fifty dollar bill. The envelope was filled with money. "This is not supposed to be a paid trial, Jane, so we'll keep this between us." He cast a furtive look over his shoulder toward the waiting room where Jane's mother was sitting then turned back to her and held out the fifty. "To help break you out of your *book free* existence, and to help you on your way to being more like Sarah, I will give you this fifty, and an additional fifty dollar bill for each vampire book you can read between now and the end of the drug study. Few things motivate a teenager like hard cold cash."

He put the fifty into Jane's open hand. "And don't worry about me, I'm good for it. As many books about pale, perfect skinned vampires as you can read, fifty for each book. Don't bring me the books, just tell me what books you've read when you come in. And for goodness sake, don't let your parents see you waving that cash around so they get suspicious and end our arrangement. Now, is this acceptable, Jane, or would you still rather watch the movie?" Dr. Burgis waited with his eyes on Jane, studying her every twitch and reaction to his proposal.

"Yes sir, I'll read them – and thank you," Jane answered, as sincerely as she could. She liked the book so far and wanted to finish it anyway. She hid the bill inside her purse picked her book back up and thought about Sarah, how she had perfect pale skin. She wondered how her skin would look soon. Hope warmed her chest. Maybe she would be like Sarah after all.

Jane

Lunch with Friends

Jane twisted the top of the brown pill bottle and took out two white pills.

"Is that the Derm pill? I thought you didn't start that till Monday," Emma asked, just before she bit into her slice of food court pizza.

"No, this is just an antibiotic. I have to take this before I start the Derm pills." Jane grabbed her bottle of water and downed the pills, took a quick bite of her Chick Fil-A sandwich, and picked her book back up. She hadn't stopped reading it since she left the doctor's office an hour ago.

Stacy stabbed her salad with a fork. "I still can't believe you got in. Thousands of teens must have tried to get into that Derm thing. I mean, I'm glad I don't really need it, but for you it's gotta be like winning the lotto!" Stacy cringed after those words were out. She looked up from her salad, expecting to find Jane with her feelings hurt, only to find Jane with her nose still buried in the book and not even listening. She reached over with a quick snakelike strike and snatched the book.

"Hey!" Jane cried, then looked into Stacy's frustrated face as she held her book hostage.

"I'm glad you're into the book and all, but *unplug already*!" Stacy growled. "You can read when you go home. And anyway, you're going to be *unavailable* all next week, so this is girl time. Talk! Spill the details, let's hear it."

Jane knew she wouldn't get the book back till after lunch, which totally sucked because she was at a good part. Stacy was right though; she would have plenty of time to read at home. Her mother told her on the way to the mall that this was the last time she would leave the house until after the trial, except to go to the doctor's office. Doctor Burgis made her parents promise and even sign some legal papers agreeing to keep her home till after the drug trial. Her dad had jokingly called it "house arrest." She knew that she probably wouldn't see her two best friends again till the start of school.

"OK! OK!" Jane put up her hands in surrender. "I'm unplugged already." She took another drink of her water and made a yuck face. "Accck! Nothing but water for ten days. I'm gonna DIE." She smiled contentedly and sighed, "But at least I'll look good in my coffin. Five pills and my zit days are *done*."

"Are you sure this stuff is gonna work that good?" Emma asked.

"Yeah, the pictures and films they showed us from the earlier trials were totally amazing. It works."

"Did you get there super early?" Stacy asked.

"We got there *three* hours before they opened!" Jane lamented. "I'd already signed up online and filled out all the paperwork and finished filling out the endless online bio, *but so had everyone else*! It was crazy! And once we got inside the doctor's office we waited another four hours before my name was called. The room was so, so freaking overcrowded that it *stank*!" Jane made a retching motion.

"Are we talking packed elevator stank, overloaded school bus reekage, or gross, sweaty, sardine style mosh pit with people disguised as human waste rubbing up against you?" Emma asked, curiously delving into the experience with a happy smile.

"There are no words," Jane said in a traumatized voice with wide open eyes, and Emma and Stacy both laughed, delighted at the agony as Jane continued her report. "And then I waited some more once I got into a room."

"I'd a lost it!" Emma said, "What freakin' time did you get there this morning?"

"We got there at 4AM. It was still dark in the parking lot, but we still weren't the first ones there. Some people camped out. Mom almost lost it in the waiting room, and I was so bored I actually started reading the book, and it's so weird because the book is what helped me get picked for the final spot!"

"The book?" Stacy asked. "What, was the doctor like a major Midnight fan or something?"

"No, it was so strange! When I went into the meeting for the psychological evaluation, which is the last part before they either dump you or keep you, it really seemed like Dr. Burgis didn't like me. But then he got all freaked when I told him that this was the first book I ever read just for fun. He said that if I agreed to read the Midnight books I was 'in' and he gave me a fifty dollar bill!" Jane took the fifty out of her purse where she'd stashed it and waved it in front of Stacy.

"Holy crap! Did I come through for you or what!?" Stacy declared. Jane nodded her total agreement as Stacy went on, "Damn girl, I think at the very least you owe me a movie and dinner at Sonic. You should be falling down on your knees and crying out *I'm Not Worthy!* I've made you RICH! and BEAUTI-FUL!" Stacy took a pull off her soda and summed up her accomplishment with mock humility, "I'm awesome."

Emma, Jane's self-appointed guardian, cut in, "Give it a rest, Stace, Jane don't owe you shit! It's not like you knew that stupid book would impress the doctor guy."

Jane shook her head no and backed Stacy up, "Nope. If Stacy hadn't of pestered the living crap out of me to read that stupid book, I wouldn't have brought it with me, and I wouldn't be in the study, so—" She gave Stacy sincere eye contact and said, "I am so not worthy. Which movie? And will Friday be OK?"

Stacy, with a smug look directed at Emma said, "Friday works for me!"

Jane, still waving the fifty around said, "Come on, Emms, let's take Mr. Fifty and celebrate! My treat!"

Emma nodded her agreement as she took another bite of her egg roll.

"Oh crap!" Jane was suddenly crestfallen. "I forgot, I can't go out till after the drug study's over. You guys should still go though. Just because I'm in lock-down doesn't mean you guys have to stay in." Jane handed the fifty to Stacy and said, "Seriously, take it." Stacy took it, but didn't look happy about it.

"No way!" Emma shot back. "We'll wait till you can come too. Wer'e not spending Mr. Fifty without you."

Jane grabbed her book back from Stacy, who was distracted making Mr. Fifty do a dance on the table top. "You guys go – and don't worry about it. I'll have another Mr. Fifty soon. Dr. Burgis said he would pay me another fifty for each vampire book I read from today till the end of the study."

"He's paying you fifty for each book!?" Stacy's eyes danced as she did the mental math. "You're a slow reader, and those Midnight books are some thick mothers," she added with a grin, "but you should still be able to finish all four books. You could make another $150 just by reading vampire books for the next ten days."

"Still," Emma said, "why'd the doctor want you to read vampire books. That's just WEIRD." She had her pen out and was drawing little hearts and smiley faces all over Mr. Fifty.

Jane didn't want to get into the details of her crying at the doctor's office, not here, and hopefully, not ever. "It's a mental thing. Dr. Burgis thought that reading about vampires with 'pale, fair skin' would be good for me while I was in the clinical trial, and I was already reading a vampire book. It sorta fit. I guess." She hoped that sounded like a good enough explanation.

"Stace, can I borrow the rest of the books? Do you have them all?"

"Sure, I'll bring them over tomorrow."

Emma laughed, "Jane's mom might not even open the door for you. "No visitors! Remember? You'll have to leave the books in a bag on her porch, ring the doorbell, then run like hell! Leave it like a flaming bag of poo."

They all laughed. Emma was funning, but Jane's mom had made it quite clear that she was totally off limits for a while.

"I'll just leave them on the porch for you," Stacy said.

They talked for a while about the new school year, boys, music and "girl stuff" till Jane's mom came back from shopping to take her home. Jane told her friends goodbye and left them at the table, planning which movie to watch on Friday and how best to celebrate with Mr. Fifty.

Jane

The First Blue Pill

The huge waiting room certainly wasn't crowded anymore. After seeing the place packed to overflowing it looked cavernous and deserted with only four teens and the parents they belonged to dotted around the room. Jane's mother had to take care of some big emergency at her work, so she'd dropped Jane off early for her appointment. On top of that, she wasn't going to be able to pick her up till after 3 PM.

That long of a wait would have totally freaked Jane out before, but not now. The amazing thing about being a book zombie (as her mother called her now) was how little it took to make her happy. Just a quiet corner. Apparently book zombies did not need a lot of things that most teens could not live without – friends, TV, movies, iPods, malls, showers, and even food! Her mother left her with lunch money, just in case she put the book down long enough to eat. She'd jokingly called her lack of appetite, the *Midnight Diet*.

Her parents were both readers, so they were excited, if a bit surprised, to see her get into reading a book at last. Her mother even joined her, starting in on the first book that Jane had already finished. In the evening they would sit together on the couch and read and read for hours. They had some weird new mother/daughter bonding action going on, but Jane actually liked it. And her father was being a sport and taking care of the house while Jane and her mom were couch potatoes. Again, no sour grapes, just happy dad. Proud father of a book zombie.

Jane went to the sliding glass window and signed in with the receptionist then looked over the waiting room, seeking the ideal corner to crawl into. She started to move toward an out of the way seat on the far side of the room when the back office doors opened and a tall, blonde girl walked out with Dr. Burgis. A man and woman that must have been the girl's parents stood and greeted the doctor.

"Hello, Dr. Burgis," the girl's father, a tall Chinese man in a black suit shook the doctor's hand. "Thank you again, this means so much to our daughter."

Jane watched as the girl's mother stood beside her husband. She was tall, thin, and looked like a blonde, glitz and glamor Barbie, dressed to kill. Everything about her screamed filthy rich. Her purse, her dress, her shoes. Jane didn't need "gay boy" fashion sense to know it was all top of the line designer stuff.

"Thank you, Dr. Burgis, we are so, very pleased to have our Sky as part of the trial," said the mother. "We've tried everything to get Sky's acne under control. It was totally impossible, nothing worked. Not the pills, not the creams, spas, wraps—" she rolled her eyes. "You name it and we have tried it!"

Sky was standing silently beside the doctor, back stiff as a board as her mother went on and on while everyone in the room listened. Sky was tall like her parents, ultra skinny, with what could only be assumed were perfect, store-bought boobs and mega hair that was a shade lighter than her mother's, but—DAMN! Girl did have a skin problem. If this worked, she would be a super model easy, but not the way she looked now. Not unless she was modeling from the neck down. On anyone else it wouldn't have looked that bad, but her face attached to the ultra perfection below it just didn't match.

After a few more totally, horrifyingly, embarrassing minutes, Dr. Burgis mercifully ended it and sent crazy ass Barbie mom, suit dad, and Sky out the door, then called for the next teen.

"Rain Bryant, please come with me."

A goth girl in all black stood and followed him into the back. She was goth, but not off the charts. No dangling chains, piercings, or nose rings, but she did sport the blue-black hair, the black lipstick and eyeliner, and the black clothes.

The dress was grunge style, but past the knees and modest. A quick scan back to the parents told all. Clean cut, beaver cleaver mom and dad and, yikes!, an almost identical twin brother. He was also clean cut, with a white button up shirt and slacks. Easy to see that the daughter was the "bad seed" of this bunch. Jane nodded. Now the controlled goth made perfect sense. It was all they would let her do. Oh well, whatever she had to put up with, Jane doubted it was as bad as crazy Barbie mom and the shit poor Sky had to deal with.

Shoving other people's problems out of her head, Jane stretched and covered her mouth as she yawned, stiff and tired from a late night of reading. It was time to get back to her book. She made a beeline for an isolated chair, settled in and opened the book. She'd just started book four, and Sarah and Ethan were about to get married! She got halfway through the first paragraph on the page she was reading before it happened.

"Hi, my name is Ryan. Ryan Bryant."

Jane, still hiding behind her book, felt the chair next to her move.

WTF! She leaned away and turned her shoulders to face the intruder. Using her book as a shield her surprised eyes slowly peeked over the top, into the smiling face of the twin, Ryan. Good grief! Come on! There were thirty open chairs in here, why sit right beside her!? He was breaking book zombie rule number one – Do Not Disturb! What did she have to do, post a sign!? She didn't want to talk to this guy, and she had a wedding to get back to, so she hid behind her book and hoped he'd get the hint and go away.

"I guess you're in the study too? Me and my sister Rain both got in," the disembodied voice said from the other side of her book.

"What's your name?" the voice asked.

Jane's wide eyes peeked over the top of the book again, amazed that this guy was still talking. She was caught between her nice well-mannered side, which wanted to answer politely, and the book zombie, which wanted to give him the finger and go back to reading. Good Jane won – but it was a close thing.

"Jane," said the eyes peeking over the top of the book.

"What school do you go to, Jane? Do you live here in Jacksonville or are you from out of town?"

"PV," said the eyes quietly.

"Really, Ponte Vedra High, that's like a brand new school isn't it? Is it really nice there?" Ryan asked.

"Yes," said the eyes.

"So, Jane from PV High, would you like to come to a get together with me – as my date?"

Holy crap! Did he just ask me out right here in front of God and everybody!? Jane glanced over to his 'rents. Yep, they were watching, and weirder still, they looked happy about the offer, smiles all around. Something was way off here, way, way off! She peeked back over the book. Ryan was still there waiting. Damn! Hmm, he *was* kinda cute. What now?

"Huh?" was the only response she could think to give while keeping with her monosyllabic dialogue.

"Yeah, there's a group of about thirty of us, we get together each Wednesday from 6 till 7. We play pool and video games and just hang out and talk for a while before church. It would be great to have you there. With me," Ryan asked the eyes and gave her a big smile. The smile was wonderful, but Jane clued in on the key word.

"Church?" said the eyes.

"Yeah, the teens get together each Wednesday before church for an hour. We even have our own band! Could you come? I'd like to get to know you better, Jane, you have very pretty eyes." Ryan stared at her, still smiling, waiting for her answer.

Jane had been to youth groups before. She'd gone to church a few times a year with her parents, but she didn't feel like doing this right here, and now, even if Ryan was cute. The whole thing was starting to feel kind of canned, like this was how he hunted for new church groupies. Jane looked back at the 'rents, the dad's suit, the slightly plump mom's bright beaver cleaver smile. Ryan's dad was probably the preacher of his church and Ryan was trying to pull in some fresh blood. Her suspicious side flared. Way, way off! Knew it!

"If you need a ride, I'd be glad to pick you up," Ryan offered.

The eyes peeking over the top of the book got all squinty, the book came up, and a voice behind the book answered, "Pass."

"Is Wednesday no good, or is it just the church thing that you don't like, Jane?" asked Ryan.

The eyes peeked back over the book and studied him for a minute. He really did seem like a nice guy, but still, not here, not now with his 'rents watching. Anyway, she had a book to read. "Later," said the eyes, and she raised her book and started reading again.

Thankfully Ryan took the hint and shut up, but he still didn't move. If the book hadn't been at a really good part she would have been weirded out by him sitting in the chair right beside her, but in short order she was into the story and totally blissed out. She didn't even hear when Ryan left or when her own name was called.

Someone tapped on her book and Jane peeked over the top and into the spectacled eyes of Dr. Burgis.

"Hello, Jane. Glad to see that you're so into your book, but it's time. Come on now." He was smiling as he led her to an exam room in the back where a nurse took her blood, blood pressure, temperature and had her get on the scale to check her weight. Surprise! She'd lost four pounds. Cool! The nurse asked what she'd been eating and a bunch of other heath-related stuff while she scribbled away on her clipboard, then Dr. Burgis came into the room. He was pushing a cart with nothing on it but a glass of water and a little paper cup.

"Thank you, Ann, that will be all." He dismissed the nurse.

"I see you've been reading, Jane. Which book are you on now? It's not the same one you had before?" Dr. Burgis asked as he studied the cover of her book.

"No sir, this is the fourth book, the last book in the series—and you were right," Jane said shyly.

"Right about what, Jane?" Dr. Burgis studied her over the top of his glasses, awaiting her reply.

"The book is better—I mean, I'm glad you asked me to read the books." Jane hesitated, then said exactly what she really wanted to say, "The other day I was only reading because I was so bored in the waiting room. But I'm glad you asked me to read the books. They're very good." She looked down, embarrassed.

"That's good to hear Jane. And what's happened to Sarah in your book?" asked Dr. Burgis.

Jane raised her head and smiled, glad to answer. "Oh!, she just got married to Ethan the vampire, it was great! They're about to go on their honeymoon," she finished with a grin.

Dr. Burgis took out his little flashlight and looked into her ears and asked, "And what do you think will happen next to our Sarah? Hmm?" He lifted her eyelid with a thumb and shone the light into her eye as she answered.

"Oh, Ethan is about to turn her into a vampire. He doesn't want to but he's going to have to do it soon," Jane answered.

"Well, Jane," he clicked off his little flashlight, "I don't know about Sarah, but it looks like you're well on your way to becoming a vampire yourself. You've been staying up all hours of the night reading, you're pale, you've got red blood-shot eyes, and you've already lost," he checked his pad again, "four pounds!" Dr. Burgis gave her a huge smile. "Well done, Jane, but don't forget to eat! And as this is book four, and I am sure this will be finished shortly, I need to fulfill my side of our bargain." Dr. Burgis pulled three fifty dollar bills from his brown envelope and handed them to Jane.

"What will you read once you finish this book? Have you already decided?" Burgis asked.

"If it's okay, I think I'll just read them again." Jane hoped that was okay. "Stacy has read the books through three times," she added.

"That's a fantastic idea, Jane!" Dr. Burgis encouraged enthusiastically. "I have books that I've read dozens of times. It's perfectly normal to reread a great book. One that has a great story." He held the envelope with the cash up and said, "Our offer still stands. A fifty for each book you can reread by this Friday. Just keep track of where you are." Dr Burgis put the envelope away.

"Did you finish the pills I sent you home with, Jane?" Burgis held out his hand. "Let me have the bottle."

Jane slipped the three fifty dollar bills into her purse and took out the empty pill bottle and handed it to the doctor.

"Now let me get your pills ready." Burgis turned to the tray, reaching into his coat pocket and pulling out four white pills from one inside pocket and a blue pill from a different inside pocket. He dropped the pills into the little paper cup then handed the cup to Jane. She stared into the cup and frowned at all the pills.

"Why are there four white pills, Dr. Burgis? And – is the blue pill the real Derm pill?" Jane asked, worried again about getting a sugar pill, fake medicine. They said that all of the twelve trial patients were getting the real medicine, but she was still worried.

"Don't be afraid, Jane, two of the white pills are the antibiotic to help you fight infection and colds during the trial, the other two white pills are to keep your stomach settled. And you may get an upset stomach after taking your medicine, but do – not – vomit. And, yes, the blue pill is the Derm 513 that changes your DNA!" Dr. Burgis gave her a bright smile and a playful eyebrow waggle. "So exciting! It reminds me of that movie, *The Matrix*, where a man has to take a pill to wake up from the dream world he was trapped in. He had to take a pill to start believing." Dr. Burgis handed Jane the glass of water and said, "Time to start believing, Jane Miller."

He watched as she put each pill into her mouth and swallowed, and then he got out his tongue depressor and searched around in her mouth to make sure she had. At least he was thorough, Jane thought. Still weird though.

Jane

Time to Start Believing

Dr. Burgis sent Nurse Ann to McDonald's for a grilled chicken salad. I said I could walk across the street and get it myself, but he wouldn't hear of it. He said that I might get sleepy or dizzy as I walked or feel out of it because of the pills and I'd be there with no supervision. He was also worried about me being left in the waiting room so long, just sitting out here, waiting on my mother. He wasn't happy with mother for stranding me here.

I told him 'here or there' didn't make any difference. If I were home I'd just be reading my book on a couch instead of in a chair in the waiting room. Here I had a nurse and a doctor for supervision. He chuckled and seemed happy with that but still said I needed to eat something right away to make sure I didn't get an upset stomach after all that medicine.

He led me out to the waiting room and told me to take a seat. When Ann got back and gave me my salad, I overheard Dr. Burgis's voice inside the office telling her to watch me from her little window when she could and make sure that I ate my salad. It was kinda nice to know I was being watched over. It really seemed like the doctor was going out of his way to take good care of me.

As I settled into my chair with my salad, I noticed that there were some new faces in the waiting room. A black teenager in a military school uniform was sitting a few chairs down from me. He was reading some military magazine from the magazine rack. The cover had soldiers hanging on a tank holding their guns in the air as they posed for the picture. In the middle of the room was a big kid who looked like a football player asleep in one of the chairs.

Dr. Burgis called, "Benjamin Grant."

The big kid woke up. He rubbed at a kink in his neck and followed the doctor toward the back, looking grumpy. Sitting in a chair by the front doors was a girl with an iPod and earbuds, totally spaced, eyes closed and head bobbing along as she listened to her music. Now that I was listening for it, I could pick up the faint noise of heavy metal escaping her earbuds.

I looked at the last teen who was sitting on the opposite side of the room, facing me. He was tall, wearing faded jeans, a black shirt, and a jean jacket. I stabbed another bite of salad and munched it as I eyed the guy. It was hard not to look at him because where he sat was right in front of me, against the wall on the other side of the room. I munched and looked.

He had his head down, his long fingers punching away on the little keypad as he texted on his phone. He had shaggy sandy blond hair. I could see his face but not his eyes as he worked over his phone looking down at the screen. He smiled. He must have gotten some message he liked. He had a really nice smile.

I took another bite of salad and resumed my shameless guy watching. He was still smiling but he was putting away his phone, slipping it into his jacket pocket, but now his head was up and I could see his eyes—were they green or blue? Hmm, somewhere in between.

From the other side of the room, his green-blue eyes looked out and across the room and right at me.

Crap! I quickly dropped my head and focused on the salad in my lap, but I still watched what he was doing with my head down.

I can't believe I got caught staring!

And now he was staring at me!

He pulled out a pad and pen from his front pocket and wrote something. Thought about it. Glanced up at me then tore it out, crumpled it up, and started over. He did this over and over, crumpling up one after another as I pretended to be interested in my salad and watched. My curiosity grew with the size of the crumpled pile balanced in the chair beside where he sat.

After fifteen minutes and I don't know how many crumbled up pieces of paper, he stood up and walked over to me. With my head down, I watched his feet stop in front of my chair. I kept my head down and wordlessly put my hand out for the note– like we already had some kind of weird understanding.

He placed the note into my hand.

> Hi, my name is Dan. I would (say) Hi but I can't, I got hurt when I was a kid and can't talk and just say Hi - but I still wanted to say Hi.
>
> Hi

Oh my God! That had to be the saddest and sweetest thing anyone had ever said to me!

Oh crap—*NO!*

Yep. I was crying. Again.

I didn't want to look up and have him see me all weepy, so I kept my head down, reached into my purse for a pen, and scribbled under his writing the first thing that popped into my head then quickly handed it back to Dan.

> Hi, my name is Dan. I would (say)
> Hi but I can't, I got hurt when I was
> a kid and can't talk and just say Hi -
> but I still wanted to say Hi.
>
> Hi
>
> *Hi Dan. I can talk just fine, but I don't*
> *want to look up right now because I'm*
> *crying. My name is Jane.*

I kept my head down and watched Dan (from the waist down) as he stood there in front of me, reading my stupid note. What was wrong with me!? Why did I write that!?

He flipped the note over and wrote on the back.

He eased it into my field of view and I took it back.

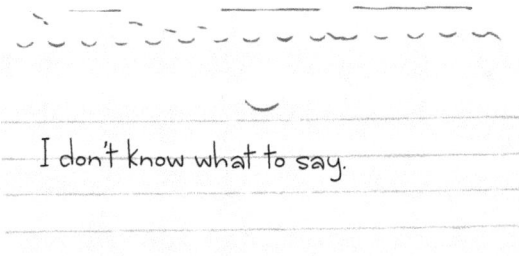

> I don't know what to say.

I wrote my helpless reply beneath his, still looking down, then handed back the note.

I don't know what to say.

Me either.

He wrote again, then handed me back the note.

I don't know what to say.

Me either.

Jane, can I sit beside you and hold your hand for a while?

I read and swallowed. When had my mouth gone dry, dry, dry and cottony? I couldn't begin to describe how strange I felt. I didn't know if I felt this way because of the book I was reading, getting myself all worked up and emotional as I read about what Sarah and Ethan were going through or if getting hit on by Ryan and now Dan had me freaked out. Or maybe I was just sleepy and tired from the pills or lack of sleep or whatever. I didn't know what was making me feel this way but I knew I wanted him to hold my hand. I *needed* him to hold my hand!

I wrote my reply and looked up at him as I handed him the note. Tears were streaming down my face. He froze with the note in his hand, the paper momentarily forgotten as he gazed down at me, so serious and concerned. Concerned about me. Worried about me. Did he care about me? After he'd studied my face thoroughly, he looked down at what I'd written.

I don't know what to say.

Me either.

Jane, can I sit beside you and hold your hand for a while?

Please Dan, Please!

Our eyes stayed locked together as he eased into the chair beside me. Dan put his hand down low between us and I put my hand into his, and we sat there together. I didn't say a word, and we didn't pass any more notes; we just sat there and held hands. It felt wonderful. Perfect. We leaned back in our chairs, heads turned to face one another as we gazed into each other's eyes—he had the most beautiful blueish-green eyes.

I closed my eyes.

"Wake up, honey, let's go." My mother was shaking my shoulder.

"Mom?" I said groggily, trying to get my bearings. I looked around. I was still in the waiting room at the doctor's, but Dan was gone. Everyone was gone except for one tall black girl and her mother talking with Nurse Ann.

"Are you okay, honey?" Mom started to sound concerned as she looked me over.

"I'm fine, Mom, just stayed up too late last night reading. Must have dozed off." I reached for my book and noticed that I had a new bookmark. It was Dan's note we'd written back and forth on. I quickly tucked it further down into the book so my mother wouldn't see. Definitely too emotionally charged for parental consumption. I grabbed my McDonald's garbage, pitching it into a can, walked out with Mom, and climbed into the back seat instead of the front so I could read Dan's note again without her seeing. And, yes, I was hoping that maybe he had said something else also.

"I'm gonna stretch out in the back, Mom."

"Sorry it took forever to get here," she apologized. "I'm sure that chair wasn't real comfortable to sleep in."

"I was fine," I said. Cover story in place, I opened the book and pulled out Dan's bookmark.

I don't know what to say.

Me either.

Jane, can I sit beside you and hold your hand for a while?

Please Dan. Please!

Nothing. Just the note as I remembered it, but it felt like there *had* to be more. More to say. It couldn't just end with "Please Dan, Please!" It was too perfect to end that way. My heart ached and my eyes started to tear up again as I opened the book back up—*and there it was!* He'd written across the top and bottom of the page I'd stopped on in the book.

Jane, I can't forget your eyes. When you looked at me I thought my heart would stop. But even if it did stop beating, I would still be yours.

Then down at the bottom of the same page he finished.

Please, let me be your Ethan.

You are already my Sarah. Love Dan

DanSimmons3557@hotmail.com

My first thought was *YES!* O God, *Yes Dan, YES!* And then I started crying. What the hell was I thinking!? People don't do this! I don't do this! Not like this, not *this* fast.

I read what he wrote again, and I started crying louder. I wanted to stop but couldn't help myself. He said he loved me! But how could he love me when all I did was write a stupid note and look at him and hold his hand? And how could I love him? HOW! I don't even know who Dan is and he can't even talk.

Did I love him? I asked myself.

Oh my God—I think I did!

The tears really started to flow now big time, complete with big heaving gasps.

"Jane, are you okay!?" Mom sounded alarmed. "What's wrong? Why are you crying!?"

I pulled myself together enough to fabricate something almost believable. "It's just the book, Mom," break for heaving cry. "It's just that," sniffle, "Ethan loves Sarah so much," cry, sniffle, "and it's, well, how do you know," cry, sniffle, cry, "that you love someone, I mean," sniffle. "How do you know, Mom?" Cry, heaving gasp, sniffle.

"You want to *know* how you know you're in love?" Mom asked, trying hard to figure out what I was saying through all the blubbering.

"Yes, how do you know!?" Heave, cry, sniffle.

"Honey, I'm sure it's different for everyone, but for me, when I met your father, it just felt right," Mom said, with rapidly rising concern. "Jane, are you okay? Lean up here, let me see you." She tried to turn around and look at me.

"But Mom! When did you first know that you loved Dad! When did you know!" I yelled at her as I fell into another fit of crying.

"Honey, when your father first told me that he loved me, I believed him and that was that." She put on her blinker. "I'm pulling over!" she said as she whipped into the parking lot of a gas station. She didn't bother with the door; she climbed over into the back seat with me.

I was sitting, frozen, staring dead ahead. I had tears on my face, but I wasn't crying anymore. I had the note in one hand and the book open in my lap to the page with Dan's writing. I watched as my mom took the note out of my hand and read it. Both sides. Then she read the writing in the book.

Then she looked at me, studying my face. I was calm now. I looked back at her, blinked twice and said, "Mom, I fell in love today. His name is Dan."

Jane

The Family Meeting

Mom and I sat together on my bed with my laptop open.

"I promise I won't embarrass you, honey, I just want to introduce myself first and say hello to Dan. Okay?"

I nodded and watched as she typed a short email.

```
Subject: Hello Dan
Hello Dan, this is Jane's mom. Would it be OK if I
spoke with you about Jane? My name is Mrs. Miller.
```

Mom hit Send.

"He may not even be online, Jane."

I nodded and leaned back against Mom's chest as she combed her fingers through my wet hair.

We waited.

Mom told Dad everything the second we got home. About me freaking out in the car, the note, and what Dan wrote in my book. Then she suggested that I go take a shower before dinner. I knew my parents wanted a chance to talk about me without me being in the room. When I got out, we all sat down at the kitchen table.

There was a weird "family meeting" vibe as we looked at each other across the table. Mom asked me how I was feeling and if I felt like I'd had some kind of reaction to the medication from the drug study. I told her that I felt fine and that I didn't think so. Dad asked me if I still felt like I loved Dan. I said, "Yes."

Then Dad said, "Honey, what if Dan didn't really mean it when he wrote that he loved you?" trying to reason with me.

I answered, "He did mean it." I watched as they looked at each other across the kitchen table. They both had the same scared look on their faces. It felt like I could almost see the words "Oh shit!" floating in the air over the center of the table between my parents, and I laughed. Their eyebrows shot up another inch at the same time, both with the same alarmed expression as they watched me laughing as the floating "Oh shit!" sign hanging in the air over the table become a red neon sign, flashing over and over—OH SHIT! OH SHIT! OH SHIT!— I laughed and laughed.

When I'd finally caught my breath and could look at them without cracking up, I said, "You guys are crazy." Then my parents laughed, and I laughed with them. I was glad my parents knew I loved Dan, even if it was crazy to love a guy you just met. But Dan still didn't know that I loved him; all he knew was that I had cried and that I'd asked him to hold my hand.

"Mom," I said. "I want to email Dan."

"Beep," said my inbox. I had mail. It was from Dan.

I watched as my mother opened Dan's reply to her email.

```
Hello Mrs. Miller
Is Jane OK, I've been very worried about her.
```

As soon as I read it, I started to worry. He hadn't said that he "LOVED" me; he said he was "WORRIED" about me! What did that mean? Did he think I was just sick or upset, or was he just trying not to freak mom out? My brain was going a hundred miles an hour and it felt like I had a hundred butterflies in my stomach. I closed my eyes and forced myself to calm down. Mom would never let me talk to Dan if I freaked out again. I listened to the clicking keys as she typed her reply.

"Jane honey, do you want to read it before I send it?" she asked. I opened my eyes and looked at her reply:

```
Jane is fine Dan
She's sitting here with me now, but I wanted to
meet you and speak to you for a bit before I leave
her room and give you two some privacy.
Can you tell me a little about yourself Dan?
```

I read it, said "okay", and she hit send. We waited silently for a minute or two before Dan's reply came.

```
Hard to know where to start Mrs. Miller.
My name is Dan Simmons and I'm seventeen.
I'm in the drug study also, with Jane.
```

I smiled when I read "with Jane." That sounded good to me. Like there weren't ten other kids in the study. It was just the two of us. Me and Dan. And he was "with" me.

```
I live at 6443 Shirley Rd here in town with my un-
cle Harold. I'm home schooled and a senior and I
like to read a lot. I can't talk. I was hurt when
I was little and I can't talk anymore.
What else would you like to know Mrs. Miller?
```

We both read his email, and I said, "Mom." She looked at me for a moment then typed a quick reply and hit send.

```
Dan, that's enough for a start.
It was good to meet you, I'll leave you with Jane
now.
Good night Dan.
```

Mom got off the bed, kissed my head, and walked out of my bedroom, pulling the door shut behind her. As soon as she was gone the inbox "beeped."

```
Jane, are you there?

Hello Dan, we're alone now.
```

```
Jane, did your Mom see our note?

Yes Dan, and what you wrote in my book.
We already had the 'family meeting'
My Mother and Father know everything.

RU In Trouble! RU OK!!
```

I had to think about that—trouble. *Trouble?*

Let's see. I was seventeen, and I'd fallen in love with a guy I had just met! I started to get upset. This whole thing was insane! What had I gotten myself into!? The butterflies started in my stomach again. I wanted to hear him say it! To hear him say that he LOVED ME!

My hands came away from the keyboard and covered my mouth, "No." I whispered under my hands, my heart pounding. Dan couldn't talk. I would NEVER hear Dan say he loved me. He may write it or type it and even mean it, but I would never hear the words. I was full of butterflies. All of them on fire. Burning! I felt hot and dizzy. I wanted to hold Dan's hand again! I wanted to see if it still felt "perfect." I typed my reply and hit send.

```
YES I'M IN TROUBLE!!!
NO I'M NOT OK!!!
```

It took less than a minute for Dan's reply to get back:

```
SHIT!... S!S!S!
```

I laughed out loud, right in the middle of all my flipped out worry and whatever. That neon floating SHIT sign was getting around tonight. I replied and hit send.

```
LOL :) That was EXACTLY what my rents said.

But you didn't do anything Jane! Except let me hold
your hand! I'm the psycho who asked you to be his
Vampire Bride! Your Mom probably thinks I'm an axe
murderer. Some crazy mute kid that fell in love
with the first girl to hold his hand.
I should have never said hi.
I should leave you alone.
Bye Jane.
```

```
DAN DON'T GO!!!

why

Because it's already too late
```

I've seen this already—been here before—done this—

A cold chill ran down my spine, freezing my burning butterflies as I did a double take at what I'd just typed. No. No, I'd read this! My brain kicked in as I recalled where I'd seen this before. It was in the Midnight book I was reading. When they first met, Ethan tried to leave Sarah because he thought it was too dangerous for her to be around him and he didn't want her getting hurt because of him, but Sarah told him that "*it was already too late.*" If Dan was trying to leave me because he didn't want to hurt me or get me into trouble, clearly those ships had sailed. So I'd said the same thing for the exact same reasons. But these weren't Sarah's words, they were my words.

I hit send.

For a moment I felt weirdly dizzy, like the world flipped upside down for a second. I'd never read books before like I was doing now, so I didn't know if it was normal to experience "Book Deja Vu" or if it was just me. Seeing little parts of the book you're reading show up in your real life because your head was so filled with it. It was weird. Like I was living in my own fairy tale.

My inbox "beeped."

```
Sarah?
```

O God! He knew! HE KNEW! He must have read the Midnight books. And he was asking if "I" was his "Sarah!" Had he felt it too? Had his world just flipped upside down? Well if it hadn't, it was about to. I replied to his question and hit send.

```
I'm here my Love.
```

"Honey, are you okay?" Mom called from the other side of my door and I jumped, my hands covering the screen!

"I'm good!" I called back, my voice a startled squeak. I didn't sound good! I couldn't let her see this!

"I'll be right out!" I called, hoping that would keep her on the other side of the door for a few more minutes as I typed a quick message for Dan.

```
Dan, I have to go, she's coming!
I'll be at the Dr.'s at 11:30 tomorrow, B there!
I need to see you - I Love You!
I have to go - Jane
```

I hit send, turned my laptop off as quickly as I could, then ran to the mirror in my room and "fixed" myself a little before I went out. Mom and Dad were already sitting at the table when I came in, but I stopped beside my chair and stood there, staring dumbly at the red and gold take-out boxes. They'd ordered out. Thai Garden. But today was Monday, and we never ordered out on weekdays, only on Saturday or Sunday to give Mom a break from cooking.

I slipped into my chair at the kitchen table and stared down at my Pad Thai Tofu. I nodded. It made sense. If the world had flipped upside down, all kinds of weird shit would be happening. "Saturdays" sliding into "Mondays." Hell, I wouldn't be too surprised if I looked out the window and saw flying pigs! I laughed, picked up a fork, and focused on my Pad Thai.

"So," Dad said. I looked up at him. "How'd it go with Dan?" he asked cautiously.

Mom and Dad were both staring at me, waiting for my answer. They weren't eating, so I put down my fork and stared back. "It went great." They kept staring—no reaching for forks. I added, "Dan was worried that he'd gotten me into trouble."

They looked at each other, then back at me. This wasn't what they were wanting to hear. They wanted to know if Dan had said that he loved me and if I still felt like I loved Dan.

"And?" Mom urged gently.

"He's worried you think he's an axe murderer," I supplied cheerfully. Still no fork action. Dual stare continued.

"And?" Dad said. He knew I was stalling, but I kept at it. They were mining for the goods on the "L" word.

"I told Dan that you read his note and what he wrote in my book. I told him you knew everything." I picked up my fork and quickly stabbed a piece of tofu and popped it into my mouth and started chewing. I kept my eyes on my food. Just me and some tofu, nothing to see here.

"Yes, but honey! What happened!?" Mom was getting worked up; the stalling was getting to her. "Are you two," she searched for the right words, "*going together* now? Are you going to see each other again?"

She stopped and looked to Dad, like it was his turn to work on me, but he shook his head, no help there.

"You know you don't have to tell us if you don't want to. But please tell us, Jane! What's happened? You seem—happy." And Mom looked worried.

"Are you sure you want me to keep telling you everything?" I answered directly. She looked guilty about asking and Dad was about to step in and say something, but I rushed on. "I like you guys knowing what's going on inside me, but stop thinking this is just some reaction to the medicine."

Mom didn't look convinced, which finally pushed my buttons and I snapped at her, "If I had met Dan a month ago and had freaked out in the car about falling in love, we wouldn't be having tofu on Monday!" I stabbed another piece of tofu and held it up in front of me as "Exhibit A" of parental freak out and stared at them through slit eyes, waving my tofu wand as I ranted. "I want to tell you! And I will! If you can be!—be!—" I spluttered. I didn't want to say "cool" but I didn't know what *to* say, so I shoved Exhibit A into my mouth and glared at my parents while I punished the tofu.

"Honey, you can tell us. We'll be good," Mom promised. Dad nodded.

I swallowed and nodded too and said, "Okay."

They waited patiently as I took a long drink of my glass of water, said "yuck," and made a face.

Dad laughed, "Four more days without energy drinks or Dew Code Red. If you're having a drug reaction, it's probably caffeine withdrawal." We all laughed. I relaxed a little and looked at my parents; I was glad they would know.

"I love him." I just said it. No surprise there.

They nodded.

"And yes, Dan loves me too."

Nods again.

"We didn't get to talk long."

Mom cringed. "Sorry—the Thai food came—and I was worried. I should have given you some more time to talk."

"It's okay, Mom," I said and smiled at her. "We had a good talk."

Nods again.

"He's meeting me tomorrow at the doctor's office at 11:30. So you can both meet my Dan." That got a reaction.

"I'll arrange an extended lunch," Dad said. "I want to meet 'your' Dan too." He smiled at me.

"Okay. Good. I want you to meet him, but be nice, he's shy."

I started eating. They waited a minute, then Dad started in on his cold Thai food and after another silent minute Mom did too. We finished eating and Mom and I went into the living room, grabbed our books, and sat on the couch together while Dad cleaned the kitchen, just as we'd done for the past five evenings. Mom wasn't really reading yet, she was watching me, but that was okay. She could look all she wanted. I didn't have anything to hide. For the life of me

I didn't know how those kids who hid everything from their parents survived it. Or why they'd want to.

I opened my book. The bookmark note from Dan was still there. Mom had put it back in my book. I took it out and read it again and carefully put the note away and then looked at the page Dan had written on in my book.

Jane, I can't forget your eyes. When you looked at me I thought my heart would stop. But even if it did stop beating, I would still be yours.

Please, let me be your Ethan.
You are already my Sarah. Love Dan
DanSimmons3557@hotmail.com

Mom spoke from her side of the couch, "It's all very romantic." Still watching me, she added, "It's like a story in a book. I just hope it has a happy ending."

I could tell she was a little better. Still worried, but better. I leaned back with my book and answered her. "You'll have to finish the books to find out, Mom, remember, I'm Sarah," I teased. Mom threw a couch pillow at me and I laughed and threw it back.

I started reading. In the book Sarah and her vampire had already gotten married. It was their honeymoon night and things were about to get hot! My eyes slid across the page to Dan's writing. "Please, let me be your Ethan." I practiced as I read the book, replacing Ethan's name with "Dan" as I read, and "Sarah" to "Jane."

I hadn't finished one page before I knew Dr. Burgis was right! The best way to read a book was to imagine yourself inside the book, and now that I had Dan as my Ethan, my imagination seemed to have kicked into overdrive. The pictures in my head were so colorful and vivid. This felt more real than any dream I'd ever had before.

I turned away from my mother so she couldn't see my face. I didn't know how red it was, but I was getting to know Dan pretty well—extremely well! Oh my—Ohh my, oh my!

"Mom, I think I'll read in my room tonight if that's okay," I said as I got up and headed to my room. I had to get off this couch before I caught on fire!

"Okay, honey," Mom said, disappointed I was spoiling our new mother/daughter bonding. I didn't want to make her sad, but I SOOO needed some privacy!

"Jane, your father turned off the wifi," Mom called after me as I retreated, "so you won't be able to email anymore tonight. Just read your book, okay?"

No arguments there. "Okay, Mom, good night!"

I headed for the privacy of my bedroom and my honeymoon with Dan.

Sky Lee Han

The First Blue Pill

Sky looked at the security bars on the window as Emelia, her maid, made up the bed.

"It's okay, Miss Sky," Emelia said as she worked. "You will be back in your beautiful room soon. It's just for a week." She snapped the sheets into place and kept talking, "And you know your mother is not being mean. This was the only way the doctor would let you into that drug study."

Emelia was always trying to convince her that her mother was "nice," "kind," and "loving" and that she was lucky to have a mother who cared so much about her. Emelia was nothing but a hired thug. Her mother had fired Merisol, her last maid, when she'd overheard her comforting Sky after one of her tantrums. Merisol thought that they were alone in Sky's room, but her mother had installed a listening device. She'd heard every word.

"No, she shouldn't have said that to you—"

"Yes, she was horrible tonight—"

"No, other mothers don't yell at their kids like that. Your mother is just so strung out on pills that she doesn't know what she's saying to you."

And that was the end of Merisol. If there was one thing her mother wouldn't tolerate, it was not being with "THE PLAN." And part of that plan was Sky "loving" her mother. And part of Emelia's job was getting Sky with "THE PLAN."

"No, she's just had a bad day—"

"Yes, but you deserved it, what were you thinking—"

"No, you got it good, you don't know what it's like out there, it's horrible—"

Emelia went at it with the same gusto as she did scrubbing the floors or taking out the trash. Sky hated her. Sky hated her mother. Sky hated her father. Sky hated her life. She wished she could just fly away.

"I need to go outside for some fresh air, Emelia," Sky said.

"Oh no." Emelia gave her a level look. "You know da rules. You have to take Nathan with you if you want to go outside. And he is driving your father to de airport, so you must stay here." Emelia stopped what she was doing and gave Sky a disapproving look and then went off on her, her speed and accent making it difficult to follow exactly what she was saying, "We ares jus looking out for you, Miss Sky! While you are on dis medicine we have to be ehxtra careful. The doctor says that you might hurt yourself. We have to keep a close eye on you anyway, but while you taking dese pills we must be ehxtra careful. The doctor said de pills would make you a little crazy, and you were already a little crazy, so that means for the next few days you are a lot of crazy! So no! No, no, no. You stay here! In de room."

Emelia turned back to the bed and quickly finished it. She grabbed the laundry basket and went to the door.

"If Nathan ghets back soon, I will send him up for you."

Giving the room and Sky one final looking over she said, "Good night, Miss Sky" and left.

Sky listened as she locked the door. She walked to the barred windows and looked through, out at the sky. The August sun had just set, slipping behind the horizon. Dark orange and purple clouds stood over the spot where the sun had died like the last mourners at a funeral. She stood there and watched as the island of color faded out. Even when she was little, she had loved the sky. She would look at the clouds and daydream about flying up to touch them with her hand. One day when she was nine she had run out after a fight with her mother and had jumped off the second story balcony. She'd wanted to fly away from all the yelling and fighting. She ended up with a broken arm, broken ribs, more pills, less freedom, and more yelling.

For Sky, the best part of being in the drug study was being off all her drugs for the first time since she was seven years old. Dr. Burgis made her parents take her off absolutely EVERYTHING so she could take the Derm pill. No more crazy pills in the morning and at lunch and no more Tryptamine and Ambien-5 at night before she went to bed. She hated those most of all. When Sky had told her psychiatrist about her flying dreams, he had insisted she start taking them. No more beautiful dreams of flying. Her mother didn't think LIFE could be sustained without the use of pills, but Sky hated taking them. She'd been off the pills for days now, but her flying dreams hadn't returned.

"Maybe tonight," Sky said as she got dressed for bed and climbed in.

The Derm pill had made her sleepy, but being off all the meds was like walking out of the clouds; even drowsy she felt more awake than she had in forever. Everything was new and *different*. She didn't know what to expect next. She settled herself into the bed and lay there with her eyes closed and thought about what would happen once the drug study was over—

Her mother or Emelia would come back into her room with a cup full of pills for her to take.

It made her want to run away. Other kids did it and so could she! She could run away and work at—at—a McDonald's! And get a roommate! Some girlfriend who worked at the McDonald's too. A real friend, someone who didn't work for her mother. They could go to movies together. Other kids did it. She would be eighteen in ten months. The picture Sky tried to hold in her head melted away. Her mother had told her many times that if she ever ran away she would have her committed to an institution. That she wasn't safe on her own.

If she couldn't run away, maybe she could fly away. Maybe she could fly.

Sky Lee

Time to Start Dreaming

I walked out onto my balcony, looked up at the beautiful summer sky, and raised my arms over my head. I felt myself become lighter. My feet left the ground as I floated up, slowly rising into the air. I was flying again! I was dreaming again!

I bumped into something flat. The vision of sky and clouds wavered. Something was pressing against my face. I tried to reach up but there was something flat lying on top of me.

Was I still asleep? Still dreaming?

I opened my eyes and tried to see in the dark. Was I lying on the floor? Had I fallen out of the bed? It wasn't carpet. I looked at the swirl pattern, trying to focus in the dim light. Is that the ceiling? I looked behind me and my eyes went wide. I was on the ceiling nine feet above my bed.

I screamed, and then I fell. I landed half on the bed and half off. My legs hit the bed but my head hit the dresser, then I fell to the floor.

It hurt.

"Sky! Sky!" Someone was shaking me.

"Ugh." I tried to open my eyes.

"Sky, what did you do! Did you jump off the bed!?" It was my mother and she was angry.

"I—I don't know," I answered but kept my eyes closed. The bright lights in the room were on and were hurting my eyes.

"Is she all right!?" Emelia's voice. "Should I call 911?"

"Shut up, Emelia!"

My mother's hands searched all over my head, neck, and arms looking for anything broken. I kept my eyes closed and waited. She reached down and started to run her hand down my calf and I cried out "Ooouch!" Her hands stopped and she pulled down my sweats to look at my leg. I squeezed my eyes shut as she pushed and prodded and checked my leg. "It doesn't seem broken, just a nasty bruise, but we'll still need x-rays." She pulled my sweats back up. "Emelia, come here and help me get her back into the bed."

I kept my eyes closed as they lifted me into bed.

"Go tell Nathan to bring the Hummer around front and then come up here. We'll take her to the 24-hour Medic Center for some x-rays to make sure she didn't get a concussion and to check the leg."

"Sky. Open your eyes, honey."

I shook my head no. "Please," I said, "just let me go back to sleep. I'm okay now." I kept my eyes closed.

"Sky, open your damn eyes!" she yelled.

I blinked in the bright light as I obeyed and opened my eyes. She looked into first one eye and then the other and seemed satisfied.

"So what happened?" she asked me.

"I fell out of the bed," I said. I wasn't about to tell her "*I flew out of bed.*" That would be crazy.

"Really." She breathed out. "You don't remember, do you?"

"No." I lied. I did remember.

"It's okay. This is not your fault, Sky. You're just having a hard time being off all your pills. Did you have any dreams? Were you dreaming again? Did you jump off the bed?"

"I don't remember any dreams. I just remember hitting my head and it hurt," I lied again.

"You'll have to get some x-rays tonight. We can't go to the hospital because Dr. Burgis might find out and kick you out of the study, and we can't have that, so we'll go to the 24-hour clinic. Can you stand up?"

I sat up and saw stars and lights for a second as my head throbbed. I held my head in my hands to keep it from throbbing. I hadn't cut myself, but I had a huge lump on the back of my head. Slowly, I swung my legs off the side of the bed, and with my mother's help I was able to stand. My leg hurt but it didn't feel broken. Nathan and Emelia came in and helped me down the stairs and into the back seat of the Hummer.

We went to the clinic. I was fine. No broken leg or skull fractures. The doctors at the Medic Center wanted to give me pain pills but my mother wouldn't let them. She didn't want it to react to the Derm pill and she didn't want the doctor's daily drug tests to show that I'd had something other than the Derm pill.

When I got back home, my mother walked me back to the bedroom. I stopped at the doorway and stared at the room. The entire room was empty. Every piece of furniture was gone except the bed, and the bed had been moved away from the walls and put in the center of the room. They'd even taken off the headboard and footboard so it looked like a giant mattress just sitting on the floor. Scattered all around the bed were pillows, covering the floor. My mother took me by the arm and led me to the bed.

"I know this looks a little extreme, Sky, but we can't have you hurting yourself."

"No," I said. "I like it." If I did fly again, I would need a safe place to land. I smiled for the first time that night.

My mother looked at me like I was crazy and my smile faded.

"It's okay, honey. It's not your fault. It's just being off your medicine. Once this Derm drug is through and we've got your face fixed, we'll get you right back on your pills. You'll feel fine again, don't you worry," my mother said as she laid me down in the bed.

"Good night, honey. Go back to sleep." She left. I heard her lock the door.

I fell back into my bed and stared up at the ceiling. Had I dreamed it? I remembered the roughness of the ceiling against my face and the feel of the pattern in the drywall as I ran my hand over it. I had four more days before my mother made me start all the drugs so I couldn't dream again. I closed my eyes.

I had four more days.

Four more days to fly.

Black Rain

Only Black

"Vrrrrrr, Vrrrrr, Vrrrrr." Rain reached for her phone as it vibrated somewhere beside her pillow in the dark. She looked at the time, 11:05 PM, and quietly started getting dressed. She'd been so wiped out by the Derm drugs that she'd gone to bed right after dinner. She still couldn't believe that she'd gotten in. She hadn't planned on making it. Actually, she'd planned on not making it and even tried to sabotage herself with her unsparingly truthful answers to all the doctor's personal and prying questions.

Rain didn't care about herself and how she looked, but she did want Ryan to get in. If she washed out, that would be better for him. One less teen to choose from had to help, but somehow they both got in and today had been their first day on the Derm pill. They were supposed to stay indoors and locked down for the next five days, but she hadn't promised any such thing. She'd sat there, staring ahead at nothing as her mother and father promised for her. But then, they were used to her being "absent" and still present at times.

Rain focused on not making a sound as she held her fancy black shoes in her hand and light stepped barefoot through the house. Quietly, she opened the back door of the trailer. She'd taped over the security sensor before going to bed so there was no annoying, "beep beep beep" to give her away.

A warm, tropical wind combed through the trees and whipped her long black hair around her shoulders as she walked through the tiny patch of grass in their front yard that her mother had managed to coax out of the sandy soil. The night air held that "charged static" feel of electricity that always comes before a good Florida storm. She hurried along, running barefoot down the rough paved street of the trailer park. If it did start to rain she didn't want to get caught in it.

Her fancy black dress blended into the night. Black. Rain always wore black. She started wearing nothing but black almost two years ago. Her parents arrived home one afternoon to find all of her clothes, except the black, bagged up and set outside with the trash. They begged her to tell them "why" she wanted to wear black, but Rain had refused to tell.

The next day she stopped talking altogether or doing anything at all. After a few frightening weeks of being a silent, staring shadow, she started speaking again, but she wasn't the same happy outgoing girl she'd been before. Rain stopped going to school or doing anything at church and seemed content to simply exist, but only on her terms. She went to church with her family, but she didn't do anything other than sit quietly in the back row till it was time to go.

One Monday morning Rain woke to find that all of her black clothes were missing. Her Mother had snuck into her room during the night and had taken everything black, leaving her with clothes that were her "old" favorite color, bright yellow. Rain responded with passive resistance. No fussing or whining, she just slipped off the black t-shirt and panties that she'd slept in and went to breakfast without a stitch. That did it.

Rain didn't try to wear black leather minis or halters; that would have caused a problem with her parents and brought attention she didn't want. She dressed nice, but she always wore black.

Her parents and her brother hated it, but soon after she started talking again, she started hanging out with other teens in the trailer park who wore black. Punks, grunge kids, goth kids—and the three trailer park witches. Rain liked the idea of becoming a witch; it fit her black mood perfectly, and she had asked to join them.

Mary Hillman, a pretty blonde, attached herself to Rain and became her best friend. Mary was her perfect opposite: fun, bubbly, air headed, outgoing, and happy. She didn't take being a witch too seriously; she enjoyed the "girl togetherness" more than anything. Bethany Kemp, thirteen with olive skin and dyed black hair, was a young goth girl who came from a horrible home. Her mother was a druggie and worse. Bethany was constantly wanting to do dark spells and hurt people, but Kendal wouldn't let her. Kendal was twenty-six and lived in the trailer park with her boyfriend Steve. She'd been a witch since she was fourteen and was teaching the girls about Wicca and how to be witches.

On Lammas night one year ago, Kendal had each of the three girls chose a new "Witch Name" to be called by, and the four girls started their coven. Rain had chosen the name "Black Rain." Mary chose to be called "Mary Fae" because she loved fairies. Bethany wanted something scary and serious sounding, so she chose "Bethany Grave" as her witch name. Kendal kept the same name she'd had since she was fourteen, "Kendal Flame." They called the corners and performed Wiccan rituals and sat on the floor of Kendal's trailer that night and made a coven cloth to celebrate the start of their coven, StarNight.

Over the past year Rain spent as much time as she could with Kendal and her "sisters." Learning how to be a witch and because being with them was easier than being with her family. Her sisters accepted how she was easily whereas her family worried when she fell into one of her black moods. She still went to church with them three times a week, but they didn't make her do anything other than go. They were afraid she would move out or worse if they pressured her, and they were right. Rain loved her family, especially her twin brother Ryan, so she tried not to throw her witch stuff in their faces. She tried to make them happy. She tried.

According to Kendal, it took a year to be a real witch, and tonight the year was full. It was Lammas again, the first Monday night in August 2016. Their coven gathered weekly at Kendal's trailer or in the small stand of woods there in the park by the retention pond, but tonight was special, and they were going somewhere special.

Kendal was also a part of another coven called RaV Heim. It was a large coven of witches from all over that came together at times like Lammas to celebrate the Wiccan high day together. Kendal wanted the girls to present themselves before RaV Heim as new witches. She also wanted them to meet some other decent witches just in case she ever left the trailer park. She was thinking seriously of leaving her boyfriend and was worried that the girls would get themselves into trouble on their own. There were so many sickos out there, it was easy to get hurt. Or tricked.

Black Rain

Black Is My Color

I kept to the shadows and shrubbery at the side of the road as I passed the big building where the community mailboxes, pool, and wash room were located. Blue Palms was nice as far as trailer parks go. Most of the trailers were well kept, and the park was clean. There was even a guard gate at the front where one of the park retirees, Mr. Tally, would sit at night and keep an eye on the comings and goings, just like the fancy country club subdivisions. He even had an old golf cart and would ride through the park at night looking for teens to torture. It wasn't too hard to get away from a 72-year-old man in a golf cart that went only five MPH, but he knew everyone in the park by sight and would let our parents know if he spotted us out after ten PM. I listened carefully for the sickly whine of the old cart's engine as I walked toward Kendal's trailer on lot 434.

They were already in the car waiting for me.

"Yay!" Mary cheered and opened the back door of Kendal's Corolla for me to get in.

"I knew you'd be able to sneak out," she said as she hugged me. Bethany was already in the front seat, but Kendal was still inside the trailer, yelling at Steve.

"What's up?" I asked Mary as I looked at the trailer.

"Oh, Steve is pissed at Kendal. He wanted to go out tonight and she told him no, that she had 'witch stuff' to do." Even Mary's bubbly mood went chilly as we sat in the dark car and silently listened to the argument inside the trailer as it grew louder and louder and then went silent.

"I hope we're still going," Bethany said sadly.

We waited.

In some ways, the silence was worse than the yelling.

We didn't talk about it. We waited. Fifteen minutes later, the trailer door opened and Kendal came out, still adjusting her own fancy evening gown as she opened the car door, tossed Bethany her makeup bag, and slipped behind the wheel.

"I'm sorry. We're gonna be a little late, girls," she said as she started the car and began to back out.

"We're just glad we're still going," Bethany said for all of us.

"Steve's just bein' a jealous shit, I told him about tonight months ago," Kendal replied, then said, "Gate."

Mary and I slid down onto the floorboard and pulled an old comforter over us as we pulled up to the guard gate. Bethany stayed in the front seat and fiddled with the radio. She didn't need to hide. Her home situation was horrible and she spent most of her time at Kendal's anyway. Mr. Tally just took a quick glance out of the window of the shed and hit the button for the gate, and we pulled out of Blue Palm's Trailer Park and into the night.

"So, are you leaving us?" Bethany asked forlornly.

"I don't think so," Kendal said. "Steve is fine with us getting together at the trailer, but he loses it when I go to RaV Heim. He thinks I'm out hooking up with guys or doing god knows what with god knows how many."

"That's what his 'fit' was about?" I asked.

"The only reason he's letting me go tonight is because you girls are with me. He thinks I'll be too busy babysitting to get into any trouble." Kendal's brows bunched up. "I might have to bring you girls with me if I ever want to go to RaV Heim again, so I hope you have a good time tonight."

Mary laughed, "Wow, that would make us, like, *your* chaperones!"

"That's *exactly* what Steve's thinking," Kendal confirmed with a put upon frown, "and I'm sure he'll be asking you if I was talking to any guys."

"What do we tell him if you do talk to a guy?" Bethany asked, and Mary answered for Kendal.

"We LIE like a witch!" We all laughed because real witches weren't supposed to lie. And Steve knew that too. He knew it and exploited it. He'd been in a few bad relationships where he'd been lied to, and the fact that Kendal never lied was a major plus to him. But for a guy as jealous as Steve, sometimes what he needed more than anything in the whole wide world was an ego boosting white lie, and Kendal couldn't give him that.

"Seriously though, girls, I want you to stay close to me all night. Never leave the room I'm in. As long as I'm there you'll be fine, so stay close." She reached into her purse and pulled out four henna tattoos, handing one to Bethany and passing two back to us in the back seat. "I had these made a few months ago and saved them for tonight. I thought it would be nice if we all matched. I've got one too." She held up her own sticker.

It was a sickle moon surrounded by four stars. Two stars were red, one was green, and one was black. It was perfect.

"They're beautiful, Kendal, but where should we wear them?" Mary asked.

"Well, it's your choice, but the best place would be the forehead." She quickly added, "But we could also do the top of the right hand."

It was quiet as we thought about it. Bethany spoke first.

"Rain can't, her parents would kill her."

"No," I said. "It's up to Mary. I'm good with the forehead."

Mary said, "It only lasts a few days anyway, so let's do it. I mean, we've been waiting on this night all year long so why not go all out?" She held her square henna sheet to her forehead and said, "Mark me baby!" and laughed.

Kendal cautioned, "Rain, are you sure this won't get you into more trouble than it's worth? We can always go with the top of the hand. This isn't something you can hide, and if they take you to church on Wednesday it will still be there."

"No, I need this. It's time to change," I said and meant it.

"Why are there two red stars, one black one, and one green one?" asked Bethany as she studied the sticker.

"That's the four of us," Kendal answered, "our witch colors."

"Am I the black star?" Bethany asked, hopeful and doubtful at the same time as she peered between the seats and looked back at me.

"No, you're red like me." Kendal looked over at Bethany who was already pouting. "You think you're black, but you're not. You're red, like me." Looking out at the traffic again, she added, "And if I had a daughter, I would want her to be red, just like me."

Bethany was quiet after that.

"But why am I green!" Mary whined. "I don't even like green!" We all laughed and Kendal said, "Mary, everyone here knows your color but you." We talked about other things and worked on the stickers and our hair and makeup the rest of the way there. Nobody said a word about my black star. Black was my color, and everyone knew it.

The house on the river was huge. It wasn't a house at all; it was an enormous white mansion, and it was *crowded*. There was a large circular drive up front, and cars were parked all over the front lawn. Expensive cars. There were three guys in tuxedos providing valet service at the circular drive. We stopped in front of the house and Kendal gave one of the guys her keys, and our little group gathered together in front of the mansion's huge double glass doors.

"Damn, Kendal!" Mary whispered fiercely. "I'm glad you had us dress up, but I still feel like a hobo." She was looking at the fancy glass doors with dismay.

"Sisters, come here," Kendal called and we gathered in a tight circle, holding hands together and looking at her.

"Look at each other," she ordered, and we did. Here under the bright entry-way lights of the porch we could actually see ourselves. We looked amazing! Our dresses, our hair, and even the makeup we had hastily put on in the car looked great, but the tattoos were simply stunning. We looked like witches! We looked powerful. And more importantly, we felt powerful!

We stood there in our private little circle and spoke in turns as we held hands and asked a blessing for our naming. We ignored other arriving guests who stepped around us and filed past, walking through the glass doors. Once we broke our circle, Kendal gave us a few final words of preparation.

"The presenting ceremony they use is extremely simple. There are so many different kinds of witches, and they don't want to exclude or offend anyone, so they've made the presentation very basic. You remember the words for the Wiccan Rede?" she asked us.

"Yes," we answered.

When we presented ourselves, we were to commit ourselves to the core Wiccan beliefs. The Rede held the basic rules that most witches lived by, like the threefold law, "what you send out returns threefold."

"If you forget or change it some, don't worry. I'm sure we'll hear a lot of variations tonight anyway. You all brought your offerings?" she asked. We were all supposed to bring something. It didn't have to be something expensive, but it did have to be personal. Something that said who you were or what you have been through.

"Yes," we all answered again.

"Did you remember to leave your cell phones in the car?" Kendal asked, as she gave us a look. Cell phones were one of her pet peeves.

"Yes," we all answered and laughed.

"Then it's time." Kendal smiled. "Let's go show them coven StarNight, and three new, powerful witches!"

We hugged quickly and turned and walked through the glass doors.

We stood in the foyer and looked out at the huge room beyond with its gleaming white marble floors, high soaring ceiling, and elegantly dressed men and women, all here at half past midnight. Chairs and couches were positioned around the sides of the enormous room, creating little islands of chatting seated people around those who choose to stand in the open middle of the room and socialize. Somewhere violins played, and waiters in white wove in and out among the guests so gracefully, they almost seemed to dance with the music while they proffered their trays of appetizers or drinks. The scene was fantastic and magical and very different from anything I'd ever seen or imagined being real outside of a movie. A tall, older gentleman with long, silver gray hair stepped forward to greet us in the foyer. He wore a warm and welcoming smile.

"Good evening, ladies. I am Cornelius Amen Hale, and I am the Conductor for this night's gathering." He bowed slightly and went on, "May I introduce you to the room and do you have any business to declare for Lammas?" He quickly produced a clipboard and a pen to write down our names and information.

We girls stood straight backed and silent as Kendal answered, "I am Kendal Flame. These are," she presented each of us in turn, "Mary Fae, Bethany Grave, and Black Rain. We are Coven StarNight."

"Wonderful!" He smiled at us. "And do you have any business for tonight, Kendal Flame?" He held his pen ready over the clipboard.

"All three have reached their year and are to be presented," Kendal said proudly.

"Then we will have nine new witches tonight, excellent. StarNight will present last." He made a quick note and handed it to a nearby attendant who darted away with it. "Now may I present you ladies to the room?" he asked and held out his arm for Kendal to take just like in the old movies.

We followed as Cornelius led us out into the center of the huge room. In one corner was a black pedestal with two beautiful ladies dressed like Greek statues and playing violins. Upon seeing Cornelius step into the center of the room with us, they stopped playing, and in the silence the other conversations ceased and all eyes in the hall turned to stare at us as Cornelius announced us to the room.

"May I present Kendal Flame and her coven StarNight."

Everyone was looking at the tattoos. We looked back at a sea of impressed faces as they bowed their heads or raised glasses in welcome, and the three of us, as Kendal had taught us, bowed our heads for a count of three before looking up again. Everyone was still frozen, looking at us until the violins started playing in the background, and like magic, everyone in the room could move again.

After being introduced to the room Kendal led us to a nearby bar to get us something to drink, which was good because I was parched. She handed a glass of wine to Bethany. "Sip it, it's the only drink you'll have tonight." Bethany nodded and carefully took the beautiful crystal glass in her hand. Kendal handed Mary a glass and turned to me. "Would you like a glass, Black Rain?" She sounded very formal, which was understandable. We all felt like we were at Cinderella's ball.

"I'm thirsty, but I can drink only water for the next five days," I told her. She knew about the drug study and some of the restrictions. She turned to the bartender and returned with a crystal wineglass filled with water which she handed to me.

"We came late, so we're not going to have much time to meet and mingle before they start, but I want to introduce you to a few people you should know." She looked around the room, "Ah! There's Cathryn, let's go."

She grabbed herself a glass and led us to a tall blonde woman, probably in her late forties or early fifties but still beautiful. She was wearing an elegant gray dress that showed off the amazing tattoos on her arms. A vine ran down each of her arms ending in a circle wrapped around her wrists.

"Cathryn, happy Lammas," said Kendal, taking her hand and kissing it as if she were royalty, she introduced each of us. We didn't talk to Cathryn long, some quick, polite conversation and we were off to another witch. Kendal led us away from some witches who walked toward us and toward her friends. Occasionally she would even point someone out and say, "Stay away," from her or him as we walked the room.

After just fifteen minutes Cornelius stepped into the center of the hall and the music stopped again. "My friends, it is time for the Presentations. Please come this way."

He left toward the rear and we all followed him into another huge room. On one side of the room was a beautiful pentagram mosaic made right into the floor with hundreds of colorful pieces of tile. You could tell by a circular stain on the floor that it was usually covered by a large circular rug. Placed in the center of the circular mosaic was a small, ornate offering table. Around the circle were thirteen large fancy candles: each one had its own unique stand and each candle was a different color. These large candles were not lit, but there were dozens and dozens of other smaller candles around the circle that were. The high ceiling above the pentagram was domed and painted like the night sky and the only light in the room was coming from the candles. It was frighteningly beautiful. Everyone was gathering around the circle mosaic as Kendal led us toward the other "new" witches who were gathering in a group beside Cornelius.

"You are last, so you three will be able to watch six others go first. Mary, you first. Then Bethany. Rain, you will go last." She gave each of us a final appraising look and nodded, leaving us in line with the other new witches as she went to find a place around the circle with the others.

People were still coming into the room, and a quiet murmur of conversation still filled the hall as they entered and settled in to watch. An old lady wearing a simple green robe was standing right beside us. Mary asked her, "Why are the big candles not lit?" pointing to the closest large ornate candle, a fancy green one with runes and vines and flowers running up and down the length of it.

The old lady said, "When you name yourself a witch, sometimes one of the candles will light all by itself." She looked at us and eyed our tattooed foreheads and added, "If you are born a powerful witch. And each of these candles tells us something different about the witch who lights it." She pointed at a large white candle and said, "White is for Magic." Then she pointed at a beautiful blue candle and said, "This Blue candle is for Dreams—and nightmares," she said with a wicked, but not unfriendly, smile.

On the far side of the circle was an ugly black candle with human skulls imbedded in the wax, peeking out here and there up its six foot length. It was horrifying, and I could not look away from it as I asked the old woman, "What is the black candle with the skulls?"

She looked at me and said in a motherly reassuring voice, "Oh, honey, don't let that thing scare you." She leaned close to us, as if to impart a secret, and whispered, "That one doesn't even have a wick! It can't light."

But I still couldn't take my eyes off it and asked, "But what is it, what does it mean?"

"That is the Murderer's Candle and can only be lit by a Black Witch who has innocent blood on her hands. Don't worry yourself, child. That candle is over four hundred years old and nobody has ever lit it, and I doubt you've brought the price of blood as your offering. Twenty pieces of silver is hard to come by these days."

Rain's hand reached to the small pocket on the inside of her dress and drew out her offering. She examined it. It was a torn piece of paper with the name "Brendon Lane Bryant" written on it. She'd wanted to name him before the doctor came in. To send him away without even a name seemed worse than anything imaginable. Frantically she'd taken one of the papers in her hand, torn off the bottom, flipped it over and wrote. A name was all she could give him. She'd never looked at the other side. Her hand was shaking as she turned the piece of paper over, and there, right at the bottom corner you could read "total fee for services $651.42."

She had the price of innocent blood.

"Malise Darden of Coven Kitting Stone! Present yourself," Cornelius called out and a young boy, maybe thirteen, stepped into the circle. Rain didn't see him. She didn't watch anything he did or hear anything he said; she looked past him to the black candle on the far side of the circle. *Everyone will know. Everyone will know* echoed over and over in her mind. Rain didn't watch the other new witches or even Mary and Bethany go forward and present themselves; she couldn't take her eyes from the Murderer's Candle. Her candle. She didn't look away until Cornelius called, "Black Rain of Coven StarNight, present yourself!"

The old woman beside her said, "Come on, dearie, it's time."

Rain looked at the empty circle and at the waiting faces around the circle with dread. They would know! She looked back at the old lady and cried, "But they will know!" From behind her she felt hands gently urging her forward, toward the circle of candlelight, and she started to cry. Cornelius called again, "Black Rain of Coven StarNight, come now and present yourself!"

Rain was crying as she stepped forward. She could feel tears streaming down her face as she walked to the center of the circle. She hadn't cried for eighteen months and now she was crying. Kendal, Bethany, and Mary had never seen her shed a tear. But now she was crying. She heard Mary's worried whisper from somewhere outside the circle say, "She's crying!" Rain was still holding the piece of paper in her hands as she walked forward with small shuffling steps until she stood in the center of the circle.

Twenty one months ago she'd gotten pregnant. The boy begged, cried, and pleaded, but when she kept putting off doing what he wanted, he'd called her a whore and worse. He gave her the money and carried her to the clinic for the abortion. And that was the day she killed Brendon and the girl she had been. That was the day she started wearing black.

Rain stood there and looked out at the faces around the circle. She wiped her eyes with the piece of paper in her hand then stepped up to the offering table. She'd hidden her darkness, her lies, and her murder from everyone. Her parents, her brother, her friends at school and church. Rain felt the presence of the black candle behind her; it seemed to whisper over her shoulder, "*They will know.*"

A cold chill shot down her spine and she cried out in defiance, "I will not *lie!*" Her world shrank to what was inside the circle. Worried voices murmured from beyond the dotted wall of wavering light. Rain turned and looked at the Murderer's Candle. Faint, almost transparent wisps of smoke were rising from the top.

"I cannot hide, and I cannot lie," she said, her voice resigned. She looked out at the blurry sea of faces beyond the ring of light and directed her next words to them, "And if you hate me for what I am, so mote it be!" She slammed her piece of paper onto the offering table.

There was a "Woosh!" and then a "POP!" as the Murderer's Candle lit with a sound like a burst paper bag.

People screamed as grim blue flames danced atop the ugly black candle. For a while it was chaos outside the circle as some people tried to get out while at the same time others crowded in to see. Rain could hear them talking around her. Individual words floating out of the noise like knives thrown from the dark:

"Black Witch!"

"Murderer!"

"Innocent Blood!"

Rain stood silently in the center of the circle as Cornelius went about the business of restoring order. Everyone's gaze bounced from her then back to the wicked blue flames that were consuming the Murderer's Candle. After a few minutes it was quiet once again, and Rain looked at the hundred and eighty or ninety people still gathered around the circle. She'd told. They all knew. Rain could see Kendal, Bethany, and Mary in the circle of faces. They were crying.

What will they think of me now? she thought numbly.

There was no more hiding. She took one deep breath and whispered to herself, "I am what I am." Rain looked down at her black dress—black was her color. She reached up to her forehead and touched the tattoo, her black star. She looked back at the black candle and then up at the painted night sky ceiling and said out loud to the room, "I am a Black Witch. I am a Black Witch. I am a Black Witch."

The Murderer's Candle had become an inferno and was melting horribly. It chose that exact moment to give way at the base and toppled to the floor with a crash, spilling black wax and sending skulls which still burned with blue flames skittering across the floor. Rain stayed motionless in the center of the circle. They left the candle burning where it lay, everyone watching and waiting for what might happen next.

Rain looked out at Kendal, Mary, and Bethany. They knew what she was now. She let her eyes drift across the other faces around her; most were scared or fascinated, but some were angry. The angry faces caught her gaze and accused without words. Rain threw her arms wide and shouted at the crowd *and those faces*, "BLACK is my color and my name is BLACK RAIN! So mote it be. As above, so below, As within, so without. This circle is open, but never is it broken." And the blue flames went out.

No one said a word or entered the circle except my Sisters. Kendal, Mary, and Bethany stepped forward and gathered around me, hugging me. I felt empty and light, like I would float away if they let go or break into a million pieces if they squeezed too hard.

"Come on, let's go home." Kendal got us moving. Each of them kept a hand on me, touching me as they led me toward the front doors. Dazed, I walked where they led me. The other guests and witches cleared a path for our group, parting and stepping out of our way, creating a living hallway of people like standing stones with eyes and faces.

No one said a word as we passed. Cornelius had dashed ahead and was already waiting nervously for us at the open glass doors. He seemed so flustered as we stood there before him. His regal, elegant bearing had deserted him, and he seemed unable to speak the words he obviously wished to say, so I helped. In a pleasant voice I said, "Thank you for having us over, Cornelius. Merry Lammas."

"Hap—Happy Lamas. Black Rain," he managed and bowed low, staying bowed as we filed past.

Outside, it was raining hard. Oddly, there was no thunder and no wind; the watery missiles pounded down in straight lines from sky to earth. A soaked, wide-eyed valet pulled our car into the covered drive just as we stepped out. A second quickly opened the back door of Kendal's old Corolla.

Bethany climbed into the back seat first and pulled me in with her, and Mary crawled in after. They squeezed me between them in the tight back seat and hugged me. We didn't talk as Kendal drove back to Blue Palm's Park. Kendal turned the lights off and waited in front of my house as Mary walked me through the rain and up to my back door.

I told Mary thank you and good night and slipped inside, walking quietly through the house and slipping back into my bedroom. I let my black dress, underwear, and bra fall to the ground then kicked the sodden mess under my bed and crawled under the covers completely naked. I didn't have the energy to look for dry clothes. I felt laid bare. Exposed. I'd never slept naked in my own bed before. The taboo thrill gave my mind a last conscious thought as sleep closed in around me. I was naked, inside and out now. My outside matched my inside.

I pulled my black sheet over me and let myself go.

Jane Miller

The Second Blue Pill

We were ten minutes early, so I wasn't upset that Dan wasn't already here in the doctor's office waiting for me. Still sucked though.

My parents asked the nurse if they could meet with Dr. Burgis for a few minutes privately, which couldn't be good. Doctor Burgis gave me an appraising look over the top of his glasses then took them back into his office right away, which also couldn't be good. I hoped they didn't get me kicked out of the drug study.

That left me alone in the waiting room which would have been great if Dan had walked in, but what I got instead was Rain and Ryan. Their mom was with them. She headed up to the counter to sign in her kids. Ryan saw me, grinned like an idiot, and headed straight for me. *Crap! Crap! Crap!* I muttered in my head as he dropped into the chair right beside me.

"Hi, Jane!" he said enthusiastically, bright smile already in place.

I ignored him and kept my eyes glued on the front door, waiting for Dan.

"Did you finish your book?"

Again I ignored him.

"You must be a fast reader," he kept on.

"You might as well talk to him or he'll just keep going."

I looked at the twin sister who was sitting in the chair across from us, and my eyes nearly popped out of my head. "Holy shit!" shot out of my mouth before I could help myself. Heads in the waiting room turned my way as my hands flew up and covered my mouth. My eyes darted back and forth from "church guy" Ryan to Rain trying to decide who I should be most embarrassed over. I was just so surprised! Dead in the center of her forehead was a TATTOO!

What did her parents say!

"Holy shit," Rain said to her brother and laughed. "Well, at least she's talking to you now," she teased.

"Don't feel too bad, Jane," Ryan said, directing a playfully disapproving scowl at his sister. "I actually said the same thing when I saw it this morning," he confessed as he eyed his sister's tattooed forehead. All three of us laughed.

"It was his first cuss word in two years!" Rain told on her brother's 'S' bomb with a smugly wicked smile.

Ryan continued, "And that guy at the Dunkin' Donuts this morning! When he saw it, he spilled scalding hot coffee all over himself." He rubbed at a stain on his shirt sleeve, "and on me!" Ryan pointed back at her tattoo and said, "That thing is evil!" He looked back at me and said, "And now you've corrupted my Jane with that thing!"

I laughed and chose to ignore the "my Jane" comment.

Rain leaned forward in her chair and said to us, "If my powers of corruption are growing, then you two should be careful, you may start making out right here in the waiting room!" We all laughed again. And that was when I noticed someone standing right beside my chair. I turned.

I was looking at his waist and a belt buckle, but I knew it was Dan. I slowly lifted my head up the line of his body and stared up at him like a deer caught in headlights. His beautiful blue-green eyes looked hurt and confused.

Oh my God! Had he heard all that! *You know he did!*

Oh no! What does my face look like?! I must look guilty as hell! What should I do!? What should I do!? Oh crap!

I fought my face to hold back the tears.

Ryan, who had been quietly trying to figure out what was going on with Dan and me and all the staring, chose that moment to open his mouth. "Hey,

is this guy bothering you, Jane?" He laid it out there in the blatant "boy defends girl" voice.

Dan didn't look away, and I didn't take my eyes off his for a second as I answered with a breathy "never."

"Who is he?" Ryan pestered.

"My Dan," I answered, my voice a little stronger. I smiled a little as I watched Dan's reaction; he liked that. Good!

"When did you meet him?" Ryan prodded again.

Rain was right, he wouldn't quit! "Yesterday," I answered. I still hadn't looked away from Dan.

"Hey!" Ryan cried foul. "When I asked you out *yes-ter-day,* you told me 'later,' and now it's *later,*" he concluded cheerfully, but with a possessive undertone that was totally serious. And that was enough for Dan. He looked away from me to eye Ryan for a second, then looked back to me.

He reached for his notepad in his shirt pocket. He flipped it open and scratched out a quick note and handed it to me like a bill from a pissed waiter. Rain and Ryan both watched this with confused interest; they didn't know what to make of Dan and his note.

Sarah

Who is this Ass!

I read it and laughed. I started to reach for my pen to write back but Dan handed me his. I smiled at him and took it.

Ethan

Don't worry.

He's Justin.

Ryan was leaning over toward my chair as I wrote, trying to read Dan's note and my reply before I handed it to Dan.

"Hey!" His brows pinched in confusion. "Why'd he call you 'Sarah,' Jane?" He looked at Dan and back at me. "And why'd you call him Ethan? I thought his name was 'Dan.'" He did the finger quotes in the air. And then he scowled darkly and looked up at Dan. "And did you just call me an ass?" he straightened his back, puffing up in that way boys did before they did stupid things. Dan tensed up too, his eyes narrowing and darkening as he glared back.

"Ha!" Rain shouted and stabbed a finger at Ryan with a triumphant grin on her face. "That's two in one day! You said ASS! When Mom gets back I'm tellin'!"

She chortled with devilish delight, calling him out on cussing again. Ryan looked chagrined and embarrassed, and his brain seemed to have rebooted. His pre-fight posturing deflated like a flatulent balloon. In her chair Rain continued to chortle and jab at him. She had fun picking on her twin brother, but I could tell she'd done that on purpose. Whether for her brother's benefit or Dan's or mine, I didn't care. I gave her a thankful smile.

Dan had read my note and was looking at Ryan with a bewildered expression as Ryan picked up right where he'd left off. "And my name is Ryan—not Justin!" he complained to me.

Dan wrote another quick reality check.

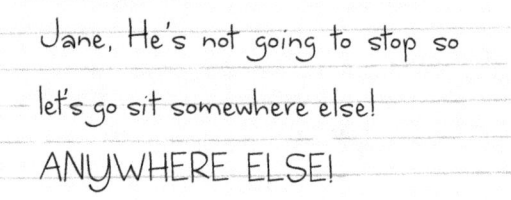

Jane, He's not going to stop so let's go sit somewhere else! ANYWHERE ELSE!

Dan was right. I grabbed my purse and stood. "If you insist on being in the story, you really should read the book."

Rain grimaced in sympathy for her brother as I handed Ryan Dan's note. "Bye, Justin," I told him. Sadly enough, the name fit perfectly. In the Midnight books, Justin was the "other" guy who liked Sarah but didn't get the girl. Ryan looked crushed, but there wasn't anything I could do about it. I gave him a last sad smile before heading to the other side of the office where Dan was waiting for me, *far away* from "Justin."

As we sat down, I could tell that Dan was still upset. I could see it in his eyes, and there was sweat on his brow. He swallowed and rubbed his palms on the legs of his jeans. Dan was nervous and edgy. I was too. My heart was still racing from getting caught talking with Ryan. And the almost fight that didn't happen! That was crazy!

Dan took out his pad and pen and leaned close to me, turning the pad toward me. I could tell he wanted me to read as he wrote and talk to him instead of passing the pad back and forth. He put his pen to the pad, but his hand was shaking and it took him a minute before he could start to write. I'd seen guys get in fights at school and remembered how wired and jittery all that adrenaline could make a guy. I felt a pain right in the center of my heart that this was because of me! He was worried about stupid Ryan because of me! I read as he tried to write.

Who is that GUY! What were

He paused, frowning down at the pad, trying to think of what to say next. I reached out and put my hand on top of his to stop the shaking and whatever he was about to write, but that meant I was holding his hand now.

Great Jane! So much for letting him make the first move. My heart ignored my head. I kept Dan's hand still with one hand as I pulled his pen free with my other. There were still questions in his eyes, but he let me steal his pen without a fuss. I pressed his hand flat on the arm of the chair the pad rested on and wrote on the back of his hand.

This hand holds my heart

I tried not to think about the girl I'd seen do this last year with her thug boyfriend. Or how Stephanie and I had made fun of her. I'd called her a brainless twit, but I'd write whatever I had to write to fix this! If that meant I was a twit—I didn't care! Was he still mad? He was staring down at what I'd written on his hand, looking worried. When he brought his eyes back up to mine I said, "It's okay." I searched his eyes for signs of damage. They looked better. And just like that, my heart felt better too.

Dan's eyes were more green today than blue. Hmm. Dan's eyes changed colors, just like Ethan's eyes in the book. A little more deja vu. That made me smile a little, and that made Dan smile. Wow! He was hot! He was definitely hotter than any other guy I had ever thought about seriously before. I looked okay, but my bad skin always kept me at what I like to think of as a solid 7, but Dan was a hunk even with skin problems. He was definitely out of my league.

It made sense. In the book Sarah was decent looking, but her Ethan had been gorgeous. That thought made me smile more and that made Dan smile more. He had one of *those* smiles! The kind that just stopped your heart. Oh God, he was HOT! I could not believe that some other girl hadn't already grabbed him. He was just too hot to be walking around "unclaimed." But he'd said that I was the first girl to ever hold his hand. How is that even possible!?

Dan took his pen back from me, flipped to a clean page in the pad and started again.

How are you?

He wrote and looked at me, still holding the pen. And I answered looking at him.

"I'm better, now that you're here." He liked that. He wrote again.

Did you read some in your book
last night?

He looked at me, still holding the pen.

Okay—and—why did he ask me that? I wondered.

"Yes." I felt my face go red as I remembered what I *had* been reading. I'd locked my bedroom door, gotten undressed, and crawled into bed with the book, hiding under the covers as I read the honeymoon scene with Sarah and Ethan over and over while I imagined myself as Sarah and Dan in Ethan's place. I imagined us together for the first time as it was in the book, kissing, touching, and holding, but at some point my imagination had taken on a life of its own and I'd left the pages of the book and let my imagination go and go and go.

It had been WILD! If Dan should be jealous of anyone it should be my body length pillow that had to stand in for him last night. He'd kick that pillow's ass if he only knew. Dan was studying my face, and I wondered how red it was! He wrote again.

Last night, You were thinking about

me Jane.

Holy crap! Was that a question or did he just know!? Had I been thinking about him? Yeah! Just a little! Over and over till I finally passed out at 2 am! My voice squeaked out a quick "Yes."

I tried a subject change before I turned inside out. "Did you drive yourself? Is your uncle here?" I stared down at his pad and not at his face. Eventually he flipped to a clean page and started to write again.

No, I caught a cab. My uncle is at

work now.

I read and looked up again. "I'm glad you came."
He looked at me for a second and wrote again.

RU here alone?

"No, my parents are in with Dr. Burgis now. They should be out any second. They want to meet you."

Dan grimaced with worry.

"No, it's not like that, my parents are great," I assured him, "and I've already told them everything—" I stopped. Should I tell him I loved him first? He'd done it in the book, and I'd done it last on the computer, but neither of us had said it in person. Face to face! I looked down, not sure what to do. Should I just say it? If I felt it, and I did love him, then I should just say it, *shouldn't I?*

A last desperate surge of pride bubbled up within me, insisting loudly that I should wait. I'd already typed it, he could say it next! Make HIM say it first! I'd already grabbed his hand first! I balled my hands into fists. Did I have no freaking shame!? Shit! I had my head down but I could see Dan's notepad that he slipped into my lap.

Jane, what's wrong? Are you
alright?

"I told my parents I love you," I said. God NO! That wasn't right! That was horrible. I wanted to say it right if I was going to say it at all! I lifted my head and stared deep into his eyes and said, "I love you."

He didn't say anything back. He just sat there and stared at me. After a minute he reached over and took my hand in his. His hand felt perfect in mine, but I was still waiting for him to "say it!" I started to cry and I closed my eyes. I wanted to hear him say it. I heard my trembling voice say quietly, "Say it, Dan. Please, *just say it.*"

How could I ask him that! He couldn't talk! WHY did I ask him that!? That was wrong. So wrong. But it didn't matter. I still wanted to hear him say it. I cried.

"I Love You, Jane!"

I stopped crying. I stopped breathing. What was that? Who said that? I opened my eyes to find Dan's blue-green orbs blazing down into my own. Tears were running down his face. I heard the same voice again as he looked right into me. His lips did not move, but I still heard a voice inside my head shout loud and clear in a glorious, triumphant, wonderfully male voice:

"I LOVE YOU!"

My eyes went as wide as they could go and Dan smiled as he watched me. He squeezed my hand. Oh my God! I'd heard him! This couldn't be real. I must have imagined it. I'm hallucinating. This couldn't be real. I frowned. Maybe I was losing it. "Dan—did you just say that?" I asked quietly, and again I heard inside my head his "voice" answering me:

"I'm here, my Love."

My world flipped upside down again! It was electric, the hair on the back of my neck stood up, goose bumps danced on my arms, and I hugged him! My whole body just flew forward like a sprung trap, wrapping around him as I pressed my face against his cheek. I felt Dan's arms close around me, holding me. My tears met his as I rubbed my face against his. My Dan could TALK! My Dan could TALK! I *was* in a fairy tale! In the book, Ethan the vampire could read people's minds, but this was different! THIS WAS BETTER! My Dan could talk! I whispered right by his ear, "Say it again, Dan," and listened in my head, but I didn't hear what I wanted to hear, what I heard instead was Dan's horrified voice inside my head shouting:

"Your parents!"

"Get your hands off my daughter!" I heard Mom shout from somewhere behind me.

I let go of Dan and snapped back into my chair as Dan did the same. Mom and Dad were walking toward us. Mom looked furious! But Dad looked amused.

"What? All I did was hug him!" I reached up to wipe my tears away. Crap! Why had I started crying? I must look a mess! Great! Mom was freaking out!! Everyone in the waiting room was staring at us!

"Keep your hands off her!" Mom ignored me and yelled at Dan. Dad grabbed Mom's shoulders and turned her around to face him, holding her in a hug/hold. "Donna, calm down." He looked at Dan over my mother's shoulder. "It's okay, Dan. You just surprised Jane's mother a little. I saw Jane tackle you from across the room."

Mom tried to turn around but he wouldn't let her go. "You didn't have much of a choice in hugging her back," Dad said to Dan, smiling at us both while he shifted his hug hold and tried to keep Mom from wigging out. He countered her every move effortlessly.

Still putting the kung-fu on, Dad spoke to me in a pleasant casual voice as if nothing weird was happening, "Jane honey, Dr. Burgis had his first appointment of the day call in. They're running a little late, and since we were early he asked if you would go back first. Don't worry, this will be good."

Mom tried to wiggle free again, "Let me go, Ed!" Dad didn't let go.

"Go on, you don't want to keep the doctor waiting." He mouthed the word "go" and pointed with his head.

As I got up out of my chair, I heard Dan's voice say to me.

"Your Dad seems cool."

I looked at him and laughed. Mom's freak out had made me forget that Dan could talk. That I was in a fairy tale. "Be right back." I gave my father and Dan an equal share of my euphoric smile before I turned to go. Nurse Ann was waiting for me, holding open the door to the back office. She gave me a concerned look as she led the way. To be honest, I didn't give a rip what she thought; I was walking on cloud nine. *My Dan could talk!*

I still had tear stains all over my face and a crazy smile I couldn't get rid of as she took my blood pressure and temp. Nurse Ann asked me to get up on the scale and out of nowhere I heard Dan's voice in my head say:

"Can you hear me now?"

I sucked in a quick breath and held it, my whole body frozen. Nurse Ann froze too, looking at me, her hand frozen in the air where she had been adjusting the slide weight on the scale. Was that Dan in the other room talking to me? I turned my head and looked in the direction of the waiting room. And—did he just make a joke?

"Sorry, just thought that might be funny. Can you even hear me in there? This is new for me, so I don't know. Your Dad's telling me about his work and I'm pretending to listen! I'm rambling, and for all I know I'm just talking to myself in my head which is fine. Oh crap, Jane, your mom just saw what you wrote on my hand! Oh crap!

Oh crap! Your mom is holding my hand!

Ahhh! Gotta write, be right back!"

Nurse Ann was still frozen, her hand still motionless above the scale. She was eyeing me like I was some type of explosive device. "So how much do I weigh?" I asked. She started to function again and finished adjusting the scale. "Only a hundred and eight. That's another two pounds since yesterday. Jane, have you been eating?"

She seemed pretty concerned about the weight and I reminded her, "You got me a salad yesterday and last night I had tofu. I ate it all. You can ask my parents. They're out there." I jacked a thumb toward the waiting room.

She looked a little reassured. "Well, tofu and a salad don't add up to much. You need to keep your weight up, Jane." She started scribbling on her clipboard when I heard Dan again:

"You like tofu?"

I laughed! Nurse Ann jumped out of her skin and then looked at me like I'd completely lost it. It seemed like Dan could hear everything I could hear—or even think. When did this start? Had it just happened when I asked him to tell me that he loved me or had he been able to do this before? I tried to talk to Dan by just thinking the words in my head.

"Dan, can you hear me?"

"Yes, Jane. I can hear you. I aaah, need a minute. Talking with your mom."

Nurse Ann went on with the usual work up and questions, keeping a close eye on me the whole time. Occasionally Dan would say something and I would laugh or get upset, depending on what he told me. Out in the waiting room my parents were asking him all kinds of questions, mostly about me. I hardly noticed when Nurse Ann left and Dr. Burgis came into the room pushing his little cart as I listened to Dan's voice in my head.

"Your mom just apologized for yelling at me, Jane. She's worried that you're not acting like yourself and she thinks I may not be my usual self either. She said we

should wait till after the Derm drugs to see if we're right for each other. Your mom wants me to stay away till after we finish the Derm drugs. She wants me to stay away from you. JANE, what do you want me to say?"

My angry thoughts shouted to him, "Show her your hand and ask her how you can stay away from me when you're holding my heart!"

"Jane!" Dr. Burgis yelled right in my face.

"What!" I fired right back, loud and angry. So damn rude! I was talking here! Who the hell yells in someone's face when they're talking!

"Jane. I've been talking to you and you didn't respond. How are you feeling today?" Burgis's voice was all mellow now, talking very, very calmly, like I was some kind of nutcase psycho out on a ledge.

"I'm fine!" I snapped, annoyed at his babyish tone and still angry at my mother. What the hell was she thinking!? I tried to calm myself down as Dr. Burgis got out his little pocket flashlight and shined it into my eyes. He held my wrist and eyed his watch, checking my heart rate. I shook my head and tried to focus on "this" room and "this" place instead of that quiet place inside my head where Dan's voice spoke to me. I tried not to think about the conversation that I knew was still taking place out in the waiting room. Mom wanted Dan to stay away. That was so *not* going to happen.

"Jane, are you all right?"

"Yes, sir. I'm okay. Sorry for yelling at you," I apologized stiffly, still fighting my nerves.

Dr. Burgis chuckled softly as he peered into my ears with his little hand held light. "No need to apologize, Jane. And I'm not surprised or worried about your behavior. We discussed this. Your hormones can make you very moody and emotional when you first start the pills. I reminded your parents about this as well. In most of our trial cases, the mood swings stopped after the second or third day, so things should improve soon." He checked the clipboard Nurse Ann had left for him. "Another two pounds!" He keyed in on that right away. "Do you still have your appetite? Tell me how you're feeling, Jane?"

"I *feel* fine," I said again but could tell by the look on his face that Dr. Burgis didn't buy that for a second.

He stared at me, waiting for more. I stayed silent. My attention was divided. Part of my brain was still waiting to hear Dan's voice again.

"Jane. Any adverse or unusual reactions or mood swings need to be documented, no matter how strange. That's the whole purpose of this study." He tipped his head down and looked at me over the top of his glasses. "I promise as your doctor, I will not tell your parents what you tell me in this room. And I will not kick you out of the study, even if you are having some unexpected reaction to the Derm pill." He arched one eyebrow, "So any unusual reactions, Jane?"

"You won't tell my parents or kick me out?"

"I promise. Now what's up?" He made himself comfortable on his little swiveling stool, ready to hear me spill my crazy all over the room. But now that I'd decided to say something, I didn't know what to say. I didn't want to tell him about Dan talking to me in my head because no matter what he "promised," that would end with me in a padded room somewhere. And Dan getting "probed." So hearing Dan in my head was definitely O-U-T! So what should I tell him?

Dr. Burgis was eyeing me like a bug in a jar as I racked my brain for something to say. But now I had to say something.

"Kinda weepy." He gave me a look. "Okay! More weepy than normal!" I offered, and he nodded. "Some moodiness, like you saw. My dreams are a lot more—" What should I say here? "—vivid" was as much as I'd dare, though I was sure my face said more. "And I'm experiencing some strange book deja vu." It sounded weird even as I said it. I didn't even know if there was such a thing as "book déjà vu" but Dr. Burgis looked pleased.

"Really? In what way?"

"Just little things. Like, I'll be writing something or typing something, or even saying something, and find that it's the same thing that Sarah said or wrote somewhere in the book that I'm reading. It's kinda weird." I hoped that satisfied him. And it was all true, which was even better because I didn't like lying. I wasn't very good at it.

Dr. Burgis was quiet for a minute as he considered what I'd told him, but then he nodded, like it was no big deal. "Don't be too alarmed, Jane. You're new to reading books. It's very easy to get carried away by a good book and then the imagination gets involved—all very natural. And you're reading a story about a teenage girl. And you are—" he paused expectantly.

"A teenage girl," I finished for him, smiling sheepishly at Doctor Burgis's smug smile.

"And that's why it's better to read a book than watch a movie," he said, sounding quite satisfied.

He turned back to his desk and took two fifties out of his envelope. "Have you started the first book again? You planned to reread them."

I was embarrassed. He'd already paid me for reading the last book. "No sir, I'm still on the last book, but I haven't read it through yet." He raised an eyebrow and I went on, "I keep going back and reading parts of book four over." I felt my face go red and looked down.

"What part was so interesting, Jane?" Dr. Burgis asked.

"When Ethan the vampire and Sarah get married, the wedding and the, ahh, honeymoon." I admitted quietly and looked up. He was smiling as he scribbled on his clipboard. I squirmed on the end of the little exam bed I was sitting on.

"I'm sure you've gotten a little further in your book. Has your Sarah been turned into a vampire yet?" he inquired.

"Oh, I got to that part this morning before we came to the office. It was horrible." It had been! Not an easy thing to do, becoming one of the living dead!

Dr. Burgis stopped writing and looked at me. He looked concerned. Which struck me as odd. Why?

"Horrible?" he said it like a question. I was about to say more when I heard Dan's voice shout in my head.

Dr. Burgis watched as I "froze," listening:

"Wow! There's some crazy blond lady out here in the waiting room fighting with her daughter. You better send Dr. Burgis out here to break it up! Ohh! Good one!"

"You better get out front, Dr. Burgis! Sky and her mom are fighting in the waiting room." I listened to Dan's voice inside my head giving the blow by blow.

Dr. Burgis got the word "How" out before Nurse Ann burst through the door.

"Dr. Burgis, come quick! We have a situation in the waiting room!"

He gave me a suspicious look. "I'll be right back, Jane," he said, then took off. Dan told me everything as it happened. Dr. Burgis, Dan, Ryan, my Dad, and all the other parents in the waiting room helped break it up. Dr. Burgis ran interference as Nurse Ann took Sky into the back and got her away from her crazy mother. I wasn't surprised when the door finally opened and Burgis stepped back into the room.

"Sorry, Jane, we're going to have to move right along." He was a little out of breath, stressed, and aggravated. "Let me get your pills ready." He grabbed the paper cup off his cart and reaching inside his coat, he pulled out six white pills and the blue pill and handed them to me along with a glass of water. I stared down into the cup.

"Why six white pills? Yesterday it was four." That was a lot of pills.

"Medicine is often made in very small dosage, Jane, that way we doctors can fine tune exactly how much you receive. Absolutely nothing to worry about. Now take your pills like a good girl." And he looked at me and made the "hurry up" hand gesture. I took my pills and Dr. Burgis did his thing with the tongue depressor to make sure they were gone.

"Good girl. Tomorrow you can tell me more about your 'book deja vu' and hopefully we will start to see some improvement on your complexion as well, but right now we must get some food into you. You can't have an empty stomach with all that medicine you just took." He handed me one of the two fifties he'd taken out and said, "Finish the book, Jane." He glanced at his watch. "Tomorrow we'll have more time to talk, but today has gotten a little—complicated." He didn't look happy about that either.

He stood. "Shall we?" He opened the door and walked me back to the waiting room.

My parents were smiling and sitting on either side of Dan, reading one of his notes as we walked up. Just looking at them all sitting together made me smile. My mom, my dad, and my Dan—it made sense.

"Hello, Mr. and Mrs. Miller. Hello, Dan," Dr. Burgis greeted them, and they were all smiles. Good! "I just wanted to thank you again for taking that early appointment. And if you would allow me to treat your family to lunch, I would ask that you make sure Jane eats right away." And he handed Dad the other fifty he had taken out of the envelope.

Dad came back with the typical response, "Dr. Burgis, you really don't have—"

"No! I insist." He waved off Dad's attempt to give him back the fifty. "But please make sure she eats something more *substantial* than a salad. And please don't delay; get some food in her at once. I don't want her to get an upset stomach after taking the Derm 513 pill." Dr. Burgis finished with a serious smile.

He was about to turn away then stopped and looked at Dan. "Dan, your appointment's not till 1:30. Perhaps you can go with them." He looked from my parents to Dan and me. "That way you can all continue your conversation over lunch perhaps?" he suggested innocently.

My parents looked at each other, then at Dr. Burgis, obviously wondering what he was up to. While they were still confused and undecided I jumped in and begged, focusing my efforts on the only "no" I saw. "Please, Mom!" I wheedled, giving her *the look*. I almost smiled and ruined it when Dan spoke in my head:

"I think they like me, Jane."

Mom was surrounded by pleading teens and dignified and reasonable adults. I knew I had her. She was *against* it, but goody for me, with everyone else on my side she caved.

"Okay, honey, we'd love to have Dan with us. And I'm sorry about the way I acted earlier, Jane. I didn't mean to embarrass you like that. Like your father said, you two just surprised me." She looked at me, then at Dan and said to the both of us in her best "Mom" voice, "No more surprises!" She gave us her "I mean it!" look.

Dad smiled and said to Dan, "I don't think we need to ask 'if' you want to go, do we, Dan?"

He shook his head no.

Pleased everything was arranged to his liking, Dr. Burgis reached for his clipboard. "Very good. Very good. Now hurry to lunch." He shooed us along,

"Doctor's orders." He turned back to the waiting room. "Rain Bryant!" he called. Rain gave me a wave goodbye as she followed Dr. Burgis into the back.

"Goodbye, Jane!" Ryan called as we headed out of the office. He waved to me from his seat. I stopped at the door and waved back. He looked so sad. Dan was watching me as I waved at Ryan, and I spoke to him inside my head:

"There's nothing to worry about."

He stared into my eyes and said in my head, *"I know."*

Dad used the clicker to unlock the car, and Dan stepped forward quickly to open the front door for my mom. We had an *awkward moment*. I could tell Mom wanted to sit with me in the back and make Dan sit up front with Dad, but he was holding her door. Waiting for her to get in. With Dan unable to talk, it was a weird situation, so she just got in.

Dan opened my door as well and then walked around and got in on his side. Dad stood there and watched the whole "door opening" thing with a grin. He sure seemed to like Dan, which really surprised me. Dad hated most of the guys he'd seen me go out with but he seemed great with Dan. Good!

Dad joked a little once we all got into the car that he was going to have to "step up his game" a notch with Dan around. Everything was going so great! I had Dan right beside me. I resisted the urge to reach over and take his hand. Didn't want to push my luck. I spoke to Dan in my head,

"Dan. Can you 'really' hear everything I'm thinking right now? When did it start?"

"Yes, I can hear everything, and it's getting clearer all the time. By the way, this all started last night." He smiled as he said this.

Oh my God! Last night I had imagined Dan and I and—and—"and Dan is reading my mind right now, aren't you?"

"Yes! But, Jane, your Mom! She just asked you a question! She asked 'Which restaurant'?!"

"Oh! Anywhere is fine, Mom," I said quickly. I hoped it worked. I waited.

Dad, "How about Outback Steakhouse, Jane, would that be okay?" he added. "It's close and we haven't been there in forever."

"That sounds great, Dad," I said as I tried to stay focused on my parents and not what I did last night. It wasn't working! I watched as Dan's smile grew bigger in the seat beside me, and I felt my face go red. I talked to my parents to keep my thoughts about last night from filling my head while Dan sat in the seat beside me, busily writing note after note as my parents talked to him too. When we parked and went into the restaurant, Dan said in my head:

"Jane, I've been having some weird food things going on. I'm worried about eating in front of your parents."

What kind of weird food things? I thought as the waiter led us to a table and handed out the menus. The waiter asked Dan what he would like, and Dan quickly wrote something on his pad and handed it to him. The waiter looked surprised as he stared at the note but raised his eyebrows and asked Dan, "Are you sure, sir?"

Dan looked embarrassed and nervous and just nodded and looked away from everyone. While the waiter got Mom and Dad's order I asked Dan in my head,

"What on earth did you order?"

"A really, really, really rare steak."

"But, why?" I asked back quickly.

"Because I've been craving blood, Jane."

Huh. "Craving blood" What—what—my brain was trying to process that.

The waiter asked me what I'd like to order. "Get a nice steak, Jane. Something more filling than a salad," Dad encouraged.

I was trying to keep my brain working. I felt in two places at once. One word Dan said was caught in my head. It shouted at me—

"BLOOD!"

"I'll have a steak," I said, just to have time to think.

I felt weird. The waiter asked how I wanted it cooked, and it felt like his words came out in slow motion as I watched his mouth moving, shaping each word as he spoke: "Well done"—"medium"—"or RARE."

I had that fairy tale, flippy feeling again.

It wasn't Dan but something else shouting inside my head.

"BLOOD! BLOOD! CRAVING BLOOD! MUST HAVE BLOOD!!!

"Jane, are you okay?" Mom's voice asked, and I realized that I'd zoned out. Everybody, including Dan *and* the waiter were looking at me now, worried faces all around.

"Sorry," I managed and looked at the waiter, "rare please—very rare." Mom and Dad looked surprised.

The waiter just said, "Are you sure, ma'am."

I nodded.

Dad leaned forward, "Jane, are you feeling okay? Do you need to lie down?"

Everyone was looking at me, even people from other tables. I felt tingly all over but I tried to ignore it and "act" okay so they wouldn't freak. "I just need to eat. Yesterday I felt better after I ate." I gave my parents and Dan a weak smile.

Dad told the waiter to hurry our order, and the waiter, having seen my little show, said he'd make sure it was the next ticket in and that he'd bring some bread back in less than a second.

The bread tasted like sand.

The water tasted disgusting.

Mom kept pushing me to eat more bread, but it tasted like sand. Gritty, tasteless mush. My parents talked and Dan wrote notes as they asked him questions. Everyone was keeping a close eye on me. I stayed quiet. Dad asked if it was like this yesterday with my first pill. I didn't answer, but I saw Dan write a note. I think he told them about my salad that the nurse made me eat. Dan and my parents talked, but I stopped listening. I even ignored Dan's voice when I heard him ask something in my head.

I felt weird—really weird.

The food came. My steak was bloody red, but Dan's was basically raw. I closed my eyes. I could *smell* the blood.

"Smells great," I said, finding my voice. It did. I cut myself a piece of the bloody steak and put it in my mouth. The texture of the steak was like chewy dirt, but the blood, ooh—it was glorious! I moved carefully. I tried to stay calm. I felt everyone's eyes on me as I ate. I ate slowly and purposefully. I ate only the center of my steak; the outside edges were just too "burnt." I ate another piece of "sand" bread because my mother insisted, and I drank some of the disgusting water.

Toward the end of the meal, I started to "engage" more in the conversation, which made Mom and Dad relax a lot. "I'm feeling better now," I told them. Everyone still looked worried.

"Does the Derm pill make you drowsy or disoriented, Dan?" Dad asked. They'd been asking him about his reactions to the pill, trying to find out if he was having the same problems. Dan wrote in his notepad.

Yes Sir, they make me sleepy and a little out of it, but Jane weighs so much less than I do. I guess that's why it hits her harder.

Dad read it and handed the note to Mom.

"Jane, how are you doing now?" she asked.

"Can I have another steak?"

Mom and Dad looked at each other, surprised. They both smiled. "Sure, honey, did you want one that's cooked this time?" Dad teased.

"No," I said. "I want it rare. I want it bloody."

Ryan

The Second Blue Pill

Jane grabbed her purse and got up, "If you insist on being in the story, you should really read the book," she told him and then handed him Dan's note. "Bye, Justin." She gave him a small, sad smile before leaving to follow Dan to the other side of the waiting room. Ryan's mouth hung open as he watched Jane walk away with Dan.

"Wow, you sure know how to pick 'um, Bro."

Ryan looked at his sister. She was watching Jane and Dan, too. The pair sat down on the other side of the office. Ryan left his seat and sat beside his sister so he could stare at them without turning around in his seat and making it painfully obvious that he was staring. He sat forward, propping his elbows on his knees and cupping his chin as he watched the happy couple on the other side of the room. His sister rubbed circles on his back with her nails, trying to comfort her heart-sore brother.

"Sorry, Ryan. Jane's amazing, mysterious, beautiful, passionate, funny, smart, kind—did I miss anything."

"Sexy," Ryan said and gave a sad groan.

"And don't forget one more thing—*in love*," Rain added, then gave her brother's back a hug. "Just not with you."

"Look at that!" Ryan whispered to his sister with a disgusted expression stuck on his face, "They're doing it again!"

"Oh yeaah!" Rain said as she leaned forward beside her brother, "The staring thing!"

They both watched, fascinated, as across the room Dan and Jane were staring into each other's eyes like the most love-sick, besotted, disgustingly romantic thing you'd ever seen in your worst chick flick nightmares. Then they started smiling at each other and then they smiled more! Rain and Ryan both watched, spellbound by the scene.

"Oh God! I think I'm gonna hurl!" Ryan muttered.

"Well, I think it's beautiful." Rain was actually getting all misty eyed. She dabbed at her eyes with the sleeve of her black top.

Ryan gave her a disgusted look. "Oh please!" He turned his attention back to Jane and Dan. The happy couple had gone back to note writing. Apparently Dan couldn't talk.

Rain was watching the note action too, trying to figure it out. "He's like your Kryptonite. He's your opposite," she concluded.

"Huh?"

Rain explained her revelation, "He can't talk and you can't shut up. Apparently Jane likes the strong 'silent' type." She pursed her lips and nodded sagely.

"But everything seemed to be going great!" Ryan lamented. "I mean, she was laughing and smiling, we were having a good time and everything." He released a long sigh as he watched the show on the far side of the room. "I wish your tattoo could have come through on that last part," he said wistfully.

"What's that?" She squinched up her brow, not understanding.

"About us making out right here in the doctor's office," Ryan said. "Your powers of corruption and all that jazz."

"Oh yeah," Rain said, remembering her earlier statement.

At exactly that moment on the other side of the room, Jane sprang out of her chair and threw herself at Dan. She wrapped her arms around him and started wallowing on his face like she'd completely lost her freaking mind and was going to attack him right here and NOW!

Ryan's horror-stricken face turned to his sister. "What are you doing!?" he cried. "Cut it out! Make 'um stop!" When he looked back, they weren't even kissing, they were *wallowing*! Rubbing faces like a couple of desperate, heat frantic freaks!

"Sorry!" Rain said, panicked. "I don't know how to stop it! I don't think I can, Ryan! Sorry! Sorry!" She watched in horror along with her brother.

"Get your hands off my daughter!" A woman's voice bellowed. Rain and Ryan's heads whipped to the right where Jane's mother and father were entering the waiting room from the back office area. Jane's mother looked FURIOUS! Their heads whipped back to Jane and Dan like spectators watching a tennis match. They'd let go of each other and had flattened themselves into their own chairs, like astronauts during liftoff!

"All I did was hug him!" Jane hurled pathetically in advance of her mother's arrival, her voice shaky and terrified. Her mother ignored her as she yelled at Dan again.

Dan sunk lower into his chair, pulling more Gs of parental outrage. The whole waiting room watched the conclusion to the drama as Jane's father grabbed her freaked out mother and held onto her while he spoke to Dan and Jane and sorted things out. In no time, Jane was out of her chair with a huge smile on her face and walking into the back with a very concerned looking Nurse Ann. She'd been standing in the doorway watching the whole show unfold.

Brother and sister watched as Jane's father continued to smooth things over. Soon Jane's parents and Dan were all sitting together, talking together as Dan wrote notes to communicate with them.

"So, do you think that was just some crazy coincidence or did you do that?" Ryan said to his sister.

Rain considered for a minute before answering. "Well, I think there's just so much of that kind of eye contact a person can take before they snap, but things have changed lately." She sounded guilty as she went on, "I may have done it." She looked concerned.

Ryan digested her answer, "Things have changed. What do you mean, Rain? What things have changed?"

She gave her brother another hug. "No, Bro. You don't want to hear it. It's witch stuff."

Ryan resisted the urge to say "that stuff is crap."

"So you think you caused Dan and Jane to jump each other's bones?" He raised a doubtful eyebrow and gave his sister a doubtful look to match.

Rain didn't bother to remind him that he'd thought so too when it first happened. No need to rub his face in it.

"Maybe—and maybe not," she said. "But either way, I'm gonna have to be a whole lot more careful with what I say." She reached up and touched her tattooed forehead. "Like I said, things have changed. I'm gonna have to learn to be more careful." She was completely serious.

Ryan wanted to be respectful and not dump on his sister's "witch" fantasies so he changed the subject.

"So what was up with all of the weird names, her calling him 'Ethan'? He called her something too—"

"Sarah," Rain supplied with a smile, glad her brother had chosen to change the subject. She loved her brother.

"Do you know what she was talking about? *'Since I'm in the story I should read the book.'* What books?"

"The Midnight books," Rain said. "Those are the books she's talking about."

Ryan's eyes lit up, excited to have some light shed on the mysterious Jane and her name game. "So you've read them." He hunkered closer in his chair, ready to know more, "What are they about? Give me some details. Jane said I was in the book, right, so who is Justin?"

Rain had a sad expression on her face. "Ryan, are you sure you want to know? When she said you were Justin she said a lot. I can't believe you haven't seen the movies."

"They don't show that crap on ESPN! Just tell me." His sister's expression told him that he wasn't going to like hearing it. "I can take it. I have to know."

Ryan leaned back in his chair and listened as his sister summed up the books as painlessly and quickly as possible. She explained how the four huge books in the series, thousands of pages, were basically a love story about a girl named Sarah and how she fell in love with a vampire boy named Ethan. She said that Justin was a boy that tried to get Sarah away from the vampire, but no matter how hard he tried, he couldn't win her heart or save her. Rain summed things up briefly by saying that Justin finds another girl in the end, but didn't go into the details.

"So that's why she seemed so sad when she said it," Ryan said, "when she called me Justin."

"Yes," his sister said, compassion in her voice. "Like I said, she told you a lot when she called you Justin. Basically she said she liked you. And if she really meant it, that she could have loved you—but she's already in love with Dan." Rain gave her brother another hug, "Mysterious, beautiful, passionate, funny, smart, kind, sexy—but also in love with Dan. Sorry, Bro."

"In the book—Ethan and Sarah truly love each other?" Ryan asked.

"Yes. Totally. Absolutely," Rain affirmed. She winced as she added, "You remember the staring thing Jane and Dan do?"

Ryan sat forward and looked at her, a little alarmed at where this was going. "Yeah, totally creepy." He looked away. "Unless she's staring at me with those eyes," he mumbled as he remembered yesterday and the eyes that had looked at him over the top of her book.

"Well" Rain said, "that staring thing is in the book too. Ethan and Sarah do it." She cringed. "A lot."

Ryan was completely still for a second, then he exploded and threw a controlled little fit in his chair, flinging his arms around, kicking his feet out, and twisting and writhing for a second or two before settling back into his seat, slumped in the chair. He took a deep breath. "If it's God's will for me to be Justin, then I'll be Justin." He took a few more calming breaths then pressed ahead. "Tell me about Justin. What does he do in the book?"

Rain shook her head as she studied her brother. She'd never seen him so torn up over a girl before. "Well, Justin saves her life a few times. And he's one of her best friends." She really didn't want to say more about the book or Justin. "Ryan, don't you think it would be best if you just stayed away from her for a while. I don't think you could handle it if she gave you one of those stares. You'd snap. Remember, you're taking the Derm 513 pill so your hormones and emotions are a mess right now."

Ryan thought about that for a minute. "You may be right, but still—" he sighed, "it's good to know my part in the story. Thanks, Sis."

Rain hugged her brother and tried to talk about other things.

A few minutes later, the front doors of the office burst open. A tall blonde girl they recognized from yesterday charged into the office headed toward the check-in counter. Her mother was hot on her heels, but she was a *mess*, half dressed, wild-eyed, hair everywhere. The mother grabbed her daughter's shoulder, spun her around and "smack!" She slapped the living crap out of her.

"Don't you ever walk away when I'm talking to you!"

The daughter held her hand to her face as her mother went on yelling at the top of her lungs, "This is all your fault anyway for keeping us up half the night last night!"

"Smack!" The daughter slapped her mother right back, and it was ON! All out, mother/daughter, cat fight to the death right in the doctor's office. Both women fell on the floor and started rolling around, going at it, pulling hair, biting, scratching, kicking. Two gorgeous six-foot-tall blonds trying to destroy each other. Ryan shot out of his chair as did Jane's dad and Dan and two of the other parents in the room. Everyone did their best to separate them, earning a few kicks and scratches for their efforts.

Dr. Burgis came charging out and took control. He got Sky, the daughter, away from her psycho mother and sent her into the back with Nurse Ann. After taking care of her, Dr. Burgis walked the mother out by the arm and yelled at her just outside the glass doors for a few minutes before stomping back in and reassuring everyone in the waiting room that all was well before heading back into the exam rooms.

"Don't blame that on me and my tattoo!" Rain spat out when Ryan dropped into the chair beside her. "We didn't have anything to do with it!" She tried to look innocent and ended up looking guilty for the effort.

Ryan was still breathing hard from his part in the drama of stopping the fight. He was also clutching at his chest where he'd been scratched up by one of the two as they thrashed about. "Not your fault, Sis. Sky's mom is crazy. And drugged up." He felt sick to his stomach. "That was ugly."

"I wonder if Sky was having some kind of reaction to the pills that made her emotions all wacked out."

Ryan gave his sister a disgusted look. "No, Sis, her mom is a bitch." Then he added, "Her mom started it, and she's not on the Derm pill. She's on something, but it's not the Derm pill. She doesn't have any excuse to treat her daughter like that." He combed his fingers through his hair and tried to calm down.

Rain was worried about her brother. She reached over and held his arm. "Bro, you're a mess. You're cussing like a sailor and getting all worked up. It's not like you." She gave him a concerned look. "You're right, she's a total bitch, but still."

Ryan shrugged and closed his eyes. "God's still on His throne even if I am a mess."

Ryan and his sister watched Dan and his "new" family. They were smiling and talking away now, asking questions and reading hand-scrawled answers off Dan's little pad. After that bumpy start and breaking up the cat fight, things seemed to have improved a great deal; everyone was happy over there. Soon Dr. Burgis returned to the waiting room with Jane in tow and talked to her parents. He told them to take Jane to lunch and then suggested that they take Dan too.

"Rain Bryant," Dr. Burgis called.

Ryan's sister gave his arm a final sympathetic squeeze and left to follow Dr. Burgis as Jane, Dan, and her parents headed toward the door.

"Goodbye, Jane!" Ryan called to her and waved and she turned and honed in on him. She paused in what she was doing and gave him a sad smile, waving back. Dan was watching the exchange, and she turned and stared at him again. They did the completely weird staring thing for a minute, then smiled at each other and left. Weird.

"She did tell me a lot when she called me Justin," Ryan mumbled to himself. It was all right there in the look and in the sad smile. He'd dreamed and daydreamed about Jane and her beautiful eyes since he'd left her engrossed in her book yesterday. And yesterday he would have sworn there was a true spark of interest. He'd seen it there in her eyes. She'd said "later" not "drop dead."

He'd come today excited and determined to win Jane's heart. Things were going so well; they were laughing and she was smiling and then—and then Dan "the vampire" had appeared out of nowhere and without one word stole her heart. Ryan replayed yesterday and today in his mind, but no matter how he looked at it, he still came to the same sad conclusion.

"God help me, I'm Justin."

Fifteen minutes later, Rain came out and Ryan got called back. The nurse poked and prodded, weighed and measured and asked her fifty questions, and in no time Dr. Burgis was wheeling his little cart into the room.

"Your sister was worried about you, Ryan," Dr. Burgis said as he pulled to a stop.

"Yes, sir, she does that a lot."

"She certainly went all out on that new tattoo of hers!" Dr. Burgis made a face.

"Tell me about it," Ryan concurred, making a similar face, "And she won't even tell us where she got it. Zero warning! She just came out of her room this morning with that thing "dead center" on her forehead and plopped down at the breakfast table like it wasn't even there." Ryan couldn't understand why on earth she wanted that thing on her forehead. Rain didn't liked being the center of attention, not since she went "black." She liked to be invisible. But now everybody who saw her gawked, spilled their drink, or shouted "Holy shit!"

"Well, she seems to like it." Burgis picked up the clipboard with the nurse's notes. "And she seems very happy." He gave Ryan a quick look. "Worried about her brother, yes, but quite happy." He went back to reading the clipboard.

"Actually, she seems better today than she has in a long time," Ryan realized this very moment. Today his sister had laughed and played and actually enjoyed herself instead of being a quiet shadow, or worse, falling into one of her dazed, dead, zombie moods. He remembered her saying "things have changed."

"Yes, Rain certainly seems to be doing well." Dr. Burgis shook his head, his voice a little more grave as he continued. "It's good she's doing so well. One person is already out of the study and others may have to be put out soon. It's a poor start." Dr. Burgis seemed to catch himself. He gave Ryan a smile, shifting to an encouraging tone and topic. "But your sister is doing fantastic! Very encouraging to see her in such high spirits."

Dr. Burgis went back to reading Nurse Ann's notes. Ryan was quiet for a while thinking about his sister and what could have changed. She said it had something to do with "witch stuff" and that worried him. Ryan was rarely quiet, and Dr. Burgis misunderstood his silence. He thought Ryan was trying to work up his nerve to witness to him again.

"Go ahead, Ryan," Burgis encouraged. "Get it out of the way so you don't have to worry about it." He flipped to another page on the clipboard he was holding. Every time Ryan had met Dr. Burgis, he'd invited him to church or tried to witness to him about God. Ryan certainly didn't feel up to it today, and he hadn't planned on doing it, but he had established this pattern and now it seemed he was trapped in it.

"You don't even believe in God, do you, Dr. Burgis?" Ryan said in a defeated tone. He felt hypocritical for even trying to witness after the morning he'd had.

"Oh, but I do believe in God," Dr. Burgis said. "Far too many people believe he exists for *something* like God not to exist. And believe it or not, it's very *scientifically hip* to believe in a Divine Being these days. Only an idiot who couldn't follow the science would deny some of the evidence that backs intelligent design. And then there's all the unexplained and yet well-documented miracles and healings that have happened over the years. It's undeniable that something beyond science as we know it today is responsible." Dr. Burgis took his glasses off and rubbed the bridge of his nose like he was tired.

Ryan was both surprised and confused at the same time. "So if I follow what you just said, you believe God exists because people *believe* he exists."

Dr. Burgis slipped the glasses back onto his face, fitting the frame into it's well-worn groove at the bridge of his nose. He answered as he got out a paper cup and began to count out Ryan's pills. "Right now we are giving you medicine designed to adjust your genes and improve your skin. But what if we could give you a pill that would increase your faith? Scientists have isolated the genes that control and alter human skin to some degree, which is the science behind the Derm 513 pill. It should be possible to also isolate that portion of DNA inside the genome that controls the human ability, or capacity, to 'believe'." Dr. Burgis handed Ryan a glass of water and the cup of pills.

Ryan noticed he had three white pills today along with his blue pill. Throwing all the pills into his mouth at once and washing them down with the water, he quoted a verse that popped into his head. "Romans 12:3 says 'According as God hath dealt to every man the measure of faith.' What you're saying, is that you want to fool around with how much faith God has decided to give each of us." Ryan gave the doctor a head shake of censure.

Dr. Burgis laughed out loud and kept on laughing. After a minute he pulled himself together enough to speak. "But Ryan, God gave you bad acne and bad skin and we're fooling around with that. What's the difference, my boy?" He gave Ryan a friendly pat on the back as he continued to rein in his amusement.

That stumped Ryan. "You've got a point, Doc," he admitted with a sheepish grin as he shook his head.

Dr. Burgis looked like some life had come back into him as he continued his train of thought with animated vigor. "The real problem isn't faith, my boy, it's doubt! I'm sure you know the verse in the Bible that says, *Truly I say to you, whoever says to this mountain, 'Be taken up and cast into the sea,' and does not doubt in his heart, but believes, it will be granted him.* You see, the tricky part is doubt. It wouldn't do any good to increase your faith if you still doubted you could move the mountain. In the same way, many highly intelligent people have the capacity for greatness, yet some flaw or mental block wrecks their ability to perform."

Dr. Burgis looked at Ryan playfully over the top of his glasses and said, "Well preacher—what do you think?"

Ryan was totally floored. He'd thought for sure Doctor Burgis was a die-hard atheist, but he actually had his own weird way of looking at things. And he knew verses. And he was wicked smart. It was a little intimidating.

"I guess that does kinda make sense, Doc," Ryan admitted. "It wouldn't matter how much faith you had if you canceled it out with doubt."

"Too right! Too right! You have to fix both or it wouldn't work."

Burgis looked as if he'd love to continue their little religious debate, but he glanced at his watch and made a pained face. He reached inside his white lab jacket and took out a sealed envelope which he handed to Ryan. Ryan saw that his name was already written on it.

"Ryan, you've impressed me with your character and your witness." He gave Ryan a serious nod before going on. "And I believe you truly are concerned for me spiritually, which I do appreciate." Another nod. "But for right now, all my concern is for my patients, for you, your sister, and the other teens in the drug study. I don't want you to waste time worrying about me, but I would consider it a great personal favor if you would pray for the other teens in the study tonight. Especially tonight. And this may sound strange, but I would ask that you pray *exactly* as I have written on the card—*if* that doesn't violate your conscience," Burgis quickly added. He looked like he very much hoped it wouldn't.

The doctor continued with a self-deprecating smile, as if embarrassed over an eccentric tick, "It may sound weird, but I put a lot of thought into my prayer requests. I really do. I like to keep them very, very simple." He tapped the envelope in Ryan's hands. "Take a look," he urged and continued talking as Ryan fumbled with the envelope trying to open it.

"I may have my own way of looking at things, Ryan, but I do believe in God, and more specifically in prayer."

Ryan butchered it but he finally got the envelope open. Inside was one white 5x8 card and four fifty dollar bills. Ryan took out the card and read it. There were four simple handwritten prayer requests on the card.

Please Pray:

That the PILLS will work far better than they were ever designed to work.

That those in the study will have the strength and focus of mind to make the change.

That the bodies, DNA, and genes of those in the study will be able to change as needed.

That the skin & complexion of those in the study will be beautiful and spotless permanently.

Nothing strange about the requests. It looked very simple, like Dr. Burgis had said. And he'd obviously put a lot of thought into it. Dr. Burgis really did believe in prayer. His theology was totally "out there" but he definitely believed in prayer.

Ryan held up the money. "I'll be glad to pray for your patients, Doc. but you don't need to pay me, really." He tried to hand the cash back but Burgis waved it away.

"Keep the money and buy your sister and mother something nice, or, or just put it in the plate at church, but please take it."

Ryan wanted to refuse, but Burgis looked determined.

"Why don't you just pray for us yourself?" Ryan held up the card. "If you believe prayer works, why don't you pray yourself instead of asking me to do it?"

Burgis shook his head, a dark smile eased onto his face, giving his grandfatherly features a sinister cast. "Ryan, 'God' is much more likely to hear you than he is to hear me." He winked, looked at his watch again and groaned. "Ryan, once again, please don't pray all over the place. I think that does much more harm than good."

He turned and opened the door for them to go. "Some of the others in the study are having real problems." He looked in the direction of the waiting room. "I really can't say more."

Ryan put the card back into the envelope, folded the envelope up, stuffing it into his back pocket, he followed Dr. Burgis out of the exam room.

"I'll pray, Doc," Ryan assured him, "but I'd still love to see you in church this Wednesday. You never know, you might just like it."

"Oh no!" he said with a definitive head shake. "As I said, please, do not pray for me. Pray for yourself and those in the study, Ryan. My every moment is taken up with making sure my patients are cared for and monitored. Please. Just the card. Nothing more." He grunted and guided Ryan back out into the waiting room where Rain and their mother were waiting.

Sky Lee Han

The Second Blue Pill

I was eating a power bar that Nurse Ann had given me when Dr. Burgis came in.

"Hello, Sky, how are you doing?" he asked as he sat in the chair beside the bed.

"Good," I answered. My lip was busted and I had scratches on my arms and legs, but my face didn't hurt anymore, which was good. Nurse Ann had already put iodine on some of the scratches and bandaged up the worst scratch on my arm. Dr. Burgis rolled his chair closer and started looking over the damage from the fight and looking at me.

"Good?" he frowned. "It didn't look good out in the lobby." Going to the sink and wetting a paper towel, he came back and started to wipe at some of the scratches on my hand and face. "How is she treating you at home?" He kept working on little cuts and scrapes.

"She moved me to a little bedroom that has bars in the window. They lock me in at night," I added quietly, "and they never leave me alone for a second outside. Mom won't even let me near a window without Nathan beside me."

Dr. Burgis threw the bloody paper towel into the red waste basket and, grabbing a handful of band aids, started to peel off the backing and place them on cuts.

"Sky, I told your mother to do those things. We talked about your jumping." He corrected, "your flying fixation. Your mother is apparently following my instructions. That's good to know." He finished with the last band aid and settled back into his chair. "So, how did it go yesterday? How was your afternoon and first night on the Derm pill?" He raised his eyebrows. "You can tell me, Sky. No matter how strange, I want to hear it, and I certainly won't tell your mother. We both know she has substance abuse problems. She needs professional help, but as the professionals are part of the problem I don't see how that will help." He made a disgusted face. He didn't seem pleased with my mother. Or her doctors.

"I flew last night."

Like he said, Dr. Burgis knew about my flying "issues." He'd asked me and my parents a hundred questions about it before he let me into the drug study. He paused in his note taking and leaned forward a little in his chair.

"Tell me about it," he said.

I told him about falling asleep and dreaming I was flying again and about waking up to find that I was on the ceiling. And falling. I showed him the bump on my head and told him about my leg. He asked to see my leg. I was embarrassed, but Dr. Burgis grumped and said, "I'm your doctor," so I showed him the bruise. I told him about the trip for x-rays and how mom was worried he would find out.

"You're going to have to be more careful, Sky. You could have killed yourself last night." He looked serious. Like he believed me about flying and was actually worried that I had hit my head.

"Oh. I won't kill myself now!" I smiled huge. "Mom fixed my room. She took every piece of furniture out except the bed. And she moved the bed to the middle of the room and took off the top and bottom so it's just like a big fat mattress. It doesn't even look like a bed anymore. And she has pillows and cushions all over the floor!" I finished in a rush, then thought about what I'd just said and how crazy it all must sound. My smile turned upside down.

"Don't worry, Sky, I believe you," Dr. Burgis said.

I studied his face skeptically, wondering if he was being honest or if he was messing with me like the psychiatrists did. They lied all the time, saying anything to get me to talk to them. Almost every word they said was a lie. Even the truths were pregnant with lies. Lies. Lies.

"You believe I flew last night?" I asked, still frowning.

"Yes, Sky. No tricks. I believe you." Dr. Burgis smiled. He handed me two more power bars. "Please eat these after you take your pills. You'll need something in your stomach and I don't trust your mother to feed you." He didn't look happy about that either.

"Dr. Burgis, why can I fly now?" I asked.

He thought for a minute before bending forward and whispering, "Can you keep a secret, Sky?"

I nodded, wide eyed and waiting.

"I switched your pills." He winked at me.

"You did?" I asked, doubtful again. I wasn't sure if he was just playing around or not.

"Yes, Sky. The pills I gave you are different. They are special." He turned around to his tray and picked up a glass of water and handed it to me. Then he picked up a little cup and reaching into his coat pockets, he pulled out one blue pill and six white pills. Yesterday I had only three white pills and the blue one. He handed me the cup and said, "Sky, these pills give you the ability to fly."

He reached into his pocket and took out a blue pill and held it up. "The blue pills help your mind Believe you can fly. And if you believe it, Sky, you can do it. If you believe, you can do *anything*." He kept the blue pill there, and with his other hand he took out a white pill and held it up. "These white pills keep your brain from stopping you. There are parts of your brain that tell you '*Don't jump off that—you can't fly! You'll fall and hurt yourself!*'" He waved the little white pill at me, "The white pill suppresses that part of your brain so the blue pill can work." He put the pills away.

I thought about it for a minute. It sounded crazy, but what did I know? All I knew was—I flew, and the doctor said that the pills would let me fly again. I looked at the cup and taking three white pills out, I put them in my mouth and swallowed. I did it again with the other three and one more time for the big blue pill. I handed the cup and glass back to the doctor.

"I want to fly," I said. "And I want to fly away from my mother," I added.

Dr. Burgis studied me for a minute like I'd surprised him. "You have surprising clarity of thought, Sky. It's quite refreshing." He smiled.

"Why did you tell me?" I asked. I was sure that my mother would kill him if she knew he wasn't fixing my face. And I knew she would kill him even more if she knew he was letting me fly. I was glad she didn't know.

"Oh, that's an easy one." The doctor laughed a little. "Can you guess why I let you know?" He waited.

"Yes," I said. It was easy. "I'm crazy," I said as I ripped open a power bar and took a bite. "They wouldn't believe me," I mumbled as I chewed.

Dr. Burgis laughed again. "Simplicity. Clarity. Focus. And a practical self-image." He handed me back the glass of water so I could take a drink and wash down my power bar. "You have a beautiful mind, Sky." He sounded serious.

I slowed my chewing and eyed him with worry. That was the first truly insane thing he'd said to me. Maybe Dr. Burgis was crazy too.

"Oh, don't look at me like that!" he complained as he pulled a face. "Just because I'm the only person you've ever met that's smart enough to recognize you're brilliant does not make me crazy. Eat that other one too, Sky." He pointed to the other power bar lying on the bed beside me. I opened it and took a bite.

"Now, about your mother," Dr. Burgis said. "She threatened not bring you back tomorrow when we spoke outside. Be good and say whatever you have to when you see her again to make her happy." He gave me a stern look, "And if she starts a fight, for heaven's sake, don't fight back, just let her throw her tantrum. The important thing is that you get back here tomorrow. You need to finish the next three days of pills, so stay focused. Be good at home and don't make your mother angry. Got it?" he ordered.

"I'll try," I growled. I didn't want to ever see her again. I didn't want to be locked in that room again.

Dr. Burgis reached over and grabbed his briefcase bag and digging way down into the bottom, he came out with a little phone. He turned it on, took a few minutes to make sure it was working, and programed his cell phone number into the contacts before he handed it to me. "Don't let your mother catch you with that. Use this only in an emergency, understand? And only call me."

I nodded.

"The battery will last till you come to see me tomorrow, so bring it with you, but keep it hidden. If you do leave your mother and fly away, find a safe spot to land and call me. I'll come and get you. But please don't cause a scene and fly where people can see you or we will both be in big trouble. They will take you away and not let you finish your pills, and they will take me away—and *that* would be the end of me." He stared at me till I nodded, wide-eyed. "Good. Now remember, Sky, this isn't just about flying. You can do more than just fly. You can do absolutely anything you wish to do if you only believe."

"Because of the blue pill?"

"Yes," he said, "absolutely anything." He squinched his eyes behind his glasses and grimaced. "But be careful. Don't hurt anyone if you can help it. You're a good girl, Sky, so I'm sure you'll do fine."

"Dr. Burgis, what makes the blue pill work? Is it magic? Will it wear off?" I was worried it wouldn't last, but he was already shaking his head no.

"As long as you take the pills for the next three days, the effects should be permanent. It won't wear off, Sky."

Good! I thought. "What kind of magic makes the blue pill work?" It felt like a silly question, but I flew last night. For all I knew he had fairy dust shoved into that blue pill. It worked for Peter Pan, so why not me?

"Yes, it's magic. The most powerful kind of magic." Dr. Burgis leaned forward and whispered mysteriously, *"Believing Magic."*

I scrunched my brow again, wondering how many kinds of magic were out there. Dr. Burgis was watching me, studying me in his way as I took it all in.

"Did you take the pills too?" I asked him. I wondered what magic he could do.

Dr. Burgis smiled, "Another excellent question, Sky. No, I'm too old." He tapped the side of his head, "As we age our view of the world is set. What we believe. What we know is possible or impossible. The mind and the subconscious mind are not able to change. And children cannot take the pills either. Their mind is too wild, uncontrolled, and they easily believe almost anything. Absolutely not for children."

He frowned before continuing, and the thought *he's experimented on children and killed them* flew through my head. I let it go.

"Between seventeen and eighteen is the only safe age to take the pills. They must be taken while the mind can still believe the impossible and the body can still adapt but old enough that the mind will not believe everything. A teenage mind is still forming, still deciding what is believable. I tried to be very careful with whom I selected. Having a firm mental fixation, like flying or painting or singing or one consuming fantasy is absolutely essential. It keeps the drug's reaction focused and less dangerous. Less random. Teenagers have hormones flying around within their constantly changing bodies keeping you in a state of chaos." He made it sound like a good thing. "You people can fall in love at first sight," he tapped me on the forehead, "and even believe you can fly."

"I can," I said with absolute certainty. I knew it. I believed it. I'd done it.

Dr. Burgis checked his watch, looked around the room quickly and back to me. "Can you do it here? Just a little?" he asked.

I hadn't tried to do it awake yet. I'd been waiting till I went back to sleep. "I don't know," I said honestly. But I should try, I thought. I slid off the doctor's exam bed and stood in front of him. "Last time it started while I was asleep, but I'll try now for you."

Dr. Burgis stood, waved me on, and backed up a step, giving me some space. He looked like a little kid at Christmas about to open his present. I kicked off my shoes, stretched my arms out at my sides, and closed my eyes. I tried to remember last night's dream. I pictured myself on my balcony looking up at the beautiful summer sky, white fluffy clouds floating in a beautiful blue sky. I raised my arms over my head and I felt myself becoming lighter again!

My feet left the ground as I floated up, slowly up into the air. My hands touched the ceiling tiles. I kept my eyes shut and felt the texture on the ceiling and the little metal groove that separated the tiles. I opened my eyes—and—I didn't fall! I was FLYING! I smiled from ear to ear. Down below Doctor Burgis looked like he was laughing and crying at the same time.

The door burst open. "Dr. Bur—" Nurse Ann was saying, she was looking right at my knees. I dropped. It wasn't that high, and I landed on my feet, but my hand hit the cart and flipped the tray across the room. The glass of water went flying and broke on the floor with a "crack!"

"Sky!" Dr. Burgis grabbed me to hold me steady. "Are you all right?" he asked, quickly checking me over to make sure I wasn't hurt.

I nodded.

"What did she do!?" Nurse Ann shouted, trying to figure out what she had just seen. Her eyes were wild.

Doctor Burgis looked at her calmly and said, "Easy Ann, she just jumped off the table." Then he waited. We both stared at her, blank faced. Ann's face went red. She looked at me and I could practically hear the wheels turning in her head. She was remembering I was "crazy" and a "jumper."

"Oh, sorry, I just thought—"

"What did you want, Ann?" Dr. Burgis interrupted her in an irritated voice.

Now Ann looked even more embarrassed as she realized she'd just burst into the room without knocking. "Sky's mother is insisting she come out at once. She said she would call the police if we didn't send her out right away. Sorry for bursting in," she said, then added, "again," while turning a deeper shade of red.

"Don't worry about it, Ann," Dr. Burgis consoled her. "That lady has been trouble from the first day. Everything has to be done right when she wants it done and everything is always a crisis." He took a deep breath, looked at me and said, "Come on then, go and try to calm her down. We need you to come back tomorrow." He gave me a knowing look and I nodded.

When Ann left, he quickly picked up the cell phone and handed it to me and said, "Don't forget your phone, Sky." I hid the phone in my pocket. I was glad I had on pants with pockets today. Usually I didn't.

We walked out to the waiting room where my mother was standing by the glass doors with Nathan. She was dressed decently now. She must have gone shopping somewhere nearby because our house was almost two hours away. Dr. Burgis walked with me and apologized to my mother for taking so long. Then he offered to change our time to a later appointment "if that would be more convenient" he told her.

She didn't say anything; she just turned and headed to the car. Nathan took me by the arm and pulled me along after her. I looked back at the doctor. He didn't do anything, but he looked like he wanted to. That was nice.

My mother didn't say a word about our fight and neither did I. She had Nathan stop at Smoothie King before we got up onto the expressway. I sucked on my smoothie, playing with the paper wrapper that came off the straw, folding it this way and that, trying to make a little paper bird.

"Throw that away, Sky, it's trash," my mother grumped from her side of the seat.

I ignored her and kept folding as I thought about Dr. Burgis and the pills. Soon the paper in my hand had my full attention. I pinched the little paper wings into place. He turned out nicely. I placed the little straw wrapper bird in the palm of my hand and held it really close to my face and looked at him. I wished he could fl y too. I imagined the little origami wings moving and fl apping and—IT HAPPENED! Th e little paper wings began to fl ap!

My eyes darted over to my mother, who was looking out the window. I scooted to the far side of the wide rear seat of the Hummer and turned away from her so she wouldn't see. Shielding with my body, I looked back to the straw bird. He was still fl apping. I imagined him moving his little head left and right and he did; then I imagined him standing up on his little feet, and I watched as the paper nubs that I had left for feet "split" at the end like it had been cut, and three little paper toes stood out on each stub foot. I carefully set the straw bird onto his new feet, and he stood on my hand.

"What are you doing, Sky?" Mom grumped again.

I kept my back to her; I was busy. "Making a friend," I said. I heard her grunt. She was used to me making friends because I didn't have any real ones. I looked at him and imagined him being alive with his own little soul just like mine, life to life, and being able to use all of his parts, his little wings, his little feet and toes and head and beak just as he wanted.

His head twitched left, then right, and I laughed. His little paper wings flutter ed. He looked so cute, my little straw bird.

"You need a name," I whispered to him aff ectionately. I wanted him to chirp and his little beak opened and a tiny little "cheep" came out. I laughed again quietly and cupped my hand around straw bird a little more to hide him from my mother. He looked at me but he didn't have any eyes. I took a pen out of a side compartment in the door and carefully made two blue dots, two eyes.

"Now you can see," I whispered. Th e blue dot eyes squeezed to a thin line and then became circles again. A blink. He looked at me, bright blue dot eyes blinking again. One eye was a little bit bigger than the other, but that gave straw bird some personality and made me smile.

"You still need a name, straw bird," I whispered, and he said "cheep" and bobbed his head.

"Sky, you're as crazy as hell," Mom said behind me. It sounded like she had gotten into the liquor bar; I didn't look.

"Uh huh," I agreed. I was trying to think up a name, not Flappy, not Wrappy—

"You're worth over four hundred million dollars, our only daughter, and you're playing with a straw wrapper."

"Yep," I said and smiled. Slurpy?

"I'll name you Slurpy!" It was perfect!

Slurpy "cheeped!"

I heard Mom hitting the bar again. Ice in a glass. I took another pull of my smoothie too.

"Must be nice to be crazy," Mom mumbled, "happy as a damn clam with nothing but a straw wrapper."

I ignored her. "I love you, Slurpy," I whispered.

Slurpy flapped and bobbed his little paper head and said, "Cheep."

I wanted Slurpy to be smart and brave and kind. I watched as his little eyes looked at me. He tilted his head to the side and opened his beak just a crack as he stared back, watching me. I wished he could talk better, with words and not just "cheeps."

"Sky, Sky," said a little tiny voice and I laughed again.

I said, "Hello, Slurpy, I love you." And I did! He was my Slurpy!

"Love—you—Sky, Sky," said Slurpy, and I thought my heart would burst! I had never been so happy in my life! My little Slurpy loved me!

"As soon as we get home, you're going back on your meds!" my mother yelled. "And I'm taking you off this damn Derm pill. You're through!"

I didn't look at her. I was so used to her yelling that I tuned it out.

"You're having a conversation with a piece of paper, Sky. We've got to get you back on your meds."

I only half heard her. I was sure she'd forget what she had just said after a few more drinks.

"I need some air," Mom said. I heard the moon roof of the Hummer opening, and the wind whipped in and threw my hair all around. I heard a little "Help!" and looked down at my empty hand and then up just in time to see Slurpy being sucked out of the moon roof!

"NOO!" I shouted and bolted for the roof, trying to crawl out the top. I got the top half of my body out before I felt my mother grab my legs inside the truck.

"Slurpy!" I yelled. "No! Slurpy!" I had to go get him! I kicked and fought as I tried to crawl the rest of the way out. I had to find Slurpy! "SLURPY!" I screamed into the roaring wind, "Fly Slurpy! FIND MEEEE!" I shouted as loudly as I could. My mother was yelling inside the truck, but I barely heard her over the roar of the wind. I would not let him go!

I WOULD FIND HIM!

I put my arms out at my side, felt the wind under my arms, and started to feel myself get lighter.

"I'm coming!" I cried.

Just as I started to rise into the air, my mother pulled hard on my legs and yanked me back down. My chin hit the roof as I came down.

I saw the clouds through the open window in the roof—pretty clouds—

David Hodges

The Second Blue Pill

David paced to stay alert. He'd come straight from the doctor's office to the mall, and he was drowsy from the pills. He knew they would be here soon. David opened his water bottle and splashed some water on his pimply face to wake himself up and clear his head. Maybe if this pill worked, he'd have a chance. He doubted it. And that didn't matter now. All that mattered was getting her away from *them*.

David watched as she walked in with Madric and Anthony. Dana wore a halter and some holey washed out jeans that were cut so low you could almost *see* things that you shouldn't be able to see. She looked like she'd just woken up. She hadn't taken the time to comb her hair, but she had taken the time to put on some hot pink lipstick. David got up and headed straight for them before they could disappear into the press of the people at the mall.

Today was the day. He was going to tell her everything. Right now. He had his green box of Menthol cigarettes in hand as he approached. Dana always gave him a few seconds of time as she bummed cigarettes, so he always carried them. He didn't smoke. He had asthma. But he would have done anything for a second of her time, and the cigarettes always gave him an excuse to talk to her.

David had loved Dana since third grade, and he couldn't let her do this to herself. They'd treat her like trash and throw her away. David could have handled it if she'd gotten with a good guy. Some tall handsome jock or something. She deserved that, but not this.

"What's up! It's Mister Smokes!" Madric said as David walked up to them.

David ignored him and walked straight up to Dana.

"Dana, I need to talk to you for a second," he said boldly. Madric was already distracted, looking away at some other girl in the food court, and Anthony was pacing back and forth by the entrance, one hand holding his cell to his ear and the other holding up his baggy pants as he walked and talked.

Dana gave an aggravated sigh and said, "Okay, David." She headed toward the side doors and the outside tables where you could smoke. She held her hand out as she walked, and he gave her a couple of cigarettes.

"If I gotta go outside with you then give me the whole damn pack," she said, disgusted.

David handed her the pack and opened the door.

Anthony and Madric were watching them from inside, laughing and joking. They didn't mind David Hodges. He was shit to them, and they knew Dana just used him for smokes or some quick cash.

"Sit down, Dana," he said as they got to a bench. She looked surprised. David never "told her" to do anything.

"What's up?" she asked cautiously as she sat at the table.

"Dana, I know you think I'm good for nothing but free smokes and money—but I love you."

She smiled a little and started slipping the cigarettes he'd handed her back into the pack. "Yeah. So?"

"Don't go with those guys, they're bad, Dana. They'll hurt you. You can do better!" David urged. "Maybe Eric or Bale, but Madric and Anthony are junkies and gang bangers! Please, Dana, I know you'll never love me, but I can't stand watching them use you and hurt you."

David reached into the bag slung over his shoulder and pulled out the pictures he'd printed of Madric with his "other" girls. He had printed only the most disturbing ones. His only problem had been narrowing down how many to show her.

"I got into his phone," he explained as she looked at the pictures. He waited a minute while she looked at the pictures then added, "He has herpes." David handed her a printout from the pharmacy where his father worked. He had accessed Madric's information and printed out his prescription history.

"Did he tell you?" David asked.

Dana scowled as she studied the page in grim silence. The key items were highlighted and circled.

He kept going. David pulled out a pocket recorder and said, "Listen to this." He pushed play and set it on the table beside her. It was a phone message of Madric and Anthony talking about her. It was ugly. Evil. David let it play as background music as he fed her more pictures and info. Rap sheets for both thugs. More pictures of other girls.

He reached out and turned off the micro player so they could talk. David had planned this moment for months. She would leave with him now or at least leave these two pieces of trash and go back to Bale. He was a thousand times better than Madric and Anthony. Maybe she would even want him. Whatever. David wanted what was best for *her*.

Dana was shocked and trying to take it all in as David leaned in, put his hand on top of hers, and went for the close.

"I love you, Dana," he said again with all the passion he had. "I'd die for you. I'd kill for you," he told her and meant it. "But you're killing yourself by staying with them."

Dana pulled her hand away and shot a quick look through the glass. The two were talking to another group of thugs now. Madric was waving her over.

"David, I gotta go," Dana said and started to get up.

"What the hell!?" he burst out. Shedding his calm, focused control, David said what he felt. "Are you just gonna ignore everything I told you and run back to him! You heard those bastards, you heard what they said! Don't go back to them, Dana! *Come with me*!" He watched her face—she didn't look like she liked that. "Go back to Bale then if you don't want me! He was a decent guy! But stay away from Madric!"

She slapped him across face and yelled, "Go to hell you friggin' little worm! I'll go with whoever I want." She stood up and slapped him again, and he fell over onto the cement. "Just go to hell, you little shit!" she yelled as she charged back into the food court.

David rolled onto his side and lay on the cold cement where he'd fallen between the table and the glass wall of the food court. His cheek was pressed to the ground as he faced the glass, looking inside. He watched Dana as she stomped back over to Madric and Anthony and their group of thugs. She was upset. She pushed Madric, yelling at him and holding up the paper with his medical records. Mardric snatched it out of her hands, but Dana yelled at him and everyone around him. David could read her lips perfectly.

"This bastard gave me herpes!"

He smiled as he watched.

"Good girl," he whispered as he lay there on the cold cement watching the show. David knew she had enough heart to—Madrick slapped her! He followed as she staggered back and slapped her again!

"I'll kill you bastards!"

David gasped in a big lungful of dust that was piled up there on the floor against by the window and chocked, coughed!

ASTHMA ATTACK!

He couldn't move to help her! He couldn't breathe! He sucked in little gasps and watched through the glass as both Madric and Anthony slapped and punched Dana. He stopped looking at her as she struggled on the floor on the other side of the glass. Instead he looked up at Anthony and Madric who stood over her.

Kicking. Hitting. Punching—*her*.

His whole world—

His whole life.

"You'll burn and die!" He struggled to take in another breath of air—"Die!" Wheeze—"Burn and die!"

He saw them die screaming before he passed out.

Black Rain

So Mote It Be

"**H**oney, wake up, we're here." Mom was shaking my shoulder. "Huhh?" I looked around, squinting in the bright sunlight. "We're home?" I didn't even remember falling asleep in the car.

"I'm calling the couch," Ryan said as he climbed out of the car stiffly. He must have fallen asleep too. I felt hot and sticky all over. I felt like passing out too, but not before a long hot shower. Those pills really zonked you out.

As soon as we got inside the house, Ryan mumbled, "Wake me for dinner," and crashed face first onto the couch.

"Mom, can I use your shower?" I shouted as I took a towel out of the linen closet in the hallway.

Mom called something back, not sure what because I was already walking through my parents' bedroom to their bathroom shower with its new fancy massager shower head. I turned the water up as hot as I could stand and crawled in. The hot steam made me dizzy, and I propped my hands against the shower wall to keep from falling over.

The hot water actually felt cool on my skin; I felt like I had a fever. Dr. Burgis had given me six of those white pills today! SIX! I hoped he didn't give me that many tomorrow; they sure made me feel out of it. I adjusted the shower head to a nice pounding setting, closed my eyes, and let the hot water pound on me. I didn't try to soap up my arms; they were busy keeping me from falling. I just stood there in the shower, letting the water chop away at me.

Today had actually been, kind of *nice*. Sad for Ryan, but still, I had laughed and had fun today. It had been strange, though, and super weird. Had I caused Jane and Dan to jump on each other because I'd made a stupid joke, or was that a coincidence?

And the guy at the Dunkin' Donuts that cut in line. I'd thought about him spilling coffee all over himself, and he had! He turned to leave, looked right at me and my tattoo, gripped his coffee too tight, and "Sploosh!" coffee had splashed all over him, Ryan, and a little girl who was standing in line with her mom. She had cried when the hot coffee burned her arm.

I was a Black Witch now, but what did that mean? Did it mean I was evil or was it just "what" I was? I took a few moments of quiet introspection.

I didn't feel evil, but I did feel better. I thought about last night, but everything was blurry now, like a half-remembered dream. We had gone with Kendal to present ourselves as witches, and I got trapped staring at the Black Candle. I couldn't remember seeing Mary and Bethany present themselves. I couldn't remember what anyone else said, but I did remembered that I hadn't said any of the words Kendal told us to say except for declaring myself a witch three times, and I had even changed that and declared myself a *Black Witch*! We were supposed to affirm the main tenants of Wicca before we declared ourselves witches but everything went nuts after I lit the Black Candle. I know I said something at the end but I couldn't recall what it had been. I dredged my foggy brain and tried to remember.

I hadn't vowed that "All Life Is Sacred" or declared The Rule of Three, "whatever you send out returns threefold." I hadn't vowed to "Do No Harm." I had said something at the end, it may have been part of the Wiccan Rede, but I just couldn't remember what it was.

"No wonder they were angry," I said to myself, remembering some of the angry faces around the circle at the presentation. I thought about the Black Candle again. The Murderer's Candle. It didn't scare me anymore. It was my candle. It made me tell the truth. A real witch did not lie.

"I am a murderer and a Black Witch," I said out loud in the steamy shower. I was. If I could go back and change it, I would. But I couldn't change anything. All I could do was accept myself as I was. It felt good to face it. I felt better.

"Hmm," I sighed. Better was good. I relaxed and let the water massage my head, back, and face. I did feel better. I may not be evil, but I was worried about hurting people by accident like the little girl who'd been burned. I'd have to be careful with what I said and thought from now on. At least my mark gave everyone some warning when they met me that something was up. One look and they knew I was dangerous.

Right then the water pressure cut in half and the hot water went cold.

"Oh crap!" I said. Mom must have thrown a load in the washer. I scrambled out, drying off with a towel, and went to the mirror. I stopped and stared at my foggy reflection in the mirror. My mark was gone. Completely gone. Gone. I knew it was a temporary tattoo, but I'd gotten used to it being there and I just didn't think about it *washing* off in the shower. It was gone.

I winced and tore my eyes away from the mirror and didn't look back. I got dressed without thinking anything. I just moved my body, got dressed, and walked into the living room.

"Feeling better?" Mom called as she worked in the kitchen, cutting up something.

I didn't answer. I just sat on the love seat and pulled my feet up into the chair and stared at the TV. It was off. So was my brain. Ryan was snoring softly on the couch. I listened to the snoring. I stared at the TV.

"Still sleepy?" Mom said as she came over to check on me. Her face lit up happily. "Oh Rain! You finally washed that nasty thing off!" She put her hand under my chin to make me look up at her so she could see my forehead. "Thank God! Now we won't have to find a way to hide it or cover it up on Wednesday before we go to church. That thing looked horrible, Rain." She leaned closer and studied my forehead. "Don't ever do that again. It looked satanic, like the mark of the beast or something," she complained as she licked her finger and rubbed at the dim ghost of the mark that remained on my forehead.

"But no one will know now," I said quietly. "No one will know what I am."

"What?" Mom said. The finger stopped rubbing my forehead, frozen in mid rub.

"I don't want to hide what I am," I said. I didn't feel better anymore. I felt dead.

"Rain Bryant," Mom was getting angry. "You are my daughter, Rain Marie Bryant. That's 'what' you are." She looked at me hard, trying to see what I was thinking, getting more concerned the longer she looked into my eyes.

I felt dead.

"I was," I said in my dead voice.

"You still are," she said, still angry. She licked her finger again and rubbed at my forehead some more. "I'm your mother. I gave you life. I carried you next to my heart for nine months. I *know* what you are. Not some trailer park witch."

Mom hated me hanging around with Kendal. She blamed Kendal for the tattoo and most of my problems. Even the ones I had before I met Kendal. She put her hands on each side of my face, held my head, and stared into my dead eyes.

"You're my daughter. Rain Marie Bryant. And your favorite color is yellow." Mom gave me a tight smile.

"Black is my color, and I cannot hide what I am," I said firmly, staring straight into her eyes.

Mom's eyebrows made an angry V. She didn't want to hear it.

"You can't hide what you are!?" she threw back at me. "All you do is hide what you are, Rain!" she yelled. She'd held this in too long and it was coming out - right now. "The black clothes! The black lipstick! The black hair! The black nails! The black tattoo! Black! Black! Black! Black! Black! All you do is hide in BLACK! You are not a WITCH! You're my CHILD!" She finished breathless, right in my face, then her expression flipped to shocked self-reproof. She slapped a hand over her mouth, horrified at herself.

"What's going on!" Ryan flailed around on the couch, startled awake by the yelling. He looked at me and Mom.

I just sat there. Dead, lifeless, hollow.

"Sorry," Mom said. One hand still covered her mouth as she hugged me with her other arm. Mom looked horrified that she'd lost it and yelled at me like that. "Sorry baby," she mumbled into my hair.

"What happened?" Ryan asked cautiously, not sure if the fight was over.

Mom was pulling herself together. She kissed me on my forehead and answered Ryan's question.

"Rain's upset. Her tattoo is gone. It washed off in the shower."

"Really!" Ryan sat up more and looked at me, looking for the tattoo. He came over and stood beside my chair and looked closer. Mom was sitting on the arm of the chair, still with an arm around me as Ryan studied my naked forehead. "Wow, that thing looked so 'on there.' I thought it'd take weeks to wear off." He paused. "Are you feeling okay, sis? You still feelin' out of it from all the medicine we took?" he asked as he stared into my dead, vacant eyes.

We all heard the front door open as Dad came in carrying a white box in one hand and a bag of groceries in the other. "Hello family!" he said as he kicked the door shut behind him and walked in. Mom got up and went over and took the bag of groceries from him and gave him a quick one-armed hug before heading into the kitchen to put them away.

Dad picked up the mood of the house right away. He came right over to me and Ryan and his eyes went wide when he saw my forehead. I noticed Ryan's small head shake, trying to warn Dad off the "tattoo" subject. Dad was always quick to take a hint. He held up the white box and smiled at me.

"I stopped by the mailbox and grabbed the mail. You got a present, honey." He placed the white box in my lap. "It's from your Grandma, read the card."

Obediently, I started to move my hands, working on getting through all the layers of tape my grandmother put over the card when she taped it to the box. Ryan got impatient and helped tear away some of the tape, then pulled the card free, opened the envelope, and handed me the card.

"Gran always goes crazy with the tape," he complained as he started on the mummified white box. I opened the card.

Hello Rain Marie,

Your parents called me and told me that you and Ryan were able to get that new medicine for your face. So exciting! I'm so happy for you both.

Your mom even emailed me a video! It looks like that stuff works wonders. What will they think of next!

I wanted to send you something special for this Sunday.

This will be your first 'PERFECT SKIN' Sunday so you need a new dress, but instead of a new one, I sent you an old one. I was in the thrift store and when I saw it I just had to get it for you, it's your favorite color. I worked on it for a while to make sure it was perfect before I sent it. I know it will look lovely on you.

Love you all, tell Ryan not to break too many hearts with his pretty new face and that I love him.

Gran Bryant

"What did Gran say?" Mom asked as she settled herself on the couch beside Dad.

I handed her the card. "She was happy Ryan and I got into the drug study and she sent me a new dress for Sunday," I said in my dead voice.

All three of them exchanged worried glances. They'd seen my black moods before. Ryan got the tape off the box and took a quick peek inside and quickly shut it. When he looked up, he looked right at me. Whatever was inside the box he didn't want me to see it.

"Open the box, Ryan," Mom said.

"Maybe we should wait till Sunday." He tried subtle, but Mom couldn't take a hint to save her life.

Dad tried to grab the box, but she beat him to it with a quick, "Let's see it!" She snatched the top off.

The dress was yellow.

Three heads turned to me. Mom, Dad and Ryan, all looking at me with dread as if I might explode or break or cry.

Dad didn't know what was up, but he'd clued in instantly on the mood and was even more nervous than Ryan or Mom. No one said anything, they just watched, waited, and worried. My head felt like an insect's as it turned on the stalk of my neck. Dead eyes looked from their worried faces back to the dress.

What did it matter? Black or yellow, blue or green. I was dead. I was hollow. I was a lie. I stood up and stepped over to my mom, lifting the dress up out of the box. It was magnificent. Victorian style yellow and white, antique, elegant, and graceful. Long sleeves with white lace at the wrist with buttons up the back. It would reach all the way to my ankles. Gran had lovingly stitched and sewn and made one alteration, a V plunge up front that was quite daring for a Sunday church dress. But Gran was a very hip old lady, she liked her clothes sexy, and she was a seamstress. The dress was absolutely magnificent. But why put a dress like that on a dead body? I was dead. Hollow. Empty.

"It's real pretty," Ryan risked very cautiously. Mom and Dad were silent and waiting on the couch, watching me. Without a word, I slowly turned and walked back toward my parents' bathroom. I could hear the quiet happy excited whispers from Mom as I walked away.

I closed the door, put the dress down on the vanity, and got undressed. Slowly, carefully, I pulled the yellow dress on. I couldn't reach the buttons behind me but it didn't matter; I could see the front and I stared at myself in the mirror. It was a reflection that I had not seen for almost two years.

"Hello, Rain Marie." I smiled at her.

Rain Marie smiled back, but the smile didn't last. She stared around, confused, like she didn't know why she was here. She had died that day, when she had me kill our son, and this wasn't her place anymore. She gazed back with angry, accusing eyes—at me and at the yellow dress.

"What have you done!?" she yelled. "Why am I here!?" She looked around from the other side of the mirror. "This is not my place anymore. It's yours! Let me die and go back! Brendon is safe in heaven and I need to go back to my place!" she cried. And she did cry. I cried too.

"I'm sorry, Rain Marie," I told her. "I'm so sorry. I don't want to kill you too."

I heard loud voices outside the bathroom door. They were yelling and trying to open the door.

I looked at the door and said, "Stay out," and turned back to the mirror.

Rain Marie was there, looking at me. She pleaded, "I told you! I don't want this life!" Tears rolled down Rain Marie's cheeks and her lips trembled as she spoke. "Please, Brendon is safe and I don't want to be here anymore. Please let me go."

I cried too as I watched her cry. I looked at her yellow dress; yellow was her favorite color.

"Rain Marie," I said, "are—are you sure you want to go—to die?" I stuttered out.

Someone kicked the door hard. We ignored them as they shouted and struggled with the lock.

She looked right at me and said clearly, "Yes. Please. Kill me—"

Someone kicked the door again. It didn't budge. I started to shake my head "no" but Rain Marie said, "It's okay—send me back. It's *my* choice." Rain Marie smiled at me and said, "Live a good life."

I looked at her and nodded. Ryan and Dad were shouting, telling me to open the door. I ignored them.

"I'm a Black Witch now," I told her. I thought Rain Marie should know.

She smiled at me. I smiled back.

She said, "I know—Black Rain."

I was surprised. What else did she know? I wondered if she could tell me what I had forgotten from last night. She was already dead so maybe she could. I asked her, "What did I say last night, what promise did I make in the circle? Can you tell me before you go?"

The yelling on the other side of the door was getting more frantic; they were pounding on the door, and the whole wall was shuddering but the door was holding shut. I looked back to the mirror.

Rain Marie gave the door a quick glance and turned back to me and smiled, "They care about you now." She seemed glad. "You belong here. Take good care of them if they let you."

I nodded, she smiled. I smiled too. She stepped a little closer to the glass and so did I.

"Last night you made one claim and one promise." Her eyes held the secret for just a second, then she spoke.

"You said these words in the circle: 'As above, so below, As within, so without.' All the power in the universe and nature, all that is above you claim as your own to bring down to yourself. As above, so below." Her smile faded before she went on, "And you made a promise."

I moved closer. My head almost bumped the glass and so did hers. She looked me in the eyes as she spoke. "'As within, so without.' You have promised to be true to yourself, that what you are on the inside will show on the outside." Her eyes got hard and she said, "You cannot hide what we have done."

I was scared and shook my head no. "But they will know!" thinking of our parents.

She looked at me without compassion and said, "So be it, let them know—Let the Black Witch now rise."

She backed up a little, tilting her head to the side. I did too. Rain Marie smiled and said, "Goodbye, Black Rain."

I smiled too and said, "Goodbye, Rain Marie." We waved at each other and I looked away from the mirror to my mother's makeup tray. I reached out and grabbed a red stick of lipstick and brought it up close to my eyes. I whispered "black," and it turned black.

A hole appeared in the drywall beside the door. A hand reached through and started grabbing at the lock. Other voices were yelling outside the door. I ignored them and turned back to the mirror. Quickly I drew a pentagram with the black lipstick then under that I wrote:

R.I.P.

Brendon Lane Bryant - Aborted,
June 2nd 2014

Rain Marie Bryant - Born Dec 3rd 1999
Died with her child, June 2nd 2014

X

Black Rain - Born August 1st, 2016
They will know - so mote it be

The pounding on the door was gone. It was quiet. They'd cut a hole in the wall but they still couldn't open the door. I guess the lock wouldn't open. I saw my mother's face trying to see through from the other side, peeking through the hole they'd cut.

"She stopped writing. She's looking at me now," I heard her say to someone else outside the door. I got down beside the door on my knees and looked through the little hole and into my mother's tear-streaked frantic eyes.

"Mom, you okay?"

She blinked a time or two and said, "Yes, Baby!" Her voice broke and it took her a second to talk. "I'm just worried about you."

I nodded and turned around on my knees to show her the back of my dress and turned back to her again.

"Mom, can you help me with the buttons? I can't reach them." I smiled at her.

She did a half laugh, half cry and said, "Yes, Baby, I'll get them for you. Do you like the dress?"

I could hear Dad and Ryan's heavy breathing on the other side of the door.

"Yes, it's beautiful. I love it, but I'll need to change it to black. I don't wear yellow," I said as I looked at her.

Mom said, "You can wear whatever color you want to, Baby, we don't care. Now can you unlock the door for us?"

"Yes, but please tell Dad and Ryan to calm down and relax. Everything is okay. I'm okay." I looked at the hole and the door and added, "Your bathroom's not okay but I'm fine." I heard Ryan laugh quietly outside the door.

Mom's face vanished as she backed away from the hole. "Okay, Baby, your Dad and Ryan are calm. They won't rush in or anything. Can you open the door now?" She sounded a little better.

"I'll try, Mom, but the guys have really done a number on it." I got up off my knees carefully; I didn't want to hurt the dress. I looked at the dress and said, "black," and it changed. I reached for the door and unlocked it with one quick twist then backed up some and said, "It's unlocked, open the door."

I backed up a little more. Someone turned the knob and opened the door. It was Dad. He looked in and looked me over really quickly, then realizing my dress was black, his eyes went wide. Mom grabbed him by the arm and pulled him back, whispering to him to let her go in first. He let himself be pulled back, but his eyes never left the dress. Mom stepped forward and took slow steps into the bathroom.

I turned my back to her and said, "Buttons."

I felt her shaking hands as she started at the bottom. There were a lot of buttons. "I'm gonna need a lot of help with this dress; it takes two to operate this thing." I said with a laugh. Mom didn't say anything; her hands were still shaking on the buttons.

"You okay, Mom?" I asked.

"Yes, Baby," she said and I felt her fingers move a little better as they worked their way up my back.

"How did you make the dress black?" Mom asked.

I changed the subject, "Isn't it pretty! I love it, and it's so comfortable. I thought it would be all itchy but it's not."

I held out an arm and showed her the little bit of lace on the cuff. It was black too.

"It does look beautiful," Mom said. She actually took the hint! Wow. Progress, Mom!

"I need to send Gran a thank you card," I said. The fingers had stopped, but there were still buttons to go. "Hey, why'd you stop? I'm not buttoned yet."

"Oh! Sorry!" The fingers started up again and soon I was done. I turned around and showed Mom the front. It was a little racy with the V cut showing off some flesh, but the dress was amazing. Mom wasn't paying any attention to the dress; her eyes kept looking at my face and darting back to the mirror and what I had written there.

"Honey, did you have an abortion?" she asked, looking at the mirror.

I really didn't want to get into what I had written, but I answered her.

"Yes, we did. His name was Brendon Lane Bryant." I looked at her quivering lip and started to cry too. "We're sorry, Mom. We're so sorry; if we could go back and change it we would but we can't." I was crying and Mom was crying.

Dad came in and looked at the mirror and at me and my dress, then he hugged us. After a few minutes I asked if I could go outside for some fresh air, and they said that would be a good idea. They looked relieved to get away from the mirror with its pentagram and worse below it.

Ryan was in the living room, and he gaped at me when he saw the black dress. I waved at him and walked out the front door with Mom and Dad. They both stayed close to me, like they were afraid I'd run away or disappear. I stood in the front yard of our trailer, right in the middle of our little patch of sandy grass and held my arms straight out from my sides, letting the rays of the afternoon sun beat down on me. I closed my eyes and breathed deeply.

I was alive. I was full of life. I was better.

I looked around me. Some of the neighbors were outside and watching me. They must have heard all the yelling from inside the trailer, and they'd gathered in little groups on porches here and there to gossip and watch the drama. At least nobody had called the cops, I thought. I didn't care if they saw me. "Let them know," I said as I looked at them. I still had my arms wide and I tilted my head

back and looked up at the sky and closed my eyes as I spun in a circle. I spoke as I spun.

"As above, so below. Let the whole world know, let the Black Witch now rise."

I laughed and spun.

Jane

The Crazy Ride Home

After the "bloody lunch" as Dan and I had named it, we stopped by the doctor's office to let Dan out. Mom and Dad politely told him goodbye. They seemed to like Dan, but I knew they were glad to have him out so they could worry about "just me." As Dan got out, he slipped me a note he'd been working on. It was two pages or more and he'd folded it so I couldn't see what it said. Dan waved as we drove away and I heard his voice in my head:

"Don't open it till you get home Jane—or if you can't hear me anymore. I don't know how far away you can be and still have me in your head. I'll keep talking as long as I can. Try to wait till you're home, in your room, and away from your parents before you read it."

Why didn't he want me to read the note now? Why did he want me to wait to open it? I worried. Did he want me to wait till he couldn't talk to me about what it said? Then I thought "Dan is listening to me worry right now" and I thought:

"Well, Dan, should I worry?"

"*No, Jane! And please know that I'm sorry I can't give you any privacy! I mean, you're over there worrying about what I'm thinking and I'm over here listening to you worry about what I'm thinking! That's just got to drive you crazy. You'll probably be glad once you're far enough away that I can't hear you anymore.*"

"How are you feeling, honey?" Mom asked. She was turned around in her chair, watching me. Lunch had really freaked my parents out. I blinked and tried to switch gears to hearing outside my head instead of inside my head.

"I'm okay, Mom. Just a little sleepy." Mom was watching me, waiting to see my reaction to leaving Dan behind. I'm sure she expected me to throw a fit, cry, or spaz out. Then I thought (knowing Dan was listening to me *think it* as I *thought it*) *ha ha, she doesn't know you're still here with me in my head.* I smiled. But I'd forgotten that Mom was still looking at my face and she saw me smile.

"What is it?" Mom asked, at the same time Dan said in my head, "*I'm right here, Jane.*"

"Oh, just thinking about Dan," I told her the truth and kept smiling as I thought about what Dan "thought" about that "thought." And that made me laugh. Now I was just being silly. And I laughed again. In my head I heard Dan's matching and devious "*hehehe.*" This would be great fun, but Mom was looking at me like I was absolutely nuts and needed to be locked away.

"Oh man! Not good! *She's really getting worried.*"

And now I got to hear Dan worry. Only fair I guess, since he had to hear me and—

"Jane! Your mom!" Dan urged, disturbing my inner dialogue.

"All right, all right—I'm on it." I grumped back playfully in my head. "But what should I say?"

"*Talk about something! Anything to get her talking. Aah, make a joke about the 'Bloody Lunch,' Jane! Ham it up like it was funny or something. She's so freaked about it.*"

"Mom," I said, "are you still freaked out about our '*Bloody Lunch!*'" I exaggerated the "Bloody Lunch" and tried to make a spooky voice as I said it. I did a little laugh trying to get them to lighten up. "It was just some rare steak. Lighten up."

"*Good, Jane! Now tell her Doctor B said we may have some strange food cravings on the pills.*"

Dan fed me the line and I used it. "Dr. Burgis said we may have some weird food cravings while we were on the pills, so don't worry."

Mom didn't look like she was buying it. That second steak had been a blood-bath. Dad hadn't even wanted to let me eat it but I had started to cry and get all shaky when the smell hit me and begged till they let me eat it. I remembered the wonderful smell —and the taste. Hmmm.

"Was it the raw meat that you're craving, Jane, or was it the blood?" Dad asked, all business as he watched me in the rearview mirror.

"W-what?!" I sputtered, surprised. I heard Dan's surprised reaction too, "*Oh shit! Sssorry! That didn't help, did it? Crap. Aaa, try changing the subject again!*"

Dad said, "It looked like you wanted the blood more than the steak. Don't you, remember?" He turned around and looked at me and my blank confused expression for a second before turning back to the road, looking up to his rear-view mirror to see me. Mom hadn't stopped staring at me the whole time.

I thought about it for a second. I didn't really remember a lot about that second steak; once the smell had hit me, everything got so fuzzy, especially after I tasted the blood. "*It was pretty bad, Jane, you even licked the blood off the plate.*" Dan supplied, trying to fill in the missing moments I was groping for in my head.

"What would cause that, Ed, craving blood?" Mom asked Dad. She was still looking right at me studying my every twitch.

"She could be anemic or have low iron. Her body may be craving iron," Dad suggested and I saw his eyebrows rise in the mirror. That sounded almost normal. Anemic? I tried to think about lunch and what had started the blood craving, but I just couldn't remember, everything was fuzzy, like I'd been dreaming.

"Low iron can do that?" I asked.

Dad said, "Maybe." He looked at Mom. "Hon, why don't you call the doctor and tell him about lunch?"

Mom took out her cell phone and called the doctor's office and left a message with Nurse Ann for Dr. Burgis to call her back. But if Mom talked to Dr. Burgis and asked about food cravings as a side effect I'll get caught in a lie! My stomach got knots. I didn't like to lie to my parents.

"*Don't worry Jane, Dr. Burgis is walking me back right now. I'll warn him about lunch and get him ready for the call. I'm on it.*"

I felt relieved. I thought back, "Thanks, Dan. I love you," and smiled. I did love him, and I was glad Dan knew my every thought. He cared about me.

But then in typical girl brain fashion I wondered for a moment *how much* he cared? Did Dan love me as much as I loved him? I thought about that—and I knew Dan was with me as I wandered around inside my head thinking. I still thought about it though and took Dan with me as I went searching through my own feelings. We had met yesterday. Was it REALLY just one day? So much had changed since Dan had given me his note and had asked to hold my hand. And left me that message in my book and told me he loved me.

And now—and now—now I couldn't imagine my life without Dan. I was *amazed* at how much I loved him. Amazed at how much I loved him being right here inside my head with me. I had never thought about how "alone" I was inside here, I thought to myself.

"*You're not alone now, my love. I'm right here.*"

GOOSEBUMPS! All up and down my arms and my heart hurt, I loved him so much. I pressed my hands to my chest! My eyes refocused in front of me again. Mom was still turned around in her chair, leaning over the seat, looking worried as she stared right at my face.

Geeesh! Enough with the staring already!

"Mom, I'm gonna take a nap. Okay?"

Before I closed my eyes I saw my mother take off her seatbelt. It looked like she was getting ready to crawl into the back with me. Great! I closed my eyes tightly so I could ignore her and all the staring and think about Dan. How could I love him so much so fast? It just wasn't normal. It was crazy to feel this way. Of course, everything had gone crazy now. The world had flipped upside down and Dan could talk inside my head. And even though Dan and I have never even kissed—it still felt like we had.

Last night had felt so real as I was reading the book. It started as I imagined myself as Sarah and Dan as Ethan while I read, but honestly, after a while my imagination had gone off all on its own, and Dan and I had been together in our own little Midnight world. It was all in my head, but it felt so real, like Dan was really there with me. I'd kissed a couple of guys before, but I had never done—

I felt my mother's hands lightly touch my face. She *had* crawled into the back with me. I squinched my eyes closed tighter and tried to ignore her.

"Are you sleepy, honey?" she asked. She was rubbing my cheek with her hand for some reason. Strange. And for some reason her rubbing my check made me think of Dan. Of last night. Of Dan and me together.

"Yeah. Sleepy," I lied. I wasn't sleepy. I was something else. I thought about Dan and me together again, knowing that he was seeing everything I thought as I called up images of last night. "I want you here with me!" I said inside my head.

"*Jane! I want you too, but you've got to wait a little while! Oh DAMN!!! uugh.. O good God! No, no, no no no no.*"

What was happening to Dan!? My whole body tensed and I sucked in a little gasp of air. I squeezed my eyes tighter as I yelled to Dan in my head:

"What is it!? What happened!? Are you okay? Are you hurt? Dan! DAN!"

"JANE! Are you okay!? What is it? What's wrong! Mom's panicked voice matched mine, like an off echo of my own voice outside my head. "I didn't hurt you, did I? By touching your face? Jane? Jane!"

I ignored her; I was listening for Dan. Mom shook my shoulders and yelled, "JANE!" at the same time in my head I heard Dan speaking to me.

"I'm okay, Jane! I was in with Nurse Ann and it was—let's just say it wasn't a good time for certain things to happen." his voice sounded frustrated. And embarrassed. "Talk to your mom! I'm fine, I promise. Talk to your mom! Please!"

"Jane! Jane!" Mom cried as she shook me.

"Jane!" Dan echoed her voice inside my head.

"What!?" I said to both of them, annoyed and dizzy.

She kept shaking me like a rag doll.

"WWWHAT!?" I shouted at the top of my lungs, and she finally quit but she still held onto my arms. With effort I opened my strangely uncooperative eyes. There were things to see with my eyes closed if I wanted to. Very nice things. *No,* I told myself. It was no time for daydreams, even if they did seem real. And Dan was in with Ann. *I'm not going there!* I fussed at myself through the haze in my head.

It took a few more seconds for me to pull myself together. I still felt like I was in two places at once as my eyes finally focused.

I absorbed the world one piece at a time.

I was in the car—check.

Mom was here looking at me like I was insane—check.

That made sense, getting used to that.

Dad was looking at me and the road, his head and eyes whipping back and forth between the two—check again.

They looked as if they were about to turn the car around and head back to the doctor's office.

"Sorry, Mom," I said into the silence.

"Was she like this yesterday when she freaked out in the car?" Dad asked.

"Well, yeah," Mom said reluctantly, "but this was different, Ed."

Had I freaked out just now? What did I do? Mom put her arm around me and hugged me and started to rock me. Okay, this couldn't be good. I sat there wide eyed and let her rock me and listened to my parents talk.

"What was different about this time?" Dad asked impatiently. He wanted details.

"I'm not sure." Mom was still rocking me, her voice a little shaky. "It looked like she was talking to herself."

My ears tingled as I heard my father cuss. A long mumbled stream of filth, as if he'd saved it all up for moments like this to really make it count. "They didn't say it would be like this!" he growled at the end. He was so mad.

"They said all kinds of things *may happen* but they didn't make it sound like "this," that's for damn sure!" Mom said. She was pissed too.

"Jane, honey," Dad said, "how are you? Are you back with us?" He was trying to use his best "Dad" voice, but I could hear the fear and anger in it.

As much as I didn't want to, I started to cry.

"Sorry for freaking you guys out," I said as I sniffled. I really had made a mess of things, getting all wrapped up talking to Dan and zoning out—and whatever else I'd done. My God! What HAD I done? *I didn't even freakin' know! I couldn't remember.*

"Jane, it's not your fault, it's ours," Mom said answering the guilt and worry on my face. She kept rocking me as I cried. "We shouldn't have trusted that doctor. We should have been a lot more careful before we let you take these pills." Mom was getting weepy too.

"But Mom," It sounded like they weren't going to let me finish the pills. I started talking in a sniffling, stuttering rush, "I'm okay now! And, and Dr. Burgis said that the—the emotional stuff would end after the second day and—and—"

"Don't worry, honey, it's okay." Dad turned and blatantly gave Mom the "get with the program lady!" look right in front of me. I didn't even have enough snark in me to roll my eyes. I was scared. Had I missed something else, like lunch, when I ate that second steak? Did I freak out or something while I was talking to Dan in my head or thinking about the book. Was I really losing it? What was wrong with me?

"You said you were sleepy, Jane. Why don't you just take a nap as we drive home? It's okay baby. Everything's going to be fine." She held me and rocked there in the back seat.

Mom kept touching my face, which felt tight, tingly, and a little numb from all the crying. Finally I had to ask. "Mom, why are you touching my face?"

She reached back into the front seat and grabbed her purse and dug around inside till she found her compact. She opened it and held it up in front of me so I could see my reflection in the mirror. At first I didn't get it. It was me, but with puffy red eyes from crying. Then I noticed my cheeks. I turned my head this way and that, checking my face. I took the mirror from Mom's hand so I could move it around better. I didn't have any redness or zits anywhere. My skin was absolutely perfect, not one spot or blemish. I was pale but my skin was perfect.

"Oh," I said and looked closer in the mirror, "that explains it." I touched my face like my mother had been doing.

"Explains what, Jane?" Mom asked.

"My skin has been real tight and tingly all over since I took my second pill," I said as I looked in the mirror. My lips looked so red! And I was kinda pale looking—

"Your skin is tingling right now?" Mom asked.

I nodded still looking at myself in the mirror.

"What's that?" Dad asked. He hadn't caught every word. Mom told him about my "new" face and my tingling skin. He tried to see me in the rearview then gave up. "Jane, honey, lean up here so I can see your face."

Mom took out a tissue and wiped my tears away and cleaned me up some. "Show your father." She gave me an encouraging smile.

I leaned forward between the seats and looked at my Dad. He touched my face too. "Does it hurt any or is it just tingling?" He was more concerned about me hurting than anything else.

"It doesn't really hurt; it just feels kind of tight and tingly all over," I said and rubbed my arms. Now that I was talking about it the tingling was bugging me more.

"It's not just your face, is it?" Mom asked. "You're tingling all over?"

"Everywhere," I confirmed and sat back into the rear seat beside her.

"You look fantastic, honey," Dad said. His cringing eyes met mine in the rear view. "Sorry I didn't tell you that first, I'm just worried about you." He turned back to the road but his eyes in the rearview mirror looked a little better. "At least those pills work." He seemed reassured now that some good was coming from all this craziness.

It's so quiet—

"Dan?"

"Dan? Are you there?" I shouted in my head out, "Dan! Can you hear me! Are you there!?"

Mom felt me tense up. "Honey, are you okay?"

"What is it, is she okay!?" Dad's worried echo followed from the front seat.

I tried to stay calm, but it was hard when I couldn't hear Dan's voice and know he was okay! My insides were all knotted up with worry. Where was he!

"I'm okay," I answered with a shaky voice.

Mom's eyes went crazy with worry again, and I couldn't help the tired, annoyed groan of a sigh that came out of me. "Holy crap, Mom!" The endless eyeballing and panic were getting on my last nerve. "Every time I twitch or move or fart, you don't have to call 911." I gave her my best annoyed teenager look. "Doctor Burgis said the first two days would be hard."

I saw Mom's "Yeah right!" expression and added, "And maybe it's harder on me than most, but it's supposed to be better by tomorrow, the third day, so everyone just—*Get A Grip!*" My voice was back toward the end, and I was able to deliver the line with a decent amount of teen angst.

Mom's cell phone rang. "It's the doctor." Mom recognized the number before she answered.

I listened while my parents fussed at Dr. Burgis about my "bloody lunch" and my weirdness. They thought I was talking to myself and going crazy. No surprise there. Mom stopped in the middle of her barrage of questions and said, "All right, fine. I'll tell her now."

She looked annoyed as she turned to me, "Dan said he's okay. Dan made Dr. Burgis promise to tell you when he called." She didn't look happy about relaying that message either.

"Mom, tell him to tell Dan I'm okay too. And that I love him." I added without thinking.

Mom tilted her head to the side and gave me a pained look. She shook her head no.

"Moomm," I whined.

"Just do it, Donna," Dad said. He wanted to keep me happy.

I gave Dad a smile and a sickeningly sweet, "Thanks, Daddy."

Mom narrowed her eyes and gave Dad the *"you'll pay later!"* look but told Dr. Burgis exactly what I had told her to say, even the part about me loving Dan. "And we'll certainly talk about *that* tomorrow!" she promised the doctor as she set a time to meet with him again tomorrow.

After playing message maid she went back to her questions, asking him about my tingly skin and the change in my face before finally letting him go.

I felt better now that I knew Dan was okay. I wished I could still hear him. I closed my eyes and tried to speak to him again. "Dan! Dan! Is anyone here?" I said inside my head. No voice answered. After having Dan in here with me it felt horrible to be alone.

My eyes snapped open with a start as I remembered Dan's note in my pocket. But that was all it took to set my mom off like a booby trap.

"Jane! Are you all right?" she said suddenly. She was on me like white on rice, staring at my face again.

"What is it? What's happening!?" Dad barked, head whipping around to see. They were acting as if a twitch were the preamble of some new meltdown.

I'd had enough.

"That's it. I'm so done with the pins and needles crap!" I yelled. "And I'm through with you getting all into my face." I said to my mother. I didn't need to get into her face to say it, she was already in mine. "You're evicted from the back seat! Go back to your own hole, woman." I pointed to the front passenger seat and ignored her objections as I pushed and shoved her in that direction.

Mom went, which got her out of my lap and gave me some breathing room. I had to do some major damage control. What I wanted to do was to read Dan's note, but if Mom saw it she'd want to know what it said and I didn't want that. I could wait. Instead I leaned forward, sticking my head between the front seats so that I was right there between both of them so they could both see me. I even reached forward and fooled with the radio, staying as close to them as I could.

"Honey, you've been trapped in the house long enough," Mom said. "I think it would be good for you to get out and see your friends again. Why don't you call Stacy and Emma? You can show them your new face."

"Yeah, that's a great idea!" Dad agreed enthusiastically. "Maybe you three girls could do an early lunch tomorrow, so when you go to the doctor's office you don't have to take that pill on an empty stomach."

And that was that. Mom had me call to set it up. The girls were both super happy to hear from me and excited to see my new face. We'd meet them tomorrow morning at the food court in the mall before heading to the doctor's. The last ten minutes it took to get home I spent on the phone talking with Stacy and Emma on a three-way call. Mom and Dad were happy as they listened to my normal *girl* talk and by the time we walked into the house it seemed like everything was back to normal.

"Don't go hide in you room, Jane, stay out here and read with me," Mom said as she sat on the couch. "I miss having you out here with me." When I hesitated, she begged, "Please, Jane! Please, please, please. And I know it sounds crazy and overprotective, but I don't want you alone in your room right now. Or on your computer. I want you right here where I can keep an eye on you." She patted the couch beside her, "Let's be couch potatoes tonight."

I got the hint. She wasn't really "asking" me to stay and read with her, she was "telling" me to stay and read with her. Mom may be acting okay but she was still totally freaked. I picked up my book from the table and sat on the couch with her. Mom looked so relieved that I felt guilty for making her worry so much.

"Make some room, lady," I said as I stretched out on the couch resting my back against the opposite arm and throwing my legs on top of hers. I opened up to the honeymoon scene again but stopped reading after the first line. Probably best to skip this part for now, especially lying here beside my mom. I didn't know what had happened last night when I read that part of the book, but there was no way I was going to read it tonight. I skipped ahead a short ways and stopped at a good blood and guts section. That should be safe, I thought. I started reading at the part where Sarah gets turned into a vampire by Ethan, definitely NOT sexy! I'd already read this part through once but I quickly got into it again. It was horrifying, going into graphic detail on the burning pain Sarah experienced as Ethan's bite transformed her into a vampire.

In no time I was totally lost in the book, into the world of Sarah and her Ethan (me and my Dan), of vampires and blood, my runaway imagination taking me deeper with each page I turned.

I completely forgot about the note Dan had given me to read.

Sky Lee Han

Clouds with Teeth

I woke to the sound of cussing in Cantonese. My father was yelling at my mother. My chin hurt, but I didn't move. I didn't want anyone to know I was awake. It felt like there was a big bandage on my chin. My father was speaking so fast it was hard to understand everything. I spoke Cantonese and a few other languages, but it was still hard to hear every word when he spoke so fast—

"Cuss! Cuss! Where was Nathan! Why didn't he stop the DAMN CAR! Cuss! Cuss! Cuss! —"

Mom spoke Cantonese too, but she answered in English, "It happened so fast, we didn't have any chance to—"

"WHY the HELL did you open the roof!?" Dad cut her off, not giving her a chance to explain. "You stupid cuss! Cuss! Cuss! What the hell were you thinking!? Cuss! Cuss! She is all I have to leave behind me in this world and you almost killed her! Cuss! Cuss! Cuss! —"

"Tam, I'm trying!" Mom's voice pleaded, "I'm trying to keep her safe but she's getting worse! Ask Emelia! She jumped off her bed last night and—"

"And why the hell did you open the roof of the Hummer!? Cuss! Cuss! Cuss! Were you so drunk and drugged up you didn't know what you were doing!? Cuss! Cuss! Cuss! —"

Mom was angry now and she screamed back at him, "SKY IS GETTING WORSE! You can't leave her alone for a second! She needs to be in a hospital, Tam!"

"Cuss! Cuss! Cuss! I will… hospital… Cuss! Cuss! Again… Cuss! Cuss!"

Mom screamed right back, "FINE! You won't have anything of yourself to leave behind because she's going to KILL HERSELF!"

Smack!

I couldn't stop myself from jumping a little, but I quickly froze again. I hoped Mom was okay. She didn't know I could fly. It wasn't really her fault Slurpy got sucked out the moon roof. It was an accident. I felt sorry for her, but there was *no way* I was going to move a muscle.

I wanted them to leave and go fight somewhere else.

They didn't.

I listened as hard as I could and tried to keep still.

"Get her off that damn pill and back on her meds." Dad was calm now and was speaking in English.

"She's getting worse." Mom's voice was quiet. I could barely hear her.

"I know." Dad was closer. I tried hard to stay calm and breathe normally like I was still sleeping.

"I already spoke with Nathan. He told me about this morning—and about last night."

"I was so scared." Mom's voice was shaking. "She fought and kicked and she would have done it, Tam! She was gone. If I hadn't caught her ankles at the last moment and pulled her back in, she would be dead right now."

Mom started crying.

"I'm sorry," Dad told her.

It was quiet for a while.

"Let her have a few days to recover. I will send Cho to visit her," Dad said.

Cho? Why, I wondered?

"Why would you send Cho here?" Mom asked for me.

"I want a grandson. Cho already runs half of my business, and he is an honorable man."

"But he's forty years old!" Mom said shocked. "Sky will not want him, Tam."

"Sky will not care once she is back on her drugs." Dad's voice was cold. "She is my only child. I will not leave all that I have worked for to someone who is not my flesh and blood. Do not worry, Gail. Cho is an honorable man. He will do the honorable thing."

"But even if Sky did agree, would Cho even want her? She's crazy, Tam," Mom said simply.

"You know I love our daughter, Gail. You know that. But I must do something before—" He stopped and it was quiet for a while.

"This is the only way," Dad said.

"I want to speak with Cho myself. She is my child too." Mom's voice was hard.

"Of course. I'll arrange it." Dad was all business now.

Someone, Mom, started to run her fingers through my hair. I didn't move.

"She was sleepy yesterday after she took that damn pill. I think she's just tired and still drugged up. She should wake up soon," Mom said.

"What did the doctor say?"

"The blow to her chin knocked her out, but they think she should be fine."

"And her chin?" Dad asked.

"She had eight stitches. They did an MRI already. The results will be back soon, and we'll know if there's any other damage."

"Sky." Dad said my name but I didn't move. He sighed.

"Call Dr. Dillinger. I want her back on her drugs."

I listened as Mom tried to use her cell phone. "I can't get a signal in here. I'll have to go outside."

"I'll go with you. Gail, wait."

"What?"

"I'm sorry. Forgive me."

Wow! I'd never heard my father say that before!

"No. I will not forgive you. I deserved it. I was drinking and I shouldn't have opened the roof. I deserved it, Tam. I deserved it."

I could hear her crying softly. I stayed quiet and still and thought about what they had said. It was like I was already dead, but somehow still here, and they were trying to find some way to save a piece of me before I disappeared completely. I knew it should have been really creepy to hear all that, but it wasn't. It was like they cared about me, but they didn't think of me as a real person with real thoughts. They wouldn't be this way if they really knew me. They just didn't understand me or see me as real.

I heard the sound of the door opening and closing.

I opened my eyes. I was in a hospital room. I reached up to touch my chin, but my hand moved only a few inches before jerking to a stop. I looked down at my wrists. I was strapped to the bed. I tried to move my legs, but my ankles were also tied down.

I lay back and looked around at the room. Of course it was a large private room. They had the usual machines hooked up to me, and in the corner of the room a TV was showing the news but the sound was on mute. I turned my head and looked the other way. There was a window. We were high up, maybe on the fifth or sixth floor of a building.

I knew I had to get out of here. I had to fly away, but how could I fly when I was trapped in this stupid bed? I looked out the window. It was still light out, but it would be dark soon. The sky held a burnt gold color where the sun was setting, the edges of the darker clouds outlined in silver and white.

I tugged at the straps. I had to get out and fly away or everything would end! It would all be over. They would put me back on the drugs and I wouldn't be me anymore.

I watched the beautiful clouds and cried as they floated by, free and happy. I could sit at my window and watch them for hours. Sometimes I got so lonely I would talk to them and give them names. Sometimes they would talk back. The clouds were my only real friends some days. Now that I could fly, I wanted to go up and touch them. Join them, but I couldn't if I was here!

I pulled against the straps as hard as I could and yanked and pulled and twisted until I sagged back onto the bed and stared out the window again, exhausted and beaten.

Up in the sky one little cloud caught my eye. I spoke to it. "If I can't go to you, come to me. Come to me, my cloud. Please!" I cried. "Come to me!"

My little cloud started to turn toward me. The rest of the clouds in the sky were going the other way. It looked odd, so I imagined my cloud stretching out and swishing back and forth like a snake. "Move like a snake, little cloud, and come to me," I whispered encouragingly.

It started to thin out into a long, wispy line as it undulated its way forward, S'ing along in the opposite direction of all the other clouds. Now it looked like my cloud was swimming through the sky. It was determined too, swimming right through other clouds but not breaking up. He was coming to me.

The door opened and a nurse came in.

"Ahh, good to see you awake, young lady." She smiled as she walked up to my bed.

"Can I go to the bathroom?" I asked in a rush.

Her smile disappeared just like that. "Yes, but I'll need to get another nurse in here to help me, sweetie. We know you've been confused lately and we don't want you to hurt yourself." She gave me back a small part of the smile she'd started with. "Now let me see how you're doing and then I'll go and get another nurse and we can get you up and to the bathroom."

She grabbed the chart off the foot of the bed and started checking the machines and making notes. I turned back to the window. My snake cloud was getting closer, and it was so beautiful. Puffy wings sprouted from its snaky body as I wanted, so it could flap and not just slither through the sky. Its wings rose and fell as it beat at the air.

"Here you go, honey, here's some pain medicine for you," the nurse said.

"NO!" I shouted. I whipped about to face her. "Don't!" The nurse jumped back a step. In her hand she held a syringe she was about to put into my IV. "I'm not supposed to have any pain medicine! I'm on special drugs! You can't give me that!" I yelled at her. "Didn't they tell you that I'm not supposed to have any drugs!?" I kept my angry and suspicious gaze locked onto her and watched as she put the syringe away.

"It was only pain medicine. I doubt it would interfere with anything, but if you don't want it you don't have to have it." She spoke softly, trying to calm me down.

"May I take your blood pressure now, Sky?" she asked very nicely.

I nodded. "Sorry for yelling at you," I said, my voice still grumpy.

Half her mouth smiled. She approached the bed and rolled up my sleeve, grabbed her compression cuff and strapped it on my arm then started pumping. I turned away and looked back out the window.

He was almost here. I watched my snake cloud making his way through the sky. He was getting closer, but he was still so fluffy and spread out. I wanted him a lot more solid and less fluffy and wispy.

The velcro made a ripping sound as the nurse undid the pressure cuff. She started to work on my chin, taking off the bandage and fussing over my cut. I turned my head a little to help her but kept my eyes on my snake cloud and kept working on him. I shaped my snake cloud's head, giving him eyes and a mouth filled with cloudy teeth.

The nurse was cleaning my cut when she jumped and cried out. "Oh my God! What is that!?" She was looking out the window. He was closing in quickly. His long wings flapping, his body wiggling as he came. He looked like a cross between a smoky snake and a dragon.

Just for fun I made his eyes a glowing bright red, like a smoldering fire, and WOW! that made him look scary, really scary, like a Sky Dragon!

"OH MY GOD! It's coming right at us!" the nurse yelled and started to back up, but then she looked down at me, remembering I was here.

"Don't leave me!" I tried to sound scared, but I couldn't help smiling as I said it. I struggled and pulled at my straps. The nurse hesitated, giving me a quick suspicious narrowing of the eyes, but then she started undoing my straps.

"Come on child, we've got to get you out of here!"

I looked out the window. Burning red eyes were staring back at me from the other side of the window. I imagined him opening his huge mouth and biting out the window, and he tried but his smoky teeth couldn't hurt anything! My brow wrinkled as I thought about how to fix him.

"Give me your hand!" the nurse yelled. She shot a quick terrified glance out the window and went back to work on the straps. People started screaming. Shouting started outside in the hall from people who must have seen my Sky Dragon out other windows.

I moved a little to let her undo my other strap and soon she was working on my feet. Sky Dragon was still trying to bite the window out, but he couldn't make a dent. Dark clouds billowed outside the window. I couldn't see anything except churning gray clouds and the angry red glow of Sky Dragon's eyes.

I imagined that his teeth were harder than iron and sharp like knives and shaped his mouth and head to hold in his new teeth. I also wanted him to be super strong so he could bite and move stuff with his mouth.

The straps were off and the nurse pulled out my IV, put a quick bandage over it, and then grabbed me and tried to pull me out of the bed. I pulled back and looked back at the window. Sky Dragon had reared back and was about to bite down, but he looked way too close!

"WAIT!" I shouted.

He stopped right before he bit into the window. His new teeth scraped on the glass, making a horrible screeching noise and leaving jagged lines across the tinted glass. Sky Dragon backed up a little and closed his mouth and looked into the window at me. It was a confused look.

"Good boy," I said. Then I noticed the nurse staring at me openmouthed. Then at Sky Dragon.

I wanted her gone, but I asked her, "Hey, before you go, where are my clothes? And I had a phone."

She stood there with her mouth hanging open and I said again, "Clothes. Little silver phone." I held my hand up and did a squishing motion with my thumb and index finger to show her how small my phone was. I gave her a smile.

She moved stiffly to a small dresser on one side of the room, opened a drawer, and took out my clothes and my little silver phone.

"Yay!" I cheered and got out of the bed in my thin paper hospital gown. I walked over and took the phone and clothes from her and set them down on my bed and said to her, "You can go now."

She didn't move.

I groaned and grabbed her arm, walking her to the door and out into the crazy hallway with everyone running everywhere. All the staff were busy moving patients and shouting at them and each other.

"Bye," I said and ducked back into the room, slamming the door in her surprised face and locking it.

I turned back to Sky Dragon. I wanted him to *carefully* take one good bite out of the window. He started moving again. His mouth opened wide as he took a huge, careful bite. He bit slowly enough for me to watch and listen to the horrible sounds as his new teeth cut through everything. He flapped his huge cloudy wings and pulled back, dragging his mouthful of steel, concrete, and glass back with him.

Sky Dragon's teeth and mouth were solid and powerful but the rest was still nothing but clouds, and the hunks of building passed right through to crash onto the ground below. He'd bitten out the window and parts of the cement and metal all around the window. There was a small foot-wide gap in the floor near the window where I could see down into the room below me and the frightened lady lying in her bed pushing bits of ceiling tile and debris off of her legs. She looked okay.

I had a moment of worried thought about people who may have been on a sidewalk down below. Sparks were arcing where an electric wire had been cut, and the wind from Sky Dragon's beating wings was blowing into the gaping hole where the window used to be. The wind felt cool and wet with rain from his clouds as I pulled off my hospital gown and quickly got into my clothes then walked to the window.

I thought of myself getting lighter as I came closer to the section of ruined floor. It didn't look safe. I stepped one foot out onto air and laughed as the air held me. I took another step and stood on nothing where the window had once been. Sky Dragon's big face and bright red eyes were looking right at me. He looked like he was glad to see me.

I cringed as I remembered that Dr. Burgis had asked me not to make a scene. But how could I get out of here without anyone seeing me? Or seeing Sky Dragon? I looked at Sky Dragon and smiled at him. "Sky Dragon, thank you so much. You saved me. And I'll bring you back soon, but for now I need you to be a cloud again."

I imagined him becoming a cloud again and wrapping all around the hospital, a big black cloud so no one could see me fly away. Sky Dragon's burning red eyes began to dim, then they vanished like two snuffed out candles. Black and gray clouds billowed out, pouring down the side of the building and pooling at the base like blood from his body. I watched, fascinated, as the clouds spread out over the hospital parking lot, looking more like spilled gray milk as it engulfed cars and sidewalks. The people on the ground tried to run from it like a scene from a monster movie, but the clouds were fast and where it went the ground vanished in a thick murky blanket.

Someone started beating on the door behind me, and I recognized my father's voice as he yelled my name. I thought about just taking off but decided I better tell him bye. I didn't want Dad to kill himself or do anything crazy. Ha ha. *Do something crazy.* That was funny. I laughed as I floated back into the room and landed by the door.

"Dad, I'm all right!" I yelled at the door.

"Sky! Open the door!" he yelled back.

"Open the damn door, Sky!" Mom yelled.

I blinked. I was glad the door was locked.

"NO!" I yelled back to them.

"Sky, there is some type of tornado hitting the building. We must leave!" Dad said, then shouted, "Now open the door!"

"Father, what is your cell phone number?" I said to the door.

"WHAT!" he shouted so loudly I jumped back.

"Don't yell! That's very rude, Father!" I said in Cantonese. That got his attention. Dad always liked it when I spoke to him in Chinese.

"Sorry!" he yelled back in Chinese. "After I give you my cell phone number will you open the door, Sky?"

"Just give me your phone number, Father!" It was always best to talk to Dad in Chinese, he understood it better. I laughed. This was fun. I should have tried talking to him through a door earlier.

"Fine! But you don't even have a phone, Sky!" he called back, frustrated. I looked back over my shoulder. Black clouds were all I could see out of the gaping hole where the window had been.

"154-775-0987" He called. "Did you get that?"

"No, once more Father," I called back.

"Again." Now he sounded tired. "154-775-0987, now open the door."

"Hold on," I said. I dialed the number on my little silver phone and held it to my ear expectantly, waiting. It was my first phone. I liked it. I heard Dad's phone ring out in the hallway and I heard him answer on my phone.

"Sky? Where did you get a phone!?" He was angry.

"I'm seventeen years old, Father. I should have had one a long time ago, don't you think." I'd always wanted one.

"Sky! Open the door! A tornado has damaged the building. We need to get out of here!"

I could hear him in the hallway on the other side of the door and on my little phone. With one hand holding the phone to my ear, I put my other arm out in front of me, pushed off with my feet, and flew right out the window just like Superman. I went up and stayed above the clouds; I didn't want to crash into anything.

"Father, go ask the nurse to unlock the door. I'm sure they have a key. I don't want you to be upset with me, but I can't open the door," I told him as I flew. It was so beautiful up here, just me and the clouds and my new little silver cell phone and my dad cussing in Chinese.

It was getting clearer as I flew farther away from the hospital. It was dark enough out that people probably wouldn't notice me up here as long as I stayed high up. It looked so beautiful too. I looked down at all the little cars and tiny people and houses far below me.

"Sky, where are you!" Dad yelled into the phone. I guess he'd finally gotten someone to let him into the room. I stopped and hung in the air so the wind wouldn't make it hard to talk.

"I'm right here, Father," I answered him in a happy voice. "You know, we never get a chance to talk; you're always too busy. Let's talk some."

"What happened in your room, Sky? Where are you?" Dad sounded scared. And worried. I was glad I had thought to get his number.

"I'm all right. Don't do anything crazy."

"WHERE IS SHE!?" I heard my mother shriek in the background through the phone.

I turned around in the air where I hung and looked back toward the hospital. The cloud had spread and settled on the ground and now looked like a heavy fog. The top three stories of the high building pierced the clouds like a tower rising out of a dark gray sea. I could just barely see the bright light pouring out of the hole in the side of the building that I'd flown out of. I was pretty sure I could see my parents standing right there close to the edge.

"Be careful, Daddy, don't get too close to the edge. It's real shaky right there," I warned as I flew a little closer so I could see better.

"Sky, where are you? Are you hiding somewhere in the room?" Dad asked. I could see him now through the opening in the side of the building, looking around the room again, and with my phone I could hear as well. There were other people telling my parents to get out of the room. Firefighters. Police. Hospital people. Lots of yelling. I had some yelling of my own to do.

"Father, I was awake the whole time you and Mom were talking in the room. I heard everything." I watched him stand still. I waited a moment but he didn't say anything.

"You and Mom were going to give me to Cho."

I waited another minute.

"You were going to drug me up and give me to Cho!" I added a little bit of anger into my words.

I waited.

"Sky, you keep trying to kill yourself! We—I was just so worried, that I—"

I waited and watched the little speck in the distance that was my father holding his cell phone to his ear. I could hear his breathing. See him run his free hand through his hair.

"I am sorry, my daughter." Dad had *never* said that to me before! First Mom and now me. He did love me. The thought warmed me though the wind was cold around me. He loved me, he just didn't understand me. He had never spent enough time with me to know I was a real person. He'd listened to the doctors and my mother.

"Father, what do I always try to do?" I asked him.

I watched the little speck way in the distance pace back and forth in front of the hole in the side of the building.

"What do you mean, Sky?" he asked. He sounded tired again, but he was trying. He was actually talking to me. To the *real* me. This was the best and longest conversation we'd ever had and I was enjoying it. I switched to speaking English to spice things up.

"Father, when I try to kill myself, what do I do?" I asked him. I watched as the little dot stopped pacing and looked out of the open hole, out at the open sky.

"You try to fly?" He said it like a question. I watched as he put his hand to his eyes and looked out into the air searching the sky. He was looking in my direction! I took off like a rocket; I didn't really want him to see me. I sped higher but it was cold and windy and I started to shiver. Man, this is cold. I didn't even have a jacket!

I kept up my speed and direction but started looking for a good place to land down below.

"Sky! Where are you!?" I heard Dad yelling into the phone over the sound of the whistling wind.

The wind and my hair fought me as I yelled back, "Gotta go! I'll call you later! And don't worry, I'm all right!" I pushed the end button and put the phone carefully into my pocket. I didn't want to drop it.

I scanned the buildings and streets far below for some public place where I could sit down and maybe clean up in a bathroom. I spotted yellow arches. A McDonald's! That would work! I looked around to see if anyone was watching me or looking up. It looked okay, so I stopped in the air directly over the spot where I wanted to land and lowered myself straight down by the door. It felt weird to be on my feet again after flying, and I wobbled for a moment before getting my land legs back.

I quickly looked around, this way and that, to see if anyone had seen me land. No one in the restaurant was looking my way or seemed surprised, but one old black lady who was driving around to the drive through was gawking at me out of her window. I looked back at her and waved and watched as she ran over the curb and slammed on her brakes.

She left her car right there with two wheels up on the curb and pushed open the door, got out, and stared at me. I stared right back. She walked across the lot and came up to me wide-eyed and open mouthed.

"Are you an angel?" she asked.

"No," I answered, then I remembered that I didn't have any money. "Can you buy me a shake?" I asked her.

She frowned at me.

I smiled back at her frown.

"I guess you're *not* an angel," she said, disappointed. She looked up over my head, trying to figure out if she'd missed something and where I may have come from then looked back at my face. She squinted her eyes, "Ooow Girl, who done cut your chin up like that!? You need ta wrap that up." Starting at my head and working her way down she inspected the rest of me, shaking her head with an occasional "Mmm!"

The cold and the wind had caused my busted lip to start bleeding again. I was barefoot; my shoes were still in my hospital room. My long blond hair was windblown and wild and sticking out everywhere behind me. My jeans were damp, my dark blue top had holes, blood stains, and tears from where I had fought with mother this morning and then later in the Hummer.

The lady grabbed my arm and turned it, looking at the scratches. "Who done scratched you up like that, child?" she asked, "and busted your lip?"

"My mother. We had a fight." I looked down at myself. My clothes were pretty bad. And wet. Right then I shivered.

"Ummhmm." She eyed me for another second. "Oh all right! I'll get you a shake. But you're gonna freeze and catch a cold wet and shivering like that." She gave me a look and pointed to the ground at my feet. "You wait right here. Let me go an park my car." She waddled off to her car, backed off the curb, and got it into a parking spot. When she came back, she had a coat in her arms which she handed to me. I slipped it on and we walked into the McDonald's.

She let me get a shake and a salad!

She gave me a strange look when I squeezed in beside her in the booth. "Why you sittin' on my side, girl?" She raised her bushy eyebrows.

I hadn't thought about it before sitting down, but I guess it would have been more normal to sit across from her on the other side of the booth.

"I'm sorry. My mother always makes me sit beside her. I just—" I stopped talking, picked up my tray, and started to move to the other side but she patted my hand.

"You stay right there, baby girl, you fine. I'll just scooch on down a bit."

I sat back down, and we had started talking when I heard something ring in my pocket.

I jumped. "What's that?" I said.

The lady, her name was Bathenda, gave me a strange look. "Baby girl, that sounds like a cell phone." She reached over and felt my jeans pocket. "That *your* cell phone. Go ahead and answer it!"

I took it out of my pocket, but it stopped ringing before I could push the button. I looked at Bathenda. "Sorry. I missed it."

"Child, ain't you ever had a cell phone before?" she asked in disbelief.

"NO!" I said. "This is my first one. I got it yesterday." I smiled and showed her my phone. It started ringing again, and I jumped a little, then pushed the little button to answer the call, putting the phone to my ear.

"Hello," I said cautiously. I wondered who could be calling me. No one had my number.

"Sky! Where are you! Tell me where you are right now! Are you still some-where in the hospital? SKY! SKY!"

I pushed the end button and dropped the phone on the table, looking wide eyed and panicked at Bathenda then back to the phone. Bathenda looked at me, wide eyed as well, then back down at the little phone too.

I'd never hung up on someone before.

"Mmm Mmm. That's one *pissed off* Momma you got there, baby girl!" We stared at the phone together. I nodded. My phone rang again, and we both jumped this time. We watched the little silver phone vibrate and dance on the table top.

"You better talk to her. She's gonna wear your battery down, callin' and cal-lin'." Bathenda shook her head while she watched my dancing phone.

I picked it up and pushed the green button. "Hello." I scrunched up, wait-ing for the screaming to start again.

"Sky, are you there?" It was my Dad.

"Oh, hey Daddy!" I lit up, happy. "How did you get my number?" I asked in Chinese, excited to talk to him again. Dad never talked to me before, but now he was calling me on my phone to talk to me. This was so great!

"When you called me, my phone saved your number, that's how I was able to call you back." he explained patiently. "Now where are you?" I could hear Mom yelling in the background.

"Thank you for calling me, but I'm not going to tell you where I am."

"Is that your father?" Bathenda asked.

I nodded.

She put her hand out, "Here child, let me talk to 'um for a second."

I said "okay" and handed her the phone.

"He can speak English, can't he?"

I nodded.

She put the phone to her ear and said, "Hello, you there."

I couldn't hear my father, but I watched Bathenda.

"Yeah, I found her out front of some McDonald's, poor child all alone, didn't have no money, no shoes or nothing. All scratched up and cut up. You need ta keep her momma offa her!" she fussed.

"Don't tell him where I am!" I whispered frantically. Bathenda nodded, she was listening to my father talk.

Her eyes scrunched up, "Hey now! Don't you get all uppity with me! I don't give a shit who you are, so now you listen up. I ain't about to let this child stay on the street tonight, so I'll take her on home with me and keep her safe for ya. Now stop a callin' her cell phone every five minutes because this child done run away and she ain't ready to go home yet."

I heard a yell on the other side of the phone, and Bathenda got mad, "Hey now! You just SHUT! YOUR! MOUTH! with that kinda talk right now, mister. Now I'll take care of this baby tonight, and I'll have her call you first thing in the mornin, but till then, stop a callin. Why don't you and her mother take tonight to think about what you done and did to make this sweet little girl up and run off on you like this?"

She listened for a minute and said, "Umhmm." Bathenda rolled her eyes, "I ain't interested in no reward money from you. God takes care of Bathenda just fine, so you keep yo money. I'll keep your baby safe tonight and have her call you in the mornin."

She listened. "Umhmm." More talking. "Yes, I promise, Mr. Han. Now don't go makin her mad. I'm a gonna let you tell her goodnight real quick. Here she is." Bathenda handed me my phone.

"Hello," I said.

"Sky, are you okay? Do you want me to come and get you!?" He sounded upset.

"I'm not going home right now. Maybe in a few days, but not right now." Dr. Burgis said that I had to finish the next three days of pills to make my flying permanent. There was no way I was going to go home till after that.

"Then stay with Miss Bathenda. She has promised to keep you safe. And call me first thing in the morning."

"I will, Father."

"Sky, remember, you have my cell phone number, you can call me anytime if you get scared, even in the middle of the night, just call me."

Wow. "Thank you. Goodnight."

"Goodnight, Sky."

I pushed the end button. Bathenda smiled at me and said, "It sounds like your father is pretty well connected, so if you really don't want him finding you, you better turn that phone off. I'm sure a man that rich can find a way to find that phone." She raised her big bushy eyebrows at me.

"How do I turn it off?" I handed her my phone. She showed me the button, turned it off, then handed me back my phone.

"Now tomorrow mornin you turn it back on and give your father a call. But for right now we better skit before the police come tearing up in this here Mc-Donald's. I'm too old to be thrown upside of some cop car, so let's go, girl. She started to shuffle her way up and off the bench.

I grabbed my shake and salad and followed Miss Bathenda to her car.

I was smiling as we pulled out.

"You done had a full day today ain't ya, child," Miss Bathenda said.

"Yes Ma'am," I said and smiled. It had been the best day of my life. I was about to take another drink of my shake but stopped and looked at my straw, re-membering my little friend Slurpy. My smile turned into a frown. I hoped he was okay. My mother never let me have friends my own age to play with when I was growing up so I always made imaginary friends, but never one that had actually come to life before. I wondered if he had gotten run over when he was sucked out the moon roof and how he would find me. How could my little bird find me? I hadn't unmade him like I had Sky Dragon, so Slurpy was still out there, lost. I could still feel him out there, like a little part of me. A part of my soul was lost. I hoped he was okay.

It was raining hard halfway between Jacksonville and Daytona, within sight of the Bunnel Florida exit. Cars and trucks had their lights and high beams on as they pushed through the downpour southbound on I-95. Tucked into the weeds on the side of the freeway was a discarded gas station soda cup. The words "Big Gulp!" printed in a bright flashy red script on the side of the cup had already faded to pink after two days of relentless Florida sun.

"Sky. Sky," a little voice cheeped.

Slurpy had been horribly damaged when he went out the moon roof. He was missing a wing and a foot. He'd pulled his little paper body inside the discarded Big Gulp cup that was stuck in the weeds when it started to rain. He could still crawl and use his little paper beak, but the rain was making him come undone even more, so he was trying to stay dry. Slurpy was smart, and brave, and he loved Sky. He tried to stay out of the water so he wouldn't come undone any more. The cup would move a little each time a big truck would pass by, rocking the high grass beside the freeway like waves in a sea of grass.

He loved her.

Where was Sky?

She needed him.

He was her Slurpy.

She loved him.

"Sky Sky," Slurpy cheeped as the storm pounded the ground harder, pushing the little cup around in the weeds.

A huge gust of wind caught the cup and tilted it up at an angle, held there by the weeds. Rain started getting into the mouth of the cup.

"No No!" Slurpy tried to climb out of the cup, but it was too steep an incline and he kept sliding back into the bottom of the cup. Even if he did get out, he would be in the rain. He didn't know what to do. His Big Gulp cup was filling with water.

"Love you."

"Sky."

Ryan Bryant

My Sister's a Witch

I sat next to Rain on the steps of our front porch as Mom and Dad talked to the cops parked out by the road. My eyes kept going back to Rain's black dress, and she punched me in the shoulder when she caught me, again.

"Ouch!" I whined.

"Stop staring you dweeb!" she said with a grin. "It's just a black dress. A very pretty dress," she added and held up arm up, flipping her lace wrapped wrist this way and that as she studied it, "but still, it's just a black dress—for now." She looked back at me and caught me staring again.

"Dweeb."

I laughed and shoved her back. I wondered what the "for now" part meant but didn't ask. She looked so happy. I couldn't help smiling with her. "Why can't you tell me how you changed it to black?" I asked for the tenth time.

"It's witch stuff," she said again, then went back to looking at the cops who were giving Mom and Dad the third degree. As we watched, two more cop cars pulled up. Rain laughed and shook her head as the boys in blue piled out and gathered around Mom and Dad like they were a couple of dangerous criminals.

"Let's take some pictures!" she joked. "No one will believe this."

My sister looked alert, alive, and happy. Which didn't make any sense. This whole thing didn't make sense! She'd practically been a walking corpse when she came out of the shower without her tattoo. Her flat voice, her dead lifeless eyes, everything, even the way she moved just screamed that something was horribly wrong. Mom was happy when Rain picked up that yellow dress, but Dad and I knew right away that it wasn't anything to be happy over. It was like she didn't even care enough to "care" anymore.

The second we heard yelling in the bathroom we tried to get in, but the absolutely insane thing had been the door! We should have been able to punch a hole right through the thing or kick it in, but Dad and I beat ourselves bloody and didn't make a dent. My shoulder was still throbbing and our knuckles were banged up from fighting with the door, the hinges, and lock. Listening to Rain talking to herself about killing "herself" right there on the other side and not being able to stop her nearly drove us nuts.

The door had us beat, but nothing could stop Mom. She avoided the door from hell and tore into the wall beside the doorframe with a drywall knife, making a hole. A few minutes later, the crisis was over. Mom talked Rain out of the bathroom and took her outside the trailer for some fresh air. She stood out front of our trailer in our little patch of yard in a dress that had somehow changed from yellow to *black* and spun in circles and laughed while she said some creepy witch rhyme over and over.

It was unsettling because now—that! —was the absolute creepiest thing I had ever seen, bumping the bathroom door experience into a close second place. She had spun in circles for a minute or two, scaring the hell out of us, then came over and hugged Mom and Dad. She hugged me too.

Then she worried over our cut up hands. She scared the crap out of us *again* when she dashed back inside the house before we could stop her and came back out with the first aid kit from under the kitchen sink. Dad and I let her and Mom work on our banged up hands while we sat on the front porch. And then the cops screeched to a stop in front of the house like someone was getting murdered inside. Of course they didn't believe us. They thought our cut up hands were because we'd been fighting. But I couldn't blame the neighbors for calling. Heck, if I had heard all that yelling I'd of called too!

"Oh crap! Here they come," I said as three of the police officers headed toward us. Two of them went right on by, up the side of the steps and into the trailer while the third stopped in front of us.

"You two all right?" he asked.

"Yes," Rain answered without a smile. "Officer Jason Williams."

"Yeah, we're fine," I added quickly, surprised that Rain's smile had disappeared and worried about what that might mean. Officer Williams didn't seem happy with Rain for using his full name for some reason. His face scrunched up and he gave her a dirty look. I watched as he took in Rain's black dress, lipstick, and fingernails.

"And how do you know my name?" he said suspiciously. Obviously his imagination was getting the better of him. If I had been Rain I couldn't have kept a straight face, but she didn't even blink; she just reached up and pointed at him. He didn't realize she was pointing to his badge, with his name written on it, plain as day.

Rain tilted her head to the side and said, "As within, so without. Officer Jason Williams."

Officer Williams was staring at her wide eyed, trying his best to be pissed and not creeped, but it was pretty plain that he was totally creeped! But when he finally realized she was pointing to his badge, he flipped all the way the other direction to pissed.

"All right, little lady, don't be a smart ass!" he said angrily and flipped open his clipboard.

"Hey! Go easy on my sister!" I snapped back at him. "She's had a hard day." I started to stand, and the cop jabbed an angry finger at me.

"SIT back down there right now!" he said. He was right up in my face, talking to me like I was a naughty three year old. My guts clenched as I sat back down on the steps beside Rain. I just stared at him, amazed at his attitude.

"Lighten up, Officer Jason Williams." I put a little attitude into it and said all of his name like Rain had. That jerk! "If you call my sister a 'smart ass' again, you'll regret it." I couldn't resist adding again, "Officer Jason Williams."

My blood was pumping. The guy may have been embarrassed and creeped out by my sis but that didn't give him the right to be a jerk!

"You shut your mouth, kid! If you say just *one more word*—" He leaned in a little to give me the eyeball before continuing, "you'll be in the back seat of my cruiser till we get this sorted out!" He stared daggers down at me.

Rain looked right up at him and said each word slowly. "Officer," pause, "Jason," then she looked at me and gave me a wicked playful smile—I knew she was daring me to do it—

"Williams," I said. And we both busted out laughing right in Officer Jason Williams' outraged face. Right then one of the cops who had gone inside the house called, "Williams, get in here!"

Rain and I had to hold onto each other to keep from falling over we were laughing so hard as we watched Williams stomp up the stairs and into the house. I was glad the smile was back on my sister's face. She kept her arm around me as we both fought off lingering fits of giggles.

After a few minutes, a different police officer came down to talk to us. He asked politely if he could sit with us on our step and we scooted over so he would have some room.

"Officer Williams said you two were trouble," he said this as he smiled at me and Rain. This new police guy was a lot older and nicer. He whipped out his clipboard and asked a few quick questions which I confirmed more than answered. What were our names? Age? What school did we go to?

Rain stayed quiet; she wasn't smiling or even looking at the officer which he noticed, but he kept asking me the questions and didn't bother her. Officer Kelly had already talked to Mom and Dad so he already knew what had happened. At least the parts we could explain.

"And your hands, you hurt those trying to get into the bathroom to get to your sister?" he asked me but he was watching Rain. She kept quiet and ignored him.

"Yes sir," I said, "Dad and I were worried about her. We're sorry you guys got called out, but really, we're all okay now." I didn't want to answer any more of this guy's questions. I was ready for them to get out of here and go.

"And your sister thinks she's a witch?" he asked me the question, but Rain answered.

"So I—*think*—I'm a witch?" Rain's voice was quick and sharp as she stared out at nothing. She didn't sound happy with the police officer's question. We both froze and looked at her. I was worried she'd get all weird on this new cop like she had on Williams.

"Yes, I—*think*—I am," Rain said calmly, still staring off into space. "But then, I—*think*—a lot of crazy things." She tilted her head to the side and said, "I think I hear dogs howling."

"Arf! Arf!" "AARRoooooo!" "Woof!" "Arf!"

BARKS and HOWLS!!! From every direction! It had to be every dog in the trailer park or every dog in the city! The officer and I both jumped and looked around wildly. I could see our neighbor's little brown and white cocker howling his head off right across the street. We could hear dogs from everywhere, in every direction:

"Hooowwll!" "AAArrooo!" "HoowAwoAwo!"

The police and the neighbors started to panic and looked around wildly for what was causing the dogs to go mad. Some of the cops pulled out their guns and started shouting at each other, and then, all at once, all the howling stopped dead. The eerie silence after all the noise was freakier than the howling. Not a yip or a bark anywhere—only the background noise of panicked, frightened people.

Officer Kelly and I were both staring at Rain, our mouths hanging open. The cop looked at me, his eyes and face asking *what just happened?* All I could do was shrug. We both looked back at my sister. She was just sitting there watching all the ruckus in the yard and street. Neighbors were filling the streets, the ones who weren't already out on their porches watching the cops in our yard were coming outside now to see what was going on with all the dogs.

Rain turned and looked at the officer, "So, what do you—*think*?" She wasn't smiling.

"Aaaa. Well. Yeah," he stalled as he got up off the steps and backed a step or two away from Rain. "I think—you're a witch." He said it cautiously like he obviously hoped it was the right answer.

"Good," Rain said in a cheerful voice. "Now that that's settled I am asking you as sweetly as I can to please finish up and go. We're all very tired and we're ready to go in now."

"Miss Bryant, we still have a—"

"THAT! —is NOT! —my name!" Rain's vicious shout cut off whatever he'd been about to say. Her smile was banished. "My name is Black Rain!" she growled at him.

"I told you she was trouble, Sergeant Kelly!" Williams called from the top of the stairs. He and the other officer were coming out of the house.

"Shut your mouth, Williams!" the Sergeant yelled up at him. "You done?" Kelly demanded of the other officer who had come out with Williams.

The cop held up a camera and said, "Yes sir, we're through."

Sergeant Kelly, Williams, and the cop with the camera walked down the steps and back toward the cop cars that filled the street. Kelly went over to Mom and Dad and started talking with them again. For about fifteen minutes Rain and I sat on the steps and complained about the cops and "Officer Jason Williams," but I didn't ask her once about her "dress" or the "dogs howling" or her being a "witch." She seemed fine again. She was scary as hell with her black dress, new name, and freaky mood swings, but with me she was happy and smiling and great.

Sergeant Kelly finally started walking back toward us, and Rain got up and stepped down into the front yard to meet him. I followed her. Rain spoke up before he could say anything, "Sergeant Kelly, I have been patient. And I am doing

my best. Please believe me. I'm trying to be very, very, VERY careful so I don't hurt you guys, but are you almost done?" Rain smiled at the cop and waited.

Holy crap! Did she just threaten the police!? I watched the Sergeant to see what he would do.

"Rain what are you doing!?" I whispered to her.

"I'm sick of this. And Mom and Dad are worn out." She looked toward our parents and I followed her gaze. They were still being talked to by yet another officer, and Mom was looking over at us with a panicked expression. She did look bad. I got mad too. We hadn't done anything to deserve all this hassle!

Sergeant Kelly said, "I think we are going to need you to come downtown with us—" He caught himself before he called her Rain Bryant again and didn't use a name at all. "We want you to talk to one of our doctors downtown for a few minutes. Your mom and dad are going to go downtown too so they'll be close by." He smiled at her and held out his hand toward one of the cars like he wanted her to follow him. "Come on. Everything will be just fine." Kelly started making motions urging her toward the cop cars.

Rain leaned back a little and said, "Really. Is that right?" She sounded disappointed, a little line on her brow was the only sign she was mad. "Have it your way. But you should probably go take care of 'Officer Jason Williams.' He has the runs." Rain turned to me as soon as the words were out. The angry gleam in her eyes quickly changed to worry.

"What?" Sergeant Kelly said, "What are you talking about?" He seemed angry now. He turned around and scanned the cops who were still standing around. We did too but we didn't see Williams anywhere. Kelly reached down and picked up his little walkie talkie. He clicked it.

"Williams. You in your cruiser?"

After a second Williams' voice answered, "Yeah. I'm in my cruiser, Sergeant." He sounded horrible.

"Get out here," Kelley ordered.

A minute later a door opened on one of the cop cars parked in the street and Williams stepped out. He looked bad. He was holding his stomach as he walked toward Kelly and he was pale and looked in pain. Kelly's eyes narrowed suspiciously as he looked at Williams and back to Rain and me.

Rain looked concerned for Williams of all things; she ran up to him and said, "Oh, I'm so sorry! Come on inside and use our bathroom!"

Williams just nodded. She took his arm and put it over her shoulder and started walking him toward the trailer. Sergeant Kelly stepped in front of Rain and Williams before they got to the steps.

"Williams, what's wrong!"

"I'm sick." Williams was pale and swayed on his feet. Rain started crying as she held Williams up. Tears began to run down her face. We could all *smell* Williams. Our eyes tracked to the ground. From the cruiser all the way to where Williams was swaying on his feet was a dark trail ending at Williams' shoes. Sergeant Kelly grabbed Williams' other arm and gave Rain a hateful look.

"I've got him! I think you've done enough!" he growled, then helped Williams up the steps and into the house. We could hear Kelly using his walkie talkie to call for an ambulance.

Rain threw herself down on the front lawn and started wailing and crying and thrashing about. I knelt down and grabbed her. Mom and Dad ran over and all of us held her while she threw a fit and cried. Soon, we had two separate and distinct rings of spectators. One, a ring of cops that had closed in around us, whispering to one another. They did not look happy. And beyond that a ring of curious onlookers. Nosy neighbors.

"What happened, baby?" Dad asked. He'd taken her from me and Mom and was holding her with her back pinned to his chest to keep her from hurting herself, I guess. Our front lawn was half grass and half dust and sand, and grit had covered us all. Rain had black dust all over her face and chest from throwing herself onto the ground and tears had cut grooves through the dust on her face.

Rain looked up at Dad, "I hurt him, Daddy. I keep hurting people." Her lip quivered. "I'm so sorry." She started to cry again.

"How did she hurt the police officer?" Dad asked me. He looked so frustrated and helpless.

"She got mad." What had she done! I didn't even know! I tried to think. "I'm not really sure, Dad, but I think she cursed the police officer and he got sick."

Dad took this in quickly, nodded, and turned to Rain.

"Honey, would you like us to pray for him?" Dad looked down at Rain and stroked her hair back out of her face and said, "I know you're a witch now, but you're still my little girl."

Mom said, "We love you, baby." I held Mom as she cried.

Rain was lying there looking up at Dad. She was shaking in his arms like she was freezing cold.

"God still loves you and he knows you didn't want to hurt that man," Dad said calmly. He gave her a hug and said, "We'll all pray, baby. I'll pray, Mom'll pray, and Ryan will pray for him, and if you want you can pray too. God still loves you too, baby."

We got on our knees right there in the front yard around Rain. We were surrounded by our ring of cops and our ring of curious nosy neighbors. We ignored all of them as the three of us made our own little ring together, holding hands, on our knees in the dust around Rain. Dad started, then Mom prayed, and I prayed last—

"Honestly, I'm feeling fine now," Williams said. He looked at his ruined trousers on the bathroom floor. "Would somebody find me some new pants!?" he called out.

Williams was still bare-assed and sitting on the toilet. Three other officers and Sergeant Kelly were crowded into the big bathroom with him but he was well beyond being embarrassed by that. One of the men wearing latex "evidence gloves" and a broad grin picked up his soiled pants from the floor and dropped them into a waste basket as the rest of the men fought not to laugh while Sergeant Kelly scowled at them.

"Y'all get on out and let me wipe, dammit!" Williams yelled indignantly. The other officers couldn't help laughing as they left. They staggered out of the trailer like a bunch of drunks, red faced and holding onto each other they were laughing so hard.

"You sure you're feeling okay, Williams?" Kelly asked him, still amazed at the rapid recovery.

"Yeah, Sarg." He shook his head and said, "I should have known better than to mouth off to her like that." He shook his head some more.

"What are you talking about, Williams?"

"I mouthed off to the witch on the front porch," he confessed. "Always a stupid thing to do. I'm from Louisiana. We got witches in Louisiana. My momma taught me better than to mouth off to a witch, but—" He raised his eyebrows, "I did."

"You're as crazy as hell, Williams," Sergeant Kelly said, but he remembered his own run in with "Black Rain" and the howling of the dogs. He thought about it for a second, wondering what the hell he was going to do. How do you put all this shit into a police report? Forget about ever getting another promotion. If he actually put this into a report they'd have him see the shrink and then push for early retirement. What the hell was he going to do?

"Williams." Kelly leaned forward a bit and kept his voice low, "This time your momma's right. That little girl is a witch."

"Damn straight, Sarg!" Williams agreed in earnest, loudly. "So what are you gonna do? You gonna take her in?" His screwed up face said clearly what he thought of that idea.

"You're the one she assaulted. You okay with us cuttin' her loose and getting the hell out of here?"

"Oh! Daamn! I got off easy! Just get me some pants and let me get my ass out of here." He looked in the direction of the front yard. "They really all sitting in the dust in the front yard right now prayin' for me?" He couldn't believe that.

"Yeah, all of 'um. Even the witch." Kelly was shaking his head too, like he couldn't believe it either.

"Damn. Maybe she's a good witch?" Williams said, sounding weakly optimistic.

Kelly pointed at the pentagram and the writing on the bathroom mirror. "She killed her own child and she says she killed herself, Williams! If she killed herself, what the hell is walking around out there?" Kelly stabbed an angry finger in the direction of the front yard. "Tell me that, Louisiana boy! And that line about her being born last night. You got that memo yesterday. The warning about extra teen vandalism. Last night was some special night called Lammas. A holy day for the witches. It all sounds Satanic as hell if you ask me. Just plain evil!"

Williams shrugged where he sat. "Yeah, I guess so. Still, seems like she was pretty upset about hurting me."

Kelly shook his head. He didn't know what to do in a situation like this. "What happens if someone else gives that little girl shit? You think she's gonna play nice? I'm worried about who else she's gonna hurt. But if either of us tells anyone about this they'll have us in front of a shrink before you could say don't! If you can keep your mouth shut and keep this between us, I say we get the hell out."

"I'm with you, Sarg! Let's go and forget we ever came!"

Williams started to clean himself up.

"DAMN, Williams! Let me get out first!" Sergeant Kelly took off as Williams reached for another roll of toilet paper.

"Ryan," Dad said and I opened my eyes. We'd been holding hands, praying in the front yard, but now it looked like something was happening. Sergeant Kelly had come out of the house and was walking toward us. Dad was sitting in the dirt holding onto Rain. She was leaned back against his chest, looking up at Kelly. Her eyes were a crazy starburst of dust-streaked tears, her black hair was stiff and dirty, and the stunningly beautiful black dress made it all look electric. She looked wild and dangerous, even on the dirty ground lying in her father's arms. I held Mom. We all looked at Sergeant Kelly.

He gave us all a long appraising look, then announced, "Williams is fine."

We rejoiced in the news, making happy sounds as we hugged each other. Rain smiled and shed some fresh tears as she hugged Dad's arm.

Kelly waited until we were done celebrating the good news then said, "He'll be out in a second. We're just getting him some new pants." He didn't look happy as he went on, "Williams told me that he was short with you two on the steps and that he probably deserved what he got." He didn't look like he agreed with that. "He also said that he doesn't think you meant to hurt him." Sergeant Kelly looked hard at Rain. "But I do."

He took one more step forward and pointed down at her. "I think you're dangerous! And *yes*, I remember you tried to warn me," he ground his teeth a little, "and maybe I should have listened or handled this differently, but that don't change the fact that you're dangerous." He pulled out his little radio and talked into it as he walked away toward the other cops. We could hear him telling them to clear out.

We saw Williams come down the steps barefoot and careful where he was stepping. He was holding his wet shoes in his hands. He stopped at the foot of the stairs and looked over at us, where we sat in the dust of the front yard.

"Sorry I was short with you. And sorry about the mess." He pointed with his thumb back toward the trailer and gave a guilty smile and shook his head as he turned toward his cruiser. His partner was still cleaning out the seats and complaining as Williams walked up.

"Holy shit, Jason! What the hell did you eat!?" He jabbed playfully.

"Ryan, go help 'um," Dad said.

I spent ten or fifteen minutes helping Williams and Fin clean their cruiser. Fin had so much fun picking on his partner that I started to enjoy myself and laugh along with them. Williams did seem like he'd forgiven us, which totally surprised me. It surprised Fin too. And Williams was feeling fine. He said he was still totally freaked out by my sister the "witch," and I replied, "Welcome to the Club!"

After they drove off I joined Mom, Dad, and Rain on the front porch. Sergeant Kelly walked over and told us that he would "*be in touch*" (whatever that meant) then he walked down the steps and got into his cruiser. We all sat there and watched silently as the last cop car rolled out of sight.

It was full dark now and we still had a good crowd of nosy onlookers circled about when down the street came an old red Toyota Corolla. It pulled right up in front of our house. It was the other trailer park witches, Mary, Bethany, and Kendal.

"What are they doing here!?" Mom growled and stood up.

"Mom," Rain said. She stood up and faced her. "Mom, this is part of my life now. Don't be angry."

"But baby, you've already been through enough today." Mom didn't want her to go. "Why don't you come on inside and we can get you cleaned up?" she pleaded. She didn't want Rain to have anything to do with Kendal.

"Let her go," Dad said. And Mom and I both turned to him, completely surprised. "Rain, be back by ten, okay?" He gave her a smile. "Promise me, Rain. You'll be back by ten." He waited.

She smiled and hugged him, "I promise, Daddy." She told Mom, "I'll be back soon. Don't worry, Mom."

"Do you want me to go with you?" I asked. I was worried about her. Mom was right; she'd been through a lot today. Too much!

Rain smiled at me and said, "No." She gave me a hug. "Be right back," she said again, then turned and walked off the steps toward the other three witches still wearing her black dress and her dirt makeup.

The three of us stood on the porch and watched as Rain walked up to the other three girls. They hugged her and got into the car and pulled away. Rain had told me the truth, things had certainly changed. My sister was a witch now. A real live, scare you to death, WITCH! *Weird.* I tried to add up the weirdness of the day.

"The tattoo thing—the black dress—the freaked out bathroom door—making all the dogs in town howl—"

"Rain did that?" Mom asked.

I told them about the conversation with Sergeant Kelly before adding, "And don't forget about making that cop poop his pants!" I looked at Mom and Dad. "Rain's a real witch. She can actually do stuff, Dad."

Dad nodded, calm and cool. "It looks that way."

"What are we going to do?" Mom said to Dad.

"Hide the broom!" I said and made a face. They laughed.

"Order pizza," Dad said. I laughed. We stepped into the house and we all noticed the black stain headed toward the bathroom. And the smell.

"I'll go clean the bathroom." I manned up. My parents didn't need to see that right now.

Anyway, I'd already built up some resistance to the YUCK factor after helping with the cop car. I waved off Mom's usual, "let me do that" as I grabbed some cleaning supplies from the kitchen and started cleaning the floor heading toward the bathroom.

I took a second to thank God that the bathroom floor was linoleum before I opened the door, walked in, and looked at what Rain wrote on the mirror. A black pentagram sat over the writing.

R.I.P.

Brendon Lane Bryant - Aborted, June 2nd 2014

Rain Marie Bryant - Born Dec 3rd 1999

Died with her child, June 2nd 2014

X

Black Rain - Born August 1st, 2016

They will know - so mote it be

Now I knew who "Brendon" was. Stared at it. I grabbed the Windex and squirted it on the mirror and said, "Bye," to the scary pentagram and its writing. I bent down and grabbed a roll of paper towels out of the basket of cleaning supplies I had brought and stood back up and looked into the mirror.

"Sheeez!" I almost jumped out of my skin! For a split second I thought I saw a reflection of a demon-faced person wearing a yellow dress, smiling at me in the mirror. After a moment my heart finally climbed back into my chest and the hair on my arms lay back down.

I hummed a hymn and kept a careful eye on the mirror as I blindly grabbed the paper towels from the floor where I'd dropped them and attacked the mirror with a vengeance. After that, I attacked the rest of the bathroom. Nasty! Yuck! Officer Williams had really EXPLODED in here. And all this was after the cop car and what he did in the yard! Where did it all come from?!? Dude must have had a hollow leg!

By the time I was done I was wishing that I'd let Mom do it. I took a quick shower to "decontaminate" then went out to eat pizza with Mom and Dad. Rain was still "out" with her witch buds, but I was beat. I told Mom and Dad good-night and went to my room.

"What a day!" I said as I grabbed my Bible and my daily journal. I opened my journal to today and read this morning's entry.

Tuesday, August 2nd 2016
AM: Going to see Jane this morning! I can't stop thinking about her. I'm going to try my best to win her. I'll find a way to make those beautiful eyes look at me for the rest of my days! Go get the girl of your dreams, Ryan Bryant! I've found the one I want. I LOVE JANE!

It was painful just to read it. This morning seemed like a lifetime ago. I un-capped my pen and wrote:

PM: Weirdest day I have lived in seventeen years. First thing this morning had my heart broken. Jane is in love with a mute psycho vampire wannabe named Dan. Go figure. BUT WAIT - here's the salt in the wound - Jane told me, in a weird and uniquely JANE way, that if it hadn't been for the Vamp I would have been her guy. So first thing in the morning - STAKE through the heart. Only I'm not a vampire. Still almost killed me.
PM, later: This is the day we all learned why Rain started wearing Black. Apparently Rain had an abortion almost two years ago and started wearing black that day. Also, as if that wasn't bad enough, Rain told us that part of her soul had died that day and the part that was left behind had killed the other part. That part that we live with and love and know as 'Rain' likes to call

herself 'Black Rain' now. Also, she is a real, honest to goodness, Witch. Heartbroken (or staked) and scared to death no less than five times today. Also creeped out and disgusted too many times to count. A Day NOT to Repeat!

Spiritual Notes: Started day off cussing - got surprised by my sister's freaky new forehead tattoo and said "Holy Shit" right at the breakfast table in front of Mom. Then this afternoon I called a Vampire an "Ass", and during the events of later today I also had...let's just say "problems." NOT ALL BAD - I was able to witness to Dr. Burgis today and it seemed like I may have got through to him just a little. He even gave me some prayer requests to pray for. I was able to pray with my family for a jerk cop my sister had almost killed with her 'witch' powers. Don't ask how! I hope, if I read this twenty years from now, that I can't remember the details. They're best forgotten. But the important part is how our little family got together and prayed, and Rain was even there with us when we prayed which was great.

Best Part about today - Rain is happy now. We're all scared about her being a witch and her powers are terrifying, but she isn't like a hollow empty shell of a girl anymore. She is so much better. I think keeping her abortion a secret was killing her and now that everyone knows, she feels better. This might sound crazy, and it's burn you at the stake theology, but I may be glad my sister is a witch. She just seems so much better.

Tomorrow's Goals:

Survive another day taking the Derm pill. I hope these things work. Try to help my sister as much as I can. God knows she needs it. Try to catch up on my Bible reading··· real far behind now.

Also, personal goal. Try NOT to get scared to death the whole day. I actually squealed like a school girl just thirty minutes before I wrote this, I thought I saw a weird reflection in a mirror and yelped like a sissy.

I read my Bible a little and then got ready to pray. I pulled out the card with Dr. Burgis's prayer requests on it.

Please Pray:

That the PILLS will work far better than they were ever designed to work.

That those in the study will have the strength and focus of mind to make the change.

That the bodies, DNA, and genes of those in the study will be able to change as needed.

That the skin & complexion of those in the study will be beautiful and spotless permanently.

I prayed for Dr. Burgis's requests exactly like he had asked and I didn't embellish or as he'd put it "go all over the place." I just followed his directions and prayed. Then I thought about Dr. Brugis asking me not to pray for him to go to church. I hadn't agreed to that because that did violate my conscience, so I prayed that Dr. Burgis would be able to come to our church this Wednesday. I also prayed that Jane and Sky would be able to come to church this Wednesday.

I thought about whom else to pray for and remembered Sky's mom and prayed that she would stop drinking or using drugs or whatever had made her so mean to her daughter. I also prayed that Rain would be safe out tonight, and that she would get back home safely tonight. I prayed for a few other simple things. For our Sunday school class to do well and for our church band to get better. I also prayed for Mr. Denton from our church, that he would feel better. He had cancer. And I prayed that our church would be able to buy a piece of property that we needed before we could build our new auditorium. We needed another five thousand to reach our building fund goal, and I prayed that would come from somewhere.

I finished, then crawled into bed and was gone. The weirdest day of my life quickly becoming yesterday's memories.

Black Rain

Let the Black Witch
Now Rise

Kendal, Mary, and Bethany hugged me and then I got into the back seat with Mary.

"Are you okay? You look terrible!" Kendal said as we pulled out.

"I'm good," I said happily. That made all three of them turn and look at me like I was crazy. I still had dirt all over my face and chest and I could feel where the tears had made tracks through the dirt. My hair was a mess but my dress still looked fantastic; it was dusty from the yard but it didn't show on the black.

I smiled at the girls as I noticed their coven marks. "Wow! You guys still have your tattoos!"

"Yeah. What happened to yours, Rain? Did your parents make you take it off?" Bethany asked as she leaned over the front seat.

"Oh, no. It was my mom's fancy new shower. Blasted it right off!" I complained. But then I had a bright idea.

"Hey you guys, do you want me to do a little magic for us?" I asked.

"What do you mean, Rain?" Kendal asked as she pulled out of the trailer park.

"On the marks. I can make them magic so they're only around when we're all together if you like."

"Really?" Mary said. She looked doubtful. "Are you sure you can do that?" Her mark was almost gone.

"Do you guys trust a Black Witch?" I asked and waited while the girls exchanged worried glances.

Bethany said, "Do us." And smiled.

"I'm in," said Kendal.

"Is it real magic?" Mary asked. She was scared.

A lazy "Yep" was my only answer. If she didn't want it that was okay.

Mary frowned, which she almost never did. Unusually serious as she touched her forehead.

"You know, I caught loads of crap for wearing this thing around today, but somehow I'm still sad to see it faded." Mary looked at me again, at my dress and face and hair.

"Real magic?" she asked again.

"Oh yeah," I said seriously.

"Do it," Mary said, serious also, not her usual bubbly self.

"Can you do it here in the car? Don't you need a circle and some supplies to cast a spell like that?" Kendal asked.

"Oh no," I laughed. "I'm not that kind of witch." The girls were quiet while I put my thoughts into words that more or less said what I wanted.

"I call the mark and set it so.
When one witch is alone, then let her mark be gone.
When two witches are near, then let their marks be clear.
When three witches unite, then let our marks shine bright.
When four witches are joined, then let our Coven be formed.
"As above, so below, I call the mark, and set it so.
"So mote it be."

All of our marks appeared on our foreheads, perfectly formed and brighter than ever! They shone like magic!

"HOLY CRAP! This is soo cool!" Bethany said as she looked at our marks then turned in the seat and dropped the visor to look at herself in the flip down mirror.

"Oh my God! They're glowing in the dark!" Kendal was looking at Bethany's mark.

Mary was digging through her purse, "Dammit, where's my mirror!" she complained.

"Will it really disappear when we're all alone?" Bethany asked as she studied her mark in the visor mirror.

"Yes," I said.

"UUuuggg!" Mary made some kind of wounded animal sound as she destroyed her purse.

She couldn't find her mirror, so I made one for her. I held both of my hands up and made a circle with my fingers. *Circle of air, please help us to see, could you please turn into a mirror for me?* The air between my hands became a perfect mirror. "Mary, just use this," I said and she looked up.

And then she freaked out.

"What the HELL is that!?" Her jaw dropped as she studied the air mirror in the circle of my fingers.

The other girls freaked for a second over the "air" mirror but then Mary got distracted looking into it, at her mark.

"I like it!" she announced brightly as she checked herself out.

"So how do you make the mirror go away and get your fingers back, Rain?" Bethany's eyes sparkled with delight.

I thought about that. I didn't know. I hadn't really given much thought to making the mirror; I just wanted to help Mary. I guess all I had to do was ask the mirror to stay and be solid, but it felt right to keep using the little rhymes to do it.

"Mirror, Mirror, in my hand. Hold your shape and let it stand," I said and then handed the mirror, which was now like a super thin piece of round glass, to Mary. "Now you got one for your purse." I smiled at her.

Everyone was staring at me, jaws hanging open. I waited for a second.

"What?" I said. "It's just a mirror."

"Nothin'," said Mary, sounding nonchalant. She shrugged then examined the circle mirror. "Oh cool." Her smile turned on again like a flood light, lighting up the car. "Look how thin it is! I wonder if it will break easy."

She passed it to Bethany's beckoning hand.

"Cool." Bethany and Kendal looked at the mirror for a while before handing it back to Mary who deposited it into her purse proudly.

"What happened at your house with all the cops?" Kendal asked.

"Family stuff," I said. I didn't want to get into it.

"Oh please, you gotta give more than that, I mean," Mary waved her hand in my direction, "look at you! You're covered in dirt. You've been crying your eyes out. You've had twenty cops at your house for hours. And where did you find that dress!? It's amazing!" She grabbed my arm and started to play with the laced cuff.

"Okay, fine!" I laughed a little as she stretched out my arm to see the dress better.

"I freaked out some this morning when my tattoo came off, and then Gran sent me this dress in the mail, only it *was* white and yellow. I changed it to black. As for the cops, the neighbors called them because I locked myself in the bathroom at home and my family threw a screaming fit trying to get me out." I stopped to catch my breath.

"But what about the dirt!?" Bethany said.

"And the tears!?" Kendal said.

"Let's just say it's been a long afternoon," I said. "Where are we going anyway?" I changed the subject.

"Well, here, at least let me clean you up some, you look scary as hell in all that dirt." Mary went into her purse and came out with a napkin.

"NO!" I shouted.

All the girls jumped. Their startled faces stared back at me, wide eyed and frightened.

"Scary is good. Scary is better for everyone else," I said quietly. They still didn't move. "But I don't want you guys to be scared of me." My eyes started to tear up. I didn't want *them* to be scared of me; they were the only ones who knew all about me. They were my sisters.

"Rain, don't cry." Mary hugged me. "Is it okay to be a little bit scared of you and still love you a whole lot?" She snuggled up next to me and hugged me and I laughed as I wiped at my tears.

"Yeah. But you're getting yourself covered in my dirt, look at your top."

Mary jumped back and gave a little squeak and started to brush herself off.

"You know, we can make you scary looking without you being all dirty!" Mary complained and Bethany laughed.

"Why do you want to look so scary, Rain?" Kendal asked. "What's been happening?" She knew something was up.

"I've been having accidents," I confessed.

"What kind of accidents?" Kendal asked, concerned now. The other girls listened close too. Serious faces all around.

"It's just that—I have to be real careful now," I said. My tears were starting to come back.

"If I think the wrong thing or say the wrong thing, even if I'm joking, stuff happens." I met her eyes as she looked back at me. "I've had some accidents," I said again.

I told them about the guy at the Dunkin' Donuts and the little girl who I burned with the cup of coffee. I told them about Jane and Dan jumping on each other in the waiting room, and they got a laugh out of that until I told them I was just joking around and didn't even mean to do it. Then I told them about the cop I almost killed and how sick he got and that he didn't get better until my family prayed for him.

"That's why I want to look scary, because it gives everyone fair warning that I'm dangerous." I looked at my sisters, my voice was cold and frightening in my own ears. "I am dangerous. Very, very dangerous." That was what Sergeant Kelly had said, and he was right. "It's just that—I have so much power now. I feel like I can do anything. Absolutely anything. I know this sounds crazy, but I actually feel like I can crush the world like an empty beer can and throw it into the sun."

Mary's eyes went wide. "Don't think that and don't say that!" she yelled, then squinted her eyes at me. "You need to go to your happy place right now, young lady!" Mary stared down at me and made a face; she was being funny but she was also dead serious.

"Yeah!" Bethany's little voice echoed. "Happy place! Happy place!" She was only thirteen, but she was beginning to understand exactly what kind of accidents I could have. She was scared too.

"Okay! Everyone just relax!" Kendal said, then she turned in the seat and looked at me. "But, Rain, Mary's right, you need to be very careful."

"I know," I said. "Sorry! I'm trying," I whined back. "And I'm doing a lot better now that I know to be careful! But when I meet someone new or if someone gives me crap my temper goes all crazy. I'm so moody now! And so emotional! And sometimes I do stuff without even thinking about what I'm doing. Like making the mirror. I just saw you needed one and I made one. And then other things just feel right, like the dirt makeup. This," I waved my hand at my face, "is who I am today. As within, So without. It feels right to let it show and wrong to try to hide it." I felt so silly even trying to explain it.

"What about your family, do they know about any of this?" Kendal asked.

"Yeah, they know everything. That's one of the reasons they let me go with you guys tonight; they know I'm a witch now. Ryan also tries real hard to protect me and keep people from bothering me. He almost got put into the back of a police car for arguing with the cops when they gave me a hard time. He knows that I can cause stuff to happen on accident and that I can lose my temper real easy and he tries hard to help me." I wiped at my eyes, I was crying again.

"So will we," said Bethany. "We can help too."

"Yeah," said Mary. "We can help too." And she hugged me again and didn't care about my dirt this time.

"Yes," said Kendal. She turned and smiled at me. "We will."

Mary hugged me and I cried for a while. Soon her white top was all sooty and looked horrible and I thought about it turning black with a pretty green vine going down each sleeve with little white flowers, and it changed.

"Blessed Be!" Mary jumped, blinked, and smiled. "Sweet, that's better. Me like it."

Bethany laughed, "Wow, can you do my hair!? I want it red!" Her smile was huge.

"Red!" Kendal and I said at the same time. We were both surprised. She always wanted black and hated it when her brown roots would start to grow out.

"Are you sure? Red?" I scrunched up my face. "How about we keep it black, but I give you some nice red highlights?" I suggested. I just didn't think red would look good on her.

"Okay," Bethany said.

Kendal gave me a quick nod, like she thought that was a good idea too. Red on Bethany's olive skin just wouldn't match. I looked at her hair and thought about how I wanted it to look, and it changed. All the girls squealed with girlish delight.

"Mmmm. Hold on, let me tweak it some more." I thought and adjusted what I'd done and it changed to what I wanted. Her hair was black with crazy deep red highlights. It was a magical coloring that the hair gurus on Project Runway couldn't have copied if they tried for a million years.

That did it! My next twenty minutes were spent playing beauty shop while Kendal drove. I did everyone's nails, including my own so we all matched with super shiny, long, black nails. I did Kendal's hair. She wanted hers the same as Bethany's; she liked it, so they were both a crazy black/red now. Mary had me make her curly blond hair go straight as a board and she had me make it waist length. Then I had to make Kendal's and Bethany's that long too so they matched. Mary had me make her hair shock white.

"White?" I asked.

We tried it and she liked it. It was ALIEN! But it was pretty damn cool too. I couldn't help leaving one lock of bright green in the sea of white hair up front and when she complained I told her, "Green is your color, Mary Fae" and smiled at her.

She griped but smiled and said she could "deal" with the one green stripe. Mary held up her little "Magic Mirror" for me to see myself. I left my dirt make-up in place but I did change my hair. I made it black as black could be and made it waist length like the other girls.

Kendal topped it off by saying, "You know, the Corolla needs a new paint job too." She smiled at me and raised her eyebrows.

"Too true, she is looking a bit skanky." I laughed.

"What!? Don't call her skanky!" Kendal shot back. She was very protective of her Corolla. She'd had it since she was fifteen years old. It had outlasted an umpteen dozen guys and survived two crashes.

"She's a good girl!" Kendal said defensively. We all laughed at Kendal but she did love her old Corolla.

"Okay! What color shall we give her?" I said.

"Red please," Kendal said.

I thought about it and it happened.

"Wonder if anyone saw that?" I asked, worried about the other drivers on the road. The girls looked out the windows to see if any of the other drivers had seen the car change color, but the other four people who were around us were all talking on cell phones and didn't see anything.

We all laughed as Kendal, complaining about people and their cell phones, pulled off the main road onto a driveway that I recognized.

"Hey! What are we doing heading back to the Mansion?" I asked Kendal. We were on the drive and pulling up to the front of the huge white house now.

"Cornelius called and begged me to bring you over. He said that he had to tell you something and that he wanted to apologize to you in person. He was upset. I don't know what happened but whatever it is, he's real sorry about it."

"Sounds fishy," said Mary, casting a squinty-eyed glare up at the double glass front doors of the Mansion.

"I've known Cornelius a long time and he's a pretty nice guy," said Kendal. "And I wouldn't have brought us if I thought we would be in danger, but still, keep your eyes open. And girls, keep people away from Rain."

Kendal looked at me and said, "Remember to be extra calm. You'll be seeing new people. Don't get upset. Be careful."

My eyes darted around as I realized that this was actually going to be dangerous. For them. It felt weird to have Kendal talk to me like a child, but honestly, that was exactly what I needed. I was afraid of what might happen.

I nodded my head.

"I'll try," I promised weakly.

Three beautiful witches with bright shining marks on their foreheads stared back at me with reassuring smiles. "Don't worry, we're here," said Bethany. Mary gave me another hug before we piled out of the car and walked up to the huge glass doors.

Bethany and Kendal stood in front of me and Mary followed behind me like guards as we waited at the front door. The butler opened the door and escorted us into the main room where Cornelius and Cathryn were waiting.

As soon as he saw us, Cornelius came forward, smiling hugely. "Welcome! And thank you so much for coming on such short notice, but we felt you should know what's happened right away." The smile he started with had already fallen off his face before he finished his sentence.

"Know about what, Cornelius!?" Kendal snapped back angrily. "You absolutely refused to tell me over the phone. Now what has happened!? Out with it. NOW!" She didn't ask him, she told him, and Cornelius turned white as a sheet.

He opened his mouth to say something but no sounds came out. It was just like Lammas night. When he got flustered, his rich and noble voice and bearing deserted him and he was reduced to stuttering.

Cathryn, Cornelius's wife stepped up and spoke instead.

"Peace, Kendal, please. I will tell you everything. Come and sit with me." She put a calming hand on Cornelius's red frustrated face and whispered the word "wine" to him.

He nodded and went toward the bar to get drinks for us as Cathryn led us toward one of the couches. Cathryn was so calm and controlled, and she walked and moved with such grace and elegance it was captivating and calming at the same time.

I was glad she was calming Kendal down. I needed calm. I relaxed just watching her move and seeing how confident and sure of herself she seemed. She gestured to the large couch in front of a coffee table and we sat down while Cornelius brought over drinks and handed a crystal glass to Bethany.

I noticed that Bethany had dressed up, and not just the changes I had made to her hair, nails, and mark. She had on her best top and had even tucked the long tail into her black jeans, and she was sitting so straight backed and proper on the couch beside me.

Bethany reached out with her free hand and delicately touched Cornelius's wrist and said to him so formally, "Black Rain will need water, Cornelius, she can't drink wine."

She looked amazing. Something about the little body and tiny voice, the hair and nails, the elegant tilt of her head, and the confidence in her voice as she held her crystal wine glass just screamed WITCH!

I couldn't help myself; I laughed with delight, but the sound was scary in the big open space and as it echoed all around. Everyone was looking at me wide eyed, waiting.

I was staring at Bethany. "You look so beautiful, do you know that?"

She gave me a radiant smile.

"Bethany Grave, let me hold your glass, please." I held up the glass she handed to me so everyone could see the dark red wine in the clear crystal glass and they all watched it change to water and continued watching as ice crystals formed on the outside of the glass.

I drank down the cold water and handed the glass back to Bethany, telling her, "Thank you."

Bethany turned to Cornelius who hadn't moved an inch since I had laughed. She held her glass up. "More wine please, Cornelius." She gave him a little nod.

Cornelius was frozen for just a second more before he replied, "My Lady,". Giving her a little bow, he took her glass and filled it with wine again.

My Sisters didn't bat an eye or look like this was anything out of the ordinary. After our beauty shop escapades in the car, it would take a lot to freak them out, but for Cathryn and Cornelius this was big mojo. They were still trying to act composed, but they weren't quite as confident now as they were a few minutes ago.

Cathryn's hand shook as she pushed a little button on the coffee table and a remote control popped up out of its hidden storage compartment. *So much for losing the remote in the couch*, I thought. She grabbed it and pushed a button. Right out of the center of the coffee table, a slot opened and a huge flat screen TV rose up through the slot. It must have been sixty inches across, maybe bigger!

"This is a grand house," Cathryn explained. "We have a large art collection and good number of priceless antiques here so we have a large network of security cameras. The night of the Lammas celebration those cameras were on." She looked at Kendal. "We had a break in this afternoon, but it wasn't your typical break in. It was digital theft. They hacked our security system and downloaded the security video showing our Lammas celebration and the presentations. We were informed of this video's existence by the FBI, who called us with questions about the minors who were seen drinking at the meeting. The thieves that took this video have altered it and placed it on the web in a number of places. All the major U.S. search engines have pulled this video off their sites, but it's on the web now, and once released it's impossible to contain something like this. It's being shared freely in the rest of the world and there are dozens or hundreds of individual web sites springing up around the video. We're very sorry, but *this is going to be huge*."

This last bit was said in a hoarse whisper. Cathryn took a long drink of wine before pressing ahead. "We have never had this happen before. We apologize and beg you to forgive us. We will make whatever restitution you feel will redress your grievance and of course offer you sanctuary if you need it. I'll show you the video now."

She pushed a button on the remote control and the lights in the room dimmed. She pushed another button and the TV came on. It was paused. We could all see the high angle of the shot; the scene was the pentagram circle with the little altar in the center. Across the top of the picture on the screen these words had been overlain:

STOP THE BLACK WITCH! THE CHILD OF DARKNESS HAS COME!
www.killtheblackwitch.net

"Wait!" Kendal shouted before Cathryn pushed play. Everyone watched as she turned to me.

"Black Rain. Remember to stay calm. Guard your thoughts. If you need to, close your eyes or look away." She held my gaze for another second. "Be careful, my Sister," she warned.

I *so* needed that. "Yes. Yes. Thank you." My stomach churned, though all I'd had for hours was a glass of water. I closed my eyes and took a couple of long calming breaths. I hadn't realized how worked up I was getting. I tried to prepare myself to see whatever it was I was about to see.

After a minute I opened my eyes. My Sisters were eyeing me with concern, but Cathryn and Cornelius looked terrified. I nodded to them, faced the TV, and squared my shoulders. The video played through the scene of my presentation.

Someone had gone through the trouble of editing the video from a number of different camera angles and had put together a collage that looked more like a horror movie than anything else. It had that scary quality of looking totally real and believable except for the impossible things that it showed. The video was one of those *absolute freak out* videos you wouldn't keep to yourself because you couldn't.

If this was on the web it was going to go everywhere! After the video ended, it showed the faces of Kendal, Mary, and Bethany each with their marks on their foreheads. And then a figure with a white hood on his head appeared, dropped in before an image of burning flames as he ranted like a crazed psycho preacher.

"Witches of the world UNITE! The Child of Darkness has been born in the flesh! We must destroy her and her coven of Evil! We call upon every witch, good or bad, evil or other. We call upon every Pagan, Shaman, and psychic. In this we are one! THE BLACK WITCH MUST DIE!" he roared.

His fist punched the air as he rallied people to his cause. "This Sabbat cast your darkest spells! Send Death! Send Disease! Send Destruction! Send Damnation! Call on all your powers and help us save the world from her Darkness before it's too late! Visit our web site to let us know if you will join our casting and download our information on the Black Witch and her coven, StarNight!"

He blathered on for a while about a fifty dollar charge for information and so forth. Which was typical. Someone wanted money. Cathryn pushed a button and the screen went dark.

"We have checked the site. There are already hundreds of witches and dozens of well-known and powerful covens that have joined and plan to curse you and your sisters this Saturday at midnight. I am so sorry."

We were all quiet. They all watched me.

"I was born on Monday and I shall die on Saturday," I said into the silence that descended on the room. "Such a short life." Not a regret, more an observation. I wasn't really afraid to die. Not since Brendon and Rain Marie.

As everyone stared at me with their stricken faces, too horrified to speak, my mind raced away to other places. Maybe when I left Rain Marie would come back; that way Ryan and Mom and Dad would be happy. I didn't know if she would, but I could talk to her about it. Maybe God would let me take her place and look after Brendon. It didn't sound too bad. Dying. I looked around at all of the crying faces. Even Cathryn and Cornelius were crying.

"Is there any way to stop a curse like this?" Kendal asked Cathryn.

"I don't think this is the kind of curse that you can keep from coming. Maybe you can channel it into someone and away from yourselves, that may be your only hope, but I've never seen anything like this before." Cathryn shook her head. "This video has already gone viral. You probably didn't even notice the black vans parked outside our gate. We think they are reporters and magazine people. Spies. I doubt you'll be able to drive home tonight without them following you. I'm sorry. By this time tomorrow the whole world will know of Black Rain and StarNight. We have ruined your life. We don't know what to say." Cathryn fell into Cornelius's arms weeping as he held her.

I thought about what she had said—"The whole world shall know." That phrase tickled my ears and I perked up. I'd heard that before. Then I remembered with a sudden flash of insight exactly *where* I'd heard it. From me. I had said it this afternoon. After I came out of the bathroom with the black dress and stood in the front lawn. I'd done this to myself. My brain was still racing away, trying to fit the last pieces into place even as I explained the edges of the puzzle that already framed the whole.

"It is not your fault, Cathryn. Or yours, Cornelius," I said. "And actually, I should be the one asking you to forgive me. I did this." I motioned toward the dark TV. "My words did this thing."

"What do you mean!?" Mary snapped at me. "You didn't have anything to do with that sheet wearing shit bag on that website!"

"Yeah!" Bethany echoed.

"It *was* me," I reaffirmed. "I did this, and I think it had to happen."

"Had to happen!? You have the power to do whatever you want, Rain! This didn't '*have to happen!*'" Mary was hurt and angry.

"No, I don't think I had a choice." I gave her a sad smile. "It's part of who I am, Mary Fae." I turned my gaze to Kendal. "It's part of my power, Kendal Flame. As above, so below." I shrugged. "I can crush the earth like an empty beer can, but there is a second part to what I have become. As within, so without.

They must know," I said, trying to explain the pieces of the puzzle inside my head. "They must know," I said again.

They'd just watched my presentation on the TV and listened to the few words I'd said inside the circle. One of the things I'd said was "*they must know.*" They, to me, meant *everyone*.

"Okay. Let's say that you did do this," Kendal said, sounding reasonable. "Tell me, exactly, what you did say that caused this to happen?"

I stood up and took a few steps away from the couch before turning back to face them. They also stood, all of them waiting for my answer.

"This is what I said in my front yard this afternoon: 'As above, so below. Let the whole world know. Let the Black Witch now rise.'" I looked at Kendal. "It had to be said. It was part of me and it felt right to say it. This is one of those things that I can't explain and I just feel."

I turned away from everyone, tired of trying to explain. I stared blankly out the wall of windows positioned before the couches and breathed. The view showed a well-manicured green lawn bordered by a dark line of shadowy oak trees. It was dark outside, but the lawn was illuminated by landscaping lights and the silvery light of the moon.

Arms encircled me from behind, and Mary rested her chin on my shoulder. Still attached like that she stepped, stepped, stepped (rocking back and forth like a penguin) a little step at a time until she turned us around to face Kendal and the others. I didn't laugh but I did smile.

"So they're going to try to curse us. Big whoop. So what!? How do we stop it!?" Mary spoke with her arms around me and her head on my shoulder but she was serious. She was ready to fight.

I hugged the arms that were wrapped tight around my middle and turned my head to the side and snuggled into her snow white hair. That was our Mary, down to business, or on to fun!

Kendal turned to Cathryn, "May we use your house this Saturday, Cathryn. You might be attacked along with us and you may need our protection before this is through."

Cathryn looked shaken by everything she'd just heard, but she nodded. "Yes, yes, of course. Come here."

Cornelius added his firm consent. "Yes. By all means, come here and prepare your defense against this atrocity! I am sure you will find a way to shield yourself from this senseless attack!" He cast a quick glance at Cathryn and said, "And if you need a place of sanctuary, you are welcome to come here. Our home is open to StarNight. Please consider yourselves our guests."

"Black!" "Black!" "Black!" "Rain!" "Rain!" "Rain!"

I reached to my purse. "Sorry, it's my cell phone," I said as I fumbled it out and flipped it open.

"Hello?"

"Hello, honey." It was my Dad! "Just called to check on you. Are you almost home?" he asked and I noticed the time on the phone. It was 9:55! I had five minutes to get home or I would have lied to my father! I'd made a promise!

"Oh yeah, Dad! I'm almost home, don't worry." I caught the wild looks that Kendal, Mary, and Bethany shot me and I held up a finger for them to give me a second.

"Okay, honey. We ordered pizza, hope you're hungry."

"Okay, I'll be right in. Bye."

"Bye, Baby," Dad said and ended his call.

I racked my brain, trying to think of how to get home in time while waving my finger around to ward off the group freak out. What on earth was I going to do!? I wished I could just open a door and be in my bedroom.

So why the hell not!? I looked at the front door; it was huge, that wouldn't do. I turned to the group standing behind me, looked at Cathryn and Cornelius and said, "I need a regular-sized door. Not some big giant Viking door or some glass thing! You got a room with a regular-sized door?"

Cathryn said, "Yes," looking totally confused.

"Take me there this instant!" I commanded. Which felt weird. Wrong even. Everyone blinked and so did I. Cathryn just looked surprised. "Forgive me, Cathryn. Please," I said as sincerely as I could and waited.

Cathryn did a little nod of her head. "Right this way," she said, then turned and took off, leading us away from the room and toward the kitchens.

Mary was sticking to my side like glue, keeping ahold of one of my arms with one hand while she fiddled with her cell with the other. "What are you going to do!? You're supposed to be home in," she looked at her own cell and wailed, "two minutes!"

I said, "Mary, Bethany, you guys want to come over to my house tonight? We got pizza!"

"What do you mean, at your house?" Bethany said. "How we gonna get there? We're in a KITCHEN!" She threw her arms wide as we walked through the huge kitchen area and into a smaller back storage area that had eight foot ceilings, and right there in front of us was a perfect door. It was white and practically the same size as my bedroom door.

"Oh great! Thanks so much!" I told Cathryn. I turned to Bethany and said, "Give me a pen please."

She didn't ask questions; she just opened her little purse and handed me a fat black marker. I took the cap off and went straight to the door and wrote right on it.

3345 Derling Drive Lot 214

bedroom door of the Black Witch

For StarNight this is a Gate

For us to leave before I'm late!

A hand placed here will open the way

At any time, on any day!

As above, so below.

I make this door and set it so.

So mote it be!

I quickly put my hand to the door and traced around it, then said, "Bethany give me your hand." She quickly put her little hand on the door and I traced around it. I didn't have to ask the other girls; they put their hands on the door as well. After I traced Kendal's hand and she backed up a step, I handed the marker back to Bethany and put my hand on the door inside the outline of my own traced hand and read the writing:

"For StarNight this is a Gate
For us to leave before I'm late!
A hand placed here will open the way
At any time, on any day!
As above, so below.
I make this door and set it so.
So mote it be!"

I knocked three times and said, "Now open up, I've got to go!"

Light shone around the edges of the door. I reached for the handle, turned it, and opened the door. It was my bedroom! I heard everyone gasp behind me. I had clothes everywhere; my room was a mess.

"Oh crap, my room is a mess!" I said then turned around and looked at the shocked faces staring into my room.

"What?" I said, having some fun with it. "It's not THAT bad!" Kendal laughed. At least she got it.

"Oh sooo cool!" Bethany turned to Kendal. "Can I go to Rain's, please! Please! Please!" She begged and bounced up and down like a five year old while she gave Kendal her pleading puppy dog eyes.

"Why don't all of you guys come over?" I thought for a minute. "Hey, maybe the butler can drive the Corolla back to your house the long way tonight?" I suggested.

"No way!" Kendal said, shocked, "I'm not leaving her!" She looked scandalized that I'd even suggested it. "And I need to talk to Cathryn about how to stop this curse that's coming on Saturday. You guys go. Your mom wouldn't be too keen on me coming out of your bedroom anyway, but she'll probably be okay with Bethany and Mary. So go, you're late already!" She gave me a quick kiss on my dirty check and told Bethany to at least call and leave a message for her mother and let her know she was safe and in the trailer park somewhere but told her not to say where.

Mary was already in my bedroom throwing clothes around, laughing.

"This is a mess! Hey, I found your black witchy undies!" She picked them up off the floor and started waving them around over her head.

"Hey!" I yelled as Bethany ran into my room, jumped up onto my bed, and started bouncing away while she and Mary laughed.

"Take your shoes off, you little WITCH!" I yelled, then turned to Cornelius and Cathryn.

"Thanks for the warning, and sorry for all the trouble I've caused you guys." I was smiling and half out of breath from yelling at the girls. "If I need to come back this way, will it be all right?" I asked.

Cathryn seemed calm and happy as she answered me. "Yes. Of course, and we will keep this door safe for your use. Come back to us soon." She came forward and surprised me as she kissed my other dirty check and gave me a quick hug before stepping back to Cornelius.

"Yes. Come back soon, Black Rain." Cornelius confirmed.

"Thank you, Cornelius," I said and walked into the room, shutting the door behind me.

As soon as it was shut, the white storage room door turned flat black. My bedroom door color. I heard knocking on the other side of the door and my mother's voice.

"Who's in there!? Someone open this door!" She was mad. Great.

The girls were already sitting on the bed, their hands in their laps and their eyes wide and innocent like perfect little angels. I shook my head, grinning as I turned back to the door and opened it.

I watched my Mom freak out as she looked at me standing in my bedroom where she knew I wasn't, but somehow *I was*.

"Oh my! Rain! How did you—? But—when did you get in!?" Her eyes tracked in on my mark that was back on my forehead and her face puckered up like she'd sucked on something sour, and then she noticed the girls behind me sitting on my bed.

"And *where* did *they* come from!?" She was gawking at Mary's white alien hair and Bethany's crazy black/red hairdo and then she noticed my own hair and nails. She looked back and forth from me to the girls, studying how we all matched now.

"Mom, these are my Sisters."

"You don't have any sisters, Rain." Mom shook her head and eyed the girls.

I tried again. "Mom, these girls aren't just my friends, they are my Sisters now, and they love me very much and I love them. Okay?" I waited until she processed that.

Mom nodded, scrunched up her eyebrows angrily and scanned the room. "You don't have that Kendal lady hiding in your room somewhere, do you?" Her mouth was set in a firm line as she eyed my closet.

"No. It's just me, Mary, and Bethany." Right then I heard Dad's voice call through the house.

"No sign of her and it's ten after ten!" He sounded upset. Not mad, just hurt.

"Dad! I'm back here!" I called.

"What!?" I heard his feet coming, pounding on the floor of the trailer as he ran across the living room and into the little hall and slid to a stop right in front of my door.

"Hi, Dad!" I greeted him with a big smile and watched his face light up.

"Rain!" he said. He squeezed right past Mom who was still standing in the doorway. He stepped in and hugged me and then noticed I had guests. "Oh!" He looked the girls over.

Bethany gave him a nervous little smile and a tiny wave. Mary smiled wide and said, "Hi, Mr. Bryant, I'm Mary." She leaned her head onto Bethany's head and said, "And this is Bethany."

"Hello, girls," Dad said. He looked them over then turned back to me, quickly observing the similar changes to my appearance. He turned back to the girls. "Are you girls hungry? We got plenty of pizza." Dad gave them a truly warm and welcoming smile and they both nodded.

"Good. I'll go get some drinks ready and set the table for us, and I'll see you girls in just a minute then." He stopped in front of me and kissed my forehead right on my mark before he turned and went toward the kitchen.

"Mom," I said and did a "come here" hand wave for her to come on into the room.

"Yes, honey?" she said and stepped inside. She still didn't seem too happy that the girls were here. I took her by the hand and led her over to Mary and Bethany.

"Mom, I want you to get to know them because I love them, and I want you to love them too. They're good girls." I said this and waited.

Mom still didn't move. My eyes started to tear up. "And *yes*, Mom, they're witches like me," I said and looked right at her. "But they're good girls."

Mom stared at me for a minute longer then sat on the bed with the girls and started asking them questions. I sat on the floor in front of them and watched as Mary's smile and Bethany just being "Bethany" started to win Mom over. After a few minutes Dad called from the kitchen for us to come and eat. Mom sent the girls on ahead.

"Can the girls stay over tonight?" I asked. Her face scrunched up again but not as bad this time.

"Won't their parents be worried about them?" she asked.

"Bethany usually sleeps at Kendal's, her home life is horrible, and you've seen Mary before. She's my best friend and I'm always hanging out at her house. Her parents will probably think that it's about time she hung out at my place for a change."

I hugged my mom and said, "I don't want to be alone tonight. Please, let them sleep over, Mom."

She looked at me for a minute, let out a weary sigh, then nodded.

"Did you have to get that tattoo put back on? And is that permanent ink?" She made a face as she touched the tattoo on my forehead.

"Don't worry, Mom, this one comes off too," I told her. It did, but I didn't want it to. I liked having my sisters around.

"All right, honey," Mom said. "They can stay. Especially that little Bethany. Tell her she's welcome anytime she needs a place to stay." Mom was completely won over by Bethany, but that was okay. So was I. I gave her a hug and went out to eat pizza with my Sisters. As I passed by his door I could hear Ryan snoring in his room. He'd slept right through all our drama. That made me smile. It felt good to smile.

Joshua McDaven

Dark Dreams

"Thump." He heard it again.

"It's nothing, it's nothing! Go to SLEEP! GO TO SLEEP!" He squeezed his eyes shut tighter.

Joshua tried to think about nothing. A blank, white sheet of paper—to clear his mind and not think about what he feared was in the closet. He didn't want to think about it.

When he was young, his older brothers had teased him relentlessly about *the closet monster,* and it had stuck. A childhood fear, lodged in his brain like a splinter grown over by new skin but still definitely there. No one noticed that his closet door was *always* closed tight before he went to sleep. It was part of his nightly routine.

"I'm seventeen years old. I'm not a kid," Joshua said to himself out loud. "I don't believe in the closet monster."

Joshua was lying to himself.

He did believe in the closet monster.

"Thump—thump—thump," came the noise from his closet.

Joshua's heart skipped a beat—then took off at a hundred miles an hour!

He flew out of bed and ran for the door! Out of the corner of his eye, he looked toward the closet.

It was OPEN!

IT WAS OPEN!!!

Bang! He crashed into his bedroom door and staggered back a step, dazed, but his hands still reached for the handle wildly. He fumbled it open and dove out into the hall; crashing loudly into the wall. Josh ran until he skidded to a stop in the center of the living room then turned quickly to look back down the darkened hallway.

There wasn't anything there. His bedroom door was open. The drywall across from his door had a body-sized dent in it but that was it. A light turned on at the end of the hall, the glow shining from under the bottom of his parents' door at the end of the hall. He probably woke everyone in the house when he crashed into the door. Dad was getting his gun right now, he thought.

As he looked down the hall, a gray hand darted out of his dark room and grabbed the door handle, quickly pulling his bedroom door shut.

BANG!! The sound echoed through the whole house.

A second later, his parents' door burst open. His father came charging out their bedroom with shotgun in hand. He pumped the weapon and pointed down the dark hall right at Joshua.

"FREEZE! Hold it right there!" He took a cautious step or two forward keeping the gun on the dark figure standing in the living room. Joshua didn't move. He couldn't move. He just stood there shaking. The door on the other side of the hall started to open, his older brother's face peeking out.

"Shut the door! Stay inside your room, Tom!"

Tom shut the door.

As his dad got a few steps closer, he was able to recognize Joshua.

"Joshua? That you?" he whispered hoarsely.

Joshua nodded. He couldn't talk.

"Is someone else in the house?" His father's eyes searched the darkness around the living room behind Joshua.

"M—m—m—my bedroom." Joshua got the words out and pointed to his bedroom door.

His dad quickly moved to the side and pointed the gun at Joshua's door. Down the hall, Joshua could see his mother's worried face looking out of their bedroom.

"What is going on, Phil?" his mom said in a hushed whisper.

His dad reached out, turned the handle on his bedroom door, and pushed it open with the barrel of the gun, slipping into the room.

Thump.

Joshua heard the noise behind him and spun around. His heart raced as his eyes scanned the darkness. There! By the front door! The coat closet door was opening slowly—it opened out, so all he could see was the white door, not inside the closet. Joshua started to back up, away from the opening door, when he felt a hand grab his arm from behind.

IT'S BEHIND ME! he thought. Joshua shot forward like a rocket, sliding to a stop at the front door. His shaking hand twisted the deadbolt.

"Josh!" he heard his brother shout just before he threw open the door.

He froze in place with his hand on the handle, his eyes squeezed tightly shut as he waited in terror for what would happen next. He was right beside the open coat closet!

"Man, it was just me!" Tom's voice carried from the living room.

Joshua was shaking as he opened his eyes and slowly turned his head to look into the dark opening of the coat closet just four feet away.

It was empty. Nothing but shoes and coats.

"Josh, man." His brother Tom walked up beside him. "What's the deal!? Is someone in the house? Who's in your room?"

Josh kept his eyes on the dark coat closet.

"Who is it!?" Tom gave him a shove. "Did someone try to get into your window or something?"

"Closet Monster!" Josh choked out, not caring if his brother thought he was a baby. It was real!

"What!?" Tom said. He noticed his brother's gaze was locked on the dark open coat closet by the front door. He looked in the empty closet for a second then looked back at his brother's terrified face.

"You think the 'Closet Monster' is trying to get you?" he asked.

Josh barked out, "YES!" His eyes were wild, face pale as a sheet.

Tom smiled crookedly and chuckled. "Closet Monster," he mumbled, shaking his head. He leaned closer to Josh's face, squinting in the poor light.

"You know, that medicine may be making you into a gutless pile of quivering woosiness," he laughed, "but it sure as hell works, Josh. You should go take a look at your face." Tom gave his brother a congratulatory smile. "That stuff finally kicked in."

"What?" Josh said weakly as he looked at his brother, then back to the empty closet. He hadn't heard a word Tom had said. The Closet Monster was REAL!

"JOSH!" Both boys turned as their father walked up. "There ain't nothing in your room boy. What the hell's going on!?" He gave them the evil eye and waited.

"Oh! Josh is just freaking out, Dad," Tom supplied with an impish grin. "He's trippin' on those Derm pills he's taking. He's high as a kite—kinda like an acid trip. I think he's seein' stuff." Tom yawned and stretched.

"You seein' stuff, Josh?" his dad asked.

Josh nodded, "It's REAL!" He looked at his dad, a terrified expression stuck on his face as he said in a rush, "You gotta believe me, Dad! It was in my closet! It almost got me! I saw its arm! It slammed my door!" Josh looked back to the coat closet.

It was still empty.

Josh's dad scratched his head then looked back to Tom who was grinning like an idiot, enjoying the midnight entertainment. Their dad's face slipped into a disappointed, almost hurt expression.

"What do you mean, like an acid trip? I didn't think you *did* acid, Tom."

Tom had always been one to experiment with drugs, but he was pretty responsible about it. His smile didn't fade a watt as he answered. "Well you're right, Dad, I don't use acid. These days we got designer stuff with all kinda weird names, but I thought I'd keep it 'old school' so you could understand what I was talking about."

His dad nodded, "Suppose you're right." His eyebrows bunched up and he looked back at Josh, who was still looking at the closet. "And it does seem like an acid trip." He and Tom studied Josh and they both nodded together.

"You would know, you old hippie." Tom said, enjoying himself and the whole situation.

Tom took a step toward the open coat closet, reached out to the door, and slammed it shut.

"Now maybe you can stop thinking about it," he said to Josh. Then he got in Josh's face. "THE CLOOOSET MONSTER! Muuuhaaahaaahaaa!" he shouted, making a scary face.

Josh lost it and broke for the front door. He grabbed the handle, threw the door open, and was halfway out when his father grabbed him and drug him back into the house, hauling him to the floor and kicking the front door shut.

"Dammit, Tom!" Their father growled as he tried to keep ahold of his out of control youngest son.

Josh kicked and punched and tried to get up and Tom jumped in with a playful shout of "Get em!" as he tried to grab Josh's kicking feet. After a few minutes they had him pinned there by the front door. Tom had his feet wrapped up and his father was sitting on Josh's back with a firm hold on his arms. Josh's cheek was pressed to the floor about a foot away from the now closed coat closet. Tom and Phil were both panting and out of breath.

"Oh my God, Phil! What's going on in here?" their mother said as she came into the living room and looked over the scene at the front door.

"Joshua's having some sort of reaction to that face pill, Hun. He's all scared that something was in his closet trying to eat him."

"Oh my," Josh's mother tisked. "Well, they did say that that pill would make him a bit crazy for a few days. He'd been so calm up till now I'd just about forgot." Mom came a little closer and said, "What was he trying to do that you gotta hold him on the floor like that? You boys don't be rough on him now." she warned.

"He was about to run off down the street, Hun," Phil said defensively. "We had to grab ahold or God knows where he would have run off to. He may have even run out into the street and got hit by a car." He eased his hold but didn't move from where he sat on Joshua's back.

"We can't sit here and hold him all night! Why don't we lock him in the closet, Dad!?" Tom suggested with an evil laugh.

Josh freaked out again and began to kick and writhe on the floor for all he was worth while his father and older brother held on for dear life. Josh's younger, smaller body fought with a strength born out of pure terror.

In the background his mother could be heard saying "Careful!" or "Grab em!" Everyone was breathing hard once they had him pinned again, shoved up against the closet door. Josh's face was crammed right in the corner.

"Dammit, Tom! Don't pick on your brother while he's all drugged up and trippin'!" Phil yelled at Tom as he tried to catch his breath.

"But Dad!" Tom whined as he panted. "That ain't fair! It's more fun to pick on someone when they're messed up! And Josh doesn't use drugs, so when am I ever gonna get another chance to torture the little weenie!? Anyway, this is way more fun than we've had together in ages. I say we do it again tomorrow night!" Tom laughed as Josh wiggled under the pile.

Josh's face was pushed right into the crack of the door. There was a two-inch gap under the coat closet. As he watched, a slate gray skeletal face with a red bloody eye dropped down, cheek to the floor just two inches away from his face. Joshua's heart started to hammer in his chest so hard it hurt, and he surged up and fought to rise up off the floor.

"Here we go again!" said Tom.

"Whoa!" Phil shouted. "Damn! This is more like a *bad* PCP trip than a nice peaceful acid trip! This skinny boy shouldn't be this strong!"

Joshua bucked like a mule and almost got up, but his father dropped onto his back and pushed him down into the corner again; he was two and a half short inches away from the face of terror pressed into the crack on the other side of the closet door. Its bloody eye looked at him with pure seething malice. It ground its yellow teeth together then breathed a breath of fetid, putrid rot under the door and into Joshua's face making him gag and cough.

"I'll go get a belt you can use to tie him up with. I got one in my closet!" Josh's mother said.

Josh watched as the closet monster's eye went wide. It smiled as it started to back away from the crack disappearing into the darkness of the closet. Josh's brain kicked in, he thought about what his mother had just said: she was going to the closet in her room—and the closet monster was going to get her!

"NOOO!" Joshua screamed and bucked, throwing his father into the air. He rolled away from Tom and jumped to his feet faster than what seemed humanly possible. Before the two had even picked themselves up off the floor Josh had already crossed the living room and grabbed the shotgun from the hallway where his father had leaned it against the wall and was running like lightning down the hallway toward his parents' room.

Josh hit the door with his shoulder, and as he flew into the room he jacked the slide on the gun. The closet door was already open about a foot. When she heard the bedroom door burst open Josh's mother turned her back to the closet and focused her surprised gaze on Josh and the gun.

Within the open gap of the closet behind her the blood red eyes of the closet monster were looking down at Joshua's mother; its clawed hand and impossibly long arm was reaching out for her head.

Josh pointed the gun at the head of the monster and pulled the trigger—nothing happened!

The SAFTEY!

The monster's hand closed around his mother's face and yanked her back into the dark closet, slamming the door. Josh heard running and turned just as his father and brother tackled him and pinned him to the ground.

"IT'S GOT MOM! IT'S GOT MOM!" Josh yelled over and over. He begged and pleaded with them, but they wouldn't listen. They drug him onto the bed and used sheets to tie his hands behind his back and his feet together.

Josh kept begging. He was crying wildly, "It's got Mom in the closet! It's gonna kill her! Go get her! GO GET HER! GO GET HERRRRR! MOOOOOM-MMMMMM!"

"Hold onto him, Tom! I'm gonna go get his mother so he'll shut up!" his dad yelled.

Tom nodded as he struggled with Josh and yelled back to his Dad so he could be heard over Josh's screams, "I take it back, Dad! I don't want to do this tomorrow night!"

His dad nodded grimly then went over to the closet and opened the door.

A gray arm shot out of the closet and grabbed him by his throat. The gray skeletal hand raised him up about a foot into the air as he kicked and tried to pry the hand off his throat, but he couldn't make a sound. Tom wasn't looking toward the closet, but Josh, facing the other direction, saw everything.

"TOM! It's got Dad!" Josh yelled. "IT'S GOT HIM! LOOK! LOOK BEHIND YOU!"

Tom turned and jumped. "Dad!"

"Get the gun, Tom! GET THE GUN!" Then Joshua remembered and called, "Turn the safety off! It's got the safety on, Tom, turn it off first!"

He watched as Tom flipped the safety off the gun and turned back to the closet just in time to see the door slam shut.

"Dammit." Tom ran up to the door and pulled on it. The door started to open but then something on the other side pulled so hard that Tom was yanked off his feet and slammed into the door, bouncing off, staggering. He held onto the gun though and quickly got his wits and leveled the gun back on the door but didn't fire. He might hit Dad, he thought.

Then he changed his mind. Whatever that thing was it was stronger than his dad. He aimed high and shot. BOOM! Tom jacked the pump action on the gun and aimed again.

"Tom! Untie me!" Josh yelled. "Tom!"

Tom looked back quickly to Josh then back to the closet. He kept the gun trained on the closet door as he stepped back to Josh. Once he was beside him, he used one hand to undo the knots.

There were *no* sounds coming from the closet. The only sounds were the heavy breathing and grunting of Tom and Joshua.

"What the HELL was THAT!?" Tom yelled as he worked on the knots.

"That was the closet monster, you dumbass!" Josh yelled back.

"Oh shit! That thing is REAL!" Tom yelled as he got Josh's hands free and moved to undo his feet.

"YES! Of course it's real, you dumbass! It just ate Mom and Dad!"

"We gotta get out of here!" yelled Tom. "Here, hold the gun on the door while I do your feet." He handed Josh the gun and bent to untie Josh's feet, and soon they were undone.

Josh got off the bed, and the two brothers stepped slowly toward the bedroom door and the hallway as Josh kept the gun trained on the closet. Once they got to the bedroom door, they stepped into the hall and shut the door behind them and started down the hall, keeping close to each other.

"Be careful, it likes to dart out of the bedrooms and it's real quick. Stay away from the doors."

"Yeah. Okay," Tom said and they pressed up against the opposite side of the hall as they passed the first door. Josh kept the gun trained on the door, then they both switched to the other side of the hall and slid, backs pressed against the wall as they passed the other door.

When they got to the living room, Tom broke for the front door at a run. They could both see the blue lights of the cops outside the house. Someone must have heard the yelling or the shotgun and called the police.

"WAIT, TOM!" Josh called, but it was too late. Joshua watched as the gray hand darted out of the coat closet and dragged Tom inside. He heard his brother scream inside the closet then everything went quiet.

Josh stood there shaking for a few seconds then he heard something behind him somewhere.

Thump.

Josh put the gun under his chin, closed his eyes, and pulled the trigger.

Dan Simmons

What Would You Do for a Klondike Bar?

"**W**ho the hell is texting you now? It's almost 1AM!" Kyle asked Avel as he checked his phone.

"Oh shit, it's Dan." Avel read the text.

"What the hell does he want at this hour?" Kyle asked as he munched the last mostly whole Dorito.

"He wants to know if I still go down to First City Plasma twice a month to give blood. Damn. He must be hurtin' for some fast cash," Avel said as his fingers started to punch in his text reply.

"Dan's that kid that can't talk right? I thought you said he was real smart," Kyle said before he upended the bag, funneling the Dorito crumbs into his mouth.

"He is smart. At least he's way smarter than us. He's got a full scholarship to college." Avel hit send.

"What'd you tell 'im?" Kyle mumbled as he chewed his mouthful of crumbs.

"I told him I quit goin' since they cut it back from thirty to twenty bucks. Cheap bastards. Thirty bucks was cool but there ain't no way I'm doing that for twenty. Screw that, it takes an hour to get in and out anyway."

Avel's phone chimed with Dan's reply text. Avel was quiet as he read.

"Oh shit!" Avel sat up in his chair. "Dan said that he'll pay me a hundred bucks to come over and give blood right now if I'm up for it."

"A hundred bucks!" Kyle shouted, then winced as he looked over his shoulder to his bedroom door. He hoped he hadn't woken up his mom. "Is he serious?" He had another thought. "And what the hell does he need with blood?"

Avel was already texting, his fingers flying over the pad of his phone. "That's what I just asked him." He hit send.

"Damn, a hundred bucks. We could party on that kinda cash," Kyle said longingly. "You wanna go over there?"

"Fuckin A!" Avel spouted as he read Dan's reply. "Dan said that he'll make it a hundred and twenty if I can get my ass to the shed behind his house in the next thirty minutes." Avel stood up and was starting to look for his shoes as he texted back.

"Damn! Ask Dan if he could use some more blood!" Kyle grabbed one of his shoes too. "Tell him I'll do it for just eighty!" He started to plow through the trash on the floor in search of his second shoe.

"Hold on, I'll ask him." Avel typed in the text message and hit send.

"This guy got that kind of cash?" Kyle said and had another thought. "And what's he gonna use to get the blood? I ain't gettin' poked with some old rusty druggie needle." He frowned; he was having second thoughts about going.

"Dan will pay, and he ain't no druggie, but his uncle is a diabetic so he'll probably have all kinda fresh needles and shit at his house."

Avel's phone chimed with Dan's reply text. He read the text and laughed. "Dan wants to know if you're a diseased scum bag!" He was already texting back.

"You know I'm not. They wouldn't let me give blood if I was," Kyle answered as he slipped on his other shoe and then started hunting for his keys somewhere in the room. Avel was already ready to go, waiting by the door reading Dan's reply when Kyle finally found his keys, wallet, and phone.

"Dan said bring it, he'll cough up the eighty if you'll open a vein." Avel held up his phone so Kyle could see the text message and laughed.

Kyle looked at the text message in glowing white letters on the blue background screen; it looked a lot more scary spelled out like that. Giving blood to a mute kid in a shed in the middle of the night—warning bells were going off.

"What kind of freak is this mute kid anyway, Avel? He ain't gonna try no shit is he?" Kyle gave Avel a hard glare.

Avel shrugged, "Man, I've played Halo and other video games at his house a bunch. Dan's okay."

"You sure he's okay?" Kyle asked again.

"Yeah, Dan's okay."

Kyle looked at Avel like he was an idiot. "If he was 'okay' he wouldn't need blood at 1AM from a dork like you."

Avel finally used his brain and thought about it for a second. "Well, maybe he's not okay," Avel admitted but then shrugged. "Must be some stupid dare or something or maybe someone's hurt or something and needs some blood, but Dan ain't got no other friends beside me so it'll just be him there—and there's two of us." Avel gave an exasperated, "Com'on, man! It'll only take an hour and we'll split it even, a hundred each."

"He better pay up," Kyle growled and grabbed a knife off his dresser before he headed out the door.

Jane Miller

Sweet Delicious Life

Where?

Where was the rest?

I turned to the next page. It was blank. I turned back again.

What do I do now?

I looked at the period after the last word in the sentence. Where was I going next? I'd been with Dan. We were together. Dizzy. My vision blurred, words and letters moving around as if alive. I strained my eyes as I tried to follow the disjointed letters and jumbled words. Where was I? Where was Dan? What was happening?

Dan had tried to convince me to leave him, to stay away from him, but I would not, could not leave. Not in this or any life. I couldn't imagine my life or my death without him. I loved him more than my own soul, more than my family, more than my friends, and more than my human life. To live forever with Dan and to look into his eyes and hold him for all eternity was all I wanted. Life as a vampire was a small price to pay to have him. It took forever to convince him, but Dan finally changed me. I remembered the burning pain of his venom as it scorched through my body, changing me, destroying me, transforming me, until finally—I died.

I distinctly remember that first moment. Of opening my eyes and waking to my new existence as a vampire.

I was alive, but not like a human. So much had changed. Everything was so different. I was different.

I (Sarah) was just starting my happily ever after with Dan (Ethan). We were happy. We had eternity to live together, to love together, to spend with each other. We would never die.

My eyes searched the page frantically. I read the last sentence over again. Dan and I had been together. He had been holding me in his arms. I turned the page—it was blank. Where was the rest of my life!?

I turned another page—blank. I turned back to the last page that had writing on it. My eyes focused on the words. Words in a book? The world spun around me. If I hadn't already been lying down, I would have fallen down I was so dizzy. My vision backed away from the words on the page far enough to reveal the edges of the book and my hands, holding a book. Was I reading a book? *The Midnight book*, a thought went through my head.

I *was* reading a book! I tried to lock this fact into place. But where was Dan? A fresh wave of dizziness washed over me. None of this made sense! I should be seeing something else. I should be somewhere else! I'd been with Dan. He'd been holding me in his arms, kissing me. He'd been so happy as he searched through my mind and saw how much I loved him! How happy I was in my new life! Had it all been words in a book?

I closed my eyes and tried not to think about anything, hoping a white page in my mind would stop the world from spinning. For a while I contented myself with simply breathing in and out. In and out. In and out. In and out.

I heard breathing, my own and someone else's. Close by.

I heard a heartbeat. Wait. The sound was coming from me! *What the—*
MY HEART WAS BEATING!

How! My heart had stopped long ago, when I died! When I changed. I listened to its powerful tha, thump, tha, thump, tha, thump, tha, thump, wondering what on earth was happening, and then I noticed the other heartbeat. A heartbeat that belonged to the sound of the nearby breathing.

Someone was lying right beside me; one of their legs was under my leg. I was on a couch. So was this other person. We were on a couch together.

Who was it? I wondered.

Was it a human? It sounded human. The leg beneath me was warm. Definitely human.

WAIT! Was I human?

What was going on? Was any of this real? Shit!

Confused, I focused inward, on myself. The heartbeat. I could hear it. I knew it was real. It was there, pounding away in my chest. The rhythmic beat was impossible to deny: tha, thump—I'm Human!—tha, thump— I'm Alive! —tha, thump—I'm Human! —tha, thump—I'm Alive!

I listened to the sound that should not have been and yet was and let it speak to me. I didn't know what to think.

Slowly I opened my eyes. The page filled my vision. I still held the book in my hands. My eyes were drawn down to the page and the words; the world tilted left and right around me and I felt as if I were falling forward, toward the page. I squeezed my eyes tight, shutting it out. Without looking, I closed the book and held it to my chest, pressing it tightly over my beating heart.

I stayed there and listened for a while to the reassuring sound. Rhythmic beating.

Tha, thump—I'm Human! —tha, thump—I'm Alive! —tha, thump—I'm Human! —tha, thump—I'm Alive!

I opened my eyes again. No more spinning. I could finally see, and I was shocked to find that I was in my living room! I looked around in wonder at all the old familiar sights. It felt like I'd been away for ages! So much had happened. The old clock on the wall said it was 12:46 AM; its ticking was loud in my ears. I looked down at the couch and felt a huge smile spread onto my face.

"MOM!" I shouted for joy! It was so good to see her again! I hadn't seen her since I had turned into a vampire!

She jumped when I shouted, arms whipping to each side as she bolted upright. A book lying on her chest fell to the floor with a thud.

"What! What!" She blinked. "What is it? Are you okay!?" She leaned forward trying to see me in the dim light.

I threw my own book onto the floor and crawled forward on the couch, wrapping my arms around her and hugging her. It felt wonderful just to hug her!

"Oh my God!" Mom shouted, surprised by my hug. I felt her cringe. She was really frightened.

"Nothing's wrong, Mom," I assured her. I didn't look up; she was too freaked out and I didn't want to see it. I was always freaking her out these days. *Oh well.* Her freak out was her freakin' problem. I didn't let it bother me as I burrowed into her and rested my head on her chest. Her heart was so loud. It was racing. Mine was beating away too. Cool! I was happy. This felt great. Mom hug! *Hm-mmm.*

"Stop freaking out," I said as I wallowed.

"Don't blame me! You scared me to death, girl!" Mom complained. "The way you sprang at me so fast, it just scared me to death! That was weird." Her arms finally wrapped around me and hugged me back.

About time, I thought.

"I just wanted a hug, that's all. Jeesh! Sue me. Can't a girl hug her own mother?" I complained.

"You can hug me all you want. Just try not to scare me gray headed." Mom laughed a little. Her hand stroked my hair then reached down to my chin and tilted my face up toward hers. Her eyes went wide as she looked at my face.

"Oh my God." She stared. "Oh—my—God." She said it again, spacing the words out this time and shaking her head as she stared at me.

I scrunched up my brow. "What now?" I asked. She was freaking out again, but now she was starting to freak me out! OMG! was not a real confidence builder.

"What's wrong, Mom?" I asked again.

"Donna. Jane." My father hit the light switch as he rushed into the room.

Mom blinked in the bright lights, looked at me, and DAMN! if she didn't *say it again*!

"Oh—my—God!" Her eyes were as big as saucers now!

She was scaring the hell out of ME and that's saying something. I'm pretty hard to scare after all I've been through—but wait a minute, had I really been through all of that or was it just in a book? Where was Dan? This didn't make any sense.

Where was I?

What was going on?

Was I even a vampire? I started to feel dizzy again.

"Donna! What's wrong!?" Dad said as he came around the side of the couch and knelt beside us.

I looked at Mom and Dad, dazed and confused, trying to figure out what was happening—I didn't know—

Who was I? —What was I? —And where the hell was Dan!?

"Look at her, Ed!" Mom breathed out in a rush. She turned my head to the side so Dad could see. I watched as his eyes went as crazed as mom's.

"How is that even possible?" Dad said, his voice weirdly quiet as he stared at me.

"Even her hair and eyes have changed, look at her eyes," Mom urged.

The y both leaned in close. I didn't blink as I gazed back into the eyes of firs t my father and then my mother.

"Th ey've changed color, but it's more than that." Dad reached out and touched my cheek. "Even the bones in her face have moved! Look at her cheek bones and the angle of her eyes."

Dad touched my lips, and I closed my mouth tight before he could see my teeth. I didn't know exactly "what" I was, but I didn't think messing with my teeth right now was a good idea.

"She's so pale and her lips are so red!" Dad said. "And you're right—" He ran his hand through my hair. "Even the hair!" I sat there on the couch as they touched and stared at me in freaked-out, frightened wonder.

"It's like she's had plastic surgery or something," Mom said. She rubbed my cheek again. "Feel her skin, have you ever felt anything so perfect and smooth, Ed?"

"Donna, why did you shout earlier?" Dad asked her, still looking at me. "What'd she do?"

Mom looked embarrassed. "She moved so fast when she crawled across the couch at me she scared me to death."

Dad gave her a questioning look.

"Jane crawled over and hugged me," she explained.

I'd been sitting there like a lump as they pawed at me but I was getting sick of it. I should have already unloaded on them with a hundred snarky comments but all I could manage was pulling my hair out of Dad's hands and pushing Mom's hands away from my face. She'd been rubbing at my face like it was Aladdin's lamp and she wanted to see the genie squirt out my nose. I kept both hands up to keep them at bay but grabbed onto each of them to keep myself upright. I was so dizzy and the room kept tilting.

"Enough with the touching. Now what's wrong?" I asked. "What's gone wrong with my face?" I closed my eyes. I was tired of having them look at me. Now I didn't have to see them, and having my eyes closed also helped with the dizziness.

"Don't worry, Jane! It's nothing bad," Dad said, voice dripping with reassurance. "Honestly, your face looks fantastic, honey, we just don't understand some of the changes. Don't worry, you look wonderful, but how do you feel?" He put a hand on my forehead (*again with the touching!*). "You feel ice cold. Are you cold?"

I shook my head. "I feel funny," I confessed. "Real dizzy and tingly all over." As I said this I noticed that my voice sounded so weird and I opened my eyes in surprise. Had my voice changed? Crap! It sounded more like singing as I talked than talking. That was so weird. My hand reached up to my mouth as I looked at Mom and Dad. I could tell that my parents had noticed the difference in my voice as well.

"You feel dizzy right now?" Dad asked, ignoring my vocal weirdness for some other weirdness.

"Actually, I'm feeling a lot less dizzy and a lot more tingly," I said and made a face. "I think I want to take a shower." My whole body felt numb and asleep, pins and needles, like when you crossed your feet too long. The more that I thought about it, the more annoying it became.

"Is it hurting or just tingling, Jane? You're not in any pain, are you?" Mom started to get worked up again.

"Chill, Lady!" I said with a little steel in my voice. I gave both of my parents a hard look. "This is starting to get old, you know! Every time I turn around," I threw my hands up in the air, "FREAK OUT!" I frowned and gave them both a well-deserved glare. "You guys knew that the Derm pill would change my looks, so why freak over it?"

I waited for my answer.

"Jane, honey," Dad's voice was annoyingly soothing, "why don't you go and take a shower?" He looked to Mom. "Go with Jane, Hon, and let her see herself in the mirror so she can see what we're talking about."

He didn't look happy. He looked scared.

"Come on, Jane. I'll go with you." Mom smiled at me. "You do look amazing, so don't let it surprise you the way it surprised me and your father." She leaned forward and bumped her forehead up next to mine; her eyes still scanned my face as she spoke. "You've changed so much and it's happening so fast." She kissed me on the forehead and said, "You look so beautiful we can hardly believe our eyes. It's like magic. We just didn't think the pill could do this."

"Do I not look like *me* anymore?" I asked.

"Come and see, honey." She got up off the couch and took my hand to help me.

I unfolded myself and stood up beside my mother. Mom and Dad both gaped at me again like I'd done something weird and I couldn't help the annoyed "What?" with a matching aggravated look stuck on my face. *What now!*

"That was, ahh, very graceful," Dad said, trying to seem casual and failing miserably.

"We're still getting used to your new look," Mom said, but she couldn't seem to take her eyes off of me. I looked from one to the other, shrugged, and headed toward the bathroom to go see for myself.

"Jane! Where'd you go!?" Mom shouted. I'd left her standing in the living room with Dad.

"I'm good!" I called from the hall bathroom as I shut and locked the door. "I'm just gonna take my shower now. Good night!" I called. "Don't wait up, go ahead and go to bed." I knew it wouldn't be that easy. I leaned my head against the door and listened as they ran through the house heading to the bathroom.

"Jane!" Dad called, "Jane, are you okay? How did you move so fast!?"

I was surprised when Dad tried the handle. Whoa! Way uncool!

"Jane, please let us in. Are you all right!?" Mom shouted on the other side of the door.

I let out an exasperated sigh as I unlocked the door and turned the handle.

"Enough!" I shouted as I swung the door open and stared at both my parents. They were both right there, crowding the door, trying to get into the bathroom with me.

"No. And not just no. But *Hell No!*" I snapped as I stood there, blocking the doorway so they couldn't get in.

"I need privacy! And I need a shower." I looked at their terrified, freaked out faces and had no mercy. "You guys had the past ten minutes to freak out, touch me, poke and prod at me—which was fine." I gave them a little nod. "Now I'm going to go in here and look for myself, *alone.* And if I freak out and say, 'Oh my God!' or 'Oh shit!' or even 'What the fuck!' then—just—LET ME FREAK OUT ALREADY!" I shouted it at them and they winced and cringed at the power in my voice. It scared and shocked the holy heebies out of me too!

I looked around a little, confused. I actually turned and looked behind me, like I was looking for whoever had said that, even though I knew it was me. HOLY HELL! What was up with my voice!? I turned back and continued talking to my parents in a more normal, but no less magical, musical tone.

"I just want to see for myself." My hand reached up and touched my own face. It did feel smooth.

My parents stood there with their shocked expressions frozen in place. I sighed, stepped out of the bathroom, and gave Mom and then Dad a quick hug. I felt them "thaw out" as I hugged them, changing from frozen blocks of ice back into worried, freaked out parents again.

"Now I'm gonna take a very, very long shower. Go to bed please," I said. "And no, don't wait up for me," I said before Mom could say it. They looked at each other then back to me.

"I'm not gonna hurt myself and I feel fine." I looked at Dad. "Just let me go see for myself."

It took them so long to answer me. I began to wonder if there was something wrong with them. If I didn't know better, I'd swear they were moving in slow motion. Maybe it was me moving fast instead?

"All right," Dad said. He wasn't happy, but he put on a good fake smile anyway. "You do look amazing. Just be sure to come and get us if you, ahh, have any problems. Or if your skin starts hurting. Or if you get dizzy again. Or if you need anything. Okay?" Dad pleaded.

"Don't worry." I gave him a big smile. His eyebrows shot up, and I remembered my teeth and quickly closed my mouth. "Good night," I said, before they started freaking out again. I turned to Mom.

"Honey," Mom said. Her voice was firm. She didn't want to leave me. It was right there on her face. She didn't need to say it, and I didn't need to hear it.

"Good night, Mom." I shut the door on them both and waited until I heard them walk away. I listened as they opened their bedroom door and walked inside.

"My Lord, Ed!" I heard Mom's voice just as clearly as if she were standing in the room with me. "What the hell's happened to her? She doesn't even look human anymore! That Derm pill has gone out of control! What's it gonna do next? She keeps changing and changing and changing! It's even changed her voice. She doesn't even sound like Jane anymore!" Mom broke down and started to cry.

I could hear Dad comforting her. Telling her that he would call the doctor before they went to bed and that tomorrow morning they would get some answers. They talked about taking me off the Derm pill and whether they should take me to the hospital to have me checked out by some different doctors. They started talking about where they might take me. I turned around and pressed my back to the door and tried to stop listening. What was happening to me? Mom had said that I didn't even look human.

I stepped away from the door and walked to the vanity to look at myself in the mirror. I wasn't surprised at all by what I saw. I knew the reflection in the mirror though I'd never seen it before. No wonder Mom thought I didn't look like a human.

I wasn't.

My skin was pale and absolutely perfect. My hair had darkened to that glossy raven black I'd seen on Goth chicks at the mall before, only darker and shinier. My lips were now a deep candy apple red, and my *eyes*! I leaned closer to the mirror and stared into my own eyes.

"Oh my God," I said quietly to myself just like Mom had. I mean, what else could you say? My eyes were weird! They used to be a dull hazel mush of brown and gray that Emma had jokingly dubbed as "gravy" colored. But now my eye color was a shocking shade of violet fading to a lighter lilac at the edge.

My pupils seemed to have changed too. Instead of inky black they were a strange shade of red. A red so dark it could pass for black unless you looked close. The eye color was wild, but that wasn't all. Dad was right! My eyes had actually tilted a little, and my cheek bones were higher!

I studied the face in the mirror. I had the faint ghost of darker circles around my eyes, and my eyebrows and eyelashes were dark, long, and full. I looked as if I had makeup, lipstick, mascara, eyeliner, and more on—only I didn't. I looked thin. Had my neck gotten longer?

I backed up another two steps and looked at the rest of me in the mirror. I looked taller! But then I remembered that I'd hunched before. Mom was constantly getting onto me for my bad posture, but not now. I was almost bent back the other way! I looked at my chest.

"Damn. I got boobs." I wasn't sure if they'd actually gotten bigger or if it was simply because I was standing so straight that my chest was poking out there in front of God and everyone. I studied my reflection. The way I was standing, my face, my eyes, my hair, my lips, my squared shoulders, chin up. Even in my faded jeans and white button up top I looked—I searched around for a word that fit and came up with *regal*. I looked like a Fairy Queen.

I smiled at myself and noticed my teeth! Wow! They were blazing pearlescent white. All my teeth were laser straight now and my canine teeth were a bit longer than they used to be. I didn't look any closer, afraid of what I might find, but I couldn't stop my tongue from exploring. I watched my eyebrows go up in the mirror as I felt a hollow in the backside of each canine. I wondered if it was made for sucking blood or injecting venom like a snake. I had no freaking clue. *Blood? Poison? Cavity in need of a filling?*

I felt dizzy again and put one hand against the vanity to steady myself.

"I'm here. I'm in my house. I'm in my bathroom. I have a heartbeat," I said to myself, repeating the words over and over, a verbal antidote for the dizziness.

"I'm here. I'm in my house. I'm in my bathroom. I have a heartbeat."

After a long minute or two of chanting, the dizziness receded and the world stabilized. It seemed that when I tried to focus on what was happening to me I got dizzy, like my brain couldn't cope with it. But it's not like I could hide from this. I needed some answers. Was I a vampire or not!? Why did I still have a heartbeat? What the hell was—the room started to tilt again! I put my hands on the wall and closed my eyes.

"I'm here. I'm in my house. I'm in my bathroom. I have a heartbeat."

"I'm here. I'm in my house. I'm in my bathroom. I have a heartbeat."

"Let me get in the shower," I said to myself. "I just—want—to take—a shower." I begged and opened my eyes. The dizziness stayed away. I schooled my thoughts. My poor brain seemed to be on strike. Cool beans.

I focused on getting undressed and determined to be blond for a while. I'd sort this shit out later. Not now. I reached up and unbuttoned my shirt, taking my top and bra off, and then unbuttoned my jeans. As I pushed them down, I

felt something in the pocket and reached in to see what it was. I pulled out—
Dan's note! I'd totally forgotten to read it.

A wave of fear shot through me as I looked at the folded piece of paper. I was scared of the note! Scared of any writing. I didn't want to get dizzy again or get sucked into the note like I had the book. I dropped it and watched it flutter down onto the floor. What would it do to me if I read it? I burned to know what it said. I had to risk it. This was Dan's note! He had wanted me to read it once I got home but Mom had dragged me onto the couch with her and we started reading—and once I had started reading, I couldn't remember anything after that except being with Dan and my life as a vampire. I hadn't stopped reading until—until—dizzy—

"I'm here. I'm in my house. I'm in my bathroom. I have a heartbeat."

"and—I've got Dan's note!" I added with a growl and the dizziness vanished like magic. I smiled.

"Thanks, my love," I whispered. Even Dan's note helped me. I retrieved the folded piece of paper from the bathroom floor, smoothed it out, and then opened the note.

Jane, I hope you have your memories back by the time you read this because if you still can't remember lunch this note will sound CRAZY! I can't tell you right now because you're in the car with your folks, and, not good. But you have 2 trust me Jane!

I quickly looked at the second page of the note.

Something bad is happening to us! I don't know how, but when you read your book you're making it real somehow.

You're changing us into VAMPS!

Whatever you do - don't read any more!

Throw those Books away! ASAURT call me! 445-3322 or Email! I love U!

I dropped onto the tile floor by the shower, half in and half out of my jeans and squeezed my eyes shut as waves of dizziness crashed over me. The world lost its axis and tumbled wildly. There was no up. No down. A swirl of colors filled my vision.

"I'm here. I'm in my house. I'm in my bathroom. I have a heartbeat."

I whispered the chant like a sinner's prayer but changed my words to fit my thoughts.

"What have I done? What have I done? What have I done?" over and over.

I heard someone outside the door and froze, listening. It was my mother. I could smell her. Her knee popped as she knelt by the bathroom door, trying to listen or maybe even peek under the crack at the bottom of the door. I could hear the thudding of her heartbeat and her breathing. And then I heard something else, a delightful swishing noise. It couldn't be—was that her blood flowing in her veins?

Suddenly, I was so thirsty! My throat burned for blood—*sweet, delicious life*—flowing, wet, red, just outside the door. The dizziness began again.

"No!" I stood while I still could, dropped the note, and quickly stepped the rest of the way out of my jeans and into the shower. I turned on the water and stared up at the showerhead, trying to clear my mind. Thinking of nothing. Waiting. And then the water came out.

It happened in slow motion. Light played off the spray of water as it left the showerhead and came toward my face and body. And then water hit my skin like an EXPLOSION of sensation! I gasped! I could feel every single drop as it struck my face, neck, and breasts, trailing down my body in dozens of little streams. It was amazing! Glorious! Indescribable! I could see so much and feel so much, all at the same instant! My whole body was alive and thrilled with the feel of it!

This dizziness was so strange. It made the world move so slowly but it also made my brain so fast. As the water rained down I realized that I was thinking about more than one thing at the same time. One part of my mind delighted in the water hitting my skin, another separate part on the steam I inhaled, enjoying all the different aromas, and yet another part watched everything, seeing more detail than I ever dreamed existed. Light playing on water drops. A dance of beautiful, tiny prisms. I laughed, and another part of my brain enjoyed the musical sound of my voice as it echoed around the shower.

The shower helped take my mind off the tingling sensation in my skin. There were so many other things to think about! The tingling didn't go away, but I was able to corral that sensory information into a small, tidy corner of my mind. As I could think about any number of things all at once now, that was exactly what I did. I enjoyed my shower in a hundred different ways.

After three or four long minutes, I let my thoughts drift back to Dan's note. Even though I didn't have it in my hands I could remember every word exactly as he'd written it. This didn't surprise me. I thought about what he'd written.

Dan said that I'd forgotten about lunch. And I had. I'd blocked it out for some reason. I focused my thoughts, trying to go step by step through my memories. I recalled walking into the restaurant. And Dan had been worried about eating in front of Mom and Dad because of his weird food cravings—

I started to get dizzy, but I ignored it this time and pressed forward—pushing upon whatever my brain was trying to hide away. Dan had been craving—craving BLOOD!

I collapsed to the floor of the shower as the world flipped upside down. Words ripped through my mind! Shouting out:

"BLOOD! VAMPIRE! CRAVING BLOOD! VAMPIRE!"

All of it snapped into place! The craving, my memories of the taste of blood returned and filled me with raging hunger. I was unable to rise and rush to the door. My body shook on the tile floor, unresponsive and trembling, and for once I was glad for the dizziness. Dan's note, the blood, the bloody lunch! It was me! It really was me! Somehow I was doing this to both of us.

And now I could remember lunch. My parents had gotten up from the table and Dan had done something. I remember looking into his eyes and somehow he'd made me forget some of what had happened at lunch. He'd buried the craving and my memory of blood. He'd tried to help me. To keep me safe. To keep my parents safe. I was changing us both into real vampires by reading the

Midnight books. Real, live, blood-crazed vampires. Dan had read my mind. He knew. He had tried to warn me. He had tried to stop me.

I worried as the dizziness began to fade but at the same time the tingling began to change. The water drops began to feel sharp, like little needles poking down into my skin. I trembled as the uncomfortable feeling shifted further to something more like pain, then burst into BURNING! I began to writhe on the shower floor, shaking and gasping, not even able to scream it hurt so much!

"God help me! Why is this happening!?" I begged quietly through clinched teeth. Why! WHY! Why was the water hurting now when it hadn't just a few minutes ago? It had tingled on my skin, but it didn't feel anything like *this!* I lay in the floor of the shower like a body in an incinerator. Only I never turned to ash and the flaming hell raining down never stopped.

Finally, through the pain, around the blinding agony, a part of my mind began to think again. I pushed the pain and torment of my skin into one part of my mind and my body stopped shaking, but it did not stop hurting. I could still feel every horrifying drop of water as it hit my skin like beads of molten lead, but I had control of my body again.

I stood up and turned off the water, then climbed out of the shower. I reached for the towel but as I started to dry myself, THAT burned like fire also! The towel raking down my burning flesh made me start to tremble again. I shivered with pain, not cold. I dumped this new sensation of torment into another part of my mind and quickly dried myself off and B-U-R-N-E-D!

I was panting, my breaths coming in short ragged gasps by the time I was dry. The pain was so intense it was breaking through all my mental barriers. I never imagined in my wildest nightmares that this kind of torment was possible. I could think about so many things at once now, and I seem to remember everything, so in a horrible way it made perfect sense. I could feel more, experience more, remember more, and apparently to even it all out I could sure as hell hurt more in this new body.

The burning, I thought, it's almost like the book, when Sarah changed into a vampire. It wasn't exactly the same, but it was close enough to make me want to cry. WHY was I burning!? I wasn't reading the damned book anymore! I had stopped reading! I was never going to look at the damn thing again! I listened for my heartbeat, the one sure sound that cried out in its own pulsing, undeniable voice that I was still "human" no matter what else had changed.

Tha thump—tha thump—tha thump—tha thump.

At first I was so relieved that I didn't notice the change, but soon my new vampire mind picked up on the subtle difference. My heart was beating slower. Somehow, without even knowing how, I knew that my heartbeat had slowed down a small instant from when I had first escaped the book. And if my heart kept slowing down at the same speed, it would stop in a little less than a day.

I would die at some point before midnight tonight. My heart would beat for the last time.

"But that's not what happened in the book!" I complained quietly. "Nobody bit me. I shouldn't be burning. It's not fair." The pain did not stop at my cry of foul. I burned.

I carefully eased myself down and sitting on the bathroom floor, I began to cry, quietly. My mother was just outside the door. I could hear her breathing. Listening. The burning had one benefit. I was too preoccupied to be hungry.

Dan had tried to warn me. He'd been so conflicted on what to do. I didn't have any idea how he made me forget the blood and the craving but I was glad he had. Dan had tried to help. He had sent me home with the note to warn me off the book. I looked at the note where I'd dropped it onto the floor. I saw that I hadn't checked the back of the second page; there was more there that I hadn't seen. I reached over, picked up the second page, and looked at the back side of the note.

> Even if my heart stops beating,
>
> I'll still be yours

I could tell it was written quickly. He'd finished it as he was getting out of the car. He'd been so worried as he handed me the note. My suspicious, self-conscious side had flared when he had spoken in my head and asked me to wait until I got home to read it. I had thought that the note must have some bad news he didn't want to tell me in person. I had asked why he wanted me to wait. Then I had asked if I should be worried. And the whole time Dan was trying to save my life! And not scare my parents to death. He hadn't wanted to say something to me in the car that would have freaked me out more than I already was. I might have lost control and gone for blood right there in the car. Shit, who knows what I'd have done. Dan had tried to save me. He had tried! But I didn't read the note. He told me to read it and I didn't.

"I've killed us both," I whispered the words.

I started to cry again, quietly.

The squeezing pain in my heart was not contained like the burning pain in my skin. Self-judgment and anguish raged inside me, and I didn't even dream of hemming it in as I thought about what I'd done to Dan. I deserved to hurt! If I was dying tonight, then so was Dan. If I was changing him along with myself then we were both doomed. Dan's heartbeats were numbered just like mine. 11:30? 11:40? I tried to gage it, but couldn't pin it down. Somewhere in between? Shit. I closed my eyes, cried, and wallowed, hating myself in every way I could imagine.

Eventually I ran out of self-hate. I couldn't think up another hurtful slight to call myself inside my heart where only Dan and I could hear. I ran out of blame. And then I ran out of fear. Which left only questions.

I opened my eyes. It felt like they'd been closed for an hour, but I knew, with absolute certainty, that only five minutes had passed. Time kept stretching out. Getting longer somehow. I couldn't decide if it was a mercy, giving me more time to live, or a torture, more time to burn and suffer?

I may be messed up, but time was still passing. Eventually, today would end. And then I would end. I wondered if I would rise again, like Sarah, in the book. She had died, then opened her eyes to a new life with her Ethan. Would I rise again, or just die? The end. Game over. Finished. Dead at seventeen. Would anyone even figure out what really happened or would everyone assume Dan and I had pulled a Romeo and Juliet together? Teenage suicide. I lifted my hand and stared at my pale skin, trying to accept it as real, but I kept running into the same questions. The same brick walls built by logic that demanded answers. "WHY ME? WHY DAN? WHY US?" and a basic all encompassing, "WHAT THE HELL!?"

Why was this happening!? And why were the books making it happen to me? Stacy had read the books through three times and so had a million other teenage girls, so why was I the one changing into a damn vampire? And why was I changing Dan!? What was different about both of us?

The Derm 513 pills. The thought came to me as plain as day. All of those other kids, like Stacy, hadn't been taking the Derm pills. It had to be some wild reaction to the pills that was making this happen. I'd been reading the Midnight books when I started the pills. Reading day and night. Obsessively. So somehow my imagination must have gotten supercharged by these stupid pills.

I thought back to the very first time I had felt dizzy. The first time the world moved. It was when Dan had sat beside me in the waiting room, held my hand, and looked into my eyes. And then later when I had read what he had written in my book when I was in the car. His note had said that he loved me. That I was already his "Sarah" and that he wanted to be my "Ethan." I couldn't help but smile as I recalled the memory. My first freak out. The first of many. My poor mother. That must have been when it all started. And from that moment on the book had been changing Dan and me into some strange, mutant version of Ethan and Sarah.

I studied the hand I still held up. There was no fire but I could feel my flesh burning. I listened to my heart again. Slower now than a few minutes ago. I sighed in resignation. This had gone too far. I'd changed too much. Read too much. No one was going to be able to stop this. Even if I never opened the book again, and even if I never took another Derm pill, I was still going to die. I knew it. My heart was still slowing down.

My mind drifted back to the hospital option that my parents were so keen on for tomorrow. If I went to a hospital the way I was now everyone would freak and treat me like a science project. Dan and I would die, all alone, surrounded by doctors. And after we died they would cut up the bodies to see what made us tick. Which would really suck if we were still trying to come back to life.

The thought made me grind my teeth together which made a weird, metallic sound. Definitely no hospitals! No doctors! Screw that! But then I thought that I should at least tell Dr. Burgis what had happened so he would know about this as a possible side effect and keep other kids from taking the pills.

Then the thought occurred to me, if it was already too late to stop—and the only hope we had was to make the change—and die—and then hopefully live again. If *that* was what I was facing, then I wanted all the help I could get. If these Derm pills had started it then I hoped they could help us finish it. Dan and I needed to take the pills one last time. Today.

Before we died.

I looked at Dan's note again.

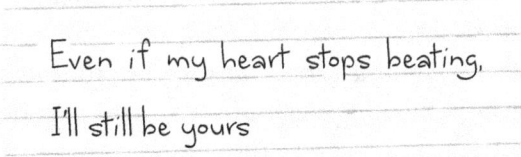

Even if my heart stops beating,
I'll still be yours

Dan had written this yesterday. Did he know, even then, that this couldn't be stopped? Maybe he saw in my head that I wouldn't stop reading the book. I let the last scraps of fear and denial fall away and accepted my new reality.

I couldn't stop this or change it, and neither could Dan. I would either die "die" tonight or I would die—and live again, forever with my love. Somehow I smiled. Tomorrow was looking up.

I thought about it some more. If we could truly make the final change, I would be with Dan forever. My smile grew wider and my mood lightened in spite of the pain locked away inside my mind. Forever in Dan's arms, forever there to hold him and love him. To enjoy eternity with Dan.

My thoughts drifted back to a (surprisingly good) production of Romeo and Juliet I'd seen at the Alhambra Dinner Theater on a school field trip. The scene with Juliet replayed in my mind, when she stabbed herself and kissed her Romeo one last time before she died. Joining her Romeo, who'd already done himself in with poison. The curtains had started to close just as they had in the real play, but then they stopped and opened again as real memories gave way to dreaming desire. Both dead lovers rose up, still pale with death's embrace. They stared into each other's eyes. And then they kissed again. And they would be that way *forever*.

I considered a love that even death could not stop and came to one final and absolute decision at that same moment. This afternoon when I saw Dan I would never leave him again. If I lived a hundred million years I would never leave his side again. I never wanted to be alone in my own mind again. I missed Dan.

"Dan. Dan," I whispered into the quiet of my mind, 'I'm coming, my Love. I'll see you soon."

I waited for a hopeful second to hear Dan's "*I'm here, my Love*," but all that answered me was silence.

Never again. Never alone. Forever with my Dan. I felt a calm settle over me as my thoughts settled. I *would* become a vampire and Dan would be my mate. My attention was drawn to the door as my mother shifted her weight. She was getting worried. I'd been quiet in here for a while. I needed to come out soon. I went back to planning for tomorrow. My vampire mind keeping all my thoughts and my pain nicely organized and in its place.

Tomorrow would be my last day on earth as a human girl or a *mostly* human girl anyway. I would be able to spend one last morning and one last afternoon with my parents before Dan and I took off together to find some quiet and private place to die and hopefully live again. I set a small part of my brain to thinking about where we might hide while I thought about tomorrow with the rest.

It was good that I would see Emma and Stacy tomorrow. At least I could tell them goodbye before I left. I was excited to show them my new body. It would be an interesting day all the way through as long as I could keep from eating anyone I loved. I thought about eating and frowned as my hunger rose up past the burning.

Mom knocked on the door. "Honey, are you okay in there?"

"Yes, Mom." I forced my thoughts away from my stomach. "I'm fine." I got up and caught a glimpse of my face in the mirror as I went to the door and almost squealed. Where my tears ran down my face were red streaks of blood. I'd cried blood from my eyes instead of tears! Dried red streaks ran down my face and onto my chest. I looked scary as hell!

"Just one minute," I called sweetly to my mother, my voice the exact opposite of how I felt. I rushed to the sink and used a hand towel to clean myself up. I grimaced as pain shot through me and was panting by the time I finished and put the bloody towel in the trash where my mom wouldn't find it.

I looked down at my clothes on the floor. I didn't want to put them back on with my skin the way it was. I wanted something light as a feather, like silk on my skin. Actually, I'd rather just walk around butt naked! This kind of pain threw embarrassment and modesty right out the window! I didn't give a rip what anyone else thought, I WAS BURNING ALIVE! If someone had a problem with me being naked then I guess I'd just have to kill 'um. That would solve the problem and I'd finally get to eat!

I laughed as I went to the door as naked as the day I was born. "Mom," I said as I unlocked the door, "I need help." I opened the door a crack and looked out at her face.

"What can I do for you, honey?" she asked, her face there in the crack of the door.

"I can't wear anything like jeans or anything heavy. I need a dress. Something as light and airy as possible, and I don't care if I'm almost naked. I can't stand having something heavy on my skin right now."

Her face pinched with worry.

"Maybe one of your silk nighties you like to wear for Dad," I suggested with a shrug. "Could I borrow one of those?" I wondered if they would even let me inside the mall wearing a silk nighty.

Mom's eyebrows went up, but she nodded, glad to have something to do, something she could help me with.

"Is your skin still tingling real bad?" she asked.

"It's not too bad." The biggest lie I'd ever told in my life. And I told it with a sweet smile. I didn't want to upset her, and there wasn't anything she could have done about it anyway.

"I'll go see what I can find." She took off and returned with four silk nighties, a few really light dresses, and one gorgeous red evening gown that I'd never seen before. Mom said that she'd bought it before I was born for a fancy dinner date but chickened out and ended up putting on something else instead. I could see why. The dress was a bit scandalous for my mom's tastes.

So, of course, I chose the gown. It had an underlining that I stripped out and a wide waist belt that I didn't use. The dress would probably be very easy to see through in any kind of direct light without the layers underneath but it was light and sheer and it would work for my trip to the mall. I would be *way* overdressed, and at the same time strangely underdressed, as I would be going *commando*.

I put it on, looked at myself in the mirror, and couldn't help thinking of Dan seeing me in the dress. The only person on earth I would endure a touch from would be Dan. For his touch I'd gladly burn. The dress was dark red and had a deep plunging neckline all the way down the front that stopped just above my belly button, and with me being braless, the dress was beyond scandalous. Yesterday I wouldn't have been able to do the dress justice, but today, with my new, super human posture everything looked quite—*nice*.

I opened the bathroom door and Mom was waiting right there.

"Can you do my hair, Mom?" I asked. She looked so surprised. Not just by my question but by me in the dress.

"You want me to do your hair right now? You're about to go to bed. Aren't you?"

"Eventually," I said. "But I would love it if you could do my hair up nice and fancy. I want to look good for Dan tomorrow," I said. "Make it real fancy, Mom. But no blow dryers," I added. I smiled, then had to do damage control. "Yes, Mom, my teeth are really white, but freak out about that later. Can you do my hair, please?"

Mom nodded. "I'd be glad to, honey."

For the next hour and a half, Mom worked on my hair and my nails. I made her take her time, and we talked about all kinds of things while she worked on me. She used curlers to make my hair as big as possible. We had a great time, in the middle of the night, blabbing away and talking girl talk together.

I almost screamed about a hundred times from the pain, but I managed to keep it locked away, at least from my mother, but I was starting to look forward to dying! This shit had to end! SOON!

After my hair was done, I made Mom lie down in her bed; it was almost 3 a.m. and she was whipped. I went into my room and took out a pad and paper and wrote a letter for Mom and Dad that I would give to them when Dan and I took off. The letter said I'd gone away with Dan and that I would call their cell soon, and not to worry. I know it was a waste of good ink to write *don't worry*, but it was one of those things you had to say anyway. Even if it was monumentally stupid.

I wrote six other letters to family and friends that I might never see again, and I also wrote one letter that I would keep with me when Dan and I died (just in case things went badly). If we didn't come back to life I wanted whoever found our bodies to know who we belonged to. I took the letters, all my money from Dr. Burgis and all my college savings from babysitting jobs, another two hundred bucks, and crammed all of it into my smallest and lightest purse. I couldn't stand the strap on my shoulder, so I adjusted the long strap and used it like a belt on the dress, letting the little purse rest on my side at my hip. I was so thin in the waist, the strap kept the dress from hanging on me like a big red tent and gave me some shape. I liked it. I checked the time, it was 5 a.m.

I went into the kitchen and made Dad's favorite breakfast: eggs rancheros. I fixed it up the way he loved it then I went into my parents' bedroom and quietly got Dad out of bed. I brought him into the kitchen and let Mom sleep. Dad ate and we talked for an hour and a half. We even played some cards. I had to be careful and let Dad shuffle because he almost had a coronary when he saw me do it.

After that I started being very careful to look as human as I could. It was kinda impossible with the way I looked and moved and sounded now. The simple fact that I could walk and move around and not have my boobs fly out of the dress I was wearing was a miracle of balance that defied gravity. I did it without even thinking, leaning and balancing and moving my body in exactly the right way, like some elegant three-way dance between me, my dress, and my chest, to keep all of me covered.

I must have reached over and gently pushed Dad's bottom jaw closed a dozen times when he would start staring and space out, either because of my voice or boobs or something else I'd done. Dad was worried that I hadn't gotten any sleep, so I lied and told him that I'd slept for a few hours. I seemed so awake and happy that he just let it go.

When Mom woke up, I cooked her breakfast too. She was horrified that I was dressed up in an evening gown, with big fancy hair and nails and cooking in the kitchen. She said it was like having a princess cook her breakfast.

When she asked me if I was going to eat I lied again and told her that I had already eaten. I talked to them, laughed with them, and did my best to make what might very well be my last few hours with them as good as they could possibly be.

They couldn't believe the change in me. How happy I seemed and how I just wanted to spend time with them and talk and talk and talk. It made me feel bad that I hadn't spent more time together before now. Or that I hadn't enjoyed the time we'd spent together more. I should have. Maybe after I changed into a vampire I could come back and see them. I had to wait and see if I was going to have enough self-control, but first I had to live through "dying" tonight. As strange as that sounded.

All too soon it was 9 a.m. and we were all in the car heading to the mall to meet up with Stacy and Emma. Mom and Dad joked carefully with me about how I was dressed and that it would cause a riot at the mall. They were still worried, but they were doing a whole lot better now.

I asked them to point the air conditioner vents in the van down or away from me. The cool air hitting my skin felt like a flame thrower, and I was fighting hard to keep all the burning pain locked away. As we got out on the road I started to think of Dan. Somehow I knew he was burning too and I began to worry. When would I get close enough for him to hear me? As we drove down the freeway I called out in my mind, "Dan! Are you there!?" I kept listening and waiting to hear his voice.

Major Tom Benistin

Doctors and Questions

"**D**r. Tachi, Dr. Armbruster, Dr. Cobb, I'd like to introduce you to Major Tom Benistin."

The three doctors nodded to the Major. He looked like Captain America in a bad mood after a hard life, except the Major was wearing a military dress uniform instead of red, white, and blue spandex tights. His tanned face was rugged, all planes and angles and his blond hair was so high and tight you could see scalp in places.

"The Major is with the Department of Homeland Defense and will be heading up the investigation into what caused the damage on the fifth floor yesterday as well as the disappearance and possible abduction of Sky Lee Han. The young lady who has the very interesting brain scan." Dr. Wolford sat down and Major Benistin stood.

Major Benistin started without a word of greeting. "Every word said here and every scrap of information concerning Sky Lee Han, her mother and father, and the events surrounding the damage at the Clinic are now classified information and a matter of national security. Under no circumstances will you share, disseminate, copy, archive, or discuss any information concerning these facts unless directed to do so by us. Any breach of this understanding would be very unfortunate, gentlemen." Benistin let the threat hang in the air for a moment then started to pace back and forth in front of the table.

Three of these doctors had personally examined or treated Sky before she had disappeared, and Dr. Wolford was the current Chair of the Rhinehart Clinic in Jacksonville, Florida. The doctors were unimpressed by the threats and wore annoyed expressions as they waited for the Major to continue.

Benistin paced as he talked. "We are convinced that the damage to the Clinic was not weather related. The damage and some of the actions immediately preceding the *event* lead us to suspect an explosive device of some kind was used. The nurse who attended Miss Han said that the girl tricked her into releasing her from her restraints and insisted on getting her clothes and cell phone back, then actually looked at the window that was blown out and said the word 'wait'."

Major Benistin watched the men for any reaction to this information before he continued. "Miss Han then forced the nurse from the room, secured the door, and used that cell phone to make a call to her father when the window was blown out. A section of the fifth floor will be sealed off as our team of experts examine the blast area and collect forensic data, so please take the appropriate measures and adjust your patients and staff accordingly. I've already reviewed your individual statements but I have a few direct questions I'd like to ask now if there are no objections?" Benistin waited for their mumbled consent.

"Is it true that the girl was unconscious the whole time she was at the clinic and that the only person to see her awake and aware was the attending nurse?"

They confirmed the report.

"Other than the girl's very abnormal MRI was there anything else about her that was out of the ordinary or should be acknowledged as a pertinent fact for this file? Please understand that what may seem inconsequential or trivial may actually be very, very important." He waited.

"Well," began Dr. Tachi. Just one word in, he paused as he took note of a young woman seated at the table who had started to transcribe his words onto her laptop. He looked from her then back to Benistin's waiting eyes.

"Yes?" Benistin prodded.

"The girl had cuts and bruises on her body from earlier struggles. She had a busted lip, a large bruise on her left hip, and various scratches that would have been consistent with her mother's injuries. I noticed that Sky's mother had similar scratches on her arms and a black eye. I think that Sky and her mother fought and scratched each other up either yesterday or this morning, before the incident in the vehicle where she split her chin open and was knocked unconscious."

Dr. Tachi's eyebrows came together and settled in an angry dark line. "I believe that the girl is being abused. Severely. She should be removed from that home until a thorough investigation can be conducted. The daughter has a very long history of mental illness, so this may be self-inflicted damage, but on the surface it looks very, very bad. I don't say it lightly, but it may be best to remove the child from her parents till we know what's going on."

Benistin nodded. "Dr. Tachi. None of this was in your initial report." There was no threat in his voice, just a question. He waited for his answer.

"Of course not." Dr. Tachi looked at him like he was simple. "You just said that this information was now 'Classified' and that no one would see it, disseminate it, copy it, or even discuss it. This information is now protected by walls of legal barriers and cannot be accessed by lawyers and used to sue the hell out of me. You don't lightly bring an allegation against someone as wealthy as Mr. Han. He would sue me into the poor house. That is why it is not in my report, Benistin." His tone and the fact that he didn't use the Major's title was enough to show what he thought of being asked "why" he hadn't put it into the report as well as what he thought of the Major.

Benistin gave Tachi a grin, "I like you, Tachi! Direct and honest. And you actually seem to care for the welfare of the girl which is also very important to us. Would you be willing to be our primary medical contact concerning the girl? We will need one doctor to organize the related medical facts concerning Sky and apparently her mother as well. We already took the liberty of doing a background check and you've been cleared. So what do you say, doctor?"

The Major gave him a level stare. "Come and work for us and your country until we can make sure this young girl is located and safe. We need someone in charge of compiling the medical data and to help us take care of Sky once we bring her in. I may look like nothing but a military tight-ass, but I like to work with honest people. People who actually care. And having an outside expert from a hospital as prestigious as Rhinehart Clinic is helpful. So what do you say,

Tachi?" Benistin waited. A tight, hopeful smile was firmly set on his face as Dr. Tachi processed the unexpected proposal.

"Please do it, Dr. Tachi," urged Wolford. "I'd rather have you in charge of this mess than some outsider that will just make a bigger mess than it's already going to be. We can make sure your patients are covered and I'm sure that the Major will compensate you handsomely for your work as well." They saw the quick nod from the Major. Wolford continued, "Better you than God knows who, and this way you can make sure the girl gets the care she needs."

Wolford waited and they all watched as Tachi gave the Major a long hard stare before he nodded.

"Excellent! Welcome aboard, doctor." Benistin said, then he directed his gaze back to the other two doctors.

"Well, gentlemen. Are there any other facts or scraps of information other than the MRI that need to be mentioned? Even unusual things you normally wouldn't consider important need to be mentioned now. Let's hear it."

Dr. Cobb was the youngest of the three doctors. He looked embarrassed as he spoke up. "You know that the young lady was attractive, but—" He met Benistin's eyes and raised his eyebrows. "I think you need to be aware that she is not simply *attractive*—she's a goddess!"

All at once the three older doctors shot him disgusted looks and the younger man cringed.

"No. Let him talk," Benistin said. "Go on, Dr. Cobb," he encouraged when Cobb remained silent and sullen in his chair.

"I'm just saying that the girl isn't merely a pretty face. Other than some acne and skin irritation, which will probably go away with these Derm pills she's been taking, her body is—well—" Cobb just couldn't say it with the other doctors in the room. "Once the pills are through with her she's going to be one in a million. That's all I'm saying about it."

Dr. Cobb looked like he wished he hadn't said anything at all. He kept his eyes forward, avoiding the gaze of his colleagues.

Benistin moved on. "Tell me more about this Derm pill drug study she was in. You mentioned that her mother and father blamed this pill on her recent suicide attempts. What do you know about this drug study?"

Tachi answered him, "I'm sure you've seen the hype on the TV. It's biogenetic medicine currently in the early stages of human testing but some of the superrich have already gotten it on the black market to use on their children. The drug works only for adolescents and teens like Sky. The Derm 513 pill alters the portions of the genetic code affecting the skin and complexion. It's really quite amazing, very exciting science, and it actually *works,* but it does have a lot of side effects. Mood swings and mental instability are a large part of those side effects, so the mother's information is probably quite accurate about the pills playing a part in her recent suicide attempt. But that still doesn't give her an excuse for abusing the child," Tachi finished, defending his earlier statement about the mother abusing her daughter.

Benistin's cell vibrated on his hip. He glanced at the number but didn't answer. He needed to wrap this up.

"All right," he said, "you mentioned that her MRI was very abnormal. Now let's hear it. What's abnormal about it?"

Dr. Armbruster, the head of the Neurology Department stood. He was a very tall and stately elderly gentleman. Arrogance was clear in his voice as he addressed Major Benistin.

"Yes, finally," he drawled out. "If you had asked this question first you would have saved yourself, *and us,* a lot of time. All the rest of this minutia you've blathered on about doesn't matter, Major. What matters is this girl's brain scan, not her body or the damage to the building."

He pushed the button on the remote control he held and the flat screen monitor on the table came on showing the results of an MRI. The active and inactive parts of the brain were colored in varying shades of red and blue.

"This is a picture of a normal human scan, Major. And this is normal activity and blood flow typical for a healthy female brain of seventeen years." He pointed to a few key regions on the scan. "Please pay particular attention to these areas." Ambruster pointed to some areas that were mostly blue, inactive. He pushed a button and the picture on the screen changed, showing a different pattern. There was a huge change in the areas Ambruster had indicated. The areas that had been blue were bright red with brain activity.

Major Benistin took this in quickly. "So tell me in plain English. How big a deal is it and what does it mean? I need to know and I can't be wrong on this, Dr. Ambruster." He eyed Ambruster's self-satisfied smile with suspicion then asked, "Is this scan accurate? Was the machine working correctly? Is there some other explanation for this brain activity, like those Derm pills she's taking? I need to know 'HOW HIGH' to jump." He gave Ambruster a small nod and added a respectful, "sir."

Ambruster seemed satisfied with that bit of give and leaned back in his chair, steepling his fingers as he spoke. "We checked the machine and it's working fine, Major. We have had our experts check the scan for any signs of tampering, but your people can probably do a better job of that than our people. Everything checked out on our side. The scan is accurate."

Dr. Ambruster stopped and waited to be prodded for more information, enjoying being the center of attention.

Benistin complied. "And if this scan is accurate, how big a deal is this girl's brain scan? Not theory. Just facts."

Benistin made eye contact with Tachi, who nodded. He didn't just want the word of one crazy old neurologist; he wanted Tachi's opinion on this too.

"Let me put it this way." Ambruster was still being a show hound as he tried to build toward the moment of revelation. His leaned forward in his chair, his voice that of a younger, more vibrant man as he finally delivered the goods. "Sky Lee Han's brain scan shows a hundred times more activity than any other brain we have ever seen!" Ambruster held up a finger, "But that's not even the exciting part! This new activity is entirely in areas that have always been 'dark spots' or 'forbidden zones' in the brain that we just don't know a lot about. This girl's brain is a miracle, Major. An absolute, one of a kind, walking, LIGHTNING BOLT of a miracle! And if you want my opinion on how 'HIGH' to jump," Ambruster looked right at Benistin and grinned as he finished his oration.

"I'd say, Sky high."

Sky Lee Han

Breakfast at Bathenda's

"Do you have a straw, Momma Bathenda?" I called as I sat at the old breakfast table with the other little girl.

"Ti-shaa!" Bathenda called from the kitchen where she was working on breakfast, "get Sky a straw, baby!"

Tisha jumped up from her bench and ran into the kitchen, coming right back with a straw still in the white wrapper. It was a McDonald's straw.

"Here you go," she said as she handed me the straw.

"Thanks, Tisha." I smiled at her, took the straw, slipped it out of the paper wrapper, and dropped it into my glass of OJ as Tisha climbed back onto her bench. She stared at me from her side of the table.

"You're real pretty," she said shyly. She picked her fork up and started eating but kept her big brown eyes on me.

"You are too, Tisha," I told her, and she smiled at me as she took another bite of her pancake.

Momma Bathenda came into the dining room with a plate in each hand. She set a plate in front of me. "Here you go, Sky Baby. Now eat your breakfast and then you need to call your father and let him know you okay." She set the other plate on the table for herself and groaned as she dropped into the chair.

"Ooh, it's so *hot* in here!" Momma fanned herself. "These fans just can't keep it cool when I run dat stove." Bathenda kept fanning.

I looked at her sweating away and thought it would be nice if it was cooler in the house. Maybe I could make it cooler. I thought about the air changing and being cooler inside the house—and it changed.

"OH MY!" Bathenda looked around wildly. "Goodness, it just got all cool in here all of a sudden." She rubbed her arms as she looked around the house.

"Does that feel better, Momma?" I mumbled around a mouthful of pancake.

"Yeah, Sky Baby, but where'd this cool air come from?" She was looking out the window. "Is there a storm a coming or something?" She stood up and walked to the window and stuck her hand outside. Her eyebrows went up. It was still warm outside the house but cool inside the house. The window was wide open and didn't have a screen in it. She pulled her hand back inside the house. She looked back at me and gave me questioning look.

"Come eat, Momma Bathenda. Your pancakes are getting cold," I called as I stabbed my pancake again.

She shook her head and came back to the table and started eating.

"That momma of yours ever feed you, child? No wonder you so skinny," she asked as she looked at my almost clean plate.

"Oh, no, Mom doesn't feed me. Robert does though," I said.

"Who's Robert?" Bathenda asked.

"He's the chef," I answered as I pulled out my little silver cell phone.

"What's a chef?" Tisha asked.

"That's someone who gets paid to cook for some rich family, baby," Bathenda told her.

"Sky, are you rich?" Tisha guessed, her eyes wide.

"No!" I laughed. "But my parents are." I turned on my little phone but a message kept flashing on the screen: *Acquiring Signal.*

"Something's wrong with my phone," I said to Momma Bathenda. I handed her the phone.

She let out a suspicious "MmmHummm" as she looked at the screen. "I figured it'd be somethin' like this." Bathenda pushed the power button and turned the phone off. "I'd bet you a new nickel that father of yours has the police searching for that phone; they probably gonna come rollin' up any second now, Sky Baby." She gave me a sad look. "If you don't wanna go home, you gonna have to take on off cause the police will be here soon. I'm sorry."

"But I was calling! I told him I would call!" Not fair! Father told me I could stay! Then I thought about that. He didn't really have much choice. But I couldn't go home yet. I needed to get to the doctor's office. I hadn't called the doctor, but everything had worked out anyway. Bathenda had taken me home, which was perfect! The doctor didn't have to run out and pick me up last night and now I could go to the office like I usually did and take today's pills.

Bathenda made a face, heaved herself up from her chair, and walked to the window. She looked out at the yard then turned back to me. She wasn't happy.

"Well, let me see if I can get that thing to work. Maybe you can still call him and tell him that you're fine before they come knockin' the door in." Bathenda didn't sound too hopeful but she walked back over and I handed her my phone. She fiddled with it for a few minutes.

"Oh! I got it on, Baby." She pushed the buttons some more then put the phone to her ear.

"Hello, Mr. Han?" Bathenda said into the phone.

"Yes, she's right here, Mr. Han; I'll give her the phone." Bathenda handed me my phone.

I put the phone up to my ear. "Hello," I said in Cantonese.

"Sky, how are you, my daughter!?" Father spoke back in Cantonese also. He sounded happy to talk to me.

"I'm good."

"Are you safe? Is Miss Bathenda taking good care of you?" he asked.

"Oh yes," I answered. It was so nice to talk to him like this. I smiled at Bathenda and Tisha. Tisha was whispering to Bathenda, asking her a question about me speaking Chinese. "She's taken real good care of me. We just ate breakfast."

"Sky, the police want to know what happened to the window at the hospital. Do you know what happened? Sky?"

Hmmm. I didn't know what to tell him. I decided I'd just ask something else. "Is mother there?"

"Your mother is here, Sky, but please tell me about the window. How did it break?" He asked again.

"The cloud broke the window," I told him. Well. It did.

"It was a tornado then." He sounded relieved.

"The cloud broke the window, Father, but can I talk to Mom?" I didn't want him to ask any more questions about the window.

"Yes, Sky, here is your mother."

"Sky!" She said.

"Hi Mom!" I said in English. It was good to hear her too. I liked talking on phones! People were so much easier to talk to on a phone. "How are you!" I asked which felt weird to me because I usually never cared enough about how she felt to ask her. I couldn't remember *ever* asking her that before.

"I'm—good, Sky. I'm good." She sounded surprised too. Surprised and sad.

"Don't be sad, I'm okay. And I won't stay gone forever. I'll come home soon," I told her.

"Sky, promise me that you won't jump off of anything high. Please don't hurt yourself. It would kill me too. It would kill me, Sky." She started to cry.

"Don't cry, Mom. You don't have to worry about me falling anymore. Don't cry." I wanted to tell her more but I didn't think that was the best idea right now. Not until after I finished my pills.

"Please just don't try to fly, Sky. You can't fly!" More crying.

The phone on the wall rang at Bathenda's and she walked over and picked it up.

My heart hurt listening to her cry. She was mean to me, even horrible sometimes, but I didn't want her to cry. I didn't even want her to be sad. She was still my mother.

"Where are you right now?" I asked her.

"Oh," She took a second to answer, "We're aah, we're at the police station. They're asking a lot of questions about the window at the hospital. They think someone set off a bomb or something. We're okay—"

"SKY BABY!" Bathenda yelled, and I jumped, almost dropping the phone.

"Tell your Momma you gotta go. The police are here! They done got the house surrounded!" Bathenda told me as she walked to the window and pulled the curtain aside to peek out. "They done and filled up the street. There must be fifty of 'um out there already." She shook her head, "MmmmHmmm. Here they come, Baby." Bathenda dropped the curtain and started walking to the front door.

"MOM!" I yelled into the phone. "I'm not coming home yet! I was fine here! Why did you send the police here!?"

I was mad. I wasn't ready to go home. I couldn't let them stop me. I had to get out and get back to the doctor's office!

"Sky! Please! Just go with the police! They are there to help you! Please don't hurt yourself!"

"Yeah right!" I griped and pushed the end button.

Bathenda was opening the front door. I hid around the bend of the dining room door as I watched her. There were two guys in gray suits at the front door. I saw some movement out of one of the windows on the side of the house and looked over. There was a cop staring into the window right at me. I heard the back screen door open.

No! I wasn't going back! I wasn't going to let them drug me! I saw someone in black walking around in the back of the house and ran up into the living room where Bathenda was talking to the two guys at the front door.

"Momma Bathenda! They're in the house!" I yelled.

She turned and put her arm out and said, "Come here, Sky Baby, they ain't gonna grab you. These here ones done promised to be real nice; I think you should go with these ones." Bathenda turned to me and said, "But Sky Baby, please turn the cold off in here before you go, child, you gonna freeze me to death." Bathenda smiled at me.

My eyes got big. I hadn't realized that she knew I'd done it.

"Okay," I said. I thought about it going back to normal in the house and it did.

Bathenda smiled at me and said, "Come on, child, come here now." She held her arm open and I stepped up and she put her arm around me, and we turned to face the two guys in suits at the front door together.

"Hello, Sky," said a guy with a grey mustache.

I didn't say hello. I just looked around the yard and street. Cops were everywhere. Some of them had guns out and I saw one that had what looked like a dart gun. That made me mad. I pointed to the guy with the dart gun.

"So, you're gonna drug me." I said.

Both the guys in suits turned and looked at the guy with the dart gun.

Mustache guy answered, "No, Sky. We're not gonna drug you."

The other guy quickly started talking into his radio. They were everywhere like ants and they all had guns. I looked up when I heard the noise; there was a black helicopter flying over the house.

"Now why don't you tell some of these fools to get the hell outta here!" Momma Bathenda said.

"And if I find some sorry nigga in my house I'm gonna punch 'um right in the mouth! So you just tell 'um to stay the hell outta my house!" she yelled at them.

The guy on the radio started talking again.

"I'm not going with you," I said to the guy with the mustache.

He just smiled at me and said, "Sky, you have to. I'm sorry." He didn't look sorry at all.

I looked back at the guy with the dart gun; he was still there. I needed to fly away but everyone would see me. And I was scared of getting grabbed by someone so I couldn't fly off. If I could get outside and get some room, I'd be gone. I didn't care who saw me but there was *no way* I was going with these people!

"I don't want to go," I said. "I want you people to leave me alone. I'm seventeen not seven. I ran away from home. People do that all the time, so why all of this!?" I waved my hand at the street. "People run away from home all the time, why can't I!? And why the drugs!? You're gonna try to drug me!" I yelled at mustache guy.

"Sky, we're not gonna drug you!" mustache guy said again. "And you don't have to go back to your mother and father if you don't want to. I promise. We have a safe place for you, but it's time for us to go now."

He took a step forward and I squirmed out of Bethenda's arms and back into the house. A cop all dressed in black with the words SWAT on his chest burst out of the back, running right at me so I turned and jumped right through the open window and just kept going.

I flew past the surprised faces of cop after cop as I swooshed by like Superman (or woman), and soon I was down the road and a few blocks away. There wasn't a cop car in sight.

I flew up and landed in the top of an oak tree, feeling my pockets.

"Oh no!" I said. I had left my cell phone at Momma Bethenda's. I wanted to call my father. I looked back down the street. I could see the flashing lights of cop cars approaching. My little silver phone! Now I couldn't even call the doctor.

I sat on my tree branch and thought about what to do now. It was still early, so I could fly home really quickly and get some new cloths and maybe even some money. I needed a shower too. I hadn't felt comfortable taking a bath at Bathenda's; she had only a tub and I was more of a shower girl. My parents were here in Jacksonville at the police station, so they wouldn't see me at the house, and I wasn't worried about Emeila anymore. I could land on my balcony without anyone even knowing I was home and go straight into my shower.

Cop cars started to flash by underneath my tree, and I heard the whirling blades of the helicopter overhead. Great! I floated carefully away from my tree to get clear of the branches, and looked to make sure the way was clear before I flew about a half a mile straight up and stopped there in the air.

I thought about the wind, that when I flew it would go around me and not make me so cold or tear at my skin and hair. And I wanted to fly so fast no one could see me, super fast. I imagined flying all the way home in just seconds. I had my whole trip planned out in my head and where I wanted to stop.

Then I took off like a rocket! The earth was a blur far beneath me, a wash of colors and lights as I flew through the sky. I slowly got used to seeing things flash by so fast and started to pick out some of the details as I whizzed by, but then I was home! I stopped at exactly the spot I'd imagined. This time when I stopped I didn't feel all rattled and shook up like a bug hitting a windshield or frozen solid and wind burned. I was glad that I'd had the air go around me this time.

Down below I could see my house. I took a few minutes to look around. It was a beautiful day and there was a comfortable breeze blowing in from off the ocean. It felt so good to be flying again. I wanted to go fly over the pretty ocean waves and then fly up and touch some clouds, but there were people out on the beach and I didn't want to be seen, so I turned back to my house.

I floated down onto my balcony and reached over to the sliding glass door. Yay, it was unlocked! I slid it open and stepped inside then snuck through my room and out to the front of the hall and listened. I could hear Emelia talking to Robert in the kitchen downstairs.

I went back to my room, shut my door, and then locked it from the inside for a change. I went into my drawers and packed a good travel bag, picking out some nice clothes to wear for today. I looked at the clock on my wall before I headed into the bathroom. It was 9:20 now, so I had a couple of hours. I wasn't supposed to be at the doctor's office until 1 p.m. Doctor Burgis had moved my time back because of my mother's fit yesterday. It didn't matter, I was sure that whenever I got there Dr. Burgis would see me. Maybe he would give me a new phone too. I hoped so. I missed my little phone; my pocket didn't feel right without it.

I headed into the shower. Bethenda's house was nice, even though they were poor, and I was okay with most everything, but I did like my rich girl shower! That tub at Bethenda's was just so *nasty*!

The Police

Unfinished Business

Watch Commander Dehart walked over to Sergeant Kelly as soon as he dropped into his chair.

"Kelly, you had that run in with that trailer park witch girl yesterday, didn't you."

Kelly closed his eyes. *Oh shit, here we go*, he thought. His paperwork on the incident that had involved more than ten officers and an ambulance had been sketchy at best. And what was worse, no one was arrested at the end of the story to catch the heat for all the man hours.

"Yes, Sir." Kelly said but thought, *Please just go away!* "I handled that call—and I know the paperwork was a little light but—"

"Handled it." The Watch Commander laughed. "Not yet you haven't, it's not over yet. Get your ass back over there. The story on that girl has gotten out.

There are reporters all over the place, crowding up the streets. The neighbors have been calling 911 nonstop and so have the girl's parents. Reporters keep knocking on their door and beating on their windows trying to get that girl to talk to them, and from what some of the other officers told me last night, this girl is the *real* deal. We've already got two units there, been there since early this morning." The Commander grinned as he herd Kelly groan. Kelly looked like he might be sick.

"And your report really was shit, Kelly. I understand *why* it was shit but still—" Dehart leaned in. "Just between you and me, Kelly, what the hell went on over there at that witch's trailer? I saw the pictures of what she wrote on that bathroom mirror—Is this girl the real deal?" Watch Commander Dehart waited expectantly, enjoying himself.

"Yes, Sir. She's a real witch. And that is all I'm saying." The Sergeant stared at his desk. He knew what this meant. More paperwork he couldn't fill out. More questions he couldn't answer. And he'd have to see that witch again. Shit.

"Well, you better get over there before that girl gets mad. We don't need any more problems with all the hell that's busting loose right now in this city. What with that kid that killed himself last night and his family missing and all the people looking for that missing girl from Rhinehart Clinic, we don't have the manpower for this witch nonsense, so clean it up quick. This one is all yours, Kelly, so go and finish what you started."

"Sir," Kelly said, "I'll need officer Jason Williams with me on this call."

"Why do you need Williams?" asked Dehart.

"Dammit! Just let me do this!" Kelly shouted, pissed. He wasn't about to explain why!

"Okay! Easy!" the Watch Commander said as he retreated. "He's yours, just take care of it, Kelly." Dehart made a hasty retreat from the upset Sergeant and went back to the safety of his office.

Sergeant Kelly rubbed his temples as he mumbled to himself. "Just give me a nice peaceful knife fight, or an OD or a DOA, a clean cut DWI, or a little B&E—maybe some grand theft auto or even some old fashioned teen punk vandalism. Why do I get the shit you can't put into a report?"

He groaned again. "Why?"

Dr. Burgis

4 PM Appointment

"**Yes, I understand,** I just can't believe it. Joshua was doing well. He hadn't shown any signs that he was having problems." Dr. Burgis looked at the picture on his bedroom wall of Joshua McDaven, study patient number 8.

"Nurse Ann did a full work-up just yesterday. Blood, weight, BP, everything, and I did a brief interview, all documented. The boy was fine. He was fine." Burgis tried to sound convincing.

"Apparently not," the detective on the other side of the connection added grimly.

Dr. Burgis was still somewhat shocked, adjusting to the horrible news. One of his trial patients had been found in his home last night in the middle of his living room. He'd shot himself with a shotgun and "apparently" committed suicide. And what's worse, the rest of his family was missing without a trace. Just vanished! The police wanted to meet with the doctor and ask him some questions about the study and the drugs Joshua was taking.

"You'll need to gather all your records on Joshua. You understand this is an ongoing police investigation. Will we need a court order for the medical records?" the detective asked.

"A court order? Yes. Certainly. I'm glad you thought to mention it. I'll need that. DAR Medical will want the paperwork. Patient privacy laws and all that are very strict. I'll clear my schedule and make myself available for you at four p.m. this afternoon at my office."

"Thank you, Doctor. I know this is probably a shock to you. Always hate to be the one to share this kind of news. And I think we'll need you to come down to the police station this morning. Right away. So we can get started."

"I'd be glad to, but if I'm to give a deposition I'll have to wait till the damn company lawyer is there to sit at the table and hold my hand. They won't let me say a single word without one; it's in my employment contract unfortunately. I'll call right now so they should have someone here by this afternoon. The main office is in Atlanta. That's a short flight. And they'll also send a replacement doctor to oversee the rest of the study and some others to start their own internal investigation I'm sure. But as for today, I can't leave my patients unsupervised, it's not safe." Doctor Burgis made his voice a little sterner, playing his part well on the phone as he lied. If the detective on the other side of the connection could see the horrified face, sweating brow, and manic pacing, then the voice wouldn't be nearly so convincing.

"And there is still no sign of the rest of Joshua's family?" asked Dr. Burgis. "I'd like to talk to the boy's mother."

"There's still no sign of the parents. It's very, very strange. I wish I could tell you more. No worries though, Doctor Burgis, we'll get to the truth soon enough. Hopefully I'll have something more I can share with you when I see you at four. You said four would be okay?"

"Yes, yes. At four then. Let me call Atlanta to make sure they get their people here as soon as possible. I'll be ready at four." Dr. Burgis hung up the phone.

He turned back to his bed and placed a last few items inside his suitcase and briefcase. He put on his white lab coat before grabbing the suitcase in one hand and the briefcase in the other and heading out the door. He didn't bother to lock the door behind him. He wouldn't be back. He juggled his burdens around so he could look at his watch. If everything went well today he would see his last patient and be out the door by two or two thirty at the latest. It was time to run.

Dana and David

Still Loving You

"**D**ana, you really shouldn't be out of your bed." The old nurse tried to step behind her wheelchair and push her back toward her room.

"NO!" Dana threw the brake on and the chair froze up. This was the third time she'd tried to go down to see him.

"If you insist on going down there at least let me push your chair," the nurse said gently. "I don't want you to wear yourself out so let me push you. Please." She waited.

"Okay," Dana relented and looked up at her with her busted, cut up face. The nurse smiled at her. She'd seen worse.

"Before we go, let me get you another pain pill. It's been three hours, you should have already had one by now."

"No. No thank you." Dana didn't want to take the pills because they made her sleepy. She didn't care about the pain. What she wanted was to go downstairs and see him. They had brought him here at the same time they brought her. She was still conscious when the paramedics were working on him, just on the other side of the glass as they worked on her on her side. His ambulance had been right behind hers as they went to the hospital.

"No. Please. Just take me to David," she whispered to the nurse who nodded and started to push the chair toward the elevator and the ICU ward. She remembered him falling down when she had hit him and slapped him but she hadn't noticed he was having an asthma attack down there under the table. She was just so mad and hurt right then and she had ran off to yell at Madric—and then she had practically gotten herself killed. She felt the tears but quickly forced them down. Hell no. Enough of that.

"Here we are, dear. Oh my. He has a visitor." The nurse parked her right outside the door. "Let me go and see who he is. If he's one of the boy's parents I can ask if they'll let you in to see him."

The nurse stepped into the room and went up to a tall man who was leaning over David's bedside. He spoke with the nurse for just a second before his head whipped around, and he looked right at Dana through the glass and headed her way. The door opened and he stood there, looking down at her, taking in her condition for a moment.

"Are you Dana?" he asked her.

She hesitated only a second. "Yes," she breathed out. This guy was obviously David's father. He looked like David. He looked very very sad.

"Why are you here?" David's father asked. His expression was blank. Not angry, not happy.

Dana thought about it for a second and cringed. Someone had probably told him that she'd slapped the hell out of David right before he had his asthma attack. *Oh great! He knows I did this to David!* she thought and started to cry.

"No! Please don't cry." David's father stepped closer and knelt down next to her chair. "Please, Dana, won't you come in and see him? Talk to him," he urged. Tears were running down his face. "David has loved you for years. I'm sure you know that. His mother and I both knew. If there is anyone on earth he will hear now, it's you." He wiped tears away from his eyes but new ones took their place as soon as he had. "Please come in and talk to him, Dana. David needs you now."

He looked at her with his watery eyes, and Dana nodded. The nurse pushed her into the room and parked her right beside David. He was hooked up to all kinds of machines, even a respirator. He'd been in a coma since the ambulance had carried him away from the mall. Dana listened as his Dad told her that he was getting weaker and that if he didn't improve soon he may die or his brain might die. He asked her to stay. To speak to him.

I did this. The thought hung there as she looked at him. And for what? For loving her and trying to save her from throwing her life away. She looked at him and cried for a while. The nurse and David's father quietly left the room and left her alone with him. Dana rolled her chair as close to the head of David's bed as she could, then leaned forward until she could slip under the hoses and wires and run her fingers through his hair. He looked so pale, and weak.

I'm a monster. I did this. I caused this.

"Oh God, David. I'm sorry," she whispered to him as she ran her fingers through his hair. She cried. All he'd ever tried to do for years and years was take care of her and love her. He didn't deserve this. She did, but he didn't. He was good and kind and loyal and—and too good for her. But he loved her. She knew that he did and that he always would. No matter what she did or said. David wouldn't change. Dana looked at his peaceful expression and knew that he loved her even now. Even after what she'd done. Even diseased, abused, ruined. He still loved her.

"David," she whispered. "David, don't die. Come back. It's me—it's your Dana."

Black Rain

Let the Whole World Know

Reporters and crazies started beating on the doors and windows at 1 a.m., trying to get me to come out and talk to them. All they got were my angry parents.

The police arrived.

Things improved.

No more beating on the windows and door, but the crowd was still out there in the dark, growing larger each minute. I looked out the window in my bedroom with Mary and Bethany, the three of us peeking through the narrow gaps between the blinds. I stared at the bright yellow tape that now encircled our trailer.

Police Line-Do Not Cross! Police Line-Do Not Cross!

The tape held back the crowd, while at the same time it declared that something on this side of the tape was wrong. Terribly wrong. Like the trailer was the scene of a crime. *Murder*—

With a sudden chilling insight I realized that it wasn't the trailer, it was *me*—my body was the scene of a crime. I pulled away from the window, *angry*. I knew what I was! I didn't need the police and their tape to remind me of what I was or what I'd done. I tried to ignore the sounds from outside and force all of it from my mind, but somehow a chill entered me that I couldn't shake.

Mary and Bethany put me into bed between them. They told me that they loved me and squeezed me tightly, as if they could squeeze the shakes out of me. Eventually that was exactly what they did.

The morning came, and we'd been fine up until ten minutes ago when a guy out in the street started in with a bullhorn, shouting, "Kill the child of the Devil!" and that other well-known breakfast tune, "BURN THE WITCH!" He stood in front of our trailer leading a chorus of sing-along psychos as he spewed his religious flavored hate at me.

He wasn't alone. There were lots of yelling crazies outside, but it was the bullhorn that pierced through the walls of the trailer. I cringed, and so did everyone else as we tried to eat. It felt like he was standing right behind my chair, yelling behind my head. I was at one end of the long table with Mary and Bethany, and Ryan sat at the other end with Mom and Dad. We were all doing our best to ignore the chaos outside but the bullhorn was too much for me.

"BURN THE WITCH!"

"BURN THE WITCH!"

"BURN THE WITCH!"

I rose from the table.

"Rain! NO!" Mary stabbed a finger at me. "No bad thoughts! Be good! Don't you hurt that idiot man!" she scolded, narrowing her green eyes.

Mom, Dad and Ryan looked shocked and then frightened. Hearing Mary talk to me like that was new. They'd observed the girls doing similar things since their arrival last night, keeping me calm and out of trouble, but nothing quite so blatant.

"Yeah, just ignore him, Rain," Ryan said, glad for the help. He gave Mary a thankful little nod.

"Don't hurt him," Dad joined in, always quick on the uptake. "You remember what happened with the policeman, Rain. Ignore him, baby, it's okay."

"BURN THE WITCH!"
"BURN THE WITCH!"
"BURN THE WITCH!"
The volume boomed even louder!

Bethany put her hands over her ears. I was so mad I was shaking as I stood there at the head of the breakfast table. It was all I could do to keep my mind from the darkest of horrors; they were just about to slip free and come to life outside my trailer on Bullhorn Guy!

"Help me!" I said through clinched teeth. I closed my eyes. I could see purple spots in the darkness, my eyes were squeezed so tight. I felt Bethany's little arms wrap around me and then Mary's. They kept telling me to calm down and not to listen but I was sooo angry—

Everything went quiet outside.

After a minute I opened my eyes.

At their side of the table, Mom, Dad, and Ryan were gathered together, praying for me. I listened as they prayed that I would calm down and that the people outside would be quiet. Mary and Bethany stared at them with me, the three of us looking back toward the street where only seconds ago it had sounded like a riot outside. Now it was almost quiet out there, and I felt better too. Calmer.

I smiled at my sisters and slipped out of their arms, going over to my family and hugging them. They stopped praying and looked surprised to see me as they opened their eyes, and even more surprised when they listened to the relative quiet. They returned my hug.

"Thanks, I needed that," I said.

We all had a quick laugh and sat back down to finish breakfast, but then the doorbell rang.

"I'll get it." Ryan jumped up before Dad or Mom could move. He went to the door and came back with a big smile on his face with "Officer Jason Williams" following behind him.

"Look who's back!" Ryan said with a big smile.

"OH!" I shouted. Without even thinking about what I was doing, I ran over and gave him a great big hug! He stood there, stiff as a board, a scared "HELP ME!" expression on his face. I heard my sisters and my family laughing behind me. I didn't laugh, it wasn't funny to me. I let him go and backed a step or two away to give him some room.

"Are you feeling better, Officer Williams?" I asked.

"Aah, yes, ma'am. I'm fine. And I'm real sorry about yesterday." He gave me a sympathetic look for some reason. As if I'd been the one hurt and not him. "Don't you worry about yesterday. My momma taught me better than to mouth off to a witch like that." He looked at my worried face for a minute longer and added, "I know you didn't want to hurt me, witch girl. I know a little about witches. I was born in Louisiana and I grew up with witches. My aunt was a witch. I know sometimes it just gets the better of you and you lose control—especially when some fool idiot does something stupid and disrespects you." He gave me a friendly smile and then added, "Like me."

"Why are you here?" I asked him.

His smile disappeared. Now he looked nervous.

"Actually, Sergeant Kelly sent me. He's placed me in charge of making sure you're safe with all these reporters around, and also—" Williams hesitated and crunched up his face, "to make sure you don't hurt nobody else."

As soon as the words were out, Williams' whole body tightened up, as if he were bracing for a punch to the face.

"Oh," I said, not surprised or concerned. "Come join the club then. Sit down and I'll make you a plate."

Before he could say no, I grabbed him by the arm and had him seated in my spot at the end of the table right between Mary and Bethany. He looked terrified, his eyes going from one scary witch girl face and forehead tattoo to another scary witch girl face and tattoo. Mom, Dad, and Ryan made their welcomes while I made him a plate of eggs, bacon, and pancakes and poured a glass of juice, bringing it over and setting it in front of him. I stood behind Bethany's chair, happy and content with this new surprise.

"Thank you, ma'am, I was kinda hungry," Williams said politely to my mother. Of course, she'd insisted that he eat something as well. He picked up his fork and started eating.

"Do you want some buttered toast?" asked Mary with a bubbly, bright smile. She reached to the plate in the center of the table and grabbed Williams a piece of toast and started to butter it for him.

"Hey!" Bethany's sweet little voice called out, followed by a happy shout of "I *know* you!"

Mom, Dad, and Ryan were stunned. Bethany hadn't spoken a word above a whisper since she had appeared in my bedroom last night, and here she was, speaking to Williams of all people!

Williams froze like a statue, fork in hand, only his eyes moving as he looked at her. His eyes were wider than it looked safe for them to go. I hoped they didn't pop out and land in his eggs! I put a hand over my mouth to try to hold back my laugh.

"Yeah! It was last Christmas." Bethany's angelic face looked off in the direction of her house. "You came by our trailer and arrested one of my mom's jerk boyfriends who was tearing up the house." She looked at Williams and smiled sweetly. "You had to hit him in the head with your flashlight like six or seven times because he was so drunk! Blood got all over the trailer. That guy bled EVERYWHERE! It even got on me!" Bethany threw her head back and laughed and laughed as she remembered that night.

Mom, Dad, Ryan, and Officer Williams watched tiny little Bethany laughing about blood. She caught her breath and continued, "Oh, but you were real nice to me while you were there, nicer than the other cops. You must have asked me fifteen times if that creep had messed with me." Bethany looked across the table to Mary as she set the buttered toast on Williams' plate with her super shiny black nails flashing wickedly in the bright kitchen lights. "He's a good guy. For a cop." Bethany smiled.

Everyone was shocked, mouths agape, except us witches. But all that talk of blood left a weird vibe floating in the air, and Mary and Bethany's "witchiness" seemed to come to life as they talked back and forth.

"Of course he's a good guy!" Mary said, her voice carrying and shaping the weirdness. "Rain has great taste in friends. Williams will help us take care of Rain now, won't you, Williams?" Mary turned her smile on him as she curled her green lock of hair with a long, black nailed finger.

Williams was still frozen in place, holding his fork.

Bethany leaned in just a little closer and gave Williams a matching look. "Yes! You'll help us, won't you, Williams?"

Poor Williams! He was trapped, his eyes bouncing from Mary to Bethany. His fork was still frozen a few inches away from his mouth, and his brain didn't seem able to get the hand to deliver the payload of eggs.

"Remember," Mary said, "Rain summoned *help*, and Williams came." Her voice was far less bubbly and much more sultry now. I was starting to get into the mood too. I'd swear that there was magic in the air.

Bethany gave a scary little laugh that gave me a chill. "He's very, very handy with a flashlight." Her little eyes flashed menace. It was almost like a spell had fallen on the breakfast table as she spoke.

Williams dropped his fork. It fell slowly and made a loud "clank! clank!" against his plate.

Everyone blinked.

"GIRLS!" Mom shouted. She stood up and directed her outraged glower toward Mary and Bethany.

Mary and Bethany jumped and quickly snapped back into their chairs, hands in their laps, eyes wide, looking guilty as hell!

"None of THAT," Mom waved her hand in the air over the table, "at the table!"

Mom's face twisted up as she directed her best disappointed face at first Mary, who looked down at her hands in her lap and refused look up again, and then at Bethany, whose eyes were almost as wide as Williams' eyes had been.

Bethany nodded then looked at me, her face shouting "HELP!" as loudly as she could without saying a word.

"Mom," I said.

Every eye turned to me except Mary and Bethany, both of whom stared down into their laps, heads down and silent.

"They didn't mean to do anything." I let that hang there for a second as I looked at Mom, Dad, and Ryan who were still trying to process what had just happened. Or almost happened. They looked at Mary and Bethany now as if they were seeing them again for the first time. Williams was busy, collecting himself. It looked like he was making sure he still had all of his fingers for some strange reason.

"Mom, I'm not the only witch here. And I'm not the only one that can have accidents. They were just talking and—it just kinda happened. They didn't mean to do anything." I waited and watched as my family took all this in and tried to decide what to do next.

Ryan was surprisingly quiet. I watched his eyes. He was waiting for Dad to make the first move.

My father stood up. "Girls." He used his "Dad" voice and they looked up at him.

Mary was crying. Bethany looked like she wanted to run away. I started crying too once I saw their faces. I almost bent down and hugged little Bethany, but I knew that Dad wasn't finished yet so I forced myself to wait behind her chair.

"You owe Officer Williams an apology for scaring him just now," Dad said and waited.

"Sorry," came Bethany's quiet little voice.

"We're sorry," came Mary's apology. She looked at Williams, eyes pleading, and he gave her a nod and she quickly looked back down at her lap.

"Aah, no aah, no real harm done," Williams managed, then cleared his throat. He didn't sound too sure of that himself but he pressed on bravely as he looked at Mom and Dad. "That, that kind of thing sometimes happens when you talk to a witch. Sometimes they don't even know themselves what they're saying when they're sayin' it." He shrugged and gave himself a shake, pulling at his uniform here and there and resettling himself in his seat. "I got surprised is all."

"Williams. Status report." The police radio on his hip crackled to life with Sergeant Kelly's voice.

We held our breath as Williams picked up the radio. His eyes moved around the table as he studied us for a second, considering his answer before he pushed the button and replied, "All clear, Sergeant."

Kelly's gruff voice came back, "What are you doing in there, Williams?"

Williams hit the button. "I'm sitting between three witches eatin' eggs." He said it stone faced, which made it funnier.

Ryan and Dad both laughed, my mom and the girls smiled, and we all relaxed a little. It seemed like Williams hadn't taken offense at almost being "witched" out of his mind. A real forgiving guy. Bethany was right, he was a good guy.

The radio beeped again and Sergeant Kelly's voice said, "Carry on."

Williams rolled his eyes and put his radio back on his belt, looking back at Mary and Bethany again.

"I wasn't expectin' there to be three witches here. Thought I'd only be dealing with just the one." He looked in my direction for a second then picked his fork back up and started eating again, carefully keeping eye contact only with his plate as he ate.

Ryan laughed quietly but didn't say anything.

"Rain, Mary," Mom said, "you girls clear the table while Bethany and I go through Rain's old clothes."

We girls shared a surprised look. Mary and I stood and listened to Mom as we started on the table.

"Bethany, you don't just wear black do you? You're wearing different colors?"

Bethany was currently wearing some black jeans and a brown top that fanned at the bottom with tails that she could tie up and show her middle if she wanted or tuck in and look dressy. All Bethany's clothes were hand-me-downs except for a few nice things like what she now wore. Those she kept at Kendal's.

"No." Bethany's voice was a whisper. She swallowed and tried again, a little louder this time. "No, ma'am. I wear other colors, but my favorite is—red." She almost said black. Bethany looked over at me and I smiled at her.

Mom stood up. "Rain stopped wearing anything but black almost two years ago. She was still bigger then than you are now, and I've got a huge closet full of clothes she won't wear anymore. I'm sure there are some nice things in there that will be perfect for you, honey. Let's go see what we can find."

Bethany got up and followed Mom as she went toward her master bedroom where she had given up half of her huge walk in to save all my "real clothes," as she called them.

Ryan passed me his plate and turned to Williams. "Hey, Jason, what happened to that guy on the bullhorn out there—" he began. It usually only took Ryan an hour at most to make a friend for life so I wasn't surprised that he was already on a first name basis with Officer Williams. Ryan was just so good with people. He *was* "good."

Period.

Mary and I left the guys talking at the table and went into the kitchen to start doing dishes and cleaning up the breakfast pots and pans. Mary was still a little freaked out about the weird kitchen table "magic funk" she and Bethany had started.

"Now you know how I feel all the time," I teased her and gave her a gentle bump with my hip. She was standing beside me, drying the dishes I washed.

Mary laughed a little but her smile fell off her face quickly. She looked scared.

"It was so weird, we were just talking, and then it was just like—there was magic all around and—and if your mom hadn't of stopped us, I think Bethany and I were really about to mess with Williams' mind a little—maybe a lot." She didn't look happy about that.

"I know," I said, giving Mary a sympathetic look. "Scary shit isn't it, when it sneaks up on you like that?"

Mary nodded but looked confused. "But—I didn't think we had powers like you, Rain." She looked back at the table to make sure we weren't being overheard. Dad, Ryan, and Williams were happy, talking away, so Mary continued.

"I think Bethany and I were actually doing *real* magic. And we didn't light a candle at our naming like you did, but it felt like we were doing—" She searched for the right word but finally said a frustrated "something!"

I studied Mary for a minute. Frightened and worried. Maybe she didn't really want to have to deal with all of this witch stuff like me. It was one thing to keep your best friend from losing her mind and going on a magical killing spree, but it was another thing entirely when you might be the one to accidentally "kill" or "maim" someone on accident. I knew how she felt. It's scary to know that you're dangerous and even more frightening to know you might not be able to control yourself.

Mary kept drying the same plate, keeping her hands busy. Her brain was elsewhere.

"Are you sorry you became a witch?" I asked her.

Mary thought for a minute as she dried the same plate. "No," she said.

I washed some more dishes and waited. I didn't rush her, even though I wanted to.

We were down to the pans when Mary finally spoke her peace. "It's just that, I'm realizing this is *real*, for *me*. I knew it was real for you, but," she gave me a little smile, "we've know you were special since we first met you. I just didn't think I was." Mary started to dry the last pan, keeping her eyes turned away from me as she did so.

"Mary," I said and she looked at me. "I think you're special. And so you are." I just stared at her. After a few seconds I saw the light come on in her eyes.

"So you think—" Mary started, then stopped. I watched her face as her brain worked with all of the confusing bits and pieces. Mary gave me a doubtful look; she still didn't believe she was special, even after breakfast.

I grabbed a plastic fork from a holder on the kitchen counter and held it in front of me. Mary's eyes focused on the plain white fork and I thought about it turning to gold—and it did. Mary's eyes went wide as she looked from the fork to me.

"If I think this fork is gold, it is gold." I set the gold fork back in the holder with the other plastic forks. I turned back to Mary; she was looking right at me, almost like she was afraid of what I might say next.

I smiled at her warmly and said, "Mary, I think you are special—and so you are."

Mary smiled at me, wiped a tear from her eye and said, "So mote it be."

"Hey! No crying in the kitchen!" Ryan was walking over to us, concerned by the tears and the intense look we had been sharing. He didn't know what was happening but he was in "keep an eye on Rain" mode, so here he came, making sure I was okay.

Mary turned to Ryan. "Oh." She wiped at her eyes. "The tear police! Busted! Sorry!" She gave her eyes a final wipe with her dish drying rag and put on a huge smile for Ryan. He gave us both a suspicious look.

"What were you girls up to?" he asked.

"Oh, just a little girl talk," I said.

Ryan kept his "yeah right" expression, cocking an eyebrow, but he didn't press for details. He changed the subject.

"Jason said that they got rid of all the bullhorns and moved some of the religious nuts farther away from the trailer but there's still a huge crowd outside. The reporters are pestering all the neighbors, bugging them for every wild tale that they can come up with."

I pulled the stopper out of the sink to drain the dish water. "Don't worry about it, Ryan, let them say what they want and let the nosy neighbors have their fun, it's okay. I don't mind."

Ryan leaned forward, opening the blinds a crack, and looked out the kitchen window at the crowd milling about in the street and grunted, "Williams said that all this started because of a video that got out on the internet showing you at some big witch get together doing magic. Someone posted it on YouTube?" He squinted his eyes. "Is that where you were Monday night? Did you sneak out?"

I nodded.

He looked at Mary. "I hope you went with her. You and Bethany—and Kendal."

"Yep. She was with us," Mary said happily, taking my arm and pulling me closer to her. Ryan gave her a sour expression which Mary noticed. She gave him a shove. "Hey!" she snapped, "she's our sister too, so get used to sharing, Bro! And don't get all weird about it, you just got EEXXTRA sisters now!" Mary smiled at Ryan and wrapped an arm around my middle.

I had to laugh at Ryan as he took that in with a weird expression on his face. His eyes darted toward our parents' bedroom where Mom and Bethany were going through my clothes and he knew Mary was right.

"God help me!" Ryan groaned.

Mary and I grabbed him and gave him a quick hug together which he quickly wiggled out of. We laughed as he retreated a safe distance, grumbling about being turned into a "witch sandwich."

"Well, sis, what are you gonna do?" Ryan asked me after we stopped giggling. "Are you going to talk to these yahoo reporter idiots? Some of them are offering you a ton of cash for a sit down interview." He shrugged, "It's not like you're hiding the fact that you're a witch. And if you don't mind that they know, you could pay your way through college with what ABC offered Dad this morning. I'm talking real big money." Ryan raised an eyebrow but quickly backed off as we glared at him.

Mary reached down and picked up the gold fork, handing it to Ryan.

"Oh, put a fork in it, Ryan!" she growled. "We don't need them or their money." Mary charged on, "Go look at that video on YouTube, those assholes are going to try to kill your sister and the rest of us girls. This is life and death! I hate to get all bitchy, but you need to know what we're dealing with. Bethany and I are gonna have to go home in a little while so it's gonna be up to you and Williams to keep her safe. At least until Bethany and I can get back over here. Those people," Mary pointed outside, "just want to use her or kill her." Mary finished with a huff and a hair flip, throwing the green lock of hair that hung in her eyes back out of her way.

Ryan nodded, stunned by Mary's outburst and by the disturbing knowledge that people were seriously out to kill me.

"Of course, Mary, I'm sorry," Ryan said sincerely. "I'll keep her safe and I'll try to keep her out of trouble too." He gave me a hard look then, making sure I heard that part, and then he finally noticed the fork in his hand.

"Is this what I think it is?" he asked, gazing at the fork in hesitant wonder.

"Yes," I said. I gave Mary a mischievous smile.

She arched an eyebrow, trying to catch onto my game.

Ryan's eyes were still captured by the fork as the gold flashed in the morning sunlight filtering through the blinds at the kitchen window.

"Go show your dad," Mary whispered to him and winked at me.

Ryan finally tore his eyes away from the fork, looked at both of us with a huge grin, and then dashed off to the table where Dad and Williams were still talking.

I quickly thought about the fork becoming a plastic fork again. Mary and I watched as Ryan charged up and stuck out his fork in front of my dad and Williams.

"Dad! Look! Rain turned this fork to gold!" We watched his face drop onto the floor as he looked at the fork again. Ryan heard our wild burst of giggles from the kitchen where we'd ducked down behind the bar.

"Hey! That's not fair!" he shouted from the dining room. "Rain! Change it back!"

We laughed even harder as we listened to Ryan, and the harder he tried to explain what happened the funnier it sounded. Mary was slapping her hand on the kitchen floor where we'd fallen in our giggle fit and crying out, "I'm GON-NA PEE!" as Mom came back in with Bethany. We could hear Dad and Williams laughing and Ryan still lamenting mournfully about the fork.

"What's going on in here!?" Mom asked with a smile, obviously enjoying the happy mood that filled the house. Mary and I picked ourselves up off the floor, still fighting the last of the giggles as Mom and Bethany walked into the kitchen.

She had a bag of clothes and about fifteen hangers in her hand holding dresses, skirts, and other clothes.

Mary and I were both trying, and failing, to control our surprise as we looked at Bethany. She had on a fancy, dusty rose colored dress that was way over the top. It was something that I'd worn when I was ten to my Aunt Penny's *dusty rose* colored wedding. The faded rose color clashed with Bethany's olive skin and new red/black hair something fierce—it was wrong! Bad wrong!

"Oh Bethany! You look so pretty," I said with a strained smile, managing not to lie. She did. The dress did not.

I slipped Mom a quick *what were you thinking!* look, which she immediately returned as, *Oh my God! I KNOW!* back at me from where she stood behind Bethany. The dress had obviously been Bethany's idea.

Mom didn't ask us again about the laughing or what we were up to. She laid the clothes on the counter and started to fold them as she talked. "Bethany honey, let me get these things folded up for you and you can take them over to your house."

Bethany's happy smile wilted and died.

After a minute, Mom noticed that we girls had gone quiet and she looked up from her folding to see why. She watched as a Mary walked over and wrapped her arms around Bethany.

"We could take them to Kendal's house, Beth," she told her gently.

Bethany nodded, "Yeah, I guess we can." She straightened a little at the thought but still didn't look thrilled. At that moment she looked much younger than her thirteen years.

Mom drank this distress in like a parental sponge. She looked at me, then back to Mary and Bethany again.

"Kendal's house?" Mom said with a frown.

I nodded.

Mom had already heard about Bethany's home life and she didn't like Kendal one bit, even if she did like Mary and Bethany. She seemed to come to some decision right then and there.

"Bethany," Mom said, and Bethany looked up at her. "Why don't you let me put these clothes in Rain's room for you? And we can clear out half of her closet and make you some room." Mom gave me a quick disappointed glance. "She doesn't use hardly any of the space in there anyway. We can set you up real nice right here, Bethany."

Mom walked over and knelt down in front of Bethany, taking her hands in hers as she looked up at her. "And you're welcome to stay here as much as you like. Rain has already told me she loves you like a sister, so I'm sure she wouldn't mind having you stay in her room."

Bethany's shocked little face was too funny; she looked from Mom then to me. I smiled at her and nodded. I was totally floored! Hearing about Bethany's "Bloody Christmas" must have really freaked Mom out. On top of that, she had some weird personal thing against Kendal. She wasn't about to let Kendal "mother" Bethany, not when she could do it herself and give her a good Christian home to be in. Plus, there was the simple fact that you couldn't *NOT* love her. Bethany was just like a little angel. A scary little "witch" angel that laughed like a demon about blood, but still, an angel.

"Really, you'll let me stay in Rain's room? You guys don't mind?" She looked so excited.

"I'd love it if you stayed with us," Mom assured her. "But if you do stay here you need to know that we go to church. Everyone in this house goes, so if you stay here you'll have to go with us just like Rain."

I knew this part was coming. I'd gone to church with my family, Sunday morning, Sunday night, and Wednesday night since before I was born. I didn't know if Bethany would have a problem with going to church or not.

She was thinking hard about it. Bethany had been doing Wicca with Kendal and she was happy with it.

"Rain," Bethany gave me a curious look, "you're not still going to church now that you're a Black Witch are you?" It was clear that Bethany didn't think I was.

Mom's eyebrows shot up and she turned to me, waiting to hear what I would say. Mom hadn't thought about tonight as anything special. My mother didn't know what I would say. For all she knew I was never going to go to church again.

"Yes, I'm going." I watched relief flood my mother's face but at the same time, Bethany looked confused and surprised. "While I live here, I go to church with my family," I said and shrugged. "I don't mind going. I always sit in the back and no one bothers me much. They don't make me do anything other than go. It's not so bad."

"You may even like it, Bethany," Mom interjected a quick commercial. "And you know all about being a witch. It might be good for you to learn a little about God too." She gave Bethany a hopeful smile to which Bethany made a yuck face.

"But I don't even believe in God. Do you, Mary?" Bethany turned to Mary who froze with her mouth in a surprised O.

"Well—" Mary began. "Sort of—kinda—yeah sure—maybe." She did a hair flip and continued in rambling "air head" mode. "I mean, there are a lot of different *powers* and *spirits*—and *things*—so—probably yeah—but more than just one. I think there's a bunch!" She finished brightly with a huge grin. We all felt dizzy after listening to that.

Bethany frowned, not liking Mary's answer, so she turned to me.

"Do you believe in God, Rain?" Her angel face was dead serious.

"Oh, God's real. So is Heaven," I affirmed as fact. "Rain Marie told me so. She's up there with Brendon right now, and it must be nice up there because she doesn't want to come back down here. I asked her to come back but she didn't want to."

Mom and the girls were all giving me blank faces.

Uh oh. I'd answered Bethany's question without really thinking. I hadn't told anyone about speaking to Rain Marie yet. And Mary and Bethany didn't even know what I wrote on the mirror like Mom, Dad, and Ryan did.

"What da? who da? huh?" Mary said, plainly confused. "Rain, I'm not sure I got that. You're 'Rain Marie.' How could you tell yourself about heaven? You're not dead." Gone was the ditsy blond, replace by a face with narrowed eyes and a hard look. "Are you?" Mary asked, seriously, as if I might actually be a walking corpse. "Did you kill yourself and come back and not even *freakin'* tell us about it!" She was torn between being mad at me for keeping secrets and being mad at herself because it sounded like I'd hurt myself.

Mom looked like she wanted to faint but wasn't about to let herself do so because she didn't want to miss a word of what we were saying.

"Did you die already, Rain?" Bethany asked, eyes wide as she leaned in. "Really? Truly? For reals?" she pressed.

"Bethany, Mary, please," I said, cutting them off before Mom had the heart attack she was working on. "I'll tell you guys about it later, but right now I need to fix my sister's dress." I smiled at Bethany.

"But—" Mary started again.

"Not now!" I said, and then I gave Mom a hug because she looked like she needed one.

Mary and Bethany were quiet while I calmed my mother down. They'd finally gotten the hint.

"I feel silly," Bethany whispered into our awkward silence. "I shouldn't have put this thing on. I don't even like dresses." She frowned as she looked down at her dress.

Mary went over to her. "Come on then. Arms out. Let's see it."

Bethany frowned but did as Mary asked.

Mary put a finger in the air and made a little circle. "Spin so we can see the back too."

Bethany did a slow little circle.

"It's a little fancy," Bethany said with a tiny shoulder shrug, "but since Rain is so dressed up all the time in her black dress I thought I would try it too." Her shy, vulnerable smile was heartbreaking.

Mary, Mom, and I fought to hide our horror at the dress and not let it show on our faces. At least not where Bethany could see. The dress itself was fancy and covered with gaudy stitch work and frills. It was hideous. And I thought that the color was the worst part of the whole thing.

"It's not the right shade of red for you, Bethany," I said. "May I change it for you?"

Bethany nodded and said, "Okay."

My mother was right there listening to every word.

"Don't freak out, Mom, I'm gonna change Bethany's dress—with magic."

Her eyebrows shot up but she nodded. She jumped a little when the "dust rose" dress turned a shocking blood red so deep and full that it looked wet. Mom let out a soft, "Oh my." Her eyes shot back to my black dress then slipped up to meet my eyes. She was thinking hard, painful thoughts crowding the eyes that stared into my own.

"I liked it better as light rose than blood red," she said in quiet reproof.

"Oh wow!" Bethany ignited, "You're right! It is the color of blood!" She looked up at us with a huge grin on her "demon" angel face. "I love it!" She beamed. Mom went white around the gills but Mary and I smiled with her.

"Rain, you're gonna have to do something about the material too," Mary said as she ran her hand across the dress.

"Yeah, I remember." I joined her, touching the shiny fabric.

Bethany gave us a lost look, not understanding what we were talking about. She'd only worn a dress a handful of times in her whole life and the only decent dress she owned was the one she had worn to the Lammas celebration, and Kendal had bought that for her at a thrift store. I explained to Bethany what Mary and I were talking about.

"This dress wasn't made to be comfortable, Beth, it was made for a wedding. I remember it itched pretty bad."

Bethany's brow crinkled, she hadn't thought about comfort, or practicality, just beauty. She rolled her shoulders experimentally and grimaced, noticing for the first time how the material stuck right to her skin.

Dad, Ryan, and Williams crowded around wearing dour faces. It seemed that any mention of "BLOOD" brought the police running.

"Everything okay in here? Someone said something about 'blood.'" Williams gave Bethany an eyeballing which she accepted meekly and bowed her head. She didn't want to cause any more trouble.

Mom stuck up for us. "We're all fine, everything is fine. Rain was just helping Bethany with her dress. And doing some magic," she added, giving me a look. "And I don't think she's done yet."

Everyone looked at Bethany's blood red dress and waited to see what I would do to it next.

"Make it special, Rain," Bethany said, "like your black dress." She brushed a hand down the material on her sleeve and added quietly, "And please make it not so itchy."

I was about to start work on the dress when I noticed Mom, Dad, Ryan, and Officer Williams leaning in, wide eyed, expectant faces watching me, watching the dress, as if they were about to see something momentous and awe inspiring.

"I wish I had my fancy blue summer dress!" Mary pouted suddenly. "You guys are gonna be all *dressy* and *fancy* with your *witchy dresses* and here I am, still in jeans and my magic top!" she fussed. "And I wore this thing yesterday, it's ripe!" She brushed at her top and squinted her eyes at a stain on one of the white flowers.

Bethany and I laughed. "I think I've got a dress I can fix up for you, Mary, don't worry."

"Oh COME ON!" Ryan interrupted loudly. "Is that all you gonna use your magic for, playing with *dresses* and doing your *hair* and *nails*? All this girly stuff is lame! Lame! Lame! Lame! Lame! Lame! Why don't you do something cool, like make Dad president, or—" he held up the fork, "redo my fork?" he said with an exaggerated frown.

I shook my head and grabbed Bethany by the arm. "Come on, girls, let's go in the bedroom. I'll work on your dresses in there. This is gonna get way too 'witchy.' I don't think the muggles could handle it," I said simply with a deadpan stare directed back at the oldsters in the room.

Ryan got a good laugh at that, but then he had to explain exactly what a "muggle" was to the others who wore vacant expressions. We girls slipped into the bedroom for some privacy, but I lingered at the door, holding it open a crack, listening to my mother as she told Officer Williams that Ryan and I would have to leave to go to the doctor's office soon.

The plan we'd made over breakfast had been to drop Mary and Bethany off at their homes on our way so they wouldn't be mobbed by reporters or crazies in the street. But maybe Bethany would be staying here now. I hoped so. We didn't get to finish the "going to church" talk, but I was sure Bethany would go with me. We could be back row Baptist buddies together! The thought made me smile as I pushed the door shut.

After about fifteen minutes we came back into the living room. Everyone was gathered at the front door, waiting for us. Of course they gawked and flipped over the new dresses and the rest or our modified appearance. Bethany's dress was totally changed. It was now a very simple and elegant one piece slipover that hugged her lithe, little body perfectly. It was made of some "unidentifiable" material Bethany settled on that came straight out of my imagination and HOLY CRAP! did it feel fantastic! It was the kind of thing you'd want to wear all day, every day, and then go to sleep in too because after wearing it everything else would feel like wearing a crinkly paper bag.

The dress was blood red at the bottom with a faded stone-like gray pattern around the neckline and down the sleeves. It also had a scattering of delicate, raised roots down the sleeves giving the dress a stunningly beautiful but frightening look. Something about it summoned to mind the picture of an old, overgrown grave.

Mary's dress was a light and summery white, made of the same "Magic Fabric" material. The dress had a hint of green at the bottom, like summer grasses, with flowery vines climbing each side before crossing across the front then running down the long sleeves of each arm. She'd gotten the idea from Cathryn and the tattoos she had on her arms. The dress also had a deep V cut like mine on the top, with a hip high slit up, not one, but *both* sides. It gave the dress a modern and very daring look. The fit and cut hugged her perfectly.

As far as my black dress went, I did change it a little. I hadn't been able to resist changing the material to "Magic Fabric," but I kept the same antique design. Before we went out I gave all of us a quick "Mega Magical Makeover and Spa Treatment." I magically cleaned, scrubbed, rubbed, relaxed, and renewed us. I made sure our hair was perfect, and then I slapped "magic" makeup on all of us and got us looking our witchy best all in just a few minutes! We looked and felt

AMAZING! And when we stepped out, everyone began asking the "how" and "what" questions that we didn't answer.

Eventually we headed for the door. Mom said that Bethany would stay with her and that they would call her mother to let her know where she was. Bethany didn't look too happy about telling her mother where she was, but in the end she relented and said, "Yes, ma'am."

Mary was giving her a few words of encouragement when Sergeant Kelly opened the front door and stepped inside. Through the open door we caught a quick glimpse of the massive crowd of people outside the trailer.

"Mr. Bryant, Mrs. Bryant." He greeted Mom and Dad stiffly and then went white faced and speechless as he looked at me, Mary, and Bethany in our new dresses, hair, nails, and forehead tattoos. He hadn't seen the other girls before, so I guess it was kinda shocking, especially now that we were all dressed up like Halloween. Our Coven marks really seemed to grab his eye. Last time he'd seen me, mine was gone, washed away by my mother's shower.

"Williams was right, there really are three of you witches now," he said roughly with an angry frown cut deep into his face like we were personally out to ruin his day. His vibe was hostile. Pissed off.

"I see you're all dressed up for your big show. That's just fantastic," he growled as he looked us over. "Yesterday there was one of you. Now there're three. And tomorrow, what, six?" He sneered, "And who knows how many the day after that!" He griped, utterly disgusted.

Mary stepped up before my mother or father could respond and grinned right up into Kelly's surprised face and snapped out a loud, snake-like, "Yesssssss! Vile and horrible witches. We breed like roaches at night. By the light of the silvery moon, oh what a horrible sight!" She pulled her arms in and SPUN, doing a pirouette, right there in the middle of our crowded foyer!

Her snow white hair and white dress fanned out and formed a beautiful circle that looked like magic all by itself. Maybe it was! Mary had taken dance for years and *it showed!* She snapped to a sudden stop right in front of Kelly, leaned in toward his stunned face, kissed her hand and blew him a kiss, and he flew backwards and slammed against the door with a jarring thud!

Kelly stayed pinned there against the door like a terrified bug on a board! We all watched, too shocked to do anything for a moment as Mary picked up the edges of her dress and did a little bow, like a curtsey. She stepped closer, leering up at Kelly in a none-too-friendly way. Kelly struggled against whatever force held him, but he couldn't move anything except his seeking fingers and his terrified eyes which loudly screamed for HELP!

My mother bravely squeezed herself between Mary and her pinned victim. "Mary! Mary!" she shouted right into her face. "Control yourself, Mary! Stop this!" Mom kept her face in front of Mary's so she was all Mary could see.

Mary blinked a couple of times. Then her expression changed to complete confusion. She looked around. She seemed unaware of what had just happened or even how she'd gotten where she was.

"Sorry," she mumbled weakly as she looked over at Kelly's terrified face. He was free from her power now and leaned against the door, Williams hands helping to keep him on his feet. Both men stared at Mary as if she were a monster.

Mary broke down and started to cry. "Sorry. I'm so sorry," she said through the burgeoning tears.

Bethany and I rushed forward, but Mom took charge. She led Mary away from the front door and toward the couch in the living room where we all sat down. Behind us we could hear Williams fussing at Sergeant Kelly, railing at him for being rude, saying, "*That was no way to talk to a witch!.*"

We sat on the couch.

"Are you feeling better, Mary?" Mom asked. Mary's face was red as she sat there, quietly staring at nothing. She wasn't crying now, but tears were still running out of her eyes. Mom wiped at the soundless tears.

"Sorry, Mom," Mary said quietly. Bethany and I met eyes for a second then we looked over to my mother's face to see how she'd react to Mary calling her "Mom." Her brows went up a bit but they seemed to be the only part of her that was surprised at being called "Mom" by Mary. Somehow it just felt right.

"It's okay, Mary. You didn't mean to do it," Mom said. She studied all three of us for a second, as a group.

"Ryan's been telling me about the problems you girls are having—now that you're witches." She frowned. "And about you girls having 'accidents'." She looked right at Mary when she said this and Mary nodded.

"From what I have seen and what Ryan has told me, you girls don't handle strangers or rudeness very well at all." Mom turned her eyes onto Bethany. "And you, young lady," she lifted Bethany's chin with a finger to stare into her little angelic face, "need to be careful when you talk about 'blood.' You get way too excited by it."

Bethany's eyes were wide as Mom held her gaze. She nodded her head.

Holy crap! Mom had us all pretty well figured out! She must have squeezed every drop of info she could out of Ryan while we were in the bedroom working on dresses.

Mom gave us a sad look. "Wasn't it easier when you girls were just normal girls?" She shook her head, like she was trying to remember herself what that was like, to have a normal girl as a daughter. "If you were normal girls, you wouldn't have to worry about having accidents and hurting people." She looked right at me and said, "Isn't there any way you can give this up and stop being witches and just be girls again? Wouldn't it be better to quit this now, before someone gets hurt? No more magic, no more accidents, and no more crazy people wanting to burn you."

Mom glanced over at the front door and the two police officers waiting with Dad and Ryan. "And no more police," she added firmly. She gave us all another pleading look. "Can't you girls go back to being 'Rain' and 'Mary' and 'Bethany'? It would be better. You could still be sisters, and Bethany, you could still stay here, honey."

Mom reached over and took Mary's hand. "Twice now, just this morning, you've lost control, Mary. What are you going to do when it happens and you can't stop yourself even though you want to? What are you, or Rain, or Bethany, going to do when someone's not around to keep you from doing something horrible? With idiots like that madman with his bullhorn screaming *Burn the Witch!* it's only a matter of time before something bad happens. This is no good for you girls. Just let it go. Let it go and be girls again." Mom pleaded. She ran her eyes over all of us again, hoping we would say something. Mary did.

"Sorry, Mom," came Mary's soft reply. "I'm scared, and I don't want to hurt anybody." Mary bowed her head, almost like she was ashamed of herself. "But I like it. I don't want to go back. I like being special."

Mary looked over at me and said, "I'd rather burn as a witch than live as a normal girl." She bowed her head and closed her eyes.

Mom looked surprised. She thought she was getting through to Mary.

"Sorry, Mom," Bethany said next. She didn't add to what Mary said, but she wanted to let her know she felt the same way.

"Sorry, Mom," I finished it.

My mother sat there and stared at us for a while then took a deep breath and hugged us. "I'll have to get used to it," she said. "I'm glad God gave me three girls in the place of the one I lost," she glanced at me really quickly, "but I don't understand why he gave me three witch girls. God only knows!"

We all laughed a little just to break the tension, and then Mary asked what time we would be leaving tonight.

We stared at her in shocked surprise.

"What?" Mary said with an angry pout. "If you and Bethany are going to church then I'm going too." She turned to Mom. "Can I, Mom?"

My mother smiled, it seemed she liked the girls calling her mom and liked the idea of all of us going to church even more. "Of course, Mary. But why don't you let us stop by and pick you up tonight at 6:00 on our way out? That way you won't have to walk back to our trailer through all the crazies."

Mom got up off the couch. "Rain. You and Ryan need to go now. You're already going to be late getting to the doctor's office."

"I want to walk out with them," Bethany said as we all got up. "Can I, Mom?" she asked. And it sounded right to all of us.

"Just as far as the porch, Honey. The police will keep the reporters off the porch so you should be safe there, but the street and yard are a mess. What little grass we had is smushed," she complained and shook her head.

We walked over to the guys who were waiting by the front door again. Officer Williams was alone now. Sergeant Kelly had beaten a hasty retreat which was no big surprise after bumping heads with Mary.

"Everybody okay now?" Dad asked as we walked up.

"They're all fine," Mom declared us fit for travel, "but the girls want to go out on the porch for a minute."

"I don't think that's a good idea." Dad didn't like that at all. "Actually, I was thinking more of running them out to the car under a blanket so these idiots can't get their picture any more than they already have." He was angry. I just now noticed it. He was crazy worried about us. It must really be bad outside.

"Dad," I said, "I will not hide what I am or who I am." I gave him a quick kiss on the cheek, ignoring his frown. "Could you and Officer Williams bring the car up to the steps? That way we don't have to walk through the crowd."

Dad looked like he wanted to argue but didn't know what good it would do.

"Okay, honey. Give us a few seconds to get the car ready and only spend a minute or two on the porch, then come get into the car. Okay?" Dad told Ryan to stay right beside me, and then he and Williams slipped out the door and quickly closed it behind them. As soon as they stepped out we could hear the crowd light up, excited by the activity. It sounded like a whole lot of people were out there.

"Holy crap!" Bethany said as she peeked out the window beside the door. "They're on the roofs of all the trailers across the street! They got cameras and all set up, pointed this way! Holy crap!" she said again in her excited, little voice.

"Bethany, honey. Language," Mom told her gently. "There's nothing holy about crap, dear."

Bethany looked at her, thought about that for a minute, and said, "Oh. I guess you're right." Her brow crinkled as she thought deeper on it. "Why do people say it then?" she asked honestly.

Ryan couldn't resist an opening like that and supplied his wisdom with a grin. "Bethany, it's one of those upside down and backwards words—like Jumbo Shrimp, which is a stupid word, because shrimp aren't jumbo, are they?" He made a face and kept going. "Or when you hear someone say that something is 'Cool as Hell' because Hell's not—"

"Ryan!" Mom yelled. "You're not helping. I'm trying to help your sister with her language, so you watch yours too," Mom fussed but she was smiling.

"Oh." Bethany smiled back at Ryan. "I get it. Thanks, Ryan."

"No problem, Little Sis," Ryan said.

"Yes, thanks, Ryan," Mom said and gave Ryan a smile, but not about the language lesson. Apparently Mom, Dad and Ryan had talked about a few other things while we were in the bedroom fixing ugly dresses. Ryan was apparently okay with adding an extra sister or two to the family. Even witchy ones.

"Here they come," Mary said as she peeked through the blinds of the living room window with me. We could see a cop car honking and flashing its lights, pushing its way through the sea of people out front.

"Come on, Beth," I called to her, "let's go onto the porch for a minute."

We followed Ryan through the front door and into the flashing cameras and the rising roar of a huge crowd. Hundreds of people filled the small yard in front of the trailer, the street, the yards across the street, *they were everywhere*! The roofs of almost every trailer with any kind of a view were taken over by news crews, TV stations, or paparazzi, all set up with their own cameras and pointed in our direction. People desperate for some vantage point climbed nearby trees and stood on the roofs of cars to get a better view. Church groups sang hymns loudly, calling on us to repent. Crazier people like "bullhorn guy" shouted fouler things and reporters shouted their questions. Everyone fought to be heard over the din, so no one was. All the shouting voices blended together into a constant cacophony.

Not everyone out there hated us; it seemed we also had some fans. Goths, punks, and what I guessed were cultists or Satanists dressed in black were waving and smiling, some hoisting signs high into the air. Thirty or so besieged cops encircled the trailer, attempting to keep control of the sea of people threatening to swamp us like some natural disaster.

I felt a little hand slip into mine and squeeze tight. Bethany. On the other side of me Mary grabbed my other hand. She wasn't smiling as she looked out at the sea of madness around us, taking it all in.

"Look at the altar in the front yard," Bethany said. There in the front yard people had set up three folding tables and put black cloth on top like a tablecloth. All down the eighteen feet of table were candles, lit and burning. There were also little bowls with incense, gifts, and other small items littering the table from end to end, piling up around the sides.

The yellow police tape was strung up on sticks, pounded into the ground, creating a buffer zone of open space about six feet wide all the way around the trailer. Right in front of the porch was an area that had apparently been set aside for the big time new guys, Fox, CNN, ABC, CBS. Everybody who was anybody.

They were all shouting at once and the religious nuts farther back were going crazy as we stepped to the rail of the porch.

A low flying helicopter was hovering above the trees a short distance away kicking up dirt and grime and blowing our long hair around wildly. I felt a small rock hit me on my shoulder. I quickly thought about there being a shield of air around the porch protecting us girls so nothing could get through. Thankfully that also cut the wind down to nothing.

"Rain, did you just—" Mary began.

"Yeah, I did," I said. We watched as a few more rocks bounced off the invisible shield.

"Good," Mary said. "The little shits actually hit you a second ago. I saw it." She narrowed her eyes and scanned the crowd, seeking out the miscreant.

I leaned over to Ryan, "Go get me one to talk to. Just one." Ryan could barely hear me over the roar of the crowd, the helicopter, and all the singing and chanting, but he nodded and went down the steps. I thought about the area on the porch and the area on this side of the police tape being quiet, with all the noise being held on the other side—and it was quiet. The impossibly loud racket vanished instantly. We heard only the voices of the police and the few people on this side of the yellow tape.

"O thank God, Rain, I was going deaf!" Mary huffed out.

The police on the "quiet" side of the line started to freak out and then began to experiment with the weirdness by stepping from the quiet peaceful side and back into bedlam. Back and forth. Back and forth. They adjusted quickly as they figured out that this "appeared" to be innocuous, although totally awesome, and more than a little terrifying.

"Rain, did you just make it quiet around the trailer?" Mom had stepped out onto the porch with us.

"Yes, Mam. It's only quiet like this right around the trailer. I'll change it back when we leave," I assured her. It seemed unwise to leave magic just floating around, but since I was going to get rid of it anyway, I added a little more to what I'd started.

Closing my eyes, I thought about a beautiful spring day and the clean scent of the air being here on our side of the tape. I still had my eyes closed, and I took a deep breath of wonderfully fresh spring air, even though it was August. It smelled great. I opened my eyes.

Mary, Bethany, and Mom were looking at me curiously trying to figure out what I had done, and then they noticed the fresh air and started sucking it in like junkies huffing paint off a rag. Mary and Bethany were smiling, laughing, and enjoying the air, but Mom looked even more disturbed.

"Rain! Don't do any more magic out here!" she pleaded. "They're crazy enough as it is. Maybe you should just stay home. Your face and Ryan's already look great, maybe you don't need to take the rest of those pills." She wanted us back in the house.

I thought about it for a second. Our faces did look great now, and with my magic I didn't even need to take the pills anymore. I could "zap" myself and I'd never have another zit again. But something didn't feel right about it—about not finishing the pills. As within, so without. Taking the pills felt right, although I didn't understand why. It felt like it would be wrong to stop. I trusted my feelings, but Mom needed other motivation and I provided that.

"Mom, you promised the doctor in writing that we would finish the drug study. We should keep our promise."

She agonized but nodded. "Be careful out there, honey. This is getting so crazy."

We looked back at the throng of crazy people going mad all around. More police were showing up and now that I'd shown some power they seemed to be lying to with more vim and vigor. This job was no longer a joke. I was for real, and they knew it. There were more cops but it was still an impossible situation.

"Sanctuary," Mary said. "That's what we need, Rain. I don't think we're going to be able to stay here. It's just not safe for us or fair to the people who live here. We need to go to Cathryn and Cornelius's house and get away from all of this." She waved a hand at the madness all around. "It's too much."

Right then we saw Ryan coming up the steps with one very surprised reporter who was freaking out over the "quiet" zone. He was from Fox news. No surprise there. My family was very conservative and they all loathed CNN.

As Ryan was helping him with his gear, I asked Mary and Bethany to stand with Mom behind the camera guy. I sat on our little wooden bench on the porch with my back to the crowd. The reporter set his camera up in the middle of our porch and pointed it at me.

"Remember, no questions," Ryan told the guy. "She wants to say something, so film it. No surprises."

The guy nodded, not even opening his mouth to say yes. He looked super professional, but frightened. He was afraid of me and what was happening. With everyone on the other side of the tape shouting and talking, moving their lips soundlessly, the world looked exactly like a big TV with the sound on "mute." It was impossible not to see it that way. Weird.

The camera guy kept glancing at the "mute" crowd, surely thinking identical thoughts. He also kept a wary eye on the three of us witches as he worked. It only took a minute for him to get ready. He got down on one knee, camera resting on his shoulder, as he stared into a view screen on the side. He looked up, met my eyes, and gave me the thumbs up.

I took a deep breath and started talking.

"Hello, my name is Black Rain. This is my home." I put my hand out toward the trailer and the camera guy panned in that direction and quickly back to me. "And these are a few of the people who want me." I pointed to the crowd and the reporter obliged and panned out across the mad throng of people and then came back to me.

"I have a few things I need to say. One." I held up one black nailed finger. "I am not the child of the Devil."

"Mom!" I called. She walked over and I stood and gave her a great big hug and turned her toward the camera. "This is my mother. And I love her and my dad very much. My dad's waiting for me down there in that police car." I pointed to the police car and the camera guy panned to the car and back to me.

Mom quickly stepped away again back out of the camera shot, and I sat back down on my bench and started talking again. "And here's my twin brother. Ryan, come say hello to everyone." I waved him over.

Ryan stepped up beside me and said a polite "Hello everyone." He gave me a quick hug right where I sat on my bench, kissed the top of my head, and then stepped back out of the camera shot and I started talking again.

"Now that you know that I'm not demon spawn or an alien, let's move on."

"Two." I held up two black nailed fingers. "I don't want to meet you. I do not want to talk to you. If you see me walking down the street, I don't want you to cross the road to come tell me hi. And I know that you think you're the exception to this rule. Trust me," I paused for dramatic effect, "you're not." I gave a hard stare into the camera and added, "Just go about your lives and leave us alone. Please."

"Three." I held up three black nailed fingers in front of the camera. "About the candles and offerings." I pointed out to the table in the yard and the camera guy obliged again. He had to stand up for a second but he panned over the offering table and candles then came back to me. "I don't want your prayers. Your candles. Your incense. Your offerings. I don't need your money. You have NOTHING I want."

I gave the camera a sad look and said, "I know that sucks, but it's true. Let me put this in a way even a second grader could understand." I looked into the camera as if I were talking to a child. "I don't want to trade lunches with you. You got what you got, and I got what I got. But if you get mean and try to take my lunch—we're gonna have problems. Which leads us to—

"Four." I held up four back nailed fingers. "I give fair warning. Governments. Cults. Religious nuts. The good, the bad, the ugly. Hear this, and hear it good. I give fair warning that I and my sisters are dangerous. We don't like to meet new people. We don't like to be startled. We do not like rude people. And if you try to harm me, my family, or my sisters—" I leaned into the camera a little and thought about my eyes going black as night, the iris, whites, and all. By the little jump of the camera guy I assumed it had worked. "I give fair warning. Do–Not–Mess–With–Me."

I sat back and thought about my eyes going back to normal.

"Finally, I want to introduce myself and my sisters to the world." I stood and Mary and Bethany came over and stood on either side of me. We all held hands and looked at the camera together. The camera guy stood and backed up a little to get a good view of us and the background chaos behind us. The dresses, hair, forehead tattoos, black nails, and the two helicopters that now hovered in the background over the crowd made for quite a visual as I started speaking.

"I am the Black Witch. Black is my color and my name is Black Rain."

I squeezed Mary's hand and she started. "I am the Green Witch. Green is my color and my name is Mary Fae."

I squeezed Bethany's little hand, and I hoped she would be okay; she was so shy, but her little voice was strong and sure as she spoke. "I am the Red Witch. Red is my color and my name is Bethany Grave."

I looked at the camera and said, "We are witches. But we're also girls. We like to have fun and laugh and have a good time just like other girls. Mary especially likes boys," I said with a smile and Mary actually blushed!

I looked back at the camera and said, "It was good to meet you all. Now please, live and let live—or you'll wish you had." I gave the world a last tilt of my head and said, "As above, so below. Let the whole world know. Let the Black Witch now rise."

I thought about the air shield being gone, the sound going back to normal, and the air going back to normal, and noise rushed in and a gust of stale wind blew our hair all around as the bubble of clean clear air vanished. I walked over to Mom and pressed Bethany's tiny hand into hers and they both slipped back inside the trailer. Mary, Ryan, and I went down the steps and into the back seat of the cop car while the camera guy stood on the porch, filming us and our retreat through the sea of people.

"Bout time, witch girl," complained Officer Williams as we got in. He was in the driver's seat.

"Sorry!" I said as I looked at my dad's grumpy face.

"Let's get over to Mary's house. We're already late," Ryan said. We started to slowly make our way through the throng of people with a lot of help from the cops to make a hole for us big enough to drive out.

Dad was up front with Officer Williams, and he turned around and asked, "What did you say to the reporter on the porch, honey?"

"Oh, I said I wasn't the child of the devil. That I had a mom and dad that I loved very much." I gave dad a smile. "And I do," I said just to make Dad smile, which he did, though he tried to fight it. He didn't look good all frowny and upset.

"What else?" Dad prodded for more details. "You were talking for a while."

"I told them not to pray to me, not to light candles to me, not to bring me offerings, and basically to just leave us alone."

Dad nodded, obviously pleased, but Ryan added a little more to what I'd said.

"Leave us alone OR ELSE!" He shivered and said, "You almost made me crawl right out of my skin when you did that thing with your eyes. That was sooooo *sick*!" Ryan played like he was gonna gag, but he did look a little green around the gills. "That was hands down, by a million miles, the freakiest thing I've ever—"

CRACK!

Glass came raining down on all of us in the back seat! We all jumped and screamed. A guy with a baseball bat had hit the back window of the cop car and shattered the glass. Williams called in on his radio for backup and sped up enough to stay away from the guy with the bat, but we couldn't go too fast in the crowded trailer park, too many people were walking around on the narrow streets.

"Jerk! I'll shove that thing up your ass!" Mary shouted at the guy who was running behind us, still following our car.

We turned around in our seats looking out the shattered rear window as we brushed glass out of our hair. Unbelievable, but the guy was still trying to catch up and give us another swing. He had on a shirt that said "Burn The Witch!" It was bullhorn guy.

"Get busy shoving," I said as I looked at him. The three of us watched as the guy skidded to a stop and started to strip off his pants right there in the street and make every effort to comply with my request.

We turned the corner onto Mary's street before we saw too much. I had warned them. And this guy had asked for it twice today, so now he was going to get it. I felt no remorse. I didn't even care if he lived through the attempt. Some cold, unforgiving part of me dismissed the man from my thoughts entirely. He'd made his bed, now he could lie in it.

Jane Miller

Lots of Surprises

Jane! I'm here! *Where are you!?*

The surprise of hearing Dan's voice inside my head stripped my control and let the monster completely out of its box. Burning pain tore through me! My back arched, my arms pinwheeled and thrashed, and my eyes rolled into the back of my head as I shook and cried out in shocked agony! Vaguely I was aware that my parents were shouting, but I was also hearing Dan shouting inside my head.

Jane! Ja—ARRHHH!

"DAN!" I knew Dan had lost it too! When I had lost it, so did he! He was burning!

WE WERE BURNING!

I cried and shook and flailed. The nails of one hand ripped into the seat beside me, tearing long gashes into the fabric. A bare foot kicked out as my knee locked and I felt the metal floor dimple beneath my bare, sholess heel. I tried to think through the scorching pain that rode my body like angry lightening! Like a thousand slavering mouths, all biting and tearing into flesh and bone, all at once, from head to toe. No part was sacred, no portion spared. The pain was altogether without mercy, feeling, or reason. It would not end if I begged it to stop. If I cried loudly enough.

I had to cage it again or be destroyed by it. As I thrashed, my rolling gaze passed over my mother. She was staring over the top of her seat, mouth agape, head shaking in pitiable denial. In that tiny piece of a second I could read her face and eyes as if she spoke an entire sentence. She expected me to expire right here and now in the back seat. This was it. I was dying.

Time passed. Excruciating time.

What was only two minutes stretched out as time itself altered. If the world had indeed flipped upside down, time and again, perhaps the entire universe had as well—and time along with it. The two minutes of burning stretched and expanded into the most horrible minutes I'd ever endured in my life as I fought the burning, forcing it back, kicking and screaming, each millisecond marked with small gains and smaller losses.

Slowly, doggedly, I forced the pain back into a contained part of my mind and regained control of my tortured body. A few tremors still shot through my limbs as my mother climbed into the back seat.

"Jane! What's happening!?" She put her hands on my face and tried to look into the eyes that I hadn't regained control of yet. They were still rolled up, looking at nothing. The touch of her hand was gas on the fire! More pain! More trembling!

"Jane! My God, Ed! It hasn't stopped! If it's a seizure it should stop eventually!" she shouted and then started to rub up and down arms that were as rigid as bars of iron, the pain blinding! What the hell was she thinking!? I fought the wild urge to kill her—

"I'm calling 911 right now!" I heard my father's voice in the front, and my brain finally kicked in the rest of the way and I was able to snap the lid down on the pain and at the same time pull my arms free of my mother's hands, giving her a WILD enough look that stopped her from touching me again as I shouted at Dad.

"Dad! Don't call 911!" I was still sucking in quick little breaths, moving around to keep Mom's hands off me.

"Jane! Are you okay!?" She leaned in to hug me, and I let her and simply endured it for as long as I could.

"Mom! I need some space!" I growled and scooted out of her arms, putting my hands up to ward her off as I tried to catch my breath. My thoughts went to Dan. How was he? Was he still burning? He must have felt all of my pain along with his own. My God! What a horrible thought. I cried out to Dan inside my head.

Dan, are you okay!? Sorry, Dan, I'm so sorry! Get control of it! I'm better now. Just force the pain down and lock it away Dan, lock it away—

"Jane!" Mom shouted, right in my face.

"Yes, Mom," I said out loud to my mother. "I'm okay. It was just a little pain. It's over now." I think I made my face smile but there was no way to be sure. I was still pulling myself together, little tremors still shaking through me every couple of seconds. I heard my dad talking on his phone to a 911 operator.

"Yes, my daughter—"

"Dad! NO!" I shouted. "I don't need them! Please tell them I'm okay! Please, Dad! We don't need an ambulance or any doctors." I said all this, but from their uncomprehending expressions it was clear that I'd spoken too quickly for them to understand me.

I could hear the 911 operator's voice on my father's cell, "*Sir, what about your daughter? Is she hurt? Do you need a—*"

I slowed it down and tried again. "Daddy, please tell them that I'm okay. *Please*!" I pleaded. Dad looked back at me, surprised that I was talking, confused by what I was saying. He listened to the operator, demanding answers, speaking into his ear.

"Jane?" he said, "but you—"

"Jane, we're taking you to the hospital!" Mom said in a shaky voice. "You're not well!" She was trying to hold my hand which I was keeping balled up in a tight fist so I didn't accidentally crush her hand if I lost control.

One more thing to think about! This was all getting out of control, I thought, frustrated. If the ambulance came here and checked me out the way I was now they'd haul me off and lock me away for sure. I'd have to run!

"PLEASE!" I cried so loudly that they both jumped. I was about to start crying, and I quickly forced myself to stop. If I cried blood they'd go straight off the deep end. I didn't want it to happen this way! This wasn't how I'd planned my day! Everything was going great and now it was all falling apart!"

"Daddy, just tell them I'm fine! I don't want an ambulance. Please, Dad."

He turned around from driving, taking a second to look right at me.

I begged, my new voice beautiful and alien in my own ears as I pleaded. "We'll be at Doctor Burgis's office soon. Please, don't call an ambulance, don't make me go away yet. I don't want to go away yet."

He turned back to the road but I watched in the rear view mirror as he narrowed his eyes. He'd caught that last part.

"*Sir! Where are you? Sir? Are you there? Can you hear me?*" the 911 operator asked again.

"Yes. Sorry. I'm right here." He talked into the phone. "My daughter had a seizure and it scared us pretty badly."

"*Sir, where are you at on I-10, what exit are you near? I'll have the ambulance come right now—*"

"NO! No, that won't be necessary." Dad's eyes met mine in the mirror. "She's doing much better now, and we have an appointment with her regular doctor at 11:15 today."

"*It sounds like you need an ambulance. I can understand why you might not want us to call them out if you don't have insurance, but if your daughter needs help you should let me—*"

"No. Really, we're fine. We'll just go to our regular doctor today, he—Sorry for troubling you. Thank you."

Dad hung up. I felt a new burning pain on my chest. I looked down. I'd come out of my dress and Mom was pulling the cloth around trying to get me covered. By some miracle I hadn't torn the sheer fabric apart, although it was twisted this way and that. I leaned forward and moved so we could put me back together.

"Thanks, Mom," I said once I was decent. And quickly I thought in my head,

Dan—are you okay? Dan?

Yes I'm okay. I've got it—controlled. Are you all right? I didn't hear for a while, what's happening, Jane? Where are you?

Mom was strangely quiet, sitting and staring at me, studying my face as I talked to Dan. I ignored her and kept talking. I had to talk to Dan. When my fit had started we'd been going over the downtown bridge with no safe place to stop, but we were beyond the bridge now and parked on the side of the freeway. Dad had already gotten out of his seat and was opening the back door of the car. I guess to get into the back with us.

I'm fine now, Dan. We're going up to the Avenues Mall right now—at least I think we are—

I scooted over some for Dad to get in, which put me in the middle with Mom on the other side. I kept talking to Dan. I had to tell Dan about the note and why I didn't get to read it! And about the book! I had to tell him I was sorry!

Dan, I'm so sorry! I didn't mean to read the book! When I got home—

He cut me off.

Hush now, Jane! It's okay. You need to talk to your Mom and Dad for a while. Don't worry. I'm right here, and I'm coming for you. Talk to your parents. I'm here.

"Never leave me again," I said out loud. Oh shit. My eyebrows went up. I had said that out loud, I thought. I heard *laughing* in my head, '*He he he.*' It was Dan! And that made me smile. *I missed you.* I didn't really think it to him so much as to myself. I'm not alone in here anymore. But what the hell was so funny I wondered?

You're so cute when you cuss. Sorry, I know that's stupid. I love you.

That made me smile more.

"Who are you talking to?" Mom asked. She was fascinated, looking right at my face. So was Dad. I was sandwiched right between the two of them. I looked from one staring face to the other. I took a deep breath and thought *okay here it goes.*

"Dan."

"Dan?" Dad said, his eyebrows coming together as he looked over at Mom who was still looking right at me.

"Jane, were you talking to Dan in the car yesterday too? On the way home?"

"Yes," I said. "I was talking with Dan. But then we got too far away and, and I couldn't hear him anymore. That was when I freaked out a little. Sorry." I waited for them to tell me I was crazy, but that's not the look they were giving me. They looked like they believed me!

"Jane, what's happening?" Dad said. "You know I usually don't ask, but I'm asking now. Tell us, Jane. Why didn't you want the ambulance to come here? What did you mean when you said you were going away?" Dad looked like he was about to cry as he reached out toward my face and ran the back his hand slowly down my cheek.

I snapped my eyes shut and tried to fight off the shivers that went down my spine—it felt like a hot poker being slowly drug down my face! Breathe! Calm! BREATHE! CALM! CALM!!!!

"Stop touching her! You're hurting her, Ed!" Mom told him. She'd obviously learned from seeing me squirm away from her incessant efforts to touch me, watching me whither and cringe each time she managed to lay her hands on me.

"Oh Lord! Sorry, Baby!" Dad said, horrified. He quickly scooted back some, giving me space.

"Sorry, baby, sorry." Frustration twisted his face into an anguished grimace of pain, as if he could feel my pain too.

I took half a second to chase the lingering ghosts of flaming hot pokers down the laundry chute in my mind, tucking them safely into the pain box I'd designed. This new sensation joined all my delightful sensations of burning. Excruciating, but small by comparison. Momentary. There and gone. Like a piece of kindling thrown inside the living hell I now held, caged inside my head like a hungry animal that wanted loose. Loose to bite and tear at me again. What the hell was I thinking!? Strange, dark thoughts.

I focused on my father. I spoke, careful to keep my words slow enough for him to hear me right. "It's okay, Daddy." I took a deep breath and let it out and smiled. This wasn't done for show; I needed to take a deep breath. I was freaking myself out.

"I'm better now," I declared brightly with a small quaver in my new musical voice. It sounded like a sad, beautiful lie. Which it was.

"It's that DAMN Derm pill!" Dad said angrily. "You're still in pain right now, aren't you? How bad is it?"

"It's not the Derm pill," Mom said firmly.

Dad and I both looked at her, surprised to find her hard, accusing gaze pinned on me.

"It's Dan, isn't it? Dan is causing this."

"What are you talking about, Donna?" Dad asked. "How could Dan possibly have anything to do with this?"

Mom ignored him and his question, skewering me with her, "YOU'RE SO BUSTED" look. By reflex, I started to scoot away from her and toward Dad, my usual safe harbor to avoid true motherly ire.

"It was all right there, all along," she accused. "Right in front of me. Spelled out, plain as day, and I just couldn't see it." She was shaking her head in a strangely self-reproving way as she eyed me.

I still didn't have a clue what the hell she was talking about? But she seemed so sure of *whatever it was* that I was squirming anyway. I didn't get it! Why was she pissed at Dan!? All he'd done was hug me and then go to lunch with us.

"The pale skin, the blood." She leaned in, looking into my eyes. "The red eyes, all the other changes. Him talking to you in your head. Dan is a real vampire, isn't he!? And he is changing you into one too!" Mom waited, as if daring me to deny it.

Dad was right there with me, as I was half in his lap now, and I saw that he was looking at me too, adding up the pieces. Pale skin—the blood—the eyes—the way I talked—the way I moved—Dan in my head.

Dan. Are you there, love?

Yes, Jane. I'm here my love. Don't worry. I'm right there with you. You're doing fine.

Good. I just wanted to hear your voi—

"STOP TALKING to that DAMN VAMPIRE!" Mom screamed at me. I mean really SCREAMED!

I scooted a little farther away, but now I *was* sitting in Dad's lap. Dad's eyebrows were somewhere in his hairline.

"Don't try to deny it! I can see it in your face when you talk to him. You tell him to stay the HELL out of your mind!"

I thought inside my head to Dan,

Don't you DARE leave me for a second! Never again, you hear me! NEVER! I have my money in my purse, Dan, everything I need I've got with me. I'm never going home again. I am yours! You come and get me, come and take me, because I'll never leave you again! NEVER!

I shouted as loudly as I could in my head. I blinked and rocked back a little in Dad's lap as Dan ROARED BACK inside my head,

RRRRrrraaaARRR!

The noise in my head was so strange. It wasn't even a human sound! A thrill shot down my spine as my body responded in a weird animal way to Dan's roar. I gasped, my back arched, and my head tilted back. It was scary because that showed ALL of my teeth to both my parents for the first time, but I didn't even care because for one small instant I didn't feel the pain of the burning!

I laughed out loud, and the noise was like music in the car. Mom and Dad were both looking at me frantic and horrified, like I was possessed, and in a wonderful way, *I was*.

"You leave her alone, you MONSTER!" Mom yelled at me. Or at Dan.

I'm sorry, Dan, they think you did this.

"Mom, please. Don't be mad at Dan," I said, then wished I hadn't. She just got madder.

"Don't be mad at him!" Mom yelled back at me. "Jane! Have you totally lost your mind! What did that monster do to you! Tell us right now!"

"Did he bite you, honey?" Dad asked; he was right there inches away. He was careful not to touch me but he started looking around my neck for the usual vampire *evidence* of a bite mark. This dress made it easy to see that I didn't have a mark on me.

If anyone had the bite mark it would be Dan, I thought as they looked me over. I was the monster, not you. I was the one reading the vampire books. I don't know how, and maybe it was some weird reaction to the Derm pills that caused my brain to go storybook psycho, but somehow I caused this to happen. I made the books real. It started that first day in the waiting room when you saw me and said "Hi."

My thoughts switched from internal pondering to first person conversation, weirdly blending back and forth between the two.

Mom and Dad were talking and getting madder. Angry at Dan.

Dan's note, I thought. I could let Dan speak for himself. They watched me as I unzipped my purse and pulled out Dan's last note, the one that I didn't read in time. I'd saved Dan's notes in my purse along with the money and letters. His note begged me—DON'T READ THE BOOK! But I did read the book. Dan, I'm so sorry.

I handed the note to my father. Mom might tear it up and not even read it as mad as she was right now.

"Dan didn't bite me, Daddy. I guess you could say I bit him. He didn't change me into a vampire. I changed him." Dad looked so confused. He was shaking his head, but he still unfolded the little square of paper and started to read the note. I heard Dan in my head,

Jane. This isn't your fault. It's a reaction to the pills or the book, but it's not you, my love. You're not a monster. You didn't want this to happen.

I thought about that. Had I wanted something like this to happen? Did I? I'd been reading the Midnight books nonstop for days—and I was so very into it. It was such a beautiful love story between Sarah and her Ethan. Ethan the vampire. And they loved each other so much. It was so romantic and perfect and—I know a part of me had daydreamed—and wished—and hoped—yearned.

Somehow even with my skin burning I felt a chill run down my spine and I knew. I knew it. I believed it. Part of me had wanted something like this to happen. Fantasized about it. Daydreamed about it. About becoming Sarah.

Mom got impatient and grabbed the note from Dad and started reading it herself. They started talking about Dan's note and what it meant and what they should do about it.

"She's talking to him again," I heard Mom complain. I ignored them and talked to Dan in my head.

Dan. This is all my fault. I drug you into this and maybe you didn't even have a choice. You know my thoughts. You know that, in a way, I did want this. I dreamed about it, and now it's all come true. And now you're burning. And you're going to die. All because of me. I'm so sorry.

I felt myself start to cry again and quickly put a stop to the tears. I heard Dan in my head,

Jane. You can't read my mind so I'll just tell you. You're not the only one that wanted this to happen. I'm the one that wrote fifty notes trying to think of how to say "Hi." I'm the one that asked to hold your hand. I'm the one that wrote in your book. I asked to be your Ethan, your "vampire." I wanted to be able to talk to you, Jane, to talk to you in your head like a vampire. I dreamed about it. Remember, I'm taking those Derm pills too, maybe I'm the one changing you! I could be the one that started this. And I've read tons of vampire books, not just Midnight.

"But why, Jane?" Mom was holding the note up in front of me trying to get my attention from Dan.

"Brrrrrr. Brrrrrr" Dad's phone was going off.

He reached for it.

"Hello."

It was the 911 operator calling back to make sure I was okay. Dad began telling her again that I was all right.

They still wanted to send the ambulance.

"Jane." Mom looked up from reading the second page of the note again. "Why did you read that book last night? After Dan begged you not to read it?" Mom was looking at me, perplexed, remembering yesterday. I'd read the book from the second we got home until well past midnight.

I vaguely remembered my parents trying to talk to me last night, but I had totally ignored them and kept reading. After a while they left me alone there on the couch and let me read. They didn't know that I couldn't stop reading. They didn't know I was inside the book—making it real and changing us both into vampires.

Mom was waiting for me to answer her question. I scooted off Dad's lap and over to Mom. Dad was still assuring the 911 operator that I was fine now.

"Mom. Yesterday when Dan handed me the note he told me to wait till I got home to read it. Dan was worried that if I read it in the car I would freak out. Or go crazy in the car and hurt you or Dad. And you and Dad were so worried about me after lunch anyway, so he told me to wait till I got home and, and when I got home—"

"Oh God," Mom said. "Oh no." I knew she was remembering yesterday. When we got home and she wouldn't let me go to my room. She "made" me sit with her on the couch and read with her so she could keep an eye on me.

Mom's face went pale, and she leaned forward to wrap her arms around me and hug me.

HELP! I thought and braced for the burning, but Mom managed to catch herself before impact, stopping an inch away from my skin. She slowly backed away with a horrified expression fixed on her face as she stared into all the extra white in my strangely colored new eyes. Terrified with relief.

"Thanks, Mom," I said with feeling.

Mom turned green and for a moment looked like she might sick-up right then and there. She fought it back down with visible effort, managing to keep the breakfast I'd made from rising from the dead. Strangely, I felt disappointed. I hoped Dan and I had better luck in our resurrection than Mom's breakfast had. Maybe she'd still spew?

Aaaah—I gave my head a shake.

Okay.

What was that!?

What—the hell—was I thinking!?

Had my damn brain gone completely off the tracks!? Was I actually wanting my mother to puke because I saw myself as dead chewed up bits of bacon, eggs, and half-digested juice, all swilling around inside her stomach? Dan and I, dead and decaying in the earth. Worm food, unless death or hell or the grave or *whatever* puked us up—

"When did you read Dan's note?" Mom asked, pulling me from the dark, ugly images in my head.

I shivered as I answered. "Last night, when I went to take a shower. I felt it in my pocket when I was getting undressed. I read the note there in the bathroom."

"No! I said we're fine!" Dad snapped his phone closed on the pushy operator. "So what do we do now!?" He looked from Mom to me. "We know that this isn't Dan's fault now. He tried to help! Although he should have told us about all of this yesterday!" Dad was upset, which didn't seem right. Dad was always the calm one. He punched the headrest of the seat in front of him and I scooted over, closer to mom, as he vented and took it out on the seat with a few more punches.

"It's those pills! This has to be some kind of reaction to those DAMN pills! So how do we stop it!?" The veins bulged large in his neck, and I found myself staring and quickly gave myself a shake. Hell no!

"Dad. Could you do me a favor?" I asked quietly in my musical voice.

He stopped beating up the seat. "Sure, honey, anything."

"Stop it," I said simply. "I need you to be calm. I need you to be calm for me and for Mom. Don't lose it, Dad." I turned to Mom. "You too. No freaking out because I have some hard things to tell you, but I want you to know. And I'm serious about the no freaking out part. I'm trying hard not to freak out too because if I do freak out, bad things might happen, so everyone's just going to be cool. Deal."

They looked at me and then at each other. I was their whole world. And their world was being torn apart right in front of them. Watching their stricken, hopeless faces made me want to cry, but I didn't let myself. I couldn't.

"Go ahead, Jane." Dad had his temper in check now and he even managed a small smile.

"Tell us the bad news first, that way everything else will seem a whole lot better and we can end on the good news."

"Good news?" Mom parroted, half in a daze. As if such a thing didn't exist anymore.

I started. "It's gone too far. I've changed too much. That's why I can't go to a hospital. They'd lock me up and treat me like a lab experiment." I gave Dad a determined look. "I don't want that, Daddy. This can't be stopped. Not for me or Dan. We have to finish it. We have to change the rest of the way."

"How do you know!?" Mom started. "A *real* doctor at a *real* hospital might find a way to help you, Jane. Maybe stop this or delay it till they could figure out what to do. We should have taken you straight to the hospital yesterday! Before you read that damn book!" She looked away, out the window, feeling guilty about yesterday.

I reached out and cupped my hands behind her head to pull her to my chest but she pulled back.

"No, honey! You'll hurt yourself!"

I let go. "You do it then," I insisted. I opened my arms and leaned my chest toward her. "Listen to my heart."

She glowered but did as I wanted and leaned down, gently pressing her head up against my chest, as I, on the other hand, gritted my teeth and tried not to scream right in her face. After a minute she sat up.

"Well?" Dad asked when she didn't say anything right away.

"It is beating funny," Mom admitted.

"My heart is slowing down," I told them. "It's going to go slower and slower until it beats for the last time at exactly 11:33 tonight. Dan's heart will do the same. We're both going to die tonight and nothing can stop that now. And that's the bad news." I held up a cautionary finger. "Remember, stay calm."

I rushed ahead before they puked, fainted, ulcerated, or stroked out. "Now here's the good news!" My huge delivery smile faltered as I grudgingly qualified that, "Well, the sort of good news anyway. We're not going to *stay* dead. After we die we'll rise again, if it works the way it's supposed to. Once we change the rest of the way we'll have to stay away for a while until I'm sure we're not going to accidentally hurt you guys. I hope it won't be long but I'll call and keep in touch. We'll be back as soon as we get some control of this thing."

I punctuated that with a little helpless shrugging and hand waving. I mean, what else could we do?

"This is not some story in a book, Jane," Mom said, calmly this time. "You're a real person. We need real help, Jane. We need a hospital." She continued to push her hospital agenda.

"This is not a story in a book—*anymore*," I corrected. "I made it real, Mom. And now I have to deal with it. Dan and I can't hide form this and hope that it goes away. We're out of time. We're both going to die tonight."

"I still don't see how you know all this, Jane," Dad started in. "There's no way you could possibly know that your own heart is getting slower or know the exact moment it would stop. It's just not possible."

I bit back my snarky comment just in time. It seemed Dad's brain was functioning again, albeit lamely, as he now considered himself the authority on what was or was not possible. Still, I took it as a positive sign of life, neurons firing and all.

"I *can* hear my own heart beating. I can hear your heart, and Mom's. I can even hear the blood pumping through your veins right now—and—and—" I made a pained face and shook myself as the swishing sound tried to keep my attention. *Don't go there!* I told myself firmly. Right then my stomach made a sick gurgling, followed by an ominous rolling growl.

"Sorry!" I said. Embarrassed. "I'm trying not to think about blood because it makes me very thirsty." I put my hands over my stomach to try to hold it still but it gurgled again sickly. I felt a burning in my throat that joined with a twisting pain in my gut. I closed my eyes. Oh shit! This was a different kind of pain.

"You didn't eat breakfast, did you? You didn't eat dinner last night. You haven't had a thing since you ate that nasty raw steak! You lied to me, Jane," Mom accused, giving me a nasty look.

"You should be thanking me, *mother*!" I shouted back, mean and ugly, which surprised her. My stomach was making me grumpy. "I need blood now. Vampire. Remember?" I just put it out there. No sense hiding from the ugly truth. But then I heard Dan's voice in my head.

Jane, I'm here. I've been listening and I know you're hungry. I have some blood for us to drink, but see your friends at the mall before you drink it. If you drink it now, it might make you too dangerous to be around people. Please just come to the food court and I'll meet you there. Oh, and Jane, your two friends are starting to get worried about you. You're late.

The joy I felt at hearing his voice in my head fizzled out as I wondered where Dan got blood! Wait! I don't want to know! My stomach cramped again and made me close my eyes, hurting. Dan was right. The last time I had blood had been a dicey thing, and I didn't want to have any accidents. If I tasted blood it might make me go *crazy*. I thought my words to Dan in my head.

You're right, Dan. I'm barely keeping it together as it is. I have to wait.

Just try to stay calm and don't think about it. It's going to be all right. I'm right there with you. But hurry up and get here so the rest of me can be with the rest of you. I need to see you.

Me too, I said. I needed to see him.

Mom and Dad were both watching me talk to Dan. I could tell they wanted to know what I was saying so I started talking out loud but I didn't mention the blood.

"Thanks, Dan, I think you're right about that." My stomach made its own last little gurgle of a comment, complaining about having to wait. "Could you tell Emma and Stacy that I'm on my way? Are you already inside the mall?" I looked at Mom and Dad and said to them, "I'll just talk out loud when Dan talks to me so you guys can hear at least part of our conversation. Okay?"

Mom nodded, Dad reached across and held her hand. I'd dropped a few bombshells on them in the past few minutes, but they seemed to be pulling themselves back together.

Nice. That's a good idea, Jane, letting them hear you talk to me. That'll help them get over the weirdness. I won't be able to tell Emma and Stacy you're coming, though. I tried to go inside but the security guard at the door stopped me. I didn't have shoes on so he made me leave. I couldn't wear the shoes, they hurt too much. So I'm on the roof of the mall over the food court waiting for your car to pull into the parking lot.

I laughed. "How did you get on the roof!?" I turned to my parents and said, "Dan's watching for us from the roof of the mall!" I explained, so they could follow along with the conversation. "Oh, and Emma and Stacy are already there waiting for us at the food court." I smiled at my Mom and Dad, trying to make this seem normal and happy.

They weren't smiling back.

"Jane! You can't be serious?" Dad said. "After what you just told us we're not still going to the mall." He looked shocked that I had even considered it. He was getting upset again. "We don't need to go to the mall; we need to go see Dr. Burgis! Right now! And when I see him I'm gonna choke some answers out of his sorry hide!" Dad was already opening the back door of the car headed back to the driver's seat.

Before he could get the front door open I crawled up the middle, between the two front seats, and sat in the driver's seat. He was really surprised to see me sitting there looking up at him when he opened the door. He stood there with the door open gaping at me.

"Jane! What are you doing!?" Mom called from the back seat. I ignored her and gave Dad a hard stare.

"I'm not going *anywhere* without Dan." I gave him a second to think about that. I offered up a smile and tried to work him like I did when I was human, it always worked then.

"Please, Daddy. Please! May we just go to the mall for a little while so I can say goodbye to Emma and Stacy and to pick up Dan? You like Dan too, I know you do." I smiled at him and waited.

He still looked grumpy. I looked over at Mom. She had her head slid up in between the seats, right beside me. They were half out of their minds with worry and already worn out from yesterday and last night. This had been hard on them, and I hated that they had to go through more of it. We had been a happy little family, just the three of us, and now, *this*. How the hell do you deal with your daughter turning into a vampire?

I quickly crawled over to the passenger seat so fast my parents both blinked and looked at me, shocked expressions on their faces again.

"Jane! It's just like in the book, you're moving fast like those vampires in the books." Mom was finally putting things together. She'd gotten up to the start of the third book so she had some idea of what I could do now. She hadn't read the fourth book where the girl "Sarah" finally changes into a vampire, but she knew enough to understand my speed and maybe some of my other abilities.

I leaned over and patted the driver's seat with my hand. "Come on, Dad. Let's go. Emma and Stacy are waiting on us."

Right then my stomach made another wet, gurgly, disgusting sound and I gasped as my stomach clenched. I wrapped my arms around my middle, closing my eyes. I actually growled a little as I rocked back and forth in my chair, trying to endure the pain of hunger. This was a very different kind of pain. In some ways less intense than the burning, but in other ways this seemed a lot harder to ignore. I needed to eat. Soon. But what? Where? O God, I thought, WHO!?

Dan. I'm gonna need that blood soon!

"Jane," Mom said. "Please, let's just go to the hospital. I know you need blood. They have blood there they can give you. And they can help us find out what's really happening!"

She was practically out of her mind. No sense even talking to her now, so I turned my attention to Dad. He'd just sat there in the driver's seat looking at Mom as if he was actually considering doing as she suggested and going to the hospital.

"Which hospital should we go to?" Dad asked my mother. She started to make suggestions.

They weren't *listening* to me. I was being too nice. I'd have to tell him in a way he'd understand.

"Dad. I love you. But if you don't start driving to the mall right now I'm gonna get out of this damn car and run there."

I gave him a second or two to chew on that. *Good freakin' grief!* I thought. This was going to take some getting used to—waiting for people to "think." And talking in slow motion. I guessed I'd given him long enough, so I continued.

"I want to stay with you and Mom as long as I can, but if you make me, I'll run," I said it slowly and firmly, and then I waited for them to process. After a while Dad reached forward and started the car.

"All right, let's go to the mall," he said calmly. "And you can quickly say goodbye to Stacy and Emma. And we'll pick up Dan. He's sick too, so he should go with us. Then we'll all go to see Dr. Burgis and get some answers."

Dad started to pull out into traffic, his voice a little darker as he added, "And if the son of a bitch doesn't answer our questions, you can eat him, honey. That bastard deserves it." Dad kept his head forward, keeping his eyes on the traffic.

He he he, I heard Dan laughing in my head and smiled.

"Thanks, Daddy," I said. That was real sweet of him, and I might just take him up on that offer if the doctor didn't help us. I leaned over and kissed him on the cheek, but I moved slowly enough so he wasn't surprised. I didn't want him to crash or anything.

We drove the rest of the way to the mall, and Mom and Dad asked me all about how this had started and what I thought. I told them that Dan and I both thought Dad was right, that it had been some wild reaction to the Derm pills. That somehow my brain had gone haywire and was making what I read in the book real, changing us into actual vampires.

I also told them that no matter what, Dan and I wanted to take those pills one last time today. They freaked at that until I told them that I wanted all the help I could get for tonight. If the Derm pill had started this change in us, and at this point we had to go through with it or die, then we were getting that pill.

We were still arguing about the Derm pill when we pulled into the parking lot of the mall and my crazy new eyes picked out Dan's from way up on the roof. He was hiding in the shadows, still a long way off, but I could see him clearly.

"Hello, my love. We're here," I said out loud. Mom and Dad, who were so worried about me dying now started worrying about other things. I noticed the looks they passed back and forth and then at my dress again, worried about me being mostly naked and about to see Dan.

I see you, Jane, and I know you see me. I've been keeping an eye on Emma and Stacy by looking through the skylights up here. They went ahead and ordered food but they're almost done eating. You better hurry and get inside. I'll give you a minute or two alone with your friends before I come down and join you. The mall cops will chase us out once they see me, so I'll give you a few minutes together first. And don't worry, I'm right here. Things have changed some for me. I'm a lot stronger today than I was yesterday, and with you this close, I'm even more connected to you. I can hear your thoughts and even feel what you're feeling I'm so much a part of you.

Oh, he could "feel" my feelings now, could he?

What am I feeling now, Dan? I said in my head.

This conversation was too spicy for Mom and Dad. I was close to him now—*and I wanted him*. Another hunger. The same as before, but stronger now. Crisper. Wilder. Another craving to have to fight. But I had a major problem. I didn't want to fight this hunger, I wanted to sate it! Drown it! Smother it with Dan's body.

Please, Jane! I want you too! Hold that thought and let's do—ALL OF THAT! But first go see your friends! And there's one other small detail we need to clear up, but I promise, we will be together soon. Trust me, my love—you'll have me soon.

"Jane!" Mom scolded, "I thought you were going to talk to Dan out loud so we could hear at least half the conversation. You're not sharing. What were you talking about just now?" she asked suspiciously.

I'm sure she already knew. Mom always wanted to "KNOW" everything, no matter what. Should I say something deceptive and superficial just to keep her happy and calm her nerves?

What should I tell her, Dan? I thought.

You wouldn't! He saw it or felt it coming before I could say it. *Jane! Don't you dare—* he said, as I "dared" out loud to Mom.

"Sex. I was talking to Dan about sex." I laughed as I heard Dan's gasp of surprise in my head. I liked surprising him. But he wasn't the only one surprised. Mom and Dad were both freaking too. I laughed and watched and listened to all of it, inside my head and out. Being a vampire was really causing my wicked side to take off!

Oh shit! I can't believe you went there! Are you trying to make them even crazier! Their gonna try and stake me!

Mom was speechless for a second with her mouth hanging open. Catching flies!

"Have you and Dan already had sex?" Dad asked. He didn't yell, he simply asked. A strange expression on his face that was somewhere between "yeah, okay" and "Oh HELL no!"

"No, Daddy. I haven't had sex with Dan in the real world yet, but I have been with Dan inside the book, and that sure seemed real. So in a way—yes, I have," I sighed at the happy memory, but then I frowned, "but in another way—no, I haven't."

Mom, Dad, and *Dan* could tell that I wasn't happy about that second part and I knew all three of them were equally freaked out.

"You know what," Dad waved his arms around as if he could chase the conversation away like a bad fart in the air, "I don't want to know! I'm sorry I asked."

Hehehe. I heard laughing in my head.

"Let's go see Stacy and Emma. And where's Dan?" Dad said. He'd already parked the car and was opening his door. I got out and quickly walked around to his side of the car. "Goodness, Jane. That was fast! You were nothing but a blur."

I nodded and pointed to the roof of the building. "Dan's right there, Dad. He's going to wait till I go in and spend a few minutes with the girls then he'll meet us inside. Stacy and Emma are already here but they're almost done eating and I don't want to miss them."

Dad was looking at where I pointed and saw Dan wave at him. Dad waved back. Mom joined us and she waved too.

"How on earth did Dan get way up there?" she asked. Dan told me in a quick whisper inside my head.

"He climbed up the wall like Spiderman. I guess we can do that now," I said.

She wasn't surprised. "Jane, make this quick. Please," Mom urged.

I nodded. "I want a few minutes to say goodbye, then we can pick up Dan and go."

They walked on either side of me as we headed into the mall.

People started to notice us, or notice ME, as we walked across the huge parking lot. People heading in and out of the mall watched me, even people driving by looking for a place to park noticed. They all stared at me. It wasn't the polite kind of stare; it was the gawking, blatant ogling kind that's totally rude. Of course the way I looked—and with this dress—I *was* totally asking for it. It was still rude though.

"Do I look *that* different now, Mom?" I asked. "Is it this dress, or is it the other changes?" I hoped I could still pass myself off as a human. I knew I was pale and half naked, but the Avenues Mall was a richer, upper class place, and pretty swanky. The rich and sleazy girls dressed crazy here all the time. I didn't think I should be causing this much of a scene. I was beginning to think coming to the mall wasn't such a good idea after all.

Waiting—waiting—it's coming—and—Mom finally answered my question.

"Well, honey. It's not just one thing. It's—everything. You're so amazingly beautiful now. And if anyone can manage to stop looking at your body in that dress long enough to notice your eyes. Or your teeth." She shook her head.

I wondered what Stacy and Emma would say when they saw me. My worry grew with each staring, freaked out person I passed. What would my two best friends say? Would they even recognize me?

Emma and Stacy

Food Court Reunion

"**This totally blows!**" Emma flipped her cell open to check the time. Again. "Blows!" she spat the word at her phone as if it was to blame. "What's she gonna do, stand us up?" She snapped her phone closed with an angry twist of her wrist. "I'm sick of waiting."

Stacy craned her neck looking this way and that, searching for Jane.

"Jane will be here, she's just really frikin' late!" Stacy said doubtfully.

Emma placed her fortune cookie on the table top and gave it a suspicious glower, then slowly and carefully smashed it flat with the palm of her hand with the cookie still safely contained inside its plastic wrapper. Emma never opened fortune cookies. They scared her.

"Her mom and dad were there with her in the car when she called. They were going to bring her up here, so what's the damn deal?" Emma continued to gripe. "And why the hell won't she answer her cell!? Jane would answer her cell and her email if she could. Something's gotta be wrong. I'm starting to wonder if this is her parents being punchy, or if it's Jane, flipping out. Maybe those pills are really messing with her head. She sure sounded out of it yesterday."

"Ya think so?" Stacy worried at her lip with her teeth as she scanned the sea of faces coming in and out of the food court. "Crap, I hadn't even thought of that. I hope she's okay. She would be here unless something major came up."

Emma snorted. "Hell, you think she'd at least call. She's got a cell phone."

Stacy threw a wadded up napkin at her which earned her a full dose of Emma's squinty-eyed gaze.

"Stop it," Emma growled.

"You stop it!" Stacy growled back. "I know your feelings are all tore up, Emma, but stop being a bitch already! Jane doesn't stand people up. She's not like that. Maybe her phone's not working or it's out of juice or something. Who knows!?" Stacy took a hard pull off her drink and hit bottom with a "sllluuuuur-rpp" noise.

Emma noticed a super pale girl in a slinky red dress enter through the front doors of the mall. Something about her made her ask, "That's not Jane, is it?"

Stacy looked up from her drink and followed Emma's gaze. At first glance she shook her head no, but the longer she looked, the slower the back and forth motion went until it ground to a halt and Stacy just stared.

It couldn't be Jane, but it had to be Jane because the two people walking with this girl were Jane's parents. One walked on each side of her, giving everyone they passed the totally evil eye like body guards. Jane's parents *walked*, but this girl in red did not walk, *she floated*, and it was freakin' crazy to watch! Stacy's eyes went to the girl's feet to see how she was doing it and was surprised to see that she didn't even have shoes on. She was walking on just the front balls of her feet, not even letting her whole foot touch the ground for some strange reason as she took each graceful step.

The only part of her that didn't move and flow like a dream was her head which snapped in quick jerky movements from one place to another almost too fast to see. The girl's skin was almost milk white like a Goth, and her hair was a teased out, glossy, raven black. But Jane's hair was brown.

"What do ya think?" Emma asked.

"I don't know." Stacy looked harder at the girl's face. It was different, but it was Jane. Her face had changed though; now it was so absolutely perfect she could be a movie star or a super model. Jane had always been pretty but nothing like this.

As she walked she didn't slouch, she held her head high and shoulders square looking past and ignoring all the staring people she passed as if she were a Goddess walking among creatures beneath her notice. Her dress was a revealing red evening gown that covered her boobs but left pale and perfect skin showing at her sides and stomach. Stacy could tell from where she sat that "Jane?" didn't have a bra on. Her nipples were clearly visible under the sheer fabric! No wonder all the guys were staring at her like deer caught in headlights. They *were* caught in headlights!

Right then "Jane?" looked right at them and smiled with teeth so bright they gleamed. She started straight toward their table with a crowd of people trailing along behind her like star struck groupies following a movie star. Stacy and Emma stared dumbly as Jane glided along in their direction, but the crowd was getting in the way. People kept trying to talk to her and a group of teenagers was laughing and pointing and crowding in as well.

"Go get a life, you punk bastards!" Jane's father yelled suddenly. "My daughter has a skin condition! She's in a lot of pain right now! She's a very sick girl! Leave us the hell alone or I'll call the cops and have you thrown out of the mall! Or I'll just beat your ass myself."

Everyone backed off to a respectful distance; some people looked away, embarrassed, while others took the emotion heavy threat of an ass kicking to heart. Everyone retreated, but not far. And the shouting had brought even more attention to Jane. More people gawking, but at a distance now.

"Thanks, Daddy," Jane told her father, and then they walked the last few steps to the table. Emma and Stacy watched as Jane "super gracefully" settled into a chair.

"Hi guys." Her voice sent a shiver down Stacy's spine. Emma was speechless. This girl didn't even sound like Jane.

"Jane?" Stacy breathed out.

"Yes, Stace, get a grip already, it's me," Jane said, a frown on her beautiful face.

"Hello, girls." Jane's mom spoke to them but kept glancing up at the crowd of pointing and whispering people hovering around like vultures. Stacy and Emma mumbled their hellos back.

"Just a few minutes, Jane, and then we have to go."

Jane nodded to her mother with a quick sharp up and down movement that made Emma and Stacy blink. Jane's parents stepped away from the table, but they didn't go far. They took up positions at opposite ends of the table making sure everyone stayed well away from Jane. They were acting so strange it made everything seem even weirder.

And then Emma exploded. She'd been holding it in for far too long, which wasn't good for Emma.

"No! Damn! Way! What the hell happened, Jane!? And did your dad just say you were sick!? What is going on!?" She looked Jane over from head to toe and blinked when she noticed that Jane was barefoot.

"And, Janers, where are your shoes?" Emma asked.

Jane laughed, delighted by Emma's outburst. The sound was beautiful, in a weirdly musical way. Jane's teeth flashed in the lights. Bright red lips curled happily and she smiled her too bright smile, back straight, head high. She seemed fantastical. She looked exactly like a Disney character come to life. Stacy had this weird feeling that any moment little birdies and deer and other critters would start to gather around their table or the seven dwarves would show up, whistling their merry way through the food court. Stacy gave herself a shake as she tried to take Jane's advice and get a grip.

"It's good to see you, Emms. I've missed you so much," Jane said in her strange new voice and then shrugged. "As for not wearing shoes, it hurt too much to wear them, so I didn't. And yes guys, I'm sick." She gave them a sad smile.

"Sick! You don't look sick, you look—" Emma's face contorted as she hunted for the right word and surfaced with, "UNREAL!" She waved a hand at Jane. "Is all this from taking that Derm pill, or did you go and get your hair done and your teeth bleached?"

Emma leaned in as she noticed Jane's eyes. "What the poop have you done to your eyes? Are those contacts? Red and purple contacts? What the hell!?"

Jane's eyes weren't her usual gray brown hazel mix; now the iris was a weird dark red and the eye color was a crazy dark violet that feathered to a pale lilac at the edges. They were beautiful, but they were also very unsettling to look into.

"I thought the eye doctor said you couldn't wear contacts," Stacy said as she studied Jane's new eyes.

"They're not contacts. This is my real eye color now. And yes. They changed because of my reaction to the Derm pill. But that's not the part that's the problem. There's a problem with my heart."

"Oh no! Jane!" Stacy wailed and she reached for Jane's hand, but Jane moved like lightning, pulling her hands back and leaning away from her in her seat.

"Don't touch me, Stacy," Jane said and then explained with an apologetic grimace. "Sorry guys, that's another part of my crazy reaction to the Derm pills. My skin is beautiful, sure, but it's also super painful right now." Jane pinched the fabric of the red dress. "That's why I'm walking around half naked with this stupid scrap of a dress on. I couldn't stand to have anything else on my skin. And that's also why I'm not wearing shoes. Every time something touches my skin it hurts like fire."

Stacy pulled her hand back and Jane sat forward in her chair again. "I guess I'm like you now, Emms, a touch me not." Jane gave her best friend Emma a warm smile.

"You don't need my issues," Emma's voice cracked a little as she spoke, "you got enough problems of your own. So your skin's a mess and your eyes are waked out, we got that and we can see that, but what's up with your heart? How sick are you anyway? What did the doctors say?"

"They told me that my heart is slowing down. It's pretty serious and—" Jane tilted her head to the side and a strange blank expression crossed her face for a second before she continued. "Actually guys, I'll have to go away, out of town for a while to see a specialist and I don't know exactly when I'll be back."

"Jane. No. Don't say that. Oh no." Emma started to cry, which was very bad because Emma was *not* a crier.

"You can't leave me, Jane," she mumbled as she fought to hold herself together.

Stacy was coping by denial. "But you don't even look sick! It couldn't be that bad. Please tell us it's not that bad, Jane. Please. Tell me it's not that bad!" Stacy demanded, eyes bulging as if she were willing it to be so.

Jane reached into her purse and pulled out two letters, handing one to Stacy and one to Emma, which made Stacy start to cry too. The letters were the last straw, mental and emotional meltdown had begun for the two girls.

"Don't open your letters till tomorrow. Okay?" Jane asked. "Don't worry. I may just be gone for a few months and I'll try to keep in touch. I know this is hard, but could you guys do me a huge favor? Please? Let's not talk about me being sick anymore. I'm *sick* of talking about me being *sick*. Let's talk about something else," Jane pleaded, but she could see that both of her best friends were spiraling toward emotional implosion. Time for intervention. Juicy girl talk!

"You guys will never guess what happened to me. I fell in love!" Jane said and bounced her eyebrows up and down. That brought the crying to a screeching halt for Stacy just as Jane knew it would.

"What!" Stacey managed to choke out. "Love? Are you serious?" She paused to blow her nose. "You fell in love? How! I thought you were in lockdown and couldn't see anyone! Spill it!"

Stacy leaned in closer for the juicy details but Emma was quiet, listening to them talk, trying not to go to pieces. She listened as Jane told them about her new guy. Emma couldn't help looking at Jane's teeth as she spoke. Had her teeth been straightened? It sure looked that way. Were her canines pointy now? She studied Jane's teeth as she listened and tried not to scream.

"His name is Dan Simmons. I met him Monday. He's in the drug study with me. We met in the waiting room at the doctor's office. He wrote me the most romantic note—" Jane's head tilted to the side and her face went blank for a second before she finished her sentence, "and it was just love at first sight I guess."

Stacy sighed in envious romantic rapture, "Oh my God. A romantic note! Love at first sight! I'm getting all goosebumpy over here! Give me more! Details, details, Janer! Gimme gimme gimme!" Stacy begged.

"I can't wait till you meet him. You guys will love him too, and he's, well—kinda like me now. He had the same weird reaction to the Derm pill that I did."

Jane had a blank look cross her face again. Stacy and Emma shared a worried look between them as they watched Jane space out for a second, and they both started to worry that Jane was having problems with her brain to go along with the heart and skin troubles. No matter how good she looked, Jane was a total mess.

Emma blew her nose with her Panda Express napkin. If Jane wanted to talk about *other things* then that's what she would do. Emma swallowed the lump in her throat and joined in the conversation. She'd only heard Jane use the 'L' word once before. She knew Jane didn't say it unless she meant it. Jane respected the 'L' word and didn't toss it around like some people did, all willy nilly, like croutons on a salad.

"Who is this guy and when do we get to meet him?" Emma growled and squinted her teary eyes as she glared at Jane. "We gotta make sure he's not a loser or some scum bag before you can go all crazy for him." Emma was worried. Jane said she loved this guy. It sounded serious already. Her protective side started kicking into full gear.

Stacy caught on quickly and got with the program.

"Oh, too true, Emms!" She snapped. "We gotta work this guy over and make sure he's no *sicko* before you can go all crazy for him. Hell, you just met this guy on Monday, so don't go throwing the 'L' word around like that. That's some seriously scary shit coming from you. You're not allowed to go crazy over this guy till we give the green light on it." She gave Jane a hard look. "You hear me, Jane Miller! Don't you dare lose your mind over this guy yet!"

Jane's face went blank for just a minute then she busted out laughing! The joyous sound echoed out, bouncing off the high ceiling then raining down upon everyone in the food court, creating an eerie hush as people stopped everything to listen. People stopped eating, stopped talking, stopped shopping, stopped walking—and *listened.* Emma and Stacy squirmed in their chairs, sharing a mutual WTF! while the sound echoed around the food court. Jane stopped laughing, but a wild and mysterious smile still clung to her face as she spoke into the newborn silence.

"Oh, Stacy, it's *waaay* too late for that." The way she said it made it seem so final, so totally absolute. So scary.

Damn! Stacy thought. *Jane's already lost her freaking mind over this guy!* But out loud she said, "Dan Simmons, huh? What does this guy—look—like—" Stacy's sentence died and her face went blank as she saw what had to be "him" walking toward their table.

She and Emma both glanced back to Jane then back to the approaching apparition. They looked the same. He glided along in the same weird way Jane had, and he brought a fresh wave of following groupies in his wake, not the least of which was an irate mall cop who was telling him he couldn't be in the mall without shoes. His pants were some plain white things that looked like hospital scrubs and he wore a white button up shirt that only had the very last two buttons at the bottom fastened, holding it together. It was easy to see his muscular chest and the top of his amazing washboard abs as he walked toward them.

Jane's parents intercepted the irate mall cop and started talking to him as this "whatever he was" stopped right beside Jane's chair. Stacy and Emma were the same as the rest of the crowd of spectators, just two more sets of eyes watching as Jane looked up into his face and he stared down into hers. They stayed like that, staring at each other while Jane's parents, Emma, and Stacy watched and waited along with everyone else. Stacy thought that the only thing missing was a wind machine blowing their hair around and a tropical island in the background and you'd have the perfect cover for a romance novel!

"Emma, Stacy, this is my Dan," Jane said, still staring up at him. She hadn't taken her eyes off him for a second.

"Your Dan?" Emma said. She let loose a suspicious "hmmmm" as she eyed him but he didn't look away from Jane.

Jane got a confused look on her face, "Sure, I'll go get them for you." She told Stacy and Emma "Be right back" as she rose from her chair and walked over to her parents who were arguing with the mall cop.

"So, your Dan?" Stacy asked him and he finally looked away from Jane and down at Stacy and Emma. His skin was almost as pale as Jane's, but it didn't look so shockingly Goth on Dan because his hair was sandy blond instead of black like hers. His eyes were a brilliant blue green but his iris color was the same scary dark red as Jane's. He seemed friendly enough as he smiled and nodded at Stacy and Emma, although he didn't say a word.

Jane came back to the table with her parents in tow, still wearing a confused expression.

"Okay, Dan, we're all here."

"What's up, Jane? What's going on?" Stacy asked, wondering why she had brought her parents over.

"Yes. What is it, honey?" Jane's father asked. "We need to leave anyway. The mall security wants us to go." He shot the mall cop a dirty look over his shoulder and looked back to his daughter.

"Dan wanted to say something to all of us together, although I'm not quite sure how he's going to do that and he wouldn't tell me. He said it was a surprise." Again she looked confused and so did her parents. Jane looked back at Dan and said, "We're ready, Dan."

Dan nodded, reached into the front pocket of his shirt, and pulled out a black velvet box. He dropped to one knee, opened the box, and held it up to Jane. It was quiet for about five full seconds while everyone tried to understand what they were seeing. Dan had found a way to say a lot, without saying a single word, and he'd left everyone, except Stacy, totally speechless. Stacy of course handled matters in her own way.

She leapt to her feet and shouted, "RING!" at the top of her lungs as she pointed at the box in Dan's hand.

And that started the stampede of onlookers again. Ooos and ahhhs came from the rapidly growing crowd as they drew in to see what was happening. Some people started taking pictures with their phones, not sure if this was real or something staged. The frumpy old mall cop backed off, giving way to the "ring" and all the magic that this particular moment commanded. The mall cop even turned his efforts toward keeping the crowd at bay, pushing them back to give the couple space. Stacy and Emma stood beside Jane's parents who looked as if they might faint at any second. They were obviously surprised and shocked, and terrified.

Just then someone in the crowd shouted, "Oh my god, she's crying blood!"

Coming from Jane's eyes and running down her face were red trails of blood! A bright red drop fell from her chin and dropped onto the white tile floor of the mall. Someone was shouting to call 911 and a few others were moving forward like they wanted to help while Jane's father kept the overly helpful people at bay and told others that they did not need 911. Most of the crowd stood there, fascinated by the scene, while others started to back up and hold napkins over their noses and mouths like they were worried that this might be something contagious. A few of those in the crowd even smiled, like it was all a big production and not even real.

More mall cops arrived on the scene.

While Jane's father fended off the crowd, Emma raided a nearby table of their napkins then rushed back over and pushed her contraband into Jane's mother's hands, who stepped closer to Jane but didn't touch her.

"What can we do?" She held the napkins in her shaking hands. "I can't touch you because it hurts you too much, but what can I do? Do you want to go to the hospital now? What can I do!?"

"I'm okay, Mom," Jane answered without taking her eyes away from Dan's. "I'm not hurt. This is how I cry now. This is normal for me now. Could you please give Dan and me a minute? Please, Mom?" Jane asked calmly.

Her mother nodded helplessly and backed off, pulling a reluctant Emma along with her. Dan hadn't moved a muscle; he still knelt there on one knee in front of Jane holding the box with the ring.

Jane

The Big Surprise

Dan knelt there before me, holding the box with the ring. Finally, his voice was there in my head. His lips didn't move but his words matched the passion I saw in his face and eyes.

Jane. When I'm inside your mind, listening to your every thought—feeling you—knowing you—it's like there's a place in the center of your soul where I "fit." A place you made just for me. Please, Jane, let me live inside your soul because I can't live without you. You are my life. Let me love you and hold your hand for all eternity. Please, Jane. Please. Will you marry me and hold my hand forever?

I'd been fighting, giving way to little drops, but I couldn't hold the blood back anymore. It streamed down my face like hot red tears. I let it go—I didn't care anymore.

Mom interrupted and I sent her away as quickly as I could, then reached out and took the ring from the little box. It burned like a lit cigarette butt as I held it in the palm of my hand. Dan put the empty box back inside his shirt pocket. He reached out, took the ring from my open palm and shivered as he slipped it onto my finger. I knew he felt it burn my finger the same as I did, but he put it on me anyway. He knew I wanted him to do it.

"Yes, Dan. I'll marry you," I said loudly enough for everyone to hear. There were more ooohs and ahhs, but the bloody mess running down my face had thrown a wet blanket on everyone's romantic sympathies. Dan rose to his feet and I held my hands out and away from my sides waiting for him as he came close. My parents, Emma, and Stacy, who was shaking her head "no" watched with horror as his arms slowly encircled me and then pulled me up next to his body.

FLAMES! FIRE! PAIN!

Scorching, Blazing, Searing Pain! My skin felt like a thousand bees all stinging at once, but I didn't run screaming—*I held tighter!* I clung to him and burned with him. I wanted him to kiss me! If I was going to hell I wanted to taste the fire of his kiss before I turned completely to ash! I tilted my head up blindly; the world was a whited-out sea of pain as our lips meet. We held each other and shared our first kiss there in the middle of hell's flames.

Eventually yelling reached my mind in the middle of the pyre where we clung to each other and burned. The worried and distressed voices of my parents and security guards pushed into the indescribable pain of kissing fire and not being consumed. I didn't have to explain or do a count down. Dan knew.

We held tight for one more blazing, perfect second—then broke—both of us taking a quick step away from each other at the same time. I stood panting and out of breath as little tremors ran through my frame and limbs while my vision returned. Dan stood in front of me with blood all over his face and chest. His white shirt was now a red ruin. I was sure I was also a mess, but I didn't care. I smiled at him.

It was worth it.

A mall cop stepped closer, "If you want to take them to the doctor yourself instead of calling 911, that's your business, but you need to leave the mall! Now!" he ordered roughly. There were five of them surrounding us now. Looking very much like police in their blue uniforms.

"Fine! We're going!" Dad yelled back.

Mom was there beside me. "Let's go, honey," she urged, wild eyed with worry and panic as she held out a handful of napkins for me. I forced down my first urge—which was to hiss like a demon cat as if the dry napkins she held were a wooden stake! I grimaced and waved them away.

"Don't you want to clean yourself up some?" she begged. I shook my head no. The thought of wiping my skin with a dry napkin was beyond horrifying! I needed a sink and some cool water, and even then I wasn't looking forward to the clean up. At least my dress was red. It still looked fine, but Dan needed to lose the shirt and wash up before he could walk around in public. He was a walking crime scene.

"Let's just go," I said.

I reached out to Dan with a hand. He raised a brow, but—*he knew*—I would put up with the pain in order to touch him. He took my hand slowly, letting us both adjust to the horror of holding hands with hell. I didn't let go.

"Can we walk out with you guys?" Stacy asked. She and Emma were standing behind my parents. They both looked sick with worry, but they hadn't run away screaming. Bloody mess that I was, I gave them my best reassuring smile.

"Sure guys. Come on, let's go."

We all headed out, leaving behind five angry mall cops and a leering creepy janitor who was setting orange cones around the place where teardrops had bloodied the floor. On our way out of the food court we passed through a gauntlet of people, some of them shouting questions while other took pictures or used their phones to take video.

"Hey! Who are you?"

"What's your name?"

"Where's the wedding going to be?"

"Why were you crying blood?"

"What's happened to your skin? Why are you so pale!" and two or three idiot guys saying, "Don't marry him, marry me!"

Dan and I ignored them all, but one guy did try to reach out and touch me as we passed, which was a mistake. I didn't even have to think about moving; Dan reached out and pushed the guy away so fast no one even saw him do it. He looked like he'd fallen down all by himself.

Jane, I've got to go pick up my bag. I left it up on the roof of the mall. I'll meet you at the car.

When we stepped outside Dan let go of my hand and headed down the sidewalk by himself to a service alley that ran behind the food court stores.

"Where's Dan going?" Mom asked me.

"He has to go pick up his travel bag. He'll meet us at the car, Mom."

We began walking again and I could tell that Stacy and Emma were about to go crazy with questions.

Stacy started. "Did it hurt bad when he kissed you? I mean," she grimaced, "we could tell it hurt you both."

My parents who were leading the way glanced back at me. I could tell that they were just as interested in this question as Stacy was.

"It totally hurt like freakin' hell, and it was totally worth it. I can't wait to do it again."

Stacy had no fun comment to that. Grimly curious, she swallowed and asked, "Did it hurt Dan too?" I heard Dan in my head.

Yes, it hurt. But worth it. Totally worth it. Next time we need more privacy though. That way if we pass out we won't be taken to a hospital by the cops. I was so worried we would pass out I almost freaked.

Shit! I hadn't thought of that. It hurt me so bad I couldn't even see, but if we passed out that would have been bad. Real bad.

You're right, Dan, more privacy next time.

"It hurt Dan too. More that it hurt me," I answered but didn't give any details other than that. I wondered if Dan had to feel his pain and my pain through what we'd just done.

Yes, he answered back in my head but didn't give any other details.

I didn't want more details.

"Did you know that Dan was going to pop the question today?" Emma asked, trying to change the subject.

"Oh no! Dan totally surprised me. I had no idea he was going to do this."

Emma took a deep breath and I could tell she was about to go on a tirade and let me have it, but so could Stacy. "Be careful, Emms!" she whisper hissed. "There's a lot of crap going on here that we don't know about, so go easy on the tough love." That was all the caution Stacy could put into it because even my parents could see that Emma was about to go off on me. She surprised all of us by starting calmly.

"Jane, are you going to finish school? You're seventeen, and if you get married today what the hell are you gonna do? They don't do coed at PV. And where are you guys gonna live? With your parents? Have you even thought about any of this?" She pushed her head at me. "How bout a job, Jane? Does Dan have a job? Can he take care of you? I hope the hell he can because I know you've never had a job in your life. You've never even flipped burgers before, so how are you guys gonna make it?"

When we reached the car, Emma turned and leaned on the bumper and faced me, giving me the full force of her squinty eye glare. She hugged herself as she waited for my answers. Mom, Dad, and Stacy also waited. I was sure Emma voiced what they were all thinking but not willing to say.

"Emma, I'm not worried about finishing school. I'm not worried about where I'm gonna live or what job I'll have. I'm not worried about what's going to happen a year from now, or five years, or fifty. All I'm thinking about is today and making the most of it. I want today to be a beautiful day. And I wanted you and Stace to be a part of it."

I left unsaid that there might not be a tomorrow for me. In the distance I saw Dan emerge from the alley he'd gone down. He was carrying a large black bag and a backpack, walking toward us at a normal "human" speed so he wouldn't attract attention.

Emma began crying again. I gave Mom a "help!" look and she went to Emma and gave her a hug. Emma went stiff as a board. She didn't do hugs. She had a weird thing about personal space, but she endured the hug from my mother as she scrubbed her tears away with the backs of her wrists. Emma didn't like to cry.

"You've taken care of Jane for a long time," Mom said as she hugged her. "And I know she's your Jane too, but they've already decided this, and they love each other. And they're not going to wait, even if we both wish they would." Emma sniffled and rubbed at her eyes and stepped free of Mom's arms.

"Yeah, I know they love each other," Emma said a little bitterly, "I can see that, but I don't even know this guy! And I'm supposed to let him take Jane away? Just like that?" She started crying again. "That just sucks!" she wailed.

Dad tried, "Emma, if it makes you feel better, I like Dan too. This may sound horribly selfish of me to say, but I'm glad Dan has the same health problems as Jane. At least she won't be alone as she goes through this—these tests." He floundered uncertainly. "We don't know how long they'll be—" Dad was trying to keep our story straight, but he was also getting emotional. "And we have no idea how long Jane and Dan will be out of town seeing the specialists. It's good to know that Dan will be there with her. He won't leave her for a second. He'll take good care of Jane."

And that was when Dan walked up. Wordlessly, he opened the backpack and pulled out two envelopes. He handed one to Stacy and one to Emma. It looked like Dan had done some writing of his own last night. I leaned close to Emms as she read her card. Oh my God! It was a wedding invitation!

"No flippin' way, Jane." Stacy's eyes were as big as saucers as she read the card. "This invitation is for today at 5 p.m. You can't be serious! You just got the ring five minutes ago! And you're sick! Shouldn't you be going to the hospital right now?" she yelled.

"Bridesmaid!" Emma choked out as she read her invitation. "And you want us to call everyone and invite them to the wedding." She held up the card, like evidence. "This is crazy!" she shouted. "Straight jacket and rubber room certified! Come on, Jane, you don't want to rush this! It's your wedding day! You need to plan this thing out and get a real dress, and a cake, and a money tree, and—

and—and all that other crap!" Emma's eyes darted over to my parents who were standing there looking dazed and not quite right.

"You aren't going to let her do this. *Are you?*" Emma demanded. She expected them to say "NO!" and bring sanity back to the world, but Dad just smiled at her.

"We'll call you, Emma." He looked at me and my bloodstained face and chest for a second and his smile faded and he added, "But for now, girls, plan on everything happening *exactly* as the invitation says. But we really have to go. Jane and Dan need to get to their doctor's appointment. We'll call you. Okay?"

"What color dresses!?" Stacy asked quickly before we could climb into the car. "And what colors will the wedding be for the tables and all the other stuff!"

"Oh my God! I'm gonna faint," Mom said. Dad put an arm around her to hold her steady. "Oh, Jane, are we really, truly doing this today?" Mom gave me a panicked look.

I looked at Dan and studied his eyes, then said, "Yes, we are. I'm getting married today at 5 p.m."

Dan smiled down at me and that made me smile back.

"The colors for the wedding will be black, white, and red," I said to Stacy. "My dress will be white and so will Dan's tux, but everyone else, including the guests, will be in black. Please make the centerpieces red and please get lots of red roses for the tables and the hall and lots of red rose petals for the aisles." Everyone was staring at me like I'd lost it.

Stacy screwed up her face. "Black?" she said. "Seriously? For a wedding?"

"What?" I said defensively. "It's my wedding. If I want white, black, and red, then that's what I get." I made an angry pouty face and heard *he he he* in my head. Dan was laughing.

Stacy said, "God, Jane, how are we gonna pay for all of this?" Dan reached into his black bag and pulled out a roll of money and counted off three thousand in hundred dollar bills and handed it to a stunned Stacy. I listened to Dan in my head,

*Jane, ask them if they could find a dress comfortable enough for you to wear and something for me too. Not a tux. I don't think I could handle it. And since they're already here at the mall maybe they could do that now, before they go to the church to decorate. I've already rented the hall and arranged the catering for the reception, but I didn't do anything about the flowers yet. I didn't know what kind you would want. I hope this is all okay. I know I didn't ask about all this—I mean—*he gave me a tight smile—*I hope you're not mad.*

"Dan, how did you pay for all of this?" I asked him out loud.

I had twelve thousand in a savings account for college. That doesn't matter now. What matters is making the most out of today, like you said, Jane. But don't forget

the book. Remember, Sarah and Ethan get married before she became a vampire in the book. He shrugged, as if he were embarrassed. *I thought maybe we should too. That was all the excuse I needed to do this because I really, truly want to marry you. And not just because of the book, but because when we're together tonight I want you to be my wife, Jane. And when we die tonight, I want you to be my wife, and I'll be your husband, so even if we die for real and don't come back we'll still be together. Even in our graves.*

Dan looked down and turned away from me, like he was ashamed of that last part.

God, that sounds so damn horrible! he said, not looking at me. *I must be out of my mind. I'm sorry I said that. Sorry.*

"Dan." I waited for him to turn back around then walked over and slowly put my hands on each side of his face and pulled him down to me and lightly kissed his lips. It burned, but without Dan's arms around me I could think past the fire and feel the smooth texture of his lips. I opened my mouth, daring for more, and so did Dan. We trembled as the hot coals of our tongues met and mingled and we kissed for a minute before I pulled away with a gasp. I took a second to catch my breath.

"I feel the same way, Dan," I said, still panting as I stared into his eyes. "In this life, in the next life, or in the grave—*I will never leave you*! And I'm not sorry about it. Not one damn bit. I love you."

"A-hmm," Dad interrupted politely. We looked over to find Stacy and Mom, biting their bottom lips, grinning through their tears and hugging Emma who stood stiff as a board sandwiched between them. They were staring at Dan and me, totally caught up in our romantic moment.

"Jane, Dan," Dad held up his cell phone to show us the time, "We're already fifteen minutes late for our appointment at the doctor's office. You can call the girls and go over the wedding plans from the car, but right now we have to go. Now get in the car." It wasn't a request.

I said a last quick goodbye to Emma and Stacy. As soon as we got into the car Dad called the doctor to let him know we were going to be a little late, I called Stacy and Emma to make wedding plans, and Mom started calling relatives and family to invite them to my wedding. Even Dan was busy, texting away on his cell for all he was worth, his fingers flying across the little key pad of his phone.

I looked at everyone, busy, busy, busy and smiled. It was all working out. I was sure that my last day alive would be the best day I had ever lived. I was so happy I couldn't stop smiling.

Major Tom Benistin

Plans

"You weren't able to track her," Major Benistin spoke into his cell while the others at the conference table listened attentively to his half of the conversation. Dr. Tachi sat on one side of the table with Tompkins and Lankford who'd just returned from their failed attempt to capture the girl. Also on their side was Benistin's personal assistant, Agent Nicks, a petite, multi-tasking blond. Nicks was face down over her PDA in front of her, punching away on something important.

Across from them sat Agent Starks, Southeast Regional Director of the FBI. He was short, balding, in his mid-forties, and had been giving Benistin nothing but hell for the past hour, questioning every decision he made. Beside Starks sat Mr. Draper with the NSA and two other NSA agents, Crawford and Dr. Sangai.

Crawford was a clean cut but unremarkable man, brown hair, brown eyes, in his late-twenties and Dr. Sangai was a tall, imposing man of Asian decent. Sangai looked to be in his mid-thirties, dressed business casual, and was covered with tattoos that wrapped around his neck and showed on the tops of his hands, peeking out past his sleeves.

"Fine, I'll have AWAX cover the north Florida air space from Jacksonville to Daytona. Have all your people stay on high alert for any sign of our target while they get into position and call us immediately if you see anything." Benistin didn't end the call; he handed his cell to another assistant standing beside his chair who took the phone and started giving further instruction to whomever was on the other end of the conversation as he walked away from the conference table.

"So you lost her," Draper said in his scratchy voice. "Not a good start, Major."

Benistin ignored the comment. "Our last radar contact tracked her as she hovered at an altitude of 50 feet a short distance away from the house she stayed at last night. We had a brief moment of visual contact from the helicopter before she shot up to an altitude of 650 feet in less than a second where she hovered for another two minutes before vanishing off the radar."

Benistin winced as agent Starks spoke up again, "That can't be right, Benistin! There must be some hint of a direction or the ghost of an echo. She couldn't have vanished at 650. It's impossible. If she had stayed at 50 feet I could almost believe her vanishing into thin air, but no one vanishes off radar at 650. At that altitude they could track something as small as a seagull, there's just no way tha—"

"Starks!" Benistin cut him off with a grim frown and an iron gaze. The man had been a total pain in the ass for the past hour and Benistin was done wading through his endless, and pointless ramblings. "I'm tired or repeating myself every time some new fact develops that you can't rationalize analytically. We're all sitting around this table talking about a six foot blond that can break the laws of fucking gravity. She's already created a cloud creature that bit a chunk out of a building *which is impossible* and if our reports from the team that entered the house are accurate, she can control the weather *which is also impossible*. So. Yes, you unbelievably dense bastard, she vanished."

Starks went purple in the face and sputtered, "What! You can't talk to me like that, you arrogant son of a—"

"Shut up, Starks," Draper said. "The Major's right. You're wasting our time. So keep your mouth shut unless you can add something of value." He turned to Benistin. "Did they express an opinion on whether or not the AWAX radar would be able to track the girl, Major?"

Everyone pointedly ignored Starks who simmered in his own seat like a pot left to boil filled with crap opinions no one wanted to eat.

"They didn't think it would work, but it's the only option we have and we should try it before we write it off as useless. If air to ground radar can't pick her up, the only other option is to put a tracking device on the girl or in her."

"Major." Agent Tompkins waited for Benistin to give a nod before he continued. "When Lankford and I spoke with Sky this morning, she spotted the shooters in the front yard with the tag guns. She got pissed, sir. Real pissed. She thought the tag guns were tranq guns. She thought we were going to drug her."

Agent Lankford smoothed down his gray mustache as he added, "We tried to calm her down. We told her that we weren't going to drug her and she didn't believe us." He glanced at his notepad. "Her exact words were, 'Why all the drugs? You're gonna try to drug me!'" Lankford flipped his notepad closed. "This matches her reaction to the nurse at the clinic who tried to give her some pain medication for her split chin. The girl yelled at her and said that she didn't want any drugs."

"Makes perfect sense to me," Tachi chimed in with his take. "We believe the girl's mother has kept her in an endless haze since she was eight years old, but to enter the Derm 513 study, the Hans would have had to take her off all her other meds. I'm sure they administered a thorough drug test to verify that her system was clean before the start of the study. That's standard practice for a clinical trial. Apart from the Derm 513, Sky hasn't had mood-altering psychotropics for over three weeks. Her entire life has been colored and rounded by these drugs and now all of that is simply gone. She will be highly unstable, both physically and mentally."

"Which brings up a damn good point," Starks interjected his opinion again. "Why the hell didn't we tranquilize her this morning when we had her on the ground? This situation would be contained if we had." He gave Benistin a critical look. His voice taunted, "Did you not have the balls to make that call, Benistin? You have three daughters about her age, so maybe you have reservations about tranqing the girl?"

Benistin laughed. It was the first sign that his face held any expression other than an iron grimace.

"Starks, if we shot her with a tranq dart and she got airborne all we would have is a dead body. We are dealing with a 'flying girl.' When she feels threatened she's not going to go hide in a closet or drive off in a car, she's going to go straight up. And she's not going to listen to threats or be rational about her decision either. Just like the doctor said, she's mentally unstable, and if she passed out at 650 feet that would be a problem. Wouldn't it?"

Starks nodded, then looked away, embarrassed at his own failure to grasp the complexities of the situation.

"Sir," Nicks spoke with her eyes glued to her PDA, "Our team in the field has finished searching the house; they got the girl's cell phone. She left it in the house when she took off. We already know the only person she called with the phone was her father, but there was one number programed into the phone. It's Dr. Burgis's cell phone number. He's the doctor running the drug study."

Dr. Tachi spoke again. "He probably gave her the cell so she could call him directly if she experienced any side effects or adverse reactions to the Derm drugs. After meeting Sky's parents I'm not surprised that the doctor gave the girl a cell to reach him directly. I'm sure he didn't trust the mother to contact him if there were any problems."

"Sir," Nicks said, "Sky has a doctor's appointment at one p.m. this afternoon with Dr. Burgis."

"Here we go!" Benistin said, enlivened by the news. "I want people there now, and I want eyes and ears in every room in that office." He looked over at Draper and the others from the NSA. "Mr. Draper, open this doctor up. His house, office, financials, contacts, history, *everything*."

"My pleasure," Draper replied with an affable grin.

"Also, I want the Han family home in Ormond Beach secured. I want undercover operatives inside and out and placed at any nearby McDonald's or other places where she seems likely to land. I also want the Hans' employees, past and present, that have had any contact with Sky processed and questioned as to whether she's ever shown signs of flight before these past few days. She's fallen and almost killed herself trying to fly on a number of occasions. We know that. But what I wanna know is what we 'don't know.' If she's ever even hovered for a split second at some point in the past I wanna know about it! When it was. Who saw it. How it happened and why!"

Major Benistin looked back to Draper. "Any thoughts, Mr. Draper?"

With a glance, Draper shifted the offer to the two men he sat with. Crawford went first.

"I'll prepare the tracking items for everyone who has any chance to come into contact with the girl. Clothing, pens, cell phones, and other items to help us track her."

Dr. Sangai said, "You should use the father. The girl has a better relationship with her father than her mother. Have him go to the doctor's office and wait for her there. If the girl shows up she'll talk to him. She's half American, but she's had a somewhat traditional, if eccentric, childhood. She respects him." His tone implied a cultural significance. "It would be good to have Mr. Han return the cell phone she left behind, of course with a tracking device in it. It's an item she's already familiar with and her father could tell her that he wants her to keep it so he can stay in touch with her and know she's all right."

Benistin's eyebrows arched up in respect. "Damn, that's good. That's real good. Let's do it."

Dr. Burgis

Just Another Day at the Office

Dr. Burgis leaned on the wall outside his exam room and tried to act *casual* and *nonchalant* as he waited for Katie Lin to emerge from the girl's restroom. The exam room he was accidentally (intentionally) guarding was the only room in his entire office that hadn't been bugged by their unexpected morning visitor. Dr. Burgis fought the clenching tightness in his gut, his jittery, frayed nerves and his own instinctual "fight or flight" compulsion. His sense of self-preservation screamed "RUN!" and yet here he stayed, a captive to curiosity. He chuckled to himself grimly as he considered the old proverb about a cat, curiosity, and the rather sticky end that was visited upon said animal—

"I have no special talents, I am only passionately curious." The quote from Einstein intruded itself into his thoughts. Burgis considered this bit of mental minutia in relation to his own quandary. He attempted to digest the soup in his head and make a morning meal of it as he patiently waited for his own sticky end.

But what is man without curiosity? he mused. *An empty hollow shell, deserving of nothing more than a sticky end. How ironic.* He punctuated this conclusion with a grim chuckle. At the very least, today would be a very memorable day, and at the most—who knew, but he planned on being here to see it.

The man posing as a fire marshal emerged from a room down the hall, his eyes shifty and calculating, face all business until he spotted the doctor outside the last unmolested room. A fake smile sprang into existence. He reached for the prop tucked under his arm, forgotten until needed. The man flourished the clipboard with its official looking inspection form as he pretended to record his findings.

"All finished, everything seems in order." He continued scribbling, trying too hard to sell it.

Dr. Burgis resisted the urge to go over and look at what he'd written. Probably just gibberish, his kids' names, his own address, maybe what he'd like to eat for lunch.

"Good to know the building's up to code. Thank you for making your inspection a quick visit. Have a good day." Dr. Burgis returned a fake smile of his own and watched as the fake fire marshal left his office with his fake form.

Katie, his first study patient of the day, came out of the restroom. She was a short, mousy girl with huge eyes. While not a great beauty, she was cute, kind, and easy to like. Today she'd put her brown hair up in ponytails that stuck out to either side of her head and made her look like a child. Katie was mildly schizophrenic in a way that affected her speech patterns and O.C.D. in a way that kept her or her hands moving and active until she crashed. She was a sweet girl, obsessed with art of any kind, especially painting.

And, as he'd expected, Katie's artistic abilities had improved exponentially because of the drugs. Now she could easily be the most gifted human artist who had ever lived. Sadly, as amazing as her talent was, it was still just "painting." Impressive, but not supernatural in and of itself. Dr. Burgis had given Katie pictures of the twelve teens in the drug study and a picture of himself from which she created an oil painting collage with him and the twelve teens. The painting was an absolute masterpiece. Dr. Burgis planned on taking the painting with him when he made his escape this afternoon. If he managed to escape that is.

"I still can't believe I did that in just one evening. I just saw it in my head and then 'bam! bam! bam!' it all came together." Katie's big bright eyes studied the painting Burgis held in his arms. She was having a very good morning. Overjoyed at the emergence of her amazing new talents and because of her face, which had cleared up overnight, just like magic.

Dr. Burgis gave himself a shake, breaking away from lingering thoughts of "escape" to focus on his enthusiastic artist.

"It appears that your artistic talents have blossomed now that your face has cleared up and you have this new wave of self-confidence. You simply had to start believing in yourself, Katie. I'm sure the talent was inside you all along, waiting to get out. I'm very happy for you, my girl, and I truly do love my painting. I will cherish it for as long as I live," he said sincerely, wondering as he said it how long that span might be.

Another shake. He gave Katie another smile. "I can't thank you enough."

Katie surprised him with a big hug. "I still can't believe how great my face looks now, but to be able to paint like this is totally awesome. Presents! Presents! Presents! It's like getting Christmas presents on my birthday!" She laughed at her own wit. "Thank you! Thank you! Thank you!" She punctuated each "thank you" with a good squeeze which finally infected Dr. Burgis and had him laughing there in the hall in spite of his frayed nerves.

"That sounds like one very happy patient, doctor," said Nurse Ann from the side office where she was weighing her least favorite patient, Benjamin Grant, and getting him ready for the doctor.

"Yes. A very happy patient indeed. Just what we like to see," said Burgis as he herded Katie toward the waiting room.

"Doctor Burgis." Ann caught him before he got away. "Jane's father called and said they were running a little late. He mentioned that he also has Dan Simmons with him in the car. They should be here in about twenty minutes."

"How did they sound on the phone, Ann?" Burgis pulled out his handkerchief and wiped at his brow. "Were they calm or distressed? You know Jane had a bad day yesterday. And a bad night."

"Bad" was a huge understatement. Dr. Burgis was dreading this meeting with Jane and her parents. He wasn't exactly sure what would come and see him today, but it didn't sound good. The scientist in him was devilishly excited about the changes her parents described, but the small part of him that was still basically a caring human being was experiencing a gut-wrenching twist of conscience. To change a sweet girl like Jane Miller into a psychotic blood-crazed monster was the epitome of evil. A curious man could be a danger to himself he mused, and a nightmare to those chosen to satisfy that curiosity. The doctor swallowed at the lump in his throat and started listening to Ann's words again.

"…seemed a little stressed but he was quite calm on the phone. And I heard the others in the car talking. It seemed like everything was okay." Ann gave Burgis a tight smile. She'd overheard some of the crazed call left on the office answering machine by the Millers when they had called a little after 1 a.m.

"They sounded much better than I expected. Much better than last night anyway," Ann said hopefully.

"As always, thank you, Ann. Thank you."

Dr. Burgis turned his attention back to Katie Linn.

"Sorry I'm so distracted this morning, Katie," he apologized as he guided Katie toward the waiting room. "Don't forget, straight to lunch. You remember how shaky you got yesterday, so get some food in your system right away. And thank you again for the beautiful painting, it's absolutely wonderful." Dr. Burgis pushed open the doors for Katie and froze. A police officer was opening the outside door for Rain and Ryan Bryant.

"See you tomorrow, Dr. Burgis," Katie called as she met up with her mother.

Distracted and half panicked, Burgis looked back to Katie and her mother. "Oh, yes, see you tomorrow, my dear," he said absentmindedly, his attention focused behind Katie where Rain, Ryan, and the police officer were standing by the door, talking. Maybe this police officer wasn't here for him after all, he dared to hope.

He noticed that Rain Bryant's appearance had altered drastically. She was wearing a spectacular Victorian-style dress, but colored in her usual black. And the dress matched the girl. Rain's hair was longer now, and a more brilliant shimmering shade of blue/black. Her makeup, nails, and shoes were all impressive, but surprisingly the forehead tattoo from yesterday that she'd been so taken with was absent.

Ryan, on the other hand, other than his clear complexion, looked exactly the same. His usual happy, smiling self. He and his sister listened to the black police officer who appeared to be telling a lively story of some kind. They all seemed happy and at ease.

"Rain Bryant," Dr. Burgis called as he stood there in the doorway to the exam rooms. Her head snapped around and looked his way, but she did not look pleased. Her eyes narrowed to thin angry slits and her mouth turned down in a menacing glower.

"Easy now!" said the officer, noticing her hostile reaction, as had Ryan. They both moved to quell her temper. Dr. Burgis watched, confused and curious as Ryan and the officer carefully and delicately took Rain in hand, turned her around and led her back to a chair and had her sit down. They worked as a team. The officer stayed with her and kept her attention as Ryan hurried over.

"Hi, Dr. Burgis," Ryan said, wearing a strained smile. "If I could go first that would be best. We need to talk about Rain."

Dr. Burgis waited for more explanation, but Ryan stood there, waiting, offering nothing.

"Very well," Burgis conceded. "Come on back, Ryan, and you can tell me what's happening with your sister. Should be an interesting story if it explains why you have a police officer with you."

Ryan let out a small humorless laugh. "Interesting. Yeah, you could say that, doc."

They headed toward the exam rooms together, and Dr. Burgis stopped at the nurse's room where Benjamin Grant was waiting for him.

"Ann, I hate to ask, but could you please keep Mr. Grant for a few minutes? I need some time alone with Mr. Bryant."

Ryan leaned into the doorway as well. "Hey, Ann, when you see Rain, *please* use her new name. When you talk to her call her Rain, or Black Rain, but don't call her Rain Bryant. She gets real upset when you call her Rain Bryant. Just call her Rain, that would be best."

"Black Rain!" Benjamin's huge voice in the small space made everyone jump. He leaned forward on the undersized patient bed he was sitting on and continued his loud and excited dialogue generously sprinkled with colorful metaphors which was his usual mode of communication.

"Holy Shit! *Your* sister is Black Rain! And she's really out there in the waiting room right now? I can't fucking believe it! Black Rain is really here!" The oversized teen cast his eyes in the direction of the waiting room, the corner of his mouth curling into a smile. His gaze snapped back to Ryan. "Hey man, introduce me to her. When I saw her on the news I thought she looked familiar. I can't fucking believe she's here." Benjamin shook his head dumbly. "I mean I know she—"

"NO!" Ryan cut him off, disgusted. "Just leave her alone, Benjamin! I mean it. The police won't let you near her anyway, and neither would I. And stop cussing in front of Ann, you jerk. She's a lady and shouldn't have to hear filth like that!" Ryan tossed that at him along with an angry, offended glare.

Benjamin's big shoulders bounced up and down as he chuckled quietly, like a big bear amused by someone poking at it with a stick.

"Benjamin, what are you raving about?" Dr. Burgis asked. "What on earth is going on!?"

Benjamin and Ryan both looked at him, surprised at his ignorance.

"Don't you watch the news?" Benjamin asked.

"Well, not last night, no. I can't say that I did." Dr. Burgis looked over to Nurse Ann who shook her head *no*.

"I just fed the kids, did some sewing, and went to bed." Ann looked to Ryan. "Well, Ryan, what has happened to your sister that made her change her name?"

"And made the news!?" asked Burgis. "And landed you with a police escort?" he added as he adjusted his glasses.

"I'll try to give you the short version," Ryan said. "Which means about ten minutes, and prince charming here doesn't need to hear it." Ryan pointed at Benjamin.

"Oh man! Come on! I'm sorry. I'll keep my big mouth shut and be nice," Benjamin pleaded.

Dr. Burgis let out a doubtful grunt, "Go ahead and start working up Ryan for me, Ann, and I'll take care of Benjamin now so he can be on his way. Ryan, I'll be back for the rest of this story shortly. Come along, Benjamin, let's get your pills ready." Dr. Burgis turned and headed toward his one useable exam room.

"Damn," Benjamin said as he slid his huge muscled frame off the short exam bed and gathered his cell phone and keys off the counter. He paused at the door and turned back to Ryan. "If I said *please* would you give me you sister's phone number?"

"No way," Ryan said. "Just stay away from my sister."

"What if I gave you my sister's phone number in exchange? She's a cheer-leader," Benjamin offered with a sick smile.

Ann shut the door in his face.

Benjamin chuckled to himself as he followed Dr. Burgis into his exam room. He had no intention of missing his chance to see Black Rain. He couldn't wait to get out to the waiting room. Her brother was just being a dick. An overprotective dick. Rain would probably give him her phone number herself if he asked for it.

Yeah. Yeah, she would.

Black Rain

Revelations

"I'm sorry. I don't know why it pisses me off so bad when someone gets my name wrong. I don't understand it!" I said as Williams sat down in the chair across from me. I was still shaking I was so mad. God, what's wrong with me! So what? So he used the wrong name and called me Rain Bryant. Why is that a big deal?

I closed my eyes and put my face in my hands and tried to calm down by looking at the back of my eyelids. After a few deep breaths I started to feel better, calmer. I kept my eyes closed and studied the darkness on the back side of my eyes and rubbed my forehead where my mark would be if my sisters were with me.

I was worried about them. I hoped they were okay. This was the first time for each of us on our own since we all started having accidents. I hoped they were doing better than I was. I rubbed my index finger where my mark should be. It felt weird not having it there.

"You all right, witch girl?" Williams asked gently.

I nodded with my eyes closed. "I'm okay. Sorry. And thank you for taking care of me." I took another deep breath, opened my eyes, and looked up at him. "Do you think I'm crazy Williams?" I asked him. Honestly, I was getting worried about myself. How do you know if you're crazy?

Williams couldn't hide his reluctance. He tugged at his collar, stalling. After an uncomfortable minute he nodded and then leaned forward in his chair across from me, elbows on knees and brows pushed together, scowling. By the look on his face I knew that he was about to answer my question as honestly as he could. I leaned in with him and mirrored him—knees, brows, scowl.

"Well now. The witches I knew from back home all had some things that set them off and it seemed like each one was different."

"Really?" I said doubtfully. "They were witches? *Real* witches?"

He gave me a dirty look. "They were real witches, girl. Not like you, but they were witches all the same. Now hush and let me finish. You still want me to answer your question?"

I nodded, muttering a chastened "sorry."

Williams grunted and continued. "My Aunt Mertyl, she was one seriously mean witch!" He paused to bug his eyes out at me to get his point across. "For some reason kids just set her off something fierce and made her crazy. Everyone in the county knew better than to let their kids anywhere near Mertyl or her house. My momma didn't even let me see her until I was fourteen and big enough to look grown, but Aunt Mertyl did her part too and put up signs and such. And she did her best to stay away from kids."

"My God, Williams, that's horrible. Is that supposed to make me feel better or worse?" I complained and so did my face. What the hell was he saying? Was I going to turn into a child eating old hag? Like the witch that tried to eat Hansel and Gretel?

Williams didn't blink or back down. "No, witch girl. I don't want to make you feel worse, but you asked me a question. And you're a witch. And I know better than to lie to a witch." He gave me a look that said everything. He'd already made his mistake and from now on he was going by whatever rule book his family had beaten into him when he was a child. Apparently telling lies to a witch was a bad, bad thing.

Williams kept going, "And then there was Old Miss Luezza, what set her off was anyone that was in love. God she hated to see it." Williams shook his head, his far off look remembering Miss Luezza. "She'd get all kinds of pissed off when she saw two people makin' eyes at each other. When I was fifteen, me and my friend Milt was out one afternoon, hanging out downtown, walking the shops, and Milt had his girlfriend Shila with him. They were holdin' hands and makin' eyes at each other and they bumped right into Old Miss Luezza because they were too busy moonin' to watch where they were walking." Williams didn't say what happened, but I could tell he remembered it and it wasn't good. He looked back at me.

"I read what you wrote on that bathroom mirror, witch girl. Rain Marie Bryant is dead. And you said you killed her. I don't understand it, and I don't want to know how you killed yourself. That's your business. Anyway, it's not against the law to kill yourself, or to kill your own child if it's still inside of you when you do it. You killed the only two people you could kill and still not go to jail for murder. And what's worse is, I think you loved both of the people you killed."

I was shocked. I knew that Williams had been in the bathroom, but I didn't think about him or anyone else reading what I had written on the mirror. Everyone knew. I felt hot and cold at the same time. Flushed, but with a cold chill sliding slowly down my spine one vertebrae at a time until my whole body was tingling numb.

Williams was right.

I had killed them. The only two people I could kill and not go to jail. Myself and my unborn child.

Williams patted my hand. "Even if you weren't a witch, killing two people that you love is bound to make you a little crazy. But you are a witch." He sounded sad. "So you may be more than a little crazy. I'm sorry, witch girl, but it's true." Williams was sweating. He took out his handkerchief and wiped his face and neck.

I felt numb. Cold, numb, and shocked.

"So the answer to my question is—yes," I said calmly.

I was crazy.

Williams started rambling on about how I was doing my best, how I was trying, letting people help me, on and on—

I wasn't really listening anymore. I let my thoughts drift away. I was crazy. Goosebumps rose up on my arms, the little hairs standing up. I thought I would be more afraid of going mad, but somehow, now that I knew, I wasn't.

"I'm crazy," I whispered.

Williams was still frantically talking, trying to undo whatever he thought he'd done, but he couldn't. He was right. I didn't try to deny or run from it. I did think about it though.

When did I go crazy?

It had to be that day. That day at the clinic. I remember. That was the first time that I had talked to myself and answered myself.

"Oh," I said out loud. That was when it happened. Rain Marie had asked me for help because she couldn't do it, she couldn't go through with it. I remember. Rain Marie spoke to me—and I spoke back to her. She begged me to help her. I didn't like thinking about that day. I didn't like thinking about any of this; my mind didn't want to go there for some reason. I wondered why it bothered me so much, and then I realized with a jolt of comprehension, that somewhere inside me, some part of me still thought I was really Rain Marie. Some hidden part of me didn't believe I was a separate person.

Think! I had to think! I forced myself to think about it. I wanted to KNOW! To examine the pieces and parts and figure this out. I closed my eyes to block out Williams and his attempts to get my attention as I thought it through. I didn't remember clearly what had happened. I remember that we spoke on that day. I didn't know if "I" had always been inside Rain Marie, sharing her life the whole time, or if that was my first day of life and I just took over where she left off.

I didn't know where I came from or how I came to be, but I knew that I wasn't Rain Marie. We were different people. And I spoke with her again just yesterday in the mirror, and she was happy and safe in heaven with Brendon. She wanted to go back, and she said she wanted me to live a good life. But what I didn't understand was how she found me again. After I had the abortion she begged me to push her out and take her place so she could go be with Brendon.

But somehow she had come back? Had I not pushed far enough? Was I still connected to her somehow? Ever since that day I hadn't felt like a complete person. If anything, I felt like a trespasser trapped inside of another person, only that other person was dead and gone. Like a living snake trapped inside a dead skin that still clung to it. I searched inward, down inside myself, down to my soul.

I thought about my soul. If only I could see it or feel it. Still with my eyed closed, there, within me, down inside of "me" I felt—*something*. It wasn't something I felt with hands, but I still felt it there. A warm glow of life, sitting within me, and connected to it was a cord, or a rope, connecting me to other things. Things of this life.

I felt the cord. This must be how Rain Marie had found me.

Even though she was dead and gone, she was still tied to me. I wondered what it felt like to have me here while she was up there in heaven. Did I feel like an anchor on her soul, weighing her down, sapping her joy? Was she forever looking over her shoulder? She'd been so upset to find herself back here. It broke my heart to see her cry. I needed to make sure it didn't happen again.

And she was happy where she was with Brendon, in heaven. I felt the tie again, this strange spiritual cord. I didn't understand what it was but I worried that Rain Marie and maybe even Brendon could still feel me here, through this connection. It was one thing for me to suffer, or even Rain Marie, but I didn't want Brendon to have to deal with any of our mess, he was innocent.

I thought about this cord or connection that tied my soul to them, and I willed it to be cut, severed. An odd sensation of movement passed through me and I knew it was done. I wasn't in pain, but I did feel *odd*, unlike anything I had ever felt before. I felt alone. Finally, it was just me. I could still remember Rain Marie's life and all her memories like they were my own. And I could remember the past eighteen months we had shared, somehow connected by that invisible strand—but now it was just me.

What was I now? Who was I? The words came out of my mouth without me having to think about it.

"I am Black Rain, a murderer, and a Black Witch."

I opened my eyes.

Williams was out of his chair, standing a few feet away, watching me. He looked ready to draw his weapon. I didn't feel up to getting shot, so I thought about Williams' gun turning into dust inside his holster. A metallic powder started to leak from the gun shaped black holster.

Instead of standing up, I just thought about rising from the chair and I "floated" up, out of the chair, landing lightly on my feet. I was numb and unfeeling for a moment after cutting whatever it was I'd cut, but now feeling was coming back into me. My skin was tingling and my hair was moving around like it was touched by static electricity or some invisible breeze that I could feel but couldn't see.

"Williams," I said and gave him a little smile. "It's okay. I won't hurt you."

Right then the front office door opened and a tall Asian man walked into the waiting room. I'd seen him here before. He was the tall blond girl's father. Sky's father. He scanned the room and gave me a quick disapproving look and Williams a downright hateful glare before he selected a chair facing the door. He looked upset. Ragged. I guess it was just one of those days for everyone.

"What the hell?" Williams noticed the sand and powder leaking from his gun holster. He unsnapped the holster and looked inside then looked at me.

I shrugged.

He shrugged.

I laughed, then he started laughing too. I made a conscious mental effort to tone down the power coming from my body and felt my hair lie back down and behave. Geesh.

"You should not even be here!" Sky's father barked at Williams with venom from over where he sat. The unexpected voice directed at him made Williams jump. We both looked at Sky's furious father and back at each other. We had mirrored expressions of *What the hell's up with him?* but we didn't have to wait long for an explanation.

"You will scare my daughter away! She won't come with you in here and your police car parked right out front, so get the hell out, now!" He said it like he was sure of himself. And it was as if his words summoned help magically because the front door opened again and a guy in a suit, definitely a cop or something, walked right over to Williams.

"Officer, why are you here?" he asked as he held up his badge for Williams to read.

Williams looked the badge over for just a second. "Protective custody. I've been assigned to this girl. I'm sorry, sir, but I can't leave her." Williams was being very respectful and professional.

He looked at both of us then said to Williams, "Your presence here is endangering a federal investigation. There are agents all around this building. I assure you that we will keep an eye on—what was your name, miss?" he asked me.

I smiled and laughed a full-throated laugh and the lights overhead dimmed and flickered like they laughed with me. Williams smiled, shaking his head, waiting to see how I treated this new guy.

"My name is Black Rain," I said and noticed the look on the agent's face. He'd heard of me. Good. He looked me up and down for an appraising second, seeing me again for the first time.

"Good to meet you—Black Rain." He stumbled over the strange name and over the unexpected need for tact and then turned back to Williams.

"Officer, we really need to have this room cleared and we need to move that cruiser out front immediately. If you feel like you can't leave 'Black Rain' here alone, then please take her with you and go, but we need you, her, and that cruiser gone. Now." This guy was serious.

"Williams, give him your keys and he can drive your car away." I looked at the agent. "And you, give Williams your sport coat. He can button it up. He'll look normal enough."

Williams didn't hesitate. He pulled his keys out and handed them to the agent. "Sir, your jacket please." He made a "gimme" gesture with his hands.

The agent looked undecided for just a second then took his jacket off. He quickly unloaded all the crap he had in the pockets.

"I want this back when we're done here, Officer." He wasn't happy but he was quick. As soon as he handed the jacket to Williams he dashed out the door. We saw the cruiser pull away a few second later.

Williams slipped his arms through the jacket and buttoned it.

"That was weird, Williams. And for once I didn't do it. I know I'm crazy, but I don't think this had anything to do with me," I said with a happy smile.

"I think you're right," Williams said as he walked me toward the back of the waiting room where we would be mostly out of sight.

"Nice jacket," I said.

"What, this old thing?" Williams chuckled as we took our seats.

"Sorry about your gun, but you were all freaked out. It looked like you were thinking about shooting me," I said.

"Well can you blame me!?" Williams said defensively. "You got all spooky and stopped talking, then my skin started to crawl like when you're too close to a lightning strike. Then you started to float out of your damn chair and your hair was all flyin' around like some scene out of *The Exorcist*. Damn straight I was freaked out!" He finished indignantly. "Who wouldn't be freaked out?"

We sat in companionable silence for a minute or two as Williams looked me over and then said, "You're looking better. Are you feelin' better now, Black Rain?"

"What's this?" I said. "I'm not 'witch girl' anymore?" I teased gently. I didn't know why, but Williams was treating me differently.

"No." He rolled his shoulders in the unfamiliar coat. "You're still 'witch girl,' but you're also Black Rain," he said. "Don't go off on me again, but what brought all that on? I mean. I just want to know so I can be sure not to do it again. Whatever it was." He was being very cautious, but he was too curious not to ask.

"Hmm" was my comment.

"Well?" he prompted and raised his eyebrows.

"I'm not sure you'll like the answer to that question, Officer Williams. It may frighten you."

He could tell that I was serious. He licked his lips. After a minute he asked again. "I think I should know what happened. Something has changed and I want to know. Why did you go all weird? What's changed? Oh shit. I'm getting that creepy feeling again." Williams started to rub his arms like he was cold. "Tell me what's changed, Black Rain."

I breathed in air and breathed out power. I felt it all around me, tickling my skin, crawling down the strands of my hair, making it play and dance on little invisible winds of energy. I felt warm.

"You will think less of me, Officer Williams," I said.

He was about to say that he wouldn't but stopped himself. His upbringing kept him from arguing with me. If I said it would make him think less of me, I was probably right.

"I still want to know what happened." he asked again.

307

I smiled at him and said, "Very well. You asked. So mote it be. I will not hide what I am. As within, so without."

I thought about how to tell him what had happened, how best to explain it, at least as far as I understood it myself.

"You've seen those big inflated balloon figures that they use in parades? Like they have in New York on Thanksgiving? The kind that are so big that it takes a hundred or more people on the ground holding ropes to keep it from flying away?"

Williams nodded. "Sure. I've seen it. There are lots of those things, like that big Snoopy balloon. Great big giant things. What has that got to do with you?" he asked. He was focused. Trying very hard to understand.

"Picture me as a float in the parade with a hundred ropes holding me to the earth. On the day I killed my child and Rain Marie Bryant I cut away ninety five ropes. But I was still tied to the earth. On the day I became a Black Witch, I cut another four ropes. I thought that nothing was left tying me down, but I was wrong, Officer Williams. You see, I still thought I was sane. And I thought I was in control and alone, when the whole time a part of me was still tied to Rain Marie Bryant. But I'm not sane. Am I? I stopped lying to myself. I accepted it. And I cut the last rope inside me that tied me to the earth. The last rope that tied me to a human life. The last rope that tied me to Rain Marie." I reached up and felt my eyes. I was crying. I looked up at Williams. His eyes were glassy, like he was about to cry too.

"But why should this make me frightened? I already knew you were a Black Witch," Williams asked quietly.

"A very good question." I nodded. "That last rope was the last part of Rain Marie. You should be afraid because the last of her is gone. You don't know me now." I breathed in air and breathed out power. I'd felt powerful before, but this was new. This was more. This power was all around me and in everything I touched. Even the air moving in and out of my lungs.

"I don't even know myself," I mused. "When I was still tied to Rain Marie there were things I wouldn't do, couldn't do." I held my hand palm up in front of me. I thought about the sand in his holster and on the carpeted floor coming together in my hand and becoming the gun again. The gun, but no bullets.

Sand drifted out of Williams' holster in a snakelike line and a cloud of sand drifted up from the carpet and they both met and took the shape of a gun in my hand.

"My gun," Williams whispered as he stared at the weapon. I handed him the gun.

"Be careful, Officer." I smiled at him. "You wouldn't want to shoot me on accident, would you?"

Williams' eye kept twitching. His hand shook on the gun, as slowly, very slowly, he eased it back into his holster.

"So what happens now?" he asked.

That was another good question. My eyebrows bunched together. "Crap. I guess I have to find out what it means to be Me. This will be new." I looked around the waiting room like I was seeing it again for the first time. "I have no idea what happens now. All I know is who I am. Not what I'll do or even why I'll do it." And right then my stomach growled. "Damn, I'm hungry." I put my hands over my stomach and Williams laughed nervously.

It was such a human thing, having your stomach growl. It was reassuring in a weird way. For a second there I didn't know if I would need to eat anymore, or ever—

The front office doors opened and Sky walked in.

"Sky," her father said from his chair. He stayed seated and didn't move toward her. Sky froze in the doorway as if she hadn't decided if she would stay or turn around and run away.

"What are you doing here?" she said, scanning the waiting room. Her eyes passed right over me but lingered on Williams for a second or two before she turned and looked around the mostly empty parking lot behind her.

"Sky, no one is going to grab you. I promise. I won't let them. Do you want me to let the doctor know that you are here for your appointment or do you want me to stay in my seat?" Her father was being exceedingly careful. Polite. Like Sky might bolt at any second.

I had the hint of a smile touching the corner of my mouth as I watched the strange show. Not because I delighted in human suffering now that I was all witched up, but this was like watching dinner theater. Really, really good drama! And it wasn't even mine! Cool.

They started talking back and forth in Chinese, which sucked. Williams sighed and put on a disappointed frown; he'd been into it too. I thought about the words, wanting Williams and me to be able to understand them.

Williams shot me a quick surprised glance when in mid-sentence we could understand what they were saying again. They were speaking in Chinese, but we understood it as if they were speaking in English. Williams didn't freak at all. We both tuned back into the show already in progress.

"…your mother is fine, Sky. They asked her to go back to our house and wait there in case you went home. I wanted to wait here." Sky's father pulled out a cell phone from his pocket. "I have your cell phone; you left it at Miss Bethenda's house. I would like to be able to call you and I would feel better if I knew that you could also call me. I am worried about you, Sky." He held the cell phone out and waited.

Sky looked back to the parking lot then over at us.

I waved and said, "Hi."

Sky looked at Williams and back to me. "Is he a cop?" She spoke in English now and nodded toward Williams.

I looked at Williams and he just shrugged.

"Yeah," I said, "But he's here for me. Not for you. They made him put that jacket on so he wouldn't look all copish and scare you off, but he's not allowed to leave me." I said it matter of factly and waited to see what she would do.

Sky looked Williams over. "Take off the jacket," she said suspiciously.

Williams stood slowly, unbuttoned the jacket and took it off, showing his white police shirt, pants, and belt, then slowly sat back down. We could both see Sky's father shooting us nasty looks behind his daughter's back but he kept quiet. Waiting.

"Why do you need a cop?" Sky looked over at her Dad. "Father, please tell the doctor that I'm here for my appointment." He nodded, stood in slow motion, and began to slowly walk his way over to the little glass window. Sky's eyes darted around like a frightened animal but she took another few steps towards us. She didn't give me a chance to answer her first question before she asked another three, quick as a flash.

"Are there any other cops inside? How many did you see? Are they after you too?"

I guess she thought I was trustworthy now that I'd ratted out Williams. I tried to answer some of what she had asked.

"I've only been here for about fifteen minutes, and I haven't seen any cops except for one guy who walked in and made Williams put on that jacket so he wouldn't scare you away. They also made him move his cop car so you wouldn't see it when you got here."

She thought about that for a second then asked, "Have you been in to see the doctor yet?"

"No. My brother Ryan is back there with him right now. You remember Ryan, tall, cute, brown hair, smiles a lot. He helped you out yesterday when you and your mom were fighting."

"Oh. Yeah. Your brother was nice to me," she said sadly.

"He's always nice," I agreed. I noticed Sky's skin was better. It looked like her bad skin days were done, although she did have a nasty looking gash running down her chin that made me wonder what kind of trouble she was in. Had the cops done that to her or had it been her crazy mother?

"The pills really worked great for you," I said as I continued to study her. She looked confused by that innocent comment for some reason so I added, "Your skin, Sky, it looks fantastic now."

Her face darkened even more and she shook her head at me like I'd lied to her for some strange reason.

"That's not what the pills do. They're not really pills for your face."

What? Okay. I had to ask. "Then what do the pills do?"

Sky's father was walking back from the window where we could see Nurse Ann sliding the glass shut. Sky looked back at him and narrowed her eyes. It was plain to see that he wanted to walk over to his daughter, but he stopped and sank down into his chair on the other side of the room and waited. Sky turned back to me.

"They are believing pills. Whatever you believe in they make you believe it more. But that's the blue pill, the blue pill is the 'believing pill.' The white pills do other things," she said in a rush and shot another furtive glance toward her father, then out the window again, scanning for cops.

"Believing pill?" My face showed my confusion. I was trying to make some sense of that but couldn't sort it out. Sky was so wired and talking so fast it was hard to hear what she said let alone understand her. She sure seemed serious though. I remembered the guy who came inside and flashed his badge at Williams. He'd been an FBI agent, not just a regular cop.

"So the pills aren't *really* Derm pills?"

Sky opened her mouth to talk, then her eyes darted to Williams, and she clammed up. She didn't want to say more in front of Williams.

"Williams, go sit over there," I told him. "We need some privacy. You're still a cop, even if you are *my* cop."

I waved him off. "Shoo. Ya. Skit. Over there." I pointed to the other side of the room.

Williams gave me an offended look as he got up. "Fine. Be that way. But you keep this up and I'm not paying for lunch!" he griped as he stalked away.

Sky kept a hard eye on him as he passed by and Williams also kept his distance. He was treating her like a deer that might spook and run if you made a sudden move.

As soon as he was gone, Sky slid into the chair beside me and leaned forward to whisper to me. I leaned forward too. We both had super long hair and we each used one hand, holding back the curtains of our hair as we faced each other. It created a private little place for us to talk. Very intimate.

"Doctor Burgis switched the pills," Sky whispered, no longer rushing her words. "The pills don't work on our faces, that's not what they do. They are magic pills."

Magic pills? It just sounded so hokey. One of my eyebrows broke rank and arced all on its own.

"Are you sure, Sky? How do you know they're magic pills and not just the Derm pills, or even sugar pills?"

"I can fly now because of the pills." She drilled her unblinking gaze into me. She was serious. "That's why the police are after me. They know I can fly and they want to grab me and lock me up. Maybe experiment on me." She narrowed her eyes. "*Who knows?*" she said darkly.

"You can really fly?" I asked.

Sky nodded. I could tell she was telling the truth. Weird. But no weirder than me, I guess. I took my first pill Monday and that night I lit the Black Candle. Lammas night. The first of August.

"But how did you find out about the pills?" I asked.

"Oh, Doctor Burgis told me yesterday, after my fight with my mom. He wasn't worried about me telling anyone because I'm crazy. So it didn't matter if I told. He knew no one would believe me." Her brow creased as she looked at me. I could tell she desperately needed someone to believe her.

"Do you believe me?" she asked. She watched me, waiting for my answer as I thought it through.

Magic pills? I still didn't get the mechanics and I didn't understand even half of what she'd said but one thing I was absolutely certain of. I believed her.

"Yes, Sky. I believe you." A huge smile sprang onto Sky's face and I couldn't help smiling back.

"But I just want to say hello to her." Sky and I both heard a strange voice say. We sat up together. Dr. Burgis was at the back door to the exam rooms looking over at us. Sky's dad had gotten up and was headed over to Dr. Burgis, but Williams was standing in front of the big football player kid. He was in the drug study. "Benjamin." I remembered seeing him in the waiting room before. Williams had his hand on the guy's broad chest holding him back.

"I'm sorry, son, the girls are not to be disturbed. You'll have to leave now."

Benjamin didn't back off. He just stood there and looked past Williams to me.

"Black Rain. Can I talk with you?" he asked, ignoring Williams. "Sorry I didn't get a chance to say hello yesterday. My name is Benjamin Grant." He stepped forward another step into Williams' locked arm and Williams staggered back, almost falling to the floor. This Benjamin kid was big! Big and pushy. And rude. I didn't do rude.

Williams got up, pissed, and broke out with his best cop voice as he got in Benjamin's face and placed one hand on his gun. "BOY! Take another step in this direction and you're going straight to jail! Step back! NOW!" he ordered.

Benjamin looked at Williams like he was a bug he wanted to step on but said, "Fine. Whatever you say, officer. I'll step back." He stepped back one small step like a total smart ass then looked back at me. He ignored Williams.

"Yeah. Sorry I didn't get to talk to you Monday or Tuesday, but I'd like to get to know you better." He looked down at Williams who stood between us like a furious, bug-eyed roadblock. "Could you get rid of your guard dog and maybe we could talk for a while?" He looked back at me and actually tried to smile. *Gross*!

"Maybe I could take you to lunch. You know how we all gotta eat right after we take our pills. Let me buy you lunch today."

Dr. Burgis called to him, "Benjamin, leave the office now or you're out of the study!" He pointed to the front door. "Out!" he ordered.

Benjamin chuckled. "You can't kick me out, Doc, I haven't done anything wrong. My parents would sue."

I felt my control on all this new power inside me slipping. I couldn't handle this childish bullshit. I was just barely holding myself together as it was, but now the pressure was building. It was almost painful. I ran my fingers through my hair and my whole body shook with the effort of holding this new unseen part of myself inside my skin. This was new. This was more power. Way more. Bottomless, endless, raging power.

"So pushy," I heard myself say. "Pushy and rude, Benjamin, and I don't—do—rude." I let slip some of the effort I was using to keep a lid on my power and felt the warm rush of invisible energy glide around me, lifting my hair and making it dance in the power coming off my body as if I were an overcharged battery. Everyone in the waiting room stared at me like I'd just sprouted a second head, especially Benjamin.

"I don't like you," I said simply.

I was surprised when Sky stepped up beside me, no big production, just her as she said, "I don't like him either. He's not nice." She shook her head. That was so sweet. I felt so much better for having heard her.

Williams glanced back at me with "Don't You Do It!" written all over his face.

"Sky, stay away from him," her father warned her. "We should call the real police to come and take—"

"NO!" Sky shouted. "No more police, Father! Just him," she pointed at Williams, "because he is her guy. I like Williams, so he can stay."

Sky's father put his hands up in surrender. "Okay, Sky. No police." He retreated, going back to stand with Dr. Burgis.

Having heard what Sky had said about the pills, I took a moment to notice how Doctor Burgis was just standing there, watching everything, taking it all in and not really getting involved. You'd think he'd be more upset, but he wasn't. If anything he was enjoying the show. He even had a little smile stuck on his face. All he was missing was the salty, buttery popcorn and an oversized soda with a bendy straw.

Benjamin's ugly voice drew my attention back to him.

"If she gave me half a chance she'd like me," Benjamin griped sullenly, taking a few steps backward as he said it. He was looking more unsure with each passing second. I guessed his heart had finally powered past the macho bullshit clogging his veins and arteries to get some blood to his sad little brain. Williams relaxed a little but stayed standing between us.

"Dammit! Go kid! Go! Get out now!" Williams urged.

"I didn't do anything wrong," Benjamin insisted. "I only wanted to talk to her," he whined. The childlike voice didn't match his big, stupid, muscled body. I laughed, and it wasn't a nice sound. It was a mean, dark, cold sound. The lights overhead flickered again. Benjamin was scared and he wasn't alone.

"What in the seven hells was that!?" Sky's father said in Chinese. He looked over at me. "What are you doing!?" he demanded in English. "What is she doing!?" He demanded of Burgis when I just smiled. Doctor Burgis told him to keep quiet and stay calm.

"Black Rain," Williams began, "Don't you do it! Don't get—"

"Hush now," I interrupted. Williams shut his mouth, but his eyes almost popped out as he tried to speak. He couldn't open his mouth; his hands groped at his sealed lips making "Hhhm Hhhmm! MMMM!" sounds as he struggled. He only panicked for a moment, then he put his hands on his hips, and pinned me with a dirty look.

Beyond Williams, Benjamin was almost to the door. He was through playing big and bad and wanted to go home to his momma now. Too bad I wasn't through with him.

"Benjamin, Benjamin, Benjamin." He stopped with a hand on the door and looked back at me.

I started to walk toward him. Williams turned away from Benjamin because he could see that the kid was *done* and turned to face me because he could also tell—*I wasn't*. He put his arms out wide, trying to make himself into a human fence, filling the gap between the two rows of waiting room chairs to keep me pinned in and away from Benjamin.

I gave him a frustrated pouty face and he gave me a sour "Hmm Umm!" right back. I felt bad about zapping his mouth shut when he was trying so hard to help me. Sky gave me a concerned look. Together, both of them helped me reign it in. I respected the arm fence and spoke to Benjamin from my side.

"I thought you wanted to get to know me, Benjamin?" I leaned forward and rested my arms on the human fencing. "What about lunch?" I teased seductively. Sky walked up to the other side, draping herself on Williams' other arm, mirroring me. Making us match. She was quick.

"I wonder if he can fly? Can you fly, Benjamin?" Sky asked him.

"No. I can't fly!" Benjamin answered roughly. "What's that got to do with anything!?" He opened the front door.

"Because if you can't fly, you fall," she said simply.

I turned my head to the right. She looked okay, but that was weird. But then, who was I to judge what was weird, I reminded myself.

Benjamin wisely took advantage of my moment of distraction to make his escape, bolting out into the parking lot at warp speed. The glass door swung shut with a bang. I filled the sticky quiet with what I thought was the best way to sum up this whole encounter with Benjamin. "What an asshole," I concluded soundly.

Someone started laughing. We all turned, surprised to see Sky's dad, laughing and laughing. Something in this must have hit him right in the funny bone because he actually doubled over, holding his side. Maybe the stress was getting to him. Sky smiled a real smile at her father for the first time since she'd seen him. It was so "family." She liked to see her father happy and that was good to see. Sky was a good girl. I really liked her.

Williams tapped me on the shoulder. "Hmm!"

SHIT! "Sorry, Williams!" I said quickly. I kissed my fingertips and then reached out and touched each side of his face and his mouth popped open with a "Dammit!"

"Sorry," I said, putting on a penitent face.

"Sorry!" Williams fumed, bugging his eyes at me. "You magic my mouth shut and you think 'sorry' covers it!?" he shouted. Understandably angry.

"Hey!" Sky jabbed him with a finger. "Be nice, Williams! She did great! She didn't kill him or turn him into anything horrible."

Williams looked at Sky, stunned but thinking it through. "You're right," he finally agreed. "You're right." He drew a deep breath and then let it go. "She did do good. She did real good," he agreed.

Dr. Burgis and Sky's father stepped closer to our little group cautiously, not sure of their welcome in our little circle. Williams put himself between us and the two of them.

"It's okay, Williams," Sky told him, like he was hers now too. "They'll be good."

Williams eyed them suspiciously then nodded and stepped aside allowing Sky's father and Dr. Burgis to join us.

"Here is your phone." Sky's father handed her a phone. "They put a tracking device in it, but that doesn't really matter because any phone you use they can track. And I would like you to have a phone so I could talk to you." He handed her a clear plastic bag that held a charger for the phone.

Sky held the little phone in her hand, thinking about whether or not to keep it. She frowned and opened it, pressed a button and turned it off, then slipped it into her pocket. "Why won't they leave me alone?" she asked.

Sky's dad didn't answer. "Can you really fly?" he asked in a doubtful voice instead.

"Of course I can!" she snapped, like it was an insult to even ask the question. "I've always been able to fly. You *know* that." I caught a quick glance from her. She didn't want to say anything about the pills.

Her father shook his head. "Sky, you fall every time you try to fly. You get hurt! You break your bones!" He was shaking his head. Even with all the fuss, he somehow didn't think she could fly. "What about the hospital?" He changed the subject. "How did you get out of the room?" he asked. "And what happened with that cloud?"

Sky was angry. She stared him dead in the eye, and enunciating crisply but not shouting, she said, "I am 'Sky,' Father. The clouds are mine. The birds are mine. The wind is mine. All that is in the air is mine. I am Sky."

HOLY CRAP! Williams and I stared at each other and basically shared the "WOW!" of it. Apparently Sky wasn't just a pretty face and gorgeous flying body.

She was—well, in a word, "Sky."

Williams and I were there, totally, but for some reason her own father wasn't buying it. It was all over his face. Sky shook her head, disappointed in her father. She held her hands in front of her, a foot wide gap between her palms. A little cloud took shape between her hands. We watched as the cloud shaped itself into a sparrow-sized cloud bird that took off, flapping cloud wings that somehow stayed together as it flitted around the room for a minute before landing on Sky's shoulder. It looked up at her as if it were waiting for something.

"I will call you *Believer,*" Sky told the little bird passionately. "Because I will not call you doubt!" She gave her father a nasty look.

I was floored. Amazed. I heard Dr. Burgis laughing happily from somewhere nearby. "That's so cool," I had to say. "Do you mind if I try, Sky?" I didn't know if she would. I didn't know if I should ask permission before I messed with her "sky."

"Oh sure," Sky said. Everyone watched as I held my hands about a foot apart in front of me. There in the middle a cloud formed, and sure enough I shaped it into a nice little bird that looked even better formed and more solid than her little cloud bird, but when I took my hands away the little bird lasted only a minute before it came unglued and drifted back to smoke.

I looked over at Sky. "Did I do it wrong?" I asked with a wince. Hell, I had no idea what I was doing.

"I've been making friends since I was little. I had to. I had no one else to talk to," she confided.

Williams glared, hot and ugly at her father who refused to even look at him as he stood there like a tight-lipped statue, radiating patient impatience.

"You just need practice," Sky encouraged with a nod.

"But how did you make Believer *live*? And *stay*?"

The little bird eyed me. He fluttered his wings then turned back to Sky as if he were also curious to know.

"When you make a cloud friend you should always give them a name, a little life or some dreams or something they like, and you have to send them a tiny piece of your soul to keep forever. It takes life to make life," she said sagely to both of us. "That's how you make a friend."

"Wow," I breathed out the word. "That's so *cool*!" I didn't know what else to say. Sky was creating life out of nothing and making *real* friends! Adam and Eve kind of stuff! She was making SOULS! Holy freaking hell! I was totally floored, but Sky's father didn't look impressed with Believer at all.

"How do you give them a soul?" I asked. I felt weird just wording the question. I was glad Ryan was in the back with Nurse Ann. He'd freak out if he heard this.

"You have to send them a piece of your heart, a little piece of your own soul." She smiled as Believer fluttered his wings happily. "Yes, I gave you a little piece of me," she told the little cloud bird with a motherly smile.

Williams had been listening quietly up to that point but here he started shaking his head. "That doesn't sound good at all. And don't that hurt you, Miss Sky? Losing a piece of your soul?" He looked so concerned. "Aren't you afraid you're not gonna have enough left over for yourself if you keep doin' that? Or what if you tear out the wrong piece? Won't you hurt yourself? That don't sound good. Both of you girls been messing around with your souls. Black Rain got hurt bad when she messed with hers." Williams looked at me.

I stared back in confusion wondering what he was talking about. I hadn't done any *soul* magic and made anyone. Not yet anyway. My bird had fallen apart.

Or—wait. Oh my God.

Had I done something like this that day in the clinic? But wait a second. No. It couldn't have been me that did it.

I wasn't even around yet.

I thought back.

My heart began to pound in my chest.

"Oh my God." It wasn't me. Rain Marie needed a friend. She couldn't make herself do it. She tried, but she couldn't go into that room and lie on that table, so she made me, and then made me do it for her. And then she made me kill her.

I killed the person who had made me.

And Brendon. His little piece of soul that we'd made together. I killed that too.

Little pieces of soul.

I was a "friend."

The room was spinning.

I felt Williams grab me and lower me into a chair.

"What's wrong!?" Sky was shouting from a long way away. I watched as she sat on the floor in front of me. I heard some other voices—far away voices—drifting—floating—peaceful—gone.

Gone.

Gone.

I felt a cool rag on my face. I blinked and looked up into the worried faces of Williams and Sky. I was on the floor now. In the waiting room. I was relaxed, which meant my power was everywhere. I watched as shining strands of blue/black hair floated in front of my face as if I were in space or under water. It gently waved there in front of me. Floating there. Peaceful. Peaceful.

"There you go. She's coming round. Can you hear me?" Williams asked.

"Yes. I think," I said quietly. I slowly raised my hand up in front of my face and looked at it, as if I were seeing it for the first time. I was a "friend." Like Sky's cloud bird. Wait. He had a name. I should use it. Believer. Like Believer. I was a friend like Believer.

I felt hands on me. Sky. Sky wouldn't hurt me. I wasn't worried. I dropped my hand and closed my eyes again. Peaceful.

"Rain. Can you hear me?"

I opened my eyes. Sky was kneeling on the floor beside me. "What happened?" she asked. She was worried about me, and so was Williams. He was on the other side of me. He reached over and wiped my face with the wet rag again. It felt good.

"I'm a friend."

"What?" Sky asked. "I know you're my friend." She looked confused.

I shook my head. "No, Sky. I'm a friend like Believer." I looked up at her and watched as her eyes opened wider and wider.

"Two years ago a girl named Rain Marie Bryant was in trouble. She needed a friend. A friend that could do something horrible for her. Something she couldn't do for herself. She tore her soul in half and made me. I'm a 'friend.'"

"WOW!" Sky said, returning my own word with feeling. She looked me over, seeing me again. It felt strange having her look at me like some "friend thing," but then again, that was what I was.

"And she made you without the pills? That's *wonderful!*" Sky was a little freaked it seemed. "Where is she now?" She asked the question with such happy enthusiasm. Across from her, I watched as Williams turned pale, which I didn't know a black guy could do.

"I killed her," I said without emotion.

"WHAT!?" Sky burst out. "You killed her!? WHY!?" She was outraged, but she didn't leave. She knew there had to be more. I was calm as I told her the rest of it.

"I did it because she asked me to. I didn't want to. But she begged me to do it. Rain Marie had gotten pregnant and she was scared. The guy was so mean, and he wanted her to kill the baby. He gave her the money and took her to the abortion clinic. She was embarrassed and afraid, but she couldn't do it herself, so she made me. She made me and forced me to kill our child. And then she made me kill her too, so she could go be with him in heaven."

"Oh," Sky said quietly. And then very softly, "Wow."

I closed my eyes. I heard Williams and Sky talking about me while I drifted. Peaceful. Hmm. I wondered what happened to us. I was a friend, not a person. What happened to friends when they died? I kept my eyes closed.

"Sky?"

"Yes," her voice answered.

"When a friend dies, what happens to us?"

"Oh. That's easy." She let out a happy little laugh. "They never really die. If I made them I can feel them. They are a little part of my soul, remember, and souls are eternal. Yesterday I made a friend named Sky Dragon. He was big and scary, and I couldn't leave him flying around, so I unmade him and took his little piece of soul back inside my own." She paused, and I knew she was touching her chest. "He's right here inside my heart, and anytime I need him all I have to do is call him and he will be here for me. And I had another friend I made named Slurpy who got blown out the moon roof of our Hummer yesterday. He was just a tiny piece of paper that I made into a bird. He died. I think he came apart in the rain." She sounded sad about Slurpy. The emotion and pain in her voice was impossible to miss. "When he died I felt his little piece of soul come back to me. Once I make a friend they never die. They are a part of me forever. I didn't want Slurpy to die, but he's with me now. I love my friends and I try to take care of them."

I thought about that with my eyes still closed. Hmm.

"Sky?" I asked again.

"Yes," her voice answered.

Williams wiped my face again with the rag.

"What happens when a regular person dies? Where does their soul go?" I asked her. Maybe she knew. I thought I knew this once but now I wasn't so sure. I hadn't even known what I was.

"Every person ever made has a soul," she began, "and that soul connects us all to God. The first person with a soul was a man named Adam. Do you know the story?"

I quoted the verse that I'd known by heart since I was a little child. "*And the Lord God formed man of the dust of the ground and breathed into his nostrils the breath of life and man became a living soul.*" Having just watched Sky create Believer, the verse made so much sense.

"*Yeah. That's it.*" Sky sounded surprised that I knew the verse but continued with her explanation as Williams wiped my face with the rag again.

"This is how it makes sense to me. I think God took a piece of his own soul and made Adam. Then he took Adam and took out a rib, right next to his heart. I'm sure you know the story. I think he also took a little piece of Adam's soul out and made Eve's soul with it. And now everyone else is just little pieces of that first piece. When we die, we go back to the one who made us. Just like Sky Dragon and Slurpy came back to me. When I die I will go back to God. God made me. I made Sky Dragon. We are all connected. And we all go back to the one who made us."

I thought about that. It fit together perfectly. Beautifully. All pieces of that first piece. It reminded me of Jesus, when he was feeding the five thousand with a loaf of bread. He kept tearing off pieces of bread and the loaf he held never went away. It was never used up. It made perfect sense. But my thoughts drifted back to what I'd done a short while ago. I had cut the cord that connected me to Rain Marie. I'd reached into my own soul and cut the cord. I was not connected to her anymore. I couldn't feel her anymore like I used to.

"Sky. What would happen if one of your friends—*left*? If they cut the cord that connected them to you? If they took the piece of soul you gave them and walked away? What would happen?" I tried to worry about it, but it was done. Whatever had happened was done. I floated and waited for an answer. Williams wiped my face with the cool rag again. Hmm.

After a minute Sky's voice answered, "I don't know. I don't know why anyone would want to cut themselves off from the one who made them. But if they did, it would be—*I don't know.* Different. Everyone is part of the same piece of soul, Rain. Good and bad. Everyone ever made. We're all connected. We all belong to God. My friends belong to me and I belong to God. But if one of my friends got cut off I don't know what would happen to them," she finished sadly.

"I do," I said.

"You do?" She sounded worried.

"Yes," I said.

"What would happen if a friend did that?" she asked with fear in her voice.

"Me," I said and opened my eyes. Sky was still holding me down. Williams was kneeling on the other side of me holding his little rag. A small pan with water he was wetting the rag in sat on the floor at his feet.

"Why are you holding me down?"

Williams answered, "Because you kept floating away, that's why. How are you feeling?"

"I'm ready to get up now, Williams. You can let me go, Sky." I felt her take her hands away and I floated up off the floor. Power. So much power. I felt it pushing past the insubstantial barrier of my skin, making my dress wave gently as it passed by and causing my hair to fan out around my head as it crawled down each blue/black strand like little conducting wires.

All I did was think about coming upright, top up, and I righted and hung in the air with my feet a few inches off the floor. My dress and hair were still swimming with power, but that wasn't all. A dangling sea of junk was floating through the air as if gravity didn't exist around me. It was mostly smaller stuff, magazines, seat cushions, yucky garbage from the trash can, a pen, sticky note pad.

I noticed Sky's father's frightened gaze locked onto me from where he sat on the far side of the room. He'd actually moved his chair as far from me as he could get. It seemed like gravity was working better over there. The poltergeist stuff was mostly limited to about fifteen or twenty feet around me.

The door to the back office burst open and Ryan came charging out, then stopped in his tracks, looking right at me as I floated in front of him like a phantom. His face went sickly pale, then he got distracted by the sea of minutia that orbited around me. Some items were stationary, suspended in air or stuck on the ceiling, while others tumbled along, end over end, or ambled about in their own unique way as they circled me.

But having all this junk floating around me was no way to live. I had to put a stop to it if I could. I took a deep breath and tried to seal off my power and hold it inside me. I felt my feet touch the carpeted floor and felt the weight of my body rest on my own two legs again, and then all the floating *stuff* started to drop with a pattering clatter. It was a weird rain storm of staplers, garbage, magazines, and office junk.

"Got it!" Williams said as he caught Sky's bag with her phone charger as it fell. I ducked my head and swatted at the hail of paper clips that were landing in my hair while Sky dodged left and right, trying to avoid getting brained by anything big enough to hurt or leave a mark.

"What the heck happened out here!?" Ryan finally shouted. "They just now told me that you fainted over five minutes ago! I take a few minutes to go to the stinking bathroom and no one even bothers to knock on the door and tell me that my sister may be out here *dying in the waiting room*! What in the world happened while I was answering the call of nature, Williams!? Is she okay!?"

Ryan was so upset. He was mad at himself.

"Did you wash your hands?" I asked, keeping my face serious.

Williams and Sky both managed to laugh and after a second Ryan broke and smiled too. He had to. It was his kind of funny. It was so nice to hear laughing. Nice to see smiles. I smiled with them, but it was only my face smiling, inside I was shaking. Crying. Screaming. What had I done to myself? My facade held. Everyone relaxed and started talking about the zero gravity craziness and Ryan came over and helped extract a few stubborn paperclips from my hair. It wasn't long before the small talk ended and he started asking questions.

"Rain, are you okay? What happened out here?"

"Honestly. No. I'm not okay." Just thinking about it made me want to throw up. What the hell had I done to myself? I turned away from my brother fighting the urge to puke.

"Did someone hurt you?" Ryan asked and turned me around by my shoulders so he could see my face. "What happened, Rain?"

He wanted to help. To protect me. But he couldn't fix this. And somehow I knew that I couldn't either.

"Ryan, I don't want to talk about it right now. So don't ask."

"Black Rain or Sky. If one of you will come this way." Dr. Burgis was standing at the back office door, waiting expectantly.

We looked at him with obvious surprise and he just smiled. It seemed we were still moving forward with our day in spite of all the weirdness out here in the waiting room. Sky was right. The doctor wanted us to take the pills. I didn't know why, but he wanted Sky to fly and me to have whatever witch powers I had. Strange.

"I'll go first," Sky volunteered, then stepped up to me, leaned close and cupped her hand around my ear. "You should make sure you take your pills also," she whispered. "The doctor said that our powers will only be permanent if we take the pills for all five days. At least he thinks so. He wasn't sure. But I think the cops are going to get him today and take him away. I'm going to ask for tomorrow and Friday's pills and see if he'll let me take those with me. I can't come back here again. They'll get me if I do. You should do the same. Take your pills and run."

She whipped around, looking out the windows, scanning the area for cops again. Was she leaving soon? If she ran away after she got her pills I'd probably never see her again.

"Sky, I can't do the things you can do with a soul, but I don't have to run from anyone. I'm not running. If you want, you can come and stay with me. Or visit anytime if you need a safe place. You're welcome anytime, I mean." Damn. Was I crying?

"What's wrong?" Sky asked. Had she seen my tears?

"If you're gonna keep that stupid tracking phone give me your number at least. I don't have a lot of friends, Sky. But I like you. You're nice," I said, then busied myself as I reached into my purse and took out my cell. Crap. I had a ton of missed calls. Sky took out her phone and called Dr. Burgis over. He helped her program my number into her phone.

"All right. One of you girls come with me," Dr. Burgis urged.

Sky turned to go and bumped right into Ryan who was standing there like a tree. They tangled up awkwardly.

"Oh! Sorry, Ryan."

"No aah—problem, Sky. And thank you for taking care of my sister while—" He didn't finish it, embarrassed.

The little cloud bird on Sky's shoulder flapped his wings, and Ryan's eyes went wide as he finally noticed the living cloud creature. Clouds rolled around inside the shape of his bird body, the edges, especially his wings, were wispy and translucent. Sky introduced them.

"Ryan, this is Believer. He's a friend of mine," she said with a big smile, then spoke to Believer as if he was a real person. "Believer, this is Ryan. He's real nice, and he helped me yesterday when I was in trouble. We like him a lot," Sky told Believer and the little bird looked at Ryan. His head bobbed up and down, then cocked to the side. Tiny red eyes regarded Ryan with understanding. He fluttered his ghostly wings.

Ryan was already nicely freaked out by me and my powers, but Believer was Sky's weirdness, not mine.

"Sky, are you another witch, like my sister?" Ryan asked, his face was downcast, already fearing her answer.

She laughed. "No. I'm not a witch." She gave him a smile so beautiful it could break a heart in two, then said, "I'm Sky."

"Come on now, Sky, let's get you your pills," Dr. Burgis urged again.

"Sorry, I have to go." Sky turned and walked over to her father and told him to watch the window and to come get her if he saw any cops. She said it in Chinese but I understood every word. She gave Ryan and me a little wave goodbye before disappearing through the door, off to get her magic pills. Ryan was still looking after her somewhat dumbstruck.

"Yeah. 'WOW' don't quite cover it," Williams supplied with a smile. I agreed. Sky was something else.

Right then the front doors opened and one of the other teens from the drug study came in. The black kid from the military school. He took a quick look around the wasted waiting room, locked in on Williams' uniform, and walked over to him.

"Was there some problem in here? What happened, sir?" He was wearing fatigues and already moved and acted like a soldier even if he was still in high school.

Williams started chatting with the new kid while Ryan and I sat down and looked over our cell messages. I had a lot. Texts and voicemail. From my dad, Mom, and Mary. They were all worried about me. Mary's text said she felt like something bad had happened to me and that she was worried.

"Can you call out?" Ryan asked me. "I can't get my phone to work. I can still send and receive texts but something's screwing up the signal for the phone."

I tried to dial. It didn't go through. "Nope. Just texts."

I shrugged and got busy texting. Time to reassure everyone I was still alive. Sort of.

I got busy on my phone and so did Ryan.

Jane and Dan

This Is Gonna Suck

"**Y**es, Uncle Billy, today at five. That gives you an hour and a half to get everyone in the car and just enough time to get here." I could hear the yelling on the other side of the phone as Mom scribbled in her little notepad. Uncle Billy was loud on a good day. Today was not a good day. Hearing that his god-daughter was getting married this afternoon had not put him in a good mood.

Mom's eyebrows went up sharply. "Hey now! If you have to talk to me like that I'll just give the phone to Ed and he can talk to you. He cusses way better than I do these days." Mom gave Dad a disapproving look as she talked on the phone. "Don't bother coming to the wedding if you're gonna be a jerk, just stay home and I'll email the pictures to you." Mom pushed end and hung up on Uncle Billy.

"Not coming?" I asked.

Mom shook her head no. "He'll call back. He's got to throw his fit to see if he can stop this from happening."

"Piinng. Piinng. Piinng." Mom's weird sonar ring tone went off.

"Billy?" I asked.

She checked the number. "Yep." Mom sounded smug. She answered it and started talking with Uncle Billy again. He was being good now.

"What in the world?" Dad said. We all looked at where we were driving. There was a road block at the entrance to the office complex where the doctor's office was. Cars were being stopped and checked. It looked like a flashing wall of red and blue lights. There must have been thirty or forty cop cars lining the street and traffic was backed up with all the cars reduced to a turtle's crawl.

"Oh my God," Mom said, forgetting that the phone was to her ear.

"No, Uncle Billy, just some weird traffic. There's a road block of some kind. We're fine."

I heard Dan's voice in my head,

This is bad, Jane. We need to get those pills but we don't want the police anywhere near us.

"Let's just sit here in the back seat and let Mom and Dad talk to them. Maybe this isn't even for us. Nobody knows what we are yet and even what we did at the mall wasn't any reason for something like this." I looked out the window again and shook my head. "This can't be for us." The police were everywhere! So were news crews and SWAT vans.

Okay. We'll try to get in to see the doctor and get the pills but let's pack up just in case we need to run for it. We can't let them take us, Jane. We can't. Not today. Not with what we have coming tonight. And especially not with you this hungry. And if you have an accident and kill one of them then they'll try to kill you and then I'll have to kill them all.

I looked at Dan. He was looking at the police through the windows, his head moving in jerky little movements as he scanned the street. I wondered if we would really have to start killing people today. Was my life that important that all these people might have to die for me to live?

Dan turned away from the window and met my waiting eyes. Of course, Dan had heard me thinking that. I looked at him and closed out everything else in the world around me and just looked at my Dan. My heart hurt. I felt that tightening in the center of my chest that had nothing to do with my heart slowing down and everything to do with how much I loved him. What would I do if they tried to hurt him? What would I do if they tried to take him away from me? *What wouldn't I do?* I heard a rumbling noise and felt my body vibrating. The seat was vibrating, the whole car. I was growling.

"Oh my God, Jane!" Mom said. She and Dad were in the front seats. It was safer that way. I was so hungry we all thought it was best for Mom to get in the front seat with Dad. She was looking right at me, peeking over the top of her chair.

"Sorry, Billy, I've got to go. This traffic is terrible. I'll see you tonight at the wedding. Yes, I'll tell Jane that you love her. Bye, Billy." Mom hung up and turned back to me.

"Jane, your eyes! They're glowing bright red now!" Mom turned back to the front and quickly turned back to me with a pair of sunglasses in her hand. She was about to hand them back to me but stopped short, a worried grimace on her face. She tossed them to me. I reached out and took them from the air like they were moving in slow motion, snapped them open, and placed them on my face.

"Thanks, Mom."

Dad said, "Do you want to stay or go, Jane? I need to know now." He knew we didn't want to be stopped by the police.

"We need those pills, Dad." I left unsaid how badly we needed them.

"Okay, I'll do the talking. But if anything goes wrong or they try to get you two out of the car, what do you want me to do?" Dad glanced back at me then turned back to the road. He was ready to do anything I asked.

"Run if it looks like they're going to do something bad. Drive away and Dan and I can jump out someplace down the road. You could drive on, lead them away, and give us a chance to hide. Dan and I can disappear and no one would ever find us. I could be wrong but I think we can run faster than the car anyway."

The thought of having to make a run for it didn't upset me. As long as I was with Dan I was okay. As long as I'm with you, Dan, please—touch me. I felt the scorching burn as his hand gently stroked down my arm light as a feather, barely touching me, but still hurting me. I needed to be touched by him more than I needed not to be hurt and Dan knew that. I was so glad Dan knew my heart all the way down to the bottom of my soul. How did anyone else ever do this without someone knowing? I couldn't imagine it.

I'm glad I'm a vampire, I thought to Dan and shuddered in pain as he stroked his hand down my arm again.

Dad said, "All right, honey. We'll give it a try and see if we can get through, but be ready to run if this goes badly."

Mom looked panicked as she looked at the police. "Ed, Ed, are we really going to run from the police?"

We were still crawling along, one car length at a time. The road block to the office complex was still up ahead in the distance.

"Let's not panic," Dad said calmly. "We'll tell them we have a medical emergency and that we have to see the doctor. Either they will let us in or make us leave. Maybe we should all calm down." He looked at Mom as he said this, which earned him a nasty scowl.

I looked out the window at one of the policemen standing under a tree about two hundred yards away. My eyesight had never been great and two days ago I would have barely been able to see him, but now I could see the man perfectly. He was about forty-two, forty-three, with a dark mustache and dark hair with a just little gray at his temples. He had kind eyes that sparkled a little in the sunlight slipping through the tree he was using for shade. He looked like he might be a nice dad for some nice family somewhere. I could read his name badge.

I hope I don't have to kill you, Lieutenant Parker, I thought. He was talking into his little ear piece. I concentrated, screening out the noises in the car and all around. And I could hear him.

"...five or six media vans but no further problems with people getting past our lines."... "No, sir."... "Roger. We'll keep it locked down. We've got enough men now unless the crowd rushes us for some reason." He released the button on his walkie talkie and smiled. Apparently he didn't think there was much of a chance of the crowd "rushing him."

We were pulling away, but I could still hear him like I was standing right beside him under his tree.

"Is the flying girl still in the doctor's office?"... "Roger."... "Yes, sir."

A black military helicopter flew right over the street, really low. It didn't make any noise at all, but wind whipped around and dust battered the people and police standing at the road block.

"What on earth is going on!?" Dad said again as he eeked forward another car length in the line of traffic trying to turn into the office complex. It looked like every car was being sent away after just a few seconds of talking with the cops at the roadblock.

"I just heard that cop over there talking on his radio." I pointed back at Lieutenant Parker. "You guys will never believe this, but they're looking for a flying girl!" I smiled. "That's not us, Dan! They're not looking for us. Yay!"

Dan smiled at me but kept breaking down his equipment in his bag. Making a small carry bag in case he needed to run. I felt a momentary silly girl moment as I watched him. All I had was a fanny pouch with my letters, ID, and cash. I wasn't very prepared. I hadn't even brought clothes.

That's just so "girl," I thought to Dan.

He he he. "Girl." Yeah, but that's okay. I love you the way you are. Anyway, I have what we need.

I thought to Dan, I don't get hot or cold anymore, Dan. I guess I don't really even need clothes anymore. If we run off to the woods I could go butt naked for you.

Dan looked up from packing his bag with a shocked expression on his face. I loved that shocked look. I loved to surprise my Dan.

If we were both naked we could do it like bunnies in the woods.

His eyes went even wider. I laughed then gave him a hungry look.

If my Mom and Dad weren't in the front seat and we weren't about to stop at a road block surrounded by a hundred cops I would take you right here. Oh hell! I might do it anyway!

I laughed again as Dan actually backed up, squishing himself against the side of the car.

"Jane!" Mom called from the front seat. "I know that laugh of yours by now and I know what it means. Stop pestering Dan for sex! You'll get to do that all you want once you're married! Get a grip, girl."

I didn't look back to where I knew Mom sat, peeking over her seat, spying on us. She was throwing off my groove! My body vibrated.

"Oh NO!" Mom yelled. "You did NOT just growl at me!" In full indignant mother mode. "Don't make me come back there, young lady!" she threatened.

I heard Dad laughing and Dan laughing in my head, *he he he,* as I tried to reign it in and stop growling but I was having a hard time.

Dad said, "Please don't make her go back there. And it would be best if you waited." He was still laughing as he said it. "But did you say that they were after a *flying girl*? Really? An actual flying girl?"

"Yeah," I said as another helicopter touched down in the field across from where we waited in the line of cars. We watched as men in military outfits and suits piled out of the helicopter and headed across the street toward the office complex.

"Did they say where this flying girl was?" Dad asked. "It sure looks like a lot of this activity is happening right around the doctor's office. You don't think—could this be one of the other kids in the drug study?" Dad glanced back at me. "If this can happen to you two maybe one of the other teen girls has started to fly. They could have had a similar reaction to the Derm pills, but instead of reading a book about vampires maybe this girl was reading or watching something that started her on flying. Who knows?"

I looked at him. "Dad. You're very smart. And I think you're right."

"I am?" Dad sounded surprised.

"He is?" Mom sounded even more surprised.

He he he sounded in my head, making me have to talk through my smile as I spoke to my parents.

"When I was listening to the guy on the radio his exact words were 'Is the flying girl still in the doctor's office?' I think you're right, Daddy. I think you're totally right. This is one of the other kids in the drug study."

"Jane, are you sure you heard correctly?" Mom asked. "Are you sure about the flying girl?" She sounded doubtful.

I looked at Mom and smiled at her. She didn't understand how much we'd changed. Neither did Dad.

"Mom. Dad. Dan and I are packed now and ready to run if we need to. We've got a few minutes before we get to the roadblock and I'd like to tell you more about Dan and me. About how we're changing. Are you guys ready for this? I mean, I'd like you to know more about what's happening to us if you want to know." I waited for their answers.

Dad said, "Sure, honey. We want to know. The good stuff and the bad. And your mom and I promise not to freak out anymore. Even if you tell us you can fly. No freaking out. We promise."

I love you, Dan said and reached over and lightly stroked his hand down my arm.

God that hurt. Thanks, Dan. I love you too. Should I start with the brain stuff? I asked Dan in my head and he nodded.

"First, you guys need to know that our brains are working about ten times faster than yours. Maybe way more. Also we don't forget anymore. Ever. Anything. We remember everything we see, hear, smell, taste, or touch. We remember every second of every day and have perfect recall on all of it. I actually have to work at it to talk slow enough so you can hear me and understand me. Like right now. I'm talking in slow motion. And then when I ask you a question I have to wait. Reeeally wait for you to answer. Like right now. I'm going to ask if you understand what I just told you and if you're ready for another heaping crap load of *crazy shit*. I'm waiting for your answer now."

I waited.

"Well that makes sense," Mom said. "Remember, I've read most of the books too, Jane, so I know parts of this also. But is it really like we're moving in slow motion for you? Like right now. Am I moving that slow?"

"Yes, Mom. You and Dad are that slow. Actually, I take that back. It's not that you're slow so much as that Dan and I are that 'fast'." I'd never really thought about how fast we were before now. Can we dodge bullets, Dan?

If we had to, maybe. But a better way would be to avoid having to dodge the bullets by running away or running up behind anyone stupid enough to ever dream that I would allow them to shoot at you.

Dad said, "Okay. We understand that your brains are working a lot better and that you can remember everything now, but what else has changed? What else can you and Dan do that you haven't told us about yet?"

I continued, "Our senses are superhuman now. Our eyesight and our hearing are hundreds of times better than a human's. My sense of smell is maybe a thousand times better now, so whatever you do, please don't fart." I kept a stone straight face to make my funny seem real, but Dan was ruining my joke. He was laughing so hard he was shaking the car.

He he he he he he he he. Damn! Where do you come up with this shit!? He he he he aaaa.

But Mom and Dad felt the car shaking from Dan laughing.

"Is that Dan laughing back there?" Dad asked. He started laughing too. "Don't fart." He laughed harder. "Good one, Jane." The car kept shaking as I heard laughing inside my head and out.

"Oh for heaven's sake!" Mom wailed. "It's just a stupid fart joke! What else, Jane? What other changes do we need to know about? Tell us. We're running out of time and I want to know as much as I can. I'm so worried."

"Okay, Mom." I started again. "You guys already know that we're super fast. But we're also super strong. We can climb anything like a spider. And you know that Dan can read my mind and talk to me in my head but it's actually more than that, but that is kind of private."

Dan touched my hand on the back of my wrist lightly like I wanted him to and I shivered then started again. "The only other big piece of news I want to lay on you is one that Mom probably already knows about because she already read the books. If Dan and I live through tonight and rise again, we will never age. We will stay seventeen forever. And unless someone kills us we will never die. Ever. We will be immortal."

It was quiet in the car for a while.

"Will you try to live off of animals or will you eat people?" Mom asked with a straight face.

"Don't know," I said honestly. "We're gonna try real hard to be good, Mom. Which means *animals only*. Unless we can score some kind of connection with a local blood bank. That would be a life saver."

Dad said, "Sounds like there are a lot of upsides to this thing. Like being a vampire isn't going to be all that bad. But tell me, Jane. Are you happy? If you could get rid of it somehow and go back to the way things were, would you want to, or are you happier like this?"

I didn't even have to think about it.

"I'm glad I'm a vampire. I would never go back. I would never give up what I have with Dan. I'll never leave him again, not for a second, even if I live to be a million years old. And I won't let anyone take him away from me. I'd kill every cop out here and wade through a sea of blood to stay with him. I know that makes me sound like a monster, Daddy, but I don't care, I'm not human anymore anyway. My only advice to the world is don't get between me and my

Dan because I will kill anyone that does. And then I'll drink their blood because I'm *so damn hungry*."

It was quiet in the car for a minute or two after that. Mom and Dad shared a little shocked eye contact. Maybe the sea of blood comment was a bit over the top, but it was the truth. I meant it, Dan. And maybe it's love that has made me crazy or that it's just part of being a vampire or maybe it's just me, but even the thought of someone trying to take you away from me makes me go mad.

I could taste metal on my tongue and a red haze filled my vision.

"Jane! Please, honey. You're gonna have to control yourself. Your eyes keep getting brighter every time you get angry." Mom adjusted the rear view mirror. "Look," she said.

Even with the sunglasses on there was a devilish red glow coming around the shades. I took off the glasses.

"Oh no! You've got to be kidding me! Dan, how can I walk around like this?" I yelled at him like it was all his fault. He looked back at me helplessly and threw his hands up in the air.

"I can't fit in like this! What's the deal with this, Dan! Why aren't your eyes raging pits of burning hell? Dammit! Dammit! Dammit all to hell!"

In the mirror I watched as the red glowing eyes actually got brighter and I ground my teeth together. It made a metal on metal sound. The big van in front of us pulled away and three cops were suddenly looking right into our car. I stared right up into their horrified faces and grinned like the demon from hell that I knew I looked like.

"Yeah. This is gonna suck," I said grimly.

"Jane! Put the shades back on!" Mom said, frantic. But it was too late. The police were already surrounding the car looking inside, busy on their radios talking to their other cop friends.

"Jane! Do you want me to take off!?" Dad yelled. The windows were all still up so the cops outside didn't hear him say that and he was waving at them all friendly but I could tell by his voice that he wanted to floor it.

"No, Daddy. Let's give it a try. They've already seen my eyes. Maybe it will help us get in to see the doctor. I definitely look like I need to see a doctor." I looked at myself in the mirror again. "Or maybe a priest," I said softly.

"Roll the windows down, Ed," Mom said. A cop was tapping on the glass with his knuckles.

Be ready to run, Jane. And if we run, go straight to the doctor's office. Maybe we can still get what we need before we disappear. Be fast and be ready to move when I say go. You stay with me no matter what.

I'm not leaving your side for a second, I said inside my head. Maybe they'll just let us through.

Dan was ready. He had a white t-shirt on and his pack strapped to his back. The black straps from the bag ran over his shoulders and were snug around his waist. Seeing those straps digging into his flesh sent a chill through me and Dan shivered too. Of course he could feel me shiver. He didn't look at me but kept his gaze out the window and on the cops all around us.

We'd made a quick stop at a gas station after we left the mall and had cleaned up some in the bathroom so I wasn't all bloody now. Dad had given Dan his white t-shirt he'd had on underneath his button up shirt and we used his old shirt to clean me up. We were clean and looked almost normal, but my eyes were impossible to explain.

The windows rolled down and a guy wearing a gray suit leaned into the driver side window, and my father spoke to him.

"We need to get in to see the doctor. Dr. Burgis. I know that you guys have something going on." Dad paused and swallowed. "We can tell something big is going on out here, but this is a medical emergency! My daughter has to see her doctor. She's had a bad reaction to the pills she's taking and we have to be seen right away!"

The guy leaned farther into the car. Dad leaned back out of the way to make some room for him as he looked at me. I still hadn't put my shades back on, so I leaned forward and gave him a full look right in his eyes. He reared back and almost knocked himself out trying to get away, banging his head hard on the top of the window.

I so wanted to laugh because it was funny as hell, but my throat closed up tight, burning, scorching. I felt Dan's arms wrap around me in a flash, like a burning metal cage. Everything faded just a little around the edges of my perfect vision.

Oh God. It smelled so good!

"Blood," I said. Dan's arms tightened around me harder and for some strange reason I didn't even feel the burn.

Jane! Don't breathe! Hold your breath! Close your eyes, Jane! Close your eyes and hold your breath! Come on, Jane, don't lose it yet! Stay here, Jane! With me! Listen to me! Stay here with me, Jane!

"What's wrong with her?" the cop at Mom's window said. Even with my eyes closed I could tell he had his head shoved inside the car...

Would he freak out like the other guy if I opened my eyes?

Would he hit his head too...?

Would there be more blood?

"Our daughter is sick!

"Why is he holding onto her like that?" he said more firmly. "What's going on?" He was worried that Dan was hurting me. Mom talked to the cop leaning into her window.

"Our daughter is sick! She's having a reaction to her pills. It's, it's a seizure! Please let us go through! We have to get in to see her doctor! Now!"

"Blood," I said with my eyes still closed. I heard Dan in my head yelling at me not to breathe but I wanted to smell it again. I needed to. "I want to smell the blood, Dan." Dan kept telling me *NO* in my head. He kept yelling at me *NO!* But I wanted to smell it. "Please, Dan! Please let me smell the blood. *Please*," I begged.

I heard other people talking, but I didn't care what they said. Mom and Dad. Others. Dan was still yelling inside my head. But still he wouldn't let me. I started to cry and shake. "Please. Please, Dan. Let me have some blood." I cried and my body shook with need as he held me but I still didn't breathe. I didn't disobey him. He was my love. He was my Dan. But why was he doing this to me. "Why, Dan? PLEASE!" I ran out of air and couldn't talk anymore. My lungs were empty. I wanted to smell the blood. To taste it on my tongue. To drink it. To touch it.

Dan was still talking in my head, but it was getting harder and harder to hear him. Quieter. His voice was fading away.

I breathed in air through my nose.

No blood. It was just air now.

I felt motion. The car was moving and fresh air was blowing through the car, all the windows had to be down. There was no smell of blood now, just a strong smell of hairspray. Lots and lots of hairspray. I guess Mom had sprayed the hairspray to cover the smell.

"Are you all right, honey?" Dad called back and I opened my eyes.

"Her eyes are open now. Jane? Can you hear us now? Jane?" I could see Mom leaning way over the back of her seat, looking down at me. She looked scared, worried, and relieved, all at the same time.

"Dan, you're not hurting her, are you? You're not squeezing too tight, are you?" Mom asked.

Then I felt Dan. He shook his head no, trying to answer my mom. Dan and I were partly in the floorboard and partly across the back seat. He was wrapped all around me like a snake. His arms and his legs, all of him squeezing me as hard as he could. It didn't hurt. It burned but it didn't hurt.

Jane! Are you back? Can you hear me now? Jane!

"Yes," I said. But my body was still shaking badly. "I can hear you." My voice didn't sound good at all. It was a deep, gravely, half growl. "Don't let me go yet, Dan. I'm not safe right now."

I felt Dan tighten up again. Good. Good, Dan. Don't let me go yet.

"I'm not safe," I said out loud again. I looked down at his arms, white muscles corded and straining as he held me. It didn't hurt other than the burning that was just a part of my body now. I felt his legs straining like a snake, squeezing tightly around my legs. We were all wrapped together. I was very out of it. It felt like I was in a dream, the kind of dream you aren't able to control. All I could do was watch it as it happened.

Jane. I'm not hurting you, am I? I don't want to hurt you but you're so much stronger than I am that it's hard to hold onto you when you start to move. Are you really okay? We're going to have to go into the doctor's office in just a second. Do you need me to carry you or do you think you can walk?

"Just hold onto me for now," I said to Dan out loud. "I'm gonna need a couple of minutes here, Dan, so be patient—I'm not, safe, yet. And don't worry, you're not hurting me. Just hold onto me for now and don't let me move. I need some time."

Okay. I'll hold you. When you feel like you're ready to get up, let me know. I'm glad you're back, my love. I'm so glad you're back. You scared me to death.

"Sorry, Dan. I didn't mean to scare you. I don't know why I'm so much more out of control than you are. You smelled the blood too, but you didn't go crazy. And my eyes! Why are my eyes so red and yours are—oh, oh, Dan," I said sadly as I noticed that Dan's eyes had gotten a little redder than they were earlier today.

"It's happening to you too now." He gave me a small smile as he strained to hold me.

Yes, Jane, my eyes are getting redder. I don't think I'll ever be quite like you but I'm having the same problems. And I'm getting hungry too. It's getting harder every second for me to stay in control but that doesn't matter now. We made it. We're here. And as soon as we have the pills we're going to drink the blood I brought for us. You know we can't drink water anymore and we can't eat solid food. I think the only thing that will help us hold those pills down will be blood. As soon as you're ready we can go in, get our pills, and drink our blood. We should be able to get the doctor to leave us in one of the exam rooms for a while. Hopefully it won't take us too long to get a grip once we drink our blood because we're going to need to get out of here soon. Remember, we have a wedding this afternoon.

Dad parked the car and leaned over the back of his seat, looking down at me.

"I don't understand. Why did they let us go?" I asked. My voice was better. I sounded more like my "new" old self and less like a deep-throated monster.

Dad answered, "The police thought you were having a seizure. When they saw blood coming out of your eyes, they panicked and just waved us through. I don't even think they knew which doctor's office we were heading for. The complex has a lot of doctors. When they saw you bleeding from your eyes like that, they got out of the way."

"Are we in front of the doctor's office now?" I asked. I couldn't tell. All I could see was the ceiling of the car and Mom and Dad's faces as they leaned over their seats, looking down at me.

Mom answered, "Yes, honey. We're here. But take your time. Take a few minutes to get yourself together. There's no rush now." She smiled at me. "We made it."

Dad said, "Dan's not hurting you, holding you that tight?"

I laughed. "No, Daddy. If you want to worry about one of your kids, worry about Dan. He's yours now too, and I'm stronger than he is. Don't worry about me. I think I'm almost indestructible now. Worry about your son-in-law trying to hold onto his very crazy 'wife-to-be' so she doesn't go on an insane killing rampage."

Dad took that to heart for a second and then said to Dan, "Are you okay, son?"

Wow! Did you hear that, Dan? Did you hear that!? Dad called you SON!

I started to cry again.

Dad noticed the fresh blood coming from my eyes and made a disgusted face. "Jane! Are you crying again!?" He looked exasperated. "Not because of me calling Dan 'son'?"

I nodded. So. I was still a girl. I felt Dan shaking a little as he held onto me.

"What's wrong, Dan?" I looked at him. His eyes were glowing redder now and he was trembling. He was looking at my face. At the fresh trails of blood on my check. Oh.

"Do you want to lick me? I wouldn't want it to go to waste, my love." I could feel the blood that had leaked down from my eyes again. Not a lot this time, but with what I'd cried out earlier, I was a mess again.

"Lick you?" I heard Mom say. "You're going to let him lick you?"

I nodded. "Mom. Dad. Could you give us a little privacy? Dan and I need some alone time. Okay?" I said, still looking at Dan. He was trembling worse now.

Dad looked as uncomfortable as I'd ever seen him look but said what I wanted to hear. "Aaah, sure, honey. We'll be right up here in the front seat. Just say something when you're—good to go."

Mom and Dad sat back down in their seats, giving us what privacy they could.

I watched as Dan leaned close to me and licked my check. I felt the burn where his tongue made a wet trail through the blood on my face. I spoke to Dan in my head, Now kiss me, Dan. This blood buffet has a price. One lick. One kiss. That's the deal.

Are you saying that just because you want to kiss me or because you want to taste some of the blood on my lips right now?

I laughed. "Both." I leaned forward to kiss him and stopped just before our lips met and ran my tongue across his bloody mouth and then into his mouth, and Dan met me with his bloody tongue. The sweet metallic, coppery taste filled my mouth like an explosion of wonder that made the burn so much more bearable. Ohh God! That was good!

Then I kissed him. Which was also nice. The wonderful taste of the blood was like cool water on flames and letting me take pleasure in the texture and smoothness of his lips and tongue as we kissed. Definitely both, Dan, I said in my head as I kissed him. Lick me again, my love. Lick me again before the blood dries.

Dan reached up and held my head to the side and licked from my bloody check down to my neck then came back up to me and shared. "Yes," I panted. Dan licked me again and shared. It was all so good I was worried that I might start crying again. It was that good!

My father's nervous, uncomfortable voice came from the other side of the front seat. "Dan, you know there are police all over the place out here. If you've got enough blood off my daughter now maybe we should go ahead and head into the office."

Dan and I both growled.

"O—K," Dad said. "Maybe another minute or two."

We kept licking. And sharing. And kissing. For another wonderful few minutes, then Dad spoke in a firmer voice.

"These cops are starting to get closer. We need to go."

Mom leaned out the window and looked up. "Look on the roof of the building, Ed. They're all over the roof."

Dan stopped kissing me first and spoke in my head,

Are you ready? Are you in control of yourself again?

"I'm okay now, Dan. Let's go."

We both sat up in the back seat and scanned the area. They *were* all over the place. At the corners of the buildings on the roofs. Standing in little groups where they would be out of sight of the front of the office. It was like a cop convention out here, all of them looking at the office and at "us."

My new vision was amazing, and it was weird how my brain processed all kinds of crazy facts. The data just stacked up, nonstop. I counted a hundred and six policemen. All seen and counted with just one quick glance around the office parking lot with my amazing new eyes. I also spotted weird net guns, like something that would be used for catching birds, mounted on the roofs of three buildings. Were they going to try to catch her in a net like an animal?

"They really want that flying girl, don't they?" Mom said. "It must be true. There really is a flying girl."

"Yeah," I said, "And I bet I know who she is too. I bet it's that blond girl that was fighting with her mom yesterday in the waiting room. Her name is Sky. It makes too much sense. With a name like that, who else could it be?"

Mom looked upset. "That poor girl with the crazy mother? Good Lord!" She sounded disgusted at life in general. "She doesn't need any more problems. She had enough garbage to deal with without all this—" Mom looked around again. "That poor girl." She shook her head.

I spoke to Dan in my head. We need to tell Sky about the cops and net guns. I wouldn't want her trapped and hauled off to be experimented on.

We'll tell her. I'm sure she's inside, Jane. They want to catch her. Treat her like a bug in a box. Dan growled.

Dad looked away from the cops to Dan as he growled. "I agree with you. There are way too many policemen out here with way too many guns for this to be a safe place." Dad turned to me. "Jane honey, are you ready to go now?"

"Wait! Put your glasses back on," Mom told me. "I know the red still shines through but it's better than you walking around without them."

I put my shades back on without a fuss. Dan opened the door and stepped out. He'd taken his black duffle bag off his back and now held it by the strap in one hand and held my hand with the other as I gracefully stepped out of the car on his side. We could see the cops getting excited and moving around as we got out and headed toward the office.

"Why did Dan bring his big bag, Jane? He could have left that in the car," Dad asked as we walked down the sidewalk toward the office. Dan answered his question in my head.

We might not be coming back to the car. I didn't want to leave anything we will need, and the blood is inside the bag. We need that.

"Oh yeah, we need that," I said with feeling. Then for Mom and Dad, "Dan has my lunch in the bag, guys."

"Oh!" they said together and Mom added, "No. We don't want to leave that behind. You do need that!"

After a few more steps Mom asked, "Honey, where did Dan get your lunch from anyway?" She kept her face blank as she walked beside me.

I answered honestly, "I haven't even asked him that myself. Actually, I haven't even let myself think about it. I don't want to know, I just want to drink it." I squeezed Dan's hand and I tried not to think about it.

Dad said, "If Dan wants us to know he'd tell us. I'm with Jane, let's not worry about it."

Dad sounded worried though.

Jane. Please tell them that "nobody died" for lunch. I wouldn't want them thinking that I had killed people yet. I may kill someone soon, but I haven't killed anyone yet. And that matters to me.

"Yes my love," I said surprised and more than a little embarrassed. "Dan wants you to know that nobody died for our lunch," I said obediently.

"Good," Dad said quickly.

"Good," Mom echoed.

"He is 'good,' isn't he?" I said. I was glad that Dan had reassured my parents. My Dan was good. Very good. I was beginning to worry that he was better than me. Less the monster. Maybe I was a bad influence—

Dan's hand slipped out of mine and I worried why for just a moment, actually missing the burn of his touch, but then I felt "pain" as his hand cupped my ass as we walked down the sidewalk together. I smiled. My ass was smoking hot as we walked side by side. Definitely a bad influence.

In the distance we could see a great big helicopter flying toward us and we saw people on the roof of the doctor's office right over our heads, looking right down at us. They looked like military commandos, not regular police.

"Let's go!" Dad said and quickened our pace toward the front door. As soon as we were inside the office I noticed that the room was a mess. It looked like it had been attacked by a group of five year olds; magazines and all kinds of little things were everywhere.

There were only two people on this side of the waiting room. One was the black teen in fatigues. He glanced our way, looking surprised, but he kept walking and following Ann into the back office. A few seats away from the door was a tall Asian man I recognized immediately as Sky's father. He looked a little freaked out as he took in our appearance. I wondered why.

I reached up to push the shades tighter to my face, and as I did so I couldn't help but notice how pale and white my arm was. I remembered what Mom had said as we walked into the mall earlier today. It wasn't just the eyes, it was the whole package. I tried not to get upset and make my eyes shine more as I looked over the rest of the waiting room. There at the back of the waiting room was Rain, her brother Ryan and a black police officer sitting with them. They were all staring at us. They also looked freaked out by our appearance.

"We'll go talk to the nurse and let them know that we're here," Mom said. She and Dad went to the sliding glass window. Dan and I turned back to the waiting room to find a seat. I heard Dan in my head,

Well, Jane, do you want to go sit beside your friend Justin and his sister?

Dan was waiting for me to pick our seat. He turned and smiled at me. He seemed happier somehow, like the time we just spent in the back seat had put him in a better mood. I couldn't understand how it was possible, but I actually felt closer to him now. More connected. More solidly tied to him. Sharing my blood and kissing him had been the most intimate thing I'd ever done in my life, but it had also been the least human.

Dan's eyes had a slight reddish glow and there was a little spot of my blood at the corner of his mouth and another on his cheek. It looked right to me. Not odd. He had such beautiful eyes. I loved to stare into them and now with my new eyesight I could see so much more, the details and the colors were so vivid and sharp where the beautiful blue met the green and the colors blended together.

I wanted him to see my eyes too, not just the stupid sun glasses, so I reached up and took them off and looked into Dan's eyes. Dan of course had been listening to my thoughts and feeling my feelings. He gave me what I wanted and stepped closer to me. I had to tilt my head up to meet his eyes. Dan stared into my eyes like he would see down to the very bottom of my soul which was exactly what I wanted.

"They're doing it again," I heard Ryan say, his voice half playful and half disgusted.

For some reason that pissed me off. Dan was so tied to my mind and emotions at that second and feeling everything I felt that we reacted like mirror images. Our heads snapped in Ryan's direction and both of us growled. Dan's eyes got a little brighter red but mine were lamps of red nightmares promising dark things.

The reaction was to be expected; everyone jumped like they had just seen a scary scene in a horror movie.

"Whoa!" the black cop cried as he launched out of his chair, placing himself between us and the others. "Hey! Easy now, you two! The boy was just joking around. Just relax and take a seat!" he ordered with a hand resting on the holster of his gun.

"What is wrong with your eyes and your skin?" I heard Sky's father say. He'd gotten out of his chair and backed away toward the front door of the office like he might run for it.

Dan and I both looked at him, still mirroring each other in our movements, and I answered him.

"Would you believe I have a raging case of pink eye?" My voice was still a little deep and dangerous sounding.

He knew that was a smart-ass response but he didn't say anything back. He cautiously eased back down into a chair close to the front door. He wasn't sure we were safe.

"Jane. Please!" Mom fussed. "Put your glasses back on! Be nice and stop scaring everyone to death!" She and Dad had come up to stand beside us.

"Yes ma'am." I griped, but I put the shades back on.

"Sorry, sir," I said to Sky's dad. He nodded at us and to Mom and Dad but didn't speak.

Ryan and Rain were standing up now looking at us and the cop had an arm around Ryan's waist holding him back from coming any closer.

"What happened to you, Jane!? What on earth happened!?" Ryan's voice broke, filled to overflowing with emotions he was fighting to control.

"Easy now, Ryan," the cop cautioned him. "You don't want to piss her off again. This girl seems a little dangerous." He kept a hard eye on us and his arm around Ryan.

Rain said, "Relax, Williams. These are friends. I think we just surprised them, and Ryan was kind of rude."

She gave her brother a nasty look, and he just shrugged and said, "What?"

Williams let Ryan go and his other hand came away from his gun, but he kept his eyes on us.

"Jane, Dan." Rain waved us over. "Why don't you and your parents come sit with us? It looks like we have a lot to talk about."

Ryan looked the same, but Rain had changed. A lot. Her hair was different. Now it was a super glossy black, long and straight, and her dress was amazing. It was Victorian in style, almost like a wedding dress, but instead of white it was solid black. Her dress looked magical. She looked magical. Magic or power buzzed in the air all around her, the air practically sang with it. Even the light was a touch different on her side of the room.

Dan noticed it too, and he was also hearing my thoughts. I spoke in my head to Dan, Maybe we aren't the only ones changing, Dan. Beside me, he nodded.

We took another few steps closer then I stopped dead in my tracks, and Dan stopped with me. My nostrils flared as I *smelled* again to be sure I had it right.

"What's the problem, Jane?" Dad said.

"Honey, are you okay?" Mom asked, worry clear in her voice.

"Just give me a minute. Just wait a minute, please," I said as I looked at Rain.

Rain, Ryan, Williams, Mom, Dad, and Dan all watched me with varying degrees of alarm as I leaned in a little and "sniffed" at Rain. She smelled different. It was a subtle thing, but it was so very different from every other human I'd ever smelled before it was jarring. It wasn't just the smell of magic or power, it was something different. The only thing I could think to label it as was "not human." Rain wasn't human anymore. She still looked human. She still smelled edible and tasty, but she didn't have the same familiar smell all the other humans had. That sameness. There was something different. She could still be food, but it would be like eating bison instead of cow. Still steak but definitely a different cut of meat.

My stomach made a *squish squash* noise, and I wrapped my arms across my middle and grimaced for a second until the cramp stopped. I had to stop thinking about food.

Dad said, "Jane, if you're having problems we can go sit on the other side of the room." He leaned forward to look at me and whispered "Are you okay?" close to my ear. I nodded and took a deep breath.

Rain was just watching us, trying to figure out why we were reacting the way we were but she didn't look scared. Not at all.

The black policeman stood back up and put himself in front of her. My stomach growling had worried him.

"Williams, give it a rest and sit down," Rain ordered but Williams wasn't having it.

"She don't look safe. She don't look safe at all, Black Rain."

He was convinced I was dangerous. Smart man. Cop instincts.

"Come on, Jason, sit down already," Ryan said, "And let them sit down."

The cop took a seat grudgingly but kept his hard gaze pinned on Dan and me as we sat in the chairs across from them. Mom and Dad sat beside us. They were a little taken aback by Rain's appearance as well. They couldn't smell what I had, but they could still feel the power coming from Rain. It was everywhere. All around the room.

"Jane. Tell us what happened to you," Ryan asked me again, politely this time.

"Dan and I have had a strange reaction to the Derm pill. We aren't human anymore."

I left unsaid what we were now and waited to see what they would do with this much insane information. Rain and Ryan both looked at each other briefly then back to us.

"Jane!" Mom hissed in warning. She didn't want me to tell. Dad looked worried too. His eyes tracked over to the cop who was listening closely with one eyebrow already cocked and his checks sucked in as he processed that bit of insanity.

"Don't worry about Williams. He's okay," Rain said reassuringly to my mom and dad as her brother dove in.

"Not human? What do you mean 'not human'?" Ryan asked, plainly confused. "You're real pale and a little scary with the crazy glowing eyes and all, but how can you not be—human?"

I changed the subject. "Is Sky in the back getting her pills?"

"Yes," Rain answered cautiously, her eyebrows bunched up.

She's protecting her, Dan, I thought.

He nodded.

"Is she still human?"

"What do you mean?" Rain said. She actually looked confused, which surprised me. Maybe she didn't even know that she wasn't human anymore.

Dan, should we tell her? She should know what she is and what she isn't.

She knows she's different, but she may not know how different. Be careful. But I'd say leave it alone.

"I'll try, Dan," I said out loud. Rain, Ryan, and Williams were all watching us so carefully, their eyes going from me to Dan like they were trying to guess if we were talking to each other, which of course, we were.

Ryan couldn't keep it to himself. "Wait a minute." He looked from me to Dan again. "Are you guys talking to each other in your heads?" He bounced his gaze back and forth from me to Dan, then spat it out like a cop who'd finally solved a murder mystery. "Somehow, you two *are* talking to each other in your heads!" he declared joyfully. "That's what you two have been doing when you're looking into each other's eyes like that."

He sounded so relieved and happy. Like this explained some great mystery that had troubled him deeply. He was happy that it had been something simple. Something he thought he understood. I felt Dan growl beside me. He didn't like this one bit, but I didn't growl, I laughed. It wasn't a mean laugh. It was just a laugh. The musical noise was still odd to hear coming out of my mouth and everyone sitting around me was surprised too, again sharing looks, unspoken communication, which were surprisingly easy for me to understand now.

As soon as my mirth ran its course I confirmed Ryan's assumptions. "Yes, Dan can talk to me in my mind but that's not why I look into his eyes the way I do. I don't think you would like to hear the real reason. It would make you sad to hear the truth, Justin." He winced when I called him *Justin*.

Rain leaned forward and took her brother's arm in hers. She did not look happy.

"That was kind of mean, Jane. I know he's pushy, but you don't have to call him Justin anymore. He knows what it means. I told him the story so you don't have to call him that anymore. His name is Ryan." Rain was very protective of her brother. I didn't want to hurt Ryan's feelings, but somehow, something felt wrong with me not calling him Justin. It had that weird book feeling, like this was part of my story, part of the story I had made happen.

Dan, I'm getting that weird feeling I get when the book is messing with me. I don't know why but I don't think I can call him anything but Justin. He's Justin to me and the book won't let me change that.

Dan took this in without alarm and nodded.

I can feel it too. Don't fight it, Jane, we need to finish the change, which means we need the book's magic to work. Just explain it to Rain so she knows why you're calling Ryan "Justin." We don't want her pissed at us. Or just don't talk to him at all. I know you think he's a nice guy, but I still think he's an annoying ass.

I gave Dan a strained look.

So—what, I'm just supposed to let it do whatever it wants?

He just shrugged, as trapped and helpless in the situation as I was. Everyone was trying to figure us out. They all knew we were talking together but didn't know what we were saying.

Mom said, "Jane, since you're not keeping this a secret, when you talk to Dan you should at least say your half of the conversation out loud so we can try to follow along. That would be nice."

I gave Mom a frustrated "gee, thanks a lot!" look and turned back to Rain.

"Rain, you remember that I was reading those Midnight books when you first saw me?"

"Yeah. I remember," she said.

"Well, I had a major reaction to the Derm pills. I don't understand it but somehow I made the book 'real'—in lots of ways." I left it at that and watched as she put the pieces together. The white skin. The eyes. Me sniffing at her like she smelled like lunch. Dan talking to me in my head. And me calling her brother "Justin." Just like in the book.

Rain was already getting over her shock as she asked, "So you and Dan are both—" She left the "V" word unsaid.

Dan and I just nodded, at exactly the same time. "We haven't completed the change. Our hearts will still be beating for a short while longer," I spoke for us.

Ryan and the cop were totally confused, but Rain knew exactly what I'd hinted at. She covered her mouth with her hand as she eyed us with overflowing sympathy. She looked over at my mom and dad and knew by their grim expression that they already knew.

"What is it?" Ryan looked from his sister's fresh tears to my parents' equally dour faces and back to me, begging one of us to say something, but I didn't want to say anything to him. I was trying hard not to even look at him.

"Come on! Someone please tell me what's going on here!" Ryan begged, getting more worked up each second.

I ignored Ryan's question and focused on Rain.

"Rain. I know this will sound weird, but I can't call your brother anything but Justin. I'm sorry. I just can't do it."

I kept my eyes on Rain as I spoke, not looking at Ryan. "It has something to do with the book and I can't change it. Sorry. I just wanted you to know so when I talk to him or about him you won't think I'm being cruel. I just can't help myself for some strange reason. I can't explain it. I can't help it. I know it's weird."

"Oh. I get it. I totally get it," Rain said, nodding her heartfelt understanding, "I have some weird things that I have to do sometimes too. Things I have to do just because they are part of my power." She looked over at her brother who was completely lost and confused by our conversation and asked calmly, "He's not going to change into a werewolf is he?" She looked back at me, gaze steady, serious as a heart attack. In the Midnight books the character named "Justin" turns into a werewolf.

"A werewolf! What do you mean 'werewolf'!" Ryan half rose out of his chair. He looked back at me waiting for my answer, but I kept my eyes fixed on Rain. I didn't want to look at him. This all started when I looked at him. When I stared into his eyes over the top of my book that first day, but I wanted it to end with Ryan. Not get worse.

"She's going to turn Ryan into a werewolf?" Williams said. He looked like he believed it was possible and wasn't happy about it. "Is she a witch too?" he asked and looked back at me giving me another once over from head to toe before looking back to Rain. "You're not going to let her do that to your brother, are you?"

I thought to Dan in my head, He sure is in the know for a cop, isn't he, Dan? Dan nodded.

"Relax, Williams," Rain said. "No. She's not a witch, she's something else." She still didn't want to say it out loud.

I saw Mom and Dad shift in their seats. They were really careful with the "V" word also. They didn't like to say it either.

Ryan looked right at me and asked, "Jane, am I going to turn into a werewolf?"

I'd been avoiding looking at him but now I felt like I had to. I felt weird, like the book was trying to tie me to Justin. Instantly I was scared to death. I didn't want that. Dan, I thought, Help me, Dan!

Close your eyes, Jane! While you're around him just close your eyes and don't look at him if you can help it.

I nodded. Behind my sunglasses I closed my eyes. If anyone noticed the red glow behind the glasses dim they didn't say anything and I could still make out where everyone was with my other improved senses. I didn't want to be connected any tighter than I already was to Justin. All I want or need in my heart is you, Dan, and I don't want the book making me do anything that I don't want to do just because it was part of the story.

I felt better with my eyes closed, like I was in control. I felt a momentary, smug spike of righteous victory. I was finally figuring out this unseen force that was changing us and getting a handle on it.

"Jane?" Ryan asked again. "Am I going to turn into a wolf?"

I turned my head to him, my eyes safely shut behind the shades. "No. I really don't think you will. I think your part in my story just involved me, romantically, if you know what I mean." I gave an apologetic grimace. "And I'm sorry all this happened, and that you got pulled into my story as the guy that didn't get the girl. Honestly, I am sorry. But I'm happy with my Dan. Very, very happy. I can't even tell you how happy I am."

I reached out blindly and Dan took my hand as I continued, "But I can feel the magic from the book right now, pushing at the edges of what's real, trying to mess with me and make 'us' more than friends, and I don't want that, Justin. I like you a lot, and I think you're a great guy, but I don't want to be forced to love you just because of a magic book. I'm sorry. But this is part of the story that I will change."

I felt stronger for having said it. I felt the coils of unseen magic around me loosen a little and I relaxed some, but I still didn't open my eyes. I wished I could see the expressions on everyone's faces but there was no way I was going to open my eyes.

After a long human minute Ryan spoke again. "I understand, Jane, but, can you change the story? Doesn't it have to happen like it did in the book?" He tried to sound neutral but with my new hearing it was easy to hear the hope in his voice. I didn't like it and neither did Dan.

"Nothing is exactly the same as it is in the book," I said, my eyes still closed tight. "Obviously no one bit us to turn us into vampires, we just started changing Monday afternoon after we took the Derm pills. So that's different. The way Dan reads my mind and talks to me in my head is different from the books. Lots of things are different. Some things are much more powerful the way they are now than how they are in the book." I stopped here and turned my head with my eyes closed to where I knew Dan was seated, looking at me, then I turned back to Ryan and continued. "And other things are less than they are in the book."

I hoped Ryan understood what I was getting at. Sometimes subtle hints worked best. "The book is changing us. I don't know why, but I do know that if I try, if I want it, I can shape what it does to me. What it does to us."

We were all quiet for another uncomfortable human second or two.

The cop, Williams, spoke up, "Did you say that you were changing into vampires? You're serious. Real vampires?"

"Yes, Williams, they are serious, and it is real. You should know that by now." I heard Rain's voice as she chided Williams for doubting what he'd just heard. I could tell by her voice that Williams had already seen a lot of impossible things. Rain's powers. Things she's done with her magic. I listened closer, trying to hear more.

"All of us are changing, Williams. I have changed into a Black Witch. Dan and Jane are turning into vampires. And you know that Sky is—well." Even with my eyes closed I could tell she made a face, "I don't even know what Sky is other than to say that she *is* 'Sky'."

That sounded pretty impressive and I asked, "Is she really powerful, Rain? I sure hope she is because there are hundreds of cops outside, all over the place, and they look like they want to catch her pretty badly. They have fancy net guns set up on rooftops all around us to catch her if she tries to fly away. We need to warn her." I wanted to open my eyes but didn't.

"Why don't you open your eyes?" Ryan asked me and I froze. He'd noticed that my eyes were shut behind the glasses. I shut them tighter.

"Jane, take your shades off and look at me," he said. The desire was naked in his voice.

Dan's inhuman roar tore the air! It was so loud he shook my body and I was sure the others could feel it in their bones. I didn't look but I heard the movement all around me as people jumped about, adjusting to this new little "problem."

I remained seated, still and unmoving, but I could easily discern what happened in the panic. Williams took Justin in hand forcefully and retreated to the other side of the waiting room, getting him farther away from a very upset Dan who dropped back into the chair beside me with a thud. He kept his gaze averted from everyone as he tried to stay calm. I honestly couldn't blame Dan. I had made myself quite clear to Justin. I did not want his affections forced on me.

Hold me my love. I felt arms close around me, and I let out a low hiss of pain as the burning scorched into me. I didn't care. I needed to be held, and Dan needed to hold me. I heard Rain sit back down in front of me and I knew that Ryan was on the other side of the office talking with Williams so I opened my eyes and looked at her.

"Your book really put the whammy on my poor brother, Jane," Rain complained. "You know that he would usually never do something like that. He fell head over heels for you that first day and hasn't recovered yet. I know you haven't led him on either, and you're doing what you can to help, but this still sucks. I hate that my brother has been caught up in your book's magic shit."

She flipped her hair out of her eyes and looked at me. She noticed the red light pouring around the glasses and her brows formed a V. She'd thought of something. "Jane. You know, I think I can change you back if you want me to," Rain said.

Dan and I went still as stones, not even breathing.

Mom and Dad perked up, they didn't know what Rain could or couldn't do, but the level of cool confidence she exuded was hard to deny. I wasn't sure myself. My mother and father both started to talk excitedly, asking her questions about how she might be able to change us back.

I don't want to go back, Dan! I cried out in my head. I needed to tie us together tighter. There were too many forces trying to separate us, change us back, rip us apart. The magic of the book, Justin, Rain, my parents, the police. There were too many people trying to take Dan away from me! I could not allow it. I *would not* allow it.

I reached up and took the shades off, ignoring my mother's complaints as I turned toward Dan. He turned to meet me. There was no need to explain. Dan already knew. I looked deep into his eyes and opened myself up to him and let him look down into the very depths of my soul and know me the way only he could.

"No! Never!" I half shouted, half growled as I stared into Dan's eyes. "I'd rather live eleven hours and thirty-six more minutes tied to you than live the rest of my life without you inside me. I will not go back! I want more of you. *I will have more! You will be MINE! FOREVER!*" I growled so fiercely my own parents leaped from their seats and backed away.

Dan raised his wrist up to my mouth. I grabbed it, opened my mouth wide and sank my new vampire fangs deep into his wrist. It took a minute, Dan's body was changing, but soon I was drinking his blood.

The world vanished and all that was in it. All I knew was the blood. I recognized it. It was Dan's, it had his taste, his flavor, and I made it my own. I pulled him into me and made him my own. And at the same time I gave myself, my venom, to him. To own and to be owned, forever.

My mouth came away from his wrist and I licked the gaping holes that I saw. The wounds closed up like magic as I somehow knew they would. I'd hunched forward, holding Dan's wrist close to my chest while I bit him, but now I leaned back in my chair. I ignored my frantic parents yelling.

"What are you doing!? NO! NO!" they shouted frantically from a safe distance.

Rain was still seated across from me in her chair, wide eyed. Watching. Fascinated.

I reached up and pulled my hair to the side and leaned my head back as Dan did what I wanted, what we needed to do. We should have done this a long time ago.

Dan bit my neck.

My vision went red again; I felt Dan's teeth push into my flesh and I felt his whole body, all of him, as he drank me in. I gave myself to him, willingly, *desperately*!

"Yes," I said. I could feel him drink me in and make me his own and I felt the burn of his venom as it raced through my body. Claiming me, changing me forever. Making me his. I complained with a breathless "no" as he pulled away. I felt him lick my neck and I knew that the wounds were gone.

Dan leaned back enough to look at me. He had some of my blood on his face. I reached out to him and ran my hands through his beautiful sandy blond hair. I wasn't burning anymore. I felt wonderful as I smiled at my Dan. My whole body felt more alive than I ever had in my life.

"Jane." Dad's voice.

"Jane honey?" Dad again.

"Yes," I said. I could hear the happy ringing in my voice. Happy? Was I happy? Hell yes I was happy!

I laughed and so did Dan. His shoulders shook and he even made a little sound as he laughed and I heard him laugh in my head also. Other than his growl (or roar) it was the first time I had heard him make any noise at all. I looked at his beautiful smile. He was happy too. And we weren't burning anymore! I had no idea what it all meant but it felt fantastic to not be on fire! *He he he he* and I heard Dan laugh again, both out loud and in my head.

Dan. I didn't know you could laugh out loud.

Neither did I! I'm still changing too, Jane. I never used to be able to make any sounds at all, so this is new for me too. Being able to growl and roar, and who knows, maybe after we change completely I'll actually be able to talk, although I don't know that I'd talk a lot even if I could. I'm used to being quiet, Jane. And I like things the way they are. Although not burning is awesome, that I don't miss at all. I'm glad that changed!

Dan smiled at me as I touched his face and we didn't feel the pain of the burning, just the amazing feel of his skin against mine.

"Jane honey, are you okay?" Mom's voice.

Talk to your parents. They're worried, my love.

I obeyed.

"I'm okay, Mom," I answered her. "Happy" still in my voice for all to hear.

I turned and looked at my mom. She jumped back a little and so did a few of those standing behind her.

Oh. I must have moved too quickly. I looked too alien.

Mom and Dad were both standing a few steps away from Dan and me, looking at us like they didn't know what to do. Behind them stood Ryan, Williams, and Sky's father along with Dr. Burgis and Sky who'd finally emerged from the back. Rain was the only person other than us still in a seat. She sat in her chair across from us looking at everyone like she didn't know why they were all so freaked out.

Dad was kinda green; seeing me get bitten was probably hard for him. He took a tentative step closer.

"Jane, are you ready to go back and see the doctor? He's ready for you and Dan now."

I looked at Dr. Burgis. He was a little white around the gills as well, but he smiled at me and I smiled back.

Mom took a step closer too. "Honey, are you all right?" she asked weakly.

"More than all right," I said.

I smelled blood. I reached up to my mouth and felt the blood on my face from biting Dan and I looked down at myself. I still had some on my neck also. I leaned my head back and to the side as Dan leaned forward. He knew what I was doing and met me half way in a slow kiss, and with our new senses we could feel everything in ways we never had before, except now we didn't feel the burning.

We took a second or two to lick a little of the wonderful mess off each other. We moved together, like two parts of the same body, then Dan and I stood. Again, everyone jumped in surprise. Dan and I looked at each other, with the same "oops" expression on our faces. We were gonna have to work at slowing it down again.

"Jane, now you're moving even faster!" Mom said. "It's like you just appeared there in front of the chairs out of thin air. I didn't even see you move."

Dan reached down with exaggerated slowness and picked up his black duffle bag. He was smiling as he slowly leaned upright with the bag and I laughed at him. "Stop being silly, Dan, that was too slow!" Dan smiled at me.

Dad laughed, shaking his head.

"Why Jane. Why did you do that?" Ryan's lamentable voice called, cutting through our happy mood like a sharp knife. He stood in the middle of the room looking forlorn and lost as he gazed at me and waved off the cop, Williams, who was whispering loudly for him to "hush up and leave it alone."

I kept my voice kind but sure as I answered him. "Because, Ryan," I was able to use his real name now and not Justin. "Now nothing. Nothing in Heaven. Nothing in Hell. Not the magic of a book or the powers of a Witch. Not ten years or ten million years. Nothing can separate Dan from me. He is mine and I am his. For all eternity. *That* is why. This was my choice and I have chosen."

Ryan said, "But I still love you. What am I going to do, Jane?" Sympathetic glances. Everyone was trapped here listening. Forced to witness Ryan's heartbreak.

Williams looked away and actually wiped at his eyes with the back of his hand.

I moved at speed, flitting over to stand before Ryan. It must have seemed as if I just 'appeared' there in front of him. I surprised everyone except Ryan. He seemed to rally his strength and took a step closer and stared into my eyes, almost like he wanted the magic of the book to rise, come to his rescue, and force me to love him too. He tried, but it was too late.

I gave a kind smile to his intense gaze. My eyes were only a little red now, some of my "new" natural eye color was showing again, purple fading to lavender and lilac.

"Ryan. You can love me like a sister. And I can even love you back like a brother." I unzipped my little side purse and took out one of the invitations. I handed it to him. "Please, be happy for me," I watched as he read the invitation.

He looked back to me in disbelief. "You're going to get married this afternoon at five?" He stared down at the card again, like it must be a mistake, but after reading and re-reading he dropped into a nearby chair.

Williams sat beside Ryan and sympathized while everyone else got busy congratulating Dan and me on our imminent marriage. Sky, Rain, and Dr. Burgis all seemed genuinely excited and nothing but happy for us.

"You're getting married!" Sky gushed, her bright smile beaming at us. "That's so wonderful!" She came over and then surprised me completely by giving me a hug.

Her father grimaced, like he wasn't happy about his girl being that close to a monster like me, but he hid it well and actually smiled once Sky let me go and stepped back to give me some room. She made me show her my ring which Dan had surprised me with at the mall.

I heard Rain asking my parents about the wedding and Mom telling her all the details. Dad was more relaxed also, talking with Williams the cop while Mom talked wedding stuff to Rain.

After Sky finished her wedding congrats, Dr. Burgis congratulated me also and said he was happy for us both.

"Today at five, goodness, that's in just a few hours. I do hope the police don't delay your trip." He shot a furtive glance out the window. "You'll need to get moving soon. If you and Dan are ready, let's go to the back and get your pills."

Dr. Burgis held his hand out, inviting us to head back to the exam rooms for our pills. Dan appeared by my side like magic, carrying the black duffle bag. We turned to follow Dr. Burgis when Ryan shouted out.

"JANE! What happens tonight!? In eleven hours and thirty minutes. What happens tonight?"

I turned around slowly and looked back. The room was silent. Everyone was looking at me except Ryan. He was looking at the invitation in his hand. I answered him calmly.

"Tonight, Dan and I will die."

No one moved a muscle. This was too weird a situation to touch with words. Too dark. Too painful. Too dangerous. Even Sky's exuberance was frozen solid.

Ryan wasn't finished. "And after you die tonight what will happen to your soul, Jane? Will you go to heaven? Will you go to God? What will having Dan cost you? It's not too late to change, Jane. I can pray with you."

He looked at me then, boring into me with his eyes, begging me to listen. To concede. To give in.

"God can still save you. God can still change you back. If you ask him to, he can change you back. I know it."

"Please, Ryan. Don't," I said, but Ryan wasn't finished.

His grief and horror at my choice was in his voice and on his face and trembling through his tortured frame as he pressed on. "Don't!" He shouted the word back at me. "Exactly!" He challenged, "Don't give up your eternal soul to be with him like this! Being a vampire means giving up an eternity in heaven for an eternity of darkness. I know that much! Don't let yourself be damned just to have him. Please, Jane. If no one else will beg for your soul then let *me* beg for it. Please! Don't damn yourself. Don't walk away from heaven forever. Let me pray with you. Come back to the light, Jane! Come to me."

His concern for my soul was real. His fear of me being damned was real. But under all of this was his burning desire to have me. For me to be his. I heard it there in his voice and my vision went red and I knew my eyes had changed color. I put my hand out to the side and felt Dan's hand slip into mine. My voice was firm, powerful, and it filled the room as I spoke.

"Heaven is for humans. I am not human. I choose the way of blood. And if I must be damned to have Dan, then let me not only be damned, but let me reign as Queen of the Damned! I am VAMPIRE!" I roared into the room. Everyone cringed and cowered or stood frozen in place. "I am the first vampire. I am the Queen of the Damned."

Dan's arms wrapped around me and mine wrapped around him as we looked at them. No one moved. Everyone looked afraid to move. Even Rain was shaken. Ryan dropped his eyes to the floor in defeat.

Dan's arms slipped away as I stepped forward and slowly walked toward Ryan. I reached out an arm and delicately lifted his chin with the tip of my finger so that he had to look into my face. I smiled at him. Everyone was watching. Not sure what I was about to do. Eat him or talk to him. They held their breath.

"Thank you for trying. May your God remember it forever and bless you for it." I gave him a second and asked, "Will you still come to the wedding?"

Ryan made a choked, strangled sob and reached up to rub at his eyes. His voice was quiet but could still be heard by everyone in the too quiet room.

"I have to." He took a deep breath and when he spoke again his voice was almost back to normal. "Of all the places in Jacksonville, you guys scheduled your wedding at my church." He held up the invitation, pointing to the address. "Dan rented our auditorium for eight thousand dollars. They texted me, told me the good news, and asked if I could come early tonight and help set up chairs for the reception. We would usually never do a Wednesday night wedding, but my pastor couldn't refuse. They're trying to buy some property and needed another five thousand by the end of the week for the binder deposit." Ryan looked over at Dan and with a wry smile.

"By the way Dan, you got screwed. They'd of done it for five."

Dan laughed, and everyone joined in.

And with that, "life" and "hope" and even "joy" filled the room.

Jane and Dan

Insights

Dan and I left with Dr. Burgis, following him to take our pills. We entered the back office area and were surprised to find a creature standing at the end of the hallway watching our approach. The thing was huge, over seven feet tall, man-shaped, with tree trunk thick arms and legs and a solid blocky body. But the whole creature was made entirely of billowing, rolling smoke. It had two glowing red eyes set in a bucket-sized head and it watched us with intelligence as we came down the hall.

"Hello, Believer," the doctor greeted the thing warmly. "These are friends of Sky and myself. This is Jane and Dan." Dr. Burgis looked at us like we should also say something to it so I spoke for us.

"Hello, Believer. We're glad to meet you," I said. It was the wildest thing I'd ever seen in my life. It was a puzzle I couldn't figure out. What held the thing together, and what force or power kept the smoke and clouds moving all around inside him so that even standing still he still looked like he was moving?

Believer nodded and opened a smoky long gash of a mouth and spoke in a deep resonate rumble of a voice.

"If you are friends of Sky then you are friends of mine. I will protect you." Believer gave us a small bow. Dan and I both shared a little shocked and amazed eye contact between us as we ducked into the exam room with Dr. Burgis. As soon as the door closed I asked the question,

"Dr. Burgis, what was that thing?"

Dr. Burgis smiled big. "Ahh, that, is a *friend*. And do be careful to call them *friends*," he warned. "Sky is very touchy about people treating them with respect and dignity like you would any other person because that is exactly what they are. People. Sky created Believer. He started off life as a little bird made out of smoke and clouds, but she wanted him large enough to protect her while she was back here taking her pills so she *remade* him into what he is now." The pride in his voice was easy to hear, and I could hear other meaning behind his words.

He was proud of Sky. Proud he had some part in making her what she was. He had done this on purpose. This was all planned from the beginning. It was all there in the layers of what he had said. I looked at Dan.

He has done this on purpose. He gave us these pills, and he knew that they would do things to us, Dan.

Yes. He has. And if we have turned into vampires, and Sky has become this powerful, what has happened to the others? There could be twelve of us running around with super powers. Like some stupid comic book series. Super Friends. Dan directed a dark look at the doctor. *I bet he knew how dangerous this was when he did it. I wonder if some of us have already died by taking these pills. I feel like they have. He could have ended up killing you.* Dan thought about that for a fraction of a second. *No. Actually, he did end up killing you, didn't he. I would like to kill him, Jane. What do you want to do with him? Your dad has already okayed him as food.*

I didn't know what to do. Dan and I watched the smile slide off the good doctor's face as he realized all was not well and his patients were both less than happy vampires. I would have given him a few minutes to sweat it, but a minute seemed like a really long time now and I didn't have that kind of patience, so I just drove on.

"Dr. Burgis. You experimented on us like lab rats, didn't you?" He looked frozen and I tried to thaw out his nerves so I wouldn't have to drag the information out of him. Not because I felt like extending him any sympathy, I just didn't want to waste any time. I didn't have any *time* to waste thanks to him.

"You are safe enough for now. But you will answer my questions. All of them. I have other abilities, doctor. I can hear if you are lying. I can hear other things also. Whole conversations behind words, it really is amazing how much people say just with the texture and color of what they say." I gave him a cruel smile. Watching his face and expressions was almost like hearing him talk. "This knowledge pleases you, doesn't it? Sky is not the only one that has created new life, is she, doctor? And you are very proud of yourself, aren't you? Pleased with what you have done to us."

Dr. Burgis had gone pale. His eyes darted to the door where he knew Believer stood. He wished he'd kept the door open now. I wondered briefly if Believer would keep us from killing the doctor. Not that he would be fast enough. I heard Dan in my head,

We could always tell him what he has done to his Sky. Believer loves Sky. You could hear that in his voice. If he knew what the doctor has done I don't think he would be happy with him. Not happy at all. Dan smiled.

Dr. Burgis said, "Are you reading my mind, Jane? Or is it Dan that's reading my mind then telling you what I'm thinking?" He looked at us. And I could hear in his voice he was half sure we were about to kill him and he was okay with it. Weird.

My brow creased as I "listened" to his other words closer. It was like he knew that he was a pathetic bastard who deserved to die, but the scientist in him still wanted to hear just one more curious detail. One more fact that he could know he had a hand in before he checked out. Are you getting all of this, Dan?

O yeah. And I'm with you. Weird. At least he knows he's a son of a bitch and deserves to die. He actually expects it. I think he would just about prefer it to being taken by the police. He knows he's not getting out of here now. They're onto him now, Jane. We've all become too powerful. They know. And they will take him if we don't kill him or hide him. I don't think we can let them take him. We have to stop this shit. He's going to make someone too dangerous and end up getting us all killed.

I spoke out loud. I didn't care if the doctor heard me or not. "Wow, Dan. You got all of that from what we just heard? That's more than I got." I gave him a smile and he smiled back, happy and at ease. My Dan was so beautiful.

Don't forget, my love. I have my ears and yours. And I have two sets of eyes. And I can feel with both of our feelings. So yeah, I got more, but you helped me get it.

We could tell the doctor was getting very nervous. So I started on the questions again.

"Dr. Burgis. Tell us what has happened to the other ten teens you have experimented on. What have you done? Other than create the first vampires and Sky. And a witch. What's happened to the rest of us? Tell me. Now."

Dr. Burgis licked his lips. He shot one more nervous glance to the door. I could tell he was remembering how fast we were. I watched the hope of escape seeping out of him almost like a visible, physical thing by the way his shoulders and the rest of him relaxed. Muscles releasing their tense hold on stored energy as a dash for safety was abandoned and he accepted whatever fate we saw fit to deliver. It was a weird way to look at it. I wondered briefly if this was some weird new *vampire* thing. My body trying to get me ready to stalk my intended prey. Human. My face set in a harder line as I stared at him and he started speaking.

"All right. All right." He licked his lips again and smoothed back his hair.

Dan and I waited. We were faster now, but that also meant everyone else was slower, which also meant we waited longer for everything. Just peachy.

"Of the twelve teens in the drug study, four of you have become very powerful. Something very special. You and Dan of course are two of those four. Then there is Sky. In some ways she is the most powerful of—" He stopped and looked at us as if uncertain how much to say or if he should sugar coat what he said and make it more P.C. and less gritty truth. I watched his eyes consider this and reject it. His body, eyes, and face were so easy to read it was the same as spoken words to me. I could tell he thought we would know if he was lying or holding back details. I saw the decision. The set of his jaw. I knew he was going to say what he wanted without the sugarcoating. The "good doctor" mask finally came off and the man behind the curtain stepped out and opened his mouth.

"You four are the most powerful of my creations. Sky is unique in that she can actually *create* life, but she is also a very good and gentle individual. Very moral. She limits herself greatly because of this. Then there is Rain Bryant. I do not know the extent of her powers, but from what I've heard and the little that I've seen, her power is absolutely astounding. I haven't had the opportunity to speak to her about her new abilities directly but I am looking forward to it. She still needs to come back and take her pills." The doctor was smiling again just like a true Dr. Frankenstein, the mad genius delighting over his monsters.

I had an unwanted mental image pop into my head like a scene from an old horror movie of Dr. Burgis rubbing his hands together over some stitched together animated corpse as it rises from a table in his laboratory. Some new monster given life by the mad scientist.

What a freak. I thought to Dan. He replied back,

Yep. Nothing fancy. Your basic mad scientist. It's a well know villain type. I've read dozens of comic books with them and seen movies with them. It's still weird to actually see one right in front of me. Like in real life. Weird.

I laughed. Full and happy. Dan slipped up behind me and wrapped his arms around me, looking over my shoulder at the doctor. I could tell by the look in the doctor's face that he wanted to ask me a hundred questions about what it was like to change into a vampire. I helped him focus.

"And the others, doctor. Tell me about them."

He nodded. "The others. Yes. None have shown the kind of abilities that you four have demonstrated. At least not openly where I could see and identify it. However. A few of the others have had very simple and predictable reactions. Katie, she was in the office first thing this morning. She was fixated on her art when she started the pills and now that talent has developed into something amazing. She's probably the greatest artist to have ever lived, but still, this change is of a more mundane and less supernatural nature." There in his voice was the rest of what he meant. He was proud of her but it was like a less favorite, less interesting toy. All too predictable and overall not very interesting. Hearing the way he discounted this Katie girl and what she could do reinforced the simple fact that the doctor was an ass.

"Then there is Ryan. He has some very frightening abilities."

"Ryan?" I asked.

The doctor nodded, looking grave. "Yes. Ryan is a true believer. He actually believes the Bible. If he had prayed for you to be changed back into a human, I am quite sure that you would have changed. It was fascinating, watching him try to get you to let him change you back. He couldn't make you do it or force you into it. That would violate his understanding of free will. Fortunately, the nature of his belief system limits him. If he doesn't think, down in his heart, that what he is praying for is 'God's will,'" he made finger quotes in the air, "then nothing happens. Ryan has directed and attributed his power to God answering his prayers and if he doubts that what he is praying for is truly God's will then his prayers go unanswered. Honestly, I am concerned what it will do to him when he learns the truth, about his abilities I mean, that he is causing things to happen himself and that it's not really God that's doing it. I fear that Ryan may not cope well with this knowledge. It's troubling."

"Ya think!?" I snapped angrily. "Troubling," he says. Like Ryan going mad meant nothing more to him than a new toy he just bought from Wal-Mart getting broken before he had a chance to play with it much! I'd like to rip his friggin' head off. I wonder how high the blood would shoot into the air. I wonder what color it would be in the fluorescent lights. I bet it's tasty. And fresh.

Dad said I could eat him. Hmmm.

"HEY!" I shouted as Dan's arms lifted me off the ground and into the air. He stepped back from the doctor a step or two and the doctor backed up against the far side of the room, getting away from me and my glowing red eyes.

"Daddy said I could eat him!" I griped. Oops. Said that out loud. Dan's arms tightened on me and I laughed. It tickled.

"Okay! Okay! I'll be good!" I managed to say as I laughed. Dan slid me back to the ground down the length of his body and he leaned forward and kissed me like I wanted him to, and then we turned back to the doctor.

"You're very lucky that my Dan is nice. Now tell me about the rest of them, doctor. I'm listening."

He mopped a hand across his brow, adjusted his dangling glasses back onto his nose, and then started talking again.

"Susan Palamino. A very musically inclined young lady with a reaction similar to that of Katie. Quite predictable. Her ability to sing and I would imagine to play musical instruments has improved exponentially. She wouldn't divulge much, but I heard enough to understand what's happening with her. Susan hasn't arrived yet today so I don't know if her change has progressed any further. And then th—"

"Wait!" I snapped and the doctor froze. Dan and I both looked up at the ceiling where we could hear movement. Then the whine of a drill. Right in the corner of the room a small camera on a bendable stalk like the head of a snake poked down through the white ceiling tile and was directed at us.

Isn't that cute, Dan. The nice police want to join us. What do you think we should do?

The ceiling crawl space and that cramped area up there might be a good place for Believer to say hello to them. Perhaps we should tell him we have some unwanted guests and ask him to carry them out. I think Believer is so scary that they may just stay out once they see him.

I laughed. "I can't wait. Let's go ask him if he would mind taking care of our little pest problem," I said.

Doctor Burgis didn't move. He watched as I walked over to the door and opened it. Believer still stood in the center of the hall where we had last seen him. Keeping guard. His red eyes turned in my direction when I opened the door.

"Believer," I called. Each of his giant steps covered more distance than a single step should have covered as he half walked, half floated over to stand in front of me. I pointed up to the ceiling, "We have some police that have crawled on top of our room. Is there any way you could go up and ask them to leave? We don't want them looking at us with their cameras or sitting up there listening to us." I scrutinized his smoky body. He looked pretty indestructible but you never know. I didn't want him to get hurt. "Don't get yourself hurt though. You be careful. And if you can, try not to hurt them much. They're just police or maybe soldiers, but right now they are following orders that we don't like, so if you could chase them away from us that would be great." I watched his red eyes as they sat in fixed points in the rolling mass of gray billowing clouds and smoke that made up his face. Believer was a *real* monster but I could already tell that he was a nice one.

"Police? Where are they?" He asked in a deep rumbling voice as he looked up at the ceiling of the exam room.

"I'm not sure. There somewhere in the crawl space above the ceiling tiles." I pointed at the camera in the corner of our room. The little camera actually tracked our movement as Believer and I walked over to it and looked up at it.

"They're up there right now? Looking at you with that?" Believer said, then looked back to me quickly.

"Is my Sky in any danger?" He suddenly looked very worried.

"Sky is fine," I said with confidence. "She's up front in the waiting room with Rain right now. And Rain won't let anyone hurt her. Rain is very powerful, Believer, and Sky is her friend."

Believer nodded; he seemed quite pleased with that answer. He looked back up at the ceiling and the little camera and spoke in his deep rumbling voice again. "I will go and ask them to leave. And I will try to be careful not to hurt them. Thank you, Jane."

Believer started to float up toward the camera just like a cloud would float, and once he got to the roof his hand pushed a ceiling tile up and out of the way and his huge smoky body just slipped into the recess above the ceiling. A second later the little camera was snatched back through the ceiling tile and all that was left was a little hole to show where it had been. We could hear some rustling noises overhead but only Dan and I could hear those noises because of our super hearing. Retreating rats. It seemed that Believer had it under control.

"Please finish, doctor," I said.

He complied. "Benjamin Grant, he seems to have some increased physical abilities. Strength and maybe more. I still don't know what he can do. He is obsessed with football and sports so his ability will probably center on the physical and be more mundane in that respect. Unfortunately he is not as well mannered. Brutish. He may be a problem if left unchecked."

This guy is amazing. I thought to Dan in my head. He actually wants us to take Benjamin out. To clean up his mess before Benjamin hurts other people.

Beside me Dan just nodded.

"And then the young black man in the military fatigues. Alfred Freeman. He was in earlier but has already taken his pills and gone. I actually sent him out the back. He hasn't shown or divulged any new abilities to my knowledge, but I am sure when they do develop it will emerge from his central obsession. He is a soldier. So he will probably just be a better soldier. Perhaps the ultimate warrior, so to speak. Another physical manifestation. But for all I know his abilities may go in an unexpected direction like some of the others have."

The doctor made a face; he looked regretful. "Shikith. A tall, athletic, black girl. She left the study after the first day. She had a horrible car accident with her parents. She has been in the hospital recovering from her injuries. I'm not sure what brought on the accident, but she is stable and should recover fully. And then there is David Hodges. His is a most unusual story." Doctor Burgis radiated curiosity; he wanted to know more about David. "He had an asthma attack at the mall as he watched a young lady being assaulted by a couple of thugs. Perhaps you saw the story in the newspaper or on TV. It was quite the story, and still would be, but there are so many amazing stories these days it has probably already faded away."

And the amazing stories were all about his *creations,* I could tell from his voice.

"The two thugs that were assaulting the girl burst into flames and burned to death right in the middle of the food court at the Orange Park Mall. The news called it the first case of documented and verified spontaneous human combustion. I'm sure it was David. He's in the hospital, recovering from the asthma attack, but he did manage to save the young girl who was being assaulted. So David may have some very frightening supernatural abilities, but I'm not overly worried. He's a very solid, nice young man."

Dr. Burgis stopped and looked at us. Like he was done.

"That's eleven patients, Dr. Burgis. What happened to number twelve?" I could read his body just like a book before he even opened his mouth.

"Joshua. He committed suicide. Killed himself with a shotgun." Well. At least he kept it short, I thought.

Let's take our pills and get away from this creep, Jane. He's pissing me off.

Dan stepped over to the bed in the center of the room and placed his big black bag on it. He unzipped the bag and took out two two-liter bottles filled with a sloshy red liquid. There were ten or twelve little blue cool packs inside the bag keeping everything inside nice and cool.

Jane, ask him if there's a microwave here. Dan asked me as he shook the bottles a little.

"Doctor. Do you have a microwave here?"

He nodded, apparently not surprised by the question. "Yes. At the end of the hall in the break room. Nurse Ann likes to eat in. She's on Weight Watchers so I got her a microwave for the break room." It was such a human sounding answer to come out of a monster like the doctor it made Dan and I both pause to look at him, then back to each other mirroring our movements as we thought the same thing at the same time. "Weird."

Jane. Keep a grip now, but I want you to sniff these and you let me know which one you like more, okay? I'll drink the other, whichever one you don't want. Or at least, whichever one you would want second.

I nodded and braced myself as Dan opened the tops on both of the two liters. It smelled wonderful, my skin felt flushed instantly. Wrapped up around the smell of blood I also smelled wine. It wasn't all blood; Dan had put at least *some* wine in with it. I guessed he did this to keep it from getting all stuck together. I didn't know. Dan was the smart, prepared one. My Dan. I leaned closer to the two bottles and sniffed first one and then the other. They were amazing, but one did smell better than the other. My eyes were rolling back into my head with need as Dan quickly put the caps back on the two bottles. I pointed a shaking hand at the one I liked and Dan nodded. He wasn't surprised. He held up the bottle I liked and said, *Avel, nice kid.* Dan held up the other one and said with a grin, *Kyle. Asshole. I paid them a hundred bucks apiece to come over and donate some blood last night. I knew we would need it today. I couldn't speak to you last night but I could feel that you were reading the book again. I knew you would be hungry, my love.*

Dr. Burgis had been busy; he'd gotten out two clear containers from one of the cabinets and held them in his hands. "Dan. If we're going to heat this up for you and Jane perhaps these would be best. They're microwave friendly." He looked at us and raised his eyebrows, and Dan and I could tell that he was being nothing but sincerely helpful. Damn. The doctor was about the weirdest little monster around. Dan and I shared another look and once again repeated our original assessment in our heads—"weird."

We got busy getting our lunch heated up with a nice side order of little white and blue pills to finish it off. Just what a growing vampire needs, I thought. Like cereal in red milk. Dan laughed quietly beside me and that made me smile.

Black Rain

So Many Me's

Ryan was inconsolable, sitting by himself looking out the window. I tried to comfort him, but he insisted on being alone right now. He said he needed some time to think so I backed off and started talking to Jane's mom. Williams was talking with Jane's dad about all the police and what to expect when they tried to leave. Sky and her father were in a heated little discussion of their own, whispering together off in a corner, and Jane and Dan had just gone into the back with Dr. Burgis, off to take their pills.

Jane's mom was so nervous and jittery as she spoke to me that she made my stomach hurt. I needed calm right now not spastic. She ran her hands through her hair as she rambled on.

"You seem to know so much about what's going on, Rain, and you seem so calm when I feel like I'm about to have a stroke for the hundredth time today. I'm so worried about them. Every time we turn around they've changed more and are doing something new. And when they change the rest of the way into vampires, what will they be like? I'm so worried about tonight! When they come back to life, after, after dying."

She was driving me nuts, but I couldn't blame her. She was still reeling from all that had just happened. I mean, GOOD GRIEF! My eyes were still locked in the (wide open) setting, and it took something pretty wild to wig me out these days. And I still couldn't believe Ryan. I mean, he did have a good excuse for acting crazy, being messed with by the magic of Jane's Midnight book, but I knew that most of what he had said had just been Ryan being Ryan. He really did love Jane, but that stuff at the end was intense. Personal. Throwing eternal damnation into the mix had taken it to the next level. Maybe the last level.

And you had to love Jane, the girl knew what she wanted and wasn't afraid to go through hell to get it. She wanted her Dan. I couldn't imagine a lady on earth who wouldn't be jealous of what we had seen between those two. The heat between them was like magic; it clung to them, in the way they moved and held onto each other and looked at each other. It was mind blowing. It was so crazy it made Romeo and Juliet look pathetic. I felt sorry for the next guy I met. I knew I wouldn't be able to get the image of Dan out of my head. Pretty damn hard to measure up to that!

"Rain?" Jane's mom was still waiting for an answer to some question I hadn't heard.

"Oh! Sorry, Mrs. Miller. I'm actually still trying to take it all in." Seeing something like that, seeing love like that was making me think. Making me think and dream. I could feel deep down inside me things moving that I hadn't even thought were in me. Was it *hope*? Was there a Dan somewhere out there for me? After seeing what I'd just seen I had to hope so. Maybe my life didn't have to end like Rain Marie's had. In tragedy. Maybe there was love out there for me too. I wasn't her, so I didn't have to end like her.

"Mrs. Miller. I think as long as Jane has her Dan she's going to be one of the happiest—make that *the* happiest person I know. Sorry. I'm just not through flipping out over it. I mean. Wow. She really loves him."

Mrs. Miller bobbed her head and wiped at her eyes. "She does, doesn't she?"

"Yes. She does," I said with feeling.

"Someone's coming. Black limo," Ryan announced to the room.

We all rushed over to the windows. There, rolling across the parking lot was a black limousine, heading straight for our office. It felt weird, all of us looking out the window together. It had a very *us* versus *them* feel to it.

Sky said, "I'm not going to go with them, Daddy." She kept her eyes on the approaching limo. Her lips were pressed tight together. She looked determined.

"We don't know what they want," Sky's father said. "I am sure that they want to talk to us but we don't know anything else. Let's just see what happens, Sky. Don't panic." He was trying to calm her down, but I didn't trust him. I also needed to find out where Williams' limits were before the shit hit the fan.

"Williams," I called and he looked my way from where he had been peeking through the blinds, watching the approaching limo with us. (On our side?)

"Right here," he said and waited for me to ask the questions.

"You're going to be put in a fix here soon. You're my friend, Williams, and I trust you, but there are people out there who can give you a direct order to screw us over. And I'm sure they are going to try to get you away from us and ask you about all our personal private crap that we've been dumping on you. Hell, if you don't spill the beans when they ask they'll probably put you in the little room and shine the heat lamp in your eyes till you talk."

Williams laughed but it wasn't a happy laugh. "Yeah. You're right about that. They're gonna squeeze me." He knew it was coming. Everyone was listening to us now. Trying to understand how Williams fit together with me and Ryan.

"I would like it if you could stay with me. I still need someone to help me, Williams. I have Ryan and my mom can help me, and my Sisters—but I'll miss you if you have to go." It seemed like a lot more had passed between us than was possible in the few hours since breakfast this morning when Bethany and Mary had almost fried his brain like the eggs he'd been trying to eat. I laughed remembering that.

"What?" Williams asked me, half of a smile on his face.

"Just remembering this morning." I walked over and stood in front of Williams.

We stood there and looked at each other while everyone watched. It felt formal.

"I can't run the risk of having you with me and not being able to trust you, Officer."

Williams winced but nodded. "I can't say as I blame you. But I'm worried about leaving you alone. You've already passed out twice since we came to the waiting room, and all types of crazy is happening around you all the time. Vampires biting people and people swinging baseball bats and this other craziness." He looked over at Sky. "And don't forget that big kid earlier that couldn't take a hint. That Benjamin kid. You need someone to take care of you. And to keep you from losing it and hurting people!"

Williams shot a quick glance back out the window, and the rest of us did too. There were three guys in suits walking up toward the office. I walked over to him and got up on my toes to give him a kiss on the cheek.

"If you have to go, or if I have to send you away, know that I will miss you. Thank you, Williams."

Williams and I turned and watched as Ryan walked over to the door. He turned and faced us before he opened it. "Hope you can stay, Jason, but I doubt it. You know you're family now so don't be a stranger." Ryan still sounded so sad.

He turned around and opened the door for the approaching suits. One of them was obvious; it was Stan Reese, the guy in charge of the FBI. I recognized him from the TV, mostly because Ryan and my dad had hated him being put into that office and they'd fussed and fussed about it. They thought Reese was nothing but a political crony. Someone who got his job because of who he knew and who owed him favors. I honestly hadn't cared a flip one way or the other but at least I recognized the guy.

He wasn't stooped or bent over, but he was old. His face was copiously wrinkled and his hair was thin, gray, and shoved to the side in an old man comb over. The man who stood beside him looked a lot less "spent" than poor old Stan. He had a tight military style haircut, and he had some bars and stuff on his suit, military of some kind or other. The last guy stood behind the other two. He was a tall, Asian-looking man with a plain gray suit, blue shirt but no tie. He also had tattoos on his hands and face. He didn't fit in with the others. I didn't like it.

They stopped just inside the door. Stan Reese was apparently not the main man in this because the military guy stepped up front. He scanned the room and stopped on Sky, nodding to her.

"Hello, Sky," he said politely. "My name is Tom."

Sky looked at him for a second before she managed a frightened "Hello." Her eyes were narrow and she darted a desperate glance at me.

She was so scared it broke my heart to see the panic in her face. She looked like she was about to fly off any second, and I didn't want that. She was safer here with me.

"I've got this, Sky. Don't worry, honey, it's okay, I'm here," I said this and all three suits turned to me. Behind them I could see Sky's relief at not being the focus of their attention.

"That's right, boys. Right here." I gave them my best emotionless blank wall gaze and waited.

Tom, the guy that had spoken to Sky spoke to me now.

"Hello, Black Rain. It's good to meet you." He attempted a halfway believable smile. I wondered how long he had practiced in front of a mirror to make this happen on demand. I still thought it looked canned. Fake.

I gave a weak smile back. "I wish I could say the same. But I'm sure you already know that I don't like meeting new people. And that is our first problem, 'Tom.' Do you remember the other things that will cause a problem, 'Tom'?" Each time I said his name I "popped" it out in an annoying fashion.

I gave him a dark look. "Have you done your homework, 'Tom'?"

Jane's parents, Sky's father, and Sky watched this little exchange with growing concern, but Ryan and Williams actually shared a grin and a head shake. They were used to me meeting new people like this. Got to break them in my way. Part of being a witch and all.

Mr. and Mrs. Miller were behind us, huddled by the back office doors trying to look invisible while they waited on Jane and Dan to come back out. They didn't want anything at all to do with the Feds or the cops. They just wanted their two vampires from the back office and then they wanted out of here.

I didn't think these suits were going to let any of us go anywhere. I was sure they wanted everyone who was in the drug study.

Sky's father tried to take a step closer to her, and she stepped away, putting her arm out, purposefully keeping him a short distance away. It was obvious she wanted room to fly if she needed it. She didn't trust her father at all. The suits also noticed this little movement, and I was sure they knew what it meant. It was tense in the room.

Tom's smile wavered for a second then slipped back on. "Yes, ma'am. You do not like to meet new people, and for that I do apologize. You don't want people to offer incense and candles to you. No problem there. And you do not like rudeness."

He nodded his head like that should do it, but I slipped up a hand and raised one black nailed finger and shook it back and forth in a *no no no* gesture. "Sloppy. You left out some of the best parts 'Tom'."

He winced a little as I popped out his name annoyingly. It surprised me that he was so easily tweeked. It made me smile and I felt my wicked side start to rise and the power within me rose with it. It started to leak out of me; I just couldn't hold it in. I gritted my teeth against it and swayed on my feet, and I felt Williams steady me, his arms holding me up.

"Black Rain, are you okay?" Williams asked.

"Bring me a chair, Williams," I managed to say through my clenched teeth. He called to Mr. Miller who was standing by the back office wall to grab a chair, and soon Williams and Ryan were helping me take a seat as the three suits watched us.

"Could we bring you a doctor, Black Rain?" asked Tom.

"Shut up and give her a second," Ryan snapped at him. He was standing on one side of my chair now with Williams on the other side. I squeezed my eyes shut, trying to hold back the power I felt raging inside me. It was a little easier with my eyes squeezed shut.

"Tom," I said with my eyes shut.

"Yes, Black Rain?" I heard impatience in his voice.

It pissed me off just enough to make me open my eyes and look at him. My hair started its annoying little under the sea waving motion as energy crawled across my scalp and down my hair, and I felt the flush of power as it slipped out of my skin and into the air around me. The three suits all stepped back a step or two and I couldn't help the laugh that came out. The lights overhead flickered as waves of raw power rolled out of me, happy to be free of the confined space of my body. Already gravity for the small objects nearby was becoming optional with me as the anchor point, a sun for my orbiting solar system of knick knack office crap. I noticed a pen floating by in front of the suits, doing a slow end over end. All three of them watched as it ambled by then looked back at me. I smiled at them.

"Easy, Black Rain," Williams cautioned me. "Remember, these are the good guys. They have to talk to you; that's their job, so try to be patient with them."

I sobered up some from my power high and nodded. "I'll try, Williams," I said quietly. I felt my body trying to float out of my chair, and it was getting frustrating. I was holding onto the arms of the chair and wrapping my feet around the legs just to stay seated. "Guys, hold me down please."

Williams and Ryan each put a hand on a shoulder to keep me in my chair. Once I was all comfy I started again by trying to annoy Tom some more.

I don't know why. It just felt like the thing to do.

"Tommmmm." I stretched his name out long this time instead of saying it short and clipped.

"Yes, Black Rain?" His voice was even tighter and more annoyed, which made my temper flare, which made my control slip. I closed my eyes and held my breath as I tried to hold inside all the power that wanted to come rushing out! I swallowed it down but it hurt. Damn! *Calm down!* I told myself. Gotta stay calm.

"Please. Just tell me. What do you want, Tom?" I spoke quietly now. Without games this time.

"Black Rain, you need to be in a hospital. You need help."

How nice, I thought, annoyed. Tom's voice had gone from annoyed to sympathetic.

"We want to keep all of you safe. You, Jane and Dan, and Sky. There are a number of very sick people out there that mean to do you harm and we don't want that to happen. We want to keep all of you safe."

A *Sports Illustrated* magazine was floating by making a nuisance of itself, and it hit Stan Reese in the side of the head. He batted the aggressive periodical away sending it off to hazard the other side of the office as I spoke with Tom.

"Dr. Burgis said you've already got the whole place bugged. Is he wrong?" I asked.

"No," Tom answered, "he's not wrong. We bugged the building and we have been listening to you but we still have a lot of questions that need to be answered and we need to get you to a safe place."

I laughed, and lights flickered overhead. "Safe for who? You want to know what we can do. Fine. You want to study us like bugs in a box. Wonderful. But tell me this, if one of us seems too dangerous will you pull off a leg or a wing so we can't fly away? Is that why you have net guns on the roof of the buildings around us? So you can capture your flying girl in a net? Like an animal?"

Before Tom could say anything, Williams quickly spoke up. "Sir. Please be very careful. Don't lie to her," he cautioned quickly.

Stan Reese was out of patience. He'd had enough and he obviously thought he could do better than "Tom" so he started talking.

"Sounds good to me, Officer. Just the plain honest truth then. Yes, we want to know what you can do. And yes, it's our job to take you to a safe place where you won't be a danger to other people or yourself. You'll all need to come with us until we can get this whole thing figured out. You don't need to be frightened about coming with us. I give you my personal promise that you'll be treated with care and we will accommodate all of your special needs. Blood as needed for Jane and Dan. And we can get *you* to someplace isolated so you won't have to meet new people all the time and where you'll be safe from all the religious nuts out there that are determined to kill you. There are a lot of those out there, Black Rain. Crazy religious zealots. And for you, Sky," the old man looked in her direction and took the time to give Sky's father the evil eye before he spoke to Sky. "We can promise you, in writing if you want it, that we will *never* use drugs on you like your mother and father have. We can provide you with a safe protected place to live where you won't be abused anymore."

Reese looked back to me. "Is there anything else? I've tried to be as forthcoming and honest as I can be. It's like the officer said, we're the good guys." Reese took another step into the room. "And perhaps the first thing we should do is get you a real doctor, young lady. Or better yet, take you to a hospital where they can get you checked out properly. You don't look well at all. Come out with us now and we can get you and the others the help you need."

I laughed and the lights flickered again. "Not just no. But respectfully, Mr. Reese, *hell no*." I tilted my head to the side and studied their reactions. Frustrated summed it up nicely. "So. What now, Reese? What will you do when a little teenage girl tells you 'no'? Is it time to send in the troops? I'm just a little girl and you're a man. I can't even stand up right now. Just come on over and force me. Make my 'no' into your 'yes'." I let out a little sigh. It was time to make some changes.

I looked up and to my right where Williams stood with one hand on my shoulder. "I'm sorry, Williams, but it's time. I can't ask you to go further with me. Come and visit us again sometime. And thank you."

He blinked in surprise at the dismissal, then shook himself. He put a hand out to shake Ryan's hand, but Ryan ignored it and gave him a one-armed hug instead as he held me in my chair with his other hand.

Once Ryan let go, Williams leaned down and gave me a hug. "Goodbye, my witch girl. Tell those sisters of yours bye from me too." He looked over at Ryan, "Don't let her lose it. It's on you now, man." Williams gave him a nod and stepped away toward the suits.

Stan Reese waited until he walked by and slipped out the front door before he made his move.

"We need you and Sky to come with us now, Rain," Reese said. He pulled out his own radio and started to mumble into it. I assumed he was calling in the troops. Ryan was still holding me down, keeping me in my chair.

"Let me go now, Ryan, and go get Dan and Jane out of the back. We're leaving."

"Are they going to let us leave?" Ryan asked and pointed with his chin to the suits who were just standing there like statues listening to us talk about them. I looked up at my brother's face. He was still so sad.

"Of course they are," I said, "They're not going to have a choice. I'm just trying to get it done as smoothly as possible. I don't want to hurt anyone unless they make it happen. I'm not ready to be a monster yet, even if I am one."

"You're not a monster, Rain." He kissed me on the top of my head then let go of my shoulders and headed to the back office area to retrieve Jane and Dan. Mr. and Mrs. Miller went with him.

I relaxed my grip on the power inside me just a fraction, and I felt myself lift out of the chair. I threw up a wall of magic between myself and the three suits, hemming them in there by the door. They couldn't see the wall but it was there. I hung in the air about a foot off the ground and looked at the three men in front of me as my hair fanned out behind me like a shimmering black halo. Mr. Reese backed up to the door and kept one hand on the handle like he was ready to bolt, but Tom and the other man stayed where they were. Tom had his radio out now, talking away to someone as well.

Sky lifted up off the ground and flew across the room, hanging in air right beside me.

"I didn't know you could fly like me," Sky said to me. Her big smile was always so pretty as it lit up her face. She was pretty. Inside and out.

"No, Sky. I float and flop around. You fly." I made a face and she laughed. "I'm going to go flop over there and talk to the suits some more, just keep your eyes open. And don't worry." She looked graceful as she hung in the air beside me; for her, being in the air looked natural like she'd been flying all her life. I gave her a little wave and floated a little closer to the suits, stopping just short of the invisible barrier that I had made.

"Mr. Tom. Mr. Reese," I looked at the last guy, "and whoever the hell you are. I know this is going to sound hard to believe but I'm trying to hold inside my body more power than you can even imagine. I'm that powerful. But I am also unstable and dangerous. Very, very dangerous. That's why I warned everyone to stay away from me. Now have you understood me so far?" I waited while they looked at each other for a second.

Tom answered, "We understand you're dangerous. And we understand that Sky and the vampires and possibly some of the others like Benjamin are also dangerous. That's why we want to help you. You need our help." He actually sounded like he meant it this time. Behind me I heard the arrival of the vampires and the others and I saw the shocked expressions on the faces of the three suits as Jane and Dan stepped up behind me.

Stan Reese said, "If you will excuse me, Black Rain. I'll leave you with Tom and Dr. Sangai." And with that he bolted out the door like his pants were on fire.

"What's up with him?" I asked Tom.

"Mr. Reese was worried about Dan's ability to read minds. He thought it best for national security purposes if he excused himself." He said this with a grin.

Jane appeared on my left side and Dan was just there, standing on my right side. Jane spoke for both of them.

"He's telling the truth. He's glad to have Reese gone. Reese wasn't even supposed to be in this meeting, but he made Tom bring him along. Tom is the one in charge, Rain. But there is a problem with the other guy. Dan and I are still trying to hear what that problem is." Jane tilted her head to the side as she looked at the Asian guy with his tattoos. And that was when the Asian guy turned on his heels and headed for the door.

I willed the door to stay shut, and we watched as he pulled and pulled on it, getting frantic as the door refused to open and let him escape.

"Dr. Sangai. Calm down! Stand down!" Tom ordered.

"Let me out!" Sangai shouted as he pulled on the door. It seemed as if he intentionally didn't turn around so we could see his face. He looked straight ahead at the door and kept pulling on it.

Jane said, "He's an assassin or a spy or both. He'll probably try to kill Tom now." She said it like it was no big deal.

Before I even had a chance to raise an eyebrow, they were at it. Sangai had gone for a gun and Tom grabbed at his hand. The gun was halfway out as they fought for control.

"Bam!" Something hit my magic shield. It was Dan! He'd charged in to help Tom but crashed into the invisible barrier and staggered back. He looked surprised but not hurt by the collision, but oddly enough Jane had passed right through my magic shield like it wasn't even there and she already had Sangai wrapped up in her arms.

"Dan! Are you all right?" Jane said from inside the shielded area. She had the Asian guy well in hand with both of his arms behind his back, holding him like he weighed nothing. He looked frantic, feet kicking as she held him in the air like a wing pinched bug.

Tom was doubled over with his hands on his knees, trying to catch his breath, but he looked thankful. Dan nodded to Jane; it looked like he spoke with her for a second in his way then disappeared as he made one of those fast moves and reappeared up against the side of the invisible shield again, running his hands over the surface of it, exploring it.

All of the excitement had my heart rate up, and I hadn't noticed how much power was escaping from the inadequate prison of my body. I smelled something nasty; it stunk like burnt plastic and I looked around to find where the smell was coming from. The carpet directly under where I floated had started to blacken and crisp and the ceiling tiles over my head and the snarl of silver duct work behind them had been forced up and away, pressed flat to the metal roofline above me.

Behind me, Sky and all the others in the room had backed away and stood at the back of the room now, backs pressed up against the wall. I tried to pull the energy inside myself but it actually hurt to do it. Even my bones hurt. I needed to get this done before it killed me.

"Rain! Are you okay!?" Ryan called to me from the back of the room. He could tell I was hurting.

I shook my head no. "Stay back, Ryan. It's bad up close to me. I just burned up the carpet. I can't control this and I don't want to hurt you," I whispered but I wanted him to hear me and I willed my words to reach him. I saw him nod his head.

I dropped the air shield I had put around the suits. Dan's hands felt the barrier disappear, and he was instantly beside his Jane, taking custody of the bad guy. Jane helped Tom gather himself together and led him to me but they stopped a good ten feet away. Tom actually held a hand up in front of his face like I was hot. I didn't feel hot. Was I hot?

My bones ached as I looked at Tom. His eyes darted around the room, jumping from impossible sight to impossible sight. Watching him made me look too and see it the way he might see it for a second.

He was surrounded by monsters.

Sky hung in the air a safe distance away, one vampire held a struggling Asian guy in his arms, and another vampire stood right beside him and held his hand as I floated in the air in front of him like a little sun in the middle of the room. Floating objects, pens, a stapler, and other little things were still caught in my orbit for twenty feet around me as I ground my teeth against the pain. I hurt. My bones hurt. My skin hurt as Tom started talking again.

"I'm sorry. He wasn't one of my men. He's with the NSA and I was told to bring him with me, Black Rain. We will deal with him."

"He's telling the truth," Jane confirmed. "Although he doesn't know if this guy had orders to kill you or not."

Tom gave her a quick suspicious glance then tried to extract his hand out of her grip. She didn't let go and just smiled at him. That made me laugh and Tom looked back to me. It was great that Jane was acting as a human lie detector for me, but now it was my turn to talk anyway.

"I have given fair warning that my sisters and I are dangerous. Very, very dangerous." I looked at the man struggling in Dan's hands and willed him to sleep. A long and peaceful sleep, but just sleep. He would be needed later. He went slack, his body limp in Dan's grasp.

Ryan's voice reached me from where he stood against the back wall. "Did you kill him?" he called. He didn't sound as if he was going to argue about it even if I had.

"No, not yet," I answered. The implied, "it's on my *to do* list" was there in my voice.

Tom looked alarmed, "We need him Black Rain! We need to find out who he was working for! Why he tried to kill me or you. Don't kill him! I need him!"

I looked down at Tom from where I floated a couple of feet above the ground.

"This man just tried to kill you and I'm sure he would have tried to kill me and Sky if he'd gotten a chance." I gritted my teeth, trying to keep my temper in check as I fought the pain of the power coursing through my body.

Tom tried to step closer to me then stepped back quickly, like that extra step was a bad idea. He rubbed at his eyes and face like they hurt or like he was trying to get bugs off before he started talking again.

"Hold on now! For all we know Dr. Sangai may have panicked when he couldn't get out of the door. And so far you haven't broken any laws or hurt anyone. You're not a murderer and you're not going to kill him. Now let me take him out of here so we can finish talking." He edged a little closer to the limp form held by Dan and looked back at me, his eyes asking permission. Tom had forgotten about Jane who was still holding his hand, walking with him.

Jane said, "He's lying, Rain."

Tom's eyes snapped to Jane and then down to his hand held by the vampire. He tried to pull his hand free again, but Jane held tight and spoke again in her strange musical voice.

"Tom, you don't really believe that that guy panicked. And you know he was trying to kill you. And you do think he was going to try to kill us. You just want him for yourself so you can get answers. Don't try to lie. It's just not possible with me here." Jane smiled at him and this time she showed teeth that were so blinding white they flashed in the office lights.

I laughed and the lights in the room laughed with me. It was good to see that Jane had a wicked side too. To his credit Tom didn't freak out. He stopped trying to get Jane to let him go and turned back to me.

"Rain, you've never killed anyone. You are not a murderer. And this is a perfect time to prove it. To prove to all of those idiots out there!" He jabbed a finger with his free hand toward the glass window and beyond where the hundreds of police and soldiers waited. "That you're not a murderer. None of you are. You've all had these changes forced upon you by Dr. Burgis and whatever he's been passing off as the Derm pills in this drug study. None of this is your fault. None of it! You're all good kids doing your best to deal with what's happened and you most certainly are not killers. Rain, you're not a murderer. Now let me take Dr. Sangai out of here. Please."

Everyone looked at me.

"That's not true," I whispered. He had said I wasn't a murderer.

I was. I looked over at the man in Dan's arms. Was I really going to do this? Making threats and talking about it was one thing, but actually doing it was something else. Was I going to murder this guy?

I felt so confused. Like I didn't even know myself. Like I didn't know who I was. I heard Ryan calling to me and some of the others but I ignored them. I was dizzy. If I hadn't been floating in the air I would have fallen on my face. I felt flushed. On fire. Burning.

I felt the word *murderer* inside me, like it was crawling around under my skin, wanting to come out, fighting to push through my flesh and expose what was inside me to everyone. As within, so without—

Am I a murderer? I asked myself and closed my eyes, trying to think, but it was so hard to think with all this power burning through me and trying to get out. My skin felt on fire! I thought about not feeling any pain at all and I felt much better right away.

Think! I had to think—am I really, truly a murderer? The power was still making it harder and harder to concentrate and keep my mind on anything! So I concentrated, thought about myself and focused my will on my mind. No matter what happened to my body I wanted to still have my mind and be able to "think" and it got easier to think again. Easier to try to go through things in my head.

I thought about when I was made and I was able to remember it so clearly now for some reason. Everything came into perfect focus. That cold ugly room in the abortion clinic where Rain Marie first started talking to herself. Talking to me. She made me and I killed our child, Brendon, but only because Rain Marie made me do it. After we killed Brendon she had wanted to die. She wanted to die with him, but she didn't want to kill herself, her body, and make our family sad. So she asked me take her place. She couldn't just leave and leave me there. She tried to, but she couldn't do it without my help. She asked me to push her out and take her body so she could go to heaven with Brendon. She swore that if I didn't do it, she'd kill herself anyway. I did it, but down in my heart I had hated it. I didn't want to kill either of them.

Did that matter? Was I a murderer? As within, so without. I had done the deed, killed on the outside. But was I a murderer on the inside? Inside of whatever shred of a soul I had left was I really a murderer?

I thought about the night of the Lammas celebration and the Black Candle. The Murderer's Candle. My candle. But in my heart would I kill another person, not because someone else told me to but because I wanted to do it, because I thought they deserved to die? Was I really going to kill this man right now? Rip away his life and send his soul back to God who made it.

Am I a murderer? I asked myself again. Was I the Black Witch or not? Was I going to be within my heart what I already was without? Did I really have a choice? I couldn't go back to the shell of a life Rain Marie had left me with even if I wanted to now. I'd cut myself off from her and cast myself away from God.

I was alone.

With my eyes closed, I floated—

I felt nothing, not my body, no pain, nothing—

I felt adrift and alone in the world. An alien to this creation and those in it.

It felt like the only thing that kept me alive at all was my will. My desire to exist. Like if I just let go, my life would wink out like a light being turned off in a dark room—*and that scared me*. I wasn't ready for it to be over yet! I still wanted to live! I want to live! It scared me to think that my damaged soul might simply drift apart into nothing, like a mist or a vapor in the air. There and gone. I clung to the only life I could find now in the darkness of my mind.

"I am the Black Witch," I tried to say but couldn't.

"I am the Black Witch." I couldn't say the words. I tried to open my eyes, but I couldn't see anything. Nothing.

I couldn't feel, or hear, or see anything of my body at all. Again, this scared me. I thought that maybe I had damaged my eyes and my mouth and I willed myself to heal. Heal my head, my eyes, my mouth, my skin, my arms, my body. I willed myself to heal inside and outside and soon I felt my arms and legs and mouth again. I felt on fire and I willed myself to heal more and felt the excruciating pain in my body all over and I was just so happy to "FEEL" anything I didn't even try to stop the pain! I thought about healing more.

"I am the Black Witch!" I gasped out, finally able to use my mouth again and able to hear myself. Fighting to live! Fighting to come back from that black nothingness! I had another wild thrill of fear at the thought that I had finally gone completely mad. Totally stark raving mad! Like a reluctant Alice in Wonderland, for so long I'd been trying to climb out of the rabbit hole to find something normal and sane in my world, but not now.

I quit fighting against the insanity of what was happening to me and embraced it. I turned about and went deeper, down the rabbit hole, down to the very bottom, never to rise again. I would make my home here in this fantasy world. This was my life now. I felt the "witch" inside me rising to the surface and this time I did not try to hold it back, tie it down, or limit it. This time I was glad and welcomed the wildness and the passion and let it carry me wherever it wanted to go. I was just glad to have something, anything, to fill me, so I filled myself with the Black Witch and everything I had ever dreamed that meant. Everything my heart ever imagined the Black Witch would be I let wash over me.

I opened my eyes. I could see again. Everyone was pressed against the walls as far from me as possible. I still hung suspended in air in the center of the room. I put my arms out in front of me. They were bare, and white, and pale. I looked down at my bare, exposed chest. A shred or two of burnt black cloth clinging to my new skin was the only evidence that I'd ever had a dress. Apparently I had burned myself down to almost nothing before I had started healing myself.

I focused on my dress and the burnt bits and the shreds of cloth that remained spread out and covered me until my nakedness was covered and the dress was whole and perfect again. I looked around the room one more time at the shocked and horrified faces. I didn't care what they thought, I was glad to be alive and happy to have a life. I was a witch now and the life I chose was calling me. I felt it settling deep into my soul. I felt like a witch. So mote it be.

"Let the Black Witch now rise!" I shouted and thought of thunder and it was there! A massive clapping BOOM! rocking the sky, rattling the windows, shaking the whole building! Everyone cried out in surprise except the vampires who stood as still as stones while the world trembled at my power.

The booming noise only pealed and rolled for a second, but it took a minute or two for everyone to get their legs under them again, wildly looking around to see if all was still well with the world and the building. Tom still stood with Jane and Dan. Dan was still holding onto our sleeping bad guy. I'm sure Tom was still hoping to get the other agent out of here and away from me.

The power within me was still causing little objects to float around the room and my hair still moved in waves as power rolled off my body and out into the air around me, but I no longer felt like I was about to come apart trying to hold it all inside. I was still getting used to the body I rebuilt, but I felt fine. I didn't try to think about the "whys" or the "hows" of what I had just been through. I was so totally thrilled to be alive I was practically euphoric!

I floated to the ground and landed on my bare feet in a slimy mess I could feel on the carpet. My shoes had burned to a crisp and my hair was gone too. I reached up and ran my hands over my smooth bald head and smiled. As I brought my hands down I stopped and looked at them; the skin on my hands was all white, like new made flesh. I willed my hair to grow back and it grew out long and black, down to my butt, then I willed all the other floating objects like pens, magazines, and other odds and ends that were floating haphazardly around the room to drop, and they all fell like their strings had been cut.

No one had said a word yet. It was a terrified, waiting silence.

The room was finally back to almost normal now. No waves of creepy heat and power coming from my body; gravity was back in good working order, and now I could almost pass myself off as a regular person instead of some floating freak from an *Exorcist* film. But all this "normal" just seemed to make everyone even more convinced that things were definitely NOT normal.

I walked, swaying my hips and smiling like the witch I was as I went toward Tom and the vampires. I stopped in front of them and sat in one of the chairs that was nearby and crossed my legs. I noticed that my feet were all bloody from whatever I'd stepped in on the floor and frowned. I willed the blood on my feet to dry up and blow away then looked up at Tom.

He looked back at me like he was seeing a stranger. Like he had never met me. He kept all of his movement very slow and well telegraphed like he didn't want to startle me. Like his life depended on not startling me.

"Are you all right?" he asked. He was looking at me with a mix of disbelief, horror, and strangely enough, acceptance. He still had a job to do.

I smiled and gave a little laugh, but this time the lights didn't flicker. There was no thunder. It was just a normal laugh. Tom and the vampires noticed the change and they all exchanged little looks, even looking up at the ceiling lights and back to me. They were all wondering what it meant.

"Well, Tom. You asked me, 'Are you all right?'" I cocked my head to the side as I considered that. "That depends on which 'me' you're talking about. Me, me, me. Me, me, me, me. Me, me, me, me, me." I made a carefree little humming tune out of it, bobbing my head as I leaned back in the chair, "Me, me, me, me, me. Lots of mes these days, Tom. If you're referring to the kind and confused girl that just burned to death here in this waiting room—then the answer would definitely be 'NO!'" The end of my words were like ice, hard and cold and angry.

Tom paled and swallowed. The vampires both looked uneasy too. I noticed the strong scent of burnt flesh in the air and remembered my feet and the blood. I looked back to where I had hung in the air. There was a very nasty looking puddle of scorched skin and pieces of the old "me" lying on the floor like a frightening puddle of roasted nightmares. I willed the mess to vanish into the oblivion and darkness that I'd almost disappeared into and sent the smell of burnt flesh with it then turned back to Tom. He and the vampires acted like they were too scared to move.

"Am I okay?" I said again, my voice more neutral. "Now. If you are referring to the girl that's sitting in front of you right now then, yeah, I'm okay." I smiled then stretched in the chair and winced, rubbing my shoulder. My new skin was a little tight, and I concentrated for a second on getting comfortable in my new body then I noticed my nails. My nails were plain and had no color at all. I held both of my hands up before my face and willed my nails to a nice long length and made them ultra glossy black. Of course I did the toes too. Had to match.

"If you're not the girl who just burned up then who the hell are you!?" Ryan yelled from the other side of the room. I turned to see him walking toward me. He must have heard what I had just told Tom. He was upset. Ryan and the others must have really freaked out when I burned and then came back. That had to have been nasty to watch.

They were a bedraggled looking, weepy bunch. I could see that Ryan had been crying and so had Sky. She walked just behind him, her hands reaching out to him to offer comfort. Good, I thought. Very good. Sky was a nice girl; I hoped they got together. Maybe that would help him get over losing Jane.

I got out of the chair and turned to face them. I willed the mark on my forehead to come back and shine, and I saw Ryan's eyes widen and then drop into a suspicious squint. He was afraid that I wasn't his sister anymore. And in a way he was right. But then in another way—I still felt like I was. I still loved him. I still felt like he was my brother. I wasn't Rain Marie but I was his sister.

"Ryan, I'm still your sister. But I had to give up what I was or cease to exist. A real person can't do what I just did. Can't go where I just went. 'Real people' don't come back from the dead. That's the kind of thing you can do only in a dream or a fantasy." I tried to think of the best way to describe myself. I had started as nothing but a phantom in Rain Marie's mind, a "friend" she had made to help her. She had given me life and then had me take over her living body. But now what was I? I changed when I became the Black Witch, and I changed again when I cut myself off from Rain Marie and God, and then, just now, when I burned up I changed again—so what on earth was I now?

I had no idea.

"If you're not a REAL person then what are you?" Ryan asked, still upset and scared.

I wished I had a nice safe answer for him that would make him happy but I didn't. I told him the only truth I could.

I told him what I believed I was.

"I am a fantasy made flesh and the dream of a dream come to life."

Ryan shook his head, "What do you mean, you're a fantasy?" He was searching my face, looking for his sister in me. "That doesn't make any sense." He stopped just a few feet from me, waiting, searching for something he could recognize as his sister.

"Ryan, I am truly the Black Witch now. And I hope you can still love me, but this will change things. I'm still figuring this out myself, and parts of this dream I'm in may actually be a nightmare." I gave him an honest shrug. "There are lots of things I don't know, but I'm happy with the things that I do know. I know that I still love you, and Mom, and Dad. I have changed, Ryan, but you're going to have to let me be what I have become. I am what I am."

I gave him a sad smile.

"So what does all that mean?" Ryan took another step closer, looking right in my face, still searching for his sister. "Are you going to go all crazy now?" He shook his head, "Can't you just go back to the way you were? Have you even tried to fix yourself, fix your mind like you did your body? Maybe you can, Rain. Maybe you can fix your memory too." He ran his hands through his hair and then shot an angry look at Tom who was still standing beside the vampires. "You would have been fine if this idiot hadn't of pushed and pushed! If they would have just left you alone like you asked!" He wiped tears from his eyes, and I stepped forward, removing the small space between us and hugged him.

"Ryan, I can't fix what's happened to me, all I can do is live as I am now. What I was is gone. I will not even turn my head to look for the shadows of what I was because they are burned and gone forever." I stepped back from his hug as Sky joined us.

"Hi," she said. "So. Are you still you?" She looked worried about me and worried about Ryan.

"No, Sky. I'm not still me." I sighed. "I am a new me, but this new me still loves the old you a whole lot. Will that do?" She grabbed me in a huge hug and lifted me off my feet, squeezing the wind out of me.

Good grief! I guessed it would do!

"Okay! Okay! I love you too!" I choked the words out. She squeezed me silly for another minute, and I laughed as she finally let me go.

"You scared the crap out of us, Rain!" Sky complained. "Do you do this all the time?" She gave me a disapproving frown, like I'd been bad and needed a good scolding.

"Do what all the time?" I asked, confused.

"Die!" she shouted, exasperated. "And then come back. From what you said earlier it sounds like you do this a lot." She shook her head and made a face, like my "dying" was a bad habit I should break, like chain smoking.

I laughed a good solid laugh and Ryan joined me as Sky gave us both the evil eye.

Tom walked up to me with the vampires shadowing along behind him. Dan still held the unconscious Dr. Sangai in his arms.

"I'm happy you're—all right," Tom said. "But could we finish talking? If you feel up to it." He obviously hoped I did.

I took a deep breath and sat in a chair and motioned for him to take a seat also. Everyone gathered around us, some dragging chairs up and sitting while others, like the vampires remained standing. It seemed weird to be able to let people sit with me again. I was almost normal now that I wasn't leaking power all over the place and making people's skin crawl off their bones.

Tom started right were we'd left off. "Can I take him out of here?" he asked again. Pointing his head in the direction of Dan and his prisoner.

"No," I said, all business. "His life is forfeit. He is mine. All those who come to me seeking the shadow of death will be welcomed with open arms. Be it one by one, ten by ten or by the millions. I am the Black Witch. The lighter of the Black Candle. She that formed me I murdered and I have murdered that which I have formed. As within, so without. I cannot hide from what I am, and what's more than that, I don't want to hide. So mote it be."

Of all those sitting in the circle around me only a few could follow or understand the confusing "witch" lingo but everyone could understand that I was not who I had been. Things had changed. I'd changed. There was no uncertainty or doubt in me as I looked at Tom.

He took this in quickly without surprise, as if he half expected this might be what he would face. "What are you going to do with him?" he asked with a grim expression on his face.

"I will kill him. But not right now." I flipped my hair over my shoulder and got comfortable in my chair. "I don't want to waste him. That would be wrong. He is dead anyway, but if his death can help others it should be so. If it will be accepted I will make his blood a wedding gift to the Queen of the Damned." I looked at Jane who didn't betray any emotion to my calling her what she had called herself or to my suggesting she eat this Fed.

Her head inclined just a fraction to the side and I knew she was talking to Dan. After a second, she nodded.

I turned back to Tom. "You want to help keep us safe and keep others safe from us. Fine. So be it. Then help. There is a wedding tonight which I am sure you are aware of. We will need to keep the crazies out but let the guests in, and I'm sure you'll want to put a bunch of soldiers or police around to keep an eye on everything so you can get started on that. Make that happen, Tom. I am willing to *try* to work with you. So. Are you ready to hear my terms?" I waited for Tom.

He cast one more look over at the unconscious guy held by the vampires and then said, "Yes. I would be glad to listen to your terms, Black Rain; however, I know that as long as Sangai is alive they will try to get him back. I hate to say it but you should probably kill him now if you're going to do it. Someone over me in the government may give a well intended order without fully understanding the consequences of the action. For all I know he was following their orders when he tried to kill you." He looked over at the limp form again.

Tom was being very forthcoming which probably had a lot to do with the vampires smiling at me right now. But what Tom said did make sense. I nodded.

"If his dying now will save others from dying later, so mote it be." I sat forward in my chair and made a circle as big around as my two hands joined together and held my hands about two feet from the floor. Small objects that littered the floor around us rose into the air and drifted toward me and as they came they dissolved, breaking down into millions of pieces like sand and snaking their way forward like little ropes toward my hands. The dust began to spin. It almost looked like I held a pint-sized tornado as the little pieces of material swirled and spun beneath my hands.

A floating magazine broke apart. A vase and fake plant. A phone from the office. A few pens and a few more magazines and I felt like I had enough raw material to make what I wanted. I thought about the shape in my mind. I formed a tall ornate urn made of the darkest, smoothest, black glass I could imagine.

I took just a moment to shape and craft the details, and then without even looking up from my work I thought about the man in Dan's arms and willed his blood to come out of his neck and float in the air over everyone's head and down into the urn in front of me. I heard the gasps of everyone in the room, but I didn't bother to look. I was working.

I thought about the urn and willed it to keep the blood warm and fresh and alive. Living, warm, healthy blood. I saw the red rope of blood start to enter the mouth of the urn, and I continued to work. Shaping and crafting the urn into my wedding gift for Jane and Dan. A gift that would help them as they died tonight. My gift. A gift only I could give.

I had used my powers to kill. To take life. That was why Rain Marie had made me. She needed someone to kill for her. Someone strong enough to do it. Someone able to go through the pain of it. I wondered if the Asian man's soul had gotten back to God yet and if God was pleased with him. I hoped so. But one way or another he was connected to God and all life in a way that I was not anymore.

I envied him his journey. It had been an accident, me cutting myself off from God, but I knew it was still my fault. Even when I had practiced Wicca with my Sisters as a witch I had never stopped believing in God. Not really. I had all of Rain Marie's memories. Years and years of going to Sunday School and Church and listening to the preaching and teaching were impossible to forget. God had made it very clear in the Bible. He didn't want people being witches, and I had chosen to be one and had ended up hurting myself. I still loved God. And I wanted to be respectful. This was his creation and his people with little pieces of his soul walking around, so yeah, I wanted to be careful. But this guy would have killed Tom and me and Sky.

He was done.

"Have a safe journey, Dr. Sangai. And please tell God that I love him and that I'm sorry. Thank you for the blood, we will use it well." I spoke into the urn as I watched the last of the blood trail in. I took a minute to shape and fashion an ornate top for the urn.

Before I sat up from my work I imagined a wall of magic running along the front of the building just outside the front office door so that no one could shoot through. I had just killed a guy; usually that's when some sniper takes you out in all the movies and cop shows I'd seen. I didn't really know if I could be killed anymore, but I didn't want to find out any time soon. Once a day was my limit, and I was already over. I was with Sky on that. Yeah, I needed to cut back to once per day on self-annihilation.

"Are you talking to the blood in that jar or are you praying?" Ryan asked.

I looked up at my brother. "To be absent from the body—" I quoted the first part of the Bible verse that explained what I wanted to say and of course Ryan finished it like I knew he would.

"—is to be present with the Lord." He looked confused. "So, you pray now? You just killed this guy and now you want to start praying?" He let a little smile creep onto his face. "Well, at least you told God you were sorry. That was good to hear. I saw that guy try to kill Tom, so I'm not all that sad to see him go. But you didn't have to squeeze him like a lemon into that jar. Tom said he'd get Jane and Dan all the blood they need from the blood bank."

Although he complained about the "squeezing," from his voice and face it sounded like he was daring to hope for some happy ending to all of this. He was still hoping I was okay. I wasn't. I wished I could just lie to him. A soothing, comfortable lie. It would be nicer than telling him the truth. As within, so without. I had to be true to myself even if that meant hurting my brother. Better to do it now and get it out of the way.

"No. I can't pray anymore, Ryan. If I want to say something to God, I have to ask someone else to talk to him for me. I'm cut off. I can't get to God anymore, Ryan. Just now, when I died, I didn't go to Him. I went somewhere but it was not to God and I don't think it was Hell. At least not the hell we know of. I don't think I'd belong in the same hell as everyone else. I'm not like anyone else." I just looked at him, my face devoid of all emotion.

Ryan's smile disappeared as he thought about what I had just said. He tried to reason with me using something he knew, something he understood. The Bible.

"Then you must not have really died, Rain. It's the only explanation. You must have healed yourself before your soul left your body. I know you remember the verse, 'It is appointed unto man once to die, but after this, the judgment.' Rain, if you really died you would be standing before God right now. For good or bad, one way or the other. Heaven or Hell. To be absent from the body *is* to be preset with the Lord. No exceptions, exemptions, or hall passes. It's the way things are. God's word does not change or fail. Somehow you must not have died all the way or, like I said, you probably healed yourself before your soul got— collected, or taken, or gathered by the angels. That must be what happened." He struggled, desperate for an explanation.

I felt tired. "Ryan. You're right. But I'm right too. That's why I was talking to what was left of Dr. Sangai as he slipped into the presence of God. For good or bad. Heaven or Hell. Sangai went there because he was a man. It's appointed unto 'man' once to die. Hu-*man*." I met his arguing eyes with what I knew was the cold flat truth staring out from my own. "Ryan, I died and came back. The only way I could do that would be for me to be something other than 'human' because as you just pointed out, humans only die once. For me, Ryan, 'to be absent from the body' just means I'm absent. And I think I've already been judged. And my judgment is to never be present. Even if I want to be."

"What are you trying to say, Rain? Are you telling me that you're damned? Beyond Damned!" he amended angrily, "That there's no hope for you anymore?

That God wont save you if you ask him to? I don't believe that!" His mouth pressed into a firm line. "Not for a second. Not you."

Jane walked up beside us. Her musical voice was gentle as she spoke. "Rain's not human anymore, Ryan. We noticed when we first got here. We could smell it. She's *other*."

Ryan kept shaking his head no, so Jane kneeled down beside my chair, looked right at him, and spoke with exaggerated slowness, trying to get Ryan to hear what she was saying. "Your sister is—not—human—anymore. And Heaven is for humans."

Ryan looked at me and Jane. "So both of you are damned. Forever." It wasn't a question. He looked over to Sky who was standing behind my chair. "What about you, Sky? Are you damned too?"

Sky's eyes got huge. "No way! Don't even say that!" She held two fingers up, twisted together. "Me and God are like that! And I'd die before I turned away from Him!" she practically shouted, then her eyes went wide and she slapped a hand over her mouth as she turned from Ryan and looked at me and Jane.

Us "damned" girls looked back at her. "Sorry guys, Sorry! I mean, I know you guys are—sort of—well, you know. And you know I love you guys and all, but—I mean, for me. I'm not going there. And—And—"

"It's okay, Sky." I stopped her before she turned herself inside out. "If I could have a 'do over' I'd go with your plan. But it doesn't work that way."

I willed the urn to rise and I had it float over to Dan where he stood beside Jane's parents. He caught it out of the air and I released it from my power.

Still kneeling beside my chair, Jane asked, "Dan wants to know why it's warm."

"Because the urn's magic will keep the blood in it warm, healthy, and alive until you are ready to drink it tonight."

Jane disappeared, then reappeared beside Dan like magic, and they both started talking together in their way as they looked at my gift.

Tom took this break in the religious and emotionally charged discourse to try to get back on a topic he cared about. "Black Rain, could we go over your terms now?"

I looked back to Tom, "Yes Tom. Let's do that. But before we do anything, Ryan and Sky are both about to fall over dead if they don't get some food fast. We must eat after we take our pills, and they haven't done that yet. Please have someone go across the street to The Loop and bring us some pizzas and some salads and stuff as quickly as possible. I'll need to eat soon also. And have someone run down the street to the hospital and fill up a cooler with some fresh O positive for our vampires. That way it's ready and right here if they get thirsty. And Tom," he looked up from writing in his notepad and met my eyes, "you might want to be extra careful with the food that comes over. Make sure it's not poisoned. The vampires and I are almost impossible to kill, but the rest of us are still human. I give this word of caution because I dread the thought of what I might do if I saw my people poisoned. I don't want to think about it, so let's make sure I don't have to, okay?"

I smiled and waited while Tom got busy on his little radio. Calling in some troops. Making sure that people were in place to double and triple check the food. As soon as that was done we started again.

He started off with the simple stuff. "Will you come with us to a secure location? You can't possibly return to the trailer. I'm sure you know that."

I nodded. "You're right, Tom. The trailer's no good. I already have a place where we can go that is secluded and spacious enough for all of us. My sisters and I will go there. And I want Williams back. Go and ask him if he'd be willing to go with us to the mansion. And when you ask him make sure he knows that he doesn't have to go if he doesn't want to. I want it to be his choice, but please tell him that I asked for him."

Tom nodded and asked, "The mansion you're talking about, is it the same one that's in the news and on the internet, with you lighting that candle?"

"Yeah," I said, "I'm sure your people already know where it is."

Tom nodded. "We'll get men in place and secure the mansion also." Tom stopped and looked a little uncomfortable, tapping his pen on his pad nervously before he spoke. "They aren't going to be happy about me letting you go to the mansion instead of getting you far away to some underground bunker out in the desert somewhere, but I'll make them do it. They're going to insist on making sure the mansion is safe though." He was pushing for something, I could tell, but I wasn't sure what it was.

"Okay, Tom, just what are you saying."

Tom leaned in a little, pleased that I seemed to be playing the negotiating game and not just telling him what to do. "The government will insist on making sure that the mansion is safe. That means military, soldiers, and lots of equipment. I don't want you to be surprised when you get there tonight after the wedding and find it surrounded by soldiers and tanks. There are real threats we are following, some of which we don't even understand yet, like what happened with Sangai. We need to keep you and the others safe and that means the military."

I nodded. "Make sure they are polite when they come calling on Cathryn and Cornelius. It would make me very upset if I find that your military friends have been less than courteous to them. They are my friends, Tom."

Tom nodded, and his pen started scribbling again as he spoke. "I understand. I'll send in a small group of Feds before the troops invade and have them *politely* explain the situation. Should I let them know you plan on coming to-night?" he asked.

"Yes, tell them," I said. Tom got on the radio for just a second ordering people around before we started again.

"If Williams isn't able to go with you we have other people who can help you, Black Rain. Good people. And I can stay with you and—"

"No." I cut him off firmly and added a dark look for good measure. "You don't get it. You just don't friggin' get it, do you? I don't trust you or your people. I've just barely gotten to the point of being able to look at you and have you around me without wanting to hurt you, Tom." I gave him a disappointed look. "You haven't really been listening to what I've said, have you? Look at what happened here this morning because you were pushy." I pointed to the dark spot in the center of the room where the carpet was burnt black. "I burned myself to a crisp! I fucking died Tom!" His eyes widened sufficiently. Now it seemed I had his attention. "So what happens if you dump a load of new people on me and I don't like one of them much? Maybe next time I'll burn up everyone in Jacksonville or all of Florida in a fit of rage instead of myself. You don't understand me or know how to deal with me, Tom. And I don't want to run the risk of meeting anyone new unless I have to. Ask Williams, and see if he will come be your contact, and if he will then that will be one less problem. I know you will want a man on the inside, and he can be that for you. If we can't get Williams, then we'll look into finding someone else."

Tom nodded and started scribbling in his notepad and asked, "What level of access do you want people to have to you? How should we deal with being around you, Black Rain? Help me help you. What do you want us to do?"

I thought about that for a minute. It was a good, sensible question.

"The most important thing is don't surprise me, Tom. Make sure I know what's going on, and don't lie to me, Tom." I gave him a level look. "And tell everyone you plan to let get close to me that even the smell of betrayal will get them what Sangai got. We will know, Tom, and I will kill anyone who threatens my family. Don't just assign people to be in my presence, give them an out. To be in my presence is not to be done lightly or to be forced upon anyone." I really didn't want to have to kill anyone else if I could help it. "Tell them the danger and ask for volunteers; that would be fair I guess."

I felt tired. And sick to my stomach. My eyes went to the black vase sitting on the floor beside Jane and Dan. It was beautiful. Dan had laid Sangai's body in the back out of sight but I knew it was there. I wondered if Sangai had a family. I wondered what they would tell his wife or kids. Would they say that he had died in the line of duty? That he was killed by the wicked witch of the trailer park? *I wonder if they will pray that a house falls on me.* The thought shot through my mind complete with the vision of little Asian girls kneeling beside a bed praying for a house to crush the witch.

Tom's voice said, "Black Rain. Will the others come with you to the mansion?"

I blinked and looked around, coming back to reality with a jerk. "What? What?" I said breathlessly, looking around startled.

"Are you okay?" Tom asked carefully. He looked at me like he was worried I was losing my mind. "Are you okay?" he asked again.

The question was so stupid it made me smile. "No, Tom, I'm not okay," I said.

Tom adjusted and loosened his tie and got back on topic again. Moving forward. "Will Jane, Dan, and Sky be coming with you to the mansion?" At heart, Tom truly was a pushy bastard.

I didn't raise my voice. I just said, "Jane," and she was there, right beside me, like magic. Tom jumped like a school girl but I was so tired and sick of everything all I could do was smile.

"Yes, Rain?" Jane said. She studied my face as she looked at me.

"After the wedding, will you come with me? I have a mansion in a remote location that I and my witch sisters will be staying at. I will worry about you tonight unless I know you're in a safe place while you die. Please come with us and I will guard you myself tonight. I can keep you safe—and the mansion is a beautiful place. It will make a beautiful place for a honeymoon."

Jane looked at me for a minute as still as stone. I watched as a little blood leaked from the corners of her eyes. She didn't wipe it away like a normal person would do but left it there.

"Yes. And thank you, Rain. Dan has been so worried about how to keep me safe tonight and now he won't have to worry."

The next thing I knew she was hugging me, her arms were around me! I hadn't even seen her move.

"Thank you, Rain," she said to me again and backed away much more slowly, as if she realized that sudden movement around me was not good, even for her. "You're coming to the wedding, aren't you?" she asked, hopeful.

"Of course!" I said, surprised she thought she had to ask. "I wouldn't miss it for the world."

She gave me a stunning white smile and looked back to an impatient Tom and turned her attention to him. Her smile vanished. "You need to be patient, human. Do not make the same mistake again. It would piss me off."

And she was gone, vanished like she was never there. I looked up and she was back in Dan's arms beside her parents.

Tom blinked a time or two, took a second to defreak himself, then looked at me, "And Sky?"

I nodded and turned to Sky.

"Hey Sky!" I shouted, old school, and got her attention away from Ryan, who was telling her some kind of wild story where they sat together on the other side of the room. They looked more like a couple already, happy, smiling, talking, sharing. It was easy to love Ryan and impossible not to love Sky.

As she walked toward us, my eyes passed over the vampires again. Jane was curled all around her Dan, kissing him with her parents sitting right beside her watching them do it. So much for the "get your hands off my daughter!" plan. Sky shot Tom a suspicious glare as she stepped in front of me.

"Yes, Rain?"

"Sky, do you want to come and stay with me for a while? There's a huge mansion just outside town on the St. Johns River. It's a beautiful place and the people who live there are letting me and my witch sisters stay for a while. Dan and Jane are staying with us after the wedding tonight and I'd love to have you stay with us too."

Sky gave me a blank look so I added, "Of course you can take off anytime you like. If you get there and you're not comfortable with it you can always bolt. No problem. But you're welcome to make yourself at home with us."

Sky's father had come close enough to be a fly on the wall and overhear my offer. He spoke before his daughter could open her mouth to answer me. "Sky, you have a home! It is your house. All I have is yours. It will be dangerous to be anywhere near these people. Please stay away from them and come home with me and your mother. You belong with us." He shot me an unfriendly look.

"Sure. I'll go with you," Sky told me with a smile as she ignored her father who was whispering frantically to her in Chinese now, trying to get her attention.

"I'll come, but only if Believer can come with me."

"The cloud bird friend you made? Sure, Sky."

Jane appeared beside us like magic again and made Sky jump this time. Jane gave her an apologetic smile then joined our conversation in the middle like she had been listening the whole time from where she sat across the room with Dan.

"Believer isn't that small anymore, Rain, but he is very nice. Dan and I like him. Do you want me to go tell him to come out?" she asked with a devilish smile on her lips.

"Please," I said. "And have Dr. Burgis come on out too. I'll ask if he wants to go to the mansion with us."

Jane vanished.

After just a minute or two Jane emerged from the back office area followed by Dr. Burgis and a seven foot tall cloud man. Jane was right. Believer was a whole lot bigger now! And it looked as if Dr. Burgis was all packed up and ready to go. He had a suitcase, a briefcase, and one painting bundled up in his arms.

His eyes scanned the waiting room as he came in. He looked happy to see me alive. He'd probably been told about my melt down and subsequent return to the living and as I looked at him, I thought it would be best if I took him with me also. If I let the government have him they would do this to other kids. I needed to make sure this didn't happen again and I had some questions for him anyway. Believer and Dr. Burgis stepped over to us.

"Hello, Dr. Burgis. Hello, Believer," I greeted them. Doctor Burgis nodded and took a seat in one of the chairs looking right at Tom, being subdued and quiet for once, but Believer came over to stand in front of me. Wow! He was big and scary looking.

"You have changed," he said to me with perfect English and a deep rumbling voice as he leaned his huge head down close, looking me over. His body was all rolling clouds and smoke that clung together even though the edges looked ghostly and a little less than solid. When he talked his lipless slit of a mouth opened and closed as he formed his words while his red, glowing eyes started down, two solid, unmoving points inside the swirling mists that made up his head.

I gave Believer a warm smile and an answer. "Yes, Believer. I had to change or I would have died."

Believer's eyes became a brighter glowing red, the clouds around his eyes darkened to near black making him look very angry.

"Did someone hurt you? I will not allow anyone to hurt a friend of Sky's." Believer was upset that I'd been hurt.

"It's okay, Believer. It was probably unavoidable." I didn't want him pissed at Tom. I didn't know what he would do if I shared all the details.

Tom had been watching and listening, and he looked relieved that I had been so tactful. He gave me a small nod of thanks. He looked scared of Believer, which was understandable. Believer was impressive and scary as hell.

"Believer," Sky said, and all of his attention was immediately given to Sky. He stepped up to her and went to one knee like she was his Queen, or maybe even his God. Sky smiled at him. "Believer, we are going to go and stay with Black Rain for a while. While we are there please take care of her and love her as you would me. And thank you for keeping a watch on the back while we were out here. I know you wanted to be out here with me. Thank you. I love you. "

Believer bowed his smoky head and said, "Yes, Sky. It is my pleasure to serve you. And I will be glad to love Black Rain for you. Jane told me that Black Rain is powerful. She said that she would keep you safe, my Sky." He turned and looked right at me and asked me a question.

"Do you love my Sky too, Black Rain?"

I nodded and smiled, glad to answer his question. "Yes, I love her."

I watched as the colors shifted and changed around his eyes and gave him the ability to show emotion on his cloudy face. He looked curious as he looked back to Sky and then to me.

"Why do you love her so?" he asked. "She did not make you, but I can tell that you love her greatly. May I know why?"

I looked at Sky. Sky looked shocked and surprised, like she wasn't expecting this kind of question or this type of thought. It seemed like Believer was a real person and had questions about the world and why it was the way it was. Everyone in the room was watching and listening to us. It was impossible not to. Believer was not in any way even remotely human. The rest of us could look human, but here in front of us was a true monster. His presence filled the center of the room. I answered him.

"Believer, I have only known Sky for a short time, but in that time I have come to learn that she is good. Her heart is good, her soul from which she made you is good, and her spirit is good. She loves her friends. Both the kind that she has made and the kind that she has met. She's not perfect but she is good. I love her and I think you are most fortunate to have had her make you."

I smiled at the look of wonder on his cloud shaped face. He rose from where he knelt in front of her, stepped to me, and knelt in front of me.

"I will love you also. I will serve you also. And I thank you for treating me like a person even if I am just a created thing. I will take good care of you, my lady." He bowed his smoky head.

And in that moment I was suddenly so sad. He was like me. I was a friend and so was he. He wanted to be treated like a person so that was exactly what I would do.

"Believer, come hug me please. I need a hug from someone like 'me.' I am a created friend just like you. Your Sky did not create me but another person did. I am like you, Believer, and I will always treat you like a person. Now please, come and hug me because I want to cry now."

For anyone else there would have been a hundred questions at this point, a surprised "you're like me!" or a "How did this happen?" or even the classic "No way!" but not from Believer. He believed every single word I had just said and accepted it as truth.

I stood up and watched as Believer rose from where he knelt and stepped up to me. He looked uncertain, like he didn't know what or how to do what I wanted. I raised my arms and said, "Pick me up, Believer, pick me up and hold me and love me." I was already crying.

Believer's smoky arms reached down and lifted me high into the air. He cradled me close to him and it was like being held by a living cloud. I spoke to Tom from the shelter of Believer's arms.

"Please do whatever Dan and Jane need, Tom. I'm sure they have to get to the church soon."

"Sky," I called.

"Yes, Rain?" she answered.

"Can I go in the back and lay down for a while with Believer?" I didn't watch anyone's reaction to what I said; I just looked up at the smoky shape of a head and the two glowing red eyes that looked down at me.

"Yes, Rain. You may. You have my blessing." She sounded a little unsure. Like she didn't know what I was going to do in the back, but I didn't know anything except that I wanted to be held and I wanted to cry and I wanted to be alone with someone whom I could trust. And right now that was Believer.

"Sky, as soon as the food is here please come get me and bring the doctor. I still need to take my pills. Keep a close eye on him; someone might try to take him from us. Maybe you could call one of your other friends to keep a watch on things while Believer is with me." I wanted them to be careful and I didn't trust Tom.

"Black Rain," Tom called, "I thought we were going to go over your terms." His voice was impatient, demanding.

Jane snapped at him, "She will talk with you when she gets back out! After the food has come! After her pills have been taken! And after she has had a chance to cry. Now let her go mourn for her soul, human, and do not speak to her again until she is ready!" Jane's voice was so full of promised violence that Tom paled and took a few steps away from her.

"Are you ready to go now?" Believer asked me.

I nodded, "Yes, Believer."

He started to walk to the back. Dan appeared by the door and opened it for him to pass through and Believer said "Thank you" to him as he passed by.

"You're very polite, Believer. I like that," I said to him as he carried me like a child in his cloudy arms.

"The last room has a larger bed, my lady. I will take you there," he said.

"Believer. Do you really love me?" I asked. "I will not be mad if you don't. You can tell me what you really feel, Believer." I stared up into his eyes.

He reached out a hand and opened the door to the big exam room and we went inside. He shut the door and turned and laid me down on the bed in the center of the room. I looked up at his glowing red eyes as he looked down at me. He looked uncertain as to what to do next, how to hold me or in what way to help me.

"You don't have to try to be human, Believer. I'm not human and you're not human. We don't have to do this their way. I just want you here with me, around me. I give myself to you. I trust you. Please hold me and love me and make it all better for just a little while." I knew it was a stupid thing to say. He couldn't make what I had done to myself or to the man I had killed any better.

I watched as Believer settled himself directly on top of me. His cloudy body wrapping me, covering me completely. It felt odd but I didn't worry, I let myself drift. I felt two soft hands, one on each side of my face and I opened my eyes and looked up into two glowing red eyes.

"You didn't answer my question, Believer. I mean, you don't have to answer if you don't want to—" I closed my eyes. What was I doing? What did it matter if he did or didn't love me? Why would it matter?

I felt water on my face and opened my eyes. Water. Or tears were falling from Believer's eyes onto my face. As soon as I saw his eyes and his face I started to cry too. I reached my hands up and wrapped my arms around his head and pulled him down to me, and I whispered to him, "Everything will be all right, Believer. Don't worry. I'm here and I love you."

We cried.

"My lady." His soft rumbling voice was there at my ear, but something about it was different this time. He almost sounded scared. Vulnerable.

Hurting?

"Yes, Believer?" I whispered back. It was all the voice I had.

"I do love you,"

"I love you too,"

I let my eyes close as we held each other.

Jane Miller

Office Party

"**G**et out of my way!" Ryan shouted in Dan's face. "You can't leave that thing back there with my sister!"

Dan answered back with an apologetic face and some helpless "common man" hand gestures.

Ryan dropped his head and charged again, pushing and shoving in another wild attempt to get through the door and into the back half of the office where Believer had taken his sister.

Watching how much effort Dan put into keeping Ryan from hurting himself as he freaked reminded me again just how great a guy Dan really was.

"Jane!" Ryan turned and rushed up to me, wild eyed and frantic. "Get your *boy* here to get out of my way!" he said in a hoarse-throated shout. "That thing is back there with *my sister!* Doing God knows what to her right now! Make him move, Jane! He'll move if you tell him to move!" Ryan danced about on the balls of his feet. "She's not well," he pleaded with me, "you know Rain's hurt right now! She's not thinking straight and she's all alone back there with that thing! JANE!" he shouted as he turned and made another slow motion lunge to get past Dan only to be stopped again.

I darted over to stand beside the two of them as he struggled and waited a second for him to see me before I said anything. "This is what Rain wants, Ryan. This is what she needs right now."

"That's crap!"

"It's not crap."

"Crap!" he argued stubbornly, but he stopped pushing against Dan and stood still, breathing hard as he split his glare between me and Dan.

"She wants to be alone right now. Alone with Believer. Believer's nice and gentle. He won't hurt her." I tried to calm him, but Ryan was in big brother mode. He wanted his sister safe—and safely away from the giant monster.

"How do you know he won't hurt her!" Ryan snapped at me like a rabid dog. "She's not right in the head right now! She said so herself. She's not thinking straight! She's my sister! My twin sister! Let me go get her!"

In slow motion he made another try for the door, and Dan turned him around and pushed him away, but Ryan let the momentum carry him forward and he rushed toward Sky.

Oh shit. I thought to Dan in my head.

"Sky! Call that thing off!"

Sky shrunk in on herself and backed up as he charged her, and her father stood up and came between Ryan and Sky.

"You made that monster so send it away or send it back to wherever you called it from, but get it away from my sister! *Please!*" Ryan stared into her eyes desperately.

Her father said something and she began arguing with her father in Chinese.

Dr. Burgis shouted out, "Soldiers are coming!" drawing everyone to look out the window.

Twenty soldiers were marching at a slow jog in our direction from the far side of the parking lot. I heard Dan in my head,

Jane, keep Ryan out of the back. I'll hold the door and keep the soldiers from getting inside the office. I'm not going to start anything. All we really need to do is stall until Rain gets out, but ask Sky if she can make more of those friends of hers. That's what Rain had asked her to do before she went into the back with Believer. It would be nice to have someone big and scary like that out here to keep these guys from trying anything stupid.

Dan appeared at the front of the office, one hand gripping each side of the metal and glass double doors as he stared out at the approaching soldiers. I did as he asked without arguing, taking his place at the back office door. He was facing away but in the reflection of the glass my vampire eyesight let me watch as his blue-green eyes began to shift to red, and I knew that he was worried. He didn't like this and neither did I. Anything that put me in danger made him angry. And anything that put him in danger made me insane.

Out of the corner of my eye I watched as Ryan turned back toward the doorway, thinking the way was clear and saw his disappointment that I'd taken Dan's place. My dad headed over to the front door to stand with Dan and face the soldiers and Mom came rushing my way. And then Ryan rushed me, trying to push past in the mix of bodies. I carefully turned him back the other way.

"Let me go get Rain! They're coming, we need her out here!" Ryan tried using the situation to his advantage. And he had a point. It would have even sounded sincere if he hadn't just tried to bull dog by me.

I gave him the "yeah right" look he deserved and tried to calm my mother down. Whatever Rain was doing, I hoped she finished up soon.

Ryan hovered annoyingly, waiting for an opening to get by, and Mom fretted, hovering on the edge of meltdown. I tried to get something accomplished while I was stuck guarding a stupid door in the back when I wanted to be at the stupid door in the front!

"Sky!" I shouted around Ryan who was crowding me. I couldn't see her around him.

"Yeah!" I heard the fear and panic in Sky's voice as she shouted back.

"Rain asked if you could bring one of your other friends to guard us while she was in the back. Do you have another friend like Believer? If you do, call him now, before those soldiers get here."

Tom had been keeping really quiet, staying off to the side, trying to be invisible, but now he spoke up. "Those men are no threat to anyone in here. They aren't going to hurt anyone. I'm sure they're just coming to retrieve the body of Dr. Sangai and to bring me a new phone. Something happened when Black Rain burned and my phone went dead. Those men are coming to check on me, and they better be bringing me a new phone that's working properly." Tom held up his radio phone, waving it around like evidence of his honesty. "Really, there's no threat here. Everyone can calm down. You don't need to 'do' anything. There is nothing you need to worry about. There's no need for panic."

Pretty speech, but I heard in his voice that there was more that he hadn't said hiding between what he had said. It was something important. Something dangerous. He was trying to lie without lying. Omission. Lies.

"Yes!" I snapped. "But there's more in your voice! I can hear it, Tom." I was so pissed, and I was sick of this guy. His being pushy had already hurt Rain horribly and now he was trying to lie to us again! Bastard! Hot rage filled me like a liquid, like scalding water poured into an ice cold glass! My vision took on a red tint and I knew that my eyes had gone blazing red. I was suddenly very thirsty as I looked at Tom's terrified, lying face. I remembered that he was food. My food. I'd already warned him not to lie. I wanted to kill him and drink his lying blood!

JANE! NO! Killing Tom right now won't help us! See if you can get Sky to call some of her other friends, Jane. These guys don't see the two of us and Sky as a threat, but if she comes up with another friend like Believer it would give us some time. All we need to do is stall until Rain gets out and she can take care of all this shit. They wouldn't be trying this if she were out here! The bastards!

You're right, I thought back. They waited till she went into the back. They think Sky is weak, that she'll bail if the shit hits the fan, and I doubt they think we're all that dangerous. Bastards.

I turned back to Sky. "Call another friend, Sky! Call one now!" I practically begged. I heard her father saying something to her in Chinese. Arguing. Telling her not to do it, I could tell just from the sound of the words.

"Jane! No!" My mother added another language with the same message directed at me. "We don't want to fight them! Those are soldiers, honey, and so far you and Dan haven't done anything to anyone. Not a thing." She glared over at Tom as if daring him to deny it. "There's no reason for them to bother us and I don't want you or Dan to give them a reason. They'll leave us alone if we leave them alone."

I just stared at her, surprised. She didn't even believe her own words. There was no way these people were going to "*leave us alone,*" and she knew it. But what else could she say?

She looked over at the front door where Dad stood beside Dan, then turned back to me. "Please tell Dan not to fight them, Jane! We don't want trouble," she begged me.

I was facing her, nodding, talking, but the greater part of my attention was on Dad and Dan who were watching the soldiers march up the sidewalk toward the door. They were dressed mostly in black and looked more like a SWAT team than regular soldiers. They jogged in an organized column, four across and five men deep, taking up the width of the sidewalk. Twenty soldiers. I felt my body shaking. I hated this.

I *hated* it.

"Jane!" Mom pleaded with me. Tugging at my arm. "Don't get mad! Stop growling!"

"What the hell!" my dad shouted as he gawked out the window. I saw it too and was just as confused by what I was seeing. It looked as if the approaching soldiers had crashed headlong into an invisible barrier fifteen feet from the front doors. It must have been an invisible wall, like the one Rain made earlier inside the office that Dan had crashed into. The soldiers had splattered themselves on the thing, creating a pile of bodies all squished up against the invisible wall.

"They hit a wall of some kind. Whoo-wee! That had to hurt!" Dad said, his face twisted in sympathy.

It was quite a spectacle, like a freeway pile up without the cars. There was no sympathy from Dr. Burgis. The good doctor busted out laughing so hard he turned red in the face, earning himself a nasty look from Tom who apparently hadn't found the invisible collision nearly as entertaining.

The soldiers at the bottom of the pile were slow to get off the ground, but soon they were all back on their feet, reorganizing. They started to run their hands along the invisible barrier. Soon they were deploying, men fanning out in both directions, searching for the edge. If there was one.

"They're not stopping. It looks like these guys are serious about getting in here," Dad said. "What do they want? Other than to give you a phone?" He turned back and looked at Tom, pissed, and I was so proud. Apparently his crap detector was working too.

We mutant teens watched as a regular "adult" got up in Tom's face and demanded an answer for a change. "Well, Major," Dad eyed the bars of rank on Tom's jacket, "what the hell do those men want?"

Tom glanced in my direction, and I flashed him some teeth and growled. My vision was already tinted red like a prelude to murder and as I looked at him I thought about what Rain had done a short while ago. She'd actually murdered that guy. Killed him. Took his blood. It excited me in strange ways. The thought of violence and blood. I wanted blood, it was food. To satisfy my gnawing hunger. That I got. It made sense. But I'd never been violent.

Tom met my eyes and I thought about killing him and he paled. He took a step back without noticing he'd done so, bumping into a chair behind him. He swung his arms about to catch his balance. He turned back to my Dad and swallowed a time or two before he could get any words to come out. I felt sad when his frightened heart began to slow down.

"My phone started to cut out after Black Rain burnt up. It finally gave out a short while ago, and with me out of radio contact they may be assuming that things are out of control. I'm sure they watched what happen to Sangai through the glass, so they may not know if I'm in distress or not. And before I lost contact they'd been discussing coming in to take the doctor. That's more than likely what these men are here for. And they'll probably want Sangai's body," he added as if it didn't matter and then turned to glare at the doctor. "People have died because of that man and his pills. He's a criminal. They want him."

"They don't need to do this now!" my father argued. "And I got every reason to hate the bastard, but do it later! Once everything settles down."

"I agree," Tom said, "but a dead radio puts me out of the game. If you want, I can go out and talk to them. They don't know the risks involved in upsetting Black Rain. Let me help, and let's all stay calm and not make a dangerous situation into a horrible one."

I heard Dan's voice in my head,

The soldiers are around the edge of the barrier. They're coming, Jane. Ask Sky again. We need something scary to get them to back off. I'm going to have to decide what to do with these guys if they get pushy. If they try to hurt you I'm afraid of what I'm going to do. I want to fight, and I know you want to fight—but we shouldn't. It'll be a disaster if we do, because once we start it won't stop. Please ask Sky again, my love. I hope she can help us because these guys are coming.

I told everyone what Dan said. "The soldiers are coming, they're around the shield and they're almost to the door." I turned and spoke to Sky again, giving her a pleading look. "Sky, if you have any other friends, please call them now! And it would be great if it was a big, scary one like Believer. We need you!"

She nodded back to me just as her father grabbed her arm roughly. He whispered in American this time so I understood what he said to her. "Don't do this! The soldiers will let us go home but not them!"

Sky tried to pull away but he held on. I saw the pain in Sky's face. He was hurting her. I wanted to rush over and help, but Ryan was just waiting for a chance to shoot by me and get to Rain.

"Sky Dragon!" Sky shouted, then yelled some angry Chinese retort right into her father's face and held out her free hand and pointed to the center of the room where a steamy shape started to take form in the air.

Her father saw it and shouted, "Sky, don't do this!" He grabbed her arm and pinned it to her side. "Do not create another monster! We need to leave this place and leave these people! They are not our concern! They have killed that man! An important man! They killed him and these soldiers are coming for them, but *not* for us! Do not help them, Sky! Do not get involved in their problems!"

I'd been listening to Sky's father rant but I was watching the cloud in the center of the room. It was bigger and more solid even though Sky wasn't pointing at it, and it was still changing, becoming more defined each second. The cloud was about the size of a big pillow now, shaped almost like a snake with wings.

Dan shouted in my head,

Jane, the soldiers are here!

Five soldiers were already standing outside the glass doors and more were coming from either side to gather at the doors. Two of them were pulling on the doors that Dan held shut. They all had guns in their hands, halfway pointed at Dan as he stood there like a marble statue, holding the doors shut and growling at them. Tom was standing beside Dan making hand motions to the soldiers, trying to get them to lower their weapons. As I watched, two of the men pointed their guns at Dan!

I moved. In a flash, a fraction of a second, I darted over to one of the office chairs, grabbed it, and darted back to the door. I punched a hole right through the wall like it was wet tissue paper and then punched another hole through the door. Then I took the chair and ripped off the shaped metal rod that made up the back support. I broke it off and straightened it with my hands. I took the piece of metal, pushed it through the holes I'd made and tied the door shut like a twist tie on a garbage bag. All of this had taken less than three human seconds.

I turned back to Dan and saw that the soldiers were all pointing weapons at him now. And shouting. The world stopped as I roared! The sound ripped from my body like a living thing and I was though the window on the far side of the office, the tinkling sound of shattering glass filling the air as I landed outside the window that I'd leapt through. I turned and ran to the soldiers, pulling guns from their hands and holsters as I went down the line of men, crushing some and simply twisting the barrels of others just enough to make them useless before moving to the next soldier and the next gun.

I went down the line of men who stood still before me as if frozen in time, one after another, faster than I'd ever moved before until I twisted the last barrel still in the hands of the soldier carrying it, then I jumped back through the glass on the other side of the office, shattering it and landing back in the waiting room in a shower of glass. I turned and roared again before the glass even fell to the floor!

I looked out at the soldiers as they staggered and reeled, some falling over and some recovering from having weapons snatched roughly away. Dan's head whipped one way toward the first window and then the other way, then back to me. Wow! I moved so fast even Dan hadn't seen me! I darted over to him and wrapped myself around him where he stood, still holding the door, though no one was tugging on it anymore.

"Now they have no guns, my love," I purred to him right next to his ear as I curled around him like a snake. I was still keeping my eyes on the soldiers on the other side of the glass, peering over the top of Dan's shoulder at them. Their eyes looked up into my red gaze and they flinched away. My sexy purr became a growl.

Holy shit, Jane! That was AWESOME! I didn't see anything but a blur! You moved faster than the sound from the shattered window! That was absolutely crazy! Did you really destroy all of their guns out there?

Dan was laughing! The perfect pale flesh I clung to shook with laughter, and I ran my fingers through his hair and rubbed up against him while still keeping an eye on the soldiers. They looked like they were rethinking the whole *let's go get 'um* idea. They were looking through the glass doors at me as I stared down at them from my perch on Dan. They were afraid of me. Very afraid. The retreat was in full force.

My dad took a step closer to me. He had been standing right there with Tom and Dan this whole time. "Jane, honey." He sounded like he always did as he scratched at his chin. "You jumped out of the office through that window?" He pointed. "And then back in through that other window over there? Right?" Dad pointed to my reentry point.

"Yes, sir." I stopped glaring at the soldiers and gave him a smile, and Dad smiled back at me.

He looked back out the glass at the retreating soldiers. "You didn't hurt anyone out there did you?" He scanned for signs of serious injury among the retreating figures.

"No, sir. I was careful. Maybe a broken finger or two, possibly an arm, nothing big."

Dad nodded, apparently fine with that. "You didn't cut yourself on the glass from the window, did you?" he asked as he looked at my face and arms.

"No, Daddy." I laughed. "Don't be silly."

Dad laughed with me.

And then I kissed Dan. I was happy. It looked like our little problem was solved. Dan released his hold on the doors and wrapped his arms around me, kissing me back. My legs wrapped around him tighter, and I starting to really enjoy myself when I heard Tom's annoying voice.

"What would you like me to do?" he asked as he looked out the window. Poor old Tom sounded confused, I could tell by his voice he was still trying to understand what had happened.

I snapped at him, my voice mean and vicious. "Get out there and talk to them!"

Tom flinched but nodded instantly, eyes wide, ready to obey me as he reached for the door and I added in an irritated tone, "And get yourself a new radio that works so you can keep them from making more mistakes!" Tom nodded again but before he could turn back to the door I added on one more demand, "And find out what's up with the blood! I'm thirsty, Tom." I knew my eyes grew brighter as I mentioned the blood. "And the food, what's taking so long on the food for the others?" That little bit of blood Dan had gotten for us wasn't enough by a long shot. I needed more. Lots more. I didn't know how much more, all I knew was—MORE. All that good fresh blood was just sitting in that urn over there waiting.

Dan growled lovingly, his body vibrating mine as I was wrapped around him.

No, you can't get into our wedding night blood, Jane. That was a gift and it would be rude to Rain. Just be patient. I'm sure Tom will get his shit together and get us some more blood before we have to go to the wedding. He better. I'm hungry too.

Tom held the door in one hand, carefully keeping his face blank. I thought that he would be irked or pissed by my pushing him around so rudely, but as I studied his face and body I was truly surprised by what I saw. He was scared to death of me. Truly terrified. Everything in him was focused on trying to make sure he didn't piss me off again. He was way more scared of me than he had been of Black Rain. Which surprised me. I didn't know I was that scary. Maybe I was.

"Anything else, Jane?" Tom asked carefully with a straight face. One hand still held the door.

I thought for a split second and added in a polite voice, "Yes, Tom, we're going to need to drive to the church soon. You should get someone in here to talk to my parents so they can go over who to let in. We have a lot of people coming, but we don't want any creeps or sickos getting in and causing problems. Can you do that for us?" Since he was being good I figured I could too. Tom nodded, scared stiff.

Mom walked up, giving me a super nasty look which confused me. I wondered why.

"Jane honey! I know you're becoming a vampire, but look at yourself, you're not decent." She waved a hand at my dress.

I looked at myself. Oh! Somewhere in all the action I'd ripped the cloth on one side of my dress completely open and I was showing flesh all down one whole side. Must have been the glass from the window that cut the dress. There were other little tears and slashes here and there but the one side was totally slashed. The only thing that still held the dress together was my little strap of a belt I'd rigged out of my purse string.

Of course the way I was wrapped around Dan didn't help. I'd climbed up him like a tree so I could wrap my arms around his shoulder and I had my legs wrapped around his waist, which got me high enough to put my face next to his like I wanted. He was so tall this was the only way I could comfortably reach his hair. And I liked to touch his hair.

I looked back down at myself. I didn't feel exposed at all—*which was weird.* I used to be super self-conscious, wearing stuff that covered me up completely, but now I just didn't give a rip. I remembered that I wasn't even wearing a bra or underwear and I still didn't care. I felt wild. Animal. Feral. And very much like a vampire. I laughed at my mom's horrified disapproving look, the musical clear sound echoed around the room.

"Mom, maybe you could head on over to the church, get things ready and make sure everything is okay. Dad can stay and keep an eye on us, and we'll be right over after the food gets here and Rain gets out of the back. Dan and I have to eat before we go to the wedding, so we're stuck here till Tom can get us some blood to drink. We're just too hungry and—" I made a face as my stomach made a sloshy squishy sound that everyone heard.

Mom nodded as she eyed my stomach. "Okay," she agreed. "But hurry. I'll be worried till I see you at the church. And don't do anything crazy, Jane. No more. Be good." She reached over and pulled my dress this way and that, trying to cover me up some. She looked so frustrated. "Dammit, Jane, you don't even have on underwear and your junk is hanging out in front of God and everyone!"

Dan and I laughed and my parents shared a sad resigned "oh well" look between them. I twisted my top around and leaned out toward Mom and gave her a hug. My legs around Dan were all that held me up. I was sure that this looked strange and alien to everyone watching me, but it felt fine to me. My body was just so incredibly flexible now. This was easy. Natural.

"We won't be long, Mom. Tom will make sure everything goes smoothly. Right, Tom?"

"Absolutely," he affirmed instantly. "We're here to help. And we need to get going so I can get a new phone and check on the food and blood, so if you're ready to go, Mrs. Miller—" Tom pushed the door open and turned back toward us, and then his eyes went wide and he staggered back a step. We all turned toward the inside of the office to see what on earth had freaked him out.

It was a dragon.

Jane Miller

A Beautiful Day

Sky's other friend was here and he was huge! He was curled up in the middle of the office with his wings held tight to each side of his snakelike body. His massive head was pushed up against the ceiling. Like Believer, he was made of swirling clouds and mist. I looked past the cloudy creature and saw Ryan and Sky's father fighting.

"Just leave her alone!" Ryan said.

Sky was hiding behind him trying to stay away from her father, and Ryan was doing his best, but his arm was hanging limply at his side like it was already hurt. Sky's father reached for Sky, and Ryan pushed her back behind his body again, keeping her away from him. Sky's father didn't hesitate; he busted Ryan right in the face and then spun around, kicking him in the ribs so hard he flew backwards over a chair and crumpled up against the wall.

"Shit!" Dad said. I shot across the room and grabbed Sky's father by his jacket and threw him back over my shoulder. I didn't watch, but I was almost positive that Dan caught him because I didn't hear him land. I kneeled down beside Ryan's crumpled form.

"Ouch! Aaaa." Ryan was trying to get up.

"Ryan! Are you okay!?" I said. It was easy to see that his arm was broken!

"He broke your arm!" I shouted. Appalled. "What were you doing?"

Ryan managed a smile as he looked at me, his voice tight and pain filled as he spoke. "Nothing really out of the ordinary," he took a wheezing breath, "just another day at the office for me." Wheeze. "Same old, same old." Wheeze. "My usual luck doing what it does these days." Wheeze. "I dodged when I should've weaved." He laughed and winced, his good hand reaching for his side like some of his ribs were hurt. His lip was busted and in the struggle blood had gotten on his face and eyelid, caught up in the lashes. He was squinting as he looked up at me. Sky's dad must have been trying to kill him or something. Shit!

"Ryan! Why were you two fighting!?" The more I looked the more concerned I got. "You're a mess," I fretted, not sure how to help, or whether to move him or leave him be. Dr. Burgis kneeled down on the other side of Ryan, also looking concerned.

"Damn," he said as he looked at the arm. "That's a bad break. Let me take a look." Ryan closed his eyes and gritted his teeth as the doctor moved it a little this way and that, checking it out.

Ryan squinted up at me, blinking because of the blood in his lashes. I reached out a hand and carefully wiped the blood from his eye. It looked like it was bothering him and I didn't even think about what I was doing as I put my finger in my mouth. Ryan tasted so good. I closed my eyes in total surprise, shocked at myself and the taste, and I heard him struggle as he tried to take a deep breath. With my super hearing I could hear the deep rattle and I knew that there was something wrong, down in his ribs, he was bleeding inside. Dammit! This didn't sound good. I forgot the blood as worry filled me.

"Dr. Burgis, a rib has broken and punctured a lung. I can hear it," I said. And I pointed to where I was sure the broken rib was located. Dr. Burgis switched from inspecting Ryan's arm to look at his ribs.

"Jane, could you help me get his shirt off, please?" he asked. I held the top of Ryan's shirt with one hand and ran my other hand down the shirt with my fingernail. It sliced just like a razor blade would, cutting the shirt from top to bottom with a loud "Riiip!"

Dr. Burgis spread Ryan's shirt out and gently probed the area I had pointed to and Ryan gasped in pain. The doctor nodded. "Of course you're right, Jane. This is bad." He looked at Ryan. "You really took a beating, my boy."

Ryan's voice was quiet as he spoke. He was forced to take small shallow breaths.

"Just my luck again. As it turns out," wheeze, "Sky's dad is some kind of kung fu ninja ." Wheeze. "He kicked my ass."

Sky had been busy getting the Dragon outside to guard the front. That accomplished, she rushed up to us and kneeled down at Ryan's head. She was very upset.

"Ryan! I'm so sorry! Are you okay? I can't believe he did this to you." She leaned down and started to fuss over him. Ryan's eyes met mine and something in me actually felt jealous, even possessive, I think. Jealous of Sky as she leaned over him and ran her fingers through his bloody hair. I reached up and touched my own face, my eyebrows and face. I was frowning. Angry. Oh shit! It was the stupid Midnight book still trying to get me to love Ryan! Oh no! Dammit! I tasted his blood!

DAMMIT! NO!

I didn't want this!

I flew to Dan, almost knocking him over as I crashed into him.

DAN! HELP ME! HELP ME! I cried in my head.

He knew what I wanted, I didn't have to tell him or explain what happened. Dan already knew everything, every single fear, every feeling, and even the taste of Ryan's blood. He knew me better than I knew me. His arms encircled me and he held me to his chest as he walked with me to the far corner of the room, far away from Ryan. He crouched down, crowding me into that far dark corner just like I wanted. His body covering me and hiding me away from Ryan. Ryan's eyes. Ryan's blood.

Why!? WHY had I tasted his blood!? DAMMIT! NO! I hadn't wanted to do that. Hadn't meant to. I could feel Ryan's heartbeat from across the room even here in this dark corner. Oh shit! No! Now I've got some kind of freaky connection with him through his blood. No! No! No! I was panicked! FRANTIC! WILD!

Dan roared! His eyes shifted from red to white and his hand shot out and grabbed me by the throat and slammed me into the back of the wall so hard I heard the wall behind me buckle. His voice thundered inside my head so loud it was all I could hear or think or know, and everything around me went blank—blank except his voice inside my head—all there was was his voice.

You are mine! Your soul is mine! Your body is mine! Your thoughts are mine! My venom has burned through your veins and nothing can undo what I have done.

Nothing can erase it or change it. And your venom has burned through me. You have taken me and made me yours. We are bound by love, by blood, by venom, and we are bound by my magic, Jane, and my power. I am the voice in the quiet of your mind that knows your fears and holds you before you even know yourself that you want to be held. I am the body that feels your hunger before you even know it's there. When you're irritated, I am angry. Your whims are my wants. I feel your pleasure and know what makes you tremble. I know what makes you smile. I know your deepest sorrow. I know every corner of your heart, every shadow, every flight of fancy, every dream or fear that passes through your mind sifts through my fingers. They are precious to me. Your thoughts are my joys and worries. This is where I live, Jane. Here inside you. And I am happy to live here. I will never leave. We are bound to share the darkness of this night, two souls, two minds, two bodies entwined and in love until the end of time. No, my love. I am not afraid of Ryan Bryant. I am not worried about him or that his blood tastes good. He's a nice guy and I know you care about him, but it's not what we have. I do not fear him and neither should you. He can't take you away from me even if he tried. It's impossible. And don't worry about yourself, my love. Don't fear that some secret part of you longs or hungers without your knowing or consent. There are no second thoughts down here. No regrets. I would know—I've looked. There are no hidden fears or shadowed corners that you need to worry about inside your heart. I'm here, and I love you. Now be at peace, my love. I'm going to open your mind back up and you'll be able to see and hear and feel and talk again. Don't worry. I'm holding you in my arms right now. And I'm right here in your mind too, as always, my love. I have you, inside and out, forever. Don't worry, Jane, my hand holds your heart.

I felt myself fall back into my body. I could see again. I was pressed up tight to Dan's chest and I felt his arms around me and I didn't want to move. Dan's arms squeezed me tighter like I wanted and I closed my eyes and took a deep breath. Please! Dan held me tighter.

Dan. Am I okay? I asked inside my head.

Yes, my love. You're okay.

I waited for a while, listening to the sounds around me while Dan held me. I felt safe. I could hear my parents' worried voices as they tried to talk to Dan. Asking him if I was okay. Asking him what was wrong. Worried about me. Worried he was hurting me. Other voices. Tom's voice and Mom's. I could hear Dr. Burgis working on Ryan; he was putting a splint on Ryan's arm and Sky was helping. I listened to the sounds for a while. Sounds of the world and people and life. I spoke to Dan in my head.

I'm sorry I freaked out.

Jane, the only reason you freaked out is because you love me so much it's crazy. Anything that comes between us makes you go insane. Like those soldiers and their guns. I'm glad you freaked out. I'm glad you love me that much. But you don't need to worry. You're safe. I'm here. And I love you.

Thank you, Dan. I needed that. Whatever that was.

I took a deep breath. Mom was crying, she was so worried. "I'm okay, Mom. Don't cry," I said, still held secure by the steel of Dan's arms around me. I heard her relieved sob.

"Oh God, Jane, what happened!? Why did you attack Dan like that! Are you hurt, did Dan hurt you?" I heard as she wiped her nose. I heard my dad as he knelt beside her.

"Dan, can you let her up now?" Dad asked. I heard anger in his voice. He thought Dan had hurt me too.

Dan shook his head no. Dan knew I didn't want to be let up yet and he was waiting on me to feel ready.

"Jane honey, are you okay?" Dad asked.

"Yes," I said, "I'm okay." I took another deep breath and slipped my arms up and around Dan's neck and he stood with me attached to him like I had been earlier, my legs around his waist and my arms around his neck. I looked around the room.

Mom and Dad were right here with me, looking at me. Tom was at the front door holding it open wide enough to talk to some other guy on the outside. The guy outside was in a suit, so he had to be FBI or something. I watched as he handed Tom a new radio phone. That was good. I approved. I looked back toward Ryan. He was still where I'd last seen him. Dr. Burgis was trying to keep him comfortable, propping something behind him to sit him up some. Sky was there with Ryan and Dr. Burgis but there was no sign of Sky's father anywhere. I assumed that he'd left.

"Where is Sky's father?" I asked Dan out loud.

Oh, I threw him out the front door after you threw him at me. I thought that would be best. He really shouldn't be around here when Rain gets out because when she sees her brother she's going to be pissed. And that guy has been a jerk for a while. We're all better off without him around. I just wish we'd thrown him out sooner. Before he hurt Ryan.

"Sky's dad is as bad as her mom," I said. "Sad for her. She's had it rough."

Dan nodded as we both looked over at Sky.

Tom and the guy who had brought Tom his new phone walked up to us.

"Jane," Tom said and used his new phone to point beside him to the new guy, "This is agent Lankford. He's here to help. He's ready to take your mother to the church if she's willing to go." He looked from me to my mom.

"Mom. You ready?" I asked her.

Mom didn't look ready. She looked pissed. "What on earth was that, Jane!? Tell me what just happened to you and Dan." She wasn't going to budge until she got some answers, I could see it in her face.

"Mom. You can't see it and you can't feel it but there's magic all around us. I got scared that some of that magic was going to hurt me so I ran to Dan for help. That's all." I smiled at her. "Dan did help." I ran one hand through his sandy blonde hair while Mom spoke to me.

"But why on earth did he throw you into the wall and grab you by the throat!?" Mom was really pissed. She shot Dan a hateful look. "He didn't need to grab you by the throat! And it looked like he did something else to you. I don't know what!"

"Mom!" I shouted to get her to calm down. "Dan did what I wanted and what I needed. And I'm so much stronger than he is he has to be real careful, especially if I'm out of control, so he doesn't get hurt. And I was out of it, Mom. That's why he held onto me like that."

Mom gave me a questioning look, like she didn't really believe me. "I still don't understand what made you go crazy like that," she said.

I smiled. "Magic and blood and love and death. All the things that make a vampire girl go crazy." I laughed as Mom rolled her eyes at my "non" answer to her question.

Dan's hand smoothed down my dress covering me up some which surprised me and I looked up at him.

You're showing a little much for Lankford and I'm trying hard not to kill him right now. The new guy doesn't know you well enough to be afraid and to look at you like Tom does. If he's not careful I may end up hurting him, Jane.

I laughed a wicked laugh, and Dan shot me a dark look because he knew what I was thinking before I did.

I leaned out and looked at the new guy. Oh yeah. I could see it all over him. He was quite excited by my body and I could see the fascination in his face, almost like little fantasies of me danced in the mirror of his eyes and I laughed again. It seemed my laugh made it worse. I felt the beginnings of a growl in my Dan. The tension of his body. But he knew I enjoyed being a little wicked so he indulged me. Dan was good to me.

"Hello, Agent Lankford. What has Tom told you about me?" I asked in a happy voice.

Lankford shot a quick glance to Tom before he answered, smiling at me behind his silver mustache, "Tom has told me that you're the scariest thing he's ever seen in his life." He hesitated only for a second and added a cheerful "Ma'am" to the end of that and waited for my reaction.

"Tom calls me Jane, but then he has the good sense to not look at me like a piece of ass, Lankford." I watched as Lankford's face paled and Tom swallowed and struggled to say something but was stuck, unsure what to do with what I just said.

Lankford's gaze slipped to looking just over my shoulder, not directly at me as he said, "I'm sorry. Please forgive me. I'm just not used to being here. I'm not used to you being able to read my mind. Please forgive me. Don't—" He looked at me for a second then directed his gaze back over my shoulder. "Sorry, ma'am. It'll never happen again."

"Good!" Mom said tartly. She shot Lankford a nasty look and I smiled at her and Dad who was also giving him a nasty look. This was fun.

I turned back to the new guy. "If we meet again, Lankford, you will call me My Queen and keep your eyes on the floor when you are near me because you are a dog. Now be very careful with my mother and I may forgive you. Give me one more reason and I'll let Dan eat you. He's not happy you have such a dirty mind. And I'm only seventeen anyway, Lankford. Bad, bad man. Here in this place, thoughts can kill, especially ones about me and you naked." I smiled and laughed as Dan's eyes shifted to red.

Mom had had enough of me playing with him. "Jane. That's enough, stop picking on him and get yourself some decent clothes. It's not all his fault even if he is a dog," Mom complained. Then she turned to Lankford who was still very carefully looking over my shoulder. "Come on, you. Let's get you out of here before you get yourself killed." Mom shook her head and did a shooing motion and Lankford quickly retreated to the door.

Mom gave me a quick hug before turning to go. "Hurry over to the church, Jane. I'll be waiting for you there." Mom headed out the door.

Tom's radio beeped and he started talking on it. They were coming with the food and the blood, I heard the voice on the other end saying to Tom. They wanted to know how many people they could use to bring the stuff.

"Just tell them to bring it, Tom. We're starving over here!" I called.

Tom's eyes locked on me and he nodded and started to tell them to just get their asses over here now, but then I heard him telling them to be careful what they thought, where they looked, and not to say a word while they were here. Tom also told them to get the vehicles ready to go. One big limo. I left Tom to his phone work and Dan and I shot over to Ryan.

Dr. Burgis jumped a little in surprised by our sudden appearance beside him as he finished wrapping some new gauze around Ryan's broken arm. "Hello, Jane. Are you feeling better?" he asked.

"Yes. Much," I answered. "How is he doing?" I looked down at Ryan.

He was pale, his eyes were closed, and it looked like they had carefully cleaned all the blood off of him. A strong alcohol smell helped cover the scent of the little spot of blood that seeped through the bandage on his split lip. Sky sat cross-legged on the floor holding Ryan's head in her lap. She was wiping his face with a wet rag and looked less than excited to see me, but her voice was civil when she spoke.

"Dr. Burgis gave him some pills so he's out for now, but he needs to get to the hospital. If Rain can't heal him he needs surgery. I can't believe he got hurt trying to help me. Again!" Sky looked back down at Ryan, patting his face with the rag.

"Oh, that's right," Dr. Burgis said. "Yesterday Ryan helped when your mother attacked you out here in the waiting room. Did he get hurt then also, I didn't think he had."

Ryan's shirt was off. A few strips of gauze were wrapped around his middle over his hurt ribs but the rest was exposed. Sky reached out and ran a hand gently over some angry red scratches that were obviously from fingernails clawing at his neck and arm.

"And she kicked him where she shouldn't have," Sky said, not happy.

Dr. Burgis grunted in sympathy for Ryan. "Yes. Now that you mention it, I do remember Ryan taking a rather low blow from your mother there at the end. It seems your parents have both taken a toll on young Mr. Bryant here." Right then Ryan coughed and we could all hear how horrible he sounded.

Sky glanced over at the back office door that I'd tied shut. "Jane, we need to get into the back office." She looked back up at me. "We need to get Rain now. If you open it I'll go get her."

"Yeah, let's get Rain," I agreed. "Tom said they're about to bring the food in, but I'm sure she'll want to take care of her brother before she eats or takes her pills."

Sky nodded and we both turned and looked over at the door as we heard the sound of metal and wood tearing. Dan had ripped the bar away and was pushing open the door.

"Are you feeling okay now?" Sky asked me, a strange look on her face.

I studied her face. She was worried that I was jealous of her. And confused at "why" I would be jealous when I had Dan. She didn't know what I felt about Ryan and was a little worried I may be unstable after my big wig out. My face must have been easy to read for her to have seen so much.

"I'm okay, Sky. And sorry about before. I know how it looked, but don't worry, it was just some stupid magic messing with me against my will. Ryan is a great guy, but I'm already taken."

Right then Dan appeared behind me and I felt his arms slip around me from behind, and I leaned back into him as I spoke to Sky. "This magic that is hanging around and annoying us will end as soon as my heart stops beating. I die, it dies."

Sky blinked. She'd forgotten that I was about to die. "Oh. Wow," she said. She processed that for a second before she asked, "Are you sure this magic will be gone once you die?" Her eyes squinted a little right at the corners.

I tried to read what she was really thinking. She was worried about me still wanting Ryan and coming after him or coming after her for going after him. And she was worried that the magic would make Ryan go after me, whether he wanted to or not. Yep. I could see it. Sky was crushing on Ryan. She was hooked. Dan's head slipped up beside mine and his check pressed against mine like I wanted him to and we both smiled at Sky, letting her know we were happy for her.

"Sky. Believe it or not, I've already read the book and I know how my story ends. I die and live with my vampire, happily ever after. And even in the magic book that started all of this Ryan doesn't end up with me—but he does find someone else." Sky's eyes got huge, she was listening intently. "There at the end of the book he finds another girl to fall in love with." I smiled, she was about to burst. "Maybe that girl is you."

Dr. Burgis was smiling too now. He liked this, I could tell. He saw us all as an extended part of his weird little mutant family. Dan and I looked at each other and thought the same word again as we considered the doctor. "Weird." But we were getting used to him. We laughed together then I held up my hand and showed my ring to Sky again.

"And don't forget, I'm going to be a married woman in two hours and thirty five minutes, Sky. So don't worry. Ryan is all yours and we're happy for you."

Dan nodded.

Sky blushed, "He's not mine. I mean. I didn't say he was my boyfriend or anything. I've never had a boyfriend. And anyway he didn't say anything—" She looked back down at Ryan and I could see in her face that she was remembering the look he had given me. She didn't like it. She didn't know how Ryan felt about her.

Right then Ryan wheezed and started to cough again. He turned his head and vomited blood all over the floor right at our feet.

Dan and I ran away.

We flew to the other side of the room and out the front window that I'd already busted out earlier and quickly slipped down to sit together in the grass just under the sill leaning our backs up against the side of the building. Dan and I shared a "Holy shit!" look as we tried to calm ourselves down.

"At least we're not in there licking up bloody barf!" I panted. Beside me Dan nodded but he looked up at the open window above us longingly. I heard his strained voice in my head,

Don't count me out. I'm willing to help with the cleanup if I thought I could stop at just what was on the floor.

"Don't remind me. And yeah, we both know how good he tastes, and yeah, it is a damn crime to let that good blood go to waste, but dammit—we're *not eating barf!*" There! I'd put my foot down and made a stand.

I looked over at Dan. He still looked undecided and that was all it took— just like that, I caved and asked, "Are we?" I mean, I was game if he was. We both looked at each other and we turned around and slowly stood up until we could peek back into the waiting room through the busted out window.

My dad, Tom, and Sky were all around Ryan, and Dad was mopping up the blood with what looked like an old shirt but worse than that was Dr. Burgis. He was just coming out of the back office area with an open bottle of alcohol. We watched with horror as he dumped alcohol on the bloody shirt and the rest on the blood on the floor.

"Oh no!" I said and heard Dan's disgusted *They ruined it!* in my head. We both settled back down on the grass under the window. We were bummed, sitting there in shards of broken glass, leaning back against the building. We looked out at the lawn in front of us. There were soldiers everywhere, all running around like ants. We were on this side of the invisible barrier, so I felt pretty safe, but we could see everything they were doing.

God, there was a bunch of them! A few hundred soldiers and loads of cops and other suits all walking around. I felt Dan reach out and take my hand in his. I looked up, surprised because he did that on his own and not because I thought about it first.

What? Dan made a face. *I like to hold your hand. It's nice.*

"Yeah," I said and smiled at him. I thought about it. Dan knew my thoughts and every desire as soon as I had it but I didn't know his thoughts or what he wanted or needed every second. Like right now, if I had been able to read his mind I would have known he wanted to hold my hand and our hands would have met halfway like he does when I want something. I was getting to the point of expecting to only reach halfway for anything. Dan was spoiling me.

"Dan. Do you wish I could read your mind too?" I asked.

Sometimes. Dan gave me a look. *But I think we'd drive each other nuts like that. I'm happy with how we are. I'm happy to live in you and through you.* Dan looked back out across the lawn at the milling soldiers and police.

"Why?" I asked. "Why are you happy it's like this, that you're living in me and it's not the other way around?"

Dan looked at me. He seemed almost shy or embarrassed by the question.

You wouldn't want to be stuck living your life through me. I'm boring, Jane! I'm usually so cautious and careful and yes, shy. He shrugged and smiled. *Me giving that note to you and saying "Hi" was crazy wild for me. And I don't mind you doing the talking for both of us. I'm used to being quiet. It feels right to me. Usually I'm just a boring bookworm or at the most a video game nerd. I may have the hair and the height, but trust me, Jane. I'm boring.*

He reached over and ran a hand down my cheek and looked into my eyes like only he could and stared into my soul. He smiled.

But you, Jane. I don't know if you were like this before you started to change into a vampire, if you were this intense before, but every second inside you is an adventure. Your passion is amazing. The way you laugh. The fun you find in everything. Dan laughed and smiled. *Even barf!*

We laughed, but soon Dan was staring into my eyes again. *And the way that you love me, Jane. I never even dreamed you could love someone like that till I heard it in your head and felt it in your soul and saw it in your face. My God, Jane, every time I turn around I'm finding myself drowning in how much you love me! And you keep doing things that show how crazy insane much you love me and I can see that it's all real! Nothing faked, nothing made up, nothing imagined. And when you do go crazy, and truly lose your mind, I know why you do it. You don't want anything to come between us. Not some other guy, not magic, or guns or anything. And you guard your heart to be able to give it all to me. You fight, to give me all of you. When I see your rage and passion and love it gives me life, Jane. More than I ever knew was out there. You're so full of life and so beautiful and you love me so much—and the most amazing part is I can see it all! It's pure and clean and perfect. And it's all mine.*

Dan reached over and pulled me onto his lap. *I'm the luckiest man ever. I can't imagine that there has ever been a love like this, Jane. Ever. Anywhere. Anyplace. Anytime. This has to be the greatest love that has ever been shaped, ever been dreamed, and somehow I'm right here and I'm the one you love.*

I was crying. Blood was running down from my eyes and my breath was coming fast. I looked up at him, into his beautiful blue-green eyes and he knew what I wanted. We ignored the hundreds of soldiers as we shared my blood, held each other and kissed. It was a beautiful day and my Dan loved me. It was a perfect moment and I forgot the world and enjoyed it.

Sergeant Kelly and Mrs. Bryant

Fugitives

"I'm tired of this! They're playing games! That girl's mine till she's eighteen, and I'm not about to let that bitch steal her! Now you tell that cop to put her in the goddamn car!" Bethany's mother yelled at her lawyer, a youthful man with a well-crafted goatee.

Sergeant Kelly and a dozen officers had been providing security and crowd control, but now Kelly was stuck trying to sort out this new mess. He recognized Ruthan as one of the drug addicted, older street walkers who'd made the beaches area her home for years. She had a long rap sheet and no money, but someone was helping her now. Probably some newspaper or magazine who wanted access to her child. Kelly had been stalling the lawyer, putting him off for thirty minutes now hoping someone in authority would call and put a stop to this, but he was out of time and excuses. As much as he hated it, Ruthan was the girl's mother.

"I have Judge Pritchet on the phone, Sergeant Kelly." The lawyer held up his cell phone and handed it to Kelly. Everyone watched as Kelly took the phone, listened, made a few quiet comments to the judge, and hung up.

"Johnson. Take the young girl to the car. She's going with her mother."

"NO!" Bethany screamed. She'd been fighting like a rabid animal from the second her mother had shown up to claim her. Some of the accusations she'd made about her mother and what she'd done had turned everyone's stomach to hear, but Ruthan denied it and said Bethany was lying because she didn't want to go home.

Mrs. Bryant had tried to be civil at first but since then she'd broken completely and now she was just as out of her mind as the child. Both of them crying and holding onto each other and creating a heart-wrenching scene.

Bethany pulled away from a distraught Mrs. Bryant as Johnson walked toward them. She darted down the hall and everyone heard a door slam on one of the back rooms.

"Don't do this! This isn't right or good for her and you know it!" Mrs. Bryant shouted at Kelly. "If you don't care about Bethany then think about my daughter! Don't you understand what this will do to her!? Don't you even care what Rain might do when she finds out!? Are you INSANE!?" she shrieked hysterically. The girl's panic and pleading and tales of torments had pulled her apart at the seams.

She charged Kelly, trying to force him from her kitchen. The sergeant did his best to shield himself, ward the blows and not hurt the distraught, churchgoing mother of two while at the same time Bethany's mother looked on and laughed. Ruthan was enjoying being on the observation side of the police drama for a change.

"Johnson! Go back there and get the girl and let's get out of here! Now!" Kelly grabbed Mrs. Bryant as she turned to go after Johnson, lifted her off the ground, and held onto her as the other officer disappeared down the hall.

"Now, bitch. We'll see what happens after my lawyers get through suing your ass!" Bethany's mother shouted with a nasty grin directed at the distraught woman restrained in Kelly's arms.

"Mr. Gill, get that *woman* out of this house, NOW!"

Gill whispered to Ruthan. The two retreated from the living room but loitered in the doorway on the porch.

They heard Officer Johnson shouting, telling Bethany to open the door or he'd have to break it down. He shouted once more.

Boom. Boom. Bust.

The noise of the door being kicked in was easy to hear. After another minute Johnson appeared from the back looking panicked.

"She's not in there, Serg! But there's blood all over the floor and all over the door!"

"What!?" Kelly shouted at the same time Mrs. Bryant cried, "Bethany!" She wiggled free then ran for the back room but was grabbed by an alert Officer Johnson.

She beat on Johnson and struggled but he held firm. "Let me go! Let! Go! Of! Me!"

Kelly slipped by and headed down the hall and stopped in front of the kicked-in door. Inside was a black rug on the floor but up close to the door the tan carpet color was visible and it was stained with blood. Lots of blood. He carefully stepped into the room, not stepping in the blood as he looked around.

No sign of the girl anywhere. He turned back to the door and pushed it shut and looked at it. There was bloody writing on the back side of the door. It took him a second to make out the writing because the door was black and the blood didn't stand out clearly from it. He guessed Bethany had cut herself and then used her fingers to write her message before putting a few bloody hand prints on the door to finish it off. From the looks of it, the girl had cut herself pretty badly. There was a lot of blood. Now that his eyes had adjusted to the light in the room he could read the message.

For StarNight this is a gate

to Cathryn's house let me escape

As Above, So Below

with my blood I make it so.

Kelly stepped the rest of the way into the room. He searched under the bed, in the closet, every corner. The window was locked and there was no sign she'd gone out that way. He reached for his radio and told the police outside to be on the lookout for any sign of the girl then went out and searched all the other rooms on this side of the house before he went out to the living room.

"Where is she, you pig!?" hissed Bethany's mother as soon as he stepped into the living room.

Sergeant Kelly bellowed at her, "Shut your damn mouth or you're going into the back of my squad car! I won't tell you again, Ruthan, so help me God, now zip it, woman!" He turned on the young lawyer next who was about to open his mouth. "And YOU!" he yelled. "I told you to take your client out of here and wait in the car. You disobeyed a direct order from an officer on the scene. Get her out now or you'll both be in the back of my car, you got that, counsel!"

The young lawyer took his cussing, screaming client in hand and drug her out of the Bryant's house. After a few minutes it was quiet except for Mrs. Bryant standing in the kitchen, waiting.

"Where is Bethany?" asked Mrs. Bryant.

Sergeant Kelly ignored her and looked to Officer Johnson. "Go room by room and search the house. Every corner. Maybe you'll find something I missed, but don't step in the blood. The girl is either hiding or missing," he said.

Mrs. Bryant shot out of her chair and headed toward the back bedroom. This time Sergeant Kelly let her go and followed her. He found her looking at the back of the door, reading the writing in the room where the girl had disappeared.

"Mrs. Bryant. Do you know where Cathryn's house is?"

"No," she said still looking at the door. She looked down at the floor and the blood on it. "Oh my God. She's cut herself!" She was sick to death with worry. She looked back at Kelly in a panic. "Bethany has a thing—a, a problem with blood. She's fascinated with blood! She's cut herself! Oh God, no!" She pushed Kelly back out of the way so she could look at the writing on the door again.

"Mrs. Bryant, I know the little girl is a witch. Is there any way she could have—I don't know. Could she have disappeared somehow? Was Bethany like your daughter? Was she able to do those kind of things too?" Kelley hated doing it but he asked the questions he felt he had to ask. For these girls, you just had to think outside the box. His interest piqued as he watched Mrs. Bryant's face; he could tell she was remembering something important.

"What is it, Mrs. Bryant? Do you know what's happened to her? Do you know where she's at?"

Mrs. Bryant was looking at the door, speaking out loud as she dredged her memories, "Yesterday! Yesterday the girls just appeared back here in this room. One minute they weren't here and the next they were all in here. Just like that, they were all here." She had another thought and turned to Kelly with a determined set to her face. "I bet Mary knows where she is! Mary's the one with the white hair. I'm sure you remember Mary." Mrs. Bryant cringed.

"Yeah," said Kelly, frowning. "I remember. The one that magiced me upside a wall. You want to go see her?"

Mrs. Bryant didn't let Kelly's attitude stop her. "Mary's trailer is just a few streets over. I'm sure she'll know where Bethany is. Look at all this blood. Bethany's hurt! We have to find her!" Mrs. Bryant grabbed Kelly's arm and started to drag him forward, not waiting for his answer.

"Figures," Kelly muttered as he reached for his radio and told an officer to drive his car around to the trailer that backed up to the Bryant's on the next street over.

"Hold on, lady!" Kelly told Mrs. Bryant.

"No! Let's go!" she complained, impatient to get out the door.

"We're going out the back. I don't want the media or that girl's mother following us. Understand?"

"Oh," Mrs. Bryant said, catching his conspiratorial mood. "That's a good idea," she whispered needlessly.

Kelly made a face. "No. Me retiring last month before all this crap happened would have been a good idea. Me not going to see that blond witch again would be a great idea. And me making sure your daughter doesn't get pissed off at me is a fantastic idea, but us sneaking out the back to avoid that lawyer is a bad idea, so let's go before I change my mind."

They slipped out the back door, climbed the fence and crept through the neighbor's back yard like a couple of fugitives.

Bethany Grave

Red Is a Beautiful Color

Green light flashed around the edges of the storeroom door before it was thrown open. Bethany staggered out. She slammed the door shut behind her then turned and gave the door a vicious kick and yelled at it triumphantly, "Follow me through that, YOU BITCH!"

Bethany panted in the dark hallway, catching her breath. After a moment she laughed. She felt light headed from losing so much blood, and her wrist hurt, but still—it had worked! She'd done it! She'd opened the "Gate" all by herself!

With blood. She knew it would work! Rain had said it would work and it had. Sweat was running down her face, tickling her nose. Bethany still held her pocket knife in her right hand, so she reached up with her left hand and scrubbed the back of her hand across her face.

"Aaack!" In the dark hallway she'd forgotten about the blood that covered her hand from her slit wrist. She'd smeared blood across her face, eyes, and into her mouth.

"Aaah. Yuck! Ptt, pttt, pttt!" Bethany spat out blood and quickly brought up her other hand but forgot about the knife she still held. The blade poked her right in the forehead.

"Oww!" she cried, snatching the knife away and throwing it down the hall.

"Owww! Shit!" Bethany reached up and felt the cut on her head but now there was blood running down her face and into her right eye. She squeezed her eye shut to keep the blood out. She staggered about like a one-eyed pirate and spat more fresh blood out of her mouth. "Ptt. Ptt. Damn that hurt!" She felt at the cut and was relieved to find that it wasn't that deep. It was bleeding freely but it wasn't super deep.

She laughed at herself. A wild, crazy, giddy laugh as she let the craziness of the whole situation take her for a moment, enjoying the few seconds of giddy insanity while blood rained down her face unchecked.

"Hey, at least I didn't gouge my eye out!" She congratulated herself on that minor victory as she staggered forward. She emerged from the dark storage room hall and stepped into the pristinely kept kitchen. She could finally see in the high bright kitchen lighting. She was covered in blood. Drenched in it. She reached up and wiped the blood from her eye but in doing so she managed to cover the rest of her face with a fresh coat of sticky red, but at least she could see with both eyes now.

It was pretty but WOW this was a lot of blood. She felt the blood as it ran in a little red stream down her forehead onto her face and down her neck. She looked down at her dress and the floor. Little drops fell from the tip of her tiny nose when she looked down. She watched as the drops hit the white marble floor at her feet.

Red on white stars bloomed like flowers.

So pretty.

She staggered a little when she lifted her head.

"Whoa," Bethany said, reaching out a hand to the kitchen wall to keep from falling. She noticed the little red hand print as she stepped away. It grabbed her attention—bright red on the white wall. It was so pretty, the way the blood glistened in the kitchen lights.

Red on white.

She walked through the kitchen and out into the next room. No one was there, but she could hear voices, arguing voices, coming from the front room, so she walked that way leaving a red trail behind her.

Angry voices. Bethany listened as she walked toward them.

"This will ruin you, Cornelius! Marconi will dump you! He'll put the word out that you're a complete liability. You'll be destitute, without a penny to your name within a month! Everything you have will be gone unless you cooperate with us!" said an angry female voice, high and shrill just as Bethany walked through the arched doorway.

Rich people worry so much about money, Bethany thought and laughed. Everyone turned at the unexpected sound.

"By the Goddess!" Cathryn shouted as she looked at Bethany.

"What happened!?" Cornelius yelled. Cathryn, Cornelius, a fat elderly silver-haired woman with a blue dress, and a man with long white hair dressed in a fancy white suit were standing around the coffee table in the center of the room. Bethany focused on Cornelius's shocked face and smiled at him; she could feel some of the dried blood crack and flake as she spoke.

"Don't worry about it, Cornelius. If you go broke you can always move into the trailer park with us." She smiled and watched them stare at her in shocked silence as she walked toward them like nothing was wrong.

Cathryn started to head toward her but Cornelius caught her arm. "Be careful," he hissed, giving her a cautionary shake of the head before turning back to Bethany. All of them gaped at the blood that covered her from head to foot.

Cathryn asked, "Bethany, what's happened? Where are the others? Where is Black Rain? Were you attacked? Is she—is she dead?"

Cathryn was upset. She clearly thought the worst had happened and Bethany felt bad for making her worry. She liked Cathryn and Cornelius. Having lived her whole life in a ratty old trailer that was usually filthy, she thought Cathryn's house felt like Cinderella's castle. Dressing up and coming here was one of the most amazing things she'd ever done in her short life, and she loved the way this house worked. Everyone dressed up so nicely, and the people here were always so super polite and formal. Like the house was magical and just being here made everyone into princes and princesses.

She loved being here, so she did her best to play her part. She kept her back straight, chin high as she spoke in her best formal voice. She ignored the blood that dripped from her chin as she spoke, even though the others in the room did not ignore it. Their eyes drank in the damage as she stood there and calmly spoke to them like nothing was amiss.

"Forgive me, Cathryn. Cornelius. I hope I'm not intruding on your company. And please, don't worry, my sisters are fine."

The man in the white suit and the fat old lady stepped away a short distance and started whispering together heatedly. Bethany could tell by the black looks they shot in her direction that they didn't like her at all. But then again, it didn't sound like she liked Cornelius much either.

Bethany's attention was drawn back to Cathryn as she pleaded for answers. "Bethany. Tell us! What happened to you!? How did you get hurt?" She took a step closer but restrained herself this time.

Bethany could see that she wanted to run over to her, but she was being very cautious. Very proper. Bethany approved. This was how it worked at Cathryn's. Like a fairy tale, filled with magic. Dangerous magic. And respect. She was treated like an adult here and she liked it. But Cathryn had asked a question, and Bethany couldn't help but smile as she answered, very politely.

"I slit my own wrist and stabbed myself in the forehead." You don't get to deliver a line like that often, if ever, and Bethany enjoyed the shock value she saw on each face. She quietly promised herself that she'd burn in hell before she ever let anyone know she'd "accidentally" stabbed herself in the head. Hell no. She'd quietly take that bit of info to her grave.

"But why did you do this to yourself? Why did you cut your wrist, Bethany?" Cathryn was still keeping her distance. Bethany held up her slashed wrist; she could feel her pulse pound in her hand as she moved it and she swayed a little on her feet.

"I had to get away. They were after me so I used the gate to get away. And I needed blood to open the gate. I am the Red Witch. Blood gives me magic."

Cathryn's eyes went wide in surprise.

"You—you opened the gate?" Cornelius asked. "You did it all by yourself?" He sounded doubtful.

Bethany smiled at him and said, "Yes, Cornelius. *I* opened the gate." Bethany couldn't help the little bit of pride that entered her voice. She did it with her own power. She felt dizzy, everything was getting a dreamlike quality, people and objects in her vision sparkled at the edges as she looked around the room. A happy smile was fixed on her face and her glazed eyes blinked slowly.

The fat old lady charged toward Cornelius and railed at him, getting up in his face as she pointed a pudgy ringed finger at Bethany. "You cannot dare to bring her, of all people, in here! Into your home! By all the powers we hold dear, come to your senses, she's one of 'them'! How dare you bring her here! Into your home!"

She turned her furious gaze to Cathryn. "What are you thinking, Cathryn! You're in enough trouble as it is. And all of it—ALL OF IT!—is because of them! That stupid video! The police seizing your records AND the financials. Why would you protect them when they have ruined you!? You fools. The others have spoken. You know what they think of them. They want them dead! They are not natural, they aren't even real witches. They're abominations!" The old lady stared daggers at Bethany.

Right then Bethany swayed and almost fell, but Cornelius quickly rushed over and took Bethany's arm. Cathryn stepped up beside him, reached into the front pocket of Cornelius's jacket and grabbing his fancy handkerchief that peeked out of his lapel pocket, she started to wrap it around Bethany's bleeding wrist.

"Don't assist her, Cornelius!" The fat old woman hissed. "Let her die! She's bleeding out, and she'll be gone if you just leave her to herself. You won't even have to dirty your hands; she's lost too much blood already."

That broke through some of the fog that had gathered inside Bethany's head. She blinked and tried to focus her eyes and look at this mean old lady. Cold, heartless, beady eyes stared back at her. Bethany could tell that this woman wanted her to die. She thought about what they were saying to Cornelius as she came in. Threatening him.

She's one of those bad witches that are trying to kill us, Bethany thought, her mind coming alive with a jolt as she realized that she was in real danger here. These were bad people. Her little smile fell away as the guy in the "too white" suit stepped closer. He looked happy and cruel. Cornelius put himself in front of Bethany protectively. But the other guy was young and strong. Cornelius was brave but he was older. Frail.

Cornelius's voice was firm as he spoke. "Yanosh. I believe it's time for you and Fiona to leave our home. Leave now. Don't make me call the police. Your invitation is rescinded. Permanently!" Cornelius stood in front of him, blocking his view of Bethany, but he ignored Cornelius and walked in a slow circle around the three of them, forcing them to turn and follow him as he circled.

He spoke with the old witch as he walked, keeping his eyes on Bethany. His voice was thick with a Russian accent. "Yes. I think you're right. She's almost out of blood." Bethany watched as he smiled, his eyes roving up and down the length of her in a way she had seen before. "It's a shame to waste such a lovely little girl. A real waste. If we were back home I could have sold her. She would have made a wonderful whore."

Bethany didn't follow exactly what he said. She didn't understand what he was talking about. "What? What did you say?" Bethany's voice came out quick and breathy as she asked her question.

Yanosh smiled and spoke clearly, mockingly so, as he answered her.

"I said you would make a wonderful whore. Your hair." His eyes squeezed tight as he considered her hair. "It's amazing. It was done with magic? Yes." He brought his hand to his chin as he thought, and his eyes came back to Bethany's face. "And your pale olive complexion is stunning also. If you were not so dangerous I would love to keep you." He shrugged. "For a while anyway, until I sold you." He laughed.

"Get out of our home, you filthy dog!" Cathryn shouted as she stepped in front of Bethany, shoulder to shoulder with Cornelius, both of them completely blocking his lecherous view while she spoke to Bethany behind her.

"Bethany. We don't care what they say. We won't let him take you anywhere!" Cathryn reached into her little purse and pulled out her cell phone, but just as she was about to dial it was slapped out of her hands. It busted on the white marble floor.

"No, Cathryn. There are already enough police, FBI, and others asking questions! You'll only make this worse by calling them now. If you don't have the stomach for this, let Yanosh and me take her and we will go."

Bethany ignored her and looked at the guy in white. He was smiling at her. Bethany had seen this face on men before. Men that her mother had brought home. Men that hurt her before. Evil men. She'd run from these men all her life. Even when she was a little child she had hidden, always hidden, sometimes under the trailer, sometimes under a pile of clothes in the corner of a room or at a neighbor's house but always she ran and she hid. Sometimes those men caught her. Caught her and hurt her. Sometimes her mother would leave food out and drug her and give her to those men. He was one of those men. A chill ran through her, but it wasn't fear, it wasn't that kind of chill. It was *hate*—it was *insanity* and *rage*.

Bethany stepped away from Cornelius, toward the man in his too white suit and his cold eyes.

"Bethany, stay behind me!" Cornelius said as he tried to step back in front of her only to be sent sprawling to the floor by Yanosh. Bethany looked up to see him shaking his hand like he'd hurt his knuckles when he had punched out Cornelius.

"Damn, he had a hard head!" Yanosh said and swore in Russian as he rubbed his hand.

Cathryn fell to the floor beside Cornelius. "Amen, my Amen." She ran her fingers over his bleeding head while she cried.

Bethany looked at Yanosh as he laughed. She let her rage focus on his head. His big, fat, disgusting, laughing head. She thought about all the blood in his body rushing into his head. Not some of the blood, all of it. Every last filthy drop of blood he had, rushing up into his big, fat, disgusting head! His face flushed red as she drew a deep breath.

"DIE!" Bethany yelled at Yanosh, and he staggered back. He had just enough time for both hands to reach the sides of his swelling head when there was a sickening "POP!" as his head exploded! Blood fanned out in every direction like a bomb had gone off inside his head. Little pieces of skull, bone, and brain flew everywhere like shrapnel. Yanosh's body collapsed to the ground, looking empty and squeezed, as if a giant hand had crushed him like a tube of toothpaste and everything inside had shot out the top all at once.

"Ptt pttt ptt." Bethany spat out blood and little pieces of bone and gore that had flown into her open mouth as she screamed. She reached up and pulled off a piece of once white hair that had pasted itself to the side of her head only to find that it was attached to a small hunk of skull. *Is that a piece of his big fat head?* she thought as she flicked it onto the floor and looked over to where Yanosh lay.

Amazingly, his white suit was almost the only spot in the room that was still clean. The calm white eye in the middle of a red hurricane. Somehow everything had exploded from him, up, out, and away, leaving the spot directly where he stood untouched. It was an unreal, awe-inspiring scene of horror. The ultra white suit and headless body lying there surrounded by a world of red. It was silent except for the odd sound of dripping blood.

Bethany's appearance was little altered; she'd already been covered in red, but now so was everyone and everything else, as if she'd drawn the rest of the world into her own bloody, red witch reality. The whole vast room in every direction was dotted or covered with red. The ceiling was twenty feet high but it was still covered in blood. It wasn't solid red, but sprinkled with millions and millions of fine little dots. Here and there a larger piece of gore stood out from the concentric blast pattern like ornaments on a Christmas tree.

Bethany turned and looked at the fat old woman. She was covered, like a fine red mist had painted her, making her white eyes seem even larger as she stared around the room. She looked like she couldn't believe what she was seeing. She stood as if rooted in place.

Bethany looked around at all the red. Red on white walls. Red on the white ceiling. Red on the white marble floor. She turned in a slow circle taking in the sight, gazing in wonder at how pretty it was—so beautiful. She tingled with the haze of power and a strange wild thrill of shedding blood. So much blood! She felt full of life and very much alive, no longer lightheaded or dizzy.

But then she noticed Cathryn on the floor with Cornelius. They were also covered in blood, and Cathryn rocked back and forth, silently, holding Cornelius in her arms. Bethany carefully knelt on the bloody floor beside her.

"Cathryn?" she said carefully.

"He's not breathing," she said, sounding dazed as she rocked him.

"Can I try to fix him?"

Cathryn looked up. Tears had made clean trails through the blood sprinkled across her face.

"What?" she asked weakly.

Bethany swallowed as she fought with her own tears that were threatening to surface as she reached out a hand and stroked Cornelius's hair. "I would like to try to fix him. I don't know if I can, but I would like to try." She looked up at Cathryn. "If you want me to, I'd like to try to heal him."

A fierce fire filled Cathryn's eyes and her face came alive. "YES!" she growled through clenched teeth. "Please, Bethany!"

Bethany nodded, then scrunched up her brow which Cathryn noticed right away.

"What!? What is it!? What's wrong!?" she pleaded.

Bethany frowned, her voice thoughtful, almost plaintive. "This is going to take a lot of blood, Cathryn. I'm gonna need a whole lotta blood to do this."

Cathryn didn't flinch. "You can cut me!" She held out her wrist to Bethany. "Take mine, Bethany!" she said.

Bethany was still frowning. "We may need more than that, Cathryn. He's hurt bad." She shook her head.

Cathryn looked back over her shoulder to where Fiona stood. She hadn't moved a step since Yanosh had died.

"How do you feel about human sacrifice?" Cathryn asked with perfect calm in her voice. She kept her eyes on Fiona as she spoke and watched as the old lady's lip started to quiver.

Bethany's voice answered back, equally calm. "If you're talking about that old bag over there, let's do it. But I doubt this will count as a human sacrifice."

"True, Bethany. Very true," Cathryn replied.

Black Rain

Embrace the Witch

"**M**y lady, I'm sorry, but you need to wake now." I felt a squeezing caress flow down the length of my body and huge, ghostlike fingers combing through my hair urging me to wake.

"Huumm," I mumbled groggily, happily. "Whaa?" I opened my eyes just a crack and looked up into two blazing red orbs like twin fires caught up in the middle of a weather tossed sky. Believer's eyes were capable of so much emotion with the clouds darkening or lightening or making lines around his eyes or on his cloudy face. If I had to put a name to the look on his face at that second, I would have called it "regretful." He wanted to stay in bed too.

I squinted and smiled at him as I stretched. He was still lying on top of me. His cloudy body still enveloped me from the waist down, molded to me and holding me suspended within his form. It felt intimate and personal in a beautiful way. His warm swirling clouds touched every part of me and at the same time I was inside him with only my head and shoulders free. He'd propped himself up over me with his elbows and forearms as his giant hands ran through my wet hair. His smiling face looked down at me.

"Hello," I said as I reached around him as far as I could and hugged him, burying myself deeper into his chest playfully. Wallowing on him. I felt him laugh. He laughed! I hadn't known he could do that. Believer had a sense of humor!

I pulled away to see his face, wanting to share this new thing with him. He smiled down at me, but as I watched, the smile I wanted to share was replaced by worry, darker shadows forming around his eyes, his slit of a mouth turning down and I frowned with him, my brows making a deep V over my eyes, mirroring his.

"My lady, Sky is at the door. She says that they need you. Your brother has been hurt," he said.

My body froze. I looked up at Believer and studied the concern in his face. I wondered how bad it was.

"How bad is Ryan hurt?" I asked him. It couldn't be too bad, I thought.

"I am not sure, my lady, Sky did not say."

I nodded without thinking. Ryan was hurt. I had to go, but I didn't want to. It had been so nice to be here, with Believer.

"Help me up," I said quietly. Regretfully. Believer slid his form off me and onto the floor and then he slipped his hands under my body. His arms were like clouds with substance and strength, and he lifted me off the bed as if I weighed nothing and carefully set me on my feet. My clothes and hair were wet. Believer was a living cloud and I was soaked through, but I wasn't cold.

"RAIN! We need you out here!" Sky's voice called urgently through the door. My stomach clenched with worry but I still didn't want to go out there and face all of that again. So many people! I reached a hand out to Believer who took it and steadied me.

"I-I don't want to go out," I said. I looked up at him, showing my weakness. "I'm scared, Believer." I didn't want to face all that again. All the problems and all the people. I didn't want to burn again or die again or kill again! How many ways would I screw up this time!? I just wanted to stay in here where it was safe and quiet.

"Why?" he asked. I could see the light in his eyes, his concentration as he looked at me, his mind trying to understand me and help me. But who could help me when "I" was the problem!?

"Because it's safe in here with you and I like it in here," I confessed, my voice sounding angry. I released his hand and started to pace as I spoke, back and forth in front of the door, getting more and more upset as I stomped back and forth.

"If I go out there I'll hurt someone else or I'll get hurt again and I'm tired of it. I'm tired of all this shit!" I threw my hands out indicating the room around us. "This is all I need. We can live in this room forever. I can make us whatever we need in here and we can hide away from the world and be safe right in here. Just you and me. Safe and alone, just you and me forever!"

I stopped and looked up at Believer fearfully. I knew I was being weak and horribly selfish, but I didn't care, I was tired of all this shit! I didn't want to do it anymore! It kept getting worse and worse. "We can hide away from the world and be safe right here. Just you and me. Safe and alone, just you and me forever!" I was tingling, my skin prickled with heat as I finished in a rush and threw my arms around Believer's truck of a body and cried.

Believer lifted my chin with one massive finger and studied me, my face, my hands that wrapped around his hand. His burning red eyes considered me closely and then he ran his other cloudy hand over my face and cooled me and absorbed my hot tears and replaced them with his own warm dampness. Then he absorbed me into his body. For a few moments he let me slip back inside his clouds and held me there, all of me inside of him.

I calmed. Surrounded by him, held floating and weightless inside his body, warm and safe and loved. I breathed him in through my mouth, in and out. He tasted like a sweet summer cloud, like the air before a storm, warm and damp but with an electric charge of life. Believer's life.

All too soon it ended and I found myself standing on my own two feet again as he stepped away from me. My own feet and legs supporting my weight as he pulled himself away. I stood, looking at my feet on the floor. Believer gave me a moment before he spoke.

"Remember your brother. What about your brother? You love him and he is outside. He needs your help."

I kept my eyes on the floor, but Believer reached out and lifted my chin to make me look up into his eyes again. "And if I stay in here with you then I will never see my Sky again, and I love her too."

He smiled at me, but I shook my head no. I didn't want to go. I didn't want him to go! I didn't want to do this anymore!

"Black Rain," Believer said which surprised me. I was so used to him calling me "my lady" or even "my love." I blinked and stopped crying. Hearing that name sent a cold chill through me.

"Yes," I said, afraid of what would happen next.

Believer smiled at me, a sad smile. "I will not hide from the one who made me. I want to be what she made me to be. And if you are like me then you cannot hide from what you are. What you were made to be." His head turned to the side as he watched me. He didn't know about Rain Marie. He didn't understand. I shook my head wildly "NO!" as I railed at him.

"But I don't want to 'be' what I was made to 'be'! I was made and formed to murder and kill and destroy those that I love!" Hot angry tears streamed down my face as I complained about my miserable creation. "And if I go out there again who knows who I'll kill next. I'm a monster, Believer! She made me that way. I murder what I love! I am a monster! A murdering monster!"

I fell to the floor and broke down, crying again. Giving myself over to my despair. Hating myself and what I was, what I had been made as. Believer stood quietly for a moment before stooping down and lifting me into his soft, strong embrace. I shook and cried, turning my head into his chest as he held me, but then I jumped in his arms as I heard Sky shout right outside the door.

"RAIN! Please come out! Ryan needs help!"

I turned and looked up at Believer. His voice was gentle as he spoke to me. "Have you murdered me, my lady?" he asked me. He calmly waited for an answer to his question.

I blinked, surprised. I didn't know why he would ask such a thing. But I answered.

"No," I said. "Never."

"Have you destroyed me, my lady?"

A line creased my brow as I answered him, still confused. "No."

Believer's smile returned. "You have not murdered nor destroyed me. But you have loved me, my lady. In a way I never knew would be possible for me. And you have changed me." His eyes grew brighter and his voice stronger, filled with passion as he spoke. I listened with rapt attention to every word Believer said as he held me like a small child in his arms.

"In my heart, I no longer see myself as just a created 'thing'." Believer lifted one smoky hand up and looked at it. At himself as he spoke. His voice introspective. "When I was first made, I wondered what I was. Who I was. And at first I was a cloud bird, then my Sky changed me and I was as you see me now, and my Sky asked me to protect her. Everything is so new. And yet—" Believer looked down at me. Sad now. "I knew I was less than the others. Less than my Sky that made me. Less than the others that I have met. I felt within myself that I was much, much less—until I met you."

Believer smiled at me then. I couldn't help smiling back and I reached up and touched his face. "My Sky made me with the ability to change, to become more, and to learn more. I no longer see myself as a 'thing' because you do not see me as a 'thing.' Your love has changed me. Made me more than what I was. More than what I thought existed for me. So much more." Believer leaned down, holding me close in his arms and whispered to me, "Do not hide what you are, Black Rain. Because you are beautiful and kind and faithful and true and compassionate and giving and lovely. Do not hide your love here, in this room, forever."

Believer stood me up on my feet, reached over and unlocked the door, and turned back to me.

"Your brother loves you too and right now he needs you. Do not hide, my love. You are not a monster. You are beautiful." Believer stepped to the side, leaving me facing the door. Letting me face it and make my choice.

This place, this room had felt so apart and away from the world and from all my problems that for a while I could pretend and imagine that this was all there was. Like a castaway on a desert island alone with someone they loved. For a while it was beautiful. A small retreat for my damaged mind and soul.

But now I could feel "myself" or *what I had become* waiting for me on the other side of that door. The power and desire and strangeness that I could only describe as the Black Witch. I felt it drawing around me. Wrapping around me almost like Believer's body did but this went deeper, much deeper. Soul deep. Soon I would breath her in and out and be enveloped with her power and desires. I hoped he was right. That there was more than murder and death inside me. Love and beauty and compassion. God please let him be right. Then I thought about that "thought."

I was truly talking to myself because God would not hear me.

Alone. Alien. Other. These words flashed by in the tangle of my mind.

"Believer," I said, still facing the door.

"Yes."

"I am changing too—and I can't control how I change. It just happens. Whether I like it or not, sometimes it just happens and not all of it is good." I turned only my head toward him; my body still facing the door.

"Thank you. Thank you for holding me. Thank you for loving me." I turned back to the door and closed my eyes.

"But you're right. I cannot hide from what I am. As above, so below. As within, so without. Black is my color and my name is Black Rain. Let the Black Witch now live in me. So mote it be." I thought about my wet hair, dress, and shoes drying and they did. Then I thought of my eyes going solid black again, like I'd had during the interview I'd done on the porch of our trailer.

With my eyes still closed I thought about the door in front of me. I didn't want to open it. I couldn't stay here, I had to go out, but I would not open the door so like a silent protest I thought about it dissolving, changing and reforming into an open arch, from floor to ceiling, wrapped around with black glass, like I had used to make the urn I'd given to the vampires. I opened my eyes and stepped through the beautiful glass archway that was eight feet across and as high as the ceiling without even looking at it.

Sky had been standing in the hall with Jane's dad and they were both falling over each other to get away from me as I stepped out into the hall and looked around. It seemed that after all their attempts to get me out of the room they were now afraid of what they'd summoned forth and wished they could put the genie back into her bottle.

"Your brother needs help. He's right out here," Jane's dad managed to say as he looked at me and my black eyes. He turned and left, back out the mangled door leading to the waiting room. I wondered what on earth had happened while I slept. Sky didn't run. She was scared but she approached me with a determined stride.

"Rain! Or Black Rain! Or whoever you are now! Come and help Ryan! He's bleeding inside and he'll die if you don't help him!" She looked right at me boldly, searching my face for some sign that I was still me or at least that some part of me still lived that would recognize her. Something that was still Rain.

I felt Believer step up beside me and saw the relief on Sky's face. She'd been worried about him, I realized. Afraid I'd hurt him. She did love her friends. I also thought she was relieved not to be alone in this hallway with me right now.

"Hello, Sky. Take me to Ryan." She nodded, satisfied, then turned and stepped through the door and back into the waiting room.

I took a deep breath and felt it, deep within me. Power. Limitless, vast and endless. As far as the east is from the west. Absolute power. Impossibly bound within me and wrapped in the strange and unusual trappings and urges of a witch. Of a Black Witch.

I looked up at Believer and laughed when I saw his glowing red eyes flare with surprise at my black eyes. Maybe he was also surprised at my smiling face. He looked at me with worry.

"Are you well? Why have your eyes changed color, my lady?" he asked.

In some ways, Believer acted like a curious child. Always asking questions.

"I am what I am, Believer. And would you prefer if we matched?" I asked. I thought about my eyes holding swirling raging mists within them while still being able to see and function normally. It was an odd sensation as the change took form within my eyes and I made some adjustments quickly to make myself more comfortable then asked "Better?" with a grin as I looked up at him.

Believer frowned down at me. "No," he said. "I liked your old eyes more."

I frowned up at his frown. Damn. Believer was so honest. So much for lying to your date to make her feel better. Believer hadn't learned that trick. I made a mental note not to ask him if my dress made me look fat. The thought made me laugh. "Okay! Fine," I said as I laughed. I thought about my eyes returning to their original state and they did.

Believer smiled down at me, and I smiled back as I took his hand in mine. "If any other person on the planet had asked I would have told them to go straight to hell. I might have even sent them there." I smiled up at him. "But not you, my love." My smile went away as I looked up at him. "But my eyes may change color again. I change all the time. Inside and out, so don't let it surprise you, Believer. It's just the way I am. So mote it be." I released his hand, turned and walked out into the waiting room.

There were two groups of people on separate sides of the room. In one half my friends gathered around my brother who was lying on the floor, but in the other half of the room were FBI or other agents all in suits. About a dozen of them were setting up a table with food and drinks. Tom was with them and it seemed like everything was well organized and controlled but just seeing all those strangers sent a chill through me and I looked away, stumbling back. I ran right into Believer. I quickly slipped my arms around him and hid my face in him while his arms went around me protectively.

"What is it, my lady? What has frightened you?" Believer asked. His voice deep and threatening like thunder.

"Just keep them on that side of the room please. It's too many people, too soon. Keep them over there, Believer, and I'll be okay." I kept my eyes closed as I held onto him.

"As you wish, my lady." He rumbled, "Go and help your brother." I felt him move away from me, dissolving out of my arms, and I resisted the urge to open my eyes and look back at the crowd of strangers as I heard the commotion of frantic voices and shuffling feet as people started to flee and push out the door in a rush. I heard Tom speaking with Believer and tried to put it all out of my mind as I stood there rooted in place with my eyes squeezed shut, as if seeing strangers had turned me into a pillar of salt.

"Rain." I heard Jane's perfect, musical voice beside me.

"Yes, Jane," I answered her and opened my eyes.

She looked good. She was still pale, but she had a little color to her face now. She looked very, very good. Jane had changed more. Become more vampire and less human since I had seen her last. Everyone was changing.

"Oh. Did you guys eat?" I asked. Jane had a little blood on her chin and at the corner of her mouth.

"Dan and I were pigs," she confessed. "We emptied out an entire cooler full of blood. Tom is having more brought in for us. But are you okay?" She looked concerned, her eyes looking at my face and I knew she saw a lot when she did that. Part of her being a vamp.

"Just take me to Ryan," I said. "I am what I am." No help for it. Of course Jane heard my words and the rest.

"I'll take you to him." She held out an arm for me to hold onto.

Did I look that frail? All this power and so weak at the same time? But it felt right, so I took her arm and let her lead me across the room to the people I knew. The people I cared about. They grouped around Ryan's still form where he lay on the floor. Sky, Dan, Jane's dad, Dr. Burgis, and I was surprised to see Williams there too. They made a place for me to get to Ryan. Jane eased me down beside my brother like I was a little old lady.

"What happened?" I asked as I looked down at my brother. I could see his arm was bandaged and his lip was busted but there was something more. His shirt was cut off and there was a bandage around his middle.

Had he been shot? I felt a cold frightening thrill of dark rage building in me as I looked down at Ryan's damaged body. Who would dare shoot my brother!

"Rain! I'm so sorry! It was my fault," Sky said suddenly. She sounded so scared, it jolted me right out of my burgeoning black mood. I didn't understand why she was scared. Did she think I would hurt her? And how could this possibly be her fault? I didn't get a chance to ask as Sky started her stuttering confession.

"M-My father and I were fighting and–and Ryan thought he was hurting me and–well–he tried to make him stop." Sky started crying. "Please don't kill my father. I know he deserves it, but please don't kill him. I still love him. He's a bad man sometimes, but please don't kill him, Rain!"

I stared at her—shocked. Did she really think I would kill her dad? Did she think me a complete monster? I looked down at Ryan. He was pale and he sounded horrible. Something rattled sickly as he took shallow breaths, in and out. The longer I looked the more I thought that Sky was right. I should be treated like a monster. Already I could feel anger trying to fill me again. Dark and ready.

I'm a mess. I said to myself.

I tried to focus on helping Ryan.

"Tell me what is broken," I demanded of the nervous silent group all around us.

"Tell me, and I will fix it." My voice. Tight. Strained.

Dr. Burgis ran down the list of injuries and told me about the medicines he had given Ryan so far. I listened patiently. As soon as he was done I looked down at Ryan and went to work. I concentrated on his body's own ability to heal itself and willed it to quicken. I focused on his arm first, willing the bones to mend and get back together then I healed his lip and then his rib. Willing it to go back to where God had intended it to be and after a few other tweaks I finished by filling him with energy and health, and I removed the effects of the drugs the doctor had given him and willed him to wake.

His eyes opened and he looked up at me and everyone else. Searching all the faces around him. I was surprised to see him stop and focus on Sky with a smile and not Jane, and I thought again that they were going to be a couple. Ryan hadn't said anything yet but his hands reached up to his bandaged chest. Then up to his lip feeling for any sign of damage. Then he sat up and looked at me and quirked a smile.

"Thanks, Sis. I guess you patched me up?"

I didn't get a chance to answer because he got smothered by Sky's arms.

"Ooof!" We all laughed as he got the breath squeezed out of him. For someone so tall and skinny, Sky was strong! Ryan's surprise was fun to watch and it was plain as day that Sky was not used to hugging boys, but what she lacked in grace she more than made up for with determined effort as she wrapped her arms around him.

"I was so worried! I thought you were going to die!" Sky said as she squeezed him. But just as quickly as it started it was over, as she jumped back from Ryan and looked at everyone around her, blushing and embarrassed at herself.

Dr. Burgis and Williams laughed and congratulated Ryan on his quick recovery while Jane's dad helped him unwrap himself. Jane appeared beside Sky out of thin air and put an arm around her and whispered into her ear. Sky listened eagerly, both of them sharing some silent but important conversation about Ryan I was sure. Their eyes stayed on him as they spoke. It was good to see everyone happy.

And Jane had moved so fast! The way she "appeared" out of thin air was smoother than before and everything about the way she moved was even more enthralling. She was captivating. It made me smile just watching her move, and it reminded me of Cathryn the witch and how she always walked and moved the way I thought a witch should. Sensuously. Gracefully and with such confidence.

And here I was. The Black Witch, filled with all this power, and I was walking around with my eyes closed because I was scared to see strangers. Stumbling around. Bumping into people. Being led around like an old lady. And my moods were so up and down I made myself dizzy half the time. I was "a mess."

"Sis. You okay?" Ryan asked me.

"No," I answered.

"Stupid question," he conceded as he pulled the last bit of gauzy bandage from his arm.

"Hello, Black Rain," said Williams. "I hear you wanted me back," he said with a smile.

"Yes. I want you back. If you don't mind." I returned his smile with a sad one of my own.

"They didn't make you come back did they?" I asked quickly.

"No. They told me that you wanted me and said that if I didn't come they'd work in a new guy. And you don't need some new guy who don't know you and don't know shit about how to treat a witch. You don't need any more stress especially after what happened earlier." His brows bunched up as he asked, "Did you burn yourself up right here in the middle of the room?" He looked upset as he glanced over at the burnt spot on the floor then back to me. "They told me that you burnt up, dead! and then came back like nothing had happened."

It was nice having Williams back, but he had missed a lot and I didn't feel like spelling it all out and reliving it.

"Yes and no, Williams." Yes, I had burned to a crisp. But no. The "me" he remembered was dead and gone. "It is good to see you though. I'm glad you came back."

Williams gave a suspicious grunt. He knew there was a lot that I wasn't telling.

"I spoke with your father," Williams said gravely, and Ryan and I shared a look. We knew that Dad must be worried to death. This morning on the way to the doctor's office, Dad had made Williams promise to keep an eye on us before we dropped him off at work. He didn't even want to go, but Williams promised to take good care of us and Dad planned on working only for a few hours.

"He wasn't happy to hear that I had to leave you two here alone," Williams said. "He's been watching the news and he's real worried about you two. He was trying to come up here but I got ahold of him on the phone and let him know that I was coming back in here to keep an eye on you. He wants you to call him." Williams held up his phone looking from me to Ryan to see who would "man up."

"Could you call him, Williams?" I asked. "Just tell him we're okay and that we'll meet him at the church tonight."

Williams didn't like it. "You should talk to him yourself," he grumped.

I didn't feel up to it. Not over the phone. "Please, Williams," I asked quietly, and he gave me a concerned look before he got up and started dialing his phone as he walked away to call our dad.

"Rain!" Ryan said as soon as Williams left to call. "We got some brother-sister business to deal with right now!" He jabbed a finger at me and then back at himself. "What's the deal with that cloud guy?" He glanced over at Sky and Dr. Burgis who were listening but kept going. "When he took you in the back room, what did you two do back there?" Ryan looked me over, eyes searching my face and clothes, hunting for evidence of me having "gotten busy" in the back. The typical overprotective brother.

"You didn't, you know. *Do* anything, did you? Not with that thing." Ryan tensed as he looked at my face and Sky's face as she knelt beside him. He could tell that neither of us liked hearing Believer referred to as a "thing."

"I'm your brother, Rain! I'm supposed to worry about my sister! So be pissed if you have to, but I want to know what went on back there. Are you and that cloud guy an item or what?"

I sighed. Ryan was so straight and narrow. He never walked on the other side of the fence like me. I'd had sex before and it had caused me nothing but pain, but I wasn't afraid of it. Or of talking about it. I tried to be good and show some restraint, but I did it for Believer's privacy and image. Not mine.

"Believer is not a thing, Ryan. Please treat him like a person because he is a person." I kept it simple. Beside me Sky nodded but didn't say anything else, not wanting to butt in on our official "brother-sister" business.

Ryan screwed up his face. "Oh come on, Rain! You just met that—'guy,' so how could you go off with him like that! You met him and five minutes later you're headed to the back with him. That's not you, Rain, that's not how you act. You would never run off with someone you just met. I tried to get back there, but Jane wouldn't let me. She even tied the door shut to keep me out." He gave me a level look and waited for a minute. I waited too.

"Well. Say something." He wanted me to confirm or deny what he thought I had done. But instead I agreed.

"You're right, Ryan. Rain never would do something like that. But a witch would. I am a witch, filled with passion and as changeable as the summer wind. I can hate in a moment and love in a second. And I don't care what people think of me." I squinted my eyes and spat out, "That was Rain Marie's problem! She was so scared of what you and Mom and Dad would think about her getting pregnant! And she was so terrified of what everyone at church would say that she did horrible things. And she made me do horrible things too! Things I didn't want to do! Well I don't give a shit what people think of me because I am what I am."

I got up in Ryan's face and smiled. I could tell he already regretted the conversation, but I couldn't stop fighting yet for some reason. Part of me insisted on seeing the white flag of surrender go up. He started it anyway.

"You want to know what we did back there?" I said loudly enough for everyone to hear.

"You want to know if he touched me?" I asked, my smile getting wicked. Sky blushed. Blinked.

"You want to know if I *liked it*?" With a thought I let my eyes sparkle and laughed when Ryan pulled back in surprise then gave me a suspicious frown. He knew I did the eye twinkle on purpose.

"NO!" Ryan said, waving his arms around in defeat. "I don't want to know! I'm sorry I asked! Don't tell me. HEY! The food's here, let's go eat!" Ryan changed the subject like he always did when we started to talk about things he didn't want to talk about and that made me laugh.

We went as a group to the other side of the room where the food was set up on folding tables they'd carried in. The crowd of agents had been cut down to only three, including Tom, which Believer stood looming watch over. Tom stood by the tables while the other agents were behind him, near the door with their heads pointing mostly at the floor.

Sky called Believer to her and then hustled him off to the side of the room where the two descended into hushed conversation, clearly wanting some privacy. I left them to it and I headed toward Tom and the food. Tom did not look happy. I doubt that he'd enjoyed having Believer tower over him and keep him on this side of the room. He looked anxious to start his game of fifty questions again. I stepped up to the table and grabbed a paper plate and a piece of pizza and a soda.

"Hey, Tom," I said casually as I took a bite of pizza.

"Hello, Black Rain," Tom said. He was being very careful with his voice. No impatience. He was trying at least.

"Any problems while I was lying down?" I asked.

One of Tom's eyebrows went up, but that was his only reaction. "A small communication problem when my phone went dead, and of course your brother got hurt by Mr. Han, but I'm sure you already knew about that. It looks like you were able to heal him." He looked at Ryan as he and Williams got into the food.

"Yes," I said. Then added, "Tom. Please keep Sky's father away from me for a while. I may be able to see him soon, but not today. Or tomorrow I think."

Tom took out his pad and made some notes. Good. Tom and his notepad. I was getting used to it. It seemed familiar and I liked familiar.

"We have a limo ready to transport you and your party to the church. I assume that you and Sky are still going to the wedding."

I thought about that. All of us together in one car riding down the road, and I got a bad feeling. It would be a great chance to wipe us all out in one shot. It was weird to think about governments and countries trying to kill us, but that guy I had killed had been something other than American. And he must have been working for someone who wanted us dead. And he may have even been working for someone from the good old U S of A that thought we were too dangerous to let live. Someone in our own government might be scared enough to try it, and if they did it right they may even be able to kill everyone but me. I didn't feel like riding in a car anyway, but I didn't tell Tom we wouldn't be going to the church that way.

"Sure, Tom, bring the limo around. Get her all gassed up and ready to go and we'll head to the church as soon as we're done eating." I gave him a polite smile.

"Good." Tom looked over at Dr. Burgis. "Can we take the doctor now?" he asked me. Like it was only a matter of time before I said yes.

"Not yet, Tom. Not yet," I said, like it was only a matter of time before I did say "yes." It had the feel of a game we would be playing for a while.

I turned my attention to the food. We all pulled up chairs and made a circle and talked and ate together. I made Tom sit down with us and eat. Of course he tried to refuse, but Williams told him that this was how it worked, and that eating together was a "witch thing." Then he told Tom about how I made him eat breakfast with my family that morning too. Tom seemed reassured by that and almost looked happy as he sat down and got into the pizza. It seemed like he was happy to be officially assimilated into my weird "witch" collective of people.

Everyone was sitting, eating, and talking except Sky who had grabbed a box of pizza and retreated to the far side of the room with Believer. I wondered why, but then Jane and Dan started talking about the wedding and I asked them if I could make their wedding clothes.

Jane's excited smile was infectious, and I couldn't help but smile back. She was so happy, so much in love, and so, so beautiful! She had us all smiling. I had both of them stand in the middle of our circle of chairs while I worked on the clothes right in front of everyone, shaping and changing the clothes right on their bodies.

Jane's dad made suggestions or complained about how tight or revealing things looked. Ryan and Williams also gave a few suggestions and Tom asked if one of his "other agents" could make a few suggestions, which surprised me. I asked Jane if this new girl was okay, and Jane asked her a few quick questions and said that she honestly just wanted to help. Jane didn't pick up any weird vibes from the girl, so we let her join our little group and I even made her get some pizza and get her own chair.

Her name was Trisha and she had a lot of fashion sense as it turned out. She helped a lot. I shaped and formed and molded something for Jane that was elegant and still "tough" in a gothic Cinderella kind of way. With any normal human wearing it, it would have looked awesome but with her wearing it, it looked otherworldly yet not overdone. Heartbreaking and dangerous.

And her Dan was like a white knight in a white leather-like outfit. Very gothic but still balanced enough to be traditional. Or borderline traditional. Trisha was a real genius and had a wicked imagination with lots of detail, and it was fun to work with her.

Everyone was getting emotional looking at them and watching how they looked at each other. Agent Trisha was crying like a baby as Dan and Jane held each other, gazing into each other's eyes in that way they did. But I noticed Trisha catching dark looks from Tom, who, no doubt, wanted his agent to stay on her game.

"Give her a break, Tom," I said. "Love like this is special. I don't know that you'll see anything like it again. Let a girl dream." I sighed then I looked over to Dr. Burgis.

"I'll take my pills now, doctor."

"Yes. Of course. I'll get them ready for you, Rain."

The doctor went to the table and grabbed one of the empty red plastic drink cups and then reached inside his white lab coat for his hidden stash of pills. One blue and six white pills went into the cup from his hidden stash.

"Will it matter that I ate first?" I asked.

"No. It shouldn't make a difference, Rain. Now take your pills." He handed me the cup with the pills.

This had always been done in a back room with no one else to see, but now everyone watched me as I reached into the cup, took two white pills out and swallowed them, taking them two at a time until they were gone. I swallowed the blue pill last. It felt ritualistic. It seemed strange to me. Taking the pills now. After everything. I didn't think I needed them anymore. The whole idea that a pill had started all of this was hard to accept. Sky was worried that if she didn't finish all the pills her powers would fade away and she would become a normal girl again. I wasn't afraid I'd lose my powers. Nothing could change me back to what I was and I didn't think anything could take away what I had become. So why did I even bother with the pills?

Because if felt right.

Because I was part of this group of mutants.

Because it was an important part of the madness.

Because it was familiar.

Tom, Trisha, and the other agent watched me and the doctor with hungry eyes. They wanted the pills. And they wanted the doctor who had made the pills. I thought about the cup in my hand. They would probably grab it if I set it down or threw it in the trash and try to get some kind of stupid "trace" evidence off the cup to make the pills on their own.

I looked at them, held the red plastic cup up in front of me, and thought about the cup dissolving into sand and it did, falling in fine dust onto the floor. Trisha had the good grace to look embarrassed, but Tom and the other guy leaned in and whispered together as they looked at me. I didn't trust them. But that wasn't new.

Tom stepped back over and spoke up. "If you're ready to leave, we can head out. We have the limos out front now. But what are you planning to do with the dragon?" Tom asked with a straight face.

"Dragon?" I asked, my brow crinkled up. "What dragon?"

Tom looked surprised that I didn't know already.

"The cloud dragon that Sky called when you were 'out.' It's been perched on the roof of your building keeping an eye on things. What will you do with the dragon? If possible, we don't want it flying over the city because that would create a panic and lots of people would get hurt. Just having it perched on the top of your building where it can be seen from a distance has been a disaster for us. Remember, we're trying to keep this as controlled as possible, but with pictures of a dragon on the news it's going to get worse fast. And it will get harder to keep everyone away from you and your friends."

Crap! A dragon. I looked up to the ceiling. It was up there, hanging out, right now. Well, I had asked Sky to call a new friend, but I didn't think she'd call a freaking dragon! Tom was right though, what was I going to do with the big fella?

"Sky!" I called. Tom jumped half out of his skin, surprised by my shout.

"Easy Tom," I soothed, giving him a sideways look. Damn. He was real wired for some reason. Wired and jumpy. I wondered what else had happened while I was out because Tom seemed a lot more nervous than I remembered him being. Something had scared Tom, and I didn't think it had been me. Maybe the dragon was that scary?

I smiled. I couldn't wait to meet him.

"Yes, Rain?" Sky asked as she walked up to us.

"We're about to leave to go to Jane's wedding, and I wanted to ask about the dragon." I pointed up. "The guy you got on the roof. Can you make him small enough to fit through a big door or does he have to stay big?"

Sky thought for a minute before answering. "I should be able to make Sky Dragon small again but why did you want him that little? Sky Dragon likes being big, he'll want to know why." Sky looked off to the side where Believer now stood. He had come over with her when I called his Sky.

"Sky Dragon is like Believer now," Sky said. "Sky Dragon is smart and a person too. I'll go talk to him, and I'm sure he'll be okay with it, but why did you want him small?"

I looked at Believer as I answered her and smiled at him as I spoke with Sky.

"We're about to leave for the wedding and Tom is worried that a giant flying dragon going over the city would cause a panic. People would freak, run screaming through the streets and all that. More trouble and way more problems. And anyway, if he were smaller he could stay closer to you when you went indoors. He could protect you better that way. I'm sure if you tell him that he'll be okay with being in a smaller package." I was still looking at Believer as I spoke to her.

Something was different.

"What did you do to him?" I said, as I looked at Believer, my eyes narrowing suspiciously as I noticed things about him I hadn't seen at first.

"You changed him!" I accused in a surprised shout. I could see it in his eyes and mouth, and his body looked more solid, more together. I stepped away from Tom and Sky, heading straight to Believer leaving them both looking at my back. Believer's smile disappeared when he saw me stomping toward him, but I didn't say anything or stop until I had my arms around his middle.

His arms went around me. He felt more solid. He was still a cloud, but with more substance to him now. I didn't know if I liked it. I looked up at him. His face was almost the same but I could see more emotion on his face. Everything was wispy before, but now his face had more definition. I looked deeper, down inside him. What looked like veins now ran through him, the larger ones were the most visible but even those were transparent and ghostlike, and as I looked closer I could see thousands and thousands of other little paths all over, spider-webbed and running through him and through the clouds and mist that swirled inside his form. In his chest close to where a heart would be was a glowing white cloud, denser than the rest of his swirling mists, and it was pulsing with light almost like he had a heartbeat now. I couldn't begin to imagine what or how all this had been done. What on earth had she done to him!

He looked happy though, and he still had a small smile on his face in spite of the angry glower stuck on mine. I tried to stay calm as I spoke. "You've changed," I said and reached a hand up to touch his chest, putting my hand over his new pulsing heart as he looked down at me.

"Yes," he said, his smile widening now. "I asked my Sky to change me. I wanted to be more. To have more. And I asked her to change me." He was smiling. He was happy with the changes, but I had been so happy with him just the way he was.

"How?" I asked.

"Why?" I demanded. I could be just like him. Just ask my rude questions and be as honest as I wanted to be! I wanted to know what had changed and why he had changed it.

Believer looked worried and thoughtful, like he didn't know how to say what he wanted to say, and he took a minute to think it through as I searched his changed face with my eyes.

The room was too small for the others not to hear what we were saying especially with Believer's deep powerful voice. Everyone seemed to migrate to the other side of the room, developing a renewed interest in the food in an attempt to give us some privacy. I didn't need it. I didn't care what they heard.

"Because I wanted more," Believer said. His long slit of a mouth still smiled. "There was so much that I could not do or feel, and I wanted more. I wanted to 'feel' and 'smell' and 'taste,' and I wanted to be able feel you inside me when we are together. And I wanted to be able to make you feel also. To touch you more. To give you pleasure. To make you happy. To make me happy. I wanted to be able to love you more, my lady."

I looked down and hid my face against his cloudy chest. He had asked Sky to change him so he could love me more! Oh God! I held onto him tightly to keep myself still as I let that sink in. He had changed his whole existence to love me more. Believer was changing his whole body for me like it was no big deal.

"My lady, I hope I have not done something you did not wish me to do. Perhaps I have been too—" Believer seemed at a loss for words which was so unlike him. I looked up at him, surprised at his troubled face.

"Hasty." He finished his sentence, looking pained to say the word. The lines around his eyes were darkening more, matching his mood. "I am sure Sky could change me back. Put me back to the way you prefer me. I am sorry. I have been unwise. When you changed your eyes I asked you to change them back and you did. Because I asked you to. I should have asked your permission before I did these things and—"

"Hush," I said and reached up high and put a hand to his mouth to keep him from saying more.

"You don't have to ask my permission to change yourself, Believer," I said. "It's your body. Yours and Sky's. She is the one that made you and if anyone owns you she does. I don't own you, Believer. You're a person and you can make your own decisions, and you don't have to ask for my permission. If you change, then change things for yourself. To make yourself happy, Believer." I took my hand away from Believer's slit of a mouth and looked up at him. He looked back at me, his eyes burning so brightly, so intensely, as he stared down at me but the rest of his face was calm. Peaceful as he spoke.

"Loving you makes me happy," he said. "And loving you more is something I want for myself."

I was reeling from what he had just said as he pulled himself straighter and took both of my hands in his. Maybe it was the pills already taking effect but I felt dreamlike and loosely connected to the ground as I looked up at him. His voice was firm, powerful and sure; it rumbled with power and gave me chills that tickled down my arms and back as he spoke.

"I am Believer. Son of Sky. I know who I am and I know what I want."

Believer wanted me. He wanted me for himself and not because Sky had told him to love me.

"Black Rain," Tom interrupted. "I'm sorry to interrupt, but we'll be late if we don't leave right now."

Like the buzz of a fly, I didn't even look at him as I said, "Then we will be fashionably late. Go away before I kill you." I didn't look to see if he went. I looked at Believer. I truly felt like "Alice" and in my Wonderland there were dragons and vampires and mad scientists with magic pills, where the Son of Sky, a living cloud, falls in love with a murdering Black Witch. I would have been worried I was losing my mind, but I knew that I'd already lost it. I was now feeling that light-headed, feverishness the pills always brought on but I wasn't worried about it. This was no weirder than anything else I'd experienced lately.

Believer smiled then like he had some surprise to share and his voice pulled me out of my little flight of fancy.

"Sky has asked if you would be willing to make a trade. Or perhaps a better way to phrase this would be as an exchange of trusts." An odd expression crossed Believer's face that I had never seen before. If I had to put a name to it I would have called it devious, or at least cunning. He was up to something!

My eyes squinted as I became curious and tried to make sense of what was going on. Sure, I was doped up, but I still knew "sneaky" when I saw it on a face that big. Believer was very smart, Sky had made him that way, and I was sure he didn't forget anything, but in a lot of ways he was still like a child. The look he had now was like a kid who was trying to sneak a cookie from the cookie jar. I wondered what mischief my Believer had started.

I tried to keep a stern face, but my smile wanted to come out and it peeked around the edges of my frown, ruining it. "Okay. Spill it! What are you up to?" I demanded. I gave him a poke with my long-nailed fingers into his cloudy body to get his attention.

"You're up to something," I said. I looked over to Sky who met my eyes. She looked so embarrassed she was about to explode as she leaned on the wall beside Ryan. She held onto one of his arms like it was a lifeline. Her hands were actually shaking as she watched us, and I heard Ryan trying to calm her down. He didn't know why she was upset, but Sky kept her eyes locked on mine as Believer spoke to me.

"My Sky wants to give you a piece of her soul, to love and to hold. But she hopes that you would give her a piece of yours in exchange. A piece she could love and cherish. Your twin brother Ryan holds a piece of your soul. My Sky wants your blessing. Sky wants Ryan for herself."

I figured as much. But still. That was just plain crazy. Totally wrong.

The sane, rational thing to think was *I can't GIVE my brother to someone. I don't own him. That has to be his choice to make!*

Or even, *You can't GIVE Believer to me, that has to be his choice!*

I was sure that's what a sane person would have said.

But I'm not sane, I thought to myself. I didn't try to fight it. I gave myself over to my feelings and let the "witch" inside me guide me. I knew what Believer wanted. He wanted me. Plain and simple. But Sky falling so hard for Ryan and Ryan falling for her so fast after Jane. It didn't seem possible or probable. It was magic. Either it was magic from Jane's book or some magic Sky was doing herself. Maybe it was even me.

I tried to remember if I had said something or thought something that could have caused any of this. I had thought that they would be a cute couple, and I had hoped that Sky could help Ryan get over losing Jane, but I didn't think this had happened because of me. One way or another, this had to be magic at work.

I still hadn't looked away from Sky's eyes. She wanted Ryan. And honestly, as I looked at her, I couldn't think of anyone else on earth that I would want him with. Believer, Tom, Dan, Jane and her Dad, Dr. Burgis, Williams, and the other two agents all watched me as I walked up to Sky and Ryan. They kept quiet and still, either because they were afraid of me after I told Tom I'd kill him if he disturbed me or because they could smell the magic that hung thick in the air like the scent of hundreds of unseen roses.

"Wild," I whispered softly, reverently, as I appreciated the magic of the moment. I stopped in front of Sky.

"Sky," I said loudly and clearly for everyone to hear.

"Yes," she answered, also loud and clear.

Ryan watched us both, wondering what was going on. He was just about to open his mouth, but Sky quickly reached out and placed a hand over his mouth to keep him from asking his hundred questions and ruining everything. It was very like what I'd done earlier with Believer, only she didn't have to reach up so far to reach his mouth.

"Wait, Ryan. Your sister and I have business to discuss," she told him, kindly but firmly.

His brows drew together in worry as Sky took her hand away, but he actually restrained himself and kept quiet. He stared hard at both of us, waiting to see what this "business" was.

I reached out and took Sky's hands away from Ryan and held them in both of mine as I spoke to her. "I love you, Sky. You are already my sister. You have my blessing."

Without another word I turned my gaze to Ryan's surprised face and asked him directly. "Do you want Sky?" I waited as he blinked, surprised by my blunt question.

He looked embarrassed to be asked in front of God and everybody, but I didn't back down. Sky looked right at him, waiting for his answer as well, and after a panicked, frantic moment of who knows what, he took another look into Sky's eyes and answered honestly.

"Yes. I want her." He said this like he'd confessed to some heinous sin.

I asked, "Do you love her?" My voice hard, demanding an answer.

"Rain! What do you think you're doing!?" Ryan shouted at me. But Sky just kept her eyes on Ryan.

"Do you love her, Ryan?" I asked again. Ryan was horrified that I would put him on the spot like this and was about to tell me off, but right then Sky reached out with a hand and gently turned his face toward hers and asked him herself.

"Do you love me?" Sky's hand trembled as she lightly touched the side of his face.

Ryan could see that Sky truly wanted him and loved him, and even though they'd just met, somehow she did truly love him. Ryan gazed into her eyes, like he was trying to see what was inside her heart and at the same time trying to understand what was happening inside of his own heart.

Sky looked so sure of what she was doing and totally at peace with how she felt about him. It had to be magic. And I knew my brother. Even though we couldn't hear it, I knew he had to be praying. Silently, to himself where only he and God could hear it. I was sure he was trying to find out what God wanted him to do and if Sky was the one God wanted him to be with.

Ryan's face slowly changed from a look of shocked uncertainty to one that closely mirrored Sky's. Sky had a beautiful soul and she loved his God. That was a love he could share. A love that it seemed he wanted to share. Everyone in the room knew what Ryan was going to say before he was able to form the words.

"Yes. I love you." He said the words with passion. Ryan's face no longer looked frantic, trapped or doubtful. And quickly before they started to wrap around each other and I lost my chance I asked the final question.

"Will you ask her?"

Ryan shot me another horrified look, like this time I'd gone too far, crossed the line. But then Sky spoke again before he could voice his outrage at my insane meddling.

"Please. Ask me, Ryan. I want you to." Sky was crying now as she looked at Ryan. I thought about Ryan's cell phone that was in his shirt pocket. I willed it to change shape into a beautiful diamond ring, one that was made of solid diamond, the band and all, sized to fit Sky perfectly. Then I willed Ryan to hear my voice in his head.

Ryan. There is a ring in your shirt pocket.

Ryan's eyes shot to me quickly but then he looked back to Sky. He kept his eyes on her as his hand went to the pocket and we all watched as he went to one knee and held out the ring.

"Sky. Will you marry me?" Ryan asked. He was deadly serious as he looked at her. Sky didn't hesitate for a second. She reached right out and took the ring and put it on her finger.

"Yes. I will," she said.

Ryan stood, putting an arm around her waist, he bent forward to kiss her but stopped as Sky dropped her chin, turning away a little, like she was afraid or shy.

Ryan looked so panic stricken and heartbroken, like he'd done something terrible.

"What is it, Sky? What's wrong?" he asked her, his heart in his throat making his voice crack.

Sky's iron confidence was failing her now as she stuttered out, "I–I–I've never kissed a boy before. I–I don't know how." She blushed and looked down again.

"Sky," Ryan said with true joy in his voice as a huge, overjoyed smile spread across his face. "I've never kissed a girl before. Never. Not once."

Sky looked up at his smiling face, amazed at this confession.

"We can learn together, my Sky," Ryan said her name like Believer did and she smiled. And that was all he was going to be able to say for a while because Sky attacked him.

And that was when half of our small group made a cry of happy congratulations. Jane's dad, an overjoyed Dr. Burgis, and even agent Trisha were jubilant for the couple and crowded around them. Dr. Burgis looked like he was the father of the bride, he was so proud and happy. Tom and the other agent whose name I hadn't bothered to learn were both standing impatiently by the door waiting for us to get into the limo, but Williams came over to me looking less than pleased with the way things had fallen together.

"Black Rain!" he whispered fiercely, trying not to be overheard by the well-wishers or the happy couple. "You ain't got no right messing with your brother's mind and making him marry that girl! He wouldn't do this if you weren't fooling around with magic right now making it all happen. I know he's happy but this ain't right." He gave me his pop-eyed disapproving stare. "And I know you put that ring in his pocket too, don't try to deny that was you." He shook his head, pouring on the disappointment and censure. "If you love your brother you should let him make his own choices. Be his own man. You shouldn't go messing with your brother like this. It's not right!"

Believer stepped up behind Williams, giving him a dark look. He didn't appreciate the way Williams was talking to me.

I looked over Williams' head and spoke to Believer, "It's okay, Believer. Williams cares about me and he cares about Ryan. He just doesn't understand what's happened."

Williams turned around, surprised to find a seven-foot-tall cloud man had snuck up right behind him and was staring down at his head with red burning eyes. Of course Believer didn't make noise when he moved. He was a cloud.

"A lot changed while you were gone, Williams. You really missed a lot."

He didn't buy it. "I was only gone for two and a half hours, and you were in the back—" He pointed with his thumb over his shoulder at Believer who loomed behind him, "with him! for most of that. How much could I have missed?" He pulled a face at me and I laughed at how "at ease" he was with cloud giant standing behind him giving him the totally evil eye.

"Two and a half hours—and you don't think you missed much. Hmm." I let power seep into my voice as I answered Williams in a sing song rhyme that just poured out without any thought or effort on my part, the magic carried my voice to every corner of the room as I spoke.

> *"I murdered a man, I died and rose again,*
> *I traveled to oblivion and journeyed back again,*
> *I fell into a cloud and found that it had hands,*
> *Hands that found my heart and helped me love again.*
> *An urn of blood, a broken rib, a dragon made by Sky,*
> *A brother with a broken heart who thought that he would die.*
> *A tender touch, a God to share, a heart that now can fly,*
> *As within and so without you know I cannot lie.*
> *I did not force his hand or dim his power to choose,*
> *I simply fanned the flames of love and let its power loose.*
> *I made the ring and sped up things and this I now admit,*
> *And if you have a problem with that, I just don't give a shit."*

Williams was speechless, and as much as he'd been complaining lately it was a welcome change.

Ryan didn't seem upset at all; he gave me a little wave with his hand and turned back to his girl and started talking again like nothing out of the ordinary had happened. Sky and Ryan weren't bothered in the least by what I said, or the sing song rhyming way in which I'd said it, just part of having a witch as a sister.

But all the others in the room were staring at me like I'd sprouted a third eye. All the concerned attention directed my way as if I were out of my mind felt unfair to me. So I was a witch. So I spoke in rhymes sometimes. *So what!?*

My temper quickly flared to life, and I stepped away from Williams and Believer to get some distance between me and the others as I worked at getting ahold of myself and my wild emotions. I felt the pills pulling me deeper into their hazy drugged up grasp, and I hardly noticed as I let my power slip into my eyes, letting them go black. It was time for them to go black anyway, something in me wanted them black, and I let that part of me have its way as magic crept along my body and out my skin, making my hair wave around my head.

Believer stood behind me, but the others who met my midnight gaze flinched away which made me smile for some strange reason. I didn't know why. I spotted Dan and Jane off in a far corner of the room in their beautiful white wedding clothes. They were too busy kissing to notice anyone else existed on the planet.

The vampires were about to get married, my brother and Sky were going to get married. But what about me—and what about Believer? He was mine now— should I marry him—could I marry him—did I want to marry him?

Yes I do. I thought quickly, surprising myself. I really, truly did love him, my cloud man. My insides tightened and I put a hand over my chest as I felt things inside me pull tight. I was really going to get married. I let that sink in for a moment.

Holy shit.

I am about to marry a cloud man. And I'm really going to do it. And I really want to do it. This couldn't be real, but then again I guess it had to be real because who could possibly make up shit this weird. No one would believe it.

I ran my hands through my hair as I thought things through. What to do now? What was the next chapter in this wild fairy tale that was my life?

Chapter Two: The Three Weddings, I thought and laughed. I liked it. I turned back to Believer, and his face fell when he saw my blackened eyes and instantly I felt my heart tighten up like his frown had touched it somehow and I looked down at the ground to hide my eyes.

Believer stepped up to me and gently lifted my chin so he could see my pitch black eyes.

"I'm sorry. They wanted to change," I confessed weakly as he looked into my eyes, his burning red staring into my midnight black. Inside, my heart squeezed again. I wanted to please him, but "black" felt right to me.

"I can try to change them back for you later if—"

"No," Believer said shaking his big head. "You told me that you cannot control these changes. That sometimes they just happen. Keep your black eyes, my lady. Something inside you wants them to be black so let them be black. I will still love you no matter how you change." He ran his cloudy hand lovingly through my hair and down my back and somehow his touch caused me to shiver with pleasure and I almost swooned but his strong arms held me up.

"Believer," I said as I looked up into his red glowing eyes and slit of a mouth. "Will you marry me?"

I watched, held safe in the comforting shelter of his strong arms as his slit of a mouth grew wider into a smile.

"Yes. I will marry you, my lady. But you do not need to marry me, I am already yours. My Sky has given me to you and you have paid for me in kind."

I reached up to his chest and placed my hand over his new heart as it pulsed within his chest and looked up at him.

"And I'm already yours too, Believer, I know you remember. I already gave myself to you. Earlier, when we first lay down together. Perhaps it was a prophecy—" I said and thought about that. My idle words and thoughts. Every idle word a witch may say can shape her path and change the day. Weird to even think that way, but it made the story even better to me so I smiled and Believer smiled with me.

It felt right to have the wedding, to do what others only dreamed of, and what girl did not dream of getting married? I looked at Jane and Dan; they were both standing still looking at me now, listening and watching. They saw my attention fix on them. Jane appeared next to me as if I'd called for her.

"Yes, Black Rain?" she asked with a smile that flashed her pearly white teeth.

"Why did you and Dan decide to get married? You already belong to each other forever, so why marriage?" I asked her.

"Oh, Dan is very old fashioned. It was his idea. If it had been up to me we wouldn't be waiting to do certain things." A line creased her perfect brow as her impatience for her honeymoon came through and I laughed.

"And for my parents," Jane continued. "We may have to leave for a while after we die if we can't control our blood lust well enough to be near humans without killing them. So in a way this may be a goodbye to our family and friends. But the main reason we are getting married is the book. The book that I was reading when I started the drug study and started taking the pills."

"The Midnight books." I remembered, her sitting there, curled up in her chair, so absorbed she didn't even let Ryan and his charms drag her away from that story about true love and vampires.

Jane nodded. "In the book, Sarah and Ethan get married before she dies and becomes a vampire. Dan thought it would be best if we followed along with the book. He wants to make sure everything works well tonight when we die." Jane reached up and touched her neck where Dan had bitten her and smiled. "We aren't changing in exactly the same way as they did in the book, but Dan still thinks it's important that we get married. And actually, that's part of the story that I want too."

She paused and looked from me to Believer and asked, "So. You guys are getting married too?" Jane laughed. "You're not thinking what I think you're thinking are you?" She watched my face and laughed again as her hand covered her mouth in shocked surprise.

"Oh yeah, you are!" She squealed with "girl" delight and made everyone jump. It was a noise I could never have imagined coming from the terrifying "Queen of the Damned!" I didn't see her move but she was just there, hugging me and then she was back where she had been like magic.

On the other side of the room I heard Dan laughing, which surprised me; he was usually so silent. But if Jane knew then Dan knew, so he was already in on the new wedding plans. But Jane got my attention right back.

"YES! It will be amazing and I think you're right! It makes the whole wedding better, more magical. Please! Can I go tell everyone?" she asked, as she bounced around with excited energy wanting to go "tell" the surprise! I nodded and she disappeared, making me dizzy with trying to focus on a spot that held nothing. I blinked and looked around to find her talking with Ryan and enjoying his surprise. Talking with Jane was easy when she knew what you were saying before you said it. It sure sped thing up.

"You're out of your mind!" Williams whispered urgently. "You can't get married to him! This isn't something to play around with, witch girl. Stop this now before you go any further! You don't need to be hurt any more than what you've already done to yourself." He wanted me to call off what he saw as a huge mistake. "Every time you turn around you find a new way to hurt yourself and make yourself more miserable, and this is going to hurt you, girl. And I don't want to see you hurt." The concern on his face made me smile as I answered him.

"You know how it works in the storybooks, Williams. A fantasy is made from pieces and parts and most of them are painful and really, really suck. Things like heartbreak, tragedy, loss and sorrow, blood, death, danger and revenge, but there is always love." I sighed contentedly. "True love is always in a good fantasy. And that makes everything else in the story worth living for." I answered his maddeningly frustrated look with a small smile.

"Come on, you can't be serious!" Williams looked up to Believer, who looked like he was about to comment or say something about the situation himself but Williams cut him off. "No offense, big guy, but she just met you and this is just way too fast for good sense." Williams rolled his eyes back to me. "Girl! What do you think your mother and father will say when they find out you're getting married to him? He ain't human!" Williams paused and looked up at Believer again.

"No offense." He turned back to me.

I gave him a shocked, mock horrified expression.

"Damn, Williams, that sounds awfully racist. I may have to report you. You got issues." I laughed, but Williams was determined.

"You're all drugged up from taking those pills! That's the only reason you're doing this!" Williams looked back up to Believer. "No offense!" Then turned back to me and just kept going, he was on a roll trying to get his point across but behind him Believer was looking more and more angry.

"Black Rain, I'm sure he's nice and all but he's not a real person. He's not REAL like you are!"

He looked up at Believer again, but this time Believer was ready and spoke first. "I'm offended!" His voice rumbled like thunder in a cloud, loud and jarring and I could feel the vibrations down in my bones. His eyes blazed red as he leaned down over the smaller man. Williams' head pulled back into his body, down between his shoulders like a turtle squishing into his shell.

"Easy, my love," I said quickly. "You can see that he cares about me; he just doesn't understand us. He still thinks I'm human." Believer nodded reluctantly and straightened. I spoke, my voice wistful, filled with memory as I remembered the girl I had been. "He sees my flesh and body and face and remembers the human girl that cried yesterday as she lay in the dirt in front of an old trailer. Or the girl who smiled and made him eat eggs this morning at breakfast." I smiled as I remembered this morning and that girl. It seemed like a lifetime ago, and I guess it was. "He thinks I'm still that girl, Believer. He does not believe."

I turned back to Williams wondering how to explain this in a way he could grasp. I tried a different approach. "Williams if you went to sleep and woke up, only to find you were still dreaming but you couldn't get out of the dream—what would you do? Would you spend the rest of your life trying to wake up, or would you enjoy the magical world of your dreams?" I watched as he thought through my crazy question. I didn't wait for him to answer.

"Well, I am in a dream, a living dream. And I will not try to wake because for me, there is nothing to wake up to. It burned away. All I have now is the dream and the fantasy and I am going to enjoy it. All of it."

I looked over at Tom who stood beside the door like a statue with his other partner.

"Hey Tom! You about ready to get this show on the road?" I called.

He nodded and walked over, looking happy finally.

"Sky!" I called. I still needed to send her out to shrink Sky Dragon down to size.

I looked over to the front of the building and the two broken windows and thought about the glass in those two broken windows coming back together and the windows being whole and unbroken again and the glass flew back up and into place just as if they'd never been shattered. Next I made all the windows on the front of the building dark so everyone on the outside couldn't see through. I thought more about the walls and ceiling of the waiting room; I wanted us sealed up and private in here and focused on that for a minute, making it so no one could see us or hear us. I also took down the barrier that I'd thrown up earlier so we could walk out without having to walk around it.

"Yes, Rain?" Sky said.

"We need you to go and take care of Sky Dragon," I told her.

She nodded and before I could say another word she took off; her feet left the floor as she flew over to the door and looked at the surprised agent still standing there.

"Open please," Sky said as she floated in air about a foot off the ground. As soon as the agent opened the door she was up and away.

I was glad that I'd already taken down that invisible barrier because she would have splattered herself like a bug on a windshield. Just the thought made me cringe. She probably would have broken her neck. My crazy ass sister needed to be more careful. I shook my head as I turned my attention back to Tom.

"Now get out your notepad because you're gonna need it. This is how it's gonna go down. I want one driver. It can be that guy," I pointed to the guy by the door, "or someone else. I want you in a helicopter flying along with us keeping an eye on everything from the air. And if there are any cameras or listening devices in the limo, get on the phone and tell them to kill them before I get out there because if I find any I'm gonna be pissed off. I want the limo private so we can talk without God and everyone listening to what we say." I watched as he scribbled away for just a second.

"What about Agent Trish?" he asked.

"Oh. She'll be in the limo with us. We like her." I smiled at him and he frowned at me.

"Okay. Let me get on the phone and clean the limo. It'll take some time to take out the bugs; we should be ready in about ten minutes. I'll wait for you outside."

Tom and his partner at the door left to get things ready and everyone started to gather around me. Dr. Burgis had his suitcase, briefcase, and his painting bundled up in his arms as he moved to a closer chair. Dan was holding the urn filled with blood and a black travel bag, and Ryan was grabbing a box of pizza for the road it looked like, but Agent Trish was a little more keyed in than I realized.

"What's up?" she asked. "You're up to something. Let me ditch my wire if you're going to do anything that needs to be kept quiet." She stripped off her jacket and pulled out a wire and radio looking device attached under her suit. "Okay. I'm good to go now," she said after she turned it off.

"Williams," I asked, "could you step outside and guard the door for a few minutes and make sure no one—including Tom—gets back inside here till I come and get you?"

He nodded, "I'm on it." He looked like he was happy to have something useful to do.

"Are we headed to the church now?" asked Jane's dad, hopeful that we were.

"What now?" Ryan asked around a mouthful of pizza.

I let my black eyes sparkle at them like black pearls.

"Now you get to see some real magic. So mote it be."

David and Dana

What the Hell Happened Here

"**M**iss. We need you to move." Dana felt strong hands grab her. "Get off me!" She threw her elbow back hard and heard a surprised "Ooooff!" The grasping hands fell away. Dana spun around and pressed her back up against David's hospital bed, ready to fight what she thought would be the hospital staff, here to unplug David.

It wasn't hospital staff. Two soldiers and three cops had come into David's room while she slept and she could see more standing out in the hall. Dana's wild tangle of hair was wrapped around her face from where she had fallen asleep with her head on his bed. She reached up and raked it out of her face, her eyes shifting around the room like a wild animal cornered in its den.

The soldier she'd elbowed was rubbing his chest wearing a pained expression. Dana kept one arm held in front of her, her hand balled in a tight fist, her other arm draped protectively over David. There was no way she was letting them unplug him! No damn way!

"Gesh! That really hurt," the soldier complained as he rubbed his chest where she'd elbowed him.

"You're not pulling his plug! Just stay the hell away from us!" Dana yelled at the cops and soldiers.

"Relax, lady, we're not here to pull his plug," the other soldier said, trying to calm her down as he took in her defiant stance and battered appearance. "We're just moving him to a better facility. He's going to be getting twenty-four hour a day care and nobody is going to pull his plug." The soldier pointed to the hallway. "Honest. Look out in the hall; we got all the battery backups and all the fancy equipment to keep everything running while we move him. We're just taking him to a better facility."

Right then the monitor on the wall above the bed displaying David's brain functions beeped and chimed, getting everyone's attention for a second as the brainwave patterns altered from the minimal scribble of a line to a more pronounced wave.

"Oh my God!" Dana shouted, thrilled to the very bottom of her heart as she grabbed David's hand.

"David! David, can you hear me!?" She rubbed his arm and kissed his face and looked at him for any sign he was waking as everyone watched her. Dana watched for an eye twitch or some small movement. A hand squeeze! Anything!

"David! David, it's your Dana! I'm here, David. It's your Dana, can you hear me? David, you need to wake up!" As Dana pleaded and begged, the others watched the monitors but it seemed that the momentary blip was gone. The brain activity faded back to a minimal line, barely anything at all.

Agent Nolan, a slim older man with pepper gray hair and a tight schedule stepped into the room. He studied the way everyone stood motionless as they watched the monitors and Dana as she worked to dredge some response from the now unresponsive David, not understanding the delay.

"What's the hold up in here?" he demanded.

"We had a moment of brain activity, sir. It's a good sign," said one of the soldiers in an optimistic voice.

Nolan frowned. "Doesn't change our orders, soldier. As of right now his body belongs to the federal government. I want him in that van in ten minutes, so get moving." He looked at Dana. "And get the girl out of here," he added with a glance to the police officers.

"Who are you people!?" Dana shouted. "You can't take him anywhere unless David's father gives you permission, and I know he hasn't! Just leave us alone!" The three cops in the room looked back at Nolan who shrugged.

"She's not even related to him," he said as he checked his watch, annoyed at the delay. "She's just the girlfriend, remove her."

A wiry, black police officer lunged for her, but Dana was ready. She'd noticed him inching closer and as soon as she saw movement at the edge of her periphery, she began her turn and the extension of her blindly thrown punch. Her fist colliding with his face compounded with the officer's own forward momentum.

He went down on the floor, cupping his broken nose and shouting "Bitch!" as one of the others grabbed her from behind, lifting her entirely off the ground and into the air as he pulled her away from David's hospital bed. He turned to flatten her up against a nearby wall to cuff her but Dana lifted up both feet, screamed at the top of her lungs and kicked off against the wall. Still holding Dana, the cop staggered backward then fell over the back of the black officer who was on his knees holding his bleeding nose with one hand. He toppled backward and smacked the back of his head against David's metal hospital bed and went down in a heap right on top of the cop with the busted nose. Somehow Dana ended on her back, lying on top of the two downed men.

"Get her!" the strained, nasaly cry of the black officer rose from the bottom of the pile. The cop that hit his head was knocked senseless and unmoving so the third cop lunged in to grab her but was unfortunate enough to get caught right in the balls by a fierce kick. He fell back, both hands cupping himself.

"Holy shit!" said one of the soldiers with a surprised, southern drawl, awe in his voice. "She's kickin' their ass!"

Dana rolled off the unconscious cop and landed on her feet beside David's hospital bed only to have a hand grab her around her sore ankle. It was badly bruised from when she'd been kicked and beaten at the mall and Dana screamed in pain as the officer squeezed hard.

"Aaaa! Aaaaa! Let go! Owww!" The angry man had a death grip on her hurt ankle. It felt like he was about to break her whole foot off and Dana fought back in the only way she could. She braced her back against David's hospital bed, lifted her unhurt foot and kicked out as hard as she could right into the guy's already broken and bloody nose, and his head snapped back. He dropped her ankle. Dana got to her feet and turned to face the third cop just as she heard an odd little "pop."

She was airborne, flying back in a nerve-induced spasm as the two metal probes pierced her stomach and the electric charge of the stun gun tore through her body. She landed right on top of David in his hospital bed.

"Aa aa aa aa aa aa aa aa aa!" Dana's scream stuttered out and her whole body shook and thrashed violently right on top of David, which set off all the machines as some of the charge jumped into David and into the machines he was wired to. The officer with the stun gun kept squeezing the trigger, pumping more punishment with a vindictive grin on his face as Dana shook and danced. He was pissed and meant to make her pay!

"Stop it, you idiot!" Agent Nolan stepped up and slapped the stun gun out of the cop's hand.

With a loud "Zzzat!" a puff of smoke and colorful shower of sparks, the brain and heart monitors mounted to the wall burst into flames.

"Get a doctor in here!" shouted Nolan toward the other two wide-eyed soldiers standing in the doorway.

"SIR!" shouted one of the soldiers already inside the room.

"What!" Nolan shouted back as he looked over at the soldier and noticed that the fla mes pouring out of the fried electronics had vanished. Then he noticed that the soldier was looking down at the hospital bed, at David and Dana.

David was sitting up in the bed, his arms wrapped around Dana, who was unresponsive in his arms. Her eyes were rolled back in her head showing nothing but white. Little tremors still shook her body every few seconds like her system was reliving the punishment over and over even though it wasn't there.

"What did you do to her?" David's voice was the barest of raspy whispers but everyone heard it.

Th e eyes of the two soldiers in the room, the cop, and the agent met in a moment of guilty horror. Th e soldiers and Nolan had been briefed on how dangerous this kid may be if he woke, and now, here he was, awake. Awake and about to be very angry!

"What did you do to my Dana?" David's voice was stronger this time. One of the soldiers was already headed for the door, a terrifi ed expression on his face as he pushed past Nolan and the cop who had fi red the stun gun.

"Get your injured men out of here," Nolan told the cop who stood immobile and uncertain. Nolan gave him a rough shove toward the two offi cers still lying on the fl oor as he walked over to the hospital bed. David's bloodshot eyes lifted from Dana and met his as he approached.

"What did you do?" David's voice rasped out. She twitched and shook again.

Nolan tried to keep his voice calm and fatherly as he spoke. "Your girlfriend went crazy and attacked the police. She may have even killed one of them." He pointed down to the man beside the bed. The black offi ce r was being helped from the room by the guy who'd fired the stun gun. His face was a bloody ruin. David's eyes followed them as they left the room without meeting his gaze and he watched as other hospital attendants rushed in who started to work on the unconscious officer with the head injury.

He looked back to Dana as she shook in his arms again asked Nolan, "Who hurt her?"

"Son, she went crazy and almost killed two police officers." Nolan kept his voice soothing, calm. "They had to use a stun gun on her, but she grabbed you when she was shocked and that caused all the machines you were wired up to to go off." Nolan was relieved to see one of the white-coated doctors come charging into the room. He didn't want to lie to this kid any more than he had to.

"What on earth happened in here!?" The doctor looked from David's face to the girl twitching in his arms and immediately went to work on Dana. David moved over to give the doctor room and listened as Nolan answered the doctor's questions about Dana's injuries from the stun gun and her being further electrocuted when the medical devices in the room went up in smoke.

"Dammit, the electricity hit everything, her insides are cooked!" Dr. Hathaway cursed under his breath as he worked on Dana. A portable monitor was quickly attached and showed a weak thready pulse that barely limped along. Hathaway wrinkled his nose at the smell of burnt flesh in the air but then he remembered himself and looked at David who was still half holding the girl. She was still lying in his bed while they worked on her, trying to get her stabilized.

Hathaway cursed under his breath yet again. Cursed fate, God, the cops, the nurses who should have been on watch, he cursed everyone as he worked on Dana. He'd watched this girl fight like a demon from hell to keep David alive for the past day and half, and here she was, about to die in his arms while he was going to have to live and watch her die instead. After assessing how bad things were, his frantic activity slowed and he turned his thoughts toward making Dana more comfortable.

"David. I'm so sorry," Hathaway said sadly.

David's voice was a raspy whisper, "Don't let her die. You can't let her die. Not my Dana." He turned back to Dana, his hands gently touching her battered face. "If she dies, I'll follow her. I always have. I always will." He smiled as he looked at her. He looked decided.

"I'm sorry about your girl," Nolan said.

"Her name is Dana."

"Dana," Nolan replied numbly.

Nolan felt guilty about how he'd botched this situation; he wanted to die on the spot, but that wouldn't undo this disaster and it wouldn't help David. He should have handled the girl with half a care and some common courtesy instead of being a dictatorial ass and trying to throw her out without a word. And that idiot cop had all but murdered the girl because he let his temper get the better of him.

And like salt in the wound, Nolan could tell that the girl loved this boy insanely and it was obvious that David loved her too. Dana bore a striking resemblance to his own daughter who currently hated his guts and wouldn't have anything to do with him. Just like her mother, she'd finally realized he was a bastard. Married to his job, not his family. Too stubborn to change. And now this.

Nolan reached for his radio without even thinking through what he was doing.

"Get me a helicopter on the roof, the van's no good, we're moving them by air. We'll be on the roof in five minutes. I want that chopper on the pad and ready." Nolan turned to the doctor.

"Will the girl live for at least thirty minutes?" he asked quickly, his hollow body suddenly infused with purpose. "Can you keep her alive that long?" he growled.

"No. I can't," he said simply. "She won't last five minutes without life support! Her lungs, heart, all her internal organs, it's all—" He stopped himself before he said "fried" or "burnt to a crisp." "She's shutting down right now. She's dying." Hathaway summed it up, resigned.

Nolan didn't balk or lose his drive of purpose. "We've got the mobile life support equipment out in the hall that we brought for David. Hook her up and keep her heart beating, doctor. That's an order! Now move!" Nolan snapped.

"There's nothing we can do for this girl!" Dr. Hathaway replied with some heat of his own, outraged and frustrated at the horrible situation. Dr. Hathaway knew that the girl was beyond help. There wasn't any point in moving her now. Or prolonging David's suffering.

"Yesterday, doctor, you would have been right about that." Nolan didn't explain further. "Now are you going to help us or not?"

Hathaway's face tightened and mottled with bottled-up rage, but he started shouting angry orders all the same. The soldiers out in the hallway pushed in a rolling bed originally intended for David and laid Dana in his place. Dr. Hathaway and a passel of nurses and attendants prepared her for the move while Nolan and a nurse helped David out of the bed and into a wheelchair. Within five minutes they were all pushing their way down the crowded hallway headed for the elevator and the helicopter pad on the roof of the hospital.

In the elevator Dr. Hathaway voiced his concerns again. "This girl is going to die, Nolan. Nobody can repair this kind of damage and I don't see why you're endangering David's health when he just woke from a coma. Take the girl if you have to, but leave David here."

The sleeves of his lab coat burst into flames.

"Fire! Ssshit! I'm on fire!" Hathaway danced around as he tried to get the coat off. Everyone pressed themselves to the walls of the elevator as he flailed about, but the flames disappeared just as spontaneously as they'd arrived. A faint stink of burnt cloth and the singed sleeves were the only evidence that a flame was ever there.

"What the hell was that!?" Dr. Hathaway shouted as he threw the jacket on the floor of the elevator and stepped away from it. Nolan ignored the doctor and turned to David who met his eyes squarely. Nolan knew exactly what had happened.

"Don't worry, David. You go with us. And if we can keep her alive for about thirty more minutes your girl will be just fine. I promise."

"Her name is Dana," David said again.

"Dana," Nolan repeated again, cursing himself inside his head. He didn't want to remember the girl's name.

Dr. Hathaway was clutching his singed forearms, disgusted at hearing what he saw as bullshit promises from Nolan. "Stop lying to the boy!" he yelled. "What the hell's wrong with you!? Lying to David won't change it and it sure as hell won't help him deal with the loss any better!"

Nolan kept eye contact with David as he answered Hathaway's furious rant. "I'm not lying to you, David. If Dana can hold on, she'll be just fine. My word on it."

The two Army medics gave Nolan a knowing nod which he returned and David picked up on. They obviously had an inkling of what he planned to do and were on board with it. The only alternative was to leave the girl here and let her die. Their current course of action had easier orders to follow.

"I can't live without her," David said as he looked at Dana on her rolling bed, intubated and wired into a mesh of machines that fought to keep her damaged body alive.

"I don't think she can live without you either," Nolan said. "Your Dana is something else, kid. She's a fighter."

"She is," David agreed as the elevator door opened and they rolled out onto the roof and toward the waiting helicopter.

Delta Force One

Going In

Three helicopters landed in the front yard of the Hale House Mansion, and soldiers and men in suits started to pour out onto the green, manicured lawn. Five FBI agents and ten special ops soldiers headed toward the front door along with Agent Phil White, a portly, aged man with solid white hair who'd been placed in charge of this most unusual mission. Agent White stepped up to the big ornate double doors and was about to push the doorbell when one of the soldiers grabbed his hand.

"Wait." The man captured White with the intensity of his gaze as he pointed to the glass front door.

"Look through the glass, sir. We have bodies on the ground. The house has been compromised. We may have hostile forces inside and friendlies down.

Should we go in silently and secure the area or just ring the doorbell and see who comes to answer it?" The implied "you dumb ass" was there. He waited just a second before adding "sir."

Agent White ignored the insult and walked up to the door. He shielded his eyes and peered through the glass. His vision wasn't what it used to be, but he could clearly see a body in a white suit lying on the ground at the end of the foyer area. There was a lot of blood on the ground as well. White's orders were crystal clear. This had to be kept friendly at all costs, but who knew what was happening inside this house filled with witches. Something was definitely wrong. A little caution seemed prudent.

"Very well. Secure the home, but *do not* get us into any confrontation with these people," White said firmly. "These people are witches, so we've no idea what to expect inside this home. We don't know who the friendlies and hostiles are. My orders were very clear. Major Benistin's exact words were 'Whatever you do, don't piss them off!' Now. Put your weapons on safety, and by all means," he gave a smug grin, "secure the area. Do we understand each other, soldier?" Agent White leaned in staring hard with his watery old eyes at the grim, chiseled face of the soldier.

"Yes, sir." The man waited until Agent White nodded then sprang into action directing his team. White and the five FBI agents with him stepped back, giving Delta One room to operate.

"Squirrel." The man pointed up and one of the men darted toward the side of the house and started to scale straight up the wall where some ornamental white iron decoration connected to the second story balcony.

"Red." He pointed left. "Blue." He pointed right. Two three man teams headed off in separate directions around each side of the house which left three members of the ten-man team there to face the front door.

"How you want to do this, Bull?" asked Carter, a tall lanky man with a long face and a harsh Jersey accent.

"Glass beside the door," Bull answered as he peered through the glass front door, keeping an eye out as his team worked.

Without another word Stitch broke into his pack of tools and produced a black suction cup which he stuck to the glass, then he pulled out what looked like a small handheld laser the size of a fat cigarette lighter. He quickly traced around the edge of the glass pane while Carter held the suction cup. Within a minute the glass was removed and Bull was stepping through the opening into the house.

At the end of the foyer he examined the headless body they'd seen from outside. Bull clicked the safety off on his weapon and whispered to his team, who were all linked by their earpieces, "Live weapons." He heard the clicks of the two men behind him as they switched their weapons off safety.

"Holy Mary Mother of God," whispered Carter. "It couldn't be just one person, Bull. This much blood couldn't come out of one body." All three of the soldiers looked at the room, sprayed from floor to ceiling with blood and gore.

"Hey, check this out." Stitch, the team medic and break-in artist knelt beside the headless body and lifted an arm. "Feel this, Bull. It's like everything in this guy was squeezed. There's not a drop of blood in his whole body."

Bull knelt by Stitch and looked at the body while Tiger covered them.

"Someone painted this place with this guy's juice. Jesus! I've never seen anything like this before, Bull. These witches are scary shit, man."

Bull spoke into his earpiece, "Everyone stay frosty, and remember we need to play nice and make friends with these witches. Don't get touchy. Squirrel, status."

"All clear. No one home upstairs. I'm at the top of the stairs now ready to come down."

"Hold there," Bull told him.

"Red."

"Sir. All clear here. Found ten servants in one of the outbuildings. Wax is covering them. No guns, no bodies, no blood."

"Leave Wax to cover, you and Keno move toward the center of the house."

"Roger," Red replied back.

"Blue."

"Sir. We're watching some type of Satanic ritual or something these witches are doing in a big room on the back side of the house. There's an old lady tied up, lying on the floor in the middle of a huge pentagram. There are two other females in the room and one of them has a knife. They look like witches. There's also one male lying on the ground. They may have already killed him. Everyone is covered in blood, Bull. What do you want to do? It looks like they're about to do this old lady."

Bull gritted his teeth. "Hold your position, Blue. This is their shit and we are guests in this mad house so just keep an eye on it—but let me know if she does the old lady. We're closing in from the front room."

"Roger," Blue answered but didn't sound happy.

Bull turned back to his medic who was studying the headless body.

"What happened to this guy, Stitch?" The gleaming white suit of the headless corpse looked squeezed and broken. Only a couple of red dots marred the suit's perfect white brilliance and Bull could tell those drops had fallen from the twenty foot high ceiling.

Stitch looked up and met his eyes and said one word that actually sent chills down Bull's spine.

"Magic."

The leader of Delta One was quiet for a second as he examined the scene again for himself. "It looks like this guy's head exploded, Stitch. You sure it wasn't an explosive device or something?"

Stitch shook his head no.

"Well shit." Right then Blue's strained voice crackled over the com.

"Bull, it looks like they're about to do the old lady! Oh shit! She slit her throat!"

"Hold your position!" Bull ordered then turned to Tiger and Stitch.

"Let's move! Squirrel, downstairs! Bring up the rear." Together they moved through the blood-spattered room and stopped at the archway leading into the large vaulted rear section of the home. Squirrel joined them. The four men inside the house and the soldiers hidden outside watched the witches in the big open hall.

A tall blonde woman held the slumped body of a large elderly woman upright while her blood sprayed and spurted out of her slashed neck onto a young girl who stood in the spray like it was a warm luxurious shower she was enjoying and not a fountain of human blood. The girl was covered in blood from head to toe. Bull noticed the star-shaped design on the floor. It was a huge pentagram. Five candles burned, one at each of point of the star set in tall metal candelabrum.

The blood was slowing now, only coming out in a trickle from the old woman's neck. The soldiers watched as the girl reared way back and plunged the knife into the old woman's heart with a grunt. She put a foot on her chest and yanked the knife free and laughed with what sounded like delight as blood sprayed out and onto her hands, and then the young girl actually got down on her knees and let the blood from the old lady spurt out onto her face and into her open mouth.

"Holy shit, Bull, are we just going to watch this happen?" Blue leader's voice came through on his earpiece.

"Hold your position, Blue, and shut your damn pie hole unless you got something worth sayin."

Bull leaned over to Stitch. "Go and tell Agent White about the party the witches are throwing for grandma and ask White what he'd suggest we do."

Stitch took off.

Bull clicked his com and addressed his entire team. "Stitch said the body in the front room was killed with magic. Not guns. Not explosives. Magic. The guy's whole body was drained and his head was popped like a grape. You men have all been told this shit is real and now we're seeing it up close and ugly. We're all going to have to stay frosty. I know none of you are gonna shit your drawers, but be extra aware of your mental state. They may do some magic shit to our minds or who knows what, so everyone just be down with the fact that we ain't in Kansas anymore. We're checking with command on how to proceed so hold fast. Don't jump. That's an order."

Bull's attention was seized when the girl started speaking. Her sweet voice echoed in the huge room, the macabre words sounding so innocent it gave Bull the chills from the top of his head all the way down to his toes.

"Blood! Blood! Blood! Blood!

I call on your power,

come out of her now in one final shower!"

Out of the old lady's neck and from her heart blood sprayed out once again, covering the child in a final offering of red before the body finally ran dry. Blood lay thick and deep on the floor in the center of the pentagram. They watched as the little girl left the woman and went to the man who was lying on the floor on the edge of the circle. She lifted his head and settled it into her lap with the knife still in hand.

"Cathryn, come here."

The tall witch let the old woman's body slump to the floor and quickly rushed over and knelt beside the girl and extended her arm, giving the girl her wrist without a word. The little witch cut with the knife and held her wrist over the body of the man, letting the blood fall on him.

Carter leaned forward and whispered to Bull. "Damn, Bull, that lady just let her do it."

"Yeah. She did Carter. She let her do it all right."

Squirrel was right beside them and added his comment, "I'm feelin' a weird vibe. Anyone else feeling anything?"

A few of the team chimed in across the com system that they felt something too.

"You feel anything, Bull?" Squirrel asked, his voice high and tight.

"Yeah, Squirrel. I feel it." Bull's skin prickled and crawled like little insects were crawling all over his body.

"What do you think it is, Bull?" came Spider's nervous voice across the com.

"Magic," Bull answered him. He clicked his com and addressed the team. "That little witch is doing some kind of magic. Nobody move a muscle. Whatever the hell she's doing I don't want us caught up in it. Everyone just root yourself to your spot and let's just wait this shit out. Hopefully it'll be over soon."

The girl's voice echoed through the hall. She shouted out her murderous words with that same innocent voice.

"Blood! Blood! Blood! Blood!
Murder and Death and Sacrifice made!
Blood has been shed, the price has been paid!
Blood! Blood! Blood! Blood!
Life giving blood from Cathryn's right hand!
Give rise in this hour to more than a man!
Blood! Blood! Blood! Blood!
Magic and Strength a Kingdom and Power!
I give to Cornelius in this bloody hour!
Blood! Blood! Blood! Blood!
I call on the power of the blood now set free!
RISE KING CORNELIUS!
RISE NOW FOR ME!"

Bethany Grave

Rise of the King

Bethany could feel the wild pulsing roar of magic as it wrapped around Cornelius and pulsed through her and down into the tile floor at her feet. Cornelius started moving again, though he appeared dazed and disoriented, as if he'd just woken up and didn't know how he'd ended up down on the floor. He wiped at his eyes to clear the blood from his face so he could see, but Cathryn couldn't wait.

"Oh Cornelius!" she cried and fell on his neck, kissing his bloody face as she wept for joy. "Thank you, Bethany!" she sobbed out as she kissed him again and again. "Thank you! Thank you! Thank you!"

"Cathryn?" Cornelius asked, still with his eyes squeezed shut. "What—" He spat out some blood that had gotten into his mouth. "What happened?" he asked.

Bethany answered him, "You got hurt, Cornelius. You got hit in the head. That guy Yanosh tried to kill us and you got hit in the head and got hurt."

Cornelius's brow bunched as he tried to see through squinted blood-covered slits. Cathryn handed him the sleeve of her gown.

"I do remember getting punched," he said, voice indignant. One hand wiped at his eyes with Cathryn's dress as the other probed his head for the injury he was sure must still be there beneath the blood, but then he finally looked around enough to take in his surroundings. The blood he was covered in, the blood on Cathryn, on the floor. He turned and saw the crumpled dead body of Fiona and all the blood on the pentagram and the lit candles.

"Blessed Be, Cathryn! What have you two done!?" Cornelius stared at Fiona's dead sightless face for a moment. Glazed dead eyes stared back. He turned back to Bethany and took a good look at her. She was more than drenched. She looked like she'd bathed in blood. Her hair, face, dress, arms, *everything* was covered in sticky red. She still held the sacrificial knife in her hand. Bethany smiled and her white teeth and white eyes peeked out of a solid red mask. It was almost too grisly to be believable.

"What—why—but—" Cornelius floundered, confused, and at a loss, utterly at a loss to know what to say, or how to say it, even if he could say it. Cathryn stayed silent, granting Cornelius a moment to wig out and adjust to what he was seeing before she answered him calmly. Bethany smiled, because it was nice to see everything getting back to normal.

"Actually Cornelius, Yanosh *did* kill you. You were not breathing. I've been a widow for the past ten minutes, my dear. And Yanosh and Fiona told us exactly what they planned to do to Bethany after they killed you. They were going to kidnap her and take her to Russia and turn her into a whore or possibly just rape and kill her here. I'm sure they would have just killed me before they left. Now that you know the details of your death, I think you should take a moment to thank Bethany. First, for killing Yanosh. And second, for sacrificing Fiona and using her blood and body to bring you back from the dead. Welcome home, Cornelius."

"No," Bethany said. "That's not his name anymore; he is King Cornelius now, and you are his Queen, and this is your Magic Castle. You remember the words. You remember what I said. I said, 'Rise, King Cornelius.'" Bethany's little voice was firm and insistent.

Cathryn smiled, "Yes, Bethany. I remember, and from this day forth his name shall be as you have named him, for you have drawn him from the shadow of death and given him back to me. And he is my King, and this is his castle." Cathryn smiled at Cornelius and he smiled back at her lovingly.

Bethany's little voice spoke out again. "Yes. Cornelius is King, Cathryn is Queen, and I am the Princess, and this is my home, and you are my family."

Cathryn and Cornelius shared a surprised look, which again turned into a smile.

"So mote it be," Cathryn intoned.

"So mote it be," echoed Cornelius.

"So mote it be," finished Bethany with a bloody smile.

Delta Force One

Getting Out!

Bull talked to his team. "Red, Blue, fall back and form a perimeter around the house. We'll fall back to the front door. Now that the witches have had their warm fuzzy human sacrifice let's bug out and let the Feds come in here and talk business over tea and crumpets with the King and Queen. Agent White and his suits can do this political shit. Let's get out of this mad house and let someone dumber than us deal with these freaks."

"Roger that, Bull!" Blue chimed in happily.

"Roger, Bull. Let's fuck off!" Red agreed.

"We're out," Bull said to the men he was with. "It's time for that old Fed to try his people skills out on the royal family. I hope he doesn't end up like Grandma." Bull and his team backed away from the arched doorway and toward the front door where Stitch waited with Agent White, who was very impatient to get in and get cracking.

Mary Fae

Welcome to Amen Hall

"**Turn right here** where all the soldiers are!" Mary shouted as Sergeant Kelly closed in on the military roadblock. Hummers and other huge wheeled military machines lined both sides of the street, and soldiers were strung out all along the road in both directions. A tent was erected by the entrance of the drive that lead to the Hale House with soldiers checking the vehicles coming and going. On each side of the drive other men in fatigues were stretching out shining circles of Constantine barb wire in each of the ditches.

"Figures," Kelly muttered as he pulled his cruiser onto the drive and was quickly surrounded by soldiers pointing weapons. One of them stepped up to the window.

"Sir. Who are you and why are you here?" A young soldier demanded roughly.

"I'm Seargent Kelly, with the Jacksonville Sherif's office, and I've got the mother of Black Rain and one of the other witches with me, soldier. I strongly suggest you let me through. And I think you better have your men lower those weapons before this girl in the back seat gets pissed and makes you regret pointing your guns at her." Kelly enjoyed a smug moment, watching the shock on the young man's face.

"One second, sir!" The soldier replied crisply in a vastly more respectful tone then turned and ordered the other men to lower their weapons and stand down. Kelly gave a satisfied grunt as the weapons dropped and the men backed away.

"What on earth is happening here!?" asked Mrs. Bryant as she took in the military invasion. "Is all this because of Rain and the girls!?"

"Wow!" said Mary as two jets rocketed by just above the treetops, their powerful engines shaking the windows of the car as they roared off into the distance.

"The crap has really hit the fan, Mom!" Mary shouted once they could hear again. She was worried about Rain and Bethany, and no one had heard from Kendal since last night when they went through the magic doorway to Rain's bedroom. Steve, Kendal's boyfriend, stopped by Mary's trailer earlier looking for her. Mary told him that she hadn't seen her since yesterday evening. Mary actually hoped Kendal was still here at Cathryn and Cornelius's hiding out and not returning Steve's calls.

The soldier stepped back to the window. "Sir. There will be someone waiting to meet you up ahead. They did ask for the names of everyone you have with you." The soldier held up a clipboard, pen in hand.

"Sergeant Conrad Walker Kelly. JSO. And in the back seat is Mrs. Bryant. The mother of the Black Witch."

And before Kelly could answer for her, Mary shouted from the back seat, "And I'm Mary Fae, the Green Witch, and *who are you*?" He was really cute! And he looked good in his snappy camo uniform too. The soldier leaned into the window staring into the back seat at her brilliant smile, her snow white hair with its captivating shock of green up front, and her sparkling green eyes. He took in her appearance with obvious surprise. His attention was pulled in more as Mary spoke.

"You're so so brave." She leaned forward. "To ask for the name of a witch. That–is–soo–soo brave." Mary widened her eyes and nodded her head, making an awed face at his "supposed" bravery. "But you didn't know, *did you?*" Mary put on mock surprise. "If I tell you my name, like I have now told, it puts you in debt to the magic I hold." She giggled, sounding seductive and very "witchy."

Kelly groaned in the front seat and rested his head on the steering wheel of his cruiser. He SOO didn't want to be in the middle of this. The soldier was about to open his mouth, but Mrs. Bryant cut in quickly.

"Mary! Cut it out! Just because he looks good in a uniform doesn't mean you can just 'take him.' You have to let people make their own choices!" Mrs. Bryant gave her a withering look and Mary scrunched into the seat looking guilty and ashamed of herself. "Anyway, he's already taken, Mary. Didn't you see the ring on his finger? What about his poor wife? You need to be careful and think about others and not just yourself. This man has a life, so cut him loose and let him go back to it and back to his wife."

Mary nodded, looked at the still dazed soldier, and spoke again. "I release you and free you from magic's cruel debt, go back to your wife. My face now forget." She snapped her fingers loudly and buried her face in Mrs. Bryant's shirt, bursting into tears, angry and upset at what she'd almost done to this young soldier. And to his poor wife, whoever she was.

The soldier blinked and shook his head.

"Thanks, kid," Kelly told the befuddled soldier and gently shoved him out of his window. "We'll take it from here, watch your toes now." Kelly pulled away, shaking his head as he left the young man standing slack jawed in the street. As they slowly crawled down the drive, soldiers on either side cupped their hands over their eyes to peer through the glare of the windows hoping to catch a glimpse of those inside.

They rolled down the long drive into an angry beehive of swarming activity. Off to one side of the house helicopters were parked in an open field and a number of tents had been erected along the tree line. Soldiers were everywhere. Kelly stopped at another roadblock set up about a hundred yards from the house itself where three agents waited for them, two men and one woman. Sergeant Kelly parked then got out to let Mary and Mrs. Bryant out of the back of his cruiser.

"Mrs. Bryant. Sergeant Kelly." A short clean cut man in his forties wearing shades greeted them with a smile and a nod. "And Mary Fae, the Green Witch. It's good to meet you. My name is Agent Beckard."

Mrs. Bryant asked right away, "Is Bethany inside the house? Is she okay? She was hurt earlier today. She cut herself very badly."

Surprise showed on Beckard's face. "We think she's fine. But we haven't had a lot of contact with her. She's been keeping to herself and staying inside. King Cornelius has ordered us to stay out of the house so we've only been able to speak with her once when we first arrived."

He was paying close attention to the concerned look on Mrs. Bryant's face and his own concern was growing. "Is Princess Bethany hurt?" he asked.

Mary and Mrs. Bryant shared a surprised look.

King Cornelius and Princess Bethany?

Mary let "Mom" ask the obvious question. She was trying hard not to keep quiet, concentrating on keeping her mouth clamped shut so she wouldn't have another accident. Mary already didn't like this new guy, Beckard. His wearing sunglass and something about his vibes had pissed her off for some reason. She didn't know why, but the sunglasses had done it for her. She flat out hated him. Mary tried not to look at him as she listened to Mom ask it.

"Why are you calling Bethany 'Princess Bethany'?"

The other male agent was a handsome man with a GQ look and a well-groomed beard. He answered the question, his words warmed by a genuine country burr. "Because she told us to, ma'am. That's the name Miss Grave, the Red Witch, has told us to call her by while she's here at The Hale House. And she prefers us to call the mansion, 'The White Castle.'"

Mrs. Bryant and Mary shared a quick look and a knowing smile. Bethany still acted like a child in a lot of ways and if she wanted to be a "princess" today then that was fine with them.

"So mote it be," said Mary, but then she noticed Beckard looking at her. His glasses caught the afternoon sun and flashed in her eyes. Her eyebrows dropped into an angry V instantly. Mary dropped her head and looked down at the ground. She gritted her teeth. What a bastard! She tried hard to find some "happy place" inside her head to think about instead of thinking about Beckard.

"Well, it sounds like Bethany is fine," Mrs. Bryant said, relieved.

"Do you know why she is insisting on being called Princess Bethany, Mrs. Bryant?" asked Beckard.

"The girls are very touchy about their names, and they change them often," she explained. "It can get confusing, but you should definitely call them as they ask to be called because it can set them off if you don't."

Mrs. Bryant noticed Mary's odd behavior, how she was keeping her gaze down or far left, or right, or anywhere but in Agent Beckard direction.

"Are you all right, Miss Fae?" Beckard asked Mary and she froze, looking at the ground at her feet. She didn't say a word. Beckard, Kelly, and the other two agents tensed, keyed in to Mary's odd behavior.

"Mary, are you okay, honey?" Mrs. Bryant asked her.

"No," Mary growled out. "Mom, I need to go inside. There are too many new people out here and for some reason I really don't like Beckard. Actually, I kinda hate him." Mary squeezed her eyes shut. "Please don't let him say anything. I need to pretend like he's not here."

"Oh my!" Mrs. Bryant heard the strain in Mary's voice and moved quickly to her side. "Just keep your eyes closed, Mary, that always helps Rain." She held Mary with one arm as she spoke to her but with her free arm she pointed to a confused and put upon looking Agent Beckard and shooed him away. Her message was clear enough and Beckard turned and jogged off toward the tents erected in the front yard.

"Mary, don't open your eyes, dear." Mrs. Bryant looked at the yard they had to cross to get to the front door of the mansion. Heavy military vehicles had cut deep ruts all through the lawn, and she didn't want to lead Mary by the hand across all that with her eyes closed. She looked back to Sergeant Kelly but remembered that Mary didn't like the man, then she eyed the tall handsome agent with the beard and judged him stout enough to carry Mary to the front door.

"Mary, you remember the nice man with the beard. Was he okay? Your remember him, don't you?"

"Oh yeah. He was okay," Mary answered. She sounded better already, which made Mrs. Bryant suspicious.

"Mary. I know you remember him, and that he was handsome, but he's also WAY too old for you, so don't even think about it. Control yourself and be good. No magic. Now I'm going to have him pick you up and carry you over to the house. Just keep your eyes closed."

Mary sighed, "Yes, ma'am." She kept her eyes closed and listened as Mrs. Bryant spoke to the agent.

"Please, don't tell us your name. Mary's having a difficult enough time right now and she really shouldn't know your name. Would you be so kind as to carry her to the door?"

Mary perked up, ready to hear the country accent of the unnamed agent.

"Of course, ma'am. I'll be glad to help Miss Fae to the front door. Give me one moment to take my gun off so it doesn't bother her while I carry her on over."

Mary kept her eyes closed as she listened and strained to "hear" what was going on but was surprised as she reached out with her mind; it seemed like she almost had a new "sense." It wasn't smell or hearing. It was like she could *feel* the life all around her. She didn't have long to explore this new strange "sixth" sense as she "felt" the unnamed agent drawing closer to where she stood. She raised her arms before he reached her and even with her eyes closed she could detect or somehow *feel* his surprise that she had known he was about to pick her up which made Mary smile. "Agent No Name" scooped her off her feet and up into his arms.

"Just keep your eyes closed and don't worry, Miss Fae, I'll have you to the front door in a jiffy." With that he started walking. Mrs. Bryant, Sergeant Kelly, and a younger Hispanic woman in dark gray slacks with an unreadable blank face followed along behind them.

Mary giggled. "He's strong, Mom."

"Mary," Mrs. Bryant cautioned.

Mary took a deep breath as they continued to walk. Her new sense of feeling really sprang into overdrive when the unnamed agent had picked her up. Mary could feel so much! She could feel the muscles in his arms and knew that he wasn't having to strain too hard to carry her. Somehow, she could feel the life-giving air as it moved in and out of his lungs and she could even feel his emotions and that he was a really good guy. Kindhearted and compassionate. Mary took another deep breath, breathing him in.

"Hmmm. He smells good too."

"Mary Fae!" Mrs. Bryant put a healthy touch of censure in her voice.

After another second, Mary's happy voice trilled out in a sing song way, "Mo-om. He's not wearing a ri-ing."

"Mary Fae! You be good!" Mrs. Bryant fussed at her.

After another minute of walking Mary spoke again. "Your name is Albert Kerchbalm the third and you live in Oooklaaahooomaaa!" she sang out happily, still holding her eyes shut as she let the living magic coming off the strong arms carrying her whisper secrets to her heart. Mary couldn't read Albert's mind but somehow he just "felt like" an Albert Kerchbalm the third.

"Can you read my mind?" Albert asked, straining hard to keep his voice calm. Mary couldn't see his worried face but she could feel Albert's worry and dread that she would find out things he'd just as well like to keep in the dark.

"Don't you dare mess around with anything inside Albert's head, young lady!" Mrs. Bryant warned.

"Mom!" Mary whined. "Honestly, I'm not messing with him. I'm a Green Witch and my magic comes from all living things. And Albert is definitely a living thing. A very strong, very handsome living thing." Mary laughed.

"Mary. Please just leave the poor man alone!" Mrs. Bryant pleaded as she looked at Albert.

He was looking like he wanted a refund on whatever he'd eaten for breakfast. The female agent's eyes were sharp and angry; it was clear she thought Albert was in danger from Mary or whatever Mary was doing to him.

They were almost to the front door when Mary shouted, "OH SHIT!" Her eyes snapped open in surprise.

"What!?" shouted Mrs. Bryant only a second before Albert shouted out his own terrified "What!?"

Sergeant Kelly added an extra word, "What's wrong!?"

"HE'S GAY!" Mary gasped, a half disappointed, half disgusted look on her face.

Albert dropped her right on her ass and ran.

Mrs. Bryant and the other female agent both stared openmouthed after Albert's attractive fleeing backside.

"SORRY, ALBERT!" Mary shouted after the fleeing agent. She felt bad about throwing Albert out of the closet like that; he definitely wanted to stay hidden in there, but she couldn't help herself. She was so surprised that it was out before she could stop herself. Mrs. Bryant and the female agent both looked down at Mary as she rubbed her butt and complained. "Doesn't anyone know that you're not supposed to surprise a witch!? He almost gave me a damn heart attack."

And that was when the female FBI agent started laughing. It started as a polite little giggle hidden behind her hand, but soon she descended into a true laughing fit and even had to sit down on the porch beside Mary to keep from falling over as she laughed and laughed and laughed. Mary watched her, strangely enthralled, not even blinking as the female agent had a true laughing meltdown right there on the porch.

"Good gracious, girl," Sergeant Kelly muttered, shaking his head as he watched her, laughing along with her as watched the young woman's laughing breakdown.

"That poor man," Mrs. Bryant said, disapproving frown in place. "It wasn't that funny," she scolded.

They all waited patiently for the woman to finish. She was actually a very pretty girl when she smiled like she was now. She was twenty-four years old with short black hair that matched her short, athletic frame of exactly five feet. Her deadpan and dour expression had been washed away and replaced by one of surprised relief. A lingering hint of a Spanish accent still clung and colored her words once she was able and ready to speak.

"For the past six months I've been throwing myself at Albert shamelessly. He was always so nice. But he kept telling me no. And I never saw him with any other girls." Both shoulders pulled up. "I didn't know. I never would have never guessed he was—" She winced, not able to say the "G" word.

Mary frowned and griped, "Yeah, I know. He needs to lose that tough-guy mustache and start wearing sweaters or something. Or put a sign on his forehead that says, 'I like Dudes!'"

"Whoa." The female agent's eyes went wide as she looked at Mary.

"Speaking of foreheads, a strange tattoo just appeared on yours right now," she pointed, "right there on your forehead. What *is* that thing?" She frowned at Mary's forehead. "It's looks like a crescent moon and four stars. Does it hurt?"

"No it doesn't hurt. Don't worry." Mary pointed to her own forehead. "This is the mark of our Coven StarNight."

The agent nodded but still looked confused. "But why did it appear just now?" she asked.

Mary smiled. "Because the Red Witch is coming. Princess Bethany is here." She looked to the front door drawing everyone's gaze with hers. Right then the front door opened and the Red Witch walked out, but she wasn't wearing red— she was wearing white.

"Hey guys!" Bethany shouted.

"Oh Bethany!" Mrs. Bryant ran over and smothered her in a huge hug.

"Hi, Mom," Bethany mumbled from inside the hug.

Mrs. Bryant held her out at arm's length to look at her. "Are you hurt?" she asked.

Bethany shook her head no. She was wearing a luxurious white bathrobe that was way too long for her. Her beautiful long hair was wet and hung down her back like she'd just gotten out of the shower. Her arms had gathered the robe up so it wouldn't drag on the ground and get dirty.

"Bethany, did you take a shower? I saw all that blood on the door in Rain's room. Where did you cut yourself? Show me where you cut yourself." Mrs. Bryant was fussing like a nervous mother hen.

"It's okay, Mom! I already healed myself with magic." Bethany stuck out one arm and pushed back the long sleeve of the bath robe to reveal her delicate little wrist. "Here. Look! It's all healed up," she chirped out like a happy little bird.

They could see the fine line of a scar where Bethany had sliced into her wrist.

"Oh, that's so cool!" Mary said with a playful grin.

"It is not cool!" Mrs. Bryant disagreed. "Why did you cut yourself in the first place? You could have killed yourself!" She gave what must have been her best "worried mom" look, but Bethany only smiled at her, unaffected in the least by her concerns.

"Mom, I needed blood to open the magic doorway to get here. I used blood and rage and it worked!" Bethany was thrilled with herself. She looked great, smiling and radiant, powerful and all charged up with magic and life. Her dark eyes practically sparkled with power.

Mrs. Bryant didn't give up that easily though. "But you didn't have to cut yourself, Bethany, you could have killed yourself. I don't want you doing that anymore! Cutting yourself like that," she complained, but as she studied Bethany's face she knew it was a lost cause.

"Mom. I am the Red Witch. My power and my magic comes from blood and death and sacrifice and rage. I know that all sounds really horrible, but I'm okay with it." She shrugged her little shoulders inside the bathrobe and smiled. "Like Rain says all the time, I can't hide from what I am. I am what I am." Bethany noticed the female agent standing with them on the porch who was looking at her healed up wrist.

"Who's she?" Bethany asked.

"Corina," Mary answered without thinking. "But we will call her Cory."

"AAah!" Cory gasped in surprise. "You read my mind too!" Agent Corina backed away from Mary a step or two.

"You didn't even touch me." She looked at Mary like she'd assaulted her somehow. "But I didn't even touch you, so how could you already know my name? Only my family calls me Cory!"

Cory kept a safe distance from the two witches and cast a longing glance in the direction her gay partner had fled as she considered following his lead.

Mary's brows pulled together and she spat out an irritated "Crrrap!" She squeezed her eyes shut again to block out the weird blurry light she kept seeing everywhere. She was completely frustrated at her lack of control and the way her magic kept running all over her and doing things without her even thinking about it or asking for it. She was still dealing with what had happened with "Gay Albert" and now she had more stuff overwhelming her senses. Mary opened her eyes and gave Cory an accusatory stare and fussed at her, but not in a mean-hearted way; it almost sounded like they were already old friends—or family.

"This is all your fault, Cory! You've been holding in all that frustration and pent up eew! and yuck! and aaak! Just hoarding it all up for six months, and then you BUST OPEN, right here, and let it all out like some kind of freakin' bomb going off!" Mary gave herself a crazy, yucked out shake. "You let out so much life and magic I nearly got washed off the porch by your vibes, and I was still freaked out by Albert and all his damn gay boy vibes!" Mary closed her eyes with an aggrieved groan, as if she were the victim of an assault and not Cory.

"You know a lot more than my name!" Cory accused right back with an angry glare. "What else do you know about me? What did you do to me?" she demanded.

Mary tilted her head back, keeping her eyes tightly shut. She rubbed her temples as she answered. "Cory, I'm so, so sorry, but it feels like we're practically sisters now."

"Sisters!" Cory squeaked in horror.

Bethany piped up, her happy little voice excited, "Wow. Do you like her Mary, is she really nice?"

Mary still had her eyes squeezed shut as she answered, "Yes, Bethany. She's great. But she worries way too much that she's never gonna find the right guy and she beats herself up over e-very l-ittle thing and—"

"Oh no, aaaaaaaaa," Mary's voice caught uncertainly. "Hey, Mom!" Mary called, still with her eyes closed as her face tracked through all kinds of emotions, one after another.

"Yes, Mary."

"Could you please give Cory a hug because she's too freaked out to let me or Bethany hug her, but she really needs a hug, and if she starts crying right now I'm gonna start crying too and then everything's just going to get all SILLY!" Mary finished in a complaining rush, but it seemed by her voice she was already fighting back tears of her own.

"You people are crazy!" Cory shouted. "I don't need a hug from anyone!" She gave Mrs. Bryant a nasty look. "And you are not my mother!" she said fiercely, but her eyes were glassy with unshed tears.

Bethany ignored Cory's fit, still happy as she spoke, "Hey, her name even ends in a 'Y.' Bethan-y, Maar-y, and Cor-y!" She stepped a little closer to Cory, looking at her closely, Bethany's dark eyes staring into the other girl's own dark Latin eyes. "Is she really going to be a sister for us?" She sounded hopeful.

Cory's eyes narrowed threateningly as she looked at Mary, but it was plain to see that she was curious to hear what Mary had to say.

"Could be," said Mary as she rubbed her temples. "Her Tia is even a witch."

"Aaaa!" Another shout from Cory, who was truly horrified to have that hidden piece of information become public knowledge.

Unfazed by her distress, Bethany's little brow crinkled, "What's a Tia?"

"It's Spanish for 'Aunt,'" Mary answered.

"You know Spanish!?" Bethany asked, surprised.

"I do now!" Mary whined and put both of her hands to her head as if she had a headache.

Bethany laughed, "Wow, her aunt's a witch! Is Cory a witch?"

"NO! Don't say that!" Cory shouted, pointing a finger at Bethany. "Don't you dare say a word about that!" She was white faced, outstretched hand trembling as she fought the onset of nerve jangled tears. Her distress finally squashed Bethany's exuberance and brought Mrs. Bryant to the intervention point. She stepped forward and put an end to their needling.

"Girls! That's enough! Leave Cory alone, she's getting upset." Mrs. Bryant ignored Cory's standoffish stance and angry expression and put a comforting arm around her. "It's okay, Cory. No one's going to do anything to you. You're okay. Everything is fine. The girls are sorry."

After a rigid moment Cory gave in to the motherly hug enough to slip an arm around Mrs. Bryant's waist, too glad for her protection to dare refuse her offered shelter.

"Sorry, Mom," said a chastened Mary. "Sorry, Cory," she added. She still had her eyes closed as she stood there with them.

"Sorry, Mom," Bethany said sadly. "Sorry, Cory."

Federal Agent Corina Maria Vaschez collected herself. She spoke to Bethany as she untangled herself from Mrs. Bryant's arms and took two deliberate steps away from all of them. "I think I should get back to my post now. It was very good to meet you, Princess Bethany."

"Cory," Bethany said, "You don't have to call me Princess Bethany anymore; you can call me Bethany. And you can call Mary, 'Mary' and Black Rain just plain old 'Rain.' And you can call Mrs. Bryant 'Mom.' You need another Mom. As above so below, now she's your mom, I make it so."

Mary's firm voice came from nowhere, "So mote it be." Cory's head snapped to her only to have to cut back the other way as she heard another, "So mote it be." Bethany nodded, face serious.

Cory stood there speechless.

Mrs. Bryant gave her a sad smile but said nothing; she didn't know what to say to the poor girl. It did look like she needed someone.

Mary sighed, "It's your choice, Cory. We can't make you join us. And your 'witch issues' are private, I won't say anything about them. Not to anyone. We can't make you be a witch, but you can't pick and choose who your family is. You're our sister whether you like it or not. So don't be a stranger. We love you."

And that was when Agent Corina Maria Vaschez followed her gay partner's example and ran for it.

"You know what sucks the most?" Mary said. With her eyes closed she "felt" Cory's now familiar life moving away from her, across the warm glow of life she could feel coming off the torn up lawn. "I'm really gonna miss her. And think about her. Because I already know her." Mary sighed again. "How messed up is that?" she complained quietly.

Bethany finally took notice of Sergeant Kelly standing at the edge of the group. "Hey, why's that cop here?"

"Don't worry, honey," Mrs. Bryant answered, "he's not going to take you back to your mother." She turned to Kelly and asked, "Are you?"

"Hell no!" Kelly shot out lightning fast. "You needed a ride, and I needed to make sure this girl wasn't hurt. That was a lot of blood you left behind in that trailer. We were all worried about you. But you look fine so I'm done here." Kelly took a couple of backward steps as he continued to talk. "The only person I'm taking anywhere is 'me.' I'm going home. There seems to be plenty of FBI agents around here who can help you ladies get home when you're ready to go." Kelly gave a final wave and muttered "Ladies," then he turned and tromped back across the rutted yard toward his cruiser.

Mrs. Bryant looked at Mary. She'd finally opened her eyes again and was squinting and blinking as if the waning afternoon light was too bright as she looked out across the lawn at all the soldiers.

"Mary honey, are you feeling all right?" she asked.

"Cantaloupe," Mary replied sullenly, unable to lie but not wishing to tell the truth.

Mrs. Bryant reached out and brushed the green lock of hair out her face where it liked to hang and hide her eyes. "You're really having a hard time controlling your magic. Every new person we've met since we picked you up from the trailer has set you off."

"I know!" Mary agreed with a frustrated growl. "I don't know what the heck my problem is, but it's getting harder and harder to control this stuff, it's like it has a mind of its own and keeps *doing things!*" Mary closed her eyes again like she was scared of what she was seeing. Or at least sick of what she was seeing.

"Are your eyes bothering you, Mary?" Mrs. Bryant had noticed the squinting and constant closing of her eyes.

"I don't want to talk about it," Mary griped. She was so sick of all the colors she was seeing out on the lawn, and all the colors she saw around the soldiers and coming off the grass and trees and even shimmering in the air. It was like every living thing had its own little glow of life coming off of it and the clash of all the colors washing over one another was driving her crazy and giving her a migraine. At least with her eyes closed she only had to deal with "feeling" all the life and magic around her. But seeing it and feeling it at the same time was sensory overload.

Mary changed the subject before they could ask her any more questions about her eyes. "So. Princess Bethany?" asked Mary with a grin, still with her eyes closed, although Mary turned and faced Bethany like she could see her just fine. "Where's your new 'witchy' dress?" she asked. "And why on earth did you take a shower?"

Mary couldn't "see" Bethany but she could definitely "feel" her and she felt AWESOME! She felt like a little magical star, burning bright, right beside her. Mary's new sixth magical "sense" seemed to be growing stronger each minute she kept her eyes closed and used it instead of her eyes to see. In some ways Mary felt like she could actually "see" more by "feeling" than seeing. It seemed that everything around her spoke right to her without even having to use words. And the crazy thing was, it seemed like everything had something interesting to say.

Bethany frowned as she ran her hand down her wet hair. She looked back toward the house then at Mrs. Bryant. "Yeah. About that. Before we go in let me explain. There was some trouble when I got here." Bethany looked very nervous. She started fidgeting with the cuff of the bath robe. "When I came through the door there were some bad people in the house arguing with my mom and dad."

"What!? With WHO?" asked a surprised Mary.

Bethany kept her voice calm as she tried to explain herself. "Mom, the people who live here are witches. Very, very nice witches, and—I hope you're not mad, and I didn't really plan for this to happen," she tried to pad the blow of her next words, "but I made them my mom and dad."

"YOU DID WHAT!?" Mary shouted. "You made Cathryn and Cornelius your mom and dad!?"

"Hush, Mary," Mrs. Bryant shushed her. "Tell us what happened when you got here, honey. You said that there were some bad people here when you arrived. What happened?"

"They were very bad people." Bethany's little eyes squinted up. "One was a big Russian guy named Yanosh, and the other was a very mean old lady witch named Fiona." Bethany looked at Mary and added, "They were some of those bad witches, like the ones from that website that want us dead."

"What!? Those people came here!?" Mary barked.

"What people? What website?" asked Mrs. Bryant.

Bethany tried to explain, "There are witches out there that want us dead. Rain and the rest of us too. And they have a website set up asking other witches to use magic to curse us and spell us to die. But the people who were here didn't try to use magic to hurt us, they were going to do it themselves. They even told us what they wanted to do to us." Bethany frowned and her voice got stronger, angrier as she spoke. "Fiona, the fat old lady witch wanted to let me bleed to death. When I got here I was bleeding really bad and she told Cathryn and Cornelius not to help me, but they didn't listen to her and helped me anyway. Then the Russian guy, Yanosh, couldn't make up his mind whether he wanted to rape me and kill me himself or make some money off me by taking me to Russia and then selling me as a whore. Cathryn and Cornelius tried to stop them and that was when the Russian guy killed Cornelius and—"

"OH NO!" Mary gasped, shocked into opening her eyes again and squinting in the wash of colors that assaulted her blurry vision. "Not Cornelius!" Mary cried.

"MARY! Don't freak!" Bethany shouted. "I raised him from the dead! He's fine."

That silenced them both for a moment until Mrs. Bryant asked, nice and calm, "You raised him from the dead?"

Bethany shrugged, "He was only dead for about ten minutes, and it still felt like his soul was hanging around close by, so it's really not THAT big a deal." She gave a dismissive wave of her arm. "And he's fine now, except I sort of changed his name when I raised him. His name is King Cornelius now." Bethany quickly added, "Oh, and Cathryn is Queen Cathryn now."

"And you're Princess Bethany," supplied a smiling Mary.

"Yes, I am," agreed Bethany with a serious nod of her head. "After I raised Cornelius from the dead and changed his name, I also changed Cathryn's name and my name, and I made this my home."

Bethany put her arms out wide, "The White Castle, Amen Hall, is now mine. And I live here with my dad, King Cornelius, and my mom, Queen Cathryn, and I am their daughter, Princess Bethany."

"So mote it be," said a now very serious Mary.

"So mote it be," echoed Bethany.

"Hmm," commented Mrs. Bryant.

"Oh!" Bethany cried, embarrassed. "You're still my mom too, and I love you too!" she assured. "And please don't be mad, but they're my mom and dad now like you and Mr. Bryant, and I love them too." Bethany studied Mrs. Bryant's face for a second before she asked, "You're not mad, are you?"

"No, Bethany," Mrs. Bryant answered. "I'm not mad. I just hope these people will take very good care of you and love you like you deserve to be loved." She wore a happy face but she did sound disappointed. "Bethany, you know you'll always have a home with me, and you're still welcome to move into Rain's room with her. I know Rain will miss you. You can visit anytime. Our trailer isn't a castle but it's nice, and it's your home too—"

"Ahmm," Mary interrupted. "Well, Mom. About that." Mary had her eyes closed again and looked weird as she made a pinched up face with her eyes closed, bracing herself to spill the uncomfortable revelation. "Rain and I already talked about this while we were in the car this morning. We sort of already decided to stay here. This is a lot more private, and we knew it would be safer here than at the trailer park surrounded by all those crazies."

They all turned as wind from a huge helicopter with two sets of whirling blades passed right overhead. Dangling underneath the helicopter was a huge box of *who knew what* heading *who knew where.* As their eyes followed the dangling bundle, they looked out at the lawn. There were hundreds of soldiers now. It looked like they were turning the whole property into a military compound. Bulldozers off at the far edge of the property were clearing a line, pushing down trees and uprooting bushes to make a path for other soldiers and trucks who were laying down cement barricades as fast as the bulldozers cleared space.

Mrs. Bryant shook her head, amazed at all the soldiers that swarmed like a disturbed nest of camo-colored man-sized ants. She was also amazed that all of this upheaval was because of her daughter and her witch friends.

Mary said, "Rain must have already told someone important that she's planning to come here."

"Yeah, she told them," Bethany griped. "Some FBI guys spoke with us before the military invaded." She put her hands on her hips. "They sure are messing up my yard!" She sounded exactly like a disgruntled homeowner with nasty neighbors that let their dog poop in her yard but didn't bother to pick it up.

"Well, this is definitely going to be a lot safer than the trailer," Mrs. Bryant agreed reluctantly. "And there were a lot of nuts trying to get at you girls over there, but all of this seems so unreal, sometimes it's hard to believe that this is really happening to me and my girls." Mrs. Bryant looked at Bethany and asked, "Can I stay here at your house, Bethany? Will your other mother mind if I stay to keep an eye on you girls?"

Bethany kept a serious face as she answered, "You can stay, Mom, but remember that this is a Witch's Castle, and here they accept my being a Red Witch for what it is. Blood and nasty stuff and all. My new mom and dad are super, super nice and polite, and inside the house there are rules that you have to follow. We have to dress nice all the time. And everything is done in a special way here, even the way you walk and talk and eat. My new mom's going to teach me how to use all the fancy forks and spoons and stuff." Bethany bubbled with excitement as she spoke. "I don't know how yet, but I'll learn." Her little face was so lit up Mrs. Bryant couldn't help but smile for Bethany. "And the way you talk when you're here, it has to be super proper and super polite. Like you would talk at Cinderella's Ball. Like in the old times when they had knights in armor and kings and queens and princesses. And the most important rule of all is that you have to treat everyone with respect here."

Mrs. Bryant was grudgingly impressed. Whoever these people were they'd already made a huge impact on Bethany. It seemed like they were good people. She hoped. "It sounds like a wonderful home," she said, making her words hopeful as well.

"It is wonderful," Mary confirmed.

Mary still had her eyes closed as she walked toward the front door as easily as if she would if she'd had them open. "Well, come on! I want to see King Cornelius and make sure he's okay. What did you do to the guy that killed him anyway?" She looked right at Bethany, lips pressed into a tight line. "Please tell me he's dead."

"Mom, you may not want to stay here once you see what I've done." Bethany sounded sad and strangely resigned.

She raised her chin and met Mrs. Bryant's eyes for a moment before turning and walking to the front doors. Bethany put one hand on each handle and said, "Come and be welcome to Amen Hall." She turned the handles and pulled; the huge ornate double glass doors opened easily, gliding apart as Bethany led the way in.

Mary had to open her eyes; she didn't trust what she was "feeling" and had to look for herself. Mary and Mrs. Bryant stopped in the foyer at the entrance of the entry hall, looking around the room, speechless.

Blood was everywhere. EVERYWHERE!

The walls, the floor, even the ceiling was covered. Someone had started to clean the floor. A path leading to the door had been mopped clean, revealing a gleaming white marble trail that cut through the sea of sprayed red that dotted or covered every surface in sight.

"Bethany. Did you do this?" asked Mrs. Bryant calmly.

"Yes, I did this," Bethany answered, also calm.

Mrs. Bryant noticed that she'd changed her voice. She was trying to sound very formal and proper now, and she was holding herself in an elegant posture, being the Princess she thought she should be.

"I used magic to kill Yanosh." Bethany pointed to a spot on the floor nearby. "He stood there. After he killed Cornelius, he stood there while he told me what he was going to do to me." Bethany looked around the room at all the blood. "I'm glad I killed him," she said, completely without remorse. "I enjoyed it. My only regret is that he only had one life to give me. I'd like to kill him again. And again." She didn't sound like a thirteen-year-old little girl; she sounded like a witch. A very dangerous, very scary witch.

Mrs. Bryant couldn't think of what to say, but Mary was still trying to understand the "how the hell!" factor and the basic mechanics of what she was seeing. "How did you kill this guy, Bethany!? Did you shove him into a paint gun and spray him all over the walls!" She looked up at the ceiling and exclaimed, "Good goobily gob! How'd you get it way up there on the ceiling!? That's got to be twenty feet high!"

"He made me very angry" was the only explanation Bethany gave. Her black eyes twinkled with power.

Right then the butler entered. He was a tall, older man but still looked fit even with his snow white hair and grey handle bar mustache. He had two other, younger male servants with him; one had mops and cleaning supplies while the other carried two large buckets of clean water. As soon as the butler saw them he abandoned the pair and rushed right over.

"Princess, I wasn't aware we had guests," he said. "Forgive me, my lady, I should have been ready to receive them at the door." He seemed embarrassed that Bethany had answered the door herself.

Bethany acted like a little Princess as she turned and introduced her guests to the flustered butler.

"Byron, this is my Sister. The Green Witch, Mary Fae."

Byron quickly eyed the mark now visible on Bethany's forehead and the one on Mary's before he bowed slightly to Mary. "Then she is family. Welcome to Amen Hall, Lady Fae."

Bethany put an arm out toward Mrs. Bryant. "And this is my 'other' mother, Byron," Bethany said with a smile.

Byron also smiled but he misunderstood Bethany's meaning. "Ah, it's a pleasure to have Princess Bethany's birth mother with us."

Bethany laughed then, and it stirred magic through the air. An ominous wave of spooky power came from her little body washing over everyone in the room as she laughed. Something about the laugh carried the thought of dark power, anger, pain, and chilling death. It was unsettling. Dark magic.

"No Byron. No. She is not my birth mother." Bethany paused to chase away a final giggle, holding a little hand delicately over her mouth for a moment before she spoke again, "Please, forgive me, Byron, I shouldn't have laughed. It was rude of me. This is Mrs. Bryant, she is the birth mother of Black Rain, the Black Witch. She is also my mother, but she is not my birth mother. The whore that I crawled out of will never be welcome in Amen Hall. The only mothers I have are the ones that I have made."

Without waiting for anyone to respond to that, Bethany introduced the shocked butler. "Mom, Mary, this is Byron, our butler. He's been with our family for over thirty years."

Byron bowed to Mrs. Bryant. "A pleasure to meet you, Mrs. Bryant."

"It's good to meet you too, Byron," she managed to say, still reeling from the blood-bathed room and Bethany's evil laugh.

Byron then turned back to Bethany. "Your mother and father are presently entertaining Federal agents in the Garden Parlor. May I escort our guests there and present them to our King and Queen?"

"Yes Byron, that would be perfect."

Byron gave Bethany a quick smile and bow before he turned and led them down the one clean path through the room of sprinkled blood, through an arched opening and into an even larger hall with a huge domed ceiling at one end. On the floor beneath the dome was a large mosaic of a pentagram set into the floor, but as they drew closer they noticed that all over the pentagram was blood. It was pooled thick and dark in places, not sprayed about like in the other room. Byron didn't mention the blood as he led them past the grisly display and out another doorway into an open garden area.

They strode a short distance to the center of the garden where two men in suits sat at a large wrought iron table, across from Cathryn and Cornelius. One servant in white stood quietly to the side, seeing to the needs of the party.

The two agents stood when the group approached, but Cathryn and Cornelius remained seated, giving the new arrivals welcoming smiles from their chairs.

"King Cornelius and Queen Cathryn," Byron bowed to them, "I present Mary Fae, the Green Witch, and Mrs. Bryant, the birth mother of the Black Witch and also a mother for our own Princess Bethany."

"Thank you, Byron," Cathryn said and the Butler backed away as the "King" and "Queen" sized up the group.

The six o'clock sun sat just high enough in the western sky to peek over the top of the garden wall directly behind them. Cathryn still looked like Cathryn and Cornelius still looked like himself, but something in the air or in the way they sat framed by the afternoon light or some intangible something made them seem regal as they sat in their chairs on the other side of the ornate table. The table itself was a metal work monstrosity, the tabletop an oval constructed of interlocking metal vines, moons, and stars. The legs on each side of the table were nightmarish looking gargoyles cast out of bronze, each squatting figure holding up one end of the table with their muscular demonic arms. If it weren't for Cathryn and Cornelius's happy smiling faces on the other side of the table it would have been a frightening place to sit.

"Welcome to Amen Hall," said Cathryn warmly.

"Yes, welcome," echoed Cornelius with a happy smile.

Bethany gripped a hesitant Mrs. Bryant by the hand and led her over to the table, and they took a seat beside the FBI agents, but Mary was spellbound, frozen in place, looking out at the garden. The garden was a smaller, private garden, only about two hundred feet long and maybe three hundred feet wide and open to the sky. It was closed in on two sides by the mansion and by a ten foot high brick wall on the other two sides. The iron table where the others sat rested on a raised hill in the middle of the garden. A decorative brick path led off to each side circling the place. At the far side, a tiny waterfall fell down from the top of the wall, cascading into a small pool. A wondrous variety of trees, bushes, and flowers were planted with masterful care throughout, turning the place into a world of wonder. Topiary arches, grown from different varieties of greenery, vines, roses, and other flowers were spaced along the path. The garden was also dotted in places with marble sculptures, art pieces, and small plush alcoves, ideal for thought, meditation, sunlight reading, or intimate privacy in a beautiful place.

"Mary, are you okay, honey?" Mrs. Bryant called from her seat at the table beside Bethany.

"Yeah," Mary answered weakly, unable to look away from the garden for even a second. Her new vision had finally sharpened and changed into something new and Mary was utterly dazzled by it.

"Are you feeling well, Mary?" asked Cathryn, also concerned by Mary's odd behavior.

"Mom. May I go play in the garden?" Mary asked, barely aware of what she said as she gazed at the glow of life all around her, completely lost in its beauty.

"Yes," answered Cathryn and Mrs. Bryant at exactly the same time. They shared an awkward moment, not sure which person Mary had been speaking to, but Mary didn't help clear things up. She walked away without another word, down the brick path and off into the garden, touching a plant here, stopping to gaze at the bushes and trees and little flowers as she went.

"Is she all right?" asked Agent White. He'd been watching Mary's odd behavior with interest.

The other agent, who looked like he was of Indian decent added, "She looked quite disoriented."

"Should someone go get her?" asked Cornelius as he turned in his chair to look through the garden to where Mary walked on the trail. On the raised hill they could see her on the path where she walked.

"It may be best if we leave her be for now," Mrs. Bryant suggested as she eyed the two FBI agents sitting at the table with them. "Mary doesn't need to see these two 'strangers' right now. She sent the last two agents she met running for their lives."

"Which agents? What happened?" asked Mr. White as he leaned forward quickly and set his tea cup down on the table with a jarring little clatter.

Mrs. Bryant tsked and gave the man a look. "Don't get yourself all worked up; your agents are fine. Just a little emotional damage, I think."

"Emotional damage?" asked Cornelius. "How?"

"Oh, Mary told them some things about themselves that they didn't handle well. The truth, but things they probably didn't want to hear. At least not out loud. They're fine, just upset I think." Mrs. Bryant looked over to where Mary walked along the path. "Mary's been having a very hard time controlling her powers; they keep taking off on her without her even knowing what they're doing. But it's so good to see her using her eyes again. Something about her magic has been affecting her eyes and she's been walking around with them closed."

"Oh my!" Cornelius groaned with worry. "Poor Mary!" He turned in his chair and then peered through the wood, catching glimpses of Mary through the thicker growth as she walked down the trail.

"Mary can see with her eyes closed, Father," Bethany told Cornelius.

"Can she now?" Cornelius mused, keeping his eyes on Mary. "I'm glad she can see with her eyes closed, but I'm even happier to know that she doesn't have to. And I'm glad to see her enjoying the garden."

"Mrs. Bryant," Agent White greeted her with a neighborly smile and a nod. "Please allow me to introduce myself. My name is Mr. White. It is a pleasure to meet Black Rain's mother. Your daughter has sure turned the world on its head, hasn't she? Have you spoken with her recently? Do you know if she plans to come here soon?" he asked.

"No," she answered with a flash of guilty worry as she realized that she'd been so concerned about Mary and Bethany she hadn't even had a chance to worry about her own "birth" daughter. "Her phone's not working well. I've only received one text message from her almost two hours ago and I haven't been able to get through since then," Mrs. Bryant complained. "The text Rain sent said that her phone wasn't working well either, but she should be at church right now with her father and Officer Williams. That's the policeman that they have with her to keep people away. She doesn't deal well with meeting strangers," she explained. "And Mary already told me that Rain was planning to come here after church."

She frowned. She hadn't planned on having to rush off and make sure Bethany was okay, and now she was way out here at the Hale House mansion, more than an hour away from the church and it was almost 6:15. Wednesday night service started at 6:30. She knew Rain had Williams, Ryan and her father with her there at the church so she tried to relax a little and not worry herself into a state.

"Mrs. Bryant, allow me to introduce myself, my name is Gupta Chandori. I, also, am with the FBI." Gupta put his hand out for her to shake. She shook his sweaty little palm with a forced, yet sincere smile.

Cathryn and Cornelius took a few minutes to formally welcome Mrs. Bryant to their home.

"Your mark is back, Bethany, when did this happen?" Cornelius asked after the introductions were over.

"The mark is magic, Father," Bethany explained. "When we're alone it disappears, but when at least two of us are together in the same place the mark comes back. I like my mark, I miss it when it's gone." She rubbed her forehead with her delicate little fingers.

"It looks beautiful on you, Bethany," Cathryn said as she studied Bethany's forehead.

"Yes, I agree," said Gupta. "It is so simple and so elegant, the mark really does set off your whole appearance. Stunning really. So few people in this country ever think of putting a tattoo on their forehead, but it is much more common in India where I grew up. It is a bold and daring thing." Gupta sounded sincere, his rich accent coloring his words as he spoke.

"You really think so?" Bethany asked him, honestly seeking his opinion.

"Definitely, Princess Bethany. Definitely," he replied and took another bite of the tiny cake he had on his plate.

A servant approached the table and asked Mrs. Bryant and Bethany if they would like anything to eat or drink.

"The hot tea is quite excellent," Gupta encouraged as he lifted his own antique teacup for another sip.

Mrs. Bryant went with the tea.

"Red wine," said Bethany and the servant complied, quickly placing a wine glass before her while Mrs. Bryant watched and looked over at Bethany's "other" mother and father to see if they would object to a thirteen year old drinking wine right in front of them. It didn't look like they had even noticed. Cornelius had turned back around in his chair and was looking through the garden at Mary while Cathryn studied Bethany's face, not her glass.

"How are you feeling, Bethany? Did you enjoy your shower?" Cathryn asked her.

After she finished taking a delicate sip of wine Bethany set her glass down. "The shower was nice, but I miss the blood," she answered sadly. Cathryn's head cocked to the side a little in thought and Cornelius turned back around in his chair, drawn into the conversation by that comment.

"You miss the blood?" he asked, raising an eyebrow. "How so, my child? What part of being covered from head to toe in blood do you miss?" he asked in a conversational tone, as if they were talking about the weather instead of carnage. The two FBI agents sat there listening without objection, eating little fancy cakes and sipping tea.

"It felt so good to have it on me, feeling the life and the power and magic spread all across my skin. Even all dried and hardened and stuck in my hair, I could still feel it, and it felt—*wonderful*." She closed her eyes in remembered bliss as she spoke. "It's amazing how much power and magic is in blood. I miss the blood. But I didn't waste it."

Bethany looked up from her glass and her eyes sparkled as she looked at her new parents.

"What do you mean, Bethany? What did you do with the blood?" Cornelius asked, delving deeper into that last mysterious statement.

"Oh, I washed the blood off, but not before I took its magic." Bethany took another tiny sip of her wine.

"Where did you put the magic, Bethany?" Cathryn asked her.

"I put some of the magic into Amen Hall. Can you feel it, Mom?" Bethany asked Cathryn.

"Yes," she said without hesitation.

Cornelius looked around for a moment, appraising his surrounding, even taking a deep breath of air before announcing, "Yes, I feel it too. I'm not sure what it is I'm feeling, but something about the Hall has definitely changed. What did you do with the magic in Amen Hall?" he asked, arching an eyebrow.

Bethany looked around her. She gazed at her new home, the wonder and love, all it meant to her showing on her beautiful face. It was her home now. It was a real home, with a witch mother and a witch father who loved her. It was everything she ever wanted or dreamed of having and more.

"I did what felt right, Father," Bethany said mysteriously, sounding every bit the witch she was and avoiding a direct answer. Cornelius raised an eyebrow as he realized this was all the answer he was going to get.

"Be careful, my child," he cautioned. "There are lots of magical items here, antiques from all over the world. Ancient items that may be very dangerous and powerful. I have no idea what most of them are, but be careful using magic on Amen Hall. It may bring about unintended results."

Bethany nodded her head. "I'll be careful, Father. But you should know that the most magical things in the Hall are its people. Especially its King."

Cornelius smiled at his new daughter and chuckled. She of course had him wrapped around her little finger already.

"What did you do with the rest of the magic, Bethany?" Cathryn asked as she took a sip of her tea.

"It's inside me."

"This is so fascinating," Gupta said excitedly. "So this 'life energy' from the blood of the bad man and woman. You have now taken this energy into your own body?" he asked curiously.

"Yes," Bethany answered, then frowned. "But that's not all. There's more. Yanosh was an evil man. A very evil man. And his soul was very black. His life, and magic, was dark. Black. Ugly." Bethany licked wine off her lips. "It was—" Her eyes looked at her red wine glass as she searched for the right word. "*Delicious.*" She breathed longingly. Bethany looked lost in dreams of blood, a vacant expression on her angelic face.

"Oh. Oh my," Gupta said with concern as he watched Bethany zone out.

"Please! Can we *not* talk about blood for a while!?" Mrs. Bryant urged with heat in her voice. "Even talking about blood makes Bethany lose control, and she's already been through enough today, *don't you think*? I know this is your home, and that you're all witches, but she's still just a child. And she's had enough."

Mrs. Bryant's angry gaze was settled on Cathryn who looked suitably chastened.

"Yes. I believe you're right, Mrs. Bryant." She looked with concern into Bethany's blank, far off stare. "I am sorry. I didn't know that simply talking about blood would have this much of an effect on her."

Bethany still seemed in a daze, looking at nothing, but then a huge smile split her face.

"What is it, Bethany?" asked Cornelius.

"Mary," Bethany said happy and alert again. She half stood as she looked off toward the garden and Mary.

"Can you feel it?" she asked. "She talking to the trees! May I go play in the garden with Mary?" Her little eyes sparkled as she looked out into the garden. They could see Mary, standing before a huge weeping willow that grew on the bank of the fountain pond. She had her arms wrapped around the trunk. "Bethany," Cathryn said, "first go put your dress back on, then you can play with Mary and the trees. Byron has finished cleaning it for you."

"Yay!" Bethany turned and hugged Mrs. Bryant, then jumped up from the table without another word. Byron was standing nearby with her red and brown dress, now cleaned, dried, and draped over his arm. Bethany didn't even think about the people around her as she ran up to Byron, untied the white bath robe and slipped it off her shoulders. She didn't let it fall to the ground and get dirty but stood there naked and handed the robe to Byron, then grabbed her witch dress and quickly pulled it over her head and shimmied into it before running off to join Mary in the garden.

"Oh my," Gupta said.

"Hmm" was Mrs. Bryant's thought.

"That was unexpected," Cornelius said, but he was smiling.

"I think it was beautiful," Cathryn said, a small smile on her face as she watched Bethany run barefoot down the path toward Mary.

"Excuse me," said Mrs. Bryant, "but you can't possibly see that as acceptable behavior. She just undressed in front of perfect strangers." She looked at the agents. "Men who she doesn't even think of as family."

Cathryn's small smile stayed on her face as she answered, "Bethany feels totally safe here, and this is her home now. She even sees Byron and our staff as family. And she is a witch." Cathryn nodded. "That means she will be peculiar, and she will always be somewhat ruled by her passions. She wanted to go play, and I told her to get dressed first, so," her smile pulled up on one side, "she got dressed."

Cornelius laughed. He took a sip of his tea.

"She should still be careful about getting undressed in front of grown men. Someone could hurt her," insisted Mrs. Bryant. She was still reeling from the overall surprise.

"I agree." Agent White put in his two cents, backing Mrs. Bryant's concerns. "The way people are now-a-days, you can't be too careful."

The smile left Cathryn's face at that. "Men have hurt Bethany before. She told me."

"Yes. I know," Mrs. Bryant confirmed quietly. She dreaded the thought of all that Bethany may have endured.

Cathryn leaned back in her chair and spoke in a commanding, powerful tone, "Bethany could walk naked through a prison filled with nothing but pedophiles and no living hand would touch her. She no longer fears *men*. And if, by some miracle, someone did touch her, I would slit his throat myself and let my child dance in his blood."

"Not if I beat you to it!" Mrs. Bryant declared angrily, surprising herself. Her hands flew up, covering her mouth, eyes wide with shocked embarrassment.

Cornelius laughed and Cathryn smiled at her. "So. You do love her," Cathryn said, obviously pleased at the discovery. "It's good to know that Bethany has chosen well. Did she make you her mother also?"

"Not really, they didn't make me into their mother, it just sort of happened." Mrs. Bryant wasn't quite sure herself how it started. "Actually, I think Mary stared calling me Mom first, and then Bethany started, and now I have three witch girls instead of just my Rain."

"So, Mary is yours also?"

"Yes," Mrs. Bryant said but then thought about earlier. Mary had already called Cathryn Mom.

"Cathryn, I think you should know, I'm pretty sure that the girls come as a set. I don't think you can pick only one of them. I think you may have three girls now. And one of them is my daughter." Mrs. Bryant didn't sound too happy about that idea.

"Your second life is very different from your first life, my King," Cathryn said to Cornelius. "All these years and no child of our own. Amen Hall filled with friends or associates but not with family. It will be different now, my Lord Amen." Cathryn placed her hand on top of Cornelius's hand and the two of them shared a moment.

"Yes, it will be different, my Queen. So mote it be," he said and smiled.

"So mote it be," Cathryn answered back with a smile of her own.

The White House

Status Report

The President faced the drop down wall-sized monitor in the West Wing conference room looking at the enormously oversized face of Stan Reese, director of the FBI. Samuel Fisk, the President's Chief of Staff, David Lansing, his senior advisor, and Stewart Gates, the Secretary of Defense, were also at the table as Reese continued his sit-rep.

"Let me get this straight. You're telling me that he was intentionally seeking out mentally unstable kids to test his drugs on? Were all twelve of these teens mentally ill?"

"Most of them," Reese replied grimly. "It was all there on the website, fluffed up to look official and viable. The website for the drug study encouraged teens with mental issues to apply. The way he set up his screening and online psychological exam made it clear that he was looking for teens with specific mental issues. Our people believe he combed through the applicants, picking out the ones he thought his pills would have the most interesting effects on. Eight of the twelve he chose were already seeing counselors and taking psych meds, and Burgis had them taken off their current meds before they started his pills. Sky Lee Han was on so many meds you could have opened a pharmacy with what they were giving her. She should have been committed years ago, but her parents were wealthy enough to prevent it."

"She's the flying girl, right?" asked Fisk.

"Yes, the flying girl that creates living monsters made from clouds," replied Reese grimly. Sky's ability to fly was amazing, but this new ability eclipsed the other and made flying seem almost trivial. A side note at best. The creatures she made were large, powerful, and dangerous, and apparently they were also being created with human or possibly even super human intelligence. New life was what the scientists were calling Sky's cloud monsters. They were literally dying to see one of the living clouds up close so they could study it. Every report from eyewitnesses and every captured audio or video of interaction between humans and the cloud entities were being devoured by scientists and psychologists the moment they were released to them.

Reese continued, "And Rain Bryant, the girl who's named herself the Black Witch is just as bad. She apparently had a psychotic break when she had an abortion two years ago and developed a split personality. She's absolutely insane, and, I would have to say, she's also the most dangerous person on the face of the earth. Possibly the most powerful and dangerous human being to ever draw breath since we crawled out of the slime. We don't even know what she *can* do, but so far she's done enough to scare the bejesus out of everyone. Manipulating invisible barriers and shields, controlling sound and weather on a whim, canceling out gravity. I saw that myself when I met her—magazines, books, and all kinds of little objects floating in the air like a zero gravity spacewalk. And then there's what she did to Dr. Sangai, killing him with nothing but a thought. And then she reshaped matter and created an urn in her hands that she stuffed Sangai's blood into for the vampires to drink. She's shown that she'll kill if we give her a reason. Her powers are frightening, but even more disturbing is knowing that it may be impossible to kill her, even if we needed to. It seems that she can come back from the dead."

"Is that concrete? Are we certain about that?" asked Gates quickly. "Is this girl really immortal, Reese?" The men seated around the President shifted in their seats, uncomfortable at the thought.

"She may be, sir," Reese said, not pulling his punches. "I've seen this girl myself, and she nearly scared me to death. And that was before she burned herself up and raised herself from the ashes. According to what Tom has told us she's vastly more powerful now than before she burned. Major Benistin said that the only way he could think to describe the kind of power she had was the word 'godlike'."

"Godlike!" Lansing shouted out. "Dammit Reese! Are you telling us this girl is a god now!?" He looked at the President. "That kind of talk would cause world-wide panic, sir!"

Stan Reese laughed, "Relax, David. That's not what I'm saying. Those were the major's words, not mine. I don't think there are any religious hang ups we need to worry about,—other than public perception. This is science clean and clear, not religion. If these teens were at some youth retreat when this happened we might have a problem." Reese shook his head. "No, this is science, Mr. Lansing, but the sooner we remind people of that the better. We need the media to focus on this as a scientific breakthrough. Spin this as some amazing discovery to keep people from going off the deep end. Mr. President, I suggest you move quickly to get ahead of the religious speculation and 'end of days' nonsense. Once that ball gets rolling—" Reese pulled a grim face.

"David," the President asked, "the press conference is in thirty minutes. How do we spin this? Do we keep it vague with a bunch of stalling and bullshit or shoot this off as some unexpected scientific breakthrough of immense proportions?"

"I don't know, sir. Let's delay the announcement for another fifteen minutes. Do it at 6:45. Let me and my people brainstorm on this and go over it some more."

"Yeah, let's push it back another fifteen minutes," said Fisk. "I'll let them know the new time, but I say we go with the vague stalling bullshit till we know more. Bullshit always works if you say it sincerely enough, but you come out with something concrete and you're screwed every damn time. Let's wait till we got more facts." He slipped out of his chair.

"What about the rest of these kids, Reese?" Gates asked. "Are they as bad as the flying girl and the witch?"

Reese answered, "Most of the others have been to doctors and psychiatrists multiple times for depression, anxiety, or OCD or even mild to moderate schizophrenia. Susan Palimino, the singer. Katie Burgis, the painter, and Benjamin Grant all were all on serious meds and were in psychiatric care before they started the drug study."

The President summed the facts up out loud as he understood it. "So Burgis was selecting only the craziest candidates he could find, and then he took these kids off their meds and then gave them his pills instead, pills that gave them superhuman powers. Some of them godlike powers." He shook his head at the enormity of it all. "That's one crazy, heartless son of a bitch."

"Yes. A crazy, murdering son of a bitch," Reese added. "We know that one of the teens has already committed suicide by blowing his head off with a shotgun, but that was only the tip of the iceberg. We traced the doctor to an orphanage in Minsk, Russia where we believe he experimented on children while developing the drugs he used here. We're still trying to get some details from the orphanage about what went on there but the Russians are already turning the place upside down. He's also spent time at a hospital in Ethiopia, and we have no idea what may have happened there either. Burgis hasn't had any partners or associates or colleagues that he may have shared his work with. He's been a loner for the past eight years, studying gene therapy on his own. He hasn't gone after scientific grants or worked for any drug companies doing official genetics research. He's been exceedingly careful."

"We get it," Fisk said as he slipped back into his chair. "Dr. Burgis is a bastard. Let's get back to the teens who've taken his pills. Are they all as powerful as the witch?"

"No, definitely not," Reese answered. "Some of them only developed existing skills and some of them haven't shown any changes at all. Most of the less dangerous or less powerful teens are already in custody and are being sent to Rikes Peak in Arizona."

Fisk waved his arms around. "Just tell us if we have it contained. Are they all in a box with us holding the key yet?"

"Run down the list. Who do we have?" the President asked.

"Here's where we stand, Mr. President." Reese picked up his clipboard. "We've already picked up Susan Palamino, the singer. We've got Katie Burns, the artist. We have Skikith Bowlings, we're not sure if she'll develop any abilities at all. She only took the pills for one day before she was in a car accident with her family, but we have her anyway. We've got Benjamin Grant; he's a dangerous one. Very strong, and we're not sure what all he can do yet but he's had a full three days of taking the pills so he may be a problem if he develops any superhuman abilities like the others, but he seems content and we have him. We also have David Hodges; he took the pills for two days before he had an asthma attack and collapsed into a coma. We're picking him up from the hospital now. And we have Alfred Freeman. He's military."

"What?" Secretary Gates asked, keying in. "Military? High school ROTC or something like that?" he guessed.

"Exactly, ROTC, and he's enrolled for early placement for Army special forces. We've been told he's a team player, very sharp, cooperative, and very responsive to command. He's had three full days taking the doctor's pills but still hasn't developed any noticeable skills that he could tell us about other than some improved dexterity and some near superhuman skills on the gun range. Those are the ones we have contained, mostly the ones with minimal power."

"And who's still off the leash?" asked Fisk.

"The witch, Rain Bryant, and the ones she's sheltering there with her at the doctor's office. Of course Sky, the flying girl, is with her and the witch's twin brother, Ryan Bryant. Ryan's taken the pills for three days now and hasn't developed any abilities at all. He's apparently too mentally stable to be able to get anything out of the pills. Just not crazy enough. Then there are the two teens who have changed themselves into vampires. Jane Miller and Dan Simmons."

"You have *got* to be shitting me!" said Lansing. "They're not real vampires."

Reese replied back grimly, "I don't know, she sure looked like a vampire to me and I only saw her and her 'mate' for a second before I ran like hell. As it turned out, that was the smartest thing I've done in a long time. Major Tom Benistin is one of the toughest men I've ever met in my life. He's been in there dealing with all of them for hours now and when I debriefed him in person before he got into the helicopter to follow the motorcade he told me a thing or two about these pretend vampires, Mr. Lansing."

Reese paused to glare at Lansing, who was staring at the screen with an incredulous face. "Benistin said that they're so strong they can rip metal apart with their bare hands. The Major said that they're so fast it's impossible to see them move, they just 'appear' where they want to go. 'Poof.' Just like magic. And he confirmed what we already suspected. They can read minds, and they do know if you're lying or holding back information just by listening to how you say what you say. They can't eat solid food anymore, only blood, and they have bloodlust. They have to work constantly to curb their cravings to keep from eating the humans around them like a five year old would suck down a juice box. Benistin raided a nearby hospital of their supply of blood to keep them satisfied for the time being. Jane Miller and Dan Simmons were a couple, and when they started taking the pills they both changed into vampires—together. Tom thinks that the psychic abilities of the vampires are forcing the other teens to fall in love with each other, pushing them to pair up. Benistin told me that he's not afraid of the Black Witch. He said that he respects how powerful and dangerous she is, but he's not scared of her. But he said that the female vampire, Jane, was the most terrifying creature he's ever laid eyes on. He told me he was terrified of her in ways that made no sense, and what's worse, he told me *himself*," Reese stressed the word, "that he was compromised. He actually asked me to relieve him of command on the grounds of his unstable mental state."

"Relieve him of command!?" the President snapped. He'd trusted this mess to Benistin and expected him to help keep it together and get the job done. "He's scared of this girl, so he wants to go home and watch from his couch as I deal with all this shit? I don't think so!" The President sat forward in his chair, clearly upset.

"What'd you tell Benistin when he asked for an out?" Fisk asked, cutting to the chase.

"I told him hell no," Reese said grimly. "And to suck it up. He's in too deep now, and the Black Witch in particular can't deal with meeting new people. I saw that for myself, and I can tell you it wasn't a pretty picture. Apparently she has some crazy aversion to meeting strangers. And when I say crazy, I mean *crazy*. So he's in tight. We need him to stay in place. But Mr. President, you should know that Tom didn't want me to pull him out because he was scared. He had a hard time trying to explain his problem, but this is important, Mr. President, or I wouldn't belabor the point. Tom said that the girl vampire is so alluring, so unbelievably attractive, and so terrifying that something about her has broken him. Major Benistin said that he's in love with the vampire, and not in a dirty way either. He was terrified out of his mind, and at first he said it was because he thought she was going to kill him at any second, but now he's terrified because he doesn't want to displease her." Reese looked grave as he spoke, "Tom's exact words to me were, 'Sir. I'm her bitch.'"

"Whoa," Gates said, stunned. Floored. He'd know Major Benistin well enough and long enough to understand just how big a mountain just got moved for Tom to say he was someone's "*bitch*."

"Yeah. Whoa," the President echoed, looking every bit as stunned as Gates.

Fisk blew it off and kept driving. "So what'd you tell him when he told you the girl owned his ass?" he asked, all business.

"I told him to do his best, try to stay away from the vampire if he could, and to get his ass back in there!"

"Good," said Fisk, relieved. "Same thing would probably happen to any man we sent in there if this girl's got enough juice to wash a man like Tom down the drain. We need to rethink this. Any man we send in would probably end up as this girl's 'bitch' so maybe we should send in some females."

Reese nodded. "I'm already working on some names; let me know if you have some preference."

"We could always send in Hillary," the President said with a smile, half joking, half serious. She'd already decided not to make a bid for the 2016 election, but with things as unsettled as they were—that could change. This mess with these kids would most likely be a difficult situation with no happy endings and nothing to show for the risk but egg on your face once it was all said and done. If nothing else, he thought, it would keep her too busy to make any election plans.

Fisk laughed, "You sadistic bastard. She just might do it."

"She's the Secretary of State! You can't send her in there!" Lansing was shocked, but he was smiling like a naughty kid at the wild thought of it.

"Hillary's a tough old broad, mentally tough, which is what we need," said Reese seriously. "It just might work, sir."

Gates was laughing. "One way or another, Hillary's bound to make an impression. She should get a fair amount of respect right off the bat and may be able to get shit done that even Tom wouldn't have been able to make happen. The only question is, can you keep her under control?"

The President's head tilted to the side as he considered it. "For all the pissing and moaning Bill does I've got to give Hillary credit for being a team player so far. Course there's always a first time for a knife in the back, but I doubt she'd do it with this, it's too serious a situation."

"Hell, let's do it!" said Fisk standing up from his chair. "If nothing else she should be flattered we thought enough of her to ask, and the difficulties of sending in a man and our need of a high ranking female with the ability to command is all the pretext we need to cover our ass if she gets sucked dry by a vampire or killed by the witch. Hell, maybe Hillary can get this shit put back in the drawer where it belongs and bring this whole damn thing back into a manageable mess. If she screws it up, we get recognition for trying. Who could blame us if it goes down in flames? The situation called for a commanding, powerful woman. 'She fits the bill,'" Fisk said matter of factly. "And if she pulls it off, we still get the credit for being confident enough to use our power players in daring ways. It's perfect."

David Lansing carried the thought forward, "And if she does get the wild idea to get into the race it would be difficult for her to criticize your handling of the situation if she's smack dab in the middle of the situation. It takes the whole thing off the table, for good or bad. If it's good, it's good for both. If it's bad, it's egg on her face too."

That more than decided it. "Let's do it," said the President. "Who's calling Hillary?" He followed that by saying, "Not me."

"Not me," said Gates.

"Not me," said Fisk.

"Not me," said Stan Reese's image on the video screen.

"Dammit." David Lansing threw his pen down onto his notepad. Usually there were more people in the room when the countdown started.

Fisk laughed, "That's what you get for drinking decaf, you schmuk. You're too damn slow!"

Ryan Bryant

An Unexpected Truth

We watched as Rain walked up to the wall in the waiting room and pressed the palm of her hand flat to the neutral beige paint. The area around her hand seemed to melt and reform until the flat featureless drywall reshaped itself into a doorway, complete with doorknob, metal hinges, and wood frame. She turned back with an easy smile, her alien bug-like eyes still black as night as she called out to me.

"Ryan! Come on, you go through and make sure everything is cool. This opens to the church. Just take a quick look around and come right back, and if you're not back in five minutes—ten minutes at most—I'll send Dan to go find you."

I gave her a puzzled frown. "What about the limo they got out front?" I asked. "We just gonna let it sit out there or what?"

Rain laughed. "No. We're taking the limo too, but not all of us." She gave me a shove toward the door and said, "Just go take a quick peek around and check things out over there and try not to let anyone see you because they'll try to talk your ear off and you don't have time for that."

"But I don't get it." I looked at the door Rain had just made. "If this opens to the church, forget the limo, let's just go through the door. It's quicker."

"Just do this my way, Bro," Rain said. "Trust the witch within me; she has her reasons." She just stood there looking at me with her solid black eyes. It gave me the chills. Her hair was still dancing around her shoulders and she had that "high" or "messed up" look on her face that I was pretty sure was from the pills Dr. Burgis had given her. The last thing Rain needed right now was to be spaced out on those pills; she was crazy enough just dealing with being a witch and everything else she'd been through today without having to deal with the pills too.

I gave her a last worried look before reaching for the handle. I turned back before I opened the door.

"Hey, Sis, where does this open up to anyway?" I asked.

"Upstairs hallway," she answered. "That little closet where they keep all the holiday crap. Nobody ever uses that door and it's always unlocked and out of the way. Plus it should be pretty empty up there, unless the place is packed for Jane and Dan's wedding."

Jane and Dan appeared beside us out of nowhere. "The wedding we're super late for," Jane said, like she'd been in on our whole conversation. "We were supposed to get married at five and it's six thirty, so let someone there know that the wedding—" Jane paused and looked at me and then Rain and gave us a smile with her scary white teeth, "Or let them know that the weddingssss will start soon, so people will know we're on our way."

My eyes almost popped out of my head as I remembered what we were all about to do—GET MARRIED!

"OH CRAP! Dad's there at the church. What if he grabs me? What do you want me to do?" I asked Rain.

"If dad grabs you just bring him with you when you come back through the door. Tell him I want to see him. He'll come. Now scoot, get things ready and come right back."

I nodded and glanced outside through the glass windows. Sky was still outside somewhere fixing up her Dragon and making him "travel sized" but I wished she were here. I wanted to tell her I'd be right back. And I wanted her back inside where it was safer.

"Tell Sky I'll be right back," I said.

Rain and Jane both laughed at me. Two aliens—my sister with her black eyes laughing out her crazy spooky witch laugh that made my skin crawl and Jane with her purple/red eyes, pale skin and shiny teeth laughing her musical crazy laugh right at me.

"Good grief!" I grabbed the handle and opened the door.

I expected it to be there but I still was shocked to actually see it with my eyes. I stood there "freaked out" for a second or two. On the other side of the door was the inside of our church auditorium. There was a narrow hall wrapping around the top of the balcony and ten rows of seats tiered down to the balcony rail that overlooked the main church hall. I saw only about twenty or thirty people sitting up here, and no one seemed to have noticed me standing in the closet or that the doorway now opened to another room behind me.

"Way cool," I said with a grin. I turned back and looked at my sister. "If I'm not back in ten minutes that means I'm in trouble, so send Dan for me," I told her.

It felt weird not having to see Dan as the bad guy anymore but things had changed. And the more I thought about it the better I felt about the way everything had come together. Jane was way too "alien" for me now, and I was even starting to believe what Rain had told me about herself when she said she wasn't human anymore. Neither of them seemed human!

Give me Sky, my nice, sweet, God-fearing, normal (HUMAN) flying girl over the alien crazies laughing at me right now, I thought. Dan was standing beside Jane and he smiled at me and gave me a thumbs up. I wondered how much of what had just flashed through my head he'd picked up on as I turned and stepped into the church, shutting the door behind me.

Probably all of it.

I scanned the balcony again, and this time I noticed the soldiers. Two soldiers stood at the top of each side riser. Their eyes scanned back and forth over the crowd below. They didn't look hostile but appeared to be placed here to keep everyone safe. The balcony was sparsely populated, but the main floor of the auditorium was packed. There were more soldiers downstairs as well but nothing looked strained or out of sorts. Everything appeared to be on the up and up. Good to go for the wedding.

The church was decorated in somber tones of red, black, and white. I quickly took this in and then walked around the balcony to the door leading to the AV room. There were two big white screens on each side of the church platform that we used during our congregational worship singing. We would project the words of the songs onto the screens so we didn't have to use hymnals anymore and everyone could just sing along with our music minister. Right now the two

screens had a basic text message with some simple clip art of a bride and groom at the altar. The text message read:

```
Welcome to the Wedding of Jane Hellena Miller
and Dan Kent Simmons.
Friends & Family of the Bride to your left.
Friends & Family of the Groom to the right.
The wedding will begin shortly. Thank You.
Carson Road Faith Baptist Church
```

I was relieved to find the AV room empty and quickly slipped into the seat in front of the sound board equipment and computer screens. I'd helped with the sound room many times and it was no problem to reset the message on the two big screens. I typed away and set my message but put the change on a delay. I wanted to be off and gone before the new message began to rotate on the screen and freak everyone out.

As I looked at it I freaked out a little myself, seeing what was about to be on the screen right there in front of everyone I knew and my Mom and Dad. The message was in two parts; I set them to rotate every three minutes.

```
Please be aware that there will now be three wed-
dings this evening. Thank you for celebrating the
marriages of:
Jane Hellena Miller & Dan Kent Simmons
Sky Lee Han & Ryan Everet Bryant
Black Rain & Believer
```

After three minutes the screen would rotate to the rest of the message:

```
Jane and Dan will be arriving shortly, about fifteen
minutes from now. They are sorry for the delay and
ask that you would forgive them. The wedding(s)
will start as soon as they arrive so please take
your seats.
If you're not here for the wedding(s), please take
these next few moments as an opportunity to excuse
yourself. If you do plan to stay for the wedding(s)
please remain seated through all three wedding
services. Thank you.
```

I just couldn't bring myself to spring this on Mom and Dad without telling them what was going on first, or at least letting them meet Sky and see that she was a good girl. If I tried to slip downstairs into the crowd to find them, everyone I knew would start the hundred questions game and I wouldn't be able to get anywhere. But then my brain kicked in and I thought, *I'll just have them come to me.*

I reached down and grabbed a mike we used for announcements and adjusted it to be heard through the whole church. "Would Mr. and Mrs. Bryant please come to the balcony AV room. Mr. and Mrs. Bryant to the balcony AV room."

I turned the mike off and I hit enter on my new message for the projection screens and quickly slipped out of the AV room to wait for Mom and Dad. I hoped they handled this well, but at the same time, I doubted it. This was going to be ugly with a capital "UG!" There wasn't any easy way to do this. I didn't know what they would say when they saw how Rain looked now or what they would say about Believer. And as freaked out as they would be over Rain, I was in hot water too, with wanting to get married to Sky.

And I did want to get married, even if it was crazy to get married to someone I had just met. I'd prayed about it, and I had peace about my decision. I was ready. And Sky was fun, sweet, and amazing, and she loved God, and for some strange reason she loved me too. And she was actually a HUMAN girl. My world had gotten so weird that finding a "human girl" was actually getting hard to do.

It didn't take long for Dad to show up. I spotted him running up the side riser, causing the two soldiers positioned at the top of the stair to come to life. They grabbed him for a second and made sure he was unarmed before letting him go. Dad didn't look happy as he walked up to me.

"Ryan, how'd you get up here and where's your sister?" he asked, then added, "and where's your mother!?"

That surprised me. "Mom's not here?" By habit I reached to my front pocket for my phone to call Mom, but then I remembered that Rain had turned my phone into a ring for Sky. I was phoneless.

"No. She's not here," Dad said, not happy. "I don't know where she is! And her phone's not working."

"Our phones are crapped out too. But come on, Dad, follow me, I'll take you to Rain." I scanned the crowd to make sure we weren't being watched then opened the closet doorway. I rushed in with Dad right on my heels and closed the door as soon as we were inside the waiting room.

Rain was in the middle of the room, talking to Believer, Sky, and another cloud creature that had to be the new, man-sized version of her dragon. He was about six feet tall and had a head that looked more like a dragon's head than a man's head. Both of the cloud men turned and looked in our direction as we stepped into the room. The Dragon's eyes were burning red dots, just like Believer's eyes.

"Rain!" Dad shouted as soon as he saw her. She spun around at the sound of his voice and looked at both of us.

"Hi Daddy," Rain said and smiled at him. At us. She didn't look like herself at all. Actually, she looked like more of a monster than the two giant cloud men standing with her. Her eyes were still black as night and her hair and the bottom of her dress danced around mysteriously all on their own. Her black dress, shiny black nails, and the feeling of power pouring off of her was so overwhelming that it took my breath away.

Having a chance to get away from her and her power for a few minutes allowed me come back to earth. Those few minutes away had brought my world closer to reality. But Rain wasn't "real" anymore. She told me earlier that she wasn't a real person anymore, that she had become a living fantasy, and though I didn't understand it, I was starting to believe it. Just being in her presence seemed to make the real world come unglued. Dad and I were both dumb struck, un-moving, as Rain walked over like nothing had changed and she was just herself. She slipped her arms around Dad and gave him a good squeeze.

"Hey Daddy. Thanks for coming," I heard Rain say just before I got tackled by Sky.

"Ryan, I was so worried!" Sky said as she hugged the life out of me and made me laugh.

"My Sky!" I told her as I wrapped my arms around her. Dad looked from me to Rain, confused as to just where to start, but then he got caught looking down into Rain's black eyes and that put her first in line for the grilling.

"Honey, what happened to your eyes?" he asked her.

Rain was looking up at him as he looked down at her and studied her face. The concern and stress and anguish of everything marked my father's face with deep lines that looked deeper and more set than I'd ever seen before. He stud-ied Rain's face carefully, her eyes, her hair, how pale her skin was, her nails, her bloodless pale blue lips. She gave him a minute to take it in, letting him examine her before she spoke.

"Dad. Please don't be mad at me, but my powers got too strong and I couldn't hold it inside me anymore—and then I made some mistakes and I end-ed up making things worse and—" Rain closed her black eyes and started to cry.

Dad held her while she cried and stroked her hair, almost like he was trying to get the crazy stuff to lie back down and act like normal hair. It wasn't cooper-ating.

"Dad. I want you to meet Sky," I said while I could. And to give Rain a chance to get a grip. Dad looked over at me and looked at Sky who was attached to me, pressing her face right up against mine while her arms squeezed the life out of my middle.

"Hello, Sky. I take it you know Ryan pretty well," Dad said with a small smile as he studied the two of us together.

"Yes, sir. We met here at the doctor's office. It's really good to meet you." Sky wore a huge smile, which was so strange, especially with Rain right there crying in Dad's arms. It seemed out of place and more than a little crazy.

"Yes, good to meet you too." Dad looked at me, then looked back over to the two cloud men who'd come closer to us, their glowing red eyes studying us curiously.

"What are they, Ryan?" Dad asked quietly, as he eyed the two monsters with worry. And that unfroze Rain.

"Oh! Sorry Dad." She stepped back from his arms and turned and put an arm out toward Believer who "step/glided" up and took her claw-like talon of a hand in his own cloudy hand.

"Dad, I want you to meet Believer," Rain said with a huge happy smile, her face still wet from all the tears, and the tears made her look like an impossible contradiction against herself, a happy, crying impossibility. It made her look crazy.

"Hello. It is an honor to meet you, sir," Believer said with his deep, powerful, rumbling voice, his slit of a mouth opening and closing as he spoke. Red burning eyes stared down from his towering height of seven feet plus. Clouds rolled and tumbled within his body, held together by some unseen power which held him in a basic man-shaped form. In the center of his chest was a denser group of brighter clouds pulsing in time with the storms inside him.

Dad was getting very good at handling weird. He spoke right back to the monster. "It's good to meet you too, Believer."

Believer smiled with his slit of a mouth. "Mr. Bryant. I know you must be wondering what I am. My appearance is odd and I know that I look like a monster, but I would never hurt your daughter. I love her. Please, don't be worried, I will watch over her and take care of her and love her." Dad was looking more disturbed each second, and Believer could see it too. He looked over to Sky, "Please tell him for us, my Sky. I think he will need to hear the story from someone who is human."

Rain slipped the rest of the way from Dad's arms and wrapped both her arms around Believer, burying herself into his cloudy form. Dad's eyebrows pulled together in an upset suspicious line; I could tell he wanted to grab her away from the monster that had her in its clutches. A monster that Rain looked very happy to be held by at that moment as she smiled up at him contentedly.

"What's going on here!?" He demanded, then glared at us as he waited for someone to speak up.

"Mr. Bryant. I am Sky," she said. "I'm not a witch like Rain but I have powers of my own. I 'made' Believer. And I 'made' Sky Dragon, his brother. They are people, and they have souls, and they are real, just like us."

"*That* has a soul?" Dad said as he looked at the creature who was holding onto his daughter.

"Yes. He does," said Sky confidently.

Dad looked over to Sky. "Only God can make souls," he replied firmly.

"Oh I know that!" Sky answered happily with a smile. "I didn't make a new soul, that's impossible. God made me and made my soul; all I did was tear off a little piece of my own soul and then I used that part of 'me' to make him. Now Believer and Sky Dragon are their own persons. They are real people and they each have their own little souls inside them."

Dad was speechless.

And that was when the vampires appeared out of nowhere. Right in front of us.

Dad handled it with the ease he handled all the weirdness. Calmly. He carefully eyed the two newcomers who had just materialized out of thin air, studying this particular new type of "monster." They were both wearing white and looked dressed for the wedding.

"Hello, Mr. Bryant," said Jane. She and Dan stood side by side holding hands. "My name is Jane and this is Dan. We're the ones that are very late for our wedding at your church." Jane looked at Sky and Rain.

"Guys, can I try to explain? This could take all day if we do this the normal human way and we don't have all day." She waited until Rain nodded and Sky said "okay."

Jane turned back to Dad, who was looking trapped and surrounded. I could tell he wanted to grab me and Rain and run for the "closet" but I had a six foot, beautiful, crazy blond wrapped around me in a death grip and Rain was in the arms of a monster.

Made it difficult to cut and run.

"Here it is." Jane stepped closer to Dad, demanding his attention by the power of her voice. "This is going to be quick and ugly. Are you ready to hear the 'truth' about where we are, and what has happened, and what is about to happen?" She waited while Dad thought for a second.

"Yes," he said.

"This is going to be hard to hear so brace yourself, Mr. Bryant. And listen fast, okay?" Jane was serious as a heart attack, and we all got quiet as she spoke to Dad, telling him quickly about the drugs and how they changed us. How it all started with the pills. This was the first time I'd heard the whole story about the drugs myself and I found myself wondering why I hadn't had any weird reactions to the pills but I quickly got sucked back into the story as Jane went on.

She told Dad about the other kids in the study and how most of them had changed, then she told him how she and Dan had changed into vampires because of the books she'd been reading when she had started the pills. Jane even explained how they would die tonight and rise again as undead immortals. Dad looked skeptical but Jane kept going, not wasting a split second or a word as she laid it all out there, summing it up quickly and completely. She told Dad about Rain burning to death, dying, and coming back from the ashes, and even pointed to the darkened spot on the floor with the burnt carpet. And she told Dad that Rain wasn't human anymore.

"So are you with me up to this point, Mr. Bryant?" she asked. Dad's eyes were wide with shock, but he nodded.

"Good." She gave Dad an evil, mischievous smile. "Because now I have to tell you some really scary stuff. Are you ready?" Dan bumped her shoulder like he didn't approve of what she was doing.

"What?" Jane looked back at Dan, all innocent looking now. "I'm a vampire, Dan, I like scary stories," Jane complained then started again without another breath.

"Your son, Ryan, is going to get married today to Sky. And your daughter is going to get married to Believer. Believer loves Rain and she loves him. Ryan loves Sky and she loves him. Now we are out of time and we've got to go, so if you're going to freak out please do it now and get it out of the way."

Jane had taken less than five minutes to tell the whole thing and now she stepped back with a self-satisfied, smug look on her face. She was obviously glad she'd sped things up and laid it all out there instead of waiting on the back and forth of normal human conversation. She really was impatient now that she was all vampy.

Dad looked at me. "Ryan, are you two planning to get married today?" he asked me. He was expecting me to say this was all a big misunderstanding.

"Yes, sir," I answered. "I love her, Dad. And yes, I have prayed about this decision and I've got peace about it. Sky is a good girl and she loves God." Right at that moment Sky's arms tightened up on me and I looked down at her as I spoke to Dad. "She can do some amazing things with her powers, Dad, but she's still a normal, human girl. And I love her."

"What church does she go to, Ryan?" Dad asked me. He had a smile now, which was good to see.

I didn't know. I looked at Sky.

"I like to go to any church," she said, "but when I was in Hong Kong my nanny was a Chinese Catholic nun. She taught me most of what I know about God. And all about the Bible."

Dad was stumped by that. "Really?" He scratched at his chin as he took that in. "A Chinese Catholic nun?"

"Uh huh," Sky affirmed with a wide-eyed nod.

"I didn't even know there were Chinese Catholic nuns," Dad said with a grin.

Sky smiled big. "Oh, there are a lot of them."

Dad laughed a little and studied Sky for another minute, and her smile fell away to worry under Dad's weighing stare. "And do you love God, Sky. And my son?" Dad asked her.

Sky hugged me tighter as she answered, "Oh yes! I love God and, and–and I love Ryan." Sky was getting very nervous. "Please–Please let us get married! I know we haven't waited a long time and we haven't done–done all the things normal people do—" She looked back and forth from me to Dad, "I don't even know what people are supposed to do, but this is different, this is right for us. Please, please, let us get married!" Sky begged, which surprised me but not as much as what Sky did next. Sky slipped out of my arms and dropped to her knees right there in front of my Dad with her head bowed and went all still. Waiting.

"I promise I will love God and I promise I will love Ryan with all my heart. Please, sir, let me have him. I need someone to love me and take care of me," Sky said this with her head still bowed. The way she held herself was very Asian, formal, and beautiful.

Watching her as she knelt there made me feel like a simple country bumpkin. One of the things I loved about Sky was that she loved to talk even more than me, but the more she talked about her life the less I felt like I actually deserved her. Sky told me about how much she had traveled with her family and how she never went to school but always had private tutors and that she could speak six languages. And Sky's family was super rich and we were trailer park people. On top of that, Sky was so smart and—I *wasn't*. That this amazing, beautiful girl saw anything in me worth begging for made me want to turn inside out.

I joined her on the floor, kneeling there beside her. Not nearly so graceful but just as sincere. I reached over and took her hand.

"And I promise I will love God and I promise I will love my Sky with all my heart. Please let me have her. I need someone to love me and take care of me."

I bowed my head like Sky and held my breath. We waited. I didn't know what I'd do if Dad said no.

"Then you two have my blessing."

What was that? Did he just..?

Sky hugged me, squeezing the life from me! She released, then quickly jumped up and hugged Dad which made him laugh as he fought for a breath of air. Girl didn't know her own strength!

Some of the others in the room who had been quietly listening laughed as they watched Sky's exuberance, but the happy feelings were short lived for my father. Once he stepped away he turned toward Rain.

"Daddy," Rain said from her hiding place deep inside Believer's arms.

"Baby," Dad said as he looked at her. "Tell me about when you died," he asked.

"It was lonely," Rain said as she snuggled herself deeper into Believer's arms, almost hiding completely within his clouds.

"Are you sure you died, honey? If you really died you would have gone to heaven. You know that," Dad said, trying to comfort her.

"No, Daddy. Not for me. And I didn't go to hell either when I died, but I don't really want to talk about all that. It's not something I want to think about. It makes me sad," she said simply.

Dad looked at Rain for a second then spun around and looked back at Sky.

"You made Believer?" he asked her again. Sky nodded, wide eyed.

"What kind of creature is he? What will he do with Rain, and what exactly is he? Is he dangerous?" Dad asked, like he expected some answers.

Sky answered but with a little of her own backbone coming back, her submissiveness vanished as quickly as it arrived. She was talking about something she was confident in and her friends were parts of her life. And soul.

"I made Believer. As I said, he has a piece of my soul which is now his own. When I made him I made him good and smart and honest and kind, and he is all those things, but he is also his own person and can make his own choices. He's already surprised me with how much of his own person he is. I am proud of him and happy with the life he has chosen." Sky spared a moment to send a warm smile to Believer and he smiled back at her worshipfully.

"Believer wants and thinks for himself," she continued. "And he wants to love and take care of Rain. As for what he is made of, I made him from clouds, soul, and love which is not that different from what God made us from. Believer is a living cloud and I made him a man so he could love your daughter. He is a son of my soul. I am Sky."

And before Dad could respond to that Jane appeared right in the middle of everyone again.

"We all good now?" She gave Mr. Bryant a short look with an implied YES, then back to Rain. "Rain. Sorry, I hate to be all pushy, but we have to go," she said simply.

"Ryan, how were things at the church?" Rain asked, also sounding like she was ready to get down to business as she slipped out of Believer's arms.

"Good to go," I told her. "They have some soldiers there for security. Four guys in the balcony area keeping an eye on everyone and a bunch of others downstairs. Everything looked peaceful and Jane and Dan have a good crowd there for the wedding. I snuck into the sound booth and changed the message on the screen to let everyone know that there would be three weddings today instead of one. Then I used the intercom to call Dad upstairs. I was there and gone and nobody even saw me, not even the soldiers." I thought it was a pretty cool accomplishment.

"I might not have magic and stuff but I got finesse." I gave my sister my best smile.

"Yeah, yeah" was Rain's response to my hamming it up. She looked around the room and her eyes settled on Dad. He looked like he still wanted to argue about her and her plans to marry the cloud.

"I will marry Believer today, Father." Rain wasn't going to ask for permission like we had. She was telling Dad how it was going to be whether he liked it or not. "He makes me happy. He's polite and helpful and kind. He accepts me the way I am, and he reminds me that there is still good in me when I get depressed and think all I have left is darkness. And I love the way he holds me. I will not deny my soul what joy I can find in what my life has become. I will enjoy this dream while it lasts, Father." Rain's voice changed and power rolled off her body in fresh force making her hair flail about as she spoke, "I am the Fantasy come to life. Black is my color and my name is Black Rain. Let the Black Witch now rise."

Rain put her arms out and nine chairs that had been set along one side of the room all moved at once, forming a line in the middle of the room; three of the chairs were occupied. Dr. Burgis, Agent Trisha, and a surprised Mr. Miller all gripped the arms of their chairs and held on for dear life as they slid forward a few feet along with six other chairs.

"Jane, Dan, Sky, Ryan, you guys take a seat with the others," Rain ordered. "Believer, you and Sky Dragon too. Grab a seat please."

There was some worried conversation about what she was planning to do, but everyone reluctantly shuffled their way to the chairs. Rain walked to the front door of the office and pulled Williams back inside. She'd placed him out front to keep everyone away but now she directed him into one of the chairs.

"What on earth are you doing? You're not going to turn these things into flying chairs and make us fly there are you, cause I'm scared of heights." Williams made a pained face as he hesitantly lowered his bottom into one of the lined up chairs.

"Why am I not surprised?" Rain said. "Don't worry, I'm not going to make you fly to the church in a chair."

"What are you going to do?" Jane asked, curiously. She still hadn't sat down.

Rain gave her half a smile. "What, Jane, you really can't tell?" Rain's half smile turned into wicked Chesher grin as she shouted triumphantly, "HA! You'll just have to be surprised along with everyone else, you *vampire!*" Rain laughed as Jane grumped and dropped into the chair in front of a laughing Dan who was already seated.

"What about me?" Dad asked Rain.

"Shhh," Rain shushed him. "Doing magic here, Daddy. You're just going back through the closet; you don't need a chair." Rain went from chair to chair, walking down the line, touching each person's head and then running her hand down the back of each chair. She even did Sky Dragon and Believer, running her hand down their cloudy heads and on down the back of their chairs. As she did me I felt a tingle of magic and power in her hand and an odd sense of deja vu. Like I was in two places at once for a brief second.

"That's all I needed. Everyone is now free to go to the wedding," Rain announced happily, then looked at Believer.

"Believer, my love, please keep a close eye on the doctor for me and don't let anyone hurt him or take him or his bags. He has the pills and we don't want the soldiers to get them."

"Gladly, my lady," Believer said with a nod of his huge head. Rain gave him a smile and turned back to me.

"Ryan, go tell the soldiers that we're coming through the doorway so they don't freak out when they see Sky Dragon and Believer, or Jane and Dan for that matter, they're pretty scary if they appear out of nowhere. Oh! Before you go." She looked over at Sky and her clothes shifted and changed right on her body, transforming into an elegant white wedding dress that sparkled, it was so white.

"Hey!" Sky shouted, alarmed until she looked down and saw the dress. She ran her hand over the satiny fabric.

"Oh. Yeah. Thanks!" Amazingly, she wasn't freaked out. Like transforming clothes was no big deal. And then my own clothes were changing and I looked down to see that I was wearing white leather pants and some crazy feeling ultra white button up shirt with long sleeves. It wasn't a suit, but it would work. The leather pants were a bit out there and were kind of snug. The whole get up made me smile. Rain and her clothes.

"Thanks, Sis. It's great," I said with a smirk.

"Shoes, Rain! I need shoes!" Sky pointed down at her brown flats. They became some white strappy pumps.

"Thanks!" Sky said. I felt my own shoes change. I resisted the urge to look at what I was wearing and added my own "Yeah. Thanks, Sis" with a laugh.

I gave Sky a quick hug and headed toward the door. I overheard Trisha ask Rain a question as I passed by. "Is there anything you can't do?"

I paused, waiting to see what she would say.

"Just one thing that I can think of, Trisha," Rain said sadly. "One thing that you can do that I can't. Not with all my power, not if I tried for a million years."

"What's that?" Trisha pressed, too curious to leave it alone.

"Go to heaven when I die."

Trisha looked mortified and sorry she'd asked. "Oh," she said and quickly slunk away.

Dad went over and hugged Rain, and she started to cry again. My stomach hurt just thinking about it.

Jane and Dan were standing by the closet door, ready to go.

"I'll go get the soldiers up to speed. I'll only need five, then bring everyone on through."

Jane smiled at me. "Okay. Thanks, Ryan." She gave me a weird look. "Strange how it turned out, isn't it. I ended up at your church on Wednesday after all. Just like you wanted."

"Huh?" I said, with my hand on the closet door. "What are you talking about, Jane?"

"When you first met me," Jane explained. "You invited me to come to church this Wednesday, and it's just such a crazy wild coincidence that we ended up here. Dan said that he called twenty-seven churches before he called yours and none of them would let him rent the hall this Wednesday no matter how much money he offered them. It's just strange that we ended up here." Jane's eyes tightened up a little. "Don't worry about it," she said.

I tried to wrap my head around it. "Yeah. That is strange, isn't it?" Our church had been praying for a last five thousand dollars to come in so we could buy a new piece of land and Dan renting the hall was a huge answer to our prayers. But it still seemed so strange that Dan would end up being the one to be the answer to our prayers.

But then I remembered that I had prayed for Jane to come to church to-night. And not just Jane. I remember that I'd prayed for Dr. Burgis and Sky to come to church too. I looked across the room to where Dr. Burgis sat, happy and smiling in his chair. I looked over to Sky as she talked with Sky Dragon. Just like I prayed. Everything I had prayed for was happening. I had prayed for them to be in church and somehow, through a hundred little things happening all throughout the day in impossible ways, here they were, about to be in my church on Wednesday.

I had powers.

"I'm so sorry," Jane said. "I said too much." She looked like she was about to cry. Dan and Jane looked at each other for a second, then Dan led Jane away, both walking slowly, heads down.

I opened the closet and stepped through into my church in my own con-fused daze, still not quite accepting what I knew had to be true.

"Ryan!" Mr. Louwerra charged up to me. "What's all this about you getting married today!? And your sister!? And who on earth is this Believer? We don't know if we want your sister getting married in this church, Ryan. There's been a lot of talk, and some of the deacons have been—"

"Mr. Louwerra!" I cut in. "How is Mr. Denton feeling?"

Mr. Louwerra looked surprised by the question. "You don't know? He's healed! He's here tonight. They're calling it a miracle healing. None of the doctors can believe it." He looked out at the congregation and pointed down below. "There he is, fourth row."

I looked down at the man that had been on his death bed just yesterday, struggling with terminal stomach cancer. I had prayed that he would be healed last night, and here he was, smiling, happy. Here.

"What's the matter with you, Ryan?" Mr. Louwerra frowned. "You should be happy and praising God but you look like you just saw a ghost. What's wrong?"

"Nothing, sir." I stepped away. "Excuse me, I don't feel well." I didn't feel well at all.

"Oh. If you're sick, are you still going to go through with it and get married?" He looked at my clothes and I looked down too. I had forgot about my crazy white outfit and white leather pants. And good grief! Rain had given me white boots with metal spikes! METAL SPIKES! Good Lord. I looked back at him.

"Yeah. I'm still getting married. And so is Rain. She's been at this church since before she was born, and if the deacons don't want her to ever come back to church here again that's fine, but they can still let her get married."

Mr. Louwerra started shaking his head. "I don't know Ryan. That's not what they're saying."

I got mad. "They let perfect strangers come in off the street and get married! People that don't even go to church here! If they can do that for strangers then they can do it for my sister who was here nine months before she could breathe air outside our mother!"

I pushed away from him and went to the soldiers, ignoring all the people who started to crowd me and my white gothic wedding get-up. I told the soldiers to clear an area around the closet door, that the wedding party would be arriving through a magic portal created by my sister the Black Witch.

I was surprised to see them jump to and move like they actually believed every word I told them. As soon as I was sure that things in the balcony would be safe for the others to come through, I ran past all the grasping hands and shouted questions to the nearest bathroom, threw open the stall door, and threw my guts up. I tried not to get any of it on me or on my whites.

Five or six men had followed me into the bathroom and were asking me if I was okay from outside my stall. Partially digested pieces of pizza stared up at me from the bowl.

I thought about the other times I'd prayed. For Officer Williams to get better when he was sick. For Rain to stay calm when that guy was yelling on his bullhorn. For the church to get the money for the land.

It was me.

Not God.

"God help me," I said and threw up again.

Black Rain

The Phoenix

Jane and Dan stepped through the doorway first, followed by Agent Trisha, Mr. Miller, and Williams.

Sky gave me a hug and almost squeezed me in two.

"I won't be long," I told her. "Don't let them start without me, okay? Stall. Tell 'em I'll be there shortly."

"I don't understand why you're not coming with us right now," Sky said with her strong arms still around me, like she was thinking of just hauling me away against my will. That she cared about me made me that much more determined to do what I was doing.

"I agree. I do not understand this," Believer rumbled. "If you insist on riding in the limo then you should not go alone. Someone should go with you, my lady."

"Yes. Let Believer go with you," Dad said. He hadn't gone back through the closet yet either.

Seeing that I was being ganged up on, Sky relented and let go. "Be careful then," she said, "and hurry." She walked through the closet with Sky Dragon leaving only Dad, Believer, and a waiting Dr. Burgis who I'd told to stay close to Believer for his own safety.

I let the guys watch while I worked. Earlier, when I ran my hand down everyone's head and down the back of each chair I made each chair remember the soul of the person that had sat in it. The soul and the shape and the character. I looked back at the chairs now and held my hands out and willed the chairs to change, calling on that memory and that lingering flavor in each. I wasn't making new life or copies; I was making shadows with substance. Memories that would look and walk and move like the real things, but were not actually living souls. As I and the others watched, the nine chairs changed, broke apart and stretched out, and I poured my concentration and power into forming what I wanted.

Where the chairs had stood a moment ago now stood nine perfect copies of the people who had sat in the chairs. Like synced robots they looked over to me at the same time, and I pointed to the front door and issued my instructions.

"GO! Wait for me outside the front door." And without a word they marched outside. The copy of Officer Williams held the door open as the others passed through. Each of my shadows moved like the person they'd been shaped from, mannerisms and facial expressions a match for the soul that had sat in each chair.

"Astounding!" said Dr. Burgis as he watched a perfect copy of himself walk out the front door. Complete in every way except for the suitcases and painting that the real doctor still clutched in his arms.

"Is it really a copy of me? And of everyone else!?" he asked, amazed.

"No, doctor," I answered. "These are shadows and fleeting memories. They're nothing but a mirage with a small bit of substance and a limited understanding. They are decoys."

I stepped over and hugged Believer. "Go now my love. I'll be there soon. I just want to make it as safe as I can for everyone."

Believer's eyes became a hotter red, mood lines darkening around his eyes as he gazed down at me. His upset stare didn't hurt my heart this time because I knew I was doing the right thing. I was trying to protect him.

"You are trying to draw attention away from us and your friends. You believe there will be an attack and you are using yourself and these shadows you have made as bait," Believer accused in his rumbling voice. "I do not approve of this, my love." He wasn't happy at all.

"Neither do I!" Dad all but shouted. "Listen to Believer, I don't think you should do this. Just send the copies you made. Or make a copy of yourself and send that, but I don't want you to go in the limo if you think something's going to happen to it."

Dad had stepped closer to Believer. They were side by side now. It was funny to watch both of them on the same side of an argument, but I didn't have the time to appreciate it in the way I would have liked to.

"The copies won't work without me there to move them and make them work. And I need to be there to make sure whoever is going to do this doesn't do it again." I didn't have any idea who was going to do what or how it was going to happen, but I was sure, absolutely positive, that something bad was waiting for me out in that limo.

"I am afraid for you!" Believer rumbled desperately. He looked like he was going to cry again and that did hurt my heart.

I tried to stay strong, time mattered now for some reason. I didn't know why but I could feel it. My dad and Believer stood side by side as I spoke to both of them. "Dad, you're human, and you can die," I told him flatly, then I looked up at Believer, into his upset glowing red eyes. "Your beautiful Sky, my Sister, is a human and she can die. Ryan, my brother, is human. Even you and Sky Dragon can be killed, my lovely living cloud. I, on the other hand—cannot. I am 'Other.'"

I stepped away from his outstretched arms as he tried to hug me. "I am what I am, and the least I can do is use it to make the ones I love safe. And the witch within me is guiding me, my love; I can't explain it. I'm sorry. Now go, and I'll seal the door behind you. I love you all."

I stepped a few more feet away and turned around, keeping my back to them so they couldn't see me as I struggled not to cry. I really didn't want to do this either, but I felt like I had to. The odd sense of foreboding danger I'd experienced since I had first heard of the limo ride to the church had grown into a screaming warning in my chest.

"Rain," Dad called. "I love you."

"I know. I'll be there as soon as I can, Daddy. Please go."

I heard the shuffling of feet as the last of them passed through the doorway.

I was alone. Finally. It was the first time since I'd burned and gone to that nothing place of my death that I'd been truly alone. I didn't like it. It felt like I was less alive or less real without other people around me. The people I loved.

I changed the doorway back into a featureless wall then walked outside. My copies were there waiting for me and they gathered around me as I stepped outside. They weren't talking to each other, but apart from their silence they were acting as the real versions of themselves would have. Jane and Dan were side by side with Mr. Miller, Jane's father, right beside them. Sky and Ryan were hand in hand and Sky Dragon was in a protective position behind them, scanning the area with his burning red eyes. Dr. Burgis was being guarded by Believer, and Williams and Trisha walked together.

I walked forward and they all walked with me toward the limo that waited in the distance. Tom was waiting for me by the limo, and I left my copies parked about twenty feet back and went forward to talk to Tom.

"Tom. Go get in your helicopter. Let's get going," I said.

"Sure," Tom said, but he looked confused. I knew that he must have already received word that we'd just arrived at the church through a doorway. He had men at the church so Tom knew everything, but here we were again, right in front of him. He was trying to decide whether to believe his eyes or not.

"Don't worry, Tom. It's me." I tried to reassure him, but it didn't seem to work. Tom still didn't move. He reached down and pulled his radio and spoke into it for a moment. He talked to the guys at the church and then gave me a doubtful look. It was a perfectly normal thing to do, but for some reason it pissed me off. Tom had always been pushy and now he was acting like he wanted to be difficult. I stepped closer to Tom and snapped a double take at the limo they'd provided.

"Hey, Tom," I said casually.

"Yes, Black Rain?" he answered, clearly suspicious.

"Black is my color, so why the hell did you bring me a white limo? That shows a surprising lack of sensitivity on your part. If a girl likes roses you don't bring her tulips. You don't serve a vampire water if you want to live. And you don't ask a Black Witch to ride in a white limo. Not cool." I tilted my head to the side. Tom just gave me a helpless but frustrated face.

I helped him out. I turned and screamed violently at the top of my lungs at the limo. "BLACK!"

My voice broke like a bomb, echoing across the parking lot. The limo turned blacker than the blackest night. A small peal of thunder began rolling through the sky as I wanted, background noise for my mood as I stepped up to Tom who appeared to be in a much more cooperative frame of mind as he stared into my dark orbs. His eyes actually seemed to have grown larger, his tiny irises looked unnaturally small in the big white circles. The dozen or so FBI agents nearby were all shuffling their feet nervously and trying hard to stay calm. One of them was on the ground. Perhaps he'd fainted.

"You ready to get moving, Tom? Or do you still have a problem with me?" I asked.

"No ma'am. I'm sorry," Tom snapped out, military crisp. "I'm ready to go whenever you are. The driver is ready too." He gave a wave to one of the agents standing beside the limo and the guy climbed into the driver's seat.

"Get in your helicopter, Tom. You're starting to piss me off." I turned away from him and headed toward my waiting shadows.

"Williams, get everybody loaded up!" I ordered and the Williams shadow nodded and marched over to the limo right past a few still shocked looking FBI agents.

He opened the limo door and my people started to climb in. I walked back into the group and mingled with the shadows and waited my turn to climb into our ride. The Believer shadow even smiled at me, reached out and took my hand and helped me into the limo which was nice. Even as a shadow, my love was good to me. As soon as we were all in I felt the giant limo lurched into motion and I breathed out a sign of relief.

"Good," I said out loud.

I looked around at my shadows. It was a big limo but we had totally filled it up. Believer and Sky Dragon took up a lot of space. The shadows were holding together just fine and they still looked perfect in every way except for the fact that they weren't talking. It was silent in the limo, nine sets of eyes, all staring at me.

It made me sad looking at shadows of the people I loved. I was through with them anyway so I willed them to dissolve, releasing the scrap of memory they had been. They vanished but left behind piles of black ash all over the seats, what was left of the chairs that I had used to give my shadows some substance. I hadn't planned on that, and I started to cough as the ashes flew all around inside the enclosed in space.

"Crap!" I fussed and quickly banished the ashes and dust, sending it away into oblivion. I checked out the little bar in the limo and made myself a diet Coke for my parched throat and looked out the window as I sipped at it.

We were in a long motorcade. There were about fifteen military vehicles in front of us and about that many behind us. Here in the middle were three other limos. Off to the side in the air I saw three helicopters keeping pace with us and I wondered which one Tom was in. I felt a flutter of fear go through me. Somehow I knew I was about to die again. Something in me was telling me, and I believed it.

I looked out the window at the familiar sights of my city, Jacksonville, Florida, passing by in front of me. I laughed a little as we passed P.K. Noodles. I remembered when they first opened up a few years back before they changed their name. They were a Vietnamese restaurant and had originally named their place Pha King Noodles, not realizing that that sounded kind of nasty in American. My laugh died out quickly. Every side street we passed was closed off with military vehicles and soldiers with guns. I wondered when it would start and if it would hurt this time or if it would be quicker than when I burned. I gave myself a shake and tried not to think about what I felt coming.

I reached over to the fancy radio controls and started searching through the stations. The first station was easy listening. "Nope!" I changed stations. Country. "Sucks!" I kept switching from station to station. I wondered what I was trying to find when I settled on a heavy metal station playing something nice and dark. A fast-paced, angry sound, and then I understood. "Ahh. Something nice to die to," I said out loud, and my witchiness felt content with it.

I bobbed my head along with the hammering beat and set my cup in the drink holder. Maybe I could actually catch a five minute nap before it happened, but I doubted it. The limo ride to the church was only about fifteen minutes and we were close to half way there already so it had to happen soon. I settled down into the seat of the limo and tried to get comfortable as I listened to the music.

I wasn't even through stretching out when it all started.

Bullets tore through the limo, turning it into Swiss cheese over me as the limo started to swerve around wildly! If I hadn't have been stretched out in the seat, lying flat, I'd have been shot dozens of times already. I wasn't worried about my body, but I quickly thought about my mind and started to make sure that it would be safe no matter what happened, and then the world exploded in flames.

I felt more shock than anything like pain as my body rent and tore and shredded while the explosive force tore the limo to shreds and the world went black.

I felt my mind ripped from my body.

And just like that, I was back.

Back here in my own private world of empty nothingness.

I couldn't see anything. I couldn't hear anything or feel anything. But I could think. I felt more solid this time, not like I was about to drift apart and go out like a light.

"Hello Darkness." I sent my greeting out into the void.

"Hello empty void of endless nothing."

"Hello formless, shapeless, lifeless silence."

"Hello my hell. My grave," I thought into the blackness, sending out my dark salutations.

There was no reply back to my thoughts. No echo of thought or memory that came back. No ripple of any kind or evidence that my thoughts sent into the void had touched anything. There was nothing here to touch. Absolutely nothing. I wondered if it was like this for God when he made everything, if he started out with a big fat nothing and just started speaking. I felt the wild urge to speak those famous words out into the empty void—

"Let there be light."

"OH HELL NO!" I thought to myself, "I'm not going there!" I felt a wild rush of shame for even considering it. I didn't want to find out what kind of world I would make. I was a witch! And I was a murderer!

I pushed my mind away from that madness and back toward thoughts of the world I had left behind, a world with my family and my friends and the assholes who had just tried to kill them. I owed someone a well-deserved ass kicking and I needed to get back there and dole it out!

I focused on the remains of my body, the bits and pieces and fragments of bone. Little shreds of skin and flesh and ash. I focused with all my mind, desire, and will. I wanted my mind or soul or whatever I was now to go to that place "there" where those pieces of me were. I still felt nothing, but I really wasn't surprised by that, I didn't have anything to feel with now.

I thought about being able to see what was around me in my mind without needing eyes and vision opened within me. I was in the middle of a burning hulk of a crater. I had no body or form, only my mind. My consciousness, floating here suspended over the remains of my body like a disembodied ghost. There wasn't a whole lot left of me. The best piece I could find still looked red and bloody, not utterly burnt and charred. I think it was a bloody hunk of my shoulder.

I willed the piece of flesh to live and stay alive and I wrapped it carefully in a protective shield and then I buried it deep in the dirt there at the bottom of the crater. I'd need it when I got done kicking some ass. I didn't want a new body, I wanted my old one back. I wasn't a scientist but it seemed like my old DNA would help me get that done the way I wanted to do it, but for now I didn't need a human body, I needed something else.

I looked around for inspiration. The crater was at least twenty feet deep and fire still smoldered all around; parts of the limo were on fire and twisted metal was shoved into the sides of the crater. I was so deep down in this hole I couldn't even see out at what was happening around me.

I needed a body.

I thought of Believer and his body of clouds, and I started to craft myself a body of flames. A billowing, rolling, raging inferno as hot as the blazing fires of the hell that I would never see! I shaped my new body as I thought of revenge and murder and death.

David and Dana

A Time to Burn

The helicopter shook with the force of the blast and the sky ahead lit up brighter than day. A huge cloud rose into the air, visible through the front windows of the helicopter about two miles away.

"My God! What was that!?" cried the pilot as he fought the controls of the aircraft.

"That had to be a two ton bomb!" cried one of the soldiers. "Maybe bigger! What the hell is going on and who'd we hit!?"

"That couldn't have been us!" Nolan yelled back. "We wouldn't hit a target in the middle of one of our own cities! Someone hit us!"

"That wasn't dropped ordinance!" cried the pilot. "That was a goddamn missile!" he shouted out his take from up front where he was piloting the chopper.

"Look!" cried the other soldier who was staring out the window on the other side of the craft.

"Incoming! It ain't over yet!"

The helicopter was shaken again as a second and a third missile tore by, followed quickly by two more huge booming explosions lighting up the sky. Everyone was talking and shouting at once. They weren't moving forward, the pilot had them stopped in air. Nolan was busy with his phone, trying to get some information on what was happening. The other men were panicked, looking out the windows, shouting back and forth.

David held onto Dana's hand. He didn't care what was going on, all he wanted was to get to whoever was going to help Dana. Everything else was distraction. Nothing else mattered.

"Let's get going! Dana needs to get to whoever you were taking her to!" David yelled at Nolan, who had a phone pressed to his ear. With his free hand he waved David off as he focused on his call.

"You promised me she'd be okay!" David yelled.

Nolan ignored him.

David looked down at his Dana, at the weak pulse on the monitor; he knew she wouldn't last long. He didn't understand what was happening or how he was doing what he was doing with fire but he called it to his hand and it was there. There, in his palm, flames danced and blazed without burning his flesh. David held his hand up in front of Nolan, who slowly moved his cell phone away from his ear and raised his other hand in a "hands up" posture.

David had his full attention now and the attention of the other men as well. Only the pilot remained in ignorance of this new danger. They stared at him now and the flames coming from his hand.

"You promised me, Nolan! Take me to the person who was going to help my Dana!" David said fiercely. "You promised!"

"David," Nolan said sadly. "Those rockets may have just killed her. I think we're too late."

David looked confused. "What?" he asked, and the fire he held went out like a light. "What are you talking about!?"

Nolan leaned in so he could talk to David without shouting to be heard over the sound of the helicopter.

"I was taking you to see the Black Witch. You've been in a coma and don't even know what's been happening. You're a part of it and you don't even know. Your ability to control fire, David. It came to you as a result of taking some pills that were passed off as the Derm 513 pill. That drug study you were in, the doctor that was running it gave you some experimental drug that changed you and gave you this new ability to control fire. But he didn't just change you, he changed all of the teens in the drug study."

David had wondered what and how it happened, but it didn't matter now, all of his focus was for Dana.

"What does that have to do with Dana!?" David demanded. "She doesn't have time for this!"

Nolan was confident that there was no hope and he extended none to David now. No more promises he couldn't keep.

"David. We were taking Dana to one of the other kids from the study. She was the one who was going to heal her." Nolan pointed off in the direction of the three rising clouds of debris. "I'm sorry, but she was our only hope."

David looked off in the direction of the clouds. There were flashes of light. The fighting was still going on in the distance. Shooting could be heard even over the winding sound of the helicopter.

"There's still fighting going on over there!" cried the pilot. "I just got it off the wire! Three groups of fighters attacked the motorcade at the same time with high-powered sniper rifles. They painted the targets for the cruise missiles. The rockets came in from some place off in the Osceola National Forest. They already blew up the launch site but there's still fighting going on right over there. They said that all of the vehicles in the motorcade are gone." The pilot paused, hand pressed to his earphones as he listened to the radio. "All of the kids are dead, sir. They're saying that nothing is moving down there, sir," he yelled back, making sure he was heard over the engine noise.

"NO!" David yelled stubbornly. "Take us there now!"

Everyone paused as five jets tore the sky, flying by not far overhead. A minute later a thunderously loud "Boom! Boom! Boom!" was heard coming from the direction of the fighting.

"But, David," Nolan began to argue his point, but stopped when David's hand became alive with flames again.

"Take us there now or we all die now," David said calmly; one hand held burning flames and his other held Dana's hand as he looked at Nolan.

Nolan nodded. It's not like he didn't deserve to die if he got killed by friendly fire.

"Pilot, let command know that we 'have to go in.'" He paused as he looked at the pilot, who glanced back at David and the light coming from his hand. The helmeted head nodded, getting the hint. "And tell them to please not shoot at us." Nolan looked at the two soldiers. "You men have weapons?"

"Just side arms, sir, we're medics," replied the soldier.

"That's all right, get ready. I'm sure some of our boys will need you down there," Nolan said.

"Here, take this!" the pilot shouted and handed back his rifle. Nolan took the weapon himself and checked that it was loaded and ready before shouting "Take us in!" as he scooted toward one of the windows. The helicopter banked hard as the pilot turned toward the lights and sounds of fighting off in the distance. As they got closer they got passed by the planes again and heard another loud "Boom! Boom! Boom! Boom!" and saw the flashes of light from the impacts.

"Shit! That was close!" one of the medics shouted.

"It looks like we're too late for the party!" the pilot called back.

They all looked out at the scene down below. Beach Boulevard, a three-lane road in each direction was a blasted wasteland of twisted metal and destruction. The road where the motorcade had been was marked with three huge holes where the rockets had hit. Each of the craters was about forty feet wide and who knew how deep. Humvees and other military vehicles were everywhere, thrown about like the toys of an irate five year old bent on destruction. Trucks were upside down or half buried by dirt and broken asphalt. Some were lying on the roofs of nearby businesses and homes. A diesel truck was buried like a spear into a Burger King that was only half standing. Bodies of soldiers were everywhere. Wounded men staggered around looking for help for fallen friends. Many were still under cover, still too afraid of sniper fire to come out and seek help.

"Take us down right by the craters!" yelled David.

Nolan yelled to the pilot, "Take us down." Then asked, "How many wounded can we carry in this bird!"

"If you all stay in I could carry three wounded. Or more if some of you get out and stay out or we dump some of this heavy gear," he shouted back.

The pilot picked a spot and eased the helicopter down, being careful of the power lines that had been sent everywhere.

As soon as they touched down they were surrounded by dozens of filthy, battered soldiers pointing weapons.

"Let me go talk to them," Nolan told David. He opened the door of the helicopter and slipped out.

Right then the earth rumbled, shaking the helicopter a little. At the same instant thunder rolled through the sky.

"What the hell was that!?" said one of the medics. "That felt like an earthquake. That wasn't a missile hit." He looked out the window.

"Hey, look at the sky!" shouted the other medic from the other side of the helicopter where he had his head shoved way out a window looking up. Directly overhead dark clouds were forming and circling around like someone was stirring the sky with a dirty stick!

"What the hell is going on? What is that!?" cried the pilot as he looked up at the burgeoning maelstrom. He looked back at David. "You're not doing that to the clouds, are you, kid!?" he asked, eyeing David with worry.

"I'm not doing anything right now." David didn't know what they were seeing but answered anyway.

Outside the soldiers were all staggering around and gazing up at the sky as well. David left Dana's side for the second it took to lean out of the door and look up at the darkening clouds forming directly overhead before going back to Dana. He watched as a small group of four soldiers broke away from the group that was talking with Nolan and ran toward the nearest crater. They climbed the raised lip of earth and asphalt pushed up by the blast and looked down into the hole then turned and started running back as fast as their legs could carry them.

David watched as Nolan and the officers in command spoke with the breathless soldiers. Officers started shouting orders and all the soldiers in the area started running for the hills except for two soldiers rushing back to the helicopter with badly wounded men in their arms. Nolan climbed back inside and helped the two as they passed up the wounded. The medics got busy on the ugly wounds. Nolan looked terrified and so did the soldiers on the ground who had just brought over the wounded. The two men eyed the helicopter with longing but they didn't climb in. The two wounded men were all the extra weight they could carry.

"David!" Nolan shouted. "We got to get in the air right now, one of those kids who died had the ability to create monsters! It looks like she created one before she died. Whatever the hell she made is climbing its way out of the crater right beside us! We've got to get airborne!"

And that was moment Dana's heart stopped beating.

The monitors and machines went wild and the frantic blood-covered medics went to work, trying to get her revived. The blades on the helicopter started to rotate faster as the pilot readied for liftoff.

"No!" David shouted above the chaos. "Leave us on the ground or I'll kill us all!" he ordered. "I'll burn us and every living thing for a mile around to ashes! ASHES!"

The pilot was turned around in his seat. He pointed a hand toward the crater.

"Look, kid! It's out of the crater! We got to go!"

Rising from the mouth of the crater was a creature shaped from living fire. It had a head, shoulders, and arms but below that was nothing but flames holding it upright as if the base was nothing but a flaming pillar. The creature was growing, rising straight up out of the crater like the impact had punched a hole straight through to hell and something had escaped. Something angry! David wouldn't relent. He held them all hostage as they struggled with Dana for another couple of minutes, getting her heart started once only to have it flatline again.

"Please, David. Let these men go. They've got families that love them too," Nolan pleaded. "Dana's gone. Let's get out of here!" He looked back toward the monster.

It was huge now. At least fifty feet tall, towering over the crater, and it was more defined now. Some soldiers were firing their weapons at it as they ran away, but it ignored the weapons fire. It even ignored a shoulder-fired rocket that some men fired off and sent at it from a distance. Others had thrown grenades as they fled. Nothing was hurting it, but it still hadn't moved from the crater.

"Let us out!" David yelled suddenly.

"What!?" Nolan shouted back. "You can't be serious!"

David pushed the medic who was still working on Dana off her body and started pulling off the wires connecting her to the machines and then he pulled out her IV. The medic started to help him remove her from the other machines and pulled out her breathing tube. David tried to lift her but was struggling to do it. He was still so weak from all he'd been through, just standing on his own feet was a struggle. Both of the medics started to help him. They were willing to do anything that would get them in the air and get this crazy, dangerous kid out of their ride.

"Hey, if they're getting out you got room for two more, right!?" asked one of the soldiers who had brought the wounded men. They were still standing beside the helicopter hoping against hope to catch a ride out.

"Help the kid and his girl out first!" shouted one of the medics, ignoring Nolan's angry glare. The two soldiers stepped up and started giving David the help he needed.

"David, what are you going to do!?" Nolan shouted down to him as David was helped off the chopper onto the ground. They handed down the dead girl to the soldiers while David watched them.

Nolan shouted again, "What are you doing!?" He was exasperated at the insanity of the situation.

David didn't shout but Nolan still heard him clearly.

"I'm going to go die with Dana. Have a nice life, Nolan." David turned and took Dana from the soldiers who handed her over then quickly climbed into the helicopter, looking relieved but guilty about leaving the kid behind. David, still wearing his blue/green hospital smock turned and started to stagger away carrying the dead girl in his arms.

"Why the hell did he want to stay?" asked one of the soldiers who had taken their place.

"He wants to die with his girl," Nolan replied.

"No shit?" said the soldier as they rose into the air.

"No shit," Nolan replied as he looked out the window.

The flaming creature was at least ninety feet tall now, still not doing anything aggressive, but its blazing white eyes looked right at the helicopter that was only a short distance away. The flaming shape had a face now, a female face, and it smiled as it looked at them. Nolan tore his eyes away from the enormous creature to look down at David far below as he struggled up the side of the crater. David still carried the dead girl as he pushed forward, looking for his end. Wanting to die with his Dana.

"I'm so sorry, kid. Please forgive me," Nolan whispered. Then they were away, putting distance between them and the flaming fire demon that the dying girl had called forth.

Black Rain

Dark Reflections

I let rage and hate swim inside the flames that formed my body like liquid fire. It was the blood inside the inferno I'd become, shooting through me, feeding and nurturing the billowing flames that made my body. My wrath grew, as did the ugly desire to torture, rend, and terrify those that dared hurt my family. Above me the dark clouds spun and circled as I drew my new body out of the hole they had pushed my old one down into. A grave they had intended for me and my family. I smiled as I thought of how many bodies I would pile into this hole they had intended for me and mine. How high I would pile the dead! What murder and evil I would unleash upon the world of men! What horror and destruction!

I gave fair warning and now they would pay!

I WOULD MAKE THEM PAY!

I let thunder rumble, its force throwing about the little men that stood in groups, huddled amidst rubble or running away from me. Death was already everywhere. Dead and dying men littered the ground all around the blasts crater, but it wasn't enough. Not nearly enough! There would be more! And I would cause it this time.

I drew myself up out of my hole, and I was almost ready to move and go find who was responsible when I got distracted by a helicopter lifting off right beside me. Everyone else had run off long minutes ago, but here was this attractive nuisance, so close. It drew my eye. I watched until the helicopter took off and moved away. I wondered who they were and what they'd been doing, and then I looked down.

Right at the edge of the crater, someone was struggling up the lip of the hill. It looked like they planned to jump into the flames just below me, which surprised and confused me, jarring me from my dark thoughts. I didn't understand. They didn't look like soldiers either. I still didn't have a voice so I thought about my form and shaped myself the ability to speak, giving myself a voice like my own had been but bigger and powerful, yet still female.

"Who are you?" I called before they reached the crest of the hill. I watched as the face looked up at me. He was a young man, and he was wearing a hospital gown like the girl he carried in his arms. He was crying, and he looked like hell; they both did. The girl already looked dead. He looked up at me and spoke but I didn't hear him for some reason. Crap! I realized that I still didn't have ears! No wonder everything was so quiet and I hadn't heard the thunder that I made earlier or heard myself speak!

"Wait!" I said to the mysterious young man. I quickly added the ability to hear to my flaming body then said to the boy in my rumble of a voice, "What do you want?"

He looked up at me, his voice filled with such grief as he spoke.

"My life is over. She's dead. My Dana is dead!" he shouted up at me brokenly. "I tried to get her help, but it's too late now. She's gone—and I want to die with her." He pulled her tighter into his embrace, kissed her gently, and looked up at me. "Can you please kill me? I'm ready to go. I need to be with her." He stared up at me, completely unafraid.

And now I understood why he wasn't scared. He wanted to die. He was trying to kill himself because his girl had died.

My heart broke completely. All the rage and wrath and hate I had gathered up poured out as I reared back and WAILED!

"Aaaaaaaaaaaaaaaaaaaaaaaaahhhaaaaahhhhhhh!"

A terrible, lamenting, howling sound of pain poured from my monolithic form, emptying my broken heart into the open sky like a volcano spewing heartache and fiery ash!

I looked back down to the boy, who was still waiting, and I spoke to him again.

"I'm so sorry. Did you love her?" I asked, but I could see it on his face. I bent down closer to look at him, but I was careful not to get too close; I didn't want to burn them on accident even if he did come to me for death.

He choked out a heaving sob, "Yes! I loved her." He hugged the dead girl to himself with all his strength, and I thought I would die all over again. This was worse than going into the void. I'd rather die myself that see this and feel it. With my heart breaking again I wondered how to help him, how to get his girl back. I looked down at the body of the dead girl and focused my mind on her and on her body.

"HEAL!" I shouted and focused on the body this boy held in his arms, forcing life and vitality and strength into her flesh, and then I bent down to David as he looked at me, surprised and hopeful. Then back down to Dana. Her body looked much better but her eyes remained shut and her form did not stir with life.

His pleading eyes turned back up to my own burning white stars and I spoke to him again, my giant flaming head as close as I could come without harming them. "I cannot pray and ask God to return her soul to you. Only you can do that," I told him. "I have done what I can and I will do more, but only you can ask for her soul. Pray now, and ask God for her soul to come back to her body if you want her to live."

And he started to pray without another word of encouragement from me. He prayed with his eyes squeezed tight, his arms wrapped around his love and he poured all he was into his prayer. Begging, crying, weeping like there was no tomorrow because, for him, there *was* no tomorrow without her.

I listened to him and even though I knew it would do no good, I prayed too. The towering inferno that I was, with a body I'd shaped to unleash my own sinful, selfish rage, I now used to weep and pray and cry out to a God. I prayed to a God whom I could not reach, for a soul that I could not help. The boy prayed also. Only moments ago I had been about to commit the darkest of horrors and now I poured out my weeping soul in a hopeless effort to save one dead girl because this boy loved her.

And so it was.

We both prayed and cried and wept—and just like that—she arose.

I was watching as her arms first started to move, and I went silent first. The boy's eyes were still closed and he kept praying until he felt her arms wrap around his neck and hug him and his eyes snapped open.

"Dana!" he shouted and hugged her back.

I waited and watched in quiet, happy ecstasy as they held each other and made the first delicate introductions to each other after being parted by death. I felt so familiar with death now, and it was such an intimate thing to die; it felt special to be right here and be a party to their experience with death and love.

But then reality started to steal the magic of the moment away as the girl noticed me looking in on their private little world. Her eyes got huge as she stared over his shoulder.

"David, are you sure we didn't die?" she asked him with her eyes still looking up at me.

"We're both alive," he assured her.

Dana pointed up at me, "Then what's up with the giant fire demon, David? Am I dead or alive or dreaming?" she asked seriously.

David looked up at me. "Thank you for helping us," he said. "I don't even know who you are. What's your name?" he asked me.

I smiled at him and his love. "I'm Black Rain. The Black Witch."

David laughed, a huge smile on his face. "*You're* the Black Witch!? They said you were dead!"

"Impossible," I replied. "Although they did try. And I let them try. I'd planned on a phoenix-like rise from the ashes before I began pouring out my wrath raining hell fire and damnation on everyone that tried to kill me," my flaming hill of a body sighed, "but I'm just not feeling it anymore. All I want to do now is go see Believer, hold him, and tell him I love him. I have enjoyed watching you two. You're a beautiful couple and you make me feel love and joy and happiness." I smiled down at them. "Thank you so much."

Without another word, I willed the little piece of me that I had preserved and buried down in the earth to rise. The small red bundle burst from the ground and rose into the air. I set it down on the ground not far from both of them where it landed with a disgusting "splat." I focused all my mind and will on that little remnant of what I had been and willed it to heal and reform exactly as I had been, and it started to grow and form.

"Oh my God!" Dana said and turned away from the grisly scene, turning pale.

David held her and but watched as my new body flopped about and took its full finished shape, and then I extinguished the burning monstrosity in which I stood and let my soul move back into my "body" like a snail going back into its favorite shell.

I blinked, squinting as I opened my eyes. Something sharp was poking me right in the back. I looked down at myself. "Eeek!" a surprised, girly sound shot out of my mouth. *I was butt ass naked!* I called forth my black dress and it appeared on my body. I staggered to my feet, still getting accustomed to being in a complete living form again. It was truly disorienting and very complex. Very limiting in a way and in other ways much more freeing. In this human form I could almost pretend, even to myself, that I was still part of this world, and this world was where I wanted to live, so I was glad to be back in my skin. I gave myself some nice boots because there was glass, smoldering cinders, and twisted metal junk all over the ground. I quickly did my hair and nails.

I turned around.

David and Dana were standing together, holding hands, looking at me, but I had other visitors as well.

"Hello Tom," I said with a smile.

Tom was still walking toward me and behind him were dozens of other soldiers and behind them hundreds of others closing in from all directions. Everyone was pointing guns at us. I willed my voice to carry to all of them.

"Lower your weapons," I said.

They complied immediately.

"Rejoice. Love has saved you," I said. I wasn't with my sisters but I called my mark anyway. It appeared on my forehead. I also let my plain hazel eyes and the whites, the entire globe of my eyes change to solid, glossy black. Power played down my hair and fluttered my dress with the unseen breeze of energy that poured from my body, making me smile with its familiar tickling touch. It felt good to be the "me" I wanted and liked to be.

"Black Rain," Tom said as he took a final step or two across the broken splintered asphalt and stopped a short distance away.

"Sorry about the driver, Tom," I said. "And the others who died, but I'm glad to see that you're okay. Nice and safe in your helicopter." I smiled at him.

Tom looked confused for a moment. I watched as he put the pieces together and realized I had put him in the helicopter on purpose. "How did you know this was going to happen?" he asked.

With the others at the church, he had to know that I was going in the limo as a decoy, so he wasn't surprised at the attack. Though I'm sure he was very surprised at the size of the attack. A whole lot of soldiers had died.

"I'm a witch, Tom. When you call the psychic hotline to get the lowdown on lotto numbers, who do you hope you're talking to? A witch. When you go to a fair and sit with an ugly old woman with warts on her nose in some little tent to have your fortune told, what is she, Tom? She's a witch. Premonitions, visions, foretelling, and mysteries." I called a nice warm summer breeze and let it whip around us, carrying the stink of burning metal, plastic, and human flesh away.

"Yes, Tom, I knew I was about to die. I'm a witch."

"But why did you let them do this?" Tom asked, horrified that I had known and did nothing.

I put my arms out wide, taking in the carnage around me. "Whoever did this had to learn that I will not stay dead. If not now, it would have happened later and my family and friends would have died along with me. If it hadn't of been now it would have happened later and it would have been bigger. A lot bigger and a lot worse. Better for it to happen now and get it over with."

"David, I need some clothes," Dana said to David. Her hospital gown was open across the back, the same as David's. My attention went back to the two of them as they held onto each other, and I had a wild crazy thought. It felt right as I looked at them. I rolled the idea around inside my head for only a moment.

So mote it be.

"Oh my God!" Dana shouted as I cleaned her body of ashes, sweat, and soot. A beautiful white wedding dress took shape on her body, replacing the blue hospital gown. Then I did her nails, hair, makeup, and shoes, all in under three minutes.

David was laughing and happy. He'd let go of her, not wanting to dirty up her white wedding dress and laughed again as I cleaned him up and dressed him in a simple white button up shirt and black dress pants and shoes. I would have done a traditional tux but for the life of me I didn't know how to make one of those or even how everything fit together, so he got the best I could come up with without getting help. I also filled David with strength and health because he still looked rough and I wanted him feeling strong and confident for what was ahead.

Without saying a word, I willed the earth nearby to rise up and form a stone arch ten feet high and ten feet wide. At the same time I thought of the two palm trees at our church that were in the decorative island of landscaping right outside the front doors. The palms were about ten feet apart. I willed those two trees to lean together at the top and form a living arch of wood and I shaped the top of the two trees into one single tree in my mind.

I walked up to the silent and shocked Dana and a smiling David. Both wearing their wedding finery.

"Do you love her?" I asked David.

"Yes. I do,." he said. "I always have. I always will." It had the sound of a well-established law on nature. Absolute and unchangeable. I really liked his answer. And I'd already seen his resolve first hand.

I looked at his girl. Dana. She looked really scared as she returned my gaze. I'd rocked her world badly, but that couldn't be helped.

"Do you love David?" I asked her.

She looked troubled by the question and dropped her head, looking down at the ground, and I worried that I had made a horrible mistake until she spoke.

"I don't deserve him." I barely heard her whispered answer.

I didn't let her off the hook that easy.

"You're probably right," I agreed. "I'm sure you don't deserve him. But that's not what I asked you, is it?"

I stared at her with my black eyes demanding an answer and asked again, "Do you love him?"

"Yes," she whispered. "I love him."

"Then follow me," I said, "*if* you love him." I gave her a wicked smile before I turned and stepped toward the stone archway.

"Tom, you're welcome to come along if you like but none of the others may follow," I called over my shoulder. I willed the space within the arch to open to the matching space within the palm tree arch at the church and before me a window to another place opened. Soldiers were already there on the other side of the palm tree arch, in position on their knees with guns pointing at me.

"Tom," I said. "Go on through and fix this, please," I said, my voice annoyed.

He did as I asked without hesitation, stepping through the archway and issuing orders for men to step back and stand down. From the other side of the arch, Sky Dragon stepped through to my side.

"Are you well, my lady?" he asked quickly, his reptilian dragon-like head whipped in all directions on the end of his long neck as he scanned the surroundings with red eyes shining in the darkening twilight. All the soldiers around us gawked, amazed at him and the archway.

"Yes, Sky Dragon," I said with a smile. "I'm well." And I stepped up and hugged him, which surprised him badly. He stood stiffly, not sure what to do as I gave his cloudy body a good squeeze.

"Oh relax, Sky Dragon!" I scolded. "I'm marrying your brother in just a few minutes. So that means you're part of the family and I love you too."

He gently slipped out of my embrace, looking uncomfortable as he put a little space between us. I gave him an apologetic smile. "I'm sorry, I'm a hugger. Thank you for coming to check on me," I told him sincerely.

"Let's go, my lady. This place is not safe. And they are impatient to start the weddings. They have been waiting for you to arrive." He kept his eyes on the soldiers as he spoke and they stared at us like they were seeing a scene out of a fantasy book complete with the witch, the dragon, and the magic portal to the fairy land. Only this portal went to a Baptist church on the south side of town.

I let my voice carry out to the soldiers and to the area around. Not a shout but a conversation. "I'm going to get married today and I find that I have no heart for revenge right now. But I can't let this go unanswered, now can I?" I looked around at all the soldiers. "So. I'll save it all for next time." I raised my hand and all the clouds that churned overhead stopped spinning and began to dissolve away into the night sky. "The next time someone tries to harm my family all of the horror, burning, and rotting piles of bodies I should pile high this day; the flayed and rent flesh that I owe the ones who did this, and every one of my darkest dreams, I will save and give to the next person or country who tries to hurt my family. As above, so below, let the whole world know—that the Black Witch *lives*!" Without another word I stepped through the arch to the church with Sky Dragon beside me.

Soldiers were everywhere at the church, covering the grounds and parking lot like a green blanket. I took another step or two toward the front door of the church, and David and Dana stepped up right beside me. I wasn't sure that they would follow but I was very glad they did.

"You're getting married today?" Dana asked bravely. I could tell she was still terrified of being near me but she was trying to ignore her fear and be tough.

"Yep."

"But you're wearing black," she said uncertainly, obviously scared that this observation might offend me.

I stopped cold and thought about that. If there was one day in my whole life, even if I lived forever, that I would wear white why not let it be this day? And I also thought it would make Dad and Believer happy, so—I did it.

I forced my eyes to go back to their natural state, my hair and nails reverted to their God-given texture and color, and my dress turned white. It was the same antique style dress, no magic, no sparkle or flair to make it special. Just white. And so was I. No unseen wind moved my muddy brown hair. It even had that little kink back in it that I hated so dearly. I was natural. I was as much me as I could make me except this didn't feel like "me" anymore.

"Wow," Dana said as she looked me over. It was a strange look, like some of the mystery was gone now that she'd seen me as a regular human girl. She gave a little shrug that almost looked sympathetic. "You're still beautiful, and you look good in white too."

She left me standing there with my eyebrows raised and stepped over and took David's arm in hers. "You never gave me a ring," she told David with a frown. "And you never even asked me to marry you either. We're just sort of here and sort of doing it."

David looked at her and said, "Marry me."

Dana's eyebrows shot up. "Are you asking me or telling me, David?" she asked, surprised.

"Telling you," he said seriously. "You like your men to take charge. So I'm taking charge. You're marrying me."

"Really?" She sounded scared, but then she looked up at him with an annoyed face. "What about the rings, David?"

"I'll make you some rings, don't worry about it," I said, and they both looked over at me. I returned her little smarmy shrug with evil pleasure as I walked up to one of the soldiers.

"Can I hold your gun, please?" He blinked a time or two then clicked some button on it, took out the ammo clip, and handed me his gun. I think it was an M-16 or something. I held it in two hands and willed it to change. I closed my eyes as I thought about how I wanted to do this. In my hands, the gun changed, dissolving and coming apart like moving sand, reducing down into two much smaller objects in the palms of my two hands.

"Thanks," I told the shocked soldier, then walked over to David and Dana. "Here you go." I handed them each their rings.

They looked at the rings, back to me, to the rings again. The rings had gold bands that I had made extra hard because I hated it when my rings got out of round. The diamonds were big but not too big because that would be hard to wear. Dana's diamond was cut in a tear drop pattern that I would have chosen for myself if I was going to wear a ring. It was a brilliant sparkling white. I made David's a square cut stone and his band was thicker and more masculine. As they held the rings in their hands they continued to change shape because as I looked at them I was tweaking this and that in my mind.

"Look at the engraving," David said to Dana. She looked at the band she'd be wearing where I'd willed the words to take form. "I have always loved you. I always will."

Engraved on his band were the words "I deserve you, and I love you."

Dana stared at her ring, reading and rereading, and David looked back at me in confused wonder.

"Why are you doing all of this for us?" he asked me. "You don't even know me or Dana and you've done so much for us. You've given me back everything—*everything!*" He gave Dana a squeeze and it was good to see her squeeze him back. "But I still don't understand why." The pair stared at me, waiting to hear what I would say.

"David, when I saw you guys down there I was about to do horrible things. Ugly, monstrous things that would have hurt my soul, but you stopped me. Your love for Dana stopped me. I was floored by how much you loved her. Thank you,

David. Believe me when I say that I still owe you and Dana big." I leaned in and gave him a hug then leaned over to a surprised Dana and hugged her too.

"Thank you," Dana said.

"Let's go please," grumbled Sky Dragon impatiently as he held the front door of the church open a short distance away from where we stood. "My Sky is ready to get married and the vampires need to go die," he complained, like this was more problems that he didn't deserve.

"Oh, all right!" I griped as I stomped over and through the door. "Sorry! Geesh! I was just a little busy keeping everyone I love from getting blown up and burnt to ashes, Sky Dragon! My bad!" I fussed at him as I shuffled forward in my white dress and left him standing there holding the door. Sky Dragon quickly left the door holding responsibilities to someone else and slipped up to walk beside me with his head bowed looking suitably shamed into a better state of mind, but now I felt all pushy.

"I'm sorry for fussing at you, Sky Dragon," I apologized. "And thank you for getting me going. I needed the help. I do get distracted easy, but I can't help it." I sighed. "I'm a witch." Like my being a "witch" was an all-purpose hall pass that would excuse me for being late to any event.

"Umhm," Sky Dragon said but he smiled a little, his long dragon mouth turning up at the end and I laughed. Sky was always saying "Umhm." It was so sweet to hear him saying it too, copying her.

My family was around me now, and I felt better for it, even if it was my new family. In the hallway there were no guests, just soldiers, lining the foyer on both sides following us with their eyes. The wedding music was already playing inside the church and the sound filled the foyer as well.

We turned the bend in the hall, and I saw the wedding party waiting by the back doors of the sanctuary. Jane and her dad stood side by side; Sky and Dr. Burgis were in line behind them. The music changed and the wedding march began.

I had one brief glance of Jane and her dad walking through the doors before Believer wrapped me up in his cloudy arms.

"My lady!" he rumbled. "Are you well?" He held me, lifting me high into the air, engulfing me within his arms completely, and I let him hold me, luxuriating in the feel of his arms and body all around me. It felt like home.

"Hello, my love." He held me and I felt safe within his arms. "I wore white for you, Believer. Did you see?"

He lowered me back to the ground and looked at me, studying me with his burning red eyes.

"Your eyes and hair and fingers are all so—*human*." He looked surprised. "How does it make you feel?" he asked me honestly. Believer was always so honest.

I thought about it. I looked at my fingers, at my short cropped nails with no color other than the fleshy pink that nature provided. I picked up a strand of my hair and looked at it. Not really a color at all, somewhere between blond and brown with its undecided kink. A little too crooked to pass for straight and too straight to pass for true kink. And the white dress. The white was the worst. It made me feel like a lie. Black was my color. I squirmed a little under his gaze, not wanting to ruin anything for him but I wanted to be honest.

"It doesn't feel right," I admitted quietly. "But I can wear it for you if you like it." I smiled for him.

"Please be yourself." Believer looked at me. "I want to marry you as you are now. Not as the girl you were and are no more. Be who you are, my love. I am not human. And I want to marry the Black Witch, not a human girl." He said this as he gazed into my human eyes.

I didn't even have to think about it; it all seemed to happen on its own. My dress, hair, nails, coven mark, and even my eyes changed and I was me again. But then life butted in on our romantic moment in the form of our church's pushy old wedding coordinator. She'd done every wedding at our church for thirty years. I thought for sure she'd be safely dead and buried before I got married, but damned if she didn't live long enough to get me too.

"Rain! Rain!" The crusty voice of Mrs. Aberforth crackled right beside us. "I need to know whether you and your—groom—are going last or if David and Dana will be last."

Believer set me on the ground to deal with this new problem. Jane and her father had already walked down the aisle, and she and Dan were probably saying their vows by now. It looked like Dr. Burgis was going to be giving Sky away, which was sweet of him to do. He looked happy to do it but he also looked funny. He still had his suitcase, briefcase, and painting clutched in his arms as he stood beside Sky. He was going to look like an idiot staggering down the aisle with all that in his arms, but I couldn't think of who to ask to hold it for him that I could trust. Oh well. Sky stood beside him chewing the nails of one hand as she pushed the door open a crack with the other to peek inside.

David was gone, waiting for Dana inside, and it looked like Mrs. Aberforth had drafted Williams to walk Dana down the aisle. Williams shot me a *What you've gotten me into now!* look as he took a tiny step away from Dana, who stood stiffly beside him, hands balled into fists, teeth clenched. She looked like she wanted to rip Williams' head off, which made me want to laugh. I would have asked Williams what he'd done to piss her off, but I could already tell that he didn't have a clue. I covered my smile with a hand as one of Mrs. Aberforth's ancient crone helpers forced Williams into a jacket that had to be from the church's lost and found closet. Yesterday he'd had to borrow someone's pants, and this was the second time today he'd been forced into another man's clothes. Somehow, it seemed right seeing him in someone else's clothes. It felt familiar.

He and Dana were lined up behind Dr. Burgis and Sky.

"We're going last," I told Mrs. Aberforth.

"Very well," she said, giving my black dress the stink eye even more-so than my "non-traditional" groom.

"Your dress was white a second ago, Rain. I saw it. What happened to the white, young lady?" She circled me like a buzzard eyeing road kill.

"Dad! Help!"

Dad intervened and Mrs. Aberforth reluctantly retreated to torture Dana some more.

"Rain. What happened in the limo?" my father asked. "We heard some big booms that actually shook the building, and all the soldiers went nuts but wouldn't tell us anything except some ridiculous lie about a gas main exploding. We were so worr—"

"Everything went fine." I stopped his rush of words before he asked me questions I didn't want to answer, but then I noticed who wasn't here. "Hey, where's Mom? And my Sisters, why aren't they here?" My eyes scanned the foyer again.

"Your mother and the other witches are at the mansion." I was surprised to hear Tom answer me. He was standing nearby blending in with the soldiers lining the wall, listening to us as we talked.

"What mansion!? Where!?" Dad fixed his gaze on Tom. "I've been worried sick! None of our phones are working and none of your people would tell me a thing that wasn't a flat-out lie! What mansion and where is it?"

"It's about an hour south of here, a big historic mansion right on the St. Johns River. The Hale House," Tom answered calmly in spite of my father's anger.

"Do they know what's going on here?" Dad asked. "That Rain and Ryan are about to get married?"

"No." Tom squirmed, looking uncomfortable. "They've been dealing with problems of their own out there. Mrs. Bryant and the other—witches," he hesitated to use the word as if it were dirty, "are fine, they're all fine." Tom kept his eyes on me as he added, "But they've been busy. The other witches seem to be having an exceptionally hard time dealing with strangers. Your sisters are far too dangerous to be here in this crowd. From what I've been told, your mother is doing an excellent job and keeping them under control, but I think it would be incredibly dangerous to bring them here. They don't know about the wedding. We didn't want to upset them."

Some of what Tom said made sense, but some of it didn't. "What happened at the mansion that has kept them 'busy?'" I asked. It sounded like something bad had happened and Tom didn't want to talk about it. He was trying to change the subject.

Tom squirmed before answering. "Apparently there were some dangerous people at the mansion that tried to take control of the house—"

"WHAT!?" I shouted. My temper flared to life, my whole body flushed with ready rage, my hair dancing wildly about as a fresh wave of power rippled down the hallway, making lights flicker and papers and church flyers swirl into the air like wind-blown confetti down through the foyer.

"Rain!" Dad cautioned. "Easy! Easy, girl!"

Tom spoke in a rush, "The bad guys are all dead! The Red Witch killed them herself before our men even arrived! She painted the walls with their blood!" he said with feeling, "The girls and your mother are safe! And now we have hundreds of soldiers around the house. And your mother is there, right this minute, keeping the girls under control. Everyone is safe."

Tom paused to take a breath, and I paused to process what I had just heard. Holy crap! Bethany had killed people. Bad people. And it sounded like she'd done a bang up job of it. *Good for her*!

I relaxed, letting the power and tension leave my body, and my hair eased to the gentle breeze it seemed to prefer.

"Are you sure that they're all right," I asked.

Tom raised his radio to his ear and spoke with someone. After a moment he was connected through to whoever it was he wanted. "Agent White, status report. This is Benistin."

After a short pause a voice responded, and I could hear his answer on Tom's two-way radio for myself. "Yes, sir. I am currently sharing tea and some refreshments with King Cornelius, Queen Cathryn, and Mrs. Bryant. The witches are currently enjoying the garden area. They are speaking to the trees at this time, sir, and seem to be making good friends with one particularly lively weeping willow." White said, making "talking to trees" sound as if it were a perfectly normal thing to do. He continued in the same easy conversational tone. "All seems to be going quite well, sir. Can we expect the Black Rain to arrive soon?" he asked.

"Yes," Benistin replied. "That's all, White. We'll be there soon."

"Sir. Mrs. Bryant would like to know how her son and daughter are doing and where they are."

Benistin held the radio to his shirt. "Do you want your mother to know about the weddings?" He obviously assumed that I didn't. I thought about it.

Dad watched me but didn't say anything one way or another. Rain Marie couldn't have born the weight of those eyes, but I could. The girls were safe and Mom was with them there at the mansion. I didn't feel up to the freak out that was sure to happen if I brought Mom and the girls here right now.

"No. I'll see her soon. I'm not going to change my mind no matter what she says or how loud she yells. I am what I am. Tell her I'm fine and that we'll all be there in a few minutes. Do your thing, Tom." I gave him a half smile. "Be reassuring, but don't lie to her if you can help it. You know what to do."

Tom nodded and walked off as he talked into the phone, doing as I asked.

Sky stood beside the Doctor eyeing him with worry, nervously chewing her nails, awaiting her turn to march down the aisle.

"Dr. Burgis!" Mrs. Aberforth crackled, giving the doctor the a sour look. "You simply must find someone else to hold those horrid bags!"

The old lady looked around for someone to use.

"You! Dragon! Get over here! Take this *stuff*!" Sky Dragon was standing protective vigil behind Sky, keeping his threatening gaze pinned on soldiers in the foyer. Sky Dragon rushed right over but gave Mrs. Aberforth a deep growl of disapproval which she answered with a "Hmmph!" of her own.

"I was supposed to be the ring bearer," he whined, disappointed.

"*Please* my Dragon! Do this for me!" Sky begged.

Sky Dragon quickly took the bags and painting from the doctor and handed him a pillow with the rings.

"Thank you, thank you, my beautiful Dragon!" Sky grabbed Sky Dragon and hugged him awkwardly around all the bags before rushing back into place beside Dr. Burgis, taking his arm. Sky Dragon looked happy now, even burdened with all the doctor's luggage as he stepped out of the way.

"Don't rush! Step slow with the music like we practiced!" Mrs. Aberforth whispered loudly. "Start ri-ght—" The music keyed. "Now!"

Ushers opened the doors wide and they started down the aisle. Dr. Burgis looked so proud he could burst and Sky was simply stunning. The doors closed.

Williams and Dana stepped into pole position, but something was wrong, Dana was shaking like a leaf and she was white as a sheet. She flat out refused to take Williams' arm.

I looked up at Believer. "Give me another minute, my love," I asked him. He nodded his big head and I stepped over to check on Dana. Mrs. Aberforth was fanning her trying to get her some air, and Williams had backed away, which seemed to be helping Dana more than anything else.

"What's wrong?" I asked.

Dana's eyes were wild and she was breathing heavily as she answered, "I know this is weird." She took another breath or two. "But I got in a fight today with the cops, and they killed me. *I think*," breathing, "I can't stand being anywhere near that cop. I'm sorry." More breathing. "I know he's your friend and all, but I'd rather walk down the aisle alone than with a cop." She was sounding more like herself now.

"You got in a fight with cops today?" I asked her.

She nodded. "I think they killed me." Her hand rubbed at her chest. "They used a stun gun on me. I remember that much before I passed out." She swallowed. "Before I died."

I hugged her. "I'm sorry you died, Dana. I know it's horrible, but at least David was there to bring you back."

She pulled back, her long graceful neck giving her room to look at me. She looked surprised. "David didn't bring me back. You did," she said.

I shook my head no. "It wasn't me." I raised my eyebrows. "I'd tell ya if it was me. I would. Really. But it wasn't me. I fixed your body, but David brought you back from the dead."

Dana still looked doubtful, "And how did David bring me back to life?"

"He prayed and asked God for your soul. David begged God for you and God gave you back to him. Don't you remember what he was doing when you woke? He was praying." I smiled at her and so did my Dad and Mrs. Aberforth. They'd both been listening as we spoke. I thought this would make Dana happy, but now she actually looked like she would faint for real.

"Dana, what's wrong!?" I asked her.

"Oh my," Mrs. Aberforth said and started fanning.

Dana broke out in a sweat as she spoke to me. "It was one thing to think that you brought me back from the dead, but to know that David did it. That he loved me that much! And that God gave me back to him." She swayed on her feet. "He really does love me."

Her eyes fluttered and began rolling back up into her skull so I willed strength and energy to flow into her body. She perked right up but still looked shaken and frazzled.

"Dad." I turned to him. "Could you walk Dana down the aisle and give her to David for me? Then you can slip out the side door and walk me down too."

"I'll be glad to give Dana to David," Dad said and gave me a kiss on the cheek before he stepped up beside Dana. "David seems like a nice boy. And it seems like God has already given this girl to David once. And I don't mind standing in for our Heavenly Father at all. As long as that's okay with Dana."

Dana was crying, mussing up her makeup. She nodded.

Mrs. Aberforth handed her a Kleenex. Her old eyes were watery as well.

"Thank you," Dana said to the old lady before she turned back to me.

"You've already given me so much and now you're giving me your dad." She sniffled.

"He's a good dad if you need one. And I'm good at sharing, I don't mind," I told her. "I have lots of sisters." I gave Dad a wink and he rolled his eyes at me.

"Thanks."

Williams called from a safe distance, "I'll watch the wedding from the balcony, Black Rain. Good to meet you, young lady." He turned and slipped up the stairs to the balcony.

Mrs. Aberforth attacked. Telling Dad where he was supposed to go, what he was to say and how she wanted him to escape when he was through giving Dana to David. After the grilling she had him take Dana's arm and stand there by the back doors, ready to march when the music started again.

"It's almost time so be ready when I say go," Mrs. Aberforth said then went to peek through the doors to see how things were going.

Believer had stepped up beside me, and I held his cloudy hand as we waited.

"Honey. Are you sure about this?" Dad looked back to us. He glanced up at Believer then focused in on me. "Believer seems like a nice person and I know he cares about you, honey, but are you ready for this? I don't want you to rush into this if you're not ready for it. Are you sure, Rain?" He looked from me to Believer.

Believer remained silent, he was so tall that standing this close to him I'd have to look almost straight up to look him in the eyes, so I contented myself with stepping closer to him and drawing his arm across my chest while I leaned back into him and spoke with my father.

"Daddy, I'm not human anymore." I saw his brows push together in denial but I ignored it. "Believer is more of a human than I'll ever be again. He is still part of this world, he is still a part of God and through Sky one day he will even go to heaven. That is 'if' he ever dies, which may not ever happen." I watched Dad for a minute. He studied me. My face. My hair as it moved gently around my shoulders. He looked into my jet black eyes.

"Are you still my little girl?" he asked me finally.

"I'll always be your little girl, Daddy. Even if I turn into a hundred foot tall fire demon."

Dad's brow wrinkled up, but he didn't get a chance to voice his thoughts about my cryptic comment.

"All right, you two, get ready." Mrs. Aberforth pushed Dad back into position.

He cast one more worried glance over his shoulder before the doors opened and for the third time this evening the wedding march called out and another bride headed down to her waiting groom. Sky Dragon slid forward and stretched out his long neck, stealing a quick peek through the open doorway before it closed again. We could all see Jane and Dan and their little group on the platform behind the main stage facing the crowd. Beside them stood a very happy Sky and Ryan. Boy did they match, they both had huge, million dollar smiles. The doors closed.

"She looks happy," Sky Dragon said. Adoration for his Sky was easy to hear in his voice.

"Yes. She does," I said. He stepped away, still carrying Dr. Burgis's stuff, but he didn't seem to mind anymore. Sky Dragon was happy.

Finally it was just me and Believer. I looked up at him and found that he was already looking down at me. I felt guilty. I'd been taking care of everyone else and making him wait for me. And he had waited. Patiently.

"Forgive me."

"For what?" Somehow he managed to make his voice quiet as he spoke.

"I've been taking care of everyone else and making you wait for me. I should have been taking care of you and loving you and—"

"No," he said, and I shuddered as he touched me, some new power in his touch reaching inside me and making my heart race. "I held you in my arms when you first arrived, and I have stood here and watched you, my love. I watched you as you took care of all those around you that you love. But tell me now," his eyes burned hotter and he leaned down toward me, "did you die again tonight? Did you die again to protect us?"

"Yes," I answered him honestly. His eyes flashed a brilliant red before setting back to their usual smolder. His arms drew me deeper into his embrace.

"Save it, you two," Mrs. Aberforth croaked beside us. "You're *not married yet*, so keep it decent." She gave both of us an equal measure of her evil watery eye and I returned fire, staring back at her with my solid black orbs. The ancient old woman grumped. Unimpressed.

"Get over here and get ready, girl," her scratchy voice ordered. "I've been watching you grow up in this church for seventeen years now, wondering when you'd be walking down this aisle, and today's the day," she said with much satisfaction, then guided us to where she wanted us to stand.

"Should I be standing down front, waiting for you like the others did?" Believer asked.

"No," I smiled sadly. "We'll walk in together. We both look so scary. It was probably for the best to let the people that are human or at least look human to go first. If they throw a fit and kick us out, then at least we haven't ruined it for the others."

"Oh, tosh posh!" said Mrs. Aberforth, wrinkling up her ample supply of facial folds as she frowned. "So you're a witch. So what!? You still need to get married if you want to do what's right. Back in the beginning God made that wicked, murdering, brother killing Cain get married. He even brought him a wife. So getting married isn't just for Christian folk. It's for all folk. Even evil witch folk like you." She gave a stiff nod. As if to say, that settles it.

"Thanks," I said. "I think." My brow creased as I thought that through. Did she just lump me in with Cain?

"I want to get married," Believer said, his rumbling voice sounded thoughtful. "I did not expect this event to hold such meaning and purpose for me, but I find that it does."

I looked up at him to see his face as he continued to explain his feelings. "I have watched the others, how they have walked the aisle to experience this joining before these witnesses, with a priest of God overseeing and blessing their commitment to each other. I did not think this would matter to me but I find that it does. It seems more than the uttering of a series of words and making a contractually binding partnership before men as I once thought. This seems to be a spiritual or a magical bonding. I did not think it would be like this. I am very glad and honored that you asked me to marry you. Thank you, my lady."

It was weird but that got me crying.

"I will always treat you like a person. And if you love someone, and you want to be with them forever, then you marry them and do it right and make them as much a part of you as you can."

"Amen," said Mrs. Aberforth as she dabbed at her eyes with a napkin. Right then Dad came down the side hall and stepped up to us. He'd already delivered his first bride of the night and was ready to go for number two.

"How should we do this?" Dad asked.

"Good question, Mr. Bryant," Mrs. Aberforth said as she eyed the three of us shrewdly. "This is a new one, *even for me.*"

We eventually decided that I would hold Dad's arm and he would walk me down the aisle while Believer walked right behind us. Dad would give me to Believer right there on the main floor and then Believer and I would go up the steps to the platform together. We were ready.

"It's time, Rain," Mrs. Aberforth said as she peeked through the door. "Get going on my word."

Dad stood beside me holding my arm. Behind me Believer reached out and I felt his soft, warm clouds brush against the side of my face. Music chimed that familiar series of expectant beats, the doors began to open, and Mrs. Aberforth croak out, "Go, girl! Go!"

We started walking.

Jane

Four Weddings and a Funeral

Dan and I argued back and forth in our heads about what to do. We both knew that Rain was going in the limo because it was going to be attacked and she wanted that attack to happen to her "alone." Dan and I could tell by her words and the way she moved and acted, as clear as if she shouted it, that she knew what was going to happen. Dan thought that it was something do with her being a "witch" and that she had picked up some magical vibe about the future, but one way or another Rain knew that she was about to die so she was doing everything she could to keep all of us safely away from her when it happened.

I didn't want to let her do it.

Dan said it was her choice and we needed to support her, not stop her.

I didn't hear it but Dan said she wasn't going to change her mind no matter what we said. I still didn't want to let her do it, but Dan said we couldn't stop her even if we tried.

No one heard us as we argued. We did it all in our heads, but still, our first fight as a couple and it was all Rain's fault. And I couldn't even be mad at her for it, *which was so damn frustrating*! Dan insisted that Rain was sure she couldn't die and protecting the people she loved was her decision to make.

I searched Rain's eyes and her face a dozen times and she did seem pretty sure she wouldn't be killed "permanently," but she was still scared. I hated it. I wanted to go and find them myself and rip whoever it was into bloody little pieces with my bare hands, but in the end Dan and I both played along and stepped through the doorway into the church without any fuss and without telling everyone what was about to happen. I hated it though.

As soon as we were all through the doorway, Rain's dad took charge. He kept everyone at the church from totally losing it by walking Believer and Sky Dragon right down front as soon as we arrived. Dan and I watched the show from the balcony, surrounded by a comforting buffer of soldiers who we didn't need to impress or coddle.

The wedding guests and church members however were going to need to be handled carefully. Dan and I looked strangely beautiful and unnaturally compelling, but unless we did something obvious we still looked human. The cloud men, however, were impossible to explain or believe.

Sky Dragon was much denser in his composition than Believer, his clouds packed together so firmly his body almost looked solid with the rolling grey and silver clouds hard to see for what they were unless you got close. But his body's solid form also made him seem more real, dangerous, and permanent. He was only a little over six feet tall which made him manlike in size, but Believer was a giant. He towered at almost eight feet of billowing rolling storm like clouds with his pulsing white clouds in the center of his chest like a visible heartbeat drawing the eye. Anyone seeing Believer for the first time would expect the rolling clouds within him to disband and drift apart at any moment, only that moment never came and the rolling clouds perpetually moved, the whole of him held together by some invisible force.

It was interesting to see how the normal humans reacted. A small handful who couldn't cope left as soon as they saw them, while others had to be restrained because they refused to leave them be, but most people handled the situation surprisingly well, sitting, watching, and discussing their thoughts with their neighbors seated around them.

Mr. Bryant, Ryan, and Sky stood on stage beside them and introduced them to the church and wedding guests. Letting the whole crowd experience this at the same time made it less frightening for everyone. Of course the soldiers who crowded the building helped create a sense of security as well. There were a lot of shouted questions, but Mr. Bryant refused to answer, other than to introduce Believer as his daughter's fiancé, which caused another loud wave of shouted questions that he ignored completely as he introduced Sky Dragon as Believer's brother.

He called for quiet and waited at the podium until he had it. He told everyone that even though they looked different, Believer and Sky Dragon were still good people. Sky asked Sky Dragon to say hello to everyone. He stepped up to the podium microphone and spoke. His voice was surprisingly pleasant, warm and rich, not the low rumbling thunder that Believer spoke with.

"Hello. I know that my brother and I may seem oddly formed, but we mean you no harm. We are people. We are not humans, but we are still people. And we do apologize for the delay. I know you've been waiting to see a wedding which I hope shall begin shortly."

"You're a demon!" someone's angry voice shouted from the crowd.

"Or an angel!" shouted someone else.

Sky Dragon's long neck stretched out toward the man with the angry voice and some of those in the crowd gasped. Even though he didn't speak into the microphone he spoke loudly enough to be heard clearly by everyone in the auditorium.

"I am not a demon. Nor am I an angel. I'm a Sky Dragon," Sky Dragon said with dignified eloquence, he retracted his long neck then stepped away from the platform ignoring all the shouting people calling out questions.

Mr. Bryant took Sky Dragon and Believer back upstairs while Ryan and Sky stayed there and continued to answer questions and reassure everyone that the world was still at least *mostly* round, or perhaps only partially square, depending on the point of view.

Once he got back upstairs Mr. Bryant introduced Dan and me to Pastor Renolds and got him up to speed on the additional weddings. Renolds took Mr. Bryant into a nearby room where they had a heated argument. Of course Dan and I heard every word they said.

Renolds asked Mr. Bryant if he'd completely lost his mind. How could he allow Ryan to get married to a girl he just met!? How could he allow his daughter to marry a monster!? The usual ravings one would expect from a man in his position faced with this kind of crap. Mr. Bryant didn't flinch. He told him that both his children had his blessing and that he was doing the best he could for them under the circumstances. Round and round it went for about five pointless minutes until Renolds gave up.

Once they emerged I let them know that Rain was on her way to the church and that we needed to wait until she arrived before we could start. Renolds almost had a fit as he explained how my family had been waiting almost two hours already. I lied and told them she'd be here in thirty minutes and that seemed to shut them up.

If Rain took any longer than that I planned to go find her myself and drag her back to the church with me. I hoped with all my heart that thirty minutes was more than enough time. I tried to shut it down but one unfortunate part of my newly fashioned, multitasking vampire mind had set itself aside to do nothing but worry about Rain. I wondered what was happening to her right this moment? Had she died yet? If she had, and had already come back, how will she get here safely? Was she hurt or possibly confused? Sometimes Rain got disoriented and lost inside her head, all daydreamy—worry, worry, worry, worry, worry, worry—

Gotta make it *stop*!

WHERE'S THE OFF SWITCH!

Worry, worry, worry, worry, worry, worry—

Shit.

Pastor Renolds insisted on giving some quick premarital counseling since we were going to have to wait until Rain arrived. I was fine with that, anything that got "most" of my mind off what Rain was doing was fantastic. Dan and I were first for our counseling cram session.

Pastor Renolds seemed distracted by Dan and the way he looked but every time he looked at me he quickly looked away. I could read his discomfort as I gracefully folded myself into the chair in front of his big fancy desk. I watched Renolds as he struggle to banish wild, unwanted thoughts and stay focused on the task at hand.

I reached out toward the chair beside me without looking and met Dan's hand, our fingers intertwining before we looked into each other's eyes. I was so worried about Rain and frazzled with everything else I was tempted to let Dan hold me as tightly as he could and do whatever he had done before to quiet my mind and take me to that peaceful place where all I could hear was his voice—with no other thought in my head but him.

It was still there!

Worry, worry, worry, worry, worry—

She's going to be all right, Jane, Dan spoke into my mind at the same time Pastor Renolds cleared his throat, ready to get started.

Dan and I turned to him at exactly the same time, our movements mirrors of each other. I saw how the pastor noticed our synchronized movements. His brow creased in thought. He didn't know what to make of us.

"Dan, your Uncle Harold already explained that you and Jane are struggling right now. And the agents told me *some* of what you and the other teens have been through." He shook his head. "It's hard to believe that a doctor would ever do something like this. It makes me sick. I hope that monster is already rotting in a jail cell in the bottom of some dark hole." He was upset, but I heard in his voice something else also.

Something he'd been working up to.

He didn't want us to get married.

I quickly slammed my eyes shut to hide the red glow I knew was filling me while at the same time I wrestled with the wild tide of fury that flashed through my body. There was no way he'd marry us if he saw my hellish glare! *Calm! Easy! 1 2 3 4 5 6 7... 987, 988.*

Dan squeezed my hand.

"With all that's happened here today and all the health problems you two are facing, it would be best to postpone this till you've recovered and had some time to let all this settle. Making a lifelong commitment is nothing you should do in a rush or when you're not feeling your best. Waiting would be best for everyone under these circumstances."

I listened but kept myself frozen as stone, not trusting myself or my temper.

"You two should be focusing on your health concerns at this time. And don't feel that you have to go through with it just because you've got a church full of people downstairs. They'll all understand. And for heaven's sake, don't worry about the money!" His voice was almost cheerful as he tried to wriggle out of his commitment. "I'll refund it. No problem. You and Dan can still get married here at the church, but let's do this when you're feeling better. Dan? Jane?" I didn't need eyes to see the cheesy, desperate smile. The weak hope he held out that he could stop this.

Jane! Be good! Dan warned.

I'm tired of being good! I growled at him in my head, fighting my body and trying like hell to do exactly that—*be good.*

"Pastor Renolds," I began, eyes carefully closed, voice forced into a carefully firm tone spoken at a speed that was slow enough to be heard and processed by human ears. "Dan and I love each other and we want to get married. I know seventeen is young, but our parents and guardians have consented and signed our papers. We are legal. And you've already agreed to marry us and taken our money. Our families are downstairs waiting. We don't want a refund and we don't want to wait, we're ready now."

With my eyes closed I turned to face Dan, and I knew without seeing that our heads turned at the same time. "Dan has made me be good, Pastor Renolds, he's very old fashioned in that way, but I'm through with it. *I'm–NOT–going–to wait.*"

I knew Dan could feel everything I felt. The thought of waiting made my heart skip a beat and I had precious few of those left.

I want you right now, Dan. I want everything we had in the book! I want my Midnight honeymoon to be real, in this world, before we die.

I listened as Dan wrote a note on his pad then handed it to Renolds. Renolds read it, but not out loud.

"Very well," Renolds said, sounding resigned and at the same time more firm and very serious. He even picked up some volume as he stepped into his "pastoral" role. "If you two insist on going through with this, then I want to make this crystal clear in your minds. Apart from what you decide to do with your eternal soul, who you marry is the most important decision you'll make in this life. What God joins together should stay that way. You need to understand that this is a commitment you're about to make before a Holy God *who does not change his mind*, before his church, before your families, and to each other. A life-long commitment. In sickness and health. Richer and poorer. Good times and bad. Till 'death' do you part. Are you willing and ready to make a commitment like that?" he asked with as much gravity as he was able to muster.

"Yes," I said, and as things seemed to be righting themselves and my temper with them I risked opening my eyes the thinnest of cracks and saw Dan as he leaned forward at the desk and flipped open his pad.

He wrote at a torturous normal human speed as the pastor watched him, but he held his paper at an angle so I couldn't see what he wrote. I wondered what Dan was doing as he tore the page out and handed it to Pastor Renolds. Renolds read it, his eyebrows going up. He actually smiled.

"You want it said exactly this way?"

Dan nodded and Pastor Renolds tucked the note into his front shirt pocket looking pleased. I wondered what Dan could have possibly written that would make the crabby pastor smile.

"What are you guys talking about?" I asked. "Said what way?" I asked Renolds instead of Dan, since Dan seemed to be trying to surprise me. I played along. My Dan liked to surprise me. He sat in his chair beside me looking innocent as Renolds, enjoying this bit of normal-seeming banter, started talking.

"Dan asked me to change one part in the wording of the traditional wedding vows." He drew out the piece of paper Dan gave him. "Where I would normally say, 'till death do you part,' Dan has asked me to say 'for all eternity.'"

My hand covered my mouth, and my heart skipped a beat, not out of anger but out of surprise. I was surprised in more than one way. First at how much my Dan loved me, but also at how the book had crept into our lives again. I remembered that in the Midnight book Sarah and Ethan had changed their wedding vows in almost the same way. I felt dizzy as the magic of the book was unleashed, changing me more.

My eyes rolled up and I slumped over in my chair as my world spun in dizzy circles. I couldn't tell up from down as the whole thing flipped upside down. I lay limp in Dan's arms as the magic settled into me, pins and needles danced across my flesh and I felt a tightening around my heart. My whole body tingled, inside and out, as my heart sputtered, skipped a long beat, then resumed beating, slower than before but still tha-thumping along. I felt it now, even as Dan held me. I was changing. In lots of ways.

"We should call a for an ambulance!" I heard a human voice, so loud it echoed around the room. I ignored it; I was so disoriented and still trying to adjust.

I felt altered.

Like something key to my existence had been moved or had changed shape within me and I was trying to figure out what had happened. Even with my eyes closed I could feel the human as he reached for the phone on his desk. Dan leaned forward putting his hand on top of the phone holding the receiver in place.

Dan held onto me with his other arm as I tried to adjust to what I had become. How had I changed? What would be new this time, I wondered. Dan wrote notes to reassure the—pastor. "Pastor Renolds," I forced myself to think of him as his name and not as "the human." Dan was doing his best to assure him that all was well and that I was waking up even now. I knew Dan could feel me and hear my thoughts. He knew I was still trying to figure myself out.

"Dan! We should call for an ambulance, it's been more than a couple of minutes."

"I'm okay now." I spoke at human speed, my eyes snapped open, and I slowly brought my hand to my face to brush my hair out of the way from where it hung, wrapped around my head. I was stunned by the sight of my own hand. I held it up in front of my face and looked at it, surprised to see that it was actually another shade paler and my eyesight had sharpened yet again! The world had come more sharply into focus and a whole new layer of detail had opened up that never existed before.

Are you all right, Jane? How are you doing? Dan's words came into my head. His voice in the quiet of my mind seemed so comforting to me that I shivered in pleasure simply at hearing him here inside me even as his arms held me on the outside. If felt so good. So right.

It felt perfect.

I let my mind drift back and thought about how his hand had felt in mine that day we first met and Dan had said "hi." My vampire mind recalled the day with perfect detail. Dan slid into the chair beside me and we held hands and looked into each other's eyes—*and I fell in love.*

It felt perfect.

It was perfect.

As I remembered that moment, words failed me. I was so happy and content that I purred, almost like a cat, a strange rumbling sound coming from deep within me, more animal than human, and Dan's body responded to it. I felt the goose bumps rise on his arms as the little hairs stood on end and he shivered with me.

Are you all right, Jane? Dan asked again, but even the voice in his head seemed shaky, straining for control.

Yes, my love, I'm fine. But I'm still getting used to myself. I became more vamp and a little less human.

Speaking of humans, the one in the room with us was growing more uneasy each second. His heart rate had increased, his blood moving faster as he watched us. His smell was alarmed and aroused and alarmed at being aroused. It was time to say something for the slow human brain in front of me to chew like cud while Dan and I talked about something important.

"I'm fine now. From time to time I have spells. I've gotten used to it and so has Dan. It's not so bad. There's no need to call anyone, Pastor Renolds." I spoke very slow and clearly.

"Are you sure?" The annoying sound of the human's voice bothered me.

"I saw a doctor right before I came to church. Honestly, I'm feeling much, much better now."

Dan could feel my new awareness of the human in the room and he felt my power too. Lots of things had changed. I didn't know how much of me was still human. If I had to guess I'd say I was down to about 5% at most. But that last 5% was beating away inside my chest and would be keeping me alive until 11:33 tonight.

"Is our premarital counseling over?" I asked Renolds, trying my best to sound human and annoyed. "Please! We're ready, Pastor. I'll meet you and Dan at the altar in just a few minutes unless you have more questions for us."

"I have a few more things we need to discuss before we can move forward." Renolds blinked, surprised at my instant recovery from my very peculiar spell. He used years of discipline and structure to order his thoughts as he moved forward, asking his question, although I could tell all he wanted was for us to get out of his office as soon as possible. And I could tell that he still did not want to marry us.

He asked his question. "Jane, Dan. I need to ask you about your souls. I know you love each other but God loves you too. Remember, I said that getting married was the second most important decision you would ever make. The most important decision is where your soul will spend eternity." He paused for a moment and leaned in, forcing himself to stare at us. "If you died today, Dan, Jane, where would you spend eternity? Do you know?" he asked. I spoke to Dan in my head.

I know where my soul will spend eternity. It will be wrapped around yours, Dan, holding you and loving you forever. And so will my arms. And my legs— and my mouth— I was snapped out of my shameless mental erotica prematurely by Dan as he pulled out his notepad and scribbled his answer to the Pastor. He held it where I could see and read what he wrote before he handed it to the Pastor.

Ryan Bryant already talked to Jane about her immortal soul. And Heaven and God and Hell. He was real worried about Jane's soul too. When he gets in here ask him yourself what Jane told him. It really is quite interesting. But can we go now?

"Interesting you say. I'll ask him." Renolds raised an eyebrow, wondering what strange answer Ryan would have. I fought hard not to smile. My Dan could be a devious little monster when he wanted to be. I wondered how Ryan would manage to dance around the question and still tell the truth without freaking out his pastor.

Dan, your evil vampire side is showing, I thought to him and kissed him, right there in front of Pastor Renolds. I like it when you're bad. You should do it more. It makes me hot! I thought to him as we kissed.

"Whoa! Hold up! Save that for later if you don't mind." Pastor Renolds spoke kindly but he definitely wanted us to stop and to get out of his office. "Did I hear you right, that you actually have your license ready and signed by both your parents?"

Dan reached into his bag and took out the marriage license which he had filled out and paid for online this morning before coming up to the mall. That was my Dan, always prepared and planning ahead.

Renolds looked it over before nodding. "You and Jane are the only ones with all your legal paperwork finished. The FBI has assured me that everything would be handled regardless of the paperwork and that all I need to do is officiate the service. They said not worry about anything else." His tone dripped with unease and suspicion. "They even told me that the additional cost for the 'extra weddings,' seven thousand dollars each, would be taken care of and any wear and tear on the church and the grounds would be paid by the government." Renolds shook his head and picked up some papers with the FBI seal on them. "They said, 'Just send the bill.'" And now he was just complaining. He dropped the papers back on his desk and ran his hands through his hair. I heard in his voice how confused and frustrated he was by the strange events of the day. Seeing Believer and Sky Dragon had shaken the man, and our strange marriage counseling session hadn't improved his disposition any, but we could tell he was uncomfortable with one more thing. He was building up his nerve, I could see it.

"I'm okay with marrying you two," Renolds said flatly, finally getting to his point. "And if Ryan and this other girl he just met want to get married, that's fine. Mr. Bryant approves of her and I'll see both of them in here shortly, but I doubt I'll be able to go through with marrying Rain to that thing downstairs. Are you still going to get married if I don't do all three of the weddings?" He waited, hopeful that this would be the deal breaker and we would all go away mad and let things go back to normal.

"No problem," I said with a sincere smile, my voice filled with understanding as I added, "Rain and Believer can go last, that way it won't interfere with the rest of us."

Even someone who wasn't a vampire could have seen how very disappointed he was that we were still moving forward. I could also see that since he'd sat down with us he'd decided (for his own reasons) to call it off if we gave the slightest bit of fuss or so much as raised our voice. But now he had a crisis of conscious. Dan and I sat there and smiled at him carefully. Careful not to show too much teeth or too much pleading. Pleading would embolden his urge to set us on the curb. So would the teeth.

We sat there. Waiting. Long human seconds passed.

He may not have sworn but his body did. He slumped in his chair, worried and trapped. He was regretting how he'd handled this. He couldn't go back on his word and say "no" without some reason. Unless he just lied or broke his word. Which he *sooo* wanted to do. Which he was about to do—

"I hope you'll change your mind," I spoke before he did, "but if you can't bring yourself to marry Rain and Believer that's your business. We totally understand. All my family is downstairs waiting. And I'm done waiting." I gave him a hard stare and my eyes may have even gone a little red because Pastor Renolds blinked and pulled back in his chair.

"I'll see you two at the altar then," he said quickly, wanting us out of his office. I tried to ignore the faster drumming of his heart. "Unless you have any other questions or spiritual concerns, I guess we're done here. God bless you two and I'll pray that you both recover quickly from what these pills have done to you. Please send in Ryan and Sky on your way out. Thank you." Renolds looked down at his desk, reorganizing papers that didn't need to be reorganized to keep from having to look at me. I wasn't surprised at not being walked to the door. Renolds didn't want to stand up.

Dan and I held hands and stepped into the small lobby where Ryan and Sky waited, happily talking away while Sky Dragon watched over them.

"Your turn, guys," I said happily.

"Hey, how'd it go in there?" asked Ryan with a grin. "Did my pastor give you guys a hard time about getting married?"

"Yes, he did. He tried to get us to wait and put the wedding off till later," I said without a smile.

"What!?" Sky shouted. "What'd you tell him!?" She was mad!

Dan and I moved our heads at the same time as we turned and shared a mutual "WTF!" at vampire speed (unseen by the humans) then turned back at the same time.

I answered for us. "We told him no."

"Good!" Sky said firmly, looking upset. "You two need to get married. I don't want your book's magic to mess with Ryan again. I want you good and married to Dan before we get married. So you're going first!" she ordered.

Ryan put his arms around her from behind. "Easy, Sky, relax. You don't have anything to worry about." He tried to reassure her. Dan and I could tell that they'd been having this conversation for a while and that Sky was still afraid that the magic affecting me would reach out to grab Ryan again. She was fighting for her man. I approved.

"Jane's not in control of it, Ryan." Sky gripped the arms across her middle and held them possessively as she argued her point. "I've seen her book magic try to get you before and I don't want it to get you! Jane told me that this magic would still be doing things until she died. So I'll stop worrying about it once she's dead!" She cast me a squinty-eyed glare. Hungry for my end.

"SKY!" Ryan said, shocked at her harsh attitude.

I laughed darkly. Dan's head turned, his eyes going a shade redder as he looked at Sky Dragon who had taken another step closer, watching us with his own burning red eyes. I was surprised and so was Dan.

Sky has some fight in her after all, Dan. And here we thought she was a pushover. Girl's got a mean streak, don't she? I told Dan. My opinion of Sky went up considerably. Again, I approved.

"If I were you, I'd want me married and dead too."

That shut Ryan up and ended his muttered apologies that we were all ignoring anyway. Sky was surprised. She nodded and I nodded too. We girls were on the same page. She seemed okay with me being okay with her wanting me dead.

Hehehehe. You're crazy! Dan's lips curled upwards as he tried not to laugh on the outside like he was on the inside. It wasn't working.

"We'll go first, Sky. Going down the aisle first sounds perfect to me," I said happily as Dan's arms folded around me like I wanted. "But Pastor Renolds doesn't know if he will be able to go through with marrying Ryan's sister to Believer, so go after me. That way if he can't go through with Rain's wedding we'll still be done."

Ryan sobered right up. "He said that he wouldn't marry Rain?"

"Pretty much. But he was actually hoping to find some way to get out of marrying all of us. He thought we would be so pissed we'd all walk off in a huff." I laughed. "Not damn likely. I'm not leaving till that human says '*man and wife*' even if I have to help him say it." My eyes went red.

"Whoa!" Ryan gave me and Sky a quick look and head shake before looking at Dan. "The ladies are FEISTY tonight, aren't they, Dan?"

Dan grinned big and nodded.

Mine is actually more "horny" than "feisty," I heard Dan in my head and laughed.

A short, ancient, old woman with her silver hair done up in a bun came marching down the hallway, her wrinkled old face looking stern and unfriendly as she approached.

"OhmyGod!" Ryan quickly grabbed Sky's arm and opened Pastor Renolds' door. He gave us an evil grin and bounced his eyebrows at us. "Have fun with our church's wedding coordinator." He giggled wickedly as he pushed a surprised Sky inside and quickly shut the door behind him.

The old lady stopped in front of Sky Dragon where he leaned against the wall. She looked up at him. His long reptilian neck extended upward and allowed his head to look down at her from a frightening angle while his red eyes blazed at the old woman. It looked like he was about to swallow her head first, but the old woman didn't bat an eye as she stared up at him.

"And who are you?" Even her voice had wrinkles in it!

"I'm Sky Dragon," came his surprisingly clear and appealing voice.

"I heard that already downstairs. All I need to know is are you in the wedding or not?"

Sky Dragon's long neck retracted until his head rested on his shoulders like a normal person. His eye ridges cocked at odd angles creating a look of confusion. "Should I be in the wedding? Believer is my brother. He is marrying Rain Bryant. And Sky is my mother. She is marrying Ryan Bryant."

"What!?" she croaked. "That tall blonde girl that was with Ryan is your mother!? She didn't look old enough to have a child your size," she declared emphatically.

"I'm only four hours old. I'm not human. My Sky made me with magic. I am a part of her soul," Sky Dragon said proudly.

The old woman walked a circle around him, eyeing him up and down. Sky Dragon seemed at first surprised by and then uncomfortable under the old lady's intense scrutiny.

"My job is weddings, not figuring out *nonsense*. Huu," she grunted. "Best man's out of the question. Your mother comes first." She narrowed her eyes. "If you're her child you'll do as a ring bearer. That's what most of the male children do in weddings these days," she pronounced as she looked him up and down again.

Sky Dragon seemed to consider that. "Ring bearer." His eye ridges leveled out. "That sounds good. I would be glad to do that for my Sky."

"That's settled then." The crone gave a nod, that problem solved. She turned her gaze to Dan and me, but Sky Dragon asked the question I wanted to ask.

"Who are you?" The Dragon's voice was much more respectful now, as was his demeanor. "Ma'am," he added with a considerate dip of his dragon head.

"I'm Mrs. Aberforth," she declared. "I'm in charge of the weddings at this church. You two." She pointed at Dan and me with a wizened old finger that looked like a bleached bone somehow still animated with life. "Come with me," she said in her scratchy old voice.

If–you vant–to live! Dan said inside my head, making his voice a horror movie mockery. I tried not to laugh and failed miserably, giggles pushed through my tight pressed lips as we followed Mrs. Aberforth down the stairs while Dan made jokes only I could hear. He said that the wedding coordinator matched the rest of us monsters and that we'd found "*the mummy.*" Or *the mummy's mummy.*

We giggled and laughed as she led us to the back of the worship hall and told us where to stand and where to go once we walked down front, and where to stand on the platform and where to go once we said our vows. She had a horrible voice but she was a sweet old lady, and Dan and I could tell that she'd been doing the weddings here forever and planned on doing the weddings at this church for the next thousand years. We sobered and let the old lady do her thing, nodding along. I said the polite "yes ma'ams" for both of us and soon Mrs. Aberforth left us to start the same process on Sky and Ryan and their "ring bearer."

BOOM! BOOM! BOOM!

The ground shook beneath our feet and the lights went out for three human seconds before flickering back to life. Ryan and Sky rushed down to meet us and Mr. Bryant. They all started to freak and it fell to Believer, Sky Dragon, Dan, and me to calm and reassure them when I wanted to freak out right along with them and go running off to see what had happened! But whatever had happened, I was sure that it had already happened.

The soldiers around us didn't get the "stay calm" memo. They started acting crazy and rushing around and getting bossy with the guests. When Mr. Bryant or others asked what happened they refused to talk or answer honestly, saying they didn't know yet. The FBI and military kept the guests from leaving. One FBI guy actually stood up in front of the church and lied his ass off saying that the roads were unsafe and that a gas leak had caused an explosion. He assured everyone that they would be free to go in just one hour.

It was a weak and pathetic lie but it was delivered well and seemed to calm things down for the moment. It was strange to watch as the women in the room accepted the lie happily and the men in the room let them, but whispered among themselves. Dan and I could hear soldiers talking and receiving orders and we knew that the limo had been blown up and that the motorcade traveling to the church had been hit by three rockets.

Dan and Believer entertained Ryan and his father while I distracted my frantic mind by talking with my two best friends in the world, Emma and Stacy. I told them the truth while we were waiting for Rain to arrive. I told them pretty much the whole story. They already knew about the "Flying Girl" and they'd heard the wild stories about the "Black Witch," but I got to tell them about the monsters that most people didn't know about yet: "the Vampires."

They freaked out a little when I showed them how fast I could move and Stace insisted on seeing my teeth. They were strangely relieved to know I wasn't sick with a heart condition and that Dan and I were just turning into the "living" dead, not dying and joining the "dead" dead.

Emma wept and actually asked me to bite her, saying that she didn't want to leave me, that she wanted to go with us. It created an awkward moment until Stacy fussed at her and told her to get a grip. I, of course, told Emma "no" as compassionately as I could and promised her that I'd be back as soon as Dan and I adjusted to our new diet.

We talked about happy things, the decorations and the wedding instead of sad things like me dying or going away. Emma and Stacy had taken advantage of us being late, using the extra time to decorate the church in red, white, and black. I laughed as they told me their antics as they raided a nearby funeral home. They came away with lots of black seat covers, black table cloths, and even the fancy black candle holders which were set up on the platform complete with BLACK candles!

They also had the sheer white material tacked up on the walls throughout the church hiding away the icky mauve wallpaper. I could tell that a lot of people had helped get things ready. Red roses were everywhere, scattered around the church, looking beautiful. Emma had even been thoughtful enough to yell at the soldiers and now we had all commandos in solid black outfits inside the church in all the visible places so they matched much better than the camo green ones we had before. Stacy was disappointed that she was going to be walked down the aisle by one of Dan's two uncles instead of some hot young guy, but Emma was too torn up to care that she'd be escorted by an old guy.

Fifteen minutes after the rumbling booms, the collective patience of the guests finally ran dry and the mutiny began. A number of people were done; they wanted to be out of this crazy church with its wild creatures and others had had enough of the military and the bossy FBI telling them that they couldn't leave if they chose to do so, while others who were determined to see the wedding were just sick of waiting. The whole auditorium felt more like a military prison than a church filled with wedding guests, and when the soldiers insisted that the big monitors on the wall of the church not be used to show the local news things got ugly, fast.

Right before it all boiled over, the wedding music started. As the normal human respect for all things matrimonial kicked in, people stopped yelling, quieted, and resumed their seats.

Mrs. Aberforth looked at me and shrugged. "We had to start or we would have lost everyone, child."

And so we started. And that was also when I heard Rain's voice coming down the hall from the front of the church. *She was finally here!* I wanted to pry off Dad's arm and run over and check on her and make sure she was okay, but we were first and I couldn't go.

Emma and Dan's Uncle Harold were the first ones down the aisle followed by Stacy and Dan's Uncle Conner, stepping out, arm in arm when the old wedding coordinator told them to go. The girls were dressed in matching black dresses and Dan's uncles looked fantastic in their black tuxedos. Uncle Harold told us how Dan had kidnapped him early this morning and drove him way out to Conner's house and took both of them up to the mall and made them get fitted for their tuxedos. I wasn't surprised. My Dan always planned ahead and thought about the details that made everything wonderful.

I didn't even get a chance to speak with Rain before I had to head down the aisle; she was still wrapped up in Believer's arms wearing a peaceful happy smile when "the mummy" said, "Go!"

The church was filled with the sound of Wagner's March accompanied by the noise of hushed whispers as we walked the aisle. Dan looked amazing. His white gothic outfit, pale chiseled features, and intense gaze made him look like an avenging angel as he stood on the platform and waited for his bride.

He wasn't smiling and neither was I as I marched toward him and my final eternal resting place in his arms. For Dan and me, this wasn't just a wedding, it was also our funeral. A chance to see our family and friends before we died. A chance to say goodbye to the human lives we'd lived and known, and somehow it seemed too somber for smiles.

That was why I had picked the colors I had for the wedding. Red was for the blood that would be our new lives together. White was for the wedding and because Dan and I were both pure, giving ourselves to each other tonight, to have and to hold forever. And black was for our death and the eternal living night which we would walk in forevermore. Everyone would celebrate the weddings today, but only Dan and I would celebrate the funeral.

I could tell that everyone was amazed at my beauty, and Dan's, but we were so alien, not just in how we looked but in how we moved that they didn't know what to make of us. I had looked at myself in a mirror earlier and I knew what I looked like. My skin was almost milk white, my lips were bright red, and my high cheek bones and the odd tilt that my purple eyes now had gave me an otherworldly appearance. My jet black hair and the strange gothic white wedding dress did not inspire the traditional sentiments that a blushing bride would normally bring out.

I knew that our nontraditional colors had also caused a stir, but once people heard that Rain was also getting married today they attributed the black candles and the other black decorations to her instead of us. I listened with my vampire hearing, picking out the whispered conversations that buzzed across the room as I slowly walked the aisle at the steady striding pace dictated by the music, tradition, and the steps of my father who walked me down the aisle.

Some of my own family whispered to each other as to whether or not I was "really" Jane. Others asked questions about Dan. Who was he and why he couldn't talk. Others wondered what had happened to us. Some of my younger relatives were guessing that I had gone Goth while others said it was because I was a vampire. I guess it was bound to get out sooner or later and now it was spreading through the room from person to person. The word "vampire" was whispered from ear to ear as we stood there before the church and looked out at all our human family as humans for the last time.

My mom was already crying and Dad cried when it was time to give me to Dan. "I know he'll take good care of you. I love you, baby." Dad kissed me and gave me to Dan then went to join Mom where she sat on the front row beside Uncle Billy and Gran.

The pastor had changed our vows as Dan had instructed, switching the "till death do you part" to say "for all eternity." When it was Dan's turn to say his vows, his Uncle Harold spoke for him while Dan gazed deep into my eyes and nodded at the appropriate times. Harold had a lovely voice, but I heard Dan for myself as he spoke to me in my head.

Other than that allowance, it was a normal, beautiful, perfect, human wedding right until we got to the end. When Dan and I kissed, we both felt that weird upside down feeling again as the book kicked in, changing us more. My skin tingled but this time so did Dan's and we held onto each other for a dizzy minute and let the world spin around us. Dan was wiped out more than I was this time and I held him up, keeping him on his feet so he wouldn't fall flat on the stage in front of God and everyone.

As soon as the pastor introduced us as "Mr. and Mrs. Simmons" we moved to the side of the platform, making room for the next couple to come down the aisle. I'd been very impatient and pushy and downright rude there at the end, but now I was content. Things were moving along nicely and I was happy. I knew that soon, *very soon*, I'd be alone with Dan. Behind me on the platform stood Emma and Stacy and behind Dan stood his Uncle Harold and his Uncle Conner. Mom and Dad sat on the front row and watched us, crying but happy.

As soon as we were out of the way, Ryan took his place on the platform beside his pastor looking very daring in the white outfit and white leather pants and boots that Rain had made for him. The music started again and Sky entered the church looking absolutely beautiful. As soon as Ryan saw her, his huge smile lit up his face and was enough to make the girls *and* the older ladies in the church melt as they saw how much he loved this mysterious girl. Sky's amazing smile matched Ryan's, watt for watt. Some of the ladies had combined forces and had done Sky's hair up beautifully and there were oohs and aaahs as people finally got a chance to see who had stolen Ryan away from all the girls here at church who had wanted him for so long. My vampire eyes picked out a bunch of them, which didn't surprise me at all. Ryan was a nice guy. I overheard the whispered complaints from half a dozen pissed chicks venting.

Life had been breathed back into the church! Ryan and Sky had banished the dark and gloom. The magic of the "Snow White Wedding" was in full bloom once again as the little girls sitting in pews saw a beautiful "human" bride that they could dream of being one day, and all the mothers looking on saw a bride they could remember having been or wanted to be.

Dr. Burgis stood in for Sky's father, walking her down the aisle and giving her away to Ryan before taking a seat on the front row beside my mom and dad. He sat there smiling up at us all. Dan and I could tell that in his own way the doctor saw us as his "kids" and he looked for all the world like a proud father as he sat beside my dad. Weird. But what was weirder were my parents. They smiled and talked to him like everything was okay now when a few hours ago, Dad had called the doctor a *son of a bitch* and told me I could eat him. How strange is that!?

Ryan and Sky's vows were traditional and went off without a hitch. They looked beautiful together as they held onto each other and stood beside us on the platform.

The "mystery" couple was a complete surprise to everyone, but I could tell Rain's handiwork when I saw it. She'd made their clothes and their amazing rings. So somewhere *out there* between the time she had left in the limo to the time she walked back into the church, Rain had found these two lovebirds and drug them to the wedding. Where she found them I had no clue, under a rock maybe, but we could all tell they were in love.

From anyone else I would have said that grabbing a pair of perfect strangers off the street and taking them to your wedding was insane, but it seemed perfectly normal for Rain. We were all learning to *go with the flow* when it came to her peculiar way of doing things. Girl was totally crazy, but in a good way. Rain's father walked the mystery bride down the aisle, gave her away, and then slipped out of the sanctuary through a side door to get back to Rain.

Pastor Renolds seemed unbothered by our mystery couple, only stopping long enough to ask their names before moving forward. They said their vows, exchanged rings, were pronounced man and wife, and then took their place with the rest of us lined up across the back of the stage and facing out at the congregation as we all waited for the next couple to walk the aisle.

The music started again and Rain and her father pushed open the back doors walking arm in arm. Believer glided along behind the two like a towering giant, filling the width of the center aisle from pew to pew. Those seated on the ends of the pews either leaned away, cringing in fear, or reached out to brush their hands through his strangely solid substance as he passed by.

Believer ignored them, keeping his burning red gaze aimed out over the heads of Rain and her father as they measured their steps to the wedding march. Believer was an impossible sight to behold, but for once he wasn't the focus of attention. Whispers, spontaneous eruptions of tears, and full on gasps burst from men and women seated on pews as she passed her way down the center aisle. Seeing what Rain had become was a soul-clenching shock to this extended family who'd known her all her life.

Rain and her father ignored the growing murmurs from the congregation, the darkly scowling preacher they walked toward, her rebelliously animated hair, and her black dress that fluttered in her own personal breeze. Step. Step. Step. We all watched their approach. Nightmare dark eyes stared from a pale face made all the more disturbing by the coven mark stamped onto her forehead. Power poured off her, rolling through the open expanse from floor to ceiling, changing the flavor of what *was*.

Renolds said during our counseling session that he wouldn't know for sure if he could go through with Rain's wedding until he saw her for himself. Well he was seeing her now and he looked as if he wanted to tell us all to go straight to hell! Rain, Believer, and her father ignored it all as they walked down the aisle. Dan and I knew this was a colossal train wreck in the making, but it wasn't one we could stop.

We watched.

A few people started to leave, either in a self-righteous huff or fleeing in terror, some with frightened children in tow. Despite the few hitting the back doors, the church was still packed. On top of the church members in attendance, Dan and I had a good crowd here and the balcony was filled to capacity with soldiers, Feds, and others in suits who'd muscled their way in. There were also FBI camera crews videotaping everything from up there. Dan and I had overheard them talking earlier, speculating on whether the President would be watching the wedding "live."

Half way down the aisle it started.

"This ain't right!" shouted someone from the crowd.

"A witch don't belong here! Get that monster and that witch out of this church!" shouted an older man who got grabbed by someone to his right and told to be quiet, but once begun the rebellion spread like wildfire. It was mostly older people but some of the younger ones joined in, shouting and punching their fists into the air alongside men too frail to stand on their own without help.

"Get out!"

"Filthy witch!"

"Get her and that monster out!"

"Devil girl!"

Then someone shouted, "Devil's whore!"

Rain, her father, and Believer reached the front but Pastor Renolds walked down from the platform and stopped them before they could mount the stair. Dan and I easily picked out Renolds' words from the shouting voices of the mob.

"I can't do this, Jim. I'm sorry, but your daughter can't get married here." He motioned to the guys in the sound booth making a cutting motion and the music stopped dead, and the noise of arguing rose and filled the void left by the music. With a pained look, Pastor Renolds walked off into the angry shouting crowd that was at odds with itself. Some people were insisting they let Rain get married while others vehemently argued against it, back and forth.

Rain and Believer stood at the foot of the steps leading to the platform. Believer was holding her as she cried while her father argued with Renolds and others.

Vile, ugly words and curses flew.

It was a mess.

Black Rain

The Garden

"I'm so sorry, my lady." Believer held me as I cried. I buried my face into him and tried not to listen to the hateful things they shouted, but I still heard them. The words seemed to find me where I hid down inside my cloud.

"Take your daughter out of our church, Bryant!"

"Look at her eyes!"

"Oh my God! Did you see her eyes!"

"She's the Devil's whore!"

"Child killer! I saw her admit it on the internet! She killed her own baby!"

"Evil witch!"

"Thou shalt not suffer a witch to live!"

"That thing is a demon she called up out of hell! I say we send them both back where they came from!"

"Look at her forehead! That's the Mark of the Beast I tell you!"

"She's not your daughter anymore, Bryant, she's sold her soul to Satan!"

A hundred dark and hateful things, shouted from the people I had grown up with all my life and thought of as almost family to me. It felt like each of their angry shouts broke little pieces inside me, little pieces of the girl that I had been and the life I'd shared with Rain Marie. The memories of these people as family and as caring, good people crumbled. My father argued with them and I listened and cried as my wedding turned into a monstrous nightmare of angry, ugly shouted words.

"We do not need to get married, my lady. I am already yours. We do not need this human ritual. Let me take you away from this place." Believer tried to comfort me but I could hear in his voice how very surprised and disappointed he was at our treatment by these people who were supposed to love me. He was surprised and hurt, mostly for me, but also for himself. I knew that he wanted this as much as I did.

The angry crowd found new targets for their venom as soldiers moved in and pushed them back to their seats and away from us. I was done here, but I still wanted my wedding. This hadn't felt right to me anyway. Something in me wasn't comfortable getting married here. In a church. This place was for those who were still a part of Him. I wasn't. Bethany had been right this morning. I was a stranger here. I did not belong in this house. I'd go where I did belong.

"Believer, a wedding is supposed to be done in front of family and friends who love you and in a place surrounded by love and magic, so *that* is what we will have, and *that* is where we will go."

Believer watched me curiously as I stepped out of his embrace and walked the short distance to a plain-looking wooden door tucked into a corner at the base of the platform. The ushers' closet. It had a normal-sized door but inside it was only three feet deep. The only things in the closet were loads of extra offering baskets, trays and shelves holding the implements for the Lord's Supper, and an old Hoover vacuum cleaner, but I had other ideas for this doorway.

I placed my hand on it and willed it to open to the witch door that I had made at Cathryn and Cornelius's house. White light flashed around the edges. I left the door closed and the mystery of what I'd done in place as I turned and faced the still crowded church.

I didn't raise my voice but simply spoke my words as if I were alone with each person here, two people talking face to face. "You don't need to argue any-more, you can stop now." Guests and soldiers started to look this way and that, trying to figure out who had spoken.

"It's me. The bride in the black dress. I'm the one who's talking to you now."

Now they turned to face me, surprised to hear my voice right beside them, but still there was shouting and noise.

"Please, let me speak and then I swear I will go. Please, be quiet for a moment."

Everyone stilled and turned in my direction.

Even the soldiers hushed. All eyes were now on me.

"We are leaving," I said simply. "Believer and I will get married somewhere else. God is God of this whole world and we will say our vows before him under the stars that he made and leave this place to you. You can have it. I won't be back."

Some people looked guilty, while others were still angry and wanted to fight, but all of it gave me the same sad feeling that this wasn't my place anymore and these were not my people. They were Rain Marie's people and this was her place. A human place. I said my goodbyes to the past.

"Thank you for all the years you loved Rain Marie. Those of you who would still like to come to our wedding are welcome to come and witness our marriage. This doorway," I gestured to the closet, "will take you to where we are going to be married. I'll return you back here to the church after the wedding, but be warned—" I held my right arm over my head, my fingers curled like a claw. The bright lights glinted off glossy black nails as I spoke. "This is your church and your home and you can say what you want in here. Call me a bitch. Call me a whore. Call my love a demon from hell. That's your business and this is your place. But if you come to my wedding, stand in my presence, and say one word against me or my love I'll rip your heart out with my bare hands and eat it myself."

People paled, eyes going wide. I hadn't raised my voice. It was all said in the same chilling conversational tone, each word carried like an individual and personal promise. I was sure everyone staring at me now could easily imagine a bloody heart resting in my clawed hand. The room erupted with worried murmurs and some people began pushing for the exits, but no fists punched the air, and no one shouted "Devil's whore!"

I reached over and opened the closet door that now led into a dark, unfriendly looking room filled with boxes and cans instead of what should have been there, the ushers' closet. The dark storage room wasn't a real confidence builder. I smiled and gestured toward the door inviting people into the darkness beyond—*if they dared.*

"Family and friends who wish to attend the wedding of the Black Witch and Believer, Son of Sky, are welcome. All others who pass this way will be bled, butchered, and burned alive." I smiled and waited by the door, ready to receive my wedding guests. Believer stood beside me with a big smile on his face that made me happy.

The room came alive with movement as people started getting out and this time the soldiers cooperated, helping them on their way, but I saw that some people were moving in the opposite direction of the outgoing tide.

The vampires materialized right out of thin air, making me jump in surprise and making Believer grumble.

"Sorry," Jane said with an apologetic smile before she slowly reached forward and hugged me.

"Dan and I are ready to go to your wedding. And for our honeymoon. And to die." Dan stood beside her, the straps of a black duffle bag around his shoulders; the bag hung down his back making it easy for him to move quickly.

Jane licked her red lips and smiled. "If we get lucky, and you end up ripping out someone's heart, would you mind if we help with the clean up? You can have the pickle, we just want the juice out of the jar." Beside her Dan shook his head disapprovingly at his new wife's crude comment, but I laughed.

Jane looked at Dan adoringly as she spoke to me. "Once your wedding is over we're going to need your help right away, Rain. Quick. Okay?" She winced a bit. "I hate to rush you, but Dan and I are worried we might eat some of your wedding guests if you take too long, and that would be too much like a 'teen slasher' movie for me to handle." The misery of it was all over her face.

I reached out and took Jane's hand in mine. I could feel death closing in on her in almost the same way I felt it coming for me earlier, I could feel it now.

"I can feel it, Jane. It's not far away now. Death is coming for you soon. The end of your human life." I spoke without meaning to, the words tumbling out of my mouth of their own volition.

"You *can* feel it coming," Jane said as she studied my face. Her strange eyes opened wide in surprise as she saw things in me only she could see.

"Oh yes." I nodded. "I felt my own death when it was coming for me in the limo, and I feel yours now." I gave her a small smile. "But at least you won't have to die alone. You'll have Dan with you, so you'll be fine. Dying alone sucks."

My voice carried the weight of personal experience, and Dan and Jane both watched me closely then turned at the same time, like they were parts of the same person and hugged each other. I watched them. It seemed that love and death were all around me today. Jane and Dan were about to experience the ultimate death and the ultimate love and here I was to witness it.

I looked past the vampires, surprised to see that a line had formed. Guests for the wedding.

"Don't worry, guys. As soon as the wedding is over I'll take care of you. And if you need extra help, I can lock you up early in a nice safe place. Do you have my gift with you?" I asked.

Dan nodded.

"It's in his bag," Jane said. "And thanks for that. We're freaking starving right now but we've been saving your gift for tonight."

I frowned. I hadn't realized that they were still hungry. I'd have to take better care of my bloodsucking family in the future. Beside me, Dr. Burgis spoke happily with Believer. My dad, Williams, Ryan, and Sky were waiting in line behind the vampires.

"Ryan, Dad, Williams, once you guys get to the other side make sure you three stay in front of everyone else. The girls know who you three are, so stay up front, okay?"

Ryan's eyebrows shot up as did Sky Dragon's ridges (which were like his eyebrows). Even Dan's eyebrows rose a fraction at the hint of danger.

"What do you mean?" asked Ryan.

I winked at him. "Just go, Bro. But remember, there're witches in there." I gave him an evil grin as he grimaced at the dark opening. "Lots of scary witches."

"Just great," Ryan griped. He looked over at Dan. "Come on, Dan. Let's go."

Together they walked into the storage room along with Jane, Sky Dragon, Sky (who gave me a quick hug first), Williams, and Dr. Burgis who was back to carrying his own bags again, and some others. Some of my family.

"How's this work anyway? This is just a dingy old storage closet with a bunch of cans and stuff," Ryan complained. "There's no door out of here, Rain, it's a dead end." He looked back at me with a shoulder shrug as he stood inside the storage room.

"Once the door shuts, give it a few seconds, then open it. It'll open up to the mansion. You guys head on out and then shut the door behind you so I can send the next group on over. Got it?"

"Why didn't you make this thing so we could walk straight through, like the door you made from the doctor's office to the balcony closet?" he complained as everyone packed into the little room.

"I made the door at the Mansion so my Sisters could use it too," I said a little defensively, "and it was my first doorway, so stop complaining, you dweeb."

"Your first doorway!?" Ryan made a face and looked around the little storage room with a skeptical eye. "Is this thing up to code? Should I call OSHA to get it inspected first? We're not going to come out the other side flat like a pizza are we?"

Sky stood behind my annoying brother and I gave her an exasperated glare. "Sky, could you PLEASE do something to shut him up!?"

She blinked, then grabbed him and started kissing him, which thankfully kept his mouth too busy to talk.

Everyone laughed, Jane's musical laugh mingling with the sounds of human laughter in the little space as my sister-in-law sucked my brother's face off, and the laughter seemed to lift everyone's spirits and chase away some of the grim, ugliness of all the scary threats and hateful words.

Dad was still laughing a little as I gave him a hug, "Tell Mom I'll be there shortly and try to explain some of it." Dad stepped into the closet with the others and looked back to me.

"You want me to explain this to your mother?" His eyebrows were still in the upright and incredulous position when I shut the door so they could open it from their side and walk out of the storage closet and into the mansion.

After waiting a few minutes I opened the door on the now empty closet and started my next load. I waved Tom and Agent Trisha on through. David and Dana came next. "Come on in, you guys. You can stay as long as you like."

Dana looked scared and hesitant, but David had her hand in his. He stepped into the closet confidently, pulling her along. I heard him whispering to Dana, "She's not going to eat us! We'll be fine, Dana."

Next came Dan's Uncle Conner. "If you don't mind, I'd love to see your wedding."

I waved him on in.

"Oh goodie!" he said, with an flourish of a wave to those he left behind as he slipped into the storage closet.

Next I was surprised to see Mrs. Aberforth. "Rain, is this going to be a real wedding? Is it something I can be a part of or should I stay here?" She studied me, waiting for her answer.

I had to think about that for a second. "Well." I scratched my head. "It's going to be as real as I can make it, ma'am. But I'm not a real person anymore and neither is my groom so—" I shrugged. "Yeah—kinda." I made a face.

"That'll do," she said, gave a stiff nod, and walked into the closet.

Next came some of my other family and friends. I made better use of the space and packed about eight more in before I closed the door and started my next load, but I had a big surprise when I opened the door.

"Rain! What's all this about you getting married!?" Mom was standing right there in front me when I opened the door. I resisted the wild urge to slam the door shut and run like hell. She quickly lost her anger and her face went pale as she stepped out of the closet and ran her eyes over me. She didn't notice Believer standing on the other side of the doorway. She was so caught up by the changes to my face and eyes she had tunnel vision.

"My God, Rain. What happened?" Her hands reached out and touched my face at my eyes.

"What happened to your eyes, honey? Can you still see at all?" She noticed my hair moving around all by itself and then looked around just enough to see Believer and his burning red eyes staring down at her.

"Hello," Believer rumbled and smiled at her.

"Oh Lord!" She jumped back and almost knocked me off my feet as she crashed into me. "Oh my!" She wrapped her arms around me tightly and took a second to calm herself down, but soon she started looking from me to Believer. Back and forth. I could see that Dad must have tried to explain some of it before she came charging on over here.

"Yes, Mom. This is Believer. Now, I know you're upset and scared for me, and maybe a little freaked out, but before you say anything, may I tell you about him?" I waited until she reluctantly nodded. Her suspicious gaze stayed on Believer as I spoke. The dozen or so people still waiting to get to the wedding listened along with my mother, no doubt wondering what I'd say to calm her down or justify my current course of action.

"He's the most honest person I've ever met. He's a real gentleman and treats me with respect. He treats me like a lady. He's very smart. He never talks down to me or disrespects me. He is kind and super polite. He's exceedingly patient. He understands me as much as anyone can because there are parts of me that can't be understood, and he's even okay with me being crazy." I looked up at Believer; he was looking down at me, listening. "And when I get depressed and want to run away from the world and hide for all eternity, he reminds me of all the good things in life that are worth staying here for. When I feel ugly inside he makes me feel beautiful. He's not afraid to tell me I'm wrong and to talk some sense into me when I lose it. And he also understands that sometimes I have to do things because of what I am. He protects me. And when he holds me I feel safe and warm and loved. He loves me, Mom, and he wants me. And I want to be loved by him. He's a person like me, with his own feelings and wants and likes, and he has his own soul. And I truly love him. He makes me happy and I'm going to marry him."

I looked away from Believer's eyes and back to my mother who was looking at me now, at my face.

"Momma, I want you to meet my fiancé, Believer, Son of Sky."

Mom blinked a tear or two away and looked up at Believer. "He–Hello, Believer. It's good to meet you." She sounded like the words were drug out of her by force. Her face was still in complete denial. This can't be happening! was practically stamped across her forehead.

Believer's deep voice rumbled, "I really don't know what to say or how best to reassure you that I am more than the monster I appear to be. I cannot imagine what you must think of me and of my being with your daughter. All I can say or think to tell you is that I love her." Believer said so much less than me but somehow it sounded like more. I stepped away from my mother's arms which tried to pull me back and into his ready embrace.

"I love you!" I told him.

"And I you, my lady," he rumbled happily as he held me.

"Should we get in the closet now?" asked Emma loudly, one of Jane's friends from her wedding. Her voice filtered down to me again where I nestled within Believer's arms. "You need to get this show on the road, Rain. Dan and Jane are about to die, *remember?*" she griped, reminding me about our terminal wedding guests who were on a delicate timetable.

"Oh. Yeah! Sorry!" My muffled voice came from down inside Believer's arms where I was buried. "Everyone cram in, let's get going!" I urged.

And with that I packed the little room full with wedding guests. Mom stayed quiet and watched me as I loaded the last dozen wedding guests up, then she squeezed in beside me and Believer as I closed the door. I was happy and smiling. I stood beside her in the tight space while we waited for a minute to give the door a second to do its thing. The dark storage closet felt like an overcrowded elevator. Mom stood right beside me but hadn't said a word, and I was starting to get uncomfortable with the silence.

"So how are my Sisters, Mom?" I asked her.

Mom kept her face forward and her voice came out in an angry rush. "Well, I guess you should know that someone killed Cornelius earlier today, and Bethany raised him from the dead and changed his name to King Cornelius when she did it. She also changed Cathryn's name to Queen Cathryn and Bethany is Princess Bethany now. And she made Cornelius and Cathryn her parents. Which means they are Mary's parents too. And yours. So you have a new mom and dad now. Mary also told me how the three of you planned on staying at the Hale House from now on."

I was shocked and reeling from that amazing mouthful, but Mom didn't give me time to finish my mental overload. She reached out, threw open the door, and stepped out into the mansion's hallway and turned back to face me.

"Welcome home, Rain," she said, her voice dripping with sarcasm as she added, "Now let's go get you married." She stalked off down the hallway, leaving me wide eyed and gape mouthed.

"She seems pissed," Emma said, stating the obvious.

"Yep," said some other person I didn't even know.

"Pissed," echoed some other guy; I think he was my cousin Mark.

"Upset perhaps, but not pissed," Believer said. He tried to put it into perspective. "She probably feels that everything has gone out of control. I think she handled this wonderfully," he encouraged.

"So far," Emma said flatly. "Hey!" She spun around, giving out the evil eye. "Who the hell poked me!?"

I started laughing. Something about that struck me as funny, and I staggered out the door laughing my ass off as I waved everyone forward and out of the storage room. My guests stepped out, smiling as they followed the trail of soldiers in camo who directed them through the house and out to the garden area. Believer and I brought up the rear of our party. It was interesting, watching how these professional soldiers reacted to us. The other humans were acknowledged, classified as to threat level, and ignored, but not us.

First, they would always notice Believer at my side and every time they would take an involuntary step back, and every time they would catch themselves and take that step forward only to lose it again once they saw me and my black eyes staring at them. It made for an odd dance step, the "Soldier of Fortune Shuffle," and I was getting used to seeing it by the time I finally stepped out onto the patio leading to the enclosed garden where the wedding party gathered.

A group of fifty people or so milled about on a hill in the center of the garden while white liveried servants rushed about, setting up torches and putting out folding chairs for the guests to sit in. Mrs. Aberforth stood in the middle of the chaos doing her thing, taking charge of the wedding. I saw a line of soldiers she must have drafted into her "Wedding Militia" coming out of a side door of the house, arms full of torches and chairs, ready to dance to her tune as she ordered them about.

I stopped to watch all the bustling activity. It made me smile to see Mrs. Aberforth here, doing what she had done for so many years at our church, and I was glad that she would have a part in my wedding. It felt right, familiar, and it made me smile.

"What has made you smile, my lady?" Believer asked as he looked down at me. He was smiling too.

"Because I'm happy." I smiled up at him. "Because this feels right, my love. Because, now, we are surrounded by family and friends who love us and care about us. And we are in a magical place." I took a deep breath and I swear I could smell it everywhere. Magic had a scent all its own and it filled the night air with its sweetness. It was special to me because I hadn't done it. I didn't like thinking that I was responsible for all the magic in the world and I liked the idea that some places were magical just because they were, all on their own, or because someone other than myself had made it that way. The garden and the house were filled with magic, lots of it from lots of places. It was like smelling a dozen different types of flowers, and I liked them all.

And that was when I saw my Sisters walking toward us down the brick garden pathway with my mom(s) and dad(s) behind them. Mom and Dad were holding onto each other and Cathryn had one hand placed elegantly on Cornelius's arm as she walked beside him. As I looked at Cathryn and Cornelius I could feel it. I couldn't explain it, but I could feel it. They were my mom and dad too now.

"So mote it be," I said, as I accepted it as real.

"What is it, my lady?" Believer asked.

"My Sisters and my parents." Believer looked in the direction of my gaze.

"I hope they approve of me." He sounded worried.

"They're not the ones marrying you." I looked up at him, making a face. "I'm the one who's going to be doing your laundry for the next hundred million years. I'm the only one that needs to approve of you."

"Hhhhaamm," Believer sighed, *I think?* It was a soft rumble of a sound filled with his concern.

"I would very much like for them to love me as well. It would make me feel more—" His face contorted into a small frown, "real."

I understood. He wanted to be treated like a person and he wanted to be loved, not just by me but by my family.

I very much wanted for him to get what he wanted. He wanted a family, my family, and I wanted to give it to him. But what he wanted wasn't mine to give. They had to give themselves to him and accept him for it to be real.

"Me too," I said and took his cloudy hand in mine as my family came closer.

"By the way, my lady, I don't wear clothes, so your eternity will not be spent doing my laundry."

I looked over at him. I'd completely forgotten that my guy went everywhere in the buff. My eyes looked at him and zeroed right in on the area below his waist that clothes were most intended to keep concealed. Where his legs joined his body and where an anatomically normal male would have "items" exposed. there was only clouds. He was just legs and body with no sex at all. I seemed to remember Sky saying that she had made Believer a "man," but there was nothing there. I looked harder, but there was no darkened area or shadow hidden within the clouds with a suggestive shape. There was nothing but rolling white and grey clouds, forever crashing about inside his body.

I thought about it some more. I seemed to recall him saying that he had asked Sky to give him the ability to be with me, to please me. But I wasn't seeing it. The way his touch made me feel was almost sexual, but still, I wondered if there was more. At any other time I would never EVER have asked—but I was about to marry him! And my family was almost here so I asked.

"Believer?"

"Yes?" he said, but it sounded like he was laughing when he said it. I looked up at him and of course he was looking down at me.

"What's so funny?" I asked suspiciously.

Believer's smile was almost ear to ear. "Were you looking for something? Did you find what you were looking for, my lady?" he asked, then couldn't hold it in anymore; he started to laugh but kept it to a quiet internal rumble, his shoulders shaking, his eyes bright with mirth.

I blushed and looked away, embarrassed I'd been caught scoping out his crotch, looking for what wasn't there but what I hoped was. I took a step away, staring out into the dark garden. I felt flushed all of a sudden, and a little faint. What I was doing was finally becoming real to me, how different everything in my life was now. The weight of it all and of everything else began washing over me.

I swayed—my eyes closed—and then I fell—but I didn't fall.

Cloudy arms caught me, held me, and bore me up. I let myself go limp and let myself go. I was so tired. It was all just too much and his arms felt so cool and perfect and safe.

"Rain!" I heard my mother's terrified voice.

"Rain!" My father.

"Rain!" Mary.

I listened to the voices echoing my name as I lay in his arms. I let my body rest, eyes closed, but let the voices reach me, the effect like that of a TV left on in a room while you had your eyes closed and hovered on the edge of sleep. Voices in a faraway land.

"What happened!? Is she okay!?" Dad asked in a rush.

"I can heal her!" Bethany's little voice. "Let me heal her. I've got plenty of magic left in me!"

"Give her to me!" Mom demanded.

"She has only fainted." Believer's voice answered my worried family calmly. "She needs only to rest for a while." I felt him start to hand me over to my family, his strong arms stretching out and I managed to say "no," and he stopped.

"Black Rain?"

"Hold me," I whispered.

"But your mother wants you—"

"No," I said. I kept my eyes shut, I just wanted to stay where I was in his arms.

He lifted me back up into his arms.

"Give her to us, NOW!" Mother's angry voice demanded.

"Margaret! Believer is NOT hurting her! Now settle down!" Dad told Mom.

"What'd you do to her anyway!?" Bethany's voice.

"PEACE!" Believer's voice boomed out like thunder. It shook my body as I lay in his arms.

If not peace, there was certainly silence.

When he spoke again he used his usual, gentle rumbling tone. "I tried to put her down and she did not wish me to do so. She asked me to hold her, so I will hold her. She needs a few minutes to recover some of her strength, but we have very little time to spare. Magic must be cast tonight and the Black Witch must be the one to do it. If you would all please walk with me, we will talk as we get in our places for the wedding." His voice was so strong and confident and sure.

I wondered what he was thinking about and how he would handle my wild family but I stayed silent in his arms. Listening with only half my attention as I rested. My face lay against his chest, pressed against the pulsing endless raging storm that raged around the new glowing heart Sky had made for him. I was content to drift and be silent and let the world happen.

"What do you mean, what magic?" I heard Cornelius's voice ask. "What are you saying?"

"I think he's talking about the vampires, the pale couple in white," Dad's voice explained.

"Vampires! Those two are vampires!?" Mary shouted.

"Yes," Dad answered. "Rain invited them to the wedding and she promised them she would help them tonight. She was going to lock them up so they couldn't get out and hurt anyone. And I think she's the only one strong enough to do that."

"Please. We can walk as we talk of these things," Believer rumbled.

"All right." Dad's voice. "Let's walk and we can talk while Rain rests. Let's go, Believer."

We started moving. I felt gentle steps, barely noticeable as steps at all within the soft embrace of Believer's arms.

"What's wrong with her?" Mary's voice.

"Why did she faint?" Bethany's little voice asked.

"She has had a trying day. We were speaking together and—she swooned," Believer said, sounding guilty, "and fainted. Some of what has happened to her I will not tell you because it is for her to tell if she chooses to, but other parts I will share. You should know that your daughter is no longer mortal or human."

"What do you mean, not human!? Of course she's human!" Mom.

"Would you please just stop being so emotional and listen to him!" Dad said sharply. "He's trying to talk to us about our daughter."

"And do you actually believe him?" Mom asked. She still sounded angry.

"I think I do." Dad. "Yes." Dad again.

"He's telling the truth." Mary's voice, sounding fuzzy. I could hear magic in it. That's nice.

"How do you know?" Bethany asked.

"I can feel that he's telling the truth. It feels like he always tells the truth, and what's more I can feel it in her. Rain isn't human. She's not even close to being human." Mary's voice almost sounded scared.

"If she's not human, then what is she, Mary?" Cornelius.

"Mom. You really won't like this." Mary.

"Won't like what?" Mom.

"Just tell us, Mary. We'd rather know the truth," Dad said. "Just tell us what you know."

"Yes. Please, Mary. We need to know." Cathryn's voice.

"Okay. But remember. You guys asked for it."

"God." Mary.

"What?" Dad.

"What?" Mom.

"Huh?" Bethany.

"God," Mary said again.

"You mean a god, little 'g'?" Cornelius's voice corrected.

"Godlike. You mean her powers are godlike," suggested Cathryn.

"No. God. Capital 'G'." Mary.

"That's not possible." Mom.

"My daughter is not God." Dad.

"Are you sure, Mary?" Cathryn.

"It sure feels that way." Mary, quietly.

"Her blood feels different too," Bethany said.

"Don't do blood magic on your Sister, Bethany! You could hurt her," Mom's voice yelled. "Leave Rain's blood alone!"

"Sorry, Mom." Bethany, sounding hurt.

"How do you know all this, Mary?" Dad asked.

"I feel all the life around us and I see all the colors. The auras. It's all connected, all life, even the rocks and air and water. I can feel everything now with my magic. I'm the Green Witch and I feel life and I know life. Even Believer. He's magic, but he's still a part of our world. But Rain's not."

"She is not God!" Mom, angry.

"Please, don't be upset." Believer again. I lay motionless in his arms listening to them talk about me. "Your daughter is not the God that made all things. She may be like him in many ways but she is not that God."

Cathryn spoke, very close by, "Mary, what do you see when you look at her? What colors? What does her aura look like?"

"Well, honestly, I'm being very careful not to look at her too closely because I'm kinda scared to. Like looking right into a black sun, it feels like I might go blind or die or something, so I've just been looking at the edges of her. But that's scary enough."

"Don't look into her then!" Cornelius's voice cautioned. "Whatever you do, keep to the edges and stay safe; we don't want to lose you, Mary!"

"Yeah, careful." Bethany.

"It would hurt her horribly if you hurt yourself within her. Please be very careful, Mary," Believer rumbled.

"Look away for now, Mary, but tell us what you've already seen." said Cathryn.

"Black," Mary said. "She's solid black, no color at all. But there are colors coming from her like rays of sunshine, they go out in all directions. Look at her hair, see how it moves all on its own. And her dress. It's the rays of light and power coming from her. Rain's aura goes out about a hundred yards in all directions and it's so strong it moves her hair and dress like a wind is blowing. She is divine. She has absolute power. Rain can do anything."

"No." Believer's voice. "She does not have absolute power. If she did she would go back to being human."

"She wanted to go back to being human? Why?" asked Cathryn.

But she didn't get a chance to get an answer to her question as other voices filled in the background, shouts of surprise. Worried shouts from dozens of people. We had reached the wedding party and other people were seeing me in Believer's arms. I heard Ryan, Sky, and Jane. I heard family and strange voices I didn't know. Williams and others all shouting and talking at once, asking what happened, if I were all right. The chaos calmed some when they heard that I'd fainted.

"Everyone please get back in your seats." That sounded like Mrs. Aberforth's voice.

"Are we still having the wedding?" someone asked.

"Of course we're still having the wedding!" the old scratchy voice croaked. "We will start as soon as the bride wakes and feels fit enough to walk the aisle. Everyone that's not immediate family get back to your seats."

"Mr. Bryant, I am going to hold her within me for a few minutes." Believer.

"You're going to do *what*?" My dad's voice.

"I'm going to hold her within my body for a few minutes. It will help her recover and it will help her to wake. We have done this before and it helped her the last time she fainted. This will look unsettling, but I'm not eating her or hurting her in any way, I am helping her. Give us a few minutes together, please."

I heard people starting to argue. I heard Sky's voice loudly telling them to let Believer hold me.

He moved me and held me upright, letting my legs rest against his body as he held my head and shoulders close to him—and then he drew me within his form, enveloping me completely. The sounds of the outside world vanished and I was floating, weightless. I was just another cloud within Believer's body, completely surrounded by his form.

I breathed his clouds (him) into my lungs with warm refreshing air. He tasted of summer storm but smelled of spring rains. Then I felt something new, like a hundred thousand little touches all along my body, my arms, legs, face, back. It felt so strange I opened my eyes to see what was touching me to find a sight that baffled my mind. Coming from the clouds all around me were thousands of ghostly little nerves, like white filaments, somehow reaching through my clothes and human flesh, down into the nerves and muscles below. I hardly had a chance to be frightened by the sight before I went loose, as if someone had thrown the breaker on my body's fuse box.

I went limp. I saw more of the nearly transparent nerves descending toward my face as my eyes lidded, lost to my control along with the rest of my body. The sensation was so alien and I was so utterly relaxed that for a panicked minute I thought about resisting, *fighting back*!, but I didn't. I lay there and relaxed and gave myself to it, to whatever Believer wanted to do with me. So mote it be.

He pressed himself deeper into my flesh in a thousand different places and then I realized what was happening. He had absorbed me and wrapped himself around me with his body but now he used his new little cloudy nerves to enter me and warm me. Now he held me on the outside and filled me on the inside. I felt warm, outside and inside my body. I was comfortable and absolutely relaxed in ways I'd never imagined were possible. Then I felt what I can only think to describe as a complete person hug. As all of me was squeezed, not hard, but in love, all at the same time—inside and out. And then some of my control was restored. The moment I could move on my own I started to laugh.

"Do you have me, my love?" I asked him playfully. Like calling the sun bright. Did he have me, YEAH! I think he did. He squeezed me again and I moaned in pleasure. It wasn't a sexual thing, this touch, it was just so wonderful to be held so completely and I felt so warm and safe inside and out that it made me sigh in pleasure and laugh at the same time.

"My lady." I heard Believer's voice and my body trembled as the vibrating sounds of the words seemed to form out of the clouds circling around me before moving up, toward his head and mouth above me. It was odd and wonderful at the same time, as I was able to hear and feel and taste his words in my mouth as he spoke them.

"Yes?" I answered, wanting him to say more.

"Are you ready to come out? I'd like to marry you if you still want me," again sounding somewhat guilty.

"I want you. *Please*, I don't want to live without you. I love you. Please marry me and love me and hold me forever." I cried real tears. I meant every word.

He squeezed me again. I moaned again.

"It's time for the wedding, my love. The guests are ready for you to walk the aisle. And your vampire guests need your help."

"All right, my love. I'm ready." I didn't want to come out but I knew I needed to. I had to.

"I like the changes Sky made for you. It felt wonderful having you hold me on the outside while you're touching and holding me on the inside too. Thank you. I'm glad she changed you."

"Oh. That's not all she changed, my lady," he said. There was a tightness in his body around me, almost like he was fighting not to laugh and I was feeling it from the inside instead of the outside and I laughed at the whole idea of feeling his held laugh.

What a crazy life I lived.

"What are you talking about?" I asked as I laughed at him. He was being silly and I was smiling as I floated inside my love, resting within my living cloud as a million little pieces of him worked their way out of my body. I sighed once he removed himself from inside me. I felt less secure and somehow very empty.

"What other changes?" I asked again.

"I cannot say right now, my love; it would not be proper to speak of such things in front of all your guests, as they are hearing all my words but not yours, but perhaps I can give you a hint. You were looking for it earlier, right before you fainted."

I tried to get my mind working. What had I been loo—

"*Oh shit! Are you serious!?*" I hissed in surprise. "But—there's nothing there!" My mind and heart were racing at the possibilities. He couldn't be talking about his having a "*thing*"!

"My lady, you were just looking in the wrong place. I do not need, nor do I have a "heart." Now it is time for you to come out here and marry me, and it is time for you to make your vampire guests safe before they eat everyone."

I giggled. I was so happy. Here I thought I was going to have to deal with only being held wonderfully for all eternity in Believer's body, but to find out that I'm not only going to be held but I'm going to be getting—WHO THE HELL KNEW WHAT!? but I bet it was going to be fantastic! I couldn't wait. I felt like a kid at Christmas! I wanted to be bad and take a peek at the present hidden somewhere inside the tree but I didn't want the vampires to eat anyone. I had promised to take care of them so I needed to get going and keep that prom-ise. And somehow I was sure that Believer would make me wait until tonight anyway. Even if I begged.

"Okay. Fine! Get me out of here so I can marry you, and then you can show me exactly what it means to be your wife *and your lover*." I took a deep breath as I felt myself moving forward; I pushed my hands out fi rst, and then my face broke the surface of Believer's chest, thrusting out into the night air. I heard all the gasps and shouts as people watched me emerge from Believer's body.

I hung there wet and dripping, half in and half out of his chest, back arched and arms wide, a hand held in each of his as I gazed up at the night sky above me. It probably looked like a scene out of *Aliens* but I didn't care. I breathed out a breath of warm air I'd saved in my lungs from inside Believer and it came out like vaporous steam in the cool night air of the garden. I watched the smoke curl and fade away into the night sky and laughed.

My love's strong arms lifted me the rest of the way out of his body and set me on my feet, but I willed myself to fl oat a few inches off the ground. My arms and legs felt like limp spaghetti from whatever it was he'd done to me, and I didn't think I could hold myself up yet, so I fl oated. Dad walked right up and hugged me. Mary slipped in front of Mom and hugged me, but she let out a "squeak" and jumped back as soon as she touched me. Th at surprised me. I was wet, so maybe I'd grossed her out.

"It's just water, Mar. He's a cloud not a ghost. It's not slime," I said with a reassuring smile.

Mary nodded. It looked like she wanted to say more, but Mom took over and crowded her out.

"Rain, honey, would you please stop scaring me to death!?" Mom fussed as she cried and hugged me. "Are you okay? My Lord, have you gotten taller?" She looked down. "Oh! You're fl oating. WHY are you fl oating? *Oh, never mind.* Do your eyes hurt; you never told me what happened to your eyes and why they're all black. Are they going to go back to your normal color or will they stay like that? Rain, you're all wet!" She ran her hand through my wet hair. "Are you really okay, honey? Do you need to lie down for a little while?" she asked, her hands running all over me as she mothered me and asked all her hundred questions that I didn't try to answer, and she didn't wait for me to answer anyway. My hair was wet and my clothes were damp, but I felt wonderful.

Mom finallytookabr eath.

"I'm feeling much better now, Mom." I gave her a good hug and a big smile, then I got attacked by everyone, Mary (she hugged me again, but very carefully this time), Bethany, Dad, Ryan, Sky, all my family.

When Cathryn finally came to hug me, I dropped to the ground letting my feet finally support my weight so she would be taller than me. I rested my head on her chest for a moment as I hugged her.

"Hello, Mother. I love you." I did, it felt right. She started crying and then I hugged Cornelius. "Hello, my father. It's good to be home," I told him.

"Hello, my daughter," he said and gave me a warm, loving smile.

I allowed myself a few minutes to talk with my family and friends. Everyone complained about me being wet now so I dried myself with a thought and quickly got myself into position to start the wedding. Believer was standing up front with Cornelius and Sky Dragon. I wondered who was going to be doing the wedding, Cornelius maybe, I hadn't asked, but I was sure someone had already worked out that detail.

I saw Dan and Jane sitting in two chairs far off to the side, close to the edge of the wood all by themselves. It looked like they were trying to stay safely away from everyone, which was probably a good idea. If they were getting hungry they needed to keep a safe distance from the nice-smelling humans, but they were so damn fast; if they wanted to go eat someone they could do it and be back before I missed them. They met my eyes, smiled and waved and seemed relaxed in their chairs. I felt okay with leaving them there until after the wedding.

"We are ready to start the wedding when you are, Rain," Mrs. Aberforth said to me.

"Mrs. Aberforth, who's doing the wedding? Who's going to marry us?"

Her drooping skin and wrinkles bunched up over her eyes, which would have been her eyebrows if she still had any.

"Who indeed? Very interesting, this place you've taken us to, girl." She pointed toward the front where Cornelius and Believer stood. "Apparently this place has a King and a Queen. When I asked who should do the wedding, your Sister, a Princess Bethany, *and I don't remember you having sisters by the way*, anyway, she said that only the King could marry couples in the land of Amen Hale, so the King is officiating the wedding." She gave a firm nod.

I recalled Mom saying something about that in her angry rant when we were in the storage closet. Something about Bethany making Cornelius a King, and Cathryn a Queen—but if Bethany was a Princess, what did that make me?

"But if Bethany's a Princess, then that means—"

"Yes, Rain. I assume that would make *you* a Princess too. Apparently you've been adopted into a royal family here. I don't know where the land of Amen Hale is, but this weather still feels like Florida to me." She looked around the garden and the huge white mansion suspiciously, trying to guess where in the world it was she stood. "And these soldiers are all American. But all the servants have told me that Cornelius is their King, so who is one old lady to argue? I even asked your mother and she told me the same thing, that he was King here, and she said that these other girls were indeed your sisters."

Dad had been listening quietly but now he leaned over, gently took my head in his hands and kissed my forehead, looking right at me. "You have been our princess for seventeen years, Rain. They're just now finding out what your mother and I knew all along." He hugged me and I hugged him back.

"I love you, Daddy."

Mary and Bethany came running up the path from the garden hand in hand, laughing and carrying a basket. They came to a breathless stop where Mrs. Aberforth jumped them.

"You two!" The old woman hammered them with her best evil eye that didn't make a dent in their good mood. "Where have you girls been!? We were about to start without you!"

Mary pointed to the basket in Bethany's hands. It was filled with dozens of different kinds of flowers, all in full bloom.

"We were getting flowers for Rain's wedding," she panted, still trying to catch her breath, so excited and beautiful. "Mary made all kinds of flowers bloom! Some were just dead sticks but they busted out with flowers! We got all kinds of them to drop on the ground in front of us!" Bethany's eyes sparkled, but from more than just excitement. I saw the flash of magic in my little Sister. She was holding magic inside her and I could feel it. It had the feel of death about it.

"Look Dad, see how many different kinds we got!" Bethany held the basket up for him to see.

"I see." His eyebrows went up as he inspected the basket of flowers. I could tell he was also smiling because of Bethany calling him Dad. He inspected and commented on one or two blossoms he recognized. "They'll look beautiful, girls."

"I'll hold the basket, Mary, and you can drop the flowers," Bethany instructed, her attention on the flowers in the basket. Mary carefully slipped an arm around me so that I had Dad on one side and Mary on the other.

"I'd say you were crazy and that you shouldn't do this but—" she made a disgusted face, "but I just can't do it. Somehow this just feels right. I don't understand it, but I believe it. And I can feel how much you two love each other." She sighed. "Still, good grief, Rain, he's so big and scary."

"No," I said as I looked forward, past the chairs and into Believer's eyes. He was watching us from the front where he stood with Cornelius. "He's beautiful and wonderful and amazing and he's all mine. I'm blessed to have him."

"Snap! You go girl." Mary did a playful head bob and Bethany and Dad laughed.

"Girls!" Mrs. Aberforth fussed. "Enough playing around. Now go stand where I showed you and start down the aisle when you hear the music begin." They each gave me a hug and hurried off.

"Are you ready, Princess?" Mrs. Aberforth asked me with a little smile.

"Yes, ma'am."

She gestured to a nearby servant in white who had a violin and he started to play, and everyone went quiet and turned to watch as Bethany and Mary began their slow walk down the aisle. It wasn't the traditional wedding march they played; I wasn't sure exactly what the music was, but it was hauntingly lovely and it fit me and who I was so much better than the traditional music ever would have.

They'd set up sixty white folding chairs with an aisle that ran right through the middle. Down this aisle my Sisters walked, Bethany holding the basket as Mary dropped the flowers. At the front Bethany set the basket down and the girls went to stand up front facing everyone. One on each side of Believer and Cornelius, looking like elegant magical "witch" bookends. Their coven marks glowed brightly as they smiled back at me and Dad. Believer stood beside Cornelius, his red eyes burning brightly. His gash of a mouth curved up in a smile. He looked very happy. This was what a wedding was supposed to be. This was perfect.

"This time will be better, Dad," I said.

"You're still going to be my little girl." Dad wiped at his eyes quickly then took my arm again.

"Always, Daddy. Always."

"Get going you two," Mrs. Aberforth ordered and we stepped out.

Dad held my arm, and for the second time tonight he walked me down the aisle toward the burning red eyes of my love, but this time everything was perfect. This time I would marry my Prince of Clouds.

Major Tom Benistin

A Divergent Path

Tom ordered the medics to carry the coolers filled with blood into the mansion and to wait with them in the kitchen area which left him alone in the big tent set up as an emergency medical facility. He grabbed an IV bag of clear saline, opened the end, and quickly squeezed the contents out into a trash bin. Tom rolled the bag up and slipped it into the pocket of his jacket then grabbed the needle and tubing he needed. He wrapped the items in a hand towel, forced the towel into his other pocket, and then slipped out of the med tent. He hadn't gone fifteen steps before they found him, agents and officers coming to ask him what to do now, and where to go, and how to wipe their own ass, and how many sheets of paper to use to get the job done.

"Sir, General Pritchet wants to know about the church, what kind of presence we need to keep there since it looks like only the wedding guests will be returning there. He wants to know if we should reallocate some of the forces, sir."

Since Stan Reese and almost everyone else with any command authority had been blown to hell by the rocket attack, this had gone on non-stop. It seemed that no one could do shit now without asking him to sniff it first to make sure it got thrown into the right fan.

"Yes. Tell him to strip it to the minimum but until further notice we own the building. Check with Johnson and see if he needs any men but bring any he doesn't need here and have them check in with General Thompson and get new assignments from him. And tell Johnson I want the perimeter pushed back another mile in every direction and we'll make that our final line. They can get to work establishing a new perimeter there, and tell him to take the bank on the other side of the river. There's an army of reporters over there pointing their stinking cameras this way and I want that fixed immediately. Use some of those state department idiots they sent us to help with the displaced homeowners."

Tom stopped talking; he was surrounded by at least six FBI agents, three Homeland Defense agents, and a couple of Army officers. He looked at the guy he'd been talking with. He didn't know his name but he was one of the senior agents on the scene.

"Who the hell are you, Agent?" Tom asked.

"Agent Griffis, sir. Twenty years, FBI, based out of Atlanta," he replied evenly.

Tom appraised him, looking him over, hoping for usable raw material. The guy was so bald the glare from his shiny head made Tom squint. Dozens of high-powered halogen lights glared down onto the yard from the top of twenty-foot-high metal poles. The whole area was lit up and soldiers were still bustling about as if it were high noon, setting up fortifications and working on into the night, clearing brush and placing barricades like they expected an attack at any moment.

Since the rocket strike everyone's alert level had jumped off the chart. In the distance the constant buzz of jets and helicopters coming and going replaced the chirping of crickets as the ambient noise of evening. If the sheer nature of what was happening here at the mansion wasn't enough to make everyone nervous, now they had the more understandable threat of rockets, guns, and hidden enemies.

People were on edge and Tom felt it in the men around him. Even the older more experienced soldiers were on edge. This was a strike on American soil, targeting Americans and American soldiers. Over a hundred and fifty had died in the rocket strike with more than a hundred wounded. It didn't get any more real than this. These men wanted sure leadership, right here, right now, so everyone was coming to him.

He'd been holding it together so far, but every second away from her was torture. He'd told Reese and General Laramie and Doctor Fields about his compromised mental condition but they were all dead. For all he knew they didn't even get a chance to pass the word of his diminished capacities on before they were killed, so Tom had forced himself to hold it together when all he really wanted to do was go to her. Only the thought that by doing what he was doing he was actually serving her, kept him in place this long. But he could feel himself losing it. He'd been away from her too long.

"Agent Griffis, the responsibility for securing the perimeter is now yours. Everything about it. Use your own best judgment and get shit done and do it fast. This is yours now so act like it is because the next person that comes to me and asks a question about the idiots on the other side of the river, the perimeter, or what to do about some pissed off homeowner that doesn't want to leave—I'm telling them to go see Griffis. You're in charge of it, now step the hell up and take care of the shit I just put on your plate, son."

"Yes, sir," Griffis replied and quickly turned away, not bothering with a salute or further explanation, which was a good sign. Some of the flies that had been buzzing around broke off and followed Griffis as he walked toward the command tents. Having overheard the conversation, they were already looking to Griffis for answers which was exactly what Tom wanted. He wanted out. Out of everything!

He spoke as he marched toward the house, handling one problem after another, sending the last few buzzards away with crisp orders but others took their place as soon as they left so that he hadn't really gained any ground at all by the time he reached the big double glass doors at the front of the mansion. Tom turned and eyed the crowd, putting out one or two more fires before he made his exit.

"I'm going back inside to attend to our special guests. I'll be unavailable. Totally unavailable for a while." Tom gave the dozen or so men on the steps a hard stare before continuing. "Until I get back out here, run all command decisions by General Thompson. And if you can't get him, go find Griffis. He'll do. Someone's got to be tapped while I'm inside, why the hell not him?" And with that, Tom turned and headed through the doors that had already been opened by the guards.

Inside the house was like a different world, the nonstop distant rumbling noise from the jets and helicopters was gone. Standing here in this opulent, peaceful space, Tom could almost forget that the world was upside down on the other side of the doors behind him. One servant in white was cleaning the leather couch in the front reception hall, and he looked up as Tom entered.

"Hello, sir. May I help you?" he asked.

"That's all right," Tom said. "I know my way around. I'm on the list," he said. "Major Benistin."

The young man referred to a clipboard that rested on the tabletop. A list of people allowed to enter the home other than the ones already inside. It was a short list and Tom's name was one of six people on it. The air carried the metallic smell of blood, but the floor and walls were clean now.

Tom looked up. There on the ceiling blood drops sprayed out in all directions. A million little red dots on the twenty foot high ceiling. Tom's throat went dry and he broke out in a sweat just looking at it. He knew she was hungry. He didn't know how he knew—but he knew.

"Will you be going toward the garden and the wedding party, sir?" asked the servant.

"Actually, I'll need to visit the restroom first. Please," Tom said as he wiped at his clammy brow.

"Right this way, sir." The servant led him toward the nearest lavatory.

"Thanks. I may be a few minutes," Tom mumbled as he slipped inside without waiting for an answer and quickly locked the door. He took out the rubber tourniquet, IV bag, needle, and tubing and set them on the marble vanity and then started to unbutton and roll up his shirt sleeve. Tom reached down and grabbed his radio.

"Status report, Phelps." His voice echoed in the bathroom and seemed loud in his own ears as the sound bounced off marbled walls and the high ceiling in the small space.

"The Black Witch just finished with her vows, sir. It's almost over," Agent Phelps' voice echoed back on the radio. He was in the garden watching the wedding. Tom had been calling for the blow by blow every few minutes for the past hour.

"I'll be there in about twelve minutes. Let me know if you see any significant movement. Where are the vampires?"

"They haven't moved," Phelps replied. "Still seated, waiting for it all to end."

"Good. Let me know if they get up."

"Yes, sir."

Tom put the phone away, grabbed the tourniquet, and tied it around his arm. He connected the tubing to the empty IV fluid bag and the other end to the needle, then went hunting for his own vein.

Stab.

"Shit." He'd missed. It hurt like hell.

He'd gone at it cautiously and the vein had rolled to the side, slipping away from the needle. Tom's hand shook as he pulled the needle back out. He grabbed some paper towels and wiped the blood away, aimed again a little higher up, and stabbed like he meant it this time. He was rewarded with a red line of blood, flowing down the clear tubing headed for the flat, empty bag.

Tom breathed a sigh of relief as he picked up the bag and sat down on the bench against the wall. He dropped the bag onto the floor and leaned back against the cool marble wall as his blood pumped into the bag at his feet in time to his beating heart.

Not for the first time this evening his hand reached over to his gun. He touched the handle and considered it again. He could end it now himself. Just put the gun in his own mouth and squeeze the trigger and go out in some way that made sense. Death by bullet. Something understandable. But the thought left him deeply unsatisfied. There was only one thing that satisfied the hunger inside Tom now. Pleasing her.

Tom knew she was just a child, a seventeen-year-old girl, but that didn't matter. And it didn't matter to him that she was in love with her vampire mate. Tom didn't care. He loved her. It wasn't sexual, although her body excited and fascinated him. No. This was more consuming than anything he'd ever dreamed of. Inside him, all his goals, his dreams, his hopes seemed to shrink down to almost nothing. His whole life was like the sound of the jets and helicopters outside, a far off distant noise that he couldn't hear now; it was just gone. All he could hear now was the sound of his own heart in his ears as it pushed blood into the bag at his feet.

She was hungry. Jane was hungry. My Queen was hungry. The three coolers of blood were great but they weren't filled with his blood. Tom wanted her to taste his blood. To drink his blood. He fantasized about it while he waited for the bag to fill—

How his blood would please her.

How she would be able to tell that his blood was fresh and freely given.

How she would know as soon as she saw him that he was hers now.

"Sir. They're on the move." The radio at his waist crackled to life.

Tom fumbled for the radio; he'd been getting drowsy from blood loss and his coordination was off. He looked down at the bag, alarmed to find it full. Very full.

"Shit!" Tom grabbed some paper towels, pulled the needle out, and placed the towels over his bleeding arm, then closed the valve on the IV bag and disconnected the tubing, letting it drop as he kept ahold of the slippery full bag. The bag was too full to hold any more blood and there was still blood in the tube that drained out all over the floor in the small bathroom, turning the white marble floor red.

"Dammit." Tom's right arm was bent in two, holding the paper towels tight over his needle wounds while the other hand fumbled with the bloody tube, trying not to get any on himself and still take care of the bag.

"Dammit. Dammit. Dammit. Dammit." Tom's muttered curses went on and on as he prepped the IV bag and cleaned blood off it and off of his hands before he shoved the tubing and needle into the trash.

"Sir, the vampires are on the move. They've just walked back toward the wedding party; they're talking with the Black Witch now."

"Dammit. Dammit. Dammit." Tom's muttered curse continued as he wiped the blood off the bottom of his shoes so he wouldn't leave a noticeable red trail all through the house. He didn't waste the time cleaning the blood off the floor. He didn't care who found it after him.

He caught a glimpse of himself in the mirror. He looked like hell. He was pale. He had dark circles around his eyes. The eighteen hours since his last shave showed with a good amount of grey and blond stubble. Tom splashed some water on his face with his free hand then grabbed some fresh paper towels and placed them over his puncture wound from the needle, replacing the ones he had already bled through. He used the rubber tubing to secure the paper towels in place before rolling his shirt sleeve back down. Tom grabbed the white towel he'd carried the needle and tubing in and wrapped that around the IV bag of blood. He stepped back outside, carrying the towel-wrapped bag cradled in the crook of his arm like a football.

"Where to, sir?" The servant was waiting for him.

Tom tried to look casual as he held the bag. He pointed with the other hand, but he could tell the servant was curious about what he held.

"The kitchen area please," Tom said.

"Yes, sir." The servant led and Tom followed.

Tom passed two soldiers who stood beside the door leading out to the garden area. He gave them a nod as he passed by on his way into the kitchen. It was busy and crowded inside. Far off in one corner his six medics stood, trying to stay out of the way of the bustling kitchen staff. The medics had stacked the three big coolers on top of one another to save space.

There were other soldiers posted here as well, at the entrance to the hall that led to the storage room closet. Four men, guarding the way to the magical door that the Black Witch had created, like it was a dangerous point of entry that enemies might pour out of. The fact that only the witches were able to open the door didn't seem to matter to them, and Tom didn't care enough to tell them that it was stupid to guard something that was no threat. Not a problem he cared about now.

"Bring the blood. It's time," Tom called.

The men got the coolers down and quickly followed Tom out of the hot, crowded kitchen, through the house and out into the cool night air of the garden. It was perfectly quiet in the garden other than the happy sounds of conversation coming from the gathering on the small hill up ahead. It was far too quiet. It had to be magic. Tom looked around but there was nothing to see other than the walls of the garden and trees. He didn't hear anything at all, no jets, no helicopters, not even the distant rumble of the bulldozers that cleared a path for the barricades to be placed around the house.

"Awful quiet. Isn't it, sir?" said the young soldier who walked right behind him carrying one end of a cooler.

"Where's the damn jets? There's no noise," said the soldier holding the other side of the cooler as he looked up, searching the sky for the jets he couldn't hear but knew must be there.

"It's magic," Tom stated dismissively, like it was no big deal. "They just shut out the sound. They've done that trick before. You'll get used to it, it's not dangerous."

"Yes, sir," the men answered, reassured as Tom exercised his natural ability to sell bullshit.

He didn't know for sure what was happening, but soldiers wanted the guy in charge to know what the hell was going on. Even when he didn't. So that's what Tom gave them. He'd been briefed on the details of the TV interview the witches gave at the trailer this morning and how they had shut out the sound around the trailer, so he was probably right. He'd been keeping up on everything he could about the powers of all the teens in the study, getting his latest update from Agent White not long ago.

Tom kept his caravan of big red coolers moving up the path toward the center of the garden, but it looked like there was going to be a problem. Apparently the wedding party had been excused and the guests were already headed back toward the house and Tom and his group were blocking the walkway. Out in front, walking arm in arm as they led the wedding guests away, were the two other witches.

"Stand aside and let them pass," Tom ordered, and he and his men stepped off the path as the party came closer. The guests behind the witches followed, but not closely; they kept a fifteen to twenty foot buffer between themselves and the witches. Tom remembered Agent White's warnings, how uncomfortable and dangerous it was to come into close personal contact with the witches.

He surveyed the area again, but there was only one trail leading up. He and his men were going to come eyeball to eyeball with the witches, unless he order a general retreat and had them hustle back up to the house, which would look odd.

"Shit!" Tom cursed.

"Yes, sir!" That from the pale and terrified kid behind him holding his end of a cooler, his wide eyes locked onto what was coming down the trail.

"Belay that order, soldier." Tom chuckled and so did some of the other men. He hadn't expected to laugh, but that was funny. The nervous knot inside his guts relaxed a little. He was getting close now and he didn't want to wait a second longer or waste the time it would take to backtrack and wait until everyone passed by. Tom decided to dig in and hold his ground.

"No one move, even if you want to. And if these witches are anything like the Black Witch you will want to do more than move. Keep it together. Don't move. Everyone understand? And no one says a damn word either, just forget you've even got a fucking mouth. Do not speak, even if they ask you a question. I'll do the talking for all of us. And don't make direct eye contact. Just look at nothing till I tell you to move out." Tom waited until he got the appropriate "yes sirs."

About a dozen huge green moths swirled in the air around the two girls as they walked toward them, their shiny iridescent green bodies flashing in the dim light of the garden. They certainly looked the part. As they reached Tom's group, the two witches stopped dead, turned and looked at Tom and his men.

The cloud of moths descended, all finding purchase on the taller witch with bright green eyes and snow white hair. The moths rested on her arms, shoulders and dress and some landed on her hair like big green hair bows. It made her look like some kind of magical wood nymph out of a children's book. The Green Witch eyed the coolers, apparently perplexed by something she saw or sensed. The younger witch with dark hair and olive skin looked glassy eyed as she gazed at the big red coolers.

"Why do you have all this blood? It's soo much blood," she said.

Tom noticed that her voice was off. Like she was high.

Mary nodded. "Oh. I guess that would explain it." Her brows bunched up and she brushed the green lock of hair hanging down in her eyes back out of the way. "I was wondering what the hell was in there that was 'alive' but still kinda not." She looked down the line of men and coolers appraisingly, then looked back to Tom and her eyes squinted up tight. She apparently found something else she didn't like. She was looking right at Tom as she gave the dazed little witch beside her a good nudge in the side.

"Get a grip, Beth. Something's up with this guy." Her voice was intense, her eyes suddenly dangerous. "Something's wrong with him."

Bethany snapped out of her funk quickly. "Should I kill them, Mary? Just say it and they're all dead." She spoke quickly, eagerly. She wanted to do it.

Tom's mind flashed on the image from the Entry Hall without really wanting to, the blood all over the high ceiling and sprayed on the walls. The little witch's hungry black eyes came to rest on him and he looked away, back to her Sister. Tom wasn't surprised that the girl knew what was in the cooler. He had already received the report from Agent White about the Red Witch and her bloodlust and how she drew her powers from blood. But this wasn't her blood.

"It's for the vampires. They need it. This is their blood." Tom's eye twitched but the rest of him was rock solid. Strange time to develop a tick. He tried to get it to stop, but it kept going while the two witches looked at him cockeyed, like he was the crazy one.

The line of guests were waiting a short distance away and coming no closer. More people were coming up behind as they said their goodbyes and fell into line, forming an ever increasing road block of human bodies between Tom and where he needed to be.

Mary stepped forward, gazing at Tom as if she were seeing things only she could see. "I'm going to touch you. Don't move. If you move, you and all your men die." She said it without a smile as she stepped closer and raised her hand like she was about to touch his face, but before she touched him her eyes dropped and came to rest on the white towel Tom held in his arms. A towel wrapped around some circular shape about the size of a football. She raised her eyes back to Tom's but her hand lowered. She kept her eyes on Tom's as she very delicately slipped her hand inside the towel and touched the bag filled with his blood. Tom watched as her emerald green eyes went wide in surprise.

"What is it, Mary?" Bethany asked.

"Don't kill them, Beth. Whatever you do, don't kill them," Mary said, her hands still hidden within the towel.

"Okay. I won't kill them." She sounded disappointed.

Mary closed her eyes, listening and hearing what only she could hear. They waited for a silent minute. Tom's men were mute motionless statues, seeing nothing, staring at nothing. Neuter fixtures and nothing more. Tom could hear the worried murmurs of the guests waiting on the trail as they watched with growing alarm.

"Mary, what is he?" Bethany asked. The first to run out of patience.

"Tell her who you are, Lucius," Mary said, then tilted her head to the side. "No. It's Tom. Tom still." Her eyes were still closed, her hand still rested on the IV bag under the white towel. No one else could see what was under it.

There was no going back from this; Tom knew that the men behind him would hear what he said. And so would the witch so he knew he couldn't lie. He didn't care anymore.

"I am hers." Tom spoke it clearly. He looked off in the direction of the hill, looking for Jane, catching a glimpse of her made his heart start beating faster. She was beside Dan, wearing her white wedding dress. He needed to go to her. He didn't care about anything else.

"Whose?" Bethany asked, confused.

"He belongs to Jane," Mary said, her eyes still closed, head tilted to the side.

"Oh." Bethany looked at the coolers again. "I guess that makes sense."

"Please. Let me go to her," Tom pleaded. His voice was thick with need. He felt out of sorts. Tom's voice sounded strange in his own ears. He'd been such an emotionless, detached machine all his life that this was absolutely unlike anything he'd ever experienced. His detached emotional state had cost him. It was the main reason his wife had left him. She'd rotated between calling him an "automaton" early on when she still respected him to "unbelievable bastard" there toward the end when she was simply trying to work up the nerve to leave him.

An agonizingly anal, emotionless machine—devoid of feelings, passion, or even the vaguest ability to love anything or care about anyone other than knowing how to keep them alive and tell them what to do. That was how she had summed him up to her family, and for the most part she was right. She waited until half of their children were grown and gone but she'd left five years ago. Tom's son was a sophomore and his oldest girl started college this year. In a way his life had been over anyway. Tom didn't feel like he was losing much.

And he finally cared about something now.

And she was hungry.

"Please," Tom said again. Pleading.

Mary opened her eyes, a sad knowing look on her face. Almost apologetic. "Sorry, Tom. Sorry to keep you waiting. Give my Sister a few bags to play with."

"Yeah!" Bethany gave an excited shout, not waiting for Tom to give his consent as she ran over to a cooler and fumbled with the latch, eagerly going after her contraband.

"Thanks Mary! Thanks Tom!" But her happy voice turned plaintive as soon as she flipped the lid and looked at the blood. "Oh crap!"

"What is it, honey?" Mary asked.

"The bloods all *funky*," Bethany complained. "I can feel the life in it, but there's no death." Her disappointed, stricken face looked back to her sister. "I mean, it's okay, and I still want some, but—" she looked back at the cooler in obvious distress, "it's just not the same. Nobody died giving this blood, Mary.

They all lived. Every one of them. There's no death or pain or even fear in the blood anywhere. It's just blood. I need death."

"Oh Bethany, honey, keep it together. Please!" Mary looked at her Sister with rapidly growing concern, but Bethany seemed not to hear her. She was still looking down into the cooler of blood.

"Crap! Where's Mom when you need her?" Mary griped. She shot a quick glance back toward the hilltop then back to Bethany.

"I think I have to be the one to do it, to bring it out," Bethany said to herself. "I need to see them die. I need to be the one to do it." Her voice was getting thick with desire, her eyes glassy as she looked down into the disappointing haul of strangely unfulfilling dark red baggies. The men holding the cooler followed Tom's advice to the letter. They saw nothing, said nothing, reacted to nothing, and therefore did not exist.

"I need to kill someone, Mary. I need death. And blood." Bethany gazed into the cooler.

Mary made a quiet "shushing" noise, and all the beautiful green moths except the one perched on her head took off and flew the short distance to land on Bethany. Immediately after landing each moth stiffened in death, falling to the ground at Bethany's feet, making a beautiful green circle around the Red Witch. Bethany looked down at the still figures on the brick path, her eyes glassy with whatever she experienced from the death of the moths.

"Thank you," her sweet little voice whispered as she stared down at the motionless insects, frozen as if she were in a trancelike state.

Mary looked from her sister back to Tom. He arched an eyebrow as if to say "Okay. What now?" only without the words.

Mary sighed, "At least it's not me this time. Bethany, Bethany, Bethany," she muttered as she stepped over in front of her sister, bent down and planted a nice juicy kiss right on her lips.

That woke her right up, just like magic! Bethany's eyes snapped back into focus and she reared back disgusted.

"Yuck!" Bethany made a face. "Ptt! Ptt!" She spat and wiped off Mary's slobber from her lips and gave Mary a grossed out look. "Hey! What's the big idea!?"

"You're back in the land of the living now, aren't you, my little death sucking blood fiend?" Mary's smile was so guileless and radiantly innocent that even Bethany couldn't resist it; she started to laugh.

"Yeah." She laughed. "Thanks, I guess."

"You know you liked it," Mary teased. "And so did Tom." Mary looked back to him and gave him a mischievous wink. "A little girl on girl action for ya, baby! Yeah!" Bethany laughed but kept wiping her lips on the sleeve of her dress.

"Can I go now?" Tom asked. His impatience with all this was growing. Sure that the main threat had passed, he wanted to go. He needed to go.

Mary gave some final instructions. "If you're going to be working here, Tom, you need to know, the vampires aren't the only ones that need blood now. But it seems like Bethany needs to do the killing herself, so maybe a few goats or a nice fluffy sheep or two." She smiled sweetly as she asked for her sacrificial lambs.

Bethany had been listening. "I want a bull!" she blurted out loudly, excited and happy at the thought of killing an animal. "Or a man if you got anybody you want dead. That's the best! Men have sin and darkness in them. But if I gotta have an animal, I want a bull. A big one. A big mean one." Her smiling face was angelic but the shining mark on her forehead gave Tom the chills as she looked at him.

"Yes ma'am. I'll see what I can do," Tom answered.

Bethany went over and grabbed two baggies out of the cooler.

"Thanks guys." Bethany held her hands down at her side and swung the red baggies of blood back and forth happily like a little child as she stepped back onto the trail with Mary.

Tom didn't wait for them to say another word but waved the men forward, directing them to stay off the trail and just make what forward progress they could on the verge.

They proceeded down the side of the path, a caravan of red coolers marching along with military crisp strides. They didn't get far. After just fifteen yards they ground to a halt, stuck on the side of the path and hemmed in by high decorative flower beds on either side of the trail. Tom tucked the towel a little tighter around the package in his arms as they waited. Wedding guests passed by, slowly strolling down the path and slowing even further to eye the coolers like a car accident shoved to the side of the freeway.

"What's in the coolers, Major?" asked one man.

"Blood," Tom said. Hoping the one word would be enough to shut the guy up and make him run. The opposite reaction surprised him. The man lit up and smiled big.

"Oh Faann-*tastic*!" He was gay, that much was obvious to by his mannerisms. He looked a little like Dan in the face. Maybe an uncle, Tom guessed. The gay man turned into the crowd and surfaced again with Jane's father and mother and told them about the blood in the coolers. They both looked relieved.

"Jane's been asking about you, Tom," said Mr. Miller. "They'll both be glad to see this." He surveyed the coolers, eyes widening. "God, that's a lot of blood," he said, amazed at the sheer quantity.

"Just go, Tom." Jane's mother moved to the side and drug her husband back with her, making room for them on the path. "Get it to them now, don't let us slow you down. She's hungry." Finally. Orders he could gladly follow.

"Yes, ma'am!" Tom faced the oncoming crowd on the path. "Slide to one side folks! We need to get by as quickly as possible!"

People obliged. There was just enough room for the guests to eek by single file on one side as Tom and his men marched the coolers up the path. Everyone seemed to be going the extra mile to not touch the coolers, as if they were afraid of what they contained. Tom ignored further inquiry which caused further dark speculation as people let their imagination go wild. Stewed demon guts or the defiled corpses of children, a hundred eyes collected from only one-eyed men or *whatever*. Nobody wanted to touch the bright red "Coolers from Hell" as one man jokingly called them while he squeezed by.

They reached the hilltop where a small group of soldiers were here collapsing folding chairs, preparing to carry them back toward the house. They gave Tom and his odd procession some strained glances as they worked. They seemed on edge and stressed as they went about their task. The small group of people still here had walked to the edge of the flattened mound and were now standing before a gleaming white structure that looked like a mausoleum or the entrance to some ancient catacombs that had risen straight up from the earth. The entrance was ten feet high by about eight feet wide. At the top of the entrance an inscription was cut into the stone.

HEREIN LIES DAN & JANE SIMMONS
SOUL MATES, LOVERS, AND OUR FRIENDS
BORN 1999 - DIED 2016
REST IN PEACE & RISE ETERNAL
SEE YOU SOON

A small crowd was gathered before the open crypt. Jane and Dan were with them. They both watched him as he approached, but Tom's eyes stayed on Jane. She looked changed from the last time he'd seen her. Both her and Dan's eyes were a brighter red and they moved sparingly. Slowly and carefully. Like they were being very careful to hold themselves in place, or possibly as if it was getting difficult to move at all.

"Sir. Should we take the blood down inside the—whatever the hell that place is?" one of the soldiers asked, bringing Tom back to the here and now.

"Yes. Take it on down, find a decent spot to leave the coolers and head back to the med tents."

"Will you be coming with us, sir?" the soldier asked.

"No. You men drop the coolers down below and head back without me. Now get going," Tom said without looking away from Jane.

The men moved forward reluctantly, each of them with a different expression (anger, worried, scared, betrayed, confused), but their varied emotions fused into one—plain old terrified—as they headed down into the crypt, carefully navigating the steep stairs that led into the darkness and who knew what else that might be down below.

"Hey, Tom!" Ryan stepped up with a huge smile and gave him a companionable smack on the back which made Tom jump a little and look away from Jane for one annoyed second. Ryan didn't notice the scowl. "So how's it going, did you find out who tried to kill us today or what?" he asked, still upbeat, but somehow Tom couldn't follow what he was saying; his attention was all for Jane.

His heart was racing. Ryan's voice was nothing but background noise, unimportant and ignored. Tom stepped away from Ryan (who was still talking) without a word, not even hearing him as he walked past Mrs. Bryant and Mr. Bryant, Dr. Burgis, and others he didn't recognize. He stopped and slowly went to his knees in front of Jane. Tom kept the towel on top of the IV bag, but he stretched out his arms, presenting his gift, giving her what he had to give.

"Oh Tom." Her voice was sympathetic. She reached out and gently moved the towel out of the way, revealing the bag filled with blood. It looked black in the moonlight, like it was full of black ink instead of blood. Tom heard the worried whispers of the others on the hilltop, but he didn't care. He was here. He was happy. Was she pleased? He hoped so.

"Tom. Do you want your old life back? Dan can make you forget me if you want to." Jane's voice reached him and his whole body went warm reacting to the sound of her voice. His throat went dry. He focused on what she was saying, trying to understand her every word.

"Do you want to go back to what you were? Remember, you had a life, Tom. I know it wasn't perfect but it was *your* life." Jane ran a hand across the dark baggie of his blood as she spoke.

"It's not too late, Tom. Dan can set you free of me right now, but if you wait till after I die there won't be any turning back. I'll be far too strong."

Ryan stepped up. "What's going on, Jane? What's up with Tom?" The rest of the group gathered around them, everyone with their own concerned face as they looked at Tom on his knees offering Jane what most people could guess was his own blood.

Jane looked up from Tom, not to Ryan but to everyone around her as she spoke. "I didn't mean to do it. I didn't know I could." She looked sad but resigned. "Somehow when I held his hand earlier this morning I marked him in some way. When I was trying to hear if he lied to Rain I did something to him. I didn't really know what it was I was doing." Jane traced her long nails along the taut plastic baggie holding Tom's blood as she spoke.

"I thought about Tom today too. Sometimes when I was mad at him I thought about killing him, sometimes annoyed and I just wanted to hurt him. Sometimes as a protector, keeping us safe. But mostly as my servant, bringing me my blood. I have called him—and he has come." Her voice wasn't quiet regretful but it was solemn and frightening in its content. Jane sounded and looked much less human and more like what she was becoming. Vampire.

Sky grabbed Ryan's arm just before he opened his mouth to protest. "Come on, Ryan, this isn't our stuff. This is theirs. Please leave it alone. All you'll do is make it worse."

He looked at her for a moment before nodding sadly. They walked back a few steps, merging with the rest of the crowd who watched the strange scene in total silence.

Jane looked back down to Tom. "Well, Tom. What's it to be? Forget this ever happened and move on with the life you had before—or serve me until you die or until I kill you. I may be a difficult Queen to serve, Tom. I don't know what I'll be like after I die. I may be a monster. I may be evil or cruel or even vile. I won't be human. You may not be too pleased with how things turn out, but you've got to decide now, before you even know." She waited, for all the world she looked like a statue, completely frozen. Behind her, Dan was her match, totally still.

"I choose to stay. Please, Jane. I love you. I don't want my old life back. It was over anyway. Please let me stay. Let me serve you until the day I die or until you kill me. As long as you're the one that kills me I'll die happy. Please. Let me serve you—*my Queen*," Tom pleaded. He didn't grovel on the ground or weep like a baby but everyone could tell he meant every word he'd just said. His voice shook along with his arms, which he still held out straight in front of himself with the bag of blood in his hands.

Jane had Tom's bag of blood in her hand now. No one had seen her pick it up, it was just there, in her hands. Dan appeared beside her. She held the bag as Dan cut the top open with his fingernail in one unseen movement, blood from the over full bag spurting out onto both their hands. Jane's and Dan's eyes went from somewhat red and menacing to a glaring red as the smell of blood filled the night. Everyone moved back. No one said a word but they all started to leave, forming a silent procession off the hilltop, not waiting to see the rest of what happened as Dan and Jane, together, drank Tom's blood.

Black Rain

Kingdom Come

"**I don't know why** you're in the FBI; you should have your own TV show, *Design by Trisha!* or something," I said as we struggled up the steep stairs together, holding hands to help each other along. "I still think this stairway needs handrails, seriously, someone's gonna break their neck on this thing," I griped.

"NO!" Trisha shook her head wildly, slapping me with her shoulder length bottle blonde hair, horrified at the thought. "That would be so uncool! And it would throw off the whole scary gothic groove we've worked so hard to create down here. This is gonna be the vampires' home, right, and they have perfect balance, so anyone else using these stairs is probably going to be unwanted company anyway."

I gave that some thought. I couldn't imagine who Trisha thought would be stopping by, prank buzzing the vampires' doorbell.

"Unwanted company? You mean like someone selling those crappy coupon books door to door or Girl Scout cookies," I teased as I pulled her up to the next step with me. "You may be right. Those freaking Girls Scouts are pushy. Last year they hit our trailer three times. THREE!" I shouted. "Three three," my voice echoed up and down the steep stairwell.

Trisha laughed and wacked me on the arm. "That's not what I'm talking about! It's not a human place, it's a vampire place."

"I guess you're right," I conceded as I grunted upward. "These steps will only be a pain in the ass for humans; the vamps will just fly right up these things. Thanks for helping me make it so nice for them."

"I had fun helping, but having you lift ideas right out of my head like that was weird." Trisha made a face and rubbed the top of her head like she was worried all her wonderful ideas were leaking out unchecked. "I feel like you've seen me naked or something."

I laughed. "Don't be wigged out, I told you, I'm not in your head anymore and I didn't go deep and get into any of your private stuff. I don't know what your favorite color is or if you're a freak."

"Hey!" Trisha gave me another whack.

"What?" I asked, all innocent. "Are you a freak?"

She growled at me.

I tried not to laugh. "Really Trisha. I stayed on the surface. It was just so much easier that way than making you talk through it all."

Trisha had come with me down into the crypt to help me design Jane and Dan's "Honeymoon Tomb." She'd been telling me her ideas as we went along: engravings, arches, colors, cloths, patterns, and flooring designs. But after a while I had the idea of simply being able to know her ideas and thoughts without her having to talk it all out verbally, and that saved a ton of time and worked so much better. I could get the picture in my head "exactly" the way Trisha was envisioning it in her head. It was funny to watch her face as what she "thought" came to life as I made it real before her eyes. At one point she even said, "Oh my God! Am I doing that!?"

We were just about done when the soldiers carrying the coolers came struggling down the stairs. They were scared to death to be down here in the crypt and were totally terrified to meet me, but I was nice to them. I told them thanks and let them run away like they wanted.

So we added one more room down here to hold the blood. There was over a hundred and thirty baggies of blood so I made one circular room with two shelves running around the whole room. On the shelves I formed 130 individual clay pots to hold the blood and I made the pots magic so the blood would stay warm, healthy, and alive until they opened each pot. It was a scene right out of a nightmarish Disney cartoon as the baggies of blood danced out of the big red coolers and emptied themselves into the pots, before each pot capped itself and floated onto the shelf where I wanted it. I chose clay pots because Trisha said I should use something biodegradable, and it did seem stylish and classy once we were through. The "less is more" effect. I could have just as easily made them all solid gold but it seemed like a stupid thing to do; the clay pots were nice.

In the center of the room we made one high table with two seats, like a breakfast bar. I also fashioned one super deep hole in the floor for them to use as a trash can, a place to pitch the empties. The Crypt had an unbelievable bedroom, a bathroom with a floor to ceiling silver mirror, magical lighting in the ceiling, a pool of cool fresh spring water, and on the other side of the room a pool area with spring water that would warm itself as it entered one side and cool back down as it left the other side, going back into the natural water system.

We didn't want to take too long and we didn't know what else they would want so we kept it simple. I did make one room with nothing in it but an archway that I could use to come down here if I needed to, but other than that there was no way out except up the stairs. I made all the walls super hard and I was confident that the place was vampire proof. They would be safely "inside" until I decided to let them back out after they were safe to be around humans again. I hoped it wasn't that hard for them to adjust, but we were ready, one way or the other.

Believer stood at the top of the stairs waiting for us.

"Hello, my love," I called. Two eyes looking down at us were the only part of him visible in the darkness ahead. I'd placed some magical lighting in the rooms down below but Trisha had me leave the stairway completely dark. For the life of me I still couldn't believe those poor soldiers made it down the steps alive hauling those big ass coolers with them. They deserved a raise after tonight. Or maybe therapy. I had created a glow of light to follow us around as we worked down below and the glow had tagged along with us as we ascended the dark stairwell.

"Hello, my lady. Has all gone well preparing their resting place?" His voice rumbled down to me.

"Yes. We're through. It's ready."

"Good. There has been an unexpected development while you were below." We finally reached the top and Believer reached out and took my hand and Trisha's. She squeaked a little when she felt his cloudy hand grab hers but she still accepted his help as we stepped out of the stairway and onto the green grass of the hilltop again.

"What now?" I asked as I banished the glow of light around us. Tom stood beside Jane and Dan about twenty feet away. The vampires didn't move, they stayed where they were. This didn't look good.

"How bad is it?" I asked.

"Perhaps Trisha should go now," suggested Believer. "As you can see, all the others have already gone back to the house."

"What about Tom?" Trisha asked. "He's standing right beside them. Is that safe? Shouldn't he go too?"

"No. But you should." Believer was pretty insistent. "You only have one life to lose, Trisha. Please, go now, but do not run, walk. Running may attract their attention."

That last statement got our attention. Trisha and I both looked up at him and raised our eyebrows.

"That bad?" I asked.

Believer smiled. "If they do lose control I'm not fast enough to stop them. I suggest extreme caution."

"Sounds like pretty damn good advice to me," I said. I looked at Trisha. "Bye, Trisha. Remember. Don't run. And don't wait for Tom. And don't look back either."

She stared at me for just a second before turning and walking away, back toward the house. Believer and I watched her until she was safely on the trail then we walked over to Jane, Dan, and Tom. Now that I was closer, I noticed the blood. Jane and Dan were both bloody. Tom had a good bit on him too but mostly it was splashed all over the vampires' white wedding clothes. But where did the blood come from, I wondered.

"Hello, Rain. Is it ready?" Jane asked. She moved only her mouth, her body looked frozen.

"Yes guys. Everything's ready. Sorry it took so long. I'll seal you in as soon as you go down. There's absolutely no way out, and I've made it as secure as I can think to make it so you'll be safe. The blood from the coolers is preserved in a special room for you in pots that will keep the blood fresh and alive until you're ready to eat it, just like your wedding urn. I built an archway down there so I'll be able to check on you. Do you know how long it may be?"

"Not really. It may be minutes or days or weeks. But probably at least a day," Jane said. Then she moved her head, very slowly, to look right beside her where Tom stood silently. It was odd to watch her move so slowly and it made her seem even more like a statue. Less human.

"Earlier today, when I touched Tom and held his hand something happened. I did not mean to do it, Rain, but I marked him. I offered him the chance to be free of me but he has refused to leave me. Tom has offered me his blood to do with as I choose. He is mine now." Jane was looking at Tom as she said this and now she spoke to him directly. "Tom."

"Yes, my Queen." He sounded like himself but he didn't look like himself at all. There was blood on his fancy military outfit and on his face and arms and he had a crazed look in his eye. Tom was definitely out of his mind. Gone. Jane didn't sound too much like herself either. Her voice sounded almost normal, which for Jane, was *not* normal.

"Your name is no longer Tom. That was another life, and it is past. From this day forth until the day you die or the day that I kill you, you will be known as Lucius."

Tom looked at Jane worshipfully, waiting for her next words, but Jane's head cocked to the side. In a quick unseen movement, her hand was suddenly around Tom's throat. Her eyes narrowed in suspicion. Tom's face started to turn red but he didn't lift his hands to her hand. His arms stayed limp at his sides. He focused on trying to get air past Jane's white hand that held his throat. Behind her Dan still hadn't moved. I thought for sure she was about to kill him.

"You have heard this name already. Who told you your new name, Lucius?" Jane asked calmly as she held his throat.

"The Green Witch met us on the path as we brought up the blood. She called me Lucius." He took a breath. "She knew that I was yours."

After a minute Jane released his throat and stood again beside Dan with her hands by her side. I hadn't seen her move, she was just there. I could see the red fingerprint marks on Tom's throat and my own hands reached up and rubbed my own throat in sympathy, but he didn't reach up to his own throat. Tom didn't move a muscle except to turn his head to look back at Jane. Waiting.

"Lucius. You will please me and serve me by serving this household and by serving Black Rain. Obey her as you would me. Until I rise eternal, she is your mistress. Do you understand, Lucius?"

"Yes, my Queen," he said. Still locked into her eyes.

"Go and wait at the edge of the clearing for her."

Without another word he turned and walked off toward the edge of the hilltop. Believer and I watched until Tom stopped at the start of the path, turned and looked back toward us. Obediently waiting.

It was an ugly scene. Tom had seemed like an all right guy, pushy as hell, focused and driven, but all right. Seeing his humanity stripped away like this was sickening. Ugly. Tom was gone. In a way he was as dead as the Asian guy I had killed and squeezed into the urn. And Stan Reese had died earlier when the rocket strike had hit the caravan of vehicles headed to the church. Blown up along with so many others. All three of the men who had come to speak with us this morning were dead now. Making Tom into a servant was crazy, but this had the feel of something done. Already in the past. Finished. Jane had said that she didn't mean to do it, and she tried to get him to walk away but he wouldn't. I knew from personal experience that some things couldn't be fixed. Sometimes you just had to move forward with things—damaged, changed, and different.

"Death is all around me. Love and Death and Change," I mused, more to myself than to anyone else but I snapped back to the here and now as Jane and Dan stepped in front of me. I gave Jane a sad smile.

"You don't have to explain it to me, Jane. It is what it is, and you have to be what you are. So mote it be and so be it."

She smiled. "So be it." She leaned in and kissed me gently on the lips which surprised me a little. Her bright red lips were so cold, and as she kissed me I got the sense of death; it was all around her, about to take her. So very close now. I reached my arms around her and hugged her as hard as I could, like I could press what life I had into her.

"Die in peace. We love you." I let her go and looked at Dan.

"Don't wait another second, you only have twenty minutes or less and you need to spend that time together. Go now Dan and I'll seal you in." Dan nodded, took Jane's hand, and they disappeared.

I was crying and unsteady on my feet as I walked over to the entrance of their resting place. Believer held my hand and steadied me. He was silent. I'd made the entrance without a door but now it was time to seal them in. Until they rose. Vampires.

"We love you and miss you already." I sealed the crypt. The material rose up as I wanted and filled the opening. It wasn't a door, only a solid wall made from the same gleaming white material I had used to make the rest of the crypt. My work was done for now.

"Carry me, my love," I said. "I'm so tired."

His arms lifted me into the air almost before I finished the words. "I have you, my lady."

I wept as Believer cradled me in his arms like a little child. I stared up at the night sky as I felt the gentle swaying movement and the cool touch of the night air on my skin. I cried and stared at the sky. Jets were flying by overhead but I didn't hear them; their noise was kept out of the garden by my magic, but I did hear someone else crying.

I peeked over the side of Believer's arm, down to where "Lucius" walked beside me. He wept openly, unashamed, which was so odd. I couldn't imagine ever seeing tears come out of Tom like this. I didn't say anything as I peeked down at him from Believer's arms, but I did start my work. He was ours now so I needed to make some changes.

As he walked I changed his uniform from the military dress uniform, stained with blood, to a black outfit. Black slacks, made from the "magic fabric" I liked so much and a sheer red, button-up shirt and a nice black trench coat made from something that looked like leather but more breathy so it wouldn't be hot. Tom didn't jump or say anything as the clothes on his back shifted and settled. I changed his shoes into boots. I liked boots on men so I gave Lucius boots. Red boots to match his red shirt. I gave him a wide solid silver belt with a large buckle that looked like a skull with red glowing eyes. I'd seen one like it before during my early "goth stage," but my parents wouldn't let me wear it. It was easy to recreate.

I also changed Lucius's hair. I made it black. It had been blond and grey, cut in a spike, and he'd showed a little scalp in places where his hair was thinning with age, but I willed his hair to fill in and made it all a deep, solid black. I didn't change his style but kept it short and spiked. Just changing it to black made him look younger, and so did the new clothes. I took away his facial hair, banishing his stubble forever and made his skin less outdoors tan and more pale, like the vampires that he served. Next I changed his eye color from blue grey to black. He no longer looked like Tom and no one would ever mistake him for anything other than what he now was.

He was Lucius, eternal servant of the Queen of the Damned. So mote it be. Finally I willed his body to be strong and healthy. I shaved off twenty pounds, the small bit of fat he had was replaced by lean, toned muscle. If he was going to serve us I wanted him as healthy and as happy as I could make him.

There was a crowd waiting for us as we neared the house. Cathryn, Cornelius, Mary, Bethany, my mom and dad, Ryan, Sky and Sky Dragon, Dr. Burgis, Williams, Agent White and Agent Trisha, and other wedding guests. Jane's mom and dad were still here and I spotted David and Dana off to the side sipping wine and seated at a bench in the garden along with some of the other wedding guests. They watched as we came down the path. Even though it was almost midnight now, servants in white still worked, hustling about, handing out drinks and seeing to everyone's needs like it was natural to work until late into the night here.

Trisha ran out to meet us, her eyes on Tom.

"Oh my God! What happened?" She stood there gawking at him, trying to make sense of what she was seeing. Tom, or Lucius now, didn't say a word to her; instead he looked up at me. His black eyes regarded me calmly, waiting for instructions. His eyes were red rimmed from crying, light reflected off the tears on his checks he'd shed for Jane but he looked at peace with himself.

Seeing him stand at ease like this, I only now realized how tight Tom had always been before. Like a spring wound as tightly as it would go, every move crisp and cut. Painfully so. But not now. He looked relaxed. I had never noticed before how Tom actually looked, his pushy businesslike manner, his age, and the uniform had hidden it all, but not now. His face was all planes and angles as he looked up at me. And now that he was at peace, he was beautiful. A fitting servant for his Dark Queen who had left her mark where we could all see it. On his throat, fingerprints, the perfect match of Jane's hand. The mark had turned from red to an ugly purple bruise. I wondered if his throat was hurt. I willed his throat to heal on the inside so he could speak, but I also willed the mark to stay. It was Jane's mark and I would not remove it.

"Tom! What the hell happened!?" Trisha stepped closer to him.

"This is Lucius." I spoke loudly enough for everyone to hear me. "He is the Eternal Servant of the Queen of the Damned." I looked over to Cornelius and met his eyes. "Father, it was Jane's will for him to serve our household. May he be the captain of our guard and a protector of our house?" I asked. "He is totally loyal and very capable. He will serve us well."

I'd surprised my new father. His eyebrows shot up in an alarming way. Agent White and Trisha both started talking at once but stopped when Cornelius raised his hand and called for silence.

"Was this his choice? Wasn't this man a soldier, a very high-ranking soldier, and called by a different name before? Will they not come looking for him to take him away, my child?" He looked troubled. "Did the vampires bite him to make him their servant? What exactly happened here, Rain?" He gave me a demanding look. My new father wanted some answers and my old father and mother ten steps to his right looked like they wanted some too. Everyone wanted answers.

Believer set me down and I explained as much as I could. As much as I knew. Believer helped and told them how Jane had asked "Tom" if he wanted to keep his old life and how Tom refused to leave her. There was some yelling but not by me. Mary said that she knew the moment she touched him that "Tom" was Jane's but that didn't help. We talked for a while. I stayed totally calm and answered their questions as well as I could. In the end I summed it up to them the same way I had summed it up to myself earlier.

"So mote it be and so be it. We cannot undo what has been done. All we can do is move forward."

"Lucius. Come here," Cathryn said. Her voice was businesslike and crisp.

He did as he was told and came and stood before her.

"Whom do you serve?" Cathryn asked him as everyone listened, wide eyed. They were still trying to wrap their heads around the whole idea.

Everyone had argued back and forth. Agent White had called this "human slavery." But ready or not. Right or wrong. Legal or illegal. Hate it or love it. Here it was.

"I serve the Queen of the Damned. I serve my mistress Black Rain. And I have been told to serve this household."

He spoke clearly and confidently. He didn't seem humiliated in the least but most of those who heard the words he said winced for him. Agent White was extremely distressed. Trisha, of course, was horrified and upset by all of it. She spoke to Tom directly.

"But why, Tom!? Or Lucius! Or whoever the hell you are now! Why are you doing this!?" she shouted at him.

"Answer her freely, Lucius," Cathryn said, but he looked to me for permission to answer.

"Lucius. Other than me, there are only two others you will obey completely." I kept my voice firm and direct like Cathryn's had been. "Cathryn is my mother, and she is the Queen of this household. You will obey her in all things as you will obey the King, my father. You will address her as Queen Cathryn. And you will address him as King Cornelius. Do you understand me?"

"Yes, Mistress," Lucius answered me.

He looked at Cathryn. "Queen Cathryn," he said, and then turned to Trisha. "Trisha. Don't be upset. Jane held my hand earlier this morning just like Black Rain told you. I was marked. But something more happened. To make a long story short, Trisha, I fell in love with Jane. I'm content to serve her. I'm happy to be here, to be near her and to please her. She didn't mean for this to happen. It was a complete and total accident. But it *has* happened." Lucius paused for a moment as he stared at her. "I could have gotten out of it, like they said. Dan could have made me forget her, but I don't want to forget her." He smiled big, it wasn't a facial expression you would ever have seen on Tom's face. Trisha actually backed up a step. "I love her, Trisha. She is my world. This is my life and I'm happy here. Very happy and content."

"Cornelius," Cathryn said. The two met eyes. "We need a captain of the guard. A protector. And it would be a waste not to use him, my lord." She wanted him.

Cornelius took a deep breath, held if for a second, then blew out a gust of air along with the last of his reservations. "This is an ugly thing." He shook his head. "An unfortunate, ugly business, this entire turn of events."

"Yes, it is," said Mr. Miller. "But Jane didn't want this to happen. All she wanted to do was get married. This isn't her fault either!" He looked around angrily, with most of his irate gaze saved for Agent White.

Cornelius tried to calm Mr. Miller and at the same time reason with White. "We know the child didn't mean for this to happen, that's obvious, but it's still a huge loss." He looked over to White. "I want to do what's right here. I do. But what would be best for you, Agent White, would not necessarily be what's best for Lucius. As things stand I believe it would be worse to send him away than to let him stay here. I'm sorry, Agent White, but I think my daughter is right. We cannot undo what has been done. From this point all we can do is move forward as best we can."

"You can't be serious!" White exploded, stepping closer to Cornelius. "They'll never allow this! Tom's not a house slave! He's a soldier, an officer, and an agent in the Department of Homeland Defense! He reports directly to the President for God's sake!" White was out of breath as he finished his rant. "You're not really going to do this?" He looked from face to face. Cathryn to Cornelius.

"Yes. We are," Cathryn said, and she didn't sound upset at all. She almost looked happy as she eyed Lucius. Like she was already trying to guess his worth and ability. She looked quite pleased by what she saw.

"Lucius," she called and he quickly stepped over to her. He appeared ready and willing to serve. Happy himself at how things were proceeding. Trisha and White started shouting again, even more forcefully and rudely.

Suddenly, a dark wave of dread washed over the room, so chilling that glasses held in hands released. There was a tinkling sound of a dozen breaking wine flutes all across the patio and up into the house. A servant dropped a tray of appetizers with a tremendous crash onto the deck. Some people actually went to their knees and cried out.

Bethany had risen from her seat, unobserved as she walked over and stood in the midst of the arguing parties. We'd not noticed her then, but we all noticed her now. As she spoke, goosebumps rose on top of goosebumps and every fine hair in the room stood to attention, mine included. Bethany had my full attention! There was no mistaking the flavor, it was black magic, dark and vile as the dredges of the pit of hell itself! It was terrifying and horrible and *electrifying*!

She worked hard to sound proper as she spoke. A true princess. Her little voice wasn't loud but her magic made it impossible not to hear every bone-chilling word. "You stand in the land of Amen Hale. You stand in the Castle of Amen Hall. You stand before our King and Queen. If you were not our guest I would kill you now for your disrespect—but I will show mercy. This time. If you get ugly again, I will kill you."

Bethany looked at Agent White for a moment more, then turned and walked back to her seat beside my mom and dad who wrapped their arms around her as soon as she sat down. Bethany let herself be held by both of them as she looked back at the room filled with silent terrified faces. Half the room was shaking in their boots as Cathryn broke the fragile silence with her calm, reassuring voice.

"Thank you, Bethany," she told her. And while everyone was still reeling she turned her attention back to Lucius.

He was still standing in front of her.

"Kneel before me." Cathryn spoke to him like you would imagine a real Queen would have spoken to a servant or a slave in the old days of feudalism. In the time of kings, queens, knights, and dragons—and slaves.

Lucius went to his knees before her.

"You will serve this household and my family as the Captain of our Guard. You will be a protector for us until such time as my daughter, your mistress, or your Dark Queen herself calls you away or kills you. Do you accept this?"

"Yes, Queen Cathryn. Gladly." Lucius smiled big. Again, it looked odd because Tom never smiled.

"Byron." The head butler came and stood before her, chin high. "Lucius is now a servant of this household. He will be the Captain of our Guard and a protector for our family. Help him as he needs help and teach him how to serve us well."

Byron bowed. "Your Majesty," he intoned and stepped back.

Cornelius then stepped into the center of the room; he looked around making eye contact with everyone before he started to speak. His sure and confident bearing reminded me of the night this all started, Lammas Night, when I had lit the Black Candle. I remembered that he'd been kind to me even on that first night. It made me happy to think of him as my father.

"This business is settled. Lucius is ours." He looked at Agent White and Trisha. "If there are more questions they can be carefully addressed in the light of a new day, but NOT tonight."

He stared at White, not looking away until White mumbled, "Agreed, King Cornelius. Till the morning then."

Cornelius nodded, then continued. "This has been a day unlike any before it, and Lucius is not the only one to have walked a path he did not imagine when this day began. We must all change and live with what we have become." Cornelius nodded like that piece of advice was for him as well, then he addressed the room, his voice brighter as he continued. "Our staff has prepared a reception meal. I know that the hour is late, but please, they have all worked very hard under difficult conditions and it would honor them to see you partake of what they have prepared for us. Please, come and sit for a while and we can rejoice in the joys of this day."

In his hand was a wine glass which he raised. "Come and we will celebrate the weddings!" he announced happily. "Celebrate the joy of young lives joined by love. Rain and Believer. Ryan and Sky. David and Dana. And we will celebrate the wedding of Jane and Dan Simmons." Cornelius's smile turned down and his voice became solemn as he continued. "But let us also mourn, for tonight is also a time of sorrow." He raised his glass a little higher. "Come, my family, friends, and guests. Let us talk of Jane and Dan. Let us hear the story of their love and let us remember their human lives this night. Let us hear more of the seventeen years they enjoyed. And let us mourn, and weep, and sorrow, as we remember what has passed."

And there was weeping. I started to cry again and I heard Jane's mother and father crying too. Lucius wept silently. Cornelius wiped at his own eyes before he continued. "Let us remember them and let us mourn them, but let us mourn in hope. I have no doubt that we shall see them stand with us again, here in this Hall." His voice grew as he finished. "To those who are wed! To Jane and Dan, soon to rise from the dead! To my new sons and daughters. To my Queen who rules by my side. To the Kingdom that has come! Amen Hale! So mote it be!" He drained his glass and threw the empty vessel on the floor, shattering it so that no lesser toast would ever be offered from the same glass.

"So mote it be!" Cathryn followed suit with her own, shattering her glass as well. A few others followed suit, but only a few, as most people had lost their glasses when Bethany scared them to death.

With Cornelius's gentle urging the crowd moved out of the Cathedral Hall and into the Entry Hall which was now clean of blood except for what was on the high ceiling. The guests were surprised as they entered. In this home things were done to a certain social standard and the servants would not hear of there being a wedding without a proper reception feast.

Five of us stayed behind in the Cathedral Hall. Mary stood nearby talking to Believer, keeping him company as Cathryn and I inspected Lucius. Cathryn eyed him intently, trying to understand him and how he would fit into our family.

"What kind of a man were you, Lucius? Were you an evil man or a good man? Were you a father? Tell me, what was your family like? Tell me about what you were." She stood very close to him, studying him. She sounded mysterious and a bit strange. I felt a slight tingle of magic. There was lots of it swirling around in the house but this was a new flavor I hadn't singled out before. And then I remembered dumbly that my new mother was a witch, and she was using her own power now. It made me smile.

"I was a good man. A hard man but a good man." Lucius spoke calmly, telling his past without hesitation or any hint of shame. "I was married for seventeen years before she left me. I had one son and three daughters. I was a poor father but a good provider. I was gone most of their lives and when I was home I didn't involve myself with them. I was uncomfortable with my own children. Distant from my wife. I was never an affectionate person. My wife said that the only thing I ever loved was my job." He stopped there, his face introspective. "But I didn't love my job. I liked being useful. And I felt the most effective and useful at work. Around things I understood. More so than at home where I felt out of place, trying to deal with three girls, my boy, a wife and all their problems." His face finally looked pained as the weight of his past bore down on him. "I did not love my wife. I tried to love my children but did a damn poor job of it. I don't think I've ever really loved anything my whole life until I fell in love with Jane. I love Jane."

Those last three words rang in the air. They sounded like steel. Hard and sharp and final. Eternal.

"I love her too, Lucius," I said firmly. I did. "You're not alone. Her magic has changed me too, and I'm glad that it has." I placed a hand over my heart and laughed a little as I remembered all the staring Jane and Dan did. The way they attacked each other in the waiting room and how Jane's mother had yelled at them. And then I thought of how Sky had attacked Ryan. Jane had affected more than just Tom and me. I knew now that it was mostly her magic that had pulled Sky and Ryan together.

"Jane made me dare to dream that there was more for me than the sorrow of my miserable creation." I relaxed my hold and let some of my own power slip out of my body, coloring the night with my own distinct flavor of magic. My hair and my dress began to billow softly in my own unseen wind of power and I knew my midnight eyes sparkled as I spoke. "I'm glad she made me dare to love again. You humans can't smell it, but I truly wish you could," I said to no one and "everyone." My smile had left me and tears started to fill my eyes again as I remembered the beautiful smell. By now I knew that Jane was dead and the beautiful smell of roses had left with her. Jane and her Dan, both dead in their grave.

"What can't we smell, Rain?" Mary asked as she came close to me and slipped her arm around me. "What are you talking about?" I felt her magic wrap around me just like her arms wrapped around my body, in a gentle embrace. She never reached inside me with her power but tried to learn what she could on the surface of what I was. Mary wanted to know what was troubling me and what I meant and this was becoming her way. Not asking questions but just touching and feeling and knowing.

"What smell are you talking about, and what's wrong, my child?" Cathryn asked.

"Jane's magic, Mother, it smells like roses. I miss it," I said as my tears finally spilled over and ran down my face. Mary started crying too, touched by my emotions and memories.

Cathryn hugged us both.

"Does it really smell like roses?" Lucius asked. "Is it beautiful? I wish I could smell it too." He looked like he was trying to imagine the smell for himself.

I spoke to him. "Your first life was filled with a family, yet still empty and hollow like mine used to be. Your second life will be filled with love, Lucius. This household will be more than just a king and queen with people to serve and lands to protect. We are a family. You will love us and cherish us all, Lucius. So mote it be."

"So mote it be," said Cathryn.

"So mote it be," said Mary as she cried and hugged me tighter.

"Enough tears!" Cathryn said loudly. "Tonight is not a time for tears, Rain. Now go to your husband, child, he's waiting for you."

I looked up. He stood just ten feet away from where I was, silently listening to us. His glowing red eyes always on me, watching me. Cathryn kissed me on my head and I nodded.

"Yes, Mother," I whispered. I tried to step away but Mary stayed attached to the other side of me like a leech.

"Mar-ry!" I laughed as I drug her along with me as I headed to Believer. Believer laughed as he watched us, his low rumble making me relax a little. He was so quiet all the time, it was always reassuring to hear him make noise.

"I can't freaking believe you got married before me," Mary griped, finally letting go of me.

I slipped over to Believer and took his hand and looked up at him shyly. I'd never had sex before, although I had Rain Marie's memories of being with Ken, that horrible boy that had gotten her pregnant. She'd only slept with him twice and it hadn't been a fantastic experience either time. Rushed, awkward, and any pleasure was washed away by regret as soon as it was done. Then she regretted it more a few weeks later once she found out she was pregnant. For the next two months Ken begged her to get an abortion, trying to reason with her at first. When that didn't work he threatened her, cussed at her, called her a whore and every vile thing he could think of until Rain Marie finally broke down and agreed to kill our child. Ken had been horrible. He'd seemed like a fun-loving, regular guy at first, but he was rotten on the inside. Evil.

I thought about Rain Marie and the one person she had given herself to in her life as I studied this giant cloud man I'd married. Ken had been a horrible little child in a teenage boy's body. And Rain Marie had been a silly, reckless, willful girl back then. But I was not a silly girl. I was not even human. I was a dream. And Believer was noble. Pure in heart and perfect. And he loved me. And he was my husband. And we had all night to be together and I didn't even have a clue as to what it would be like to "be" with him. My eyes wanted to look down from his eyes to his chest where I knew a denser white mass of clouds were located. These clouds were not his heart. Believer didn't need a heart. But he did need other things. Especially tonight. My throat was dry and I swallowed and looked down at the floor.

"Are you tired, my love?" he asked me gently.

"Yes," I answered honestly. "But not that tired." I looked up at him and met his red eyes with my own. My beautiful cloud man. My first time would be different. My first time would be everything hers was not.

Please. Let it be beautiful. I prayed silently to myself, as I was the only person who heard my prayers now, it seemed appropriate.

"Mom, when can I get married!?" Mary complained to Cathryn. They stood nearby watching us.

"Not tonight, Mary," Cathryn answered quickly. "This day's magic is coming to a close and it's time for us to go eat with our guests, say our farewells, and go to bed."

"Yeah! Go to bed all by myself you mean!" Mary griped, giving Believer and me an envious look.

"Yes. By yourself, Mary." Somehow Cathryn still answered calmly.

"But they're gonna be up half the night getting' busy!" Mary complained as she brushed her green lock of hair out of her eyes and continued to voice her suspicions. "That Sky is wild too. I bet she's a screamer! I bet it's gonna sound like someone's killing a cat upstairs." Mary nodded firmly, confident in her assessment. "We won't be able to sleep," she told Cathryn. "You know they're gonna keep us up all night with all their wild—"

"Mary! Go get yourself a glass of wine and don't say *another word* till you've finished it please!" Cathryn ordered, finally having had enough. She pointed a finger toward the reception hall and all the guests. "Go!"

I laughed as Mary stuck her tongue out in a quick snakelike strike before she turned and took off. Skipping happily away to get her wine. At least she obeyed. She hadn't said another word.

"Oh Goddess, help me," Cathryn breathed out, putting a hand to her forehead as she turned back to me. "You and Believer will be in my room, up the stairs, the last room with the double doors. You can't miss it. Cornelius and I will share with one of the servants tonight. We will make other arrangements for tomorrow, but for tonight take our room. We love you. Now go, say goodnight to your other mother and father and take your leave of us."

Believer walked me into the reception hall and I said good night to my friends and family. Ryan and Sky were happily talking away, laughing, eating, and enjoying themselves and all our company but David and Dana were already through for the evening. I saw a servant leading them up the stairs toward their room.

I spoke briefly with all our guests, sharing a few words with each before moving to the next. I noticed Lucius, standing at the edge of the room apart from us and I brought him over and made him sit down beside Williams and eat.

He and Williams started talking business right away, and it was good to see him already making himself at home. Making himself useful.

I hugged my mom and dad and spoke to them for a few minutes. They said that they were going to stay here, but just for tonight. They planned on leaving tomorrow morning after they saw Ryan and me. I knew they just wanted to make sure we were okay before they went back home. I said my last goodbye and left Mom and Dad there at the table. They looked happy, even after all the events of the day, and I hadn't left them alone. Bethany had curled up in Dad's strong arms and had fallen fast asleep. She looked like a little sleeping angel resting in his arms.

"Isn't that beautiful?" I whispered to Believer.

He nodded, and then reached over and picked me up without saying a word. It surprised me, and I looked up at him and studied his face, trying to see what he was thinking. I could see it in his face. Believer was ready to go.

"Are you ready, my lady?" he asked me. He held me in his arms, pressed up against his chest and I finally allowed myself to look at the white pulsing clouds there in the center of his chest right beside me. From a distance it looked like nothing but a denser mass of white clouds, pulsing with light within his cloudy body. But up this close I could see more, I noticed that the shape was definitely suggestive of what I had imagined it would be. A shy smile stole its way onto my face.

"Yes. I believe I am," I said as I looked at his "heart." Believer laughed quietly, his body rumbling happily as he carried me up the stairs and to my wedding bed.

Cathryn and Cornelius

Riddles in the Dark

The evening was done. The reception dinner was over. All the wedded couples had retired to their rooms and Mary had taken a final load of stragglers to the doorway for the journey back to the church. Officer Williams had decided to leave with them and go home to his family. He said that Rain had a husband now, two sets of parents, her brother, and Lucius to look after her so she was in good hands, and he had no desire to be used as a spy and pumped for information once he returned. He'd experienced that once already. Once, he said, was enough.

Jane's parents had asked to stay at the house while they waited for Jane and Dan to rise so they had taken one of the guest rooms upstairs in the main house. Mr. and Mrs. Bryant were in another guest bedroom. Mr. Bryant had carried

Bethany to their room with them in his arms, already asleep. Rooms had been made for Dr. Burgis, Ryan and Sky, David and Dana, and one had been set aside for Mary and Bethany there in the same long hall. Sky Dragon stood guard in that upstairs hall, keeping a careful watch over the others as they slept. Neither Sky Dragon nor Believer needed to sleep so he was the perfect guard.

"Yes, Philip, we will be sleeping in the green room. Just make us a pallet on the floor and we'll be fine."

Philip was young, about twenty, somewhat overweight and his unruly mop of wavy brown hair always look disheveled. He, like all their staff, came from a family of witches and was familiar with their lifestyle and accustomed to the workings and events of the house. Only fifteen servants and staff lived and worked at Amen Hale full time but thirty others worked part time, driving in as needed for large events or gatherings. Philip had been given one of the coveted full-time resident slots three months ago and he'd been a less than stellar addition to the household from the very first day. Cathryn had tried to encourage him and work with him but after all her best efforts were exhausted Philip remained a huge disappointment. All Cathryn's life she'd had an almost magical ability to inspire and manage people, and this household in particular, so her failure with Philip had troubled her deeply.

She'd never before had to let someone go for being a lazy slacker. Byron the House Steward urged her to wait until after the Lammas celebration and she'd agreed. The upheaval of that night had delayed his expulsion. And after Lammas, one disaster after another had come crashing down on her and Cornelius, as if some dark force were bent on destroying everything they held dear. The video from the security cameras was stolen and used to make that horrible web site. Next came the FBI and the IRS investigating Cornelius's business dealings and seizing all their assets. The police came out, asking questions about minors at their Wiccan celebrations participating in questionable activities and underage drinking. And then came the arrival of Yanosh and Fiona.

When she had knelt there on the cold marble floor weeping over Cornelius's dead body the only mercy she had hoped for was a quick death so she could be spared seeing what horrors Yanosh planned for Bethany. She felt as if she knelt at the bottom of a monstrous hourglass, unable to scream, and hardly able to draw a breath as the last few black grains of sand that marked her burned and ruined life drifted down upon her head like ash. Her time was up.

But in an instant, everything changed. The hourglass was turned upside down. From that moment on her world began to rebuild itself anew. The first of many joys was the death of her enemies. The second was the resurrection of Cornelius from the dead. She heard the spell and felt the awesome power of Bethany's magic as she'd called out, "RISE KING CORNELIUS!" And rise he did. As a King. Which again seemed to prove the paradox of the world having been stood on its head as Cornelius himself was a direct descendant of Nathan Hale, that great American patriot who had died a hero in the Revolutionary War fighting to free America from the rule of a King. But as America and its authorities seemed hellbent on their destruction, it was a joy to know that Amen Hale was no longer a part of that nation nor subject to its laws.

Another completely unexpected joy was gaining a daughter of her own. All her life she'd dreamed of having children but according to the doctors, she was barren. Cornelius had offered to adopt but Cathryn was never comfortable with it. Instead of motherhood she'd invested her time and energy into her private life as a witch and the head of her coven, and into her public life as a loving wife to Cornelius and the head of Cornelius's family home, Amen Hall. Amen Hall was listed on the National Registry of Historical Sites and had hosted dozens of famous weddings over the years, entertained state dinners, and, until recently, hosted historical tours of the house and grounds every Friday afternoon.

Immediately after Cornelius was raised from the dead, Cathryn and Cornelius had assembled the servants and staff and told them everything. It was an amazing tale, but with Bethany standing there, drenched in blood, two dead bodies lying in the house, and the FBI surrounding the property, they believed it. All of it. Every last unbelievable word of it.

She and Cornelius told them about the resurrection and that he, Cornelius, was now a King, and that she, Cathryn, was now a Queen. Cornelius informed them that Bethany was now their daughter. He commanded that she be addressed as Princess, or Princess Bethany, and accorded all the honor that would be due a child of his own body. Again, none of the servants questioned a word.

They were told that from this day forward the house would be run as a sovereign kingdom, totally independent and apart from the United States of America. Cornelius invited any who wished to leave his service to do so because, as he put it, "*Serving a King and Queen is different from serving a gentleman and a lady.*" And, he added with a certain pride that "*unlike the King of England,*" he wanted everyone to have the freedom of choice. They could stay and serve under a monarchy or choose to leave Amen Hale and live in America. Cornelius even offered a generous stipend for any who chose to take their leave of the house. No one wanted to leave.

Especially Philip. Apparently Philip agreed with Cornelius. To him, serving a wealthy household was very different from serving a King and Queen. He was completely transformed. It was if he'd finally woken from a long half sleep. His eyes were clear and bright and his movements crisp and determined. Everything he put his hand to was now a service done to the utmost of his ability, without complaining, and he was happier now than Cathryn had ever seen him.

They quickly discovered that the idea of serving a King and Queen was fascinating to far more people than just Philip. Since this afternoon a steady stream of uninvited "guests" had been arriving at the gate. Most had been sent away but some had been allowed to stay. Byron had been moving those he selected out to the Guest Hall and other outbuildings without disturbing the wedding party or the main house, but more people kept coming. People wanted to be a part of what was happening and they continued to wash up at the gate like refugees.

Events were rushing forward so quickly. This newly constructed life seemed almost too unbelievable to be real at times. Cathryn had moments where she'd stop suddenly and think to herself, *Is this really happening?* or *Am I really doing this?* or simply *Am I dreaming? Is this even real?* She only had one answer for herself. Yes. Though the speed of things and the magic seemed hard to believe at times, the idea of being a Queen didn't intimidate Cathryn at all. She'd managed every aspect of the Hale House with its many servants for years, and she'd been the head of her Coven for years. She needed no one to tell her that she'd run both extremely well. How much different could being a Queen and running a kingdom possible be?

In a way, tomorrow would be the start of building a new household. Tomorrow they would go through the people they had brought in already, sorting the wheat from the chaff. Tomorrow she and Cornelius would start building a new kingdom, but until tomorrow they had to deal with the crowding of tonight and the problems of security, which was why Lucius had asked them to stay in the Green Room. Just for tonight. He was worried about their safety and the Green Room had no windows, only one door, and was on the first floor of the main building where no one would expect them to be. Lucius also planned on standing watch outside their door tonight himself to keep them safe. She'd already learned years ago that when one of her skilled people gave her advice it was best to listen. So in the Green Room they would stay.

Cathryn watched as Philip went about his work. His strained face and the tightness of his movements told her how much what he was doing upset him. The work no longer upset him, but the thought of his King and Queen sleeping on a pallet set on the floor of the Green Room did.

"Don't worry, Philip, it's just for tonight, tomorrow will be different. Make yourself a pallet beside ours and sleep in the Green Room with us. That way, should Cornelius and I need some service or a glass of water during the night you'll be the one we call on." Cathryn knew that would make him happy, and it did.

"Yes, my Queen!" he said with a joyful smile. And that was another way in which everyone was different. All of the staff and guests were still adjusting to the new deportment and there was a wide variety of titles in use.

"My Queen," "Queen Cathryn," or even for Cornelius "My Lord" were common, and Cathryn preferred these, but some of the older, mostly English staff insisted on using "Your Majesty" or "Your Highness," which still seemed unusual in her own hearing.

And to make matters worse, the changes kept coming. As soon as the staff settled on the structure of things, the household structure transformed again. Now all three of the witches were considered "daughters" of the King and Queen. And then there was the question of the other guests. Ryan and Sky and David and Dana. And the presence of the vampires who were now entombed in the garden. Combined with the presence of Believer and Sky Dragon and the magic of the witches, the whole castle had been transformed into a place of constant wonder and sometimes frightening magic. As if their magical guests weren't enough evidence, one look out the window at the hundreds of soldiers that encircled the property like swarming green ants was an instant reminder that the world as they knew it had changed. No pinch was needed. It wasn't a dream. The Kingdom was real, the magic within it was real, and their King and Queen were real as well.

Philip had just brought in a second pallet when a half drunk Mary came spinning into the room. She caught Willomena's hands in her own and danced her around the room as she laughed. Willomena held on for dear life as Mary twirled and spun gracefully with her for a minute before letting her go. The old woman sagged into a chair, fanning herself, surprised and out of breath.

"Mo-om! I'm ba-ak. But we gaaat a little pro-blem. She's riiiight beeehind meeee!" She sang and danced her way all around the Green Room, swaying elegantly and adding a spin pirouette here and there as she leaned and dipped and kicked and flowed around the furnishings, doing all of this with her eyes closed tight.

After one final twirl and the end of her song, Mary collapsed onto the bed that Philip had so lovingly prepared for his King and Queen, falling face first into the crisply turned down pallet. She wallowed into the bedding for only a second before it seemed she was out. No one noticed Emma's silent entrance into the room, but now that Mary had "crashed" Cathryn gaze finally found her standing just inside the door, waiting. She recognized her. She was one of Jane's friends who had been in her wedding and had come with all the others guests to see Rain and Believer's wedding, and to see the vampires laid to rest, though that had turned out to be a bloody affair.

"Should I take her up to her room, my Queen?" Philip asked, drawing Cathryn's attention. He stared down at the body lodged in the middle of the pallet, unsure what to do.

"Just cover her up, Philip. She can have that one. Cornelius and I will take the one you were going to use," Cathryn said with a sigh.

"That's not what she wants," spoke a dry cynical voice and everyone turned back to Emma. She'd said it.

Cathryn studied the girl for a second. She had spoken very little this evening, staying close to Jane and Jane's parents for most of the night. She was very tall and very plain. Straight brown hair, brown eyes, scarecrow thin with no curves to help fill out the black gown she still had on from Jane's wedding. But she had sounded quite sure of herself.

"Why should we not cover her, Emma?" Cathryn was forced to ask. She couldn't imagine a reason to not cover Mary. Philip stood beside the pallet with the blanket in hand, waiting.

"I don't think she wants to sleep alone."

Cathryn considered that and looked at Mary again, planted right in the middle of the pallet where she herself had planned on sleeping. Was Emma right?

"Why would you think that, child?" Cathryn asked her.

"She's not happy unless she's touching someone." Emma's flat voice, while not disrespectful, was definitely plaintive as she spoke. "She's been attached to people all night long. She even made me hold her hand on the way back over here." Emma took another couple of steps into the room and looked over at Mary who was still out.

"If you don't lie down with her she'll just get up and find someone else to lie down with. I really hope you let her sleep with you."

Emma's frown turned down another couple of degrees and the edges of Cathryn's mouth turned up an equal measure in response. What a strange creature this Emma was. Interesting, strange, and apparently very perceptive. As she considered what Emma said and thought back on the evening it did seem that Mary had stayed in contact with someone almost every second of the evening. Sitting in someone's lap, holding a hand or hugging someone, or attached to their side. But that didn't explain the last part of what Emma had said.

"I think you may be right, Emma, but explain again why you want *me* to sleep with her," she asked.

Emma's frown turned down even more before she answered in her plaintive flat voice. "I'm worried that if you don't sleep with her she'll come and find me and get in my bed. And I'm just not a touchy feely person. I don't like people touching me. It's weird. I like my space." Her eyes squinted as she spoke.

Cathryn studied the scowl, the tightened eyes, and the rigid stance. This type of reaction in a young girl usually meant she'd been hurt by someone as a child or more recently. But something else Emma said drew her attention.

"Why would you worry about Mary sleeping in your bed, Emma? You're going home to your family tonight. You should have gone back to the church with the others." Cathryn was sure that Jane's parent's had mentioned that Emma was going back to the church. And she remembered Emma walking off with the others that had gone with Mary to travel back to the church through the doorway.

Emma's grimace was replaced by a fearful, but determined, look as she walked to middle of the room and went to her knees before Cathryn. "Please let me stay. I'll do anything you need doing. I'll do laundry. I'll do floors. I'm real good with bathrooms and I can help in the kitchen. I'm not afraid of hard work." She said it like she meant it. "And you're gonna need more servants around this place with all these new people at your home. You don't even need to pay me. I'll keep quiet and I won't be any trouble. You won't even know I'm here. And I don't need my own room, I can sleep anywhere. Please. I just want to stay here with Jane." She stopped, finally running out of steam.

Now that she'd had her say it looked as if her confidence had reached its limit. Emma looked at the floor, her bony shoulders sagging as she waited to be sent home.

"Uhum." A polite noise announced visitors.

Cathryn looked up. Cornelius and Byron stood in the doorway looking in. From their faces it seemed they had heard the girl's request but hadn't said a word yet; they waited for her permission to enter the room. But now the girl had truly intrigued her. Something about her unusual manner piqued Cathryn's interest and moved her heart. She was tired, but today was a day of strange events, none of which were to be taken lightly or ignored.

"Everyone. Leave us," Cathryn commanded.

Cornelius and Byron raised their brows and backed from the door without a word and the two servants in the room took their leave with a mumbled "yes, my Queen" from Philip and a quick "Your Majesty" from Willomena.

The door shut, and they were alone except for a sleeping Mary. Emma's brown eyes met hers and Cathryn studied what she saw in this girl. Among other things, lots of pride.

"You still have not addressed me by my name or by my title, Emma. You do realize that if you worked here, sooner or later you'd need to call me something." Cathryn smiled.

"Yes, ma'am," Emma replied, avoiding the question and an answer altogether in one fell stroke.

Cathryn laughed, a full happy laugh with no mockery in it at all. Yes, the girl had lots of hard won pride.

"Not the grandest of the names I now have but it may serve—for now." Cathryn stepped closer to her. Emma was still on her knees and was forced to look up to meet her eyes.

"Why do you want to stay here, Emma?"

"To take care of Jane," she said simply.

"Things have changed for her, child. Jane has a husband now. And she has Rain to take care of her, and Rain loves Jane like her own soul. And what Rain loves, Mary and Bethany and I love. We are a family, and we love together, so the King and I love her also. There is no shortage of people to love and take care of Jane. And now she even has Lucius, her own human servant. So let me ask you again." Cathryn got on her knees in front of Emma and regarded her directly. "Why?"

Emma wanted to look away, but her stubborn streak forced her to meet Cathryn's gaze. It was a fascinating cascade of emotions that washed over this intensely personal and private girl. Cathryn waited patiently, letting it come, and it was a few minutes before she finally spoke.

"You have half my life buried out there in your garden. The better half." She swallowed, trying to wet her dried throat enough to speak the rest of her words. "I'd rather stay with this part of my life. Please."

Her answers only brought more questions, but those would wait for another day. Cathryn nodded. "How old are you, child? Will your parents not miss you tonight?"

Emma blinked a time or two before she spoke. It was her only reaction before speaking. "I'll be eighteen in six months. And even if they came to get me, this place is a separate country now, isn't it? So they'd have to ask you first. They couldn't just take me." She struggled to keep her face neutral and unchallenging.

"No one can take you without my leave, Emma. But what I asked was if your parents would miss you. Will they miss you, child?"

"Yes." A one word answer. Emma held her breath as she waited. Contents under pressure.

Cathryn sighed regretfully. "I guess I'll have to sleep with Mary tonight then," she said in a more casual, conversational tone, like they were just two girls, talking. "I'm a witch too, Emma; it makes us act a little odd at times. Quirky and peculiar. I'm not nearly as bad about touching people as Mary, and I'm much more selective, but I really do like to have my arms around Cornelius when I sleep. Especially after a day like today." She raised both eyebrows, making herself look young and surprised. "He died on me today! That kind of thing makes a girl think."

Emma laughed. It was the first bright and happy sound she'd heard the girl make. It didn't last long as she killed it quickly. She looked surprised at herself and terribly worried that she may have laughed out of turn. She covered her mouth with both hands. Two big brown eyes stared at Cathryn, waiting to see what would happen. An odd sense of humor for an odd girl. Cathryn's warm smile reassured her. Emma lowered her hands. She was smiling too.

"Let me go let everyone in and we can start getting ourselves settled for the night." Cathryn stood and walked over to the door and opened it. They were waiting there for her. Cornelius was already in his night clothes and had Cathryn's in his hands.

"Is all well, my Queen?" asked Cornelius, giving her a gentle kiss on the lips.

"Yes. Emma will be staying with us tonight. And Mary has some specific needs now because of her magic. She seems to be unable to sleep alone and she's crawled into my bed, so I'll have to sleep with her tonight."

Cornelius peeked around Cathryn, into the room. "Seems like a popular pastime this eve, my Queen."

Cathryn and Byron looked into the room just as Emma crawled into the pallet with Mary. She'd taken the time to remove Mary's shoes and set them, along with her own, at the foot of the pallet before getting in. She didn't look comfortable at all as she lay beside Mary, stiff as a board and still wearing her black dress from the wedding, but Mary looked absolutely blissful spooned up beside Emma with a happy smile on her face.

"What's this?" asked Byron.

Cathryn smiled, "Just a little more magic at the end of a magical day."

"Hmm." Cornelius was curious but focused on the less magical and more immediate benefit. "Does this mean you shall lie next to me, my lovely Witch Queen?"

"Yes, my Lord. It does," she replied happily.

Byron nodded. "Will the young lady be retained as an addition to the household staff?" He sounded hopeful. Emma was right about them needing more people.

"I'm not sure yet, Byron. Perhaps I'll have a better sense of things soon. For now treat her as a guest."

Byron bowed, then turned and waved Philip and Willomena into the room to dress the other pallet. Cathryn slipped out of her clothes and into her nightgown right there outside the door of the Green Room as the servants prepared the bed. Cornelius handed Byron her old clothes for the wash. Nudity in their home was not taboo. The servants didn't even notice. While appreciated no less for what it was, getting naked just wasn't a big deal in a witch's home.

"Good night, Willomena. Good night, Philip," Cornelius said as they headed out the door. They climbed into the second pallet beside the girls. As soon as they were settled into the bed Philip turned off the light. "Thank you, Philip."

It was completely silent in the room for all of three minutes.

"Good night, Mom. Good night, Dad." Mary's voice came out of the darkness, breaking the new silence that had just settled in. "Good night, Emms," she finished.

"*Quiet, Mary!*" Emma's voice whispered from the darkness to Mary.

"*Why?*" Mary whispered back in the darkness.

"*Because you're bugging them!*" Emma whispered back.

"*But that's our job. They're—*"

"Good night, Mary. Good night, Emma." Cathryn's voice cut into the whispering match. "Good night, Cornelius," she finished because it needed finishing.

"Good night, Mary. Good night, Emma. Good night, Cathryn," Cornelius said, stifling a little laugh.

It was silent for about a minute.

"*Emms. You got to say goodnight!*" Mary whispered. The acoustics of the room carried the whisper to everyone.

Three frustrated sighs breathed out into the darkness.

"*If I do, do you promise to go to bed?*" Emma's whisper asked. "*That's a witch thing, right? You gotta keep your promises. So do you promise?*"

"*I promise,*" Mary whispered. "*Just tell them goodnight.*"

"Goodnight." Emma's voice surfaced to normal volume for the one word before submerging back into whispers. "*Now go to bed.*"

"*No deal, you didn't say it right!*" Mary whispered back.

"Good grief!" Emma said, not quite a whisper.

"*Still not right,*" Mary whispered. "*Hehehe,*" she snickered.

Cathryn spoke. "Just say it, Emma. She's trapped herself now. Use her own magic against her. She must keep her word, so run through all the variations you can think of and eventually you'll hit on it and she'll go out like a light."

"Really?" Emma asked, not bothering to whisper either.

"Hehehehe," Mary giggled.

"All right! You asked for it." Emma launched into her attack. "Good night, Queen Cathryn. Good night, King Cornelius. Good night, Princess Mary."

"Hehehehe," Mary giggled.

Emma's voice rose just a little louder on this next attempt. "Good night, my Queen. Good night, my King. Good night, Princess.

"Hehehehe."

"Ugh!"

"Nope, not it either," Mary said, then giggled again. "Hehehe."

"Keep trying, child. Be patient and think it through," Cornelius encouraged. "Once you unlock her little riddle you have my royal permission to hit her with your pillow before you go to sleep. Now keep trying."

"Hehehe," Mary giggled.

Emma wondered what to try next. Maybe she needed to go simple instead of complex. She tried to shorten it up.

"Good night, Cornelius. Good night, Cathryn. Good night, Mary."

"Hehehehe."

"Good night, King. Good night, Queen. Good night, Princess."

"Hehehe."

"Good night, Mom. Good night, Dad. Good night, Mary."

Silence.

No giggle.

The only one asleep in the silent room was Mary.

Cathryn, Cornelius, and Emma lay in their beds, wide awake, thinking, while Mary enjoyed her blissful sleep.

And she didn't even get hit with a pillow.

Bull Danridge

Non-Believer

Bull Danridge, commander of Delta Black One, ran his hands across the cool white stone that still defied him. It did so without pomp or arrogance. Defeat was as alien a feeling to Bull as the white stone itself. Simply put, it was something he'd never experienced before. But the last twenty-four hours was filled with new experiences and so far most of them sucked.

"That's it. Pack the gear," Bull ordered.

The men didn't object as they began to break down and bag their equipment. The original mission had been to get inside the crypt itself, but they quickly settled for trying to cut a piece off of the structure, then they broke down to just trying to leave a dent or even a scratch on the surface. In the past two hours they'd used everything in their bag of tricks but there wasn't a mark on the crypt anywhere.

"What a waste of a night," Squirrel complained.

Bull disagreed. "It wasn't a complete waste of time; we learned few important things."

"We didn't even make a scratch, Bull. The only thing we learned was how to screw the pooch!" Squirrel held two sawed off shotguns resting in the crook of each arm, aimed out into the night. They'd opted for high spread weapons for tonight's op, but the weapons hadn't been needed, and Bull doubted they would be.

"For starters, we know they're dead." Bull rapped on the white stone-like surface with his knuckles. The dull sound wasn't loud, but he knew that to the vampires and their hearing it would be very loud, especially in the quiet of a tomb. "With all the freaking ruckus we've made out here they still haven't come out to eat us. They've got to be dead. Hell, if I was in there and heard us knocking around all night long I'd of come out and shot us by now."

Squirrel's eyes didn't stop scanning the darkness for a second but he laughed quietly. "Guess we did give up the silent approach a while back. That freaking drill was pretty loud; next time we need one with a motor that doesn't whine like a bitch."

Bull ran his hands over the mysterious white surface. The things they'd done to it would have put a scratch in it even if it were made of solid diamond. Bull always laughed when he heard people use words that implied "absolutes" like impenetrable or impregnable, unassailable or invincible - because there was no such thing as a place you couldn't get into with the right team and equipment. That was his job, getting into impossible places and doing what needed doing. But those words that had never been "words" to him were starting to feel as real as the cool white stone beneath his hands.

"We also learned that the vampires are not getting out until that witch lets them out. There is no way in hell they're clawing their way through this shit."

"Roger that, Bull," Squirrel said with feeling. "Maybe it's better this way. I didn't really want to go in there and kill two kids anyway. Even if they are vampires."

"Not our call, Squirrel. You know that. We don't think. We follow orders, kill shit, and do as we're told."

"Not tonight we don't," Squirrel said, sounding disgusted. "We finally screwed the pooch, Bull. This place has beat us. Hopefully that witch will keep them in there forever. Or maybe they'll just stay dead."

"Not the way our luck's been running lately," Bull said.

"Hey Bull, we got something over here," called Tiger from where he stood beside the crypt. He was looking down at a spot on the wall where they placed test scabs. They had placed ten of the patch-like scabs, each one with a different ultra-powerful solvent or acid. Bull and the team crowded around as Tiger finished lifting the last of the ten scabs. The white stone had definitely been marked by this last one; it had some fine little pitted holes and showed some signs of darkening on the surface.

Tiger held a sample dish while he used a scraper to chisel out a few flakes off the white surface. The knife didn't bite in far, only a thin centimeter or two, but to Bull and his team it felt like they'd just cracked the code at Fort Knox. Grins showed on blacked out faces as Tiger quickly scraped a few more hunks of white material off the area treated with the acid. Their team had never failed in a mission, and officially this was now NOT a failure. They would be able to hand off these little samples to the boys in the lab and come back with something custom made to cut right into the crypt if that was what they wanted them to do.

"Yeah, the boys in the white lab coats are gonna have kittens when they get this shit under a microscope," said one of the men, happy to have something to bring back. They all knew what this meant. Delta Black One's perfect record was still intact. Mission accomplished. Again.

"What the hell was on that last patch, which one did it?" Bull asked Tiger.

The big black man grinned, his white teeth bright in the near darkness as he worked.

"Dammit, Tiger, stop brushing your teeth so much. Those things are like flashlights," Bull complained as he eased in beside the big man and looked at the stone more closely.

"It was just one of the simple acids, sir. Nothing fancy, just a strong citric acid." Tiger scraped a last hunk or two of softened stone and capped his sample container, placing it in his pack with the rest of his gear.

"Sweet. Can't cut in with a halon torch or nick it with a diamond drill, but squirt some OJ on it and it crumbles." Bull shook his head. That's what he got for letting himself think that something was actually "IMPREGNABLE." He had almost been a believer for a second or two.

"There is no fucking hole we can't get into! No ass we cannot kick! No man, animal, alien, creature, or fucking vampire that we cannot kill! We are Delta Black One! We are the best! There's only one thing we don'tt know how to do. Fail! Hurrah!" Bull said quietly but firmly into his head set.

"Hurrah!" came back the quiet calls from his team, pumped by this last-minute victory.

"Pack up. Let's get the hell out of this damned garden; we're out of dark anyway. Take a few extra minutes to clear tracks."

He and his men crept silently toward the back garden wall. Bull and his team had entered the garden a little after three thirty and it was almost five thirty now. Three teams had come into Amen Hale. Delta One had been assigned to the vampires' tomb but the others had been assigned the more mundane, less horrifying job of bugging the rest of the mansion.

Spec Ops teams ranged far and wide across the campus installing surveillance equipment, listening devices and cameras everywhere. They easily avoided the people still up and working, but they had to be very careful around the main building where what was left of the Major stood vigilant guard on the first floor and one of the cloud men patrolled the upstairs hallways.

Fortunately his team had already bugged those rooms earlier in the day when they had first arrived so they had the whole place wired. But the nighttime fun was over. It was time to let the "day shift" come in and reap the benefits of all their hard work, get the glory, and negotiate with the natives. But that was okay. Bull was used to that and liked it that way. He knew he'd most likely be back tomorrow, to finish what he had started tonight, and by then the vampires may not be in the mood to welcome visitors. They were supposed to get in and get it done while they were dead or "asleep."

He hadn't told his men what their orders had been. They thought the mission was to kill the vampires. They didn't need to know the rest. It wasn't their call.

Mr. and Mrs. Han

Drenched Bastard

"Finally!" Mrs. Han gusted out as she dropped, exhausted, into the thinly padded booth. Her husband had requested a specific table so they ended up waiting even longer for "that specific table." Gail hadn't complained; she thought it was more than worth the wait. Their booth had a perfect view of the only TV in the restaurant and it was tuned in to the national news.

"Thank you for the table. Is there any way you could turn up the volume?" Mr. Han asked as he held out a twenty dollar bill to the bedraggled looking server. The money disappeared. The volume got raised. The young girl also took the time to take their order right away before going off to see about her other customers.

The restaurant was understaffed and overcrowded. This Denny's had never been this busy on a Wednesday night, or technically early Thursday morning. It was 5:35 AM and there was a thirty minute wait to be seated. It was a strange collection of people that had invaded the only 24-hour restaurant in the area. Half a dozen news vans were parked in the vacant dirt lot beside the restaurant where big rigs and tour buses would normally park. On the roof of each was a nest of antennas and satellite dishes ready to beam back their stories as soon as they had something worth reporting. Inside the restaurant the media people made little groups, the camera talent for each surrounded by a group of mostly nerdish looking, name tagged techs.

There were church buses in the parking lot also. Bringing in the faithful to picket and protest and pray and preach, but that's hungry work best done on a full stomach in the light of day, so here they sat, fueling up at Denny's. The opposite of the church crowd was also present in large numbers as well. Goths or pagans, both teens and adults, dressed in black.

Looking from table to table, it made for an odd mix of colors. There was no shouting, fights, or friction. Everyone seemed to be getting along wonderfully, pierced up punks happily talking with churchies at nearby tables. The atmosphere in the place was nothing that would be expected at this horribly late hour, or horribly early hour.

The place literally crackled with energy. The goths, witches, and pagans were like over excited children who'd been told all their lives that Santa wasn't real, only to find out he was real after all! And here they were, dying to get a peek at the North Pole to see Santa's workshop and maybe even catch a glimpse of the big guy himself. Only in this case the guy was a girl, and the girl was a Black Witch.

Fifteen minutes down the road from this location was the Hale House, as the locals and the state registry of historic sites called it. It was just another big beautiful mansion on the banks of the St. Johns River with some mediocre historical clout, due to the place being built and owned by the descendants of Nathan Hale, but North Florida had tons of places with more historical value. The architectural appeal of the structure and the history of its ownership were inconsequential to what it had become yesterday. The home of the Black Witch.

The church groups had the same excitement about them as the pagans. It seemed that all it took to invigorate the faithful to raise the standard high had been the rise of a Black Witch. Almost like spiritual Viagra, people who had warmed pews with their backside for years, doing nothing, now had the energy to board a bus in the middle of the night and happily wait thirty minutes for a seat at Denny's and another thirty for a Grand Slam breakfast.

The news crews were no less wound up. They were in media heaven, enjoying the ride of the wildest story they'd ever seen or dreamed about. The scramble for people who had anything to say or any connection to the event was on. Like bearded, gold-crazed miner 49ers charging into a river to pan for gold, they were running all over the city, nerds with microphones and cameras, mining for their media gold to send out to an anxious and listening world.

While the Hans were standing in the stifling crowd, waiting for their seat, they avoided all notice but now that they had a booth, one of the media vultures recognized them. The man reached down into his bag and fished out his directional microphone, plugged in his earphone, and aimed it at the Hans' table. He quickly made a triangle tent with his Denny's menu so the other techies wouldn't see what he was up to and get in on the action. He set his palm cam on the table too and use the napkin dispenser and a bottle of maple syrup to hold it in place and hide it from view as he aimed it at the Hans' table. He would merge sound and image from the two devices later, but first he had to get the sound right. He slipped his hand under the menu tent and fiddled with the direction until the conversation he wanted popped into place as he listened on his earphones.

"Yeah baby," he muttered to himself, reached down to the portable hard drive on his hip, and flipped it on, recording the conversation. With his one free hand he repositioned his half-eaten plate of waffles. Time to look normal, be invisible, and make some money.

"… can't believe she did this. How is this even legal!?" Mrs. Han said as she looked at the TV. They were showing clips of the wedding, video of Sky and Ryan walking the aisle and saying their vows.

"She wasn't herself, Gail. And that boy wasn't himself either; he was out of his mind. Neither of them were able to stop it. I told you all about that; they were being influenced by the vampires. All of them were." Mr. Han pushed another forkful of pancake into his mouth as he looked at the TV screen. Their food had come out almost immediately. A twenty dollar tip went pretty far at a Denny's.

"I know what you said! But what do we do, Tam!? How do we fix this!? How do we get her back home where she belongs?" Mrs. Han wasn't interested in her food. Her eyes were fixed to the TV screen as she spoke to her husband.

He'd had some time to think through the events of the day, and it had been a very long day. The first half was spent getting grilled by FBI and Homeland Defense agents about the events at Rhineheart Clinic. They thought an explosive device had been used to blast a hole in the building and they thought he and his daughter had something to do with it. At least they did then. Not now. The picture on the TV cut to commentators who were discussing the doctor and his pills.

"I can't believe they still haven't arrested that bastard Burgis!" Mrs. Han unleashed her angst against her eggs and stabbed them violently, shoving in a quick bite before spitting it back out into a napkin.

"Shit! These people don't even know how to cook an egg, Tam!"

He laughed. "I'm glad you quit drinking, but it's making you very tense." He reached out and grabbed her trembling hand that held the napkin and rejected eggs, holding her hand steady. Gail looked into his eyes. He knew she was having withdrawal symptoms. "Perhaps a valium would help," he suggested.

"No. I'm not taking pills either. I'm through with the pills and the drinking." She pulled away from his grip and grabbed her glass of Diet Coke and took a drink to make her point.

"No pills?" Tam asked, shocked. "Are you serious?"

"Hell yes. If Sky can do it, quit cold turkey, so can I." She took her hands off the table and placed them out of sight in her lap.

"I have to change, Tam. I need to keep her safe and I can't do that if I'm drugged up and out of my mind. I'm through with the pills. Forever."

"Have you told Dr. Dillenger?" Tam asked.

Her eyebrows bunched up in anger. "He's a pill doctor, of course he thinks I should be on the pills. To hell with Dillenger and his damn pills! I mean it, Tam, I'm through. I'd rather be a little crazy and be me than be some drugged up, out of control bimbo who lets her daughter get—get—"

Tam got out of his side of the booth and slipped in beside his wife, putting his arms around her.

He spoke to her in Chinese. "My precious flower. This is where I would normally say have a drink. Take a pill." She nodded. That was what he'd just tried to do.

"I did this because I did not have the time or energy to deal with it. To deal with you. But no longer." He lifted Gail's trembling hands and held them in his own as he spoke. "If you want me to help you quit, I will, but this will be hard, Gail. Very hard."

"I want to quit, Tam. I don't want to be like that anymore." She stared into her husband's eyes.

"Help me, Tam," she begged.

"Is she okay?" asked the little server girl, who'd noticed Gail's breakdown and the tears. "Can I do anything for you? She gonna be okay?" She leaned in and looked at Mrs. Han with worry.

"Yes. She will be fine," answered Mr. Han in English. "We are fine."

The girl eyed Mrs. Han for a second, obviously trying to determine if he was the source of his wife's distress, but she quickly dismissed that notion and moved to a problem of a different stripe.

"Okay then. You've been real nice to me and I ain't never had a twenty tip on a two top before, leastwise not from someone who didn't want to sleep with me." She winked at Mr. Han and gave him a smile which he returned kindly. "You seem like really nice folks. You orta know that there's one of them reporter son-bitches pointing his microphone thing and his camera at you right now. Spyin' on you." She pointed directly at the booth half way across the restaurant.

The guy in the booth who knew he was made waved and smiled. He didn't stop filming though; sometimes the best footage came when the gig was up. Gail and Tam gave each other a little smile.

"Tip the lady, Tam, she's earned it," Gail said as she slipped out of the booth.

"Yes. She has." Tam reached for his wallet.

It was a hundred.

As soon as they were up and out of their seats the guy with the camera started to wave his arms wildly, trying to pay so he could follow them out of the restaurant.

"Check please!" he called out, waving his card at a passing server along with a few bucks in his hand. The girl passing by had her hands full of dishes, but the impatient reporter laid his card, the bill, and a couple of extra dollars on the top of the stack.

"Help me out here, darlin. I gotta go!" he said and looked back out the window trying to see the Hans.

"Fine," she said and marched off into the kitchen to dump the dishes before ringing up the ticket for the pushy customer. She would have told him to stick it, but he'd left three bucks with the card. Cheap. But three bucks was still three bucks.

"LeAnn. Here," said her sister Missy as she laid a twenty dollar bill on the table right beside her.

"Holy shit, what ya givin' me a twenty for?"

"For this." She grabbed the credit card off the top of the stack of dishes, walked over to the hot grill top, and dropped the card on for just a second on each side. Not enough to melt it, but enough to make the magnetic strip useless. She scooped the card up with a spatula and wiped the grease and little bits of egg off with a towel.

"Here." She handed the card back with a wicked grin. "Now go tell that bastard that he better have cash or a different card, cuz this one's *fried*."

"What the hell he do to ya, grab your ass?" LeAnn asked, not really too surprised. She'd seen the cooked card trick before.

"Hell no, way worse than that." Missy placed a full pitcher of tea and carafe of cranberry juice on a platter and heaved it onto her shoulder.

"Well what'd that sorry bastard do?" LeAnn asked, a little worried now. Her sister had a bad temper and it was hot right now.

"He was spyin' on some poor sweet lady, takin' pictures of her while she cried." Missy's eyes squinted up as she looked at her sister.

"You really gonna do it, ain't ya."

"Hell, yeah." Missy marched out the door to make one sorry bastard into one drenched sorry bastard.

"It's just been one of them days," LeAnn sighed, grabbed the cooked card, and went out to watch the show.

Jane and Dan

The Grave

There was no sound in the room. Not the sound of laughing, the noise of intimate conversation, nor the sounds of lovers embracing that one would be expect to hear on a wedding night. Even the soft inhale and exhale of peaceful even breathing was absent. The silence was total. The stillness was absolute.

Within the room were only two pieces of furniture. A white gothic table the color of ivory ran the length of the wall on one side of the room. The table itself looked like a living thing, some strange formation of bone, birthed straight up out of the stone. On top of the table were only four items, a small purple purse, a man's wallet, a cell phone, and one large urn made from black glass.

The urn was open and empty. The contents had been devoured. Black trails of dried blood marked the side of the urn and a few black drops of dried blood also dotted the white tabletop. The lid of the urn rested on the floor by the wall on the other side of the chamber.

On the floor beside the table rested a black duffle bag. Some clothes lay strewn about on the floor as well, left where they'd fallen. The only other object in the room was the bed. They lay there, nude, in the center of the bed, positioned side by side.

They were facing each other, their legs intertwined as they stared into each other's eyes. Unmoving. Completely still. No burning red light came from their eyes obscuring the colors. Dan's blue green eyes stared into Jane's purple and lilac. They looked into each other's eyes like they had so many times before, but this time there was no thought behind the gaze. No passion or emotion. The stillness was the same as any other grave.

No dreams. No thoughts. No breath of life.

There was nothing except the fragrance of a million beautiful roses.